PENGUI...

THE SPANISH...

R. H. Mottram was born in Norwich in 1883, and educated there and in Lausanne. He spent most of his life in East Anglia, where many of his later novels are set. He started work as a clerk in the local bank, and in 1904 he met John Galsworthy (about whom he was later to write the intimate portrait *For Some We Loved*) who encouraged his literary ambitions. He served with the Forces in France from 1914–19, and in 1924 published *The Spanish Farm* (filmed as *Roses of Picardy*). His first novel, *The Spanish Farm*, won the Hawthornden Prize (1924) and featured a preface written by Galsworthy. Its sequels, *Sixty-Four, Ninety-Four!* (1925) and *The Crime at Vanderlynden's* (1926), were equally successful and in 1927 the three were published as *The Spanish Farm Trilogy*.

R. H. Mottram wrote some sixty books altogether, including *Our Mr Dormer* (1927), *The English Miss* (1928), *Flower Pot End* (1935), *The Gentleman of Leisure* (1948), *Over the Wall* (1955), *Musetta* (1960) and *Happy Birds* (1964). In 1966 he was awarded the honorary degree of Doctor of Letters by the University of East Anglia. R. H. Mottram died in 1971.

R. H. Mottram

# The Spanish Farm Trilogy

1914-1918

Penguin Books

Penguin Books Ltd, Harmondsworth, Middlesex, England
Penguin Books, 625 Madison Avenue, New York, New York 10022, U.S.A.
Penguin Books Australia Ltd, Ringwood, Victoria, Australia
Penguin Books Canada Ltd, 2801 John Street, Markham, Ontario, Canada L3R 1B4
Penguin Books (N.Z.) Ltd, 182–190 Wairau Road, Auckland 10, New Zealand

*The Spanish Farm* was first published by Chatto & Windus 1924; *Sixty-Four, Ninety-Four!* by Chatto & Windus 1925; and *The Crime at Vanderlynden's* by Chatto & Windus 1926

*The Spanish Farm Trilogy, 1914–1918* first published by Chatto & Windus 1927
Published in Penguin Books 1979

Copyright © The Executors of R. H. Mottram, 1927
All rights reserved

Set, printed and bound in Great Britain
by Cox & Wyman Ltd, Reading
Set in Linotype Pilgrim

Except in the United States of America,
this book is sold subject to the condition
that it shall not, by way of trade or otherwise,
be lent, re-sold, hired out, or otherwise circulated
without the publisher's prior consent in any form of
binding or cover other than that in which it is
published and without a similar condition
including this condition being imposed
on the subsequent purchaser

# Contents

| | |
|---|---:|
| The Spanish Farm | 7 |
| D'Archeville | 163 |
| Sixty-Four, Ninety-Four! | 175 |
| The Winner | 381 |
| The Crime at Vanderlynden's | 387 |
| The Stranger | 533 |

# The Spanish Farm

*To My Wife*

*Part One*
# LA PATRIE EST EN DANGER

*Part One*
# La Patrie est en danger

A farmer stood watching a battalion of infantry filing into his pasture. A queerer mixture of humanity could not have been imagined. The farmer wore a Dutch cap, spoke Flemish by preference, but could only write French. His farm was called Ferme l'Espagnole – The Spanish Farm – and stood on French soil. The soldiers were the usual English mixture – semi-skilled townsmen, a number of agricultural and other labourers, fewer still of seafaring and waterside folk, and a sprinkling of miners and shepherds, with one or two regulars.

The farmer, Mr Vanderlynden, Jerome, described in the Communal records as a Cultivator, sixty-five years of age, watching his rich grass being tramped to liquid mud under the heavy boots of the incoming files, and the shifting of foot-weary men as they halted in close column, platoon by platoon, made no protest. This was not merely because under the French law he was bound to submit to the needs of the troops, but also because, after twelve months' experience, he had discovered that there were compensations attached to the billeting and encampment of English. They paid – so much per officer or man – not always accurately, but promptly always, and what would you more in war-time? The Spanish Farm was less than twenty kilometres from the 'Front', the actual trenches, whose ground-shaking gun-rumble was always to be heard, whose scouting aeroplanes were visible and audible all day, whose endless flicker of star shells made green the eastern horizon all night. The realities of the situation were ever present to Mr Jerome Vanderlynden, who besides could remember a far worse war, that of 1870. Moreover, the first troops passing that way in the far-off days of 1914 had been French, and had wanted twice as much attention, and had never paid, had even threatened him when he suggested it.

\*

Standing with his great knotted earthy fists hanging by his side, as the khaki stream poured and poured through the wide-set gate, he passed in review the innumerable units or detachments that had billeted in the Spanish Farm or encamped in its pastures. Uncritical, almost unreasoning, the old peasant was far from being able to define the difference he had felt when the first English arrived. He had heard tell of them, read of them in the paper, but was far from imagining what they might have been like, having no data to go on and no power of imagination. He had been coming in from getting up the last of the potato crop of 1914 when he had found flat-capped, mud-coloured horsemen at his gate. Sure that they were Germans (the Uhlans had been as near as Hazebrouck only a few weeks before), he hastily tied the old white horse in the tombereau, and had gone forward cap in hand. But his daughter Madeleine had already met the soldiers at the gate. A widower for many years, Jerome Vanderlynden's house was kept by his youngest child, this Madeleine, now in her twentieth year. To say that he believed in her does not do justice to his feelings. She had been the baby of the family, had had a better education than he or his sons, at a convent in St Omer; added to all this, plus her woman's prestige, was the fact that she inherited (from heaven knows where!) a masterful strain. What she said (and she was not lavish of words) was attended to. Whether it were education, inspiration, or more probably an appreciation beyond the powers of her father, that told her that English cavalry officers would agree with her, it is certain that she started with those first squadrons of the Cavalry Division a sort of understanding that she would never have attempted with French troops. They paid her liberally and treated her respectfully, probably confusing her in their minds with English farmers' wives to whom they were in the habit of paying for hunt damage. They had money – officers and men wanted to supplement their rations and the horses' forage. Madeleine had eggs, coffee, soft bread, beer, fried potatoes, beans, oats. She could and did wash collars and shirts better than the average soldier servant. It took her some time to understand that every English officer required many gallons of water to wash in, at least once a day. But once she had grasped that too, she attended to it, at a small charge.

\*

And now it was October, 1915; more troops than ever, especially infantry, were in the Commune, and an interpreter had warned Jerome Vanderlynden that he would have a whole battalion in the farm. He made no remark, but Madeleine had asked several questions. More awake mentally than her father, it had not escaped her close reading of the paper that a new sort of English troops were coming to France. They were described indifferently as 'Territorials' and as 'New Army' or 'Kitchener's Army', and neither Madeleine nor indeed the newspapers of the Department du Nord knew of any difference between them and the Territoriaux of the French system. Madeleine put them down as second-line troops and stored the fact in her vigilant mind.

She came and stood beside her father, as the 10th Battalion Easthamptonshire Regiment broke up and moved off to its billets. Two of the sadly depleted companies went to adjacent farms, two remained on the premises. The officers – of whom only twelve had survived the Battle of Loos – were busy with non-coms, going through nominal rolls, lists of missing men or damaged equipment, trying to disentangle some sort of parade state and indent for replacements.

Madeleine did not bother about them. She said to her father: 'I am going to find the Quarta-mastere!'

She found him, standing amid his stores in the hop-press, and knew him by his grey hair and white-red-white ribbon. She had long ago inquired and found out that this rank in the English Army were chosen from among the old soldiers, and were quickest at getting to business. It had been explained to her that the white-red-white ribbon was for length of good conduct, and secretly tolerant of men's foibles as of a child's, she stored this fact also, for identification purposes.

In this instance the Mess President having been killed, the old ranker, Lieutenant and Quartermaster John Adams, was acting Mess President, and doing nearly every other duty in the disorganization and readjustment that followed the tragic bungle of the New Army's first offensive.

He greeted her with his professional aplomb: 'Good day, Maddam, dinner for twelve officers; compris, douze!' He held up the fingers of both hands and then two fingers separately.

'All right!' returned Madeleine in English. 'Where are their rations?'

He replied, 'Ah, you're sharp!' and called to his storekeeper, 'Jermyn, officers' rations to Maddam and tell the mess cook!' He went on to bargain for other things – beds for the Colonel, the Adjutant and himself – and in the course of the argument Madeleine informed him that according to General Routine Orders there was to be no smoking in the barns and no insanitary practices, that all gates must be kept closed, and no movables removed. Handing him her price list, she withdrew to her long coffin-shaped stove in the brick-floored kitchen.

\*

Dusk settled down on the Spanish Farm – autumn dusk – with swathed mists on the small flat chocolate-coloured fields, richest and best tilled in the world – now bare of crops. The brilliant colours of the last hop-leaves and of the regular rows of elms that bordered each pasture were hidden, but the tops of the trees towered above the mist-line into that wide blue vault that the old painters loved, nowhere wider than in the Flemish plain. The Spanish Farm stood on the almost imperceptible southern slope of the sandy ridge that divides in some degree the valley of the Yser from that of the Lys, whose flat meadows lay spread out, almost from Aire to the factory smoke of Armentières, at a slightly lower level to the south. Northward, behind the house, the ground rose very gradually in fertile field and elm-encircled pasture. Westward, black against the last glow of the sunset, two little 'planes droned their way from the aerodromes round

St Omer towards the eastern horizon where the evening 'hate' was toned down by the distance to the low boom of 'heavies', the sharper note of the field guns, the whip-lash crack of rifles and machine-guns, and the flatter squashed-out reports of mortars and grenades.

The house itself was a single-storied building of immensely thick walls of red brick – much as the settlers under Alva had left it three hundred years before – except for enlargement of windows and re-thatching – though the existing thatch was so old that wallflowers tasselled its ridge from one octagonal spoke-tiled chimney-stack to the other. Originally a simple block with door in the middle, outbuildings had been added at each end, giving it the form of an unfinished quadrangle, the gap towards the south, enclosing the great steaming midden of golden dung. Completely surrounded by a deep wide moat, access to it was only possible by a brick bridge on the southern side, guarded by a twenty-foot extinguisher-roofed 'shot' tower, whose loopholed bulk now served for tool shed below and pigeon-loft above.

Further outbuildings stood outside the moat, a few to the north in the smaller pasture behind the house, but a long broad range of cowshed, stable, and hop-press stretched into the ten-acre 'home' or 'manor' pasture.

Never, since Alva last marched that way, had the old semi-fortress been so packed with humanity. Two companies, which even at their present weakness must have numbered over three hundred men, were getting rid of their arms and equipment and filing round to the north pasture where the cookers flared and smoked, and the cooks, demoniac in their blackened faces and clothes, ladled out that standard compost that, at any time before nine in the morning was denominated 'coffee', at any hour before or after noon 'soup', until the end of the day, when, as a last effort, it became 'tea'. Derisive shouts of 'Gyp-oh!' intended to convey that it was accepted for what it was – yesterday's bacon grease, hot water and dust from the floor of a lorry – greeted it, as it splashed into the tendered mess-tins of the jostling crowd.

*

Within the house, in the westward of the two principal rooms, Madeleine, with Berthe, most useful of the Belgian refugees about the place, had got her stove nearly red hot, and was silently, deftly handling her pots and dishes, while the mess cooks unpacked the enamelled plates and cups and carried them through to the other room where the table was being set by the simple process of spreading sheets of newspapers upon it and arranging the drinking-cups, knives and forks thereon. Bread being cut, there only remained for 'Maddam', as they called Madeleine, to say that all was ready, so that the brass shell-case in the passage could be used as a gong. The Colonel appeared, and the Adjutant, both regular soldiers, masking whatever they felt under professional passivity. There were no other senior officers; the only surviving Major was with a captainless outlying company. The two companies in the farm were commanded by lieutenants. The junior officers were all Kitchener enlistments. Some of them had hoped to spend that night in Lille.

The conversation was not so brilliant as the meal. In many a worse billet, the Easthamptons looked back to their night at Spanish Farm. Everyone was dog tired and bitterly depressed. The Colonel only sat the length of one cigarette. Adams took his food in his 'bunk'. The junior officers clattered up the narrow candle-lit stair into the loft where two of them had a bedstead and two others the floor. The Adjutant was left collating facts and figures, with the Doctor, who was going through his stores. To them came the runner from the guard-room (improvised in a tent at the brick pillared gate of the pasture).

'Reinforcement officers, sir!'

There entered two rather bewildered young men who had passed during the previous forty-eight hours through every emotion from a desperate fear that the 'victory' of Loos would end the war without their firing a shot, to sheer annoyance at being dumped at a railhead and told to find a battalion in the dark. They had lost everything they had except what they carried on them, and were desperately hungry.

The Adjutant surprised even himself at the cordial greeting he gave the two strangers – untried officers from a reserve battalion he had never seen. He knew nothing of their history or capabilities, but the sense of more people behind, coming up to fill the gaps, warmed even the professional soldier's trained indifference. He got up, and went to the door of the kitchen, calling for 'Maddam' and repeating 'Mangay' in a loud voice to indicate that further refreshment was required.

Madeleine had just finished, with Berthe, the washing and cleaning up of her cooking utensils, and was about to go to bed in her little single bedroom that looked out over the northern pasture. She was just as inclined to cook another meal as a person may be, who has already worked eighteen hours and expects to rise at half past five in the morning. Nor was there anything in the stare of the shorter, fair-haired new arrival, with his stolid silence, to encourage her. But the taller and darker of the two asked her in fair French if she could manage an omelet and some coffee. They regretted deranging her, but had the hunger of a wolf and had not eaten since the morning. Whether it was being addressed in her own tongue, or the fact that the young officer had hit on the things that lay next her hand and would not take five minutes, or whether it was something in the voice, Madeleine acquiesced politely, and set about providing what was asked.

The Adjutant stared. He was not accustomed to interpolations in foreign tongues in his orders. But this young officer was so obviously unconscious of offence, and the interference so opportune, that there was nothing to be said. He talked to the new-comers as they supped, and, apologizing for having to put them in the little ground-floor room with the orderly officer, retired to his own.

Silence and darkness fell upon the Spanish Farm, only broken by the steps of the sentries, the change of guard, and the dull mutter and star-shell flicker from the line, and for some hours all those human beings that lay in and around the old house, lost consciousness of their hopes, fears, and wants.

\*

## THE SPANISH FARM

English officers and men who billeted in the Spanish Farm (and practically the whole English Army must have passed through or near it at one time or another) to this day speak of it as one of the few places they can still distinguish in the blur of receding memories, one of the few spots of which they have nothing but good to tell. In part this may be easily explained. The old house was comparatively roomy, well kept, water-tight. There was less overcrowding, no leaking roof to drip on one's only dry shirt – and besides, though the regulations were more strictly observed here than anywhere, that very fact gave almost an impression of home – order, cleanliness, respect ruled here yet a little – but perhaps there is another reason – perhaps houses, so old and so continually handled by human beings, have almost a personality of their own: perhaps the Spanish Farm that had sheltered Neapolitan mercenaries fighting the French, Spanish Colonists fighting Flemish, French fighting English or Dutch – and now English and Colonials fighting German – perhaps the old building bent and brooded over these last of its many occupants – perhaps knew a little better than other houses what men expected of it.

\*

Madeleine thought no more of the War, and the population it had brought to the Spanish Farm, until half past seven, when the mess orderlies began to prepare breakfast. Obstinately refusing to allow anyone to touch her stove, she cooked that incomprehensible meal of oat-soup ('porridge' they called it!), and bacon and eggs, after which she knew they ate orange confiture. She, her father, and the farm hands, had long taken their lump of bread and bowl of coffee, standing. Her attention was divided between the hum of the separator in the dairy and her washing drying on the line, when she heard her father's voice calling: 'Madeleine, leinsche!' ('Little Madeleine!'). She called out that she was in the kitchen.

The old man came, moving more quickly than usual, voluble in Flemish, excited. The soldiers had moved out all the flax-straw lying in the long wooden drying-shed behind the house,

## LA PATRIE EST EN DANGER

on the pasture, and all the machines, reapers and binders, drills and rakes. Moreover, they had taken for firewood hop-poles that had been expressly forbidden.

Madeleine washed her hands at the sink, saying she would see about it. But she was saved the trouble. Her father went out into the yard, unable to keep still in his impatience, and she heard him in altercation with old Adams. They drifted into the mess-room. As she was drying her hands, there was a knock on the kitchen door, and she saw her father ushering in the dark young officer of the evening before. Her brow cleared. She had not the least doubt she could 'manage' the young man.

The young man surpassed expectations. Madeleine found it unnecessary to keep to her rather limited English. His French, while not correct, was expansive. He admitted her version of the farmer's rights under Billeting Law, but would not accept the sum, running into hundreds of francs, which Jerome Vanderlynden, typical peasant at a bargain, asked for compensation. It appeared that the quiet-looking young man knew something of flax culture and more of agricultural machinery. He quoted within a very little the cost of re-stacking the flax, oiling the machinery, with the price of two burnt hop-poles. He offered forty francs.

Old Vanderlynden made his usual counter: 'What if I go to Brigade Headquarters about it!'

'Then you will get nothing at all. They are too busy, and we move on today!'

The old man laughed and slapped his leg.

Madeleine, knowing by experience that the officer had been authorized to spend fifty francs (a sum which appealed to the English, being recognizable as a couple of sovereigns), began to respect him, took the money, and signed the receipt.

Left alone, old Jerome remarked that the young man was very well brought up. Madeleine was looking carefully through her pots and pans to see that nothing had disappeared into the big mess-box.

From the window she saw the battalion paraded, and watched them move off, as she passed hastily from room to room, counting things. Her father was round the outbuildings. The last to go was old Adams with the wagons. A great stillness fell on the old farm, the litter of papers, tins and ashes, and all the unmistakable atmosphere of a crowded place suddenly deserted.

\*

The day following the departure of the battalion was fine and still. Even the Front was quieting down. After the early midday meal of soup and bread, Madeleine put on her second-best frock, washed, did her hair, spent a little time over her hands, and putting on her fur but no hat, picked her way over the cobbles, and left the farm by the main gate.

She walked with the ease of a person of perfect health, who knew what she wanted and where she was going, and who had habitually no time to stroll, no need to think. The clumsiness of a life of hard physical labour had been corrected by a good education, and she might well have passed, in her dress that had so evidently been best, and was going to be everyday, for an English girl. Only the boots and the hatless head marked her for a follower of the continental tradition, though her strong ankles and round neck would have well supported the low shoes and simple felt or straw of an outdoor English woman.

She said nothing to her father or to the farm-hands as to her errand. No one inquired. For a long while, ever since she had left the convent school, she had been mistress of her own actions and of other people's. Old Vanderlynden, if he ever spoke of her to others, used not the peasant's usual 'Ma fille' – 'my little girl', but 'Ma demoiselle' – 'my young lady'. Her dress indicated nothing, for etiquette forbade her going beyond the farm in her old worn 'every-day' and apron, clogs and upturned sleeves. Old men and women and children were ploughing, manuring and weed-burning in the fields bordering the hedgeless road. She spoke to no one, and no one spoke to her. She met them all once a week, at Mass, and that was sufficient. One or two of them, glancing at her straight figure and level, unswerving gait, glanced at each other and grinned. The usual surmises were probably made, for it was known that she was keeping company with none of the young men of her generation before they were hurried off to the War – and it was plainly unnatural that a good-looking young woman with a dowry should not be sought in marriage. These surmises were all the more interesting because nothing definite was known.

Some hundreds of yards before reaching the Lille–Calais road, Madeleine passed under the shadow of one of those little woods of oak, crowning a small conical hill, that constitute the only untilled plots of the hard-worked Flemish border. Like its counterpart in all the neighbouring parishes, this wood also was called the 'Kruysabel' or Poplar-cross, on account of the crucifix that hid in its highest and thickest part, where its five 'rides' met in a tiny clearing. To the south of this clearing was a little hunting shelter, brick, with mock-Gothic windows and leaded lights, encircled by a timber-pillared veranda, on which the thatch of the eaves descended, in the worst style of Lille garden-furnishing ('rustic work' in England). After entering the wood by a wicket, it was to this erection that Madeleine mounted a soft squashy 'ride' between impenetrable walls of oak sapling, planted as close as it would grow, and cut regularly, section by section, according to age, so that little could be seen but slim straight grey-green stems on all sides.

Arrived at the little clearing on the summit, the girl took out a key and entered the hunting shelter. The ornamental porch led straight into a dining-place almost filled by the long table surrounded by benches. The porch and windows filled the north wall, a great open brick-hearth with fire-dogs, the western. Opposite was a long rack of antlers, false or real, for greatcoats, guns and bags. On the remaining side was a partition pierced by two doors. The apartment was clean and well kept – nor was this wonderful to anyone who could have seen Madeleine produce feather brush and duster, and go carefully along the pine-board wainscot, round mouldings and window-ledges, and along the frames of the photographs of many a jolly party – photographs in which a man, appearing variously from middle age to past it, moustached and whiskered in the fashion of his youth

– which must have been the fall of the Second Empire – and a youth who passed to manhood in the newest group – were surrounded by male companions who tended to be less and less hairy the newer the picture – and women in every fashion from crinolines to gaiters and deerstalkers – live horses and dogs and dead birds and beasts, on a background of hunting shelter and trees. Madeleine hardly paused to gaze at one, but passed on, chasing spiders, fly marks, dust, and looking for damp or wormholes. She was far from being a person to stand in front of a photograph while there was work to do.

Next she opened the left-hand door and peered into the little kitchen almost filled by the vase-and-coffin-style stove, at which she and others had cooked many a hot-pot and lapin-chasseur. All was in order here, and she only glanced to see that no invading hand had touched the stacked fuel, and that the iron-ringed flagstone that opened on a diminutive cellar had not been removed. She left the kitchen. Before the other door some little animation gleamed through the naturally passive, almost defensive expression – behind which she habitually concealed her thoughts. Entering this third apartment, a little upholstered lounge, twelve feet square, she closed the door softly and stood a moment without moving. It had been originally a gun-room, but the present Baron, her father's proprietor, owner of two thousand hectares of shooting of which this shelter was the centre, had turned it into a withdrawing-room for ladies, as their presence at the shooting parties became more and more usual. A divan ran under the curtained windows, west and south, a tiny fireplace was beside the door, while a corner had been carved off the kitchen for toilet purposes. Otherwise it was pine boarded and upholstered in plaited straw like the rest of the building. But the straw-surfaces were covered with cushions, mats and covers, chiefly Oriental, and all collected, like the Flemish china on the walls, and the fancy photographs, 'Kruysabel by Moonlight', 'Morning in the Woods', etc., etc., by Georges, the present Baron's son.

\*

## LA PATRIE EST EN DANGER

It was this very Georges – spoiled, lovable, perverse, self-indulgent, whose taste and personality penetrated and overcame the rococo-rustic architecture and upholstery – that Madeleine had met in this very room, every time she could and he would, all that summer that led up to the declaration of war. How many times they had spent the Catholic five to seven o'clock – she protected by endless subterfuges and evasions – he coming easily of right – she was far from counting. Nor did she cast back in her mind to the commencement of the thing. Indeed, there had been nothing remarkable about it. It happened like this:

Her father was the old Baron's chief tenant and head gamekeeper (as that office is understood in France). She had known Georges as a thin, dark-eyed, imperious, tyrannical boy. As a girl she had helped carry the materials of the midday feast, that, cooked and served at the Kruysabel, was the converging-point of the morning drives of the Baron's shooting parties. The last shoot of the spring of 1914 had finished in darkness, and she had been left, as usual, to clear up. Her basket packed, the place all squared-up and tidy, she had stood by candle-light, munching a strip of buttered spiced-bread and finishing, careless of the dregs, the last of a bottle of Burgundy that her Flemish soul loved as only a Flemish soul can. She had caught Georges' prominent brown eyes on her, more than once during the day, as she moved about, waiting at table. Conscious of looking her best, this had pleased her, beneath her preoccupation with her duties of cooking and serving. Moreover, she had a good day's work behind her (the Baron paid well if he was satisfied), and the Burgundy warmed her heart.

She heard footsteps behind her, and a tune hummed, and knew instinctively who it was. She kept quite still. Instinct told her that this was the most effective thing to do. Two arms, under hers, bent her backwards, and Georges fastened his lips to hers. Self-controlled, she neither called out nor resisted. Careful, even grudging in everything, when she gave, she gave generously, no half measures. That was how it had started. The most natural thing in the world. It had gone on in spasms of passion, and interludes, as far as she was concerned, of cool efficient concealment. Georges was a little younger, far less healthy in mind or body, probably less strong, physically, than she. There may have been an undercurrent of almost maternal feeling on her part, and certainly not the least illusion as to the consequences of being found out. And no one had found out.

*

But now, as she stood in the empty room, on this October afternoon of 1915, she was as far from ruminating on the beginnings of the affair as she was from the neo-classic tower of Merville Church, visible fifteen kilometres away, in the pale sunshine, through a gap in the branches. She had to stop for a moment to get used to the atmosphere, as a diver adjusts himself to the pressure of a lower level, but it was an unconscious pause; then, pressing her lips together, she dusted and swept, opened the windows, banged mats and covers. Not that she hoped by the elaborate preparation of a room unused these fifteen months, and destined to be empty many another, to charm back the man through whom alone that room interested her. Madeleine's point of view was much simpler. Her father had charge of the shooting. She had automatically undertaken the care of the shelter. Having done so, unasked and unpaid, as part of the general unwritten arrangement between her father and the Baron, she could be trusted to go through with it, whatever happened.

Her task finished, she straightened her back and stood, hands on her hips, looking at nothing. From somewhere beyond Estaires, Givenchy or Festubert perhaps, came the sound of guns; some petty incident of the four-hundred-mile year-long battle was dragging out its squalid tragedy. Her lips moved, formed the words 'Bêtes – sales bêtes!' which meant so much more than 'dirty beasts' and something more immediate than 'foul brutes' in English. No sound came. All that feeling of hers was too deep down to struggle into active expression through her habitual reserve and acquiescence with current manners. Not hers to criticize or revolt, hers only to feel, to feel with all the depth of a narrow, obstinate nature. Anyone might have supposed that she was thinking of the Germans who had killed one brother, and held another prisoner since Charleroi. Could she have been induced to express herself, she might have said, from mere habit of convention, that she meant the Germans. But it was deeper than that, so deep as to be almost impersonal.

Years before, when she was but a little girl, she had stood by the bedside of her mother, dying for want of proper medical attention, the fees for which had been grudged until it was too late. Her mother had said: 'Pray to the Virgin, now that you are alone!' She had answered, sobbing: 'I will pray, and I will take care of father and brothers, and they of me!' 'Pray to the Virgin!' the mother repeated. 'She is the only one that will take care of you!' That unique effort of expression of a life worn down with toil, and given up to save expense, had sunk into Madeleine's mind, been confirmed by the teaching of the convent school, where the nuns seemed to be perpetually clearing up the mess men made of things. When the war came Madeleine dumbly recognized it for a thing that men did. She had none of the definite sex-antagonism of an English suffragist, was affectionately tolerant of her father and brothers, and constructively tender to Georges, would have loved to have surrounded him with perpetual comfort and indulgence. But in the bulk, men were always doing things like this war. Her smouldering, almost sulky resentment had not decreased one particle during the fifteen months that had passed. For her, the day of mobilization had been catastrophic. Georges, grandson of an ennobled 'industrialist' and of bourgeois blood of the official classes, surprised everybody, surprised Madeleine, surprised perhaps himself. The manifesto 'La Patrie est en danger' had just been issued. He seemed to have swallowed its sentiments whole. His papers arrived, and found him in uniform – he was (of course) in the cuirassiers. He mounted and rode off. Like so many others, the indolent expensive young man lost all thought of anything except what he deemed 'duty'.

Madeleine, who knew as well as anyone that his depot would be at Lille, had taken her stand, that August morning, just inside the gate of the Kruysabel. She had chosen that place for easy concealment, and she knew he must pass that way; she was prepared to give him anything he might want. He passed her at a trot, looking rather fine in his regimentals, and well mounted. He raised his hand to the salute, but did not draw rein. She had gone home and taken up her work where she had laid it down.

Going about the endless jobs of a farmer's daughter, her slow-moving temper had risen and risen. She knew Georges, his impulses, his absorption in the matter that held him for the moment, his spoiled thriftlessness. He would rush into military life, engulf himself in it, never thinking for a moment to take his fill of happiness first. He would not write. She hoped he would not. There would be no means of keeping the arrival of his letters secret from the whole village. Nor would she write to him. She made no bones over social distinctions, upheld them rather. He was the young master. It was not for her to write. This left a great ache in her, for which she presently found a partial cure. It came to her as she was packing up parcels of small luxuries for her brothers. She packed a third one, more carefully than the first two. As the billeting of English troops on the farm became increasingly regular, she managed to vary and improve that third parcel, obtaining from the – to her – sumptuously overstocked canteens and private presents of the men in khaki – tinned stuff, toilet wares, and the beautiful English cigarettes Georges loved. She posted this third packet from Hazebrouck each weekly market day, for however well known she was to the farming community, she was a stranger to the small postal and other officials of the railway town. She comforted herself that if anything (it was always called 'anything' by the women of the War, whatever their nationality) had happened to Georges the parcel would be returned. She was far from picturing the trenches to herself. So, with steady, profitable work at the farm, now a camp and barrack as well, with a weekly parcel to send, and a weekly visit to the shelter at Kruysabel, the interminable months had passed. People – her father with one son dead and one a prisoner – her sister, down in Laventie, within bullet-range of the trenches – got accustomed to the war.

But not Madeleine.

*

So, as she stood in the fading light of the October sunset, resting a moment before she returned to the farm, there was nothing petty or personal in the grim set of her features, the slow-burning anger of her eyes. She might have posed there for a symbolic figure of Woman contemplating Fate. She stood straight in her neat, almost careful dress, bought with one eye on looks and one on usefulness, solid well-kept boots and stockings, thick but without hole or wrinkle. Large boned, but so close-knit that she did not look disproportionately broad, her figure, kept in check by hard work and frugal feeding, promised to grow thick only with middle age. Anyone looking at her face would have said, 'What a handsome woman', not 'What a pretty girl.' There was something below the surface that kept the red lips closed in their firm line, the round chin lifted, the grey eyes and level brows serene. Her dark hair, which she kept, while at work, tied in a duster, was neat and smooth. Her skin had the pallor of health.

That internal quality that made her simple shapeliness so much more interesting than any trick of dimple, glance, or elaborate preparation and high colour, was, like anything else worth having, the gradual distillation of the hard-lived generations gone before. How much of it came from the cultivators who had hung on to that low ridge between the marshes and the sea, as French and Norman, English, Burgundian and Spaniard swept over it, and how much from the Spanish blood of Alva's colonists who had held the old block-house-farm amid all the unfriendliness of climate, native inhabitants, and chance, none can now say.

Jerome Vanderlynden had a hook nose and beady brown eyes. Madeleine rather took after her mother, a Delplace of Bailleul, in her straight nose and fair complexion. But there it was, outwardly, obstinacy; inwardly – something more. It was that 'something more' that clouded her smooth forehead and flashed in her stabbing, side-to-side stare. She never even dreamed of envying the properly married women who had received official and private recognition of the trouble the War had brought them. Nor did she stop to pity the hundreds of thousands of women of irregular position, who had been abandoned on the outbreak of hostilities, without resources. Her feeling, if almost impersonal, was simple, direct. This War, this 'Bêtise', this great Stupidity had taken Georges from her. She would be even with it. She put away her duster and brush, wrapped herself in her fur, and locking up, descended the ride to the wicket without glancing at the scuttling rabbits, crossed two arable fields by their narrow grass borders, and so through the north pasture entered the house by the plank bridge and the scullery door. Hanging her fur in her room, she slipped on her long blue apron, went to the kitchen, and began doing the next thing.

\*

Nearly a week passed before the advance-party of a new battalion, consisting of an interpreter in the blue uniform of the French Mission and an English officer, rode into the courtyard. They were received by Madeleine, who gave them coffee and began to explain herself in English as usual, as to what she was disposed to do, and charge, and the rules she expected to be observed. The Englishman was the usual square, blond, sheepishly-grinning grown-up boy, who nodded and said 'All right' whenever there was a pause. The interpreter was a middle-aged commercial traveller for a colonial house, who talked glibly and respectfully, while under the table his foot pursued Madeleine's. The arrangements completed, Madeleine left the two, who had obviously lunched well in Hazebrouck or Cassel, to measure up and ticket the various rooms, barns, and stables, according to their requirements.

It was again her day for the Kruysabel, and she went to her room, slipping off her apron and her stained and mended dress, to tidy herself. Her room was a small cell-like apartment looking out across the moat to the north pasture. The distempered walls were marked with damp, but the tiled floor was clean and the places round the window where the plaster had come away were hidden by short curtains. Before this window, which was in a corner, stood a chest of drawers, bearing the cheap deal looking-glass and an old inlaid box containing the girl's few treasures. The remaining wallspace of the outside wall was filled by the great wooden bedstead, above the head of which was a little china bracket carrying the inevitable sprig of box-tree. The bed came so far down the little room that there was only place for a wooden chair between its foot and the door, on the other side of which stood a tall press, reaching to the ceiling, and a wooden washstand, surmounted by a shelf that held the relics of Madeleine's first communion under a glass bell, such as used to be seen in England encasing Dresden clocks. The washstand just allowed for the drawers to open.

Thus, as she did her hair before the glass in the window, Madeleine could see her door softly opened, to admit the interpreter, who had drawn off his boots and tiptoed in, his brown eyes gleaming greasily at the sight of her bare arms and neck, muttering: 'What luck!' The words died on shaking lips and the creased eyelids fluttered over downcast eyes, as she turned in cold fury: 'Get out of my bedroom!'

He hesitated, and catching the ewer of common white china she slung it forward with the force of muscles accustomed to tossing swedes to feed the mashing-machine. It broke on his forehead, cutting his eyebrow and deluging him with water. With a gasp he was gone.

She called to Berthe to bring a swab and broom. When the mess was cleared: 'That imbecile of an interpreter!' she said.

'It is a dirty type,' grunted the philosophic Berthe. Madeleine forgot the incident.

She recalled it, however, before the new battalion had been under the roof of the Spanish Farm many hours. They broke every rule, stole, destroyed, trespassed, and worst of all, left open the gate from the pasture to the 'plain' (the level range of arable), so that the cattle got out and had to be chased back. Madeleine, having expostulated with N.C.O.s and men, finally appealed to the Major, who sent for the Adjutant. The latter, not allowing for Madeleine's English, said bluntly that the interpreter had informed him that the people were Germans in disguise, and would be the better for a lesson.

Madeleine interposed with such energy and point that the officers promised, in order to get rid of her, to issue orders. Not believing in stones left unturned, Madeleine also wrote to the Chief of the French Mission at Cassel. Then an idea struck her. She looked in her account book, where under the heading 'Easthamptonshire Regiment' she had noted the name of the dark young officer who spoke French so well, Lieutenant Geoffrey Skene. She wrote to him as well, asking if he would come over and intercede with the troops.

\*

The day after, the battalion left, the Major giving her twenty francs for wood burnt, fowls and eggs. As there had been over twenty officers in the mess and nearly nine hundred men in the battalion, Madeleine added up the billeting and mess money and was content. She received an acknowledgement of her letter from the French Mission, but nothing else. Again peace and emptiness fell on the Spanish Farm.

Again, nearly a week elapsed, when Madeleine, stirring the midday soup, saw an officer ride into the courtyard. She called to her father, who was sorting haricots. He went out and returned with Lieutenant Skene.

Madeleine did not understand the English and it did not worry her. She had indeed required this young man to deal with a difficulty, but the need had passed. Still, he might be useful, and she invited him to stay to lunch, calling to Berthe to kill a fowl, while her father got up a bottle of Burgundy. She heard politely a long explanation as to the receipt of her letter, and the impossibility of replying sooner, owing to conditions prevailing in the trenches. She understood what was said, but paid little heed, not being interested. She had found this young man so far 'well brought up' and 'malin', 'sharp at money' in contest with her father. She now began to see that he was 'serviable', 'willing'. This thought, striking against her eternal preoccupation with Georges, kindled a spark.

It was when the young officer mentioned that he lay in the trenches next some French troops that the spark caught, flamed, became an idea. She showed nothing, of course, presiding with her usual competence at the long Flemish midday meal, which

LA PATRIE EST EN DANGER

she felt to be his due, after having got him to come so far on his useless errand. But as the four courses followed one another, and a carafe of beer gave place to more Burgundy, she was thinking. Her father went back to work, leaving the Lieutenant smoking over his coffee and glass of Lille gin.

She began to question him with infinite caution, trying to find out what his strange view of life might be. She made up her mind, after rallying him (as was rather the fashion) on his conquests of her sex in France, that he was very innocent, well brought up, sharp at money, willing, and now she added in her mind, 'rather a child', 'un peu enfant'. It did not displease her. On the contrary, it was all to the good. She rather expected the English to be like that. He did not take the subject up and feign interest in her, as a Frenchman would have done, but remained serious. She was therefore obliged to say right out what was in her mind. It was to ask him, next time he went up to the trenches, next to the French troops, to try and obtain news of Georges for her. She had heard that his regiment was in the northern sector. She formed no idea of the trenches, of the camps and resting places next to them. She simply said what she wanted. Once the words were out she had to use all her self-control. The sound of her request, the speaking aloud of what had been going round and round in her mind for so long, brought a rush of feeling such as she had not experienced since the first day of mobilization. She bit her lips to keep back tears and sobs. Then she was glad to hear the Lieutenant promising to do what he could. There was some difficulty about it, apparently, she was not curious to understand. She was glad she had asked the Englishman, realizing now how the thing sounded, and what a tale a Frenchman would have made of it. All she cared about now was for the young man to go – she was aching with the effort of restraint – and get her the news she wanted. She had no clear idea what. She pictured in a dim way Georges sending a message that he was all right, and making an appointment to meet her, in St Omer – Calais – where he liked. Further than that her imagination could not take her.

She thanked the young man cordially, and offered him more

gin. He refused, and went away, assuring her that he was at her service in this as in other matters. She forgot him before he was out of the yard, and fearing that she would cry – a thing she had not done since she was a tiny girl – she went to her room. But she did not cry. She sat on the wooden chair at the foot of the bed, her hands on the wooden rail, her face upon her hands. Nothing happened. She soon went back to her work, for her feelings were even worse in that little room of hers than in the big kitchen where she had so much to do. Gradually her heart ceased to thump, her eyes to smart. But she had taken the first active step towards getting Georges back – towards that recovery of anything taken from her, that was her deepest instinct. And she knew she would not stop at any first step – not she!

\*

It took more than a mere European war twenty miles off to interrupt the regular life of the Spanish Farm. Troops came and troops went, and Madeleine watched them, watched the payments made by the messes for extra accommodation and cooking, and the weekly payments through the Mairie for billeting and stabling, watched the storing of the crops, the thrashing, the milking, the feeding of the fowls. Every week she went to market, sold what she could, bought as little as possible, and sent her parcel, surreptitiously, from the post office. She neither heard nor saw anything of Georges. She neither heard nor saw anything of Lieutenant Skene. But, sure enough, on the first opportunity, she was obliged to try to get news of Georges.

It happened, as winter came on, that 'the château' had need of some things, eggs, and hare pâté – nowhere so good as at the Spanish Farm – and Madame la Baronne wanted some sewing done, rather special, better than any of her women could do. A message came via the Baron, who shouted from horseback, as he rode by, to Vanderlynden, at work in the plain. Old Vanderlynden handed it on to Madeleine, as he bent in an attitude half of prayer, half a crouching ape's, over the midday soup.

Madeleine nodded and told him to put in the horse – not that she could not have done it, but she must clean herself. Accordingly, half an hour later, there might have been seen issuing from the yard of the Spanish Farm, over the brick bridge, along the earth road that divided the manor pasture, out by the brick-pillared gate on to the road, surely the oldest, most repaired of high black gigs, drawn by an old white horse whose sonorous walk took it along at perhaps two miles an hour. Framed in the dark aperture of the hood, upright, expressionless, sat Madeleine, bareheaded, but in her best dress, holding the reins in a gloved hand, basket between her feet. Silent, expressionless, she may have been, but when she turned into the Lille–Calais road and met a string of English transport, limbers and wagons, it was noticeable that the Quartermaster-Sergeant, after glancing at her face, instead of shouting to her to get out of the way, turned in his saddle and shouted to the drivers, 'Right o' the road!'

She came to the village and crossed the empty Grand' Place, where the old houses stared unchanged over the notice-boards of the offices of the Head-quarters of an English Division, and the church, newly faced with red brick, showed the zeal of the pious Flemings. Turning sharply out of this, she mounted, at the snail pace of the old white horse, a steep street between little houses of people who had retired to live on about the equivalent of forty pounds English per annum (as people do in France). It ended in a great eighteenth-century iron grille, the entry to the château. The central gates stood open and she drove straight along a road deep between high banks covered with shrubs, which followed for some fifty yards the old line of the moat, until she came under the back part of the château where a broad terrace of gravel separated the basement offices from the kitchen garden. Leaving the old horse, with perfect confidence, looking down his nose into a laurel bush, Madeleine took her basket on her arm, and entered the great square kitchen.

One of the things that renders life so easy in France is the absence of change. Anywhere outside Paris, and often in it, change seems to have worn itself out, and to have ceased. In that remote corner of Flanders, Madeleine had no shyness, hesitation, or doubt, in entering the house of her father's landlord and her lover's mother. She would not have dreamed of entering by the front. No less would she have thought of leaving the house without seeing Madame la Baronne in person. She was not alone in this. The establishment was ruled by a lean, gaunt, grey-moustached person, discernible to be of the female sex only by her clothes, named Placide. Just as for Madeleine, so for Placide, life was an easy riddle. She knew her place to a hair's breadth, between God, and her master and her mistress, on the one hand, and the servants, tenants, tradespeople on the other. The great square block of a house, the main building of the older castle, whose wings had been thrown into its moat, whose forecourt had become flower gardens in the revolution of 1790, went on its way way under her iron rule, undisturbed by wars. The presence of a mess of English officers in the Baron's quarters, east of the main staircase, the absence of young Master Georges, of all the men-servants, and of some of the women who had gone to work on farms, did not throw Placide out of her stride. When Madeleine entered, she was standing with her back to the dresser with its shining pots and pans, telling a maid-servant her duties. The following conversation ensued:

'Good morning, Madeleine, how goes it?'

'Good morning, Placide, not too badly!'

'You have brought the things!'

'Here they are.'

'What will you have to take?'

'Nothing, thank you!'

'Come, a glass of beer, a cup of coffee!'

'Nothing, thank you all the same!'

'But you will say "Good day" to Madame!'

'Why yes, if Madame wishes it.'

This little formality, for both speakers had said just those words hundreds of times and knew them by heart, being over, Placide went to see if Madame were free to see Madeleine, and Madeleine sipped coffee as though she had not refused it, and gossiped with the girls.

She was then ushered through the paved and plastered back

## LA PATRIE EST EN DANGER

passage, smelling of all the game that had been carried through it, and of all the corks that had been drawn in it, to the front hall floored with black and white stone, on which stood heavy old furniture, a little of each period and a good deal of 1860 to 1870, between walls that were painted in landscape as a background to the plaster statues of classical deities and symbolic figures of the virtues, holding lamps. From this, the high double doors opened into the drawing-room or salon, where Madame sat since the use of Monsieur's apartments by English troops had forced her to relinquish her boudoir to serve as his bedroom.

Madame la Baronne d'Archeville had been married when the Empress Eugénie was the first lady of Europe, and taking marriage very seriously, had never tried to change since. Although she had neither the height nor carriage of her imperial example, she continued in 1915 doing her hair and wearing her clothes as she had begun, and the effect was all her own. Herself of high bourgeois blood, she had married when told to, without demur, the Baron, who, son of an army contractor and, so he said, great-grandson of an emigré of 1792, had re-purchased with money made out of républiques and empires, what those empires and républiques had taken from his ancestors, real or imaginary.

The room in which Madame sat looked like it. Originally the banqueting hall of the small feudal castle from which the château had grown, it ran from back to front of the modernized building, with two tall windows looking on to the kitchen garden behind, and two others, opposite, looking on to the flower garden in front, and over trees and village roofs into the rich undulations of the plain. The great beams that held the roof were visible, but below them the walls that had been panelled were papered cream and gold. Against this background hung two rows of pictures, the upper row smallish and very dark, displaying, as far as could be seen, grim old men in more or less armour, and stolid ladies in stuffs, laces and jewels hardly less resisting. The lower row was composed of portraits of whiskered men in uniforms of recent eras, and women, all in evening dresses of the nineteenth century, varied by landscapes, some good, some too good to be true, in pairs. Below the pictures were marble slabs on gilt brackets, tables shining with brass inlay. The floor space was occupied with curly armed, heavily stuffed chairs and settees. It was a room into which the Second Empire seemed to have burst in flood, washing up the drift of earlier ages, and to have ebbed, leaving a carpet shiny from use.

But to Madame la Baronne, and Madeleine, no such thoughts occurred. To Madame it was her salon. To Madeleine it was Madame's salon. To Madeleine, Madame said:

'Good day, Madeleine. All goes well at the farm?'

'Yes, Madame la Baronne. I hope that the health of Monsieur and Madame is good, and that there is good news of Monsieur Georges.'

She stood, square planted and upright, not quite so near the door as a servant, not quite so near Madame's chair as a visitor. She was perfectly conscious that on her left, in the curve of the grand piano, was a red, blue and white draped easel on which was a picture in oils of Georges, as a boy, in a white sailor suit, lips parted, eyes staring a little, evidently just going to say, 'I want so-and-so,' in his spoiled way. But she spoke his name without tremor, and heard the reply:

'Thank you, we are well; we have no news of my son, but that is good news, is it not?'

'Yes, Madame. I have brought the things.'

'Very well. Placide will pay you. Good day.'

'Good day, Madame la Baronne, and thank you.'

Backing with a curtsy to the door, she let herself out, took her money from Placide, received her basket with her cloths and terrine, jerked up the head of the old white horse, and drove back to the farm. She had got what she wanted – the assurance of no ill news of Georges.

\*

That evening, in the lamp-lit salon, after Madame had said, 'There is nothing more; good night, Placide,' there was silence only broken by the Baron puffing his cigar. He supported the war very badly. He was too old to serve and was prevented from fishing or shooting by English water-supply officers, who dammed up and filtered his waters, and by French Gendarmerie Commandants, who stopped his supplies of cartridges. At last he exploded:

'Nothing ever happens in this cursed war. You, what have you done to-day?'

Madame la Baronne replied, after a moment's silence that was partly protest at his manners and partly some tiny instinctive defensiveness, 'I have seen Madeleine Vanderlynden!'

'Ah, she brought the ham and the hare pâté!'

'Yes.' Madame was struggling with that tiny instinct – could not quite catch what it prompted – her feeling only materialized into the words:

'She has bold eyes!'

'It is a fine girl. Probably she knows it!' qualified the Baron, and mused.

Madame mused too. But the necessity, forced upon her early in married life with the Baron, of shutting one's eyes and ears to what men did and said about women, prevented her connecting Madeleine's composure with her own family. She could only fall back on her stock complaint.

'She will never be like her mother, that poor Sylvie!'

But irritation had supervened with the Baron: 'You're not obliged to receive the girl!'

'One has to do what one can for one's people. They wouldn't like it if one didn't say a word to them when they come with things.'

'Do what you like so long as I have hare pâté,' yawned the Baron. 'Ugh, this war, I do nothing but yawn and sleep!'

'I pray!' said Madame to herself, and rose to go to the little 'chapel' in the turn of the stairs to do so.

\*

Madeleine had no theory of the Irony of Fate. She had a merely hard experience of it, gained from watching crops and prices.

Reassured as to Georges' safety by what she had heard at the château, she took what comfort she could.

Three days after her visit, she was sewing and mending by the kitchen stove, using the light of the dying sunset to the last glimmer. There were no English troops in the farm on that day, and outside were the sounds of her father putting up the horses, on a background of damp late-autumn silence, and behind that, the muffled vibration of the eternal battle, that made the window-panes tremble ever so little.

Suddenly there came the sound of whistling – the last bars of the well-worn tune:

> 'Madelon – lon – lon
> Madelon donne-moi ton cœur!'

and shouted greetings. Then her father's slouching tread and a brisk military stride. Then her father's voice:

'Mad'leine, here is Victor Dequidt, home on leave!'

She got up, pushed the ever-ready coffee-pot over the heat of the fire, and greeted the guest. He was the son of a neighbouring farmer, and if she ever bothered her head about such things, Madeleine was perhaps conscious deep down in herself that he liked her more than a little. They had played together as children, grown to adolescence together, had experiences in common, wandering in the Kruysabel. But ever since her mother's death had forced her to early maturity, Madeleine had been very busy, then, with Georges, very busy and very happy, and since the War, very busy and preoccupied. Any memories of Victor hardly disturbed the surface of her mind. If he liked to follow her about with his blue eyes, and pay her small compliments, why, let him. Most men looked at her, so might he. She poured him out coffee, and some of the rum she had got from the quartermasters of various English units, and listened politely, but without interest, to his talk.

It was the usual talk of men on leave. All that he said was being said in English, French, German, Italian, during years, whenever men got home for a few brief days. It was about food, railways, jokes, old acquaintances – never about the cosmic murder in which they were engaged, or their daily decreasing belief that they might escape alive. In the middle of the commonplaces that she had heard from different lips a hundred times in that kitchen, Madeleine heard the words:

'It was a good job, that stretcher-bearing business at the hospital, miles from the line – good food – a bunk to sleep in at night, and who do you think was the last stretcher-case I carried?'

Silence. Old Vanderlynden was not good at guessing. Madeleine was bored. Victor went on:

'Why, the young Baron Georges!'

Silence again. Old Vanderlynden, who could hardly see to fill his pipe, said:

'It's as dark as a nigger's back in here!' and held a paper spill to the candle on the mantelshelf.

Madeleine cried with a stamp of her foot:

'Don't light up! don't light up!'

Her father obediently lit his pipe, knocked out the half-burnt spill against the fireplace and put it back.

Victor, disappointed at the way his anecdote was received, said gallantly:

'One sees you are a good housekeeper, and not one to burn good money!'

But Madeleine was just succeeding, by sheer will-power in swallowing – swallowing down It – the maniacal desire that had come rushing up from her heart into her head – the strong frenzy of a strong nature – bidding her catch up the great steel harl from the hearth and smash in the heads – not so much of her father and Victor, but of these two men – prototypes of all the other careless, mischievous, hopeless men, that had let Georges be hurt in their insane war. She swallowed, and the fury of that instant was gone, battened down, under control. She replied to Victor in a steady off-hand voice:

'Oh no, we have plenty of candles from the English. After all, you might as well light up, Father!'

As he did so, the old man asked:

'What had he the matter with him, the poor young baron?'

'He had become consumptive, owing to the life.'

As the candle took heart and shone, Madeleine's courage rose to meet the necessity for showing nothing and finding out everything which she deliberately courted. Sure of herself, she said gently:

'To which base-hospital did you say he was going?' She saw her mistake in a moment. She was not so completely mistress of herself as she had thought. No hospital had been mentioned. But there was nothing subtle about Victor. He was only too pleased to have interested her. He replied:

'The English hospital in tents at Naes' farm, there beside the St Omer line. Ours are full.'

His gossiping talk flickered on like the candle flame – dim and alone. Madeleine and her father said scarcely a word, the former deliberately, wanting to be alone, the latter lacking the habit of speech. As no interest was shown and no further refreshment offered, Victor eventually rose to go. They bade him good night at the door, locked up, and turned to their rooms, with their usual brief word of nightly affection. The old man was snoring directly. Madeleine lay for hours on her back, her eyes burning at the dim ceiling of her little room, her legs and feet straight and rigid, hands clasped on her thumping heart. Surely he was a lucky man for whom she planned and schemed and longed so in her short, hard-earned time of rest!

\*

The next day Jerome Vanderlynden and Madeleine set out in the dark early morning and reached Hazebrouck before most of the market had forgathered. This the old man understood and agreed to. One got one's own price by this means from people who were in a hurry. What he did not understand was why Madeleine had on her very best instead of her second best that she usually wore to market, without a hat. Incurious and incapable of challenging her decisions, he said nothing. The stuff sold well. By eight o'clock the basket and receptacles were almost empty. Then Madeleine said:

'We must go and see the young baron.'

'What do we want to go tra'passin' over there for?'

'Because Victor may be wrong. The Baron and Madame had not heard the other day.'

'That's their affair.'

'If it's true, they'll be glad enough to know.'

'It will cost something.'

'Leave the money to me.'

She had made up her mind and she was going. Independent as were few girls of her sort, she was too conventional to risk the journey alone. That would be to court scandal. So her father must come with her.

At the station they got into some difficulty about tickets. The line was almost entirely military. The grey-haired Commissioner was an acquaintance.

'What are you going to do there, you two?'

Madeleine pushed before her father.

'We are going to see a wounded relative in hospital!'

'Well, you can have privilege tickets. All you want is the certificate of the Mairie.'

Madeleine knew better than to argue on such a point. She drew the old man outside.

'Get down to the "Golden Key" and come back with the cart. Look sharp!'

'Why not drive all the way?'

'Twenty kilometres there and twenty back; we should not be home all night, and supposing an English regiment comes to the farm when I'm not there?'

One of the great advantages Madeleine possessed over her father was that she could think so much quicker. The old man had fetched the cart, Madeleine had done her shopping, and they were two kilometres on the road home before he had thought of the next objection:

'What are you going to say to Blanquart?'

Blanquart was the schoolmaster and secretary of the Mairie.

'That I want a certificate that we have relatives at the war.'

'But that won't get you a cheap ticket to visit the young baron in hospital?'

'You leave it to me.'

Obedient, the old man left it.

Blanquart was not at the Mairie, he was measuring fields for an 'expertise,' a professional assessment.

Leaving the cart on the road, Madeleine lifted her best skirt and stepped over the clods to him. He was busy and interested in his job, and didn't want to be dragged home to the Mairie. At her suggestion he wrote the certificate on the next fair page of the big square pocket-book he was covering with figures. He was not very curious about the matter. The Vanderlyndens were the best-known family in the parish. The loss of the two boys was no secret. He was asked every day for the endless certificates, questionnaires, lists and returns by which France is governed: 'You are going to join the Society of the Friends of the Prisoners of War, I suppose?'

Madeleine let him suppose, only murmuring that one did what one could in such times.

He wrote: 'I, Anastasius Amadeus Blanquart, Secretary of the Mairie of the Commune of Hondebecq, certify that Vanderlynden, Jerome, cultivator, has male relatives mobilized for military service,' and signed.

'Now you'll want the official stamp. Ask my little Cécile. She knows where it is.'

'Perfectly. And we thank you many times.'

'There is nothing. Always at your service.'

'Good day, Monsieur Blanquart.'

Sure enough, at the schoolhouse, also in all Flemish villages the office of the Mairie, little Cécile Blanquart was proud to affix the official stamp, with its 'République Française, Commune de Hondebecq' inscription in violet ink.

So back went the old gig, down the same road it had just come. In the distance rumbled the battle. Each side of the hedgeless road with its grassy stone pavé and 'dirt' paths, the rich heavy lands gleamed with moisture in their nakedness, in the pastures the last leaves of the elms fluttered down upon thick grass that soaked and soaked. Flanders, the real Flanders, the strip of black alluvial soil between the chalky downs of France and the gravelly or stony waste border where the Germanic peoples begin, was preparing herself for another fruitful year, as she had, time out of mind, in war and in peace, paying as little attention to this war as to any other of the long series she had seen. And across her breast, on that Route Nationale that a French Emperor had built with stone from Picardy, went old Vanderlynden, child of her soil, inheritor of her endless struggle, and Madeleine, the newer, more self-conscious, better-educated generation, perhaps even more typical of her country than her father, showing the endless adaptability of her mixed border race, absorbing the small steps of human progress, and emerging even more Flemish than before.

The old man, in his black suit and high-crowned, peaked Dutch cap, sat almost crouching on the seat of the gig, knees nearly as high as his chin, wrists on knees, dark eyes fixed on the road ahead, speaking from time to time to the old white horse, who paid no attention nor varied its wooden shamble. Madeleine, whose clothes were almost those of a modern girl of the towns, sat upright, hands folded in her lap, head erect, in face and figure just another of those strongly built, tranquil, slightly 'managing' Madonnas of the pictures of the old Flemish painters, if ever Madonna had so grim an immobility, such a slow-burning, unquenchable spark in the grey eye.

They reached the "Golden Key", put up the horse and gig, and walked to the station. There was a train in ten minutes. They each took a bowl of coffee and slice of bread, not at the station buffet where the tariff was aimed at the hurried traveller, but at the little café outside, where the small ill-paid world employed at a French station gets itself served for twenty centimes a time less than other people. Then Madeleine went with her certificate, her own and her father's identity cards, and her hand full of small notes, to the booking-office.

'Two third-class privilege tickets to Schaexen Halte, and return, to see a wounded relative!'

The booking-clerk took the papers and looked at them.

'This is no good,' he muttered through his decayed teeth.

Madeleine, with all the contempt of the comparatively free

and wealthy farmer's daughter for the small railway official, and all the cunning of one who deals with beasts and the law, held her peace.

The booking-office clerk was in that category of age and infirmity which alone in those days could exempt a man from mobilization. He worked fifteen hours a day in a pigsty of an office, whose glazed wicket made a perpetual draught. He was easily flustered.

'You asked for two privilege tickets to go and see a wounded relative in hospital.'

'That is what I said!'

'This certificate is incomplete!'

Madeleine said never a word, but leaned calmly on the ledge of the wicket, making herself look as stupid as she could, by letting her lower lip droop. Behind her a queue was forming. Already there were cries of: 'Come on!' 'The train goes in five minutes,' and a wag, 'They are making a film for the cinema!'

Tears of exasperation came into the little man's eyes and his hand began to tremble. He stamped his foot.

'Write the name of the relative you are going to visit.'

'I have no pen.'

Men were hammering on the partition and women were saying, 'Are we going to miss the train in addition to all our other miseries?'

The booking-office clerk flung his hairy crossed-nibbed pen at Madeleine. She took it, and wrote in the margin of Blanquart's certificate the name of her dead brother, carefully using the Flemish script, which the railway people, mainly pure French, could not read. The paper was seized; the cards of identity, the privilege tickets, the change were thrust into her hands. She moved away, counting her change and smiling a very little to herself, and giving just a glance each to the English military policeman and the French gendarme at the platform entrance, both amused spectators of the scene. Behind her, the booking-office clerk kept chewing over the words 'sacred peasants', 'swine's luck', and other expressions of feeling, as he jabbed the

LA PATRIE EST EN DANGER

date on tickets and served them in frenzied haste to the crowd that besieged his wicket.

On the wooden benches of the third-class compartment old Vanderlynden and Madeleine found many an acquaintance. There were cries of: 'How goes it, Madeleine?' 'Jerome, what are you jolly-well doing here, since when did you live St Omer way?'

\*

Madeleine, who had foreseen this contingency, nudged her father, and replied for both:

'We have a little business to attend to,' having made up her mind that no one would guess what it was. She was right. Thus she set running the right stream of vague gossip. For weeks after, the news ran through all the surrounding communes, and flowed back to Hondebecq, that she and her father had been to St Omer by train. It circulated from the inn of 'Lion of Flanders' to the restaurant 'The Three Crown-pieces', even descended to mere estaminets like the 'Return from the Congo' and the 'Brave Sapeur-Pompier'. No one could make it out. Victor Dequidt soon rejoined his regiment, and if he mentioned the young baron, no one except Madeleine was curious enough to ask which hospital he had gone to. Nor did anyone know of Madeleine's particular interest in him. At last, when the tale got to the café-restaurant 'de la Gare et de Commerce', one of the graziers or bullock merchants who used that more business quarter of the village was able to propound a theory. There was an English Forage Officer at St Omer, and he had his depot just exactly at Naes' farm, by the new sidings the English had had to make at Schaexen Halte for their hospital, so as to be out of the way of the bombing. No doubt old Vanderlynden had worked the trick all right with that officer (who was buying large quantities), and done well out of it. The certificate of having mobilized relatives that Blanquart had given in such a hurry (and which, of course, was known through Cécile and the other school-children), might be on account of Marcel Vanderlynden, or might be merely a blind. The original paper on which Madeleine had written her brother's name remained in the archives of the station until all were burnt in the bombardment of December 1917.

\*

Descending at Schaexen Halte, Madeleine and her father made their way to the block of white marquees and tents that almost filled the manor pasture of Naes' farm. In spite of the fresh air, the smell of anaesthetics and disinfectants hung over the duckboard paths and cindered drives, and mingled with the odour of cooking maconochie and the smoke of a giant incinerator that, never quenched, burned the daily load of discarded clothing and bandages, filthy with human refuse and trench mud. Near by, in the corner where Naes used to grow his maize, was a small neat cemetery of little mounds with inscribed wooden crosses, destined to grow with the years into a bigger area than the hospital and the sidings together, until lawyers had to argue out the compensation due to Naes for the expropriation. At this point luck deserted Madeleine, for no sooner had she and her father got into conversation with an orderly, than up rolled a convoy of a dozen ambulances, out ran all the available orderlies, and the whole place hummed like a railway station. There was no getting an answer to a question, and the pair were obliged to step into the nearest tent to avoid being run over. They found themselves, in the peculiar half light of such places, before a wooden table at which a sergeant was writing hurriedly. At Madeleine's question he called over his shoulder:

'What about these civilians, sir, are they allowed?'

A young doctor came in from somewhere behind, buckling on a belt. He spoke kindly in French, but was obviously preoccupied. There had been some French casualties in the hospital, he thought, but it had not been his tour of duty, and they had been passed on at once.

'Besides,' he added, 'all next-of-kin are informed if it is a serious case, and you will soon hear for certain.'

Aware of the truth of this, and of her false position, Madeleine did not press the matter. She knew the English were queer about such things. So were the French, but she understood their sort of queerness and sympathized with it, not the English sort.

The officer and sergeant went outside, and began examining, questioning, listing, sorting the long line of stretchers, each with its pale, patient face above dirty blankets, a line that grew faster than it could be dealt with. Madeleine drew her father outside and sent him off to the halte on the railway, to drink a glass of beer. She herself pried about among tent-pegs and ropes, canvas flaps and damp twilight. She managed to get into one big tent with iron beds in rows, and was going from one to the other when she was stopped by a girl of her own age, in the ugly grey and red uniform and beautiful white coif of English nurses. The girl said:

'Défendu!' She spoke with a queer accent.

Madeleine had a flash of inspiration:

'I am looking for my fiancé, a French soldier,' she said in English. The girl's eyes melted.

'I'm so sorry, there are no French here, all gone!' She called an orderly to 'show the lady out!'

Madeleine tried to question him, but all she got was: 'Straight down the cinder track you'll find the road!' and 'Now then, mum, get on, 'ow the 'ell am I to evacuate these bloody blessays with you in the gangway. 'Tisn't decent, besides!'

She made a detour and tried once more, but only once. She pushed her way into a tent behind some screens, and peeping over, saw a sergeant-major, followed by bearers with a stretcher covered by a Union Jack. They put it on the iron table, lifted the flag and began fetching water, unbinding and washing the helpless thing. She slipped away behind the screens unnoticed. She tried no more. She did not connect the dead body with Georges. She could not imagine him dead. But it was unlucky. Deep down some superstition was touched.

\*

She rejoined her father, and they caught a train that got back to Hazebrouck at four. Suddenly she wished to be alone, felt a necessity for a moment to gather herself for the next stroke, as it were. Her father had not said a word since the hospital, but she wanted him to go away. She sat in the salle d'attente and sent him for the horse and gig. She stared in front of her at the gathering shadows, between the sand-bagged windows. She heard the feet of the old horse, the rattle of the gig-wheels. Then suddenly her father appeared with Lieutenant Skene. She had not thought of him, but she thought fast enough now. Quickly, using the word 'fiancé' for Georges, she explained her plight. He was the same well-brought-up, handy, decorous young officer. In a moment he had broken into the Railway Transport Office, pushed aside the corporal, possessed himself of the telephone and was trying to get something definite from the hospital as to Georges's destination after leaving the place. He came back disappointed; they could not trace the name.

Meantime, the fighting half of her spirit had got its breath, and cutting short his apologies, she went rapidly on to the next thing. Could he get her a lift in a car or lorry to the English base to which alone, so he said, casualties passing through English clearing-stations would go? In a moment she saw her mistake, she had asked too much, had run across some inexplicable – to her, unreasonable, prejudice in the young officer's mind. She knew well enough that it was forbidden for civilians to travel in British vehicles, but had counted hastily on his position as an officer and her powers of persuasion. He began to use commonplaces, to inquire how she was getting on with the troops at the farm. Briefly, tartly, she replied she must be getting home, and rose to go. She did not bother about the look of concern on his face, but turning to say good-bye from the gig, as it got slowly in motion, she reflected that it was foolish to throw away possible friends and their help, and called to him, 'Come and see us soon.' He made a gesture and she accepted the fact that he was rather taken with her. He would be.

Driving home in the twilight, however, she had only one thought – rather one feeling. This war had dealt her a blow. She admitted that, on the day's doings, she was worsted. Was she going to give in? Not she! Silent beside her father, up the road between the silent fields, one process only was going on in her. A hardening, a storing-up of strength. Done? She was only just beginning!

\*

She had plenty of time for reflection as the winter wore on. Madame la Baronne did not send down to the farm for anything special enough to be made a pretext for a visit to the château. Moreover, though she longed to go and ask boldly what had happened to Georges. and was only prevented by a sure knowledge of his resentment if she exposed herself and him in that way, yet she was able to tell herself with confidence that if the very worst had happened, it would have got known – would have filtered out through the servants, through Masses announced in church, through mourning worn by the Baron and Madame. But there were no rumours, no horror-stricken whispers, no sign of black in Madame's dress or in what the Baron called his 'sports' (indicating clothes of material that meant to be Scotch tweed, colour meant to be khaki, cut meant to be that of an English gentleman out shooting – but which failed at all points, as Frenchmen's clothes so often do). So far, so good.

There existed in Madeleine, as in so many women of those days, the queerest contradiction. Fearing daily and desperately the very worst – death to their loved man – they never could believe in it happening, often even when it did actually happen, as was usual in those years. Relieved, respited at least from the major anxiety – for Georges must be in hospital or depot somewhere, and out of the fighting, Madeleine began to be a prey to a lesser – to know what had happened to him? which led her curiosity to explore the unknown at least once a day.

\*

Meanwhile, the war that had dealt her that private blow was gentle with her. The English kept on increasing. Seldom was the farm without its happy-go-lucky khaki crowd, whose slang, mixed with Indian words learned from old regular soldiers, and cheerful attempts at anglicized French phrases, Madeleine learned and used, as she learned the decorous politeness of the older officers, the shy good humour of the younger ones. Many a good sum did Blanquart pay her for billeting, many a neat bill did she receipt for anxious Mess Presidents. It was a queer education for a girl of her sort. At the convent school she had committed to memory certain facts about England and its people, not because they interested her, but because she soon discovered that it was easier to do lessons than to be punished for not doing them, and because her scheming mind knew by practice, if not by theory, that knowledge is power. And now she was having an object-lesson in very deed.

All the communes lying close to the line, whose population had been decimated by general mobilization, were being repeopled by English-speaking men and women, in billets and horselines, rest-camp and hospitals, aerodromes and manoeuvre grounds. Night after night she heard the winter darkness atremble with traffic on the road, and learned to know it as the sound of 'caterpillars' (which she took to be the name of some new kind of road engine, and was not wrong) bringing up guns and yet more guns. This was interesting, comforting, profitable, there were no dull hours, no sense of danger, and plenty of money to be made. But it had an indirect effect which Madeleine saw clearly enough, if she did not trace the connection very closely. The more ships were torpedoed by German submarines, the fewer ships there were. The more English there were, the more ships were wanted. Therefore the still fewer ships to import foodstuffs. Therefore appeals from deputies, maires, publicists, parliamentarians of all sorts, praising, cajoling, inciting the 'honest peasants' to grow more and more food. The greater waxed the importance of the question, the more the endless bargaining and speculating to which she and her father, instinctively prone, needed little encouragement.

Jerome Vanderlynden and all his sort – all backed up by wives and daughters, more or less like Madeleine – hung on to their produce for better and better prices. Subsidies had to be granted, taxes eased, bounties promised, facilities given. Then they would go on and grow some more – and then hang out again for greater and greater benefits. Beet, haricots, potatoes, wheat, barley, oats, all served their turn. Flax doubled in price, and doubled again. Hops were worth their weight in gold. Chicory had to be the object of special legislation. The farmers learned slowly, but surely. There was no brisk, open 'business as usual' propaganda – and no need for it. The dour old men, and quiet, careful women and girls, were not likely to miss the opportunity. The atmosphere was right. If death and disaster come tomorrow – 'gather ye rosebuds while ye may'. Gathering rosy thousand-franc notes is even better. And who would blame an old man with one son dead and one a prisoner, with his barn full of English soldiers who smoked pipes and set lighted candles among the straw as they wrote home, not to mention the ever-present possibility of shells – like all the farms Armentières way – or bombs – like all those towards St Omer.

\*

As a side issue, the social position of the peasant farmer began to improve. He had been accustomed to brief spells of flattery at election times – not to the wave of adulation that now engulfed him. He began to look the whole world in the face, and fear not any man. But many a man began, if not to fear him, at least to seek his good offices. Besides all the politicians, the contractors, the endless train of semi-public opportunists the War had created, the easy-going world of retired middle-aged people that are to be found in every French Department, suddenly discovered that the only way to remain easy-going was to get the farmer to befriend them. Everything from coals to chicken meal, from bread to cotton was being rationed. That facile plenty which is the basis of the French provincial middle class was threatened. Thus, as 1916 advanced, and the long sordid epic of Verdun began to string out its desperate incidents, the Baron Louis d'Archeville, walking round his shooting with the air of a child gazing at a birthday cake it has been forbidden to touch, bowler hat, 'sports', camp-stool, all complete, stumped over the pavement of the yard, and found Madeleine putting her week's washing through the portable wringer.

## THE SPANISH FARM

Having it in his mind to ask for wooden logs, eggs, ham, and anthracite, he naturally began:

'Ah, good day, Madeleine, pretty as ever!'

'Good day, Monsieur le Baron.'

'And this brave Jerome, he goes well? A glass of beer? I shall not say no!' He sat down on a wheelbarrow and waited for her to call her father.

Old Jerome came at Madeleine's cry of 'Papa, kom ben t'haus!' from picking over his seed potatoes.

Madeleine, who wanted the men out of the way, let it pass for politeness that she took the carafe of beer and two hastily washed glasses into the kitchen, swabbed the table and invited the Baron to place himself. She went back to her wringer, leaving the door into the scullery open. One never knew. She had kept her secret in her heart ever since her visit to the English hospital. She had no news, and had been able to think of no new way of getting even with the War, but she had forgotten nothing, forgiven nothing, renounced nothing.

Old Jerome, who, even a year before, would have stood in the Baron's presence until told to be seated, now sat down beside his landlord without apology.

The baron did not remark on this, but said: 'Then, you have your farm all full of English?'

'They do damage enormously.'

'Very likely, but you have the right to be paid!'

'They pay, but they do damage all the same.'

Old Jerome was not going to let go a possible advantage.

The Baron, whose feelings against the English had been cool from 1870 until Fashoda, then violent until the idea of the Entente and its meaning had filtered into his unreceptive mind, had just been reading propagandist literature, 'The English Effort', and so forth, designed for just such as he. Expanding with the new ideas he had received, he reviewed the situation at some length, dwelling on England's immense resources of material, untouched reserves of men, all that cheerful unknown which was so comforting in face of unpleasant known facts of the growing wastage of France.

Jerome added one remark born of the unaccustomed way money was now handed about. 'Besides, they are rich!' which led the Baron on again, along the path pointed out by yet another pamphlet he had been reading, on the subject of the new war loan.

Much of the verbiage and all the argument was lost on old Jerome. He was thinking of his sons and poured out another glass for himself and the Baron. 'It's a grievous business, this war,' he sighed. 'You must feel that as much as I.'

The Baron did not miss the allusion, blinked a moment, for what is one to say to a man who has two sons, one of whom is dead and for ever gone, and the other a prisoner, with uncertain prospects. He concluded that the most comforting thing was to talk of his own son. Besides, he preferred to.

'At last we have news of Georges. He has written to us, you will never divine from whence!'

He waited a moment, but old Jerome was not good at guessing. In the scullery the wringer was no longer creaking as it turned, and the splashing of water and the soft flop of the clothes into the tin pail had ceased.

'He has written from Monte Carlo. It seems that the army surgeons found he was making himself a bad chest, and sent him to the south for convalescence. He is being marked inapt for service, but he still wishes to do his part, and they will put him in this French Mission with the English Army as Officer-Interpreter. One day or another, we may see him here, if he is attached to a division that passes this way.'

In the scullery Madeleine was standing over the wringer, allowing herself to smile ever so little. Within her breast her blood was dancing to the tune 'I knew it, I knew it!' Now, that terribly serious Georges of the day of mobilization that she did not understand and for whom she could do nothing would be changed back to the gay Georges (Monte Carlo, she had heard him speak of it, could see and hear him doing so now) that she did understand, and who would want her. The Baron was talking of other things now, of how the French would take it easy, and how the English would come in and finish the War. It was quite their turn. One had made sufficient sacrifices. Could Jerome let him have – this, that, and the other? She paid little heed. Her father bargained a bit, then acquiesced. She thought it fitting, when the Baron rose to go, to come to the door of the kitchen and say:

'Au revoir, Monsieur le Baron.'

'Au revoir, Madeleine, remain young and pretty, it is all one asks of you!'

\*

She on her side asked little. She would get Georges back. She was sure now. The days might pass, nothing happen, no news come, but she was sure, sure as though he had written giving the date of his arrival.

Spring came – never more beautiful than in Flanders, where beauty can only exist on a basis of utility. It came shyly, a northern spring. The sodden greyness of the marshland winter on flat hedgeless fields gave way to cold and fitful sunshine that shone on rich young green everywhere, while the black dripping leaves of the elms in the dank pastures seemed blurred in vapour, that, upon examination, proved to be but a profusion of tiny light-coloured buds. And then something happened. It began happening so far away and so high up among the principalities and powers of this world that it was weeks before Madeleine felt its effects.

As the horrors of Verdun dragged on, the wastage that was obvious to so mediocre an observer as the Baron began to be acutely felt at the more sensitive Great Head-quarters. So much so that Great Head-quarters of France insisted to British Great Head-quarters that something must be done. British Great Head-quarters, well groomed, well mannered, had a long way then still to go before it should shake off its slightly patronizing attitude towards its ally. It merely said that something should be done when it was ready. Great Head-quarters of France, doubting when that time would come to a people who had to be so well groomed and well mannered, insisted still harder. British Great Head-quarters replied good-humouredly, 'Oh, very well then!' It became known that there was to be a British offensive in the Somme. Gigantic rearrangements were necessary, and among the million schemes, orders and moves, was the establishment of Corps Head-quarters at Hondebecq. This necessitated a lot of room, and the mere fighting troops had to be pushed farther out. Thus Madeleine, one fine morning early in March, only just saved herself from dropping a saucepan of boiling soup. An officer-interpreter, in the uniform of the French Mission, had ridden into the yard. She knew the uniform well, had seen many such a one, but since the Baron's last visit it meant to her only one person. Her emotion, kept well under, was gone in a flash. She saw directly, as the officer dismounted, it was not Georges. He came from the new Corps Head-quarters to say that no more infantry would be billeted at the farm. Instead, she would be expected to house the Corps Salvage Officer.

Madeleine knew little and cared less as to what this might mean, except as it affected the work of the farm. She waited, and in a few days an elderly gentleman appeared who had the tall angular figure, whiskers, and prominent teeth of French caricatures of English people of the nineteenth century. With him came a gig, a motor-car, three riding horses, servant, groom, chauffeur and sundry dogs. He surveyed the room offered him coolly enough, had some alterations made in the position of bed and washstand, but warmed in his manner at once when he discovered, in the course of a few hours, that Madeleine could speak really resourceful if slangy English, and understood about his cold bath. He had had such difficulty, he told her, and the French were so dirty. Madeleine smiled (for he had passed her estimate for accommodation and cooking without a murmur) and took him under her wing. There was something about him that she dimly associated with what her father might have been, in totally different circumstances – a mixture of helplessness and partiality to herself. She mended his bed-socks and filled his india-rubber hot-water bottle almost with affection. He on his side would often say words which she took for endearment, in what he conceived to be French – was less trouble than

THE SPANISH FARM

the ever-changing battalion messes, and paid, in the long run, nearly as much. She was glad to have the barns freed from everlasting fear of fire, and to get them empty before the summer. The space which the Salvage required she had Blanquart measure up, and charged at the rate laid down in the billeting regulations. It came to nearly as much as housing infantry.

\*

This old gentleman, by name Sir Montague Fryern, and his 'salvage dump' were merely concrete evidence which slowly revealed to Madeleine what was going on. The idea of 'salvage' had been imposed upon English fighting formations unwillingly, from somewhere high up and far off, some semi-political Olympus near Whitehall. Divisional and Corps Staffs knew better than to resist. They thought it silly and superfluous – the war was trouble enough, and already much too long and dangerous for the average regular soldier, without having to economize material as well. But, wise with eighteen months of such a war as they had never dreamed of, and hoped never to see again, they had found out that the way to deal with these mad ideas invented by people at home, was to acquiesce, and then to side-track them. So when pressed for the third time for reasons why they had not appointed a Salvage officer, the Corps Staff now functioning at Hondebecq looked at one another, and some one said jokingly, 'Let's make old Fryern do the job!'

The baronet had been almost a national joke. In 1914 dapper old gentlemen in London clubs had said:

'Heard about old Fryern?'

'No!'

'He's joined up as a private in the R.A.M.C.'

Some one said it was to avoid commanding a battalion, some that it was to escape scandal or a writ, others that it was merely 'just like old Fryern!' In the course of a year he had become notorious for prolonging officers' convalescence with illicit drink and the King, it was said, had insisted on his taking a commission. Too eccentric to be put in a responsible position, and insisting on not remaining in England, he had drifted about Divisional, and then Corps Head-quarters until this heaven-sent opportunity housed him in a suitable nook. A man of unexpected resource, no sooner had he understood what was required of him than he began to gather at the Spanish Farm the most miscellaneous collection of objects ever seen together since Rabelais compiled his immortal lists of omnium gatherum. A field-gun, a motor-car, other people's servants, several animals, French school books, Bosche pamphlets, sewing machines, ploughs and tinned food; nothing came amiss to him. What good he did, no one could say. Little of the stuff was reissued and served the purpose of economy, but when Dignitaries from British Great Head-quarters came down to see Corps Head-quarters and said to its old friends: 'I say, Charles, you were awfully slack about that Salvage Order, you know!' the old friends were able to answer:

'Well, we aren't now; you come and see old Fryern's dump after lunch – say about three!'

'What, old "Chops" Fryern?'

'No other, I assure you!' and so on.

*

It happened, only a week or so after Sir Montague's arrival at the farm, that a lorry stopped in the yard. There was nothing unusual in that. They did so at all hours of the day and most of the night. The English, so wits said, fought on rubber tyres. Old Jerome, leaning on his hoe, type of primitive man drudging with his primitive implement to wring a subsistence from inscrutable Nature, often stood to watch these powerful, docile servants of a younger age, that could do the work of ten men and four horses in half an hour. He was doing so now, and Madeleine, if she thought about it at all, thought like this: 'Poor old father, he's making old bones; it's the boys he misses,' when she saw Jerome drop his hoe and run to the lorry to help out a woman with a shawl over her head.

In another moment Madeleine had no doubt. It was her sister Marie from Laventie. In a moment she was out. The men on the lorry, with the queer, dumb, unexpected kindliness of the poorer Englishman, were handing down Emilienne, Marie's little girl, in a sort of frozen stupor of cold and fright. Madeleine ran to take the child, while her father helped Marie, who seemed dazed, into the house. Round the kitchen stove, quickly stoked until the top shone red, Madeleine plied them with the inevitable coffee, and presently with slabs of staunch farm bread.

Jerome stood by, the mere helpless male in the face of calamity. It was he who said first:

'What is it, my girl?'

At first Marie could only say, 'O, my God!' and rock herself. But presently, reviving under the influence of food and drink, and the still more potent surroundings of safety in that familiar, warm old kitchen, where she had grown up, began to tell of the daily increase in shelling and bombing. In her half-empty farmhouse, with the glass long gone from its shuttered windows, and the machine-gun bullets in its walls, relics of the first engagement with the Germans in 1914, she had billeted some English Engineers. The sector had been quiet ever since Neuve Chapelle, a year before. Suddenly, as the English sat with her around the fire, the shell had come. It had fallen in the doorway of the farm and had flung half the house upon the soldiers. Marie, protected by the solid brick chimney-piece, as soon as she got her breath, had scrambled under the debris to the room where Emilienne was crying to her. The door was jammed by a fallen beam. Some soldiers had run from a neighbouring billet, had broken in the door and got the child out. How they had all tramped up the road, shells ahead, shells behind, shells falling each side, with the sky red and the air rocking with the English artillery retaliation, she could not tell. At last, at a dump of some sort the Engineers had put her on a lorry that had taken her to Strazeele. Farther than that they could not go; it was the limit of their Corps area. Marie and Madeline had been educated by the past eighteen months, and knew better than to expect a lorry to go outside its Corps area. So Marie had had to walk, with the child in her arms, to Caestre, where she had found, thank God! plenty of lorries running back from railhead. On hearing her tale, an officer had allowed her to get into one that was going to Hondebecq, and she had easily persuaded the driver to go as far as Spanish Farm.

At this point there was a tap on the door, which was opened by a khaki-clad figure, with a sheepish face and unmistakable Cockney accent.

'Beg parding, mum, but 'ow's yer little gal?'

'Give them something to take, they had been so —' she used the untranslatable word 'gentil', for which 'decent' is perhaps the nearest equivalent. But Marie meant what the word perhaps originally meant – human as against inhuman, civilized as against barbarous.

Madeleine took out mugs of coffee and rum, and was rewarded by a cheerful, 'Thank ye, kindly, miss, and here's the very best!'

Madeline came back, stepping softly. Emilienne had sunk into a deep, heavy sleep, interrupted by twitching and muttering, in the chimney corner. Giving her a glance, Madeleine clasped her hands.

'O Marie, all your things! The brass bedstead, the beer glasses, the clock!'

Marie shook her head, tears ran down her face.

Above her, old Jerome, caring little for women's fallals, muttered: 'Thank God, the little one was spared!'

Like all other incidents of the War, there it was. Shells fell, something was destroyed. One went on as well as one could. That was the history of the past eighteen months, was to be the history of another two years and a half – just a perpetual narrow margin of human survival over all the disasters humanity could bring upon itself. Not that the Vanderlyndens took the large impersonal view. Marie and Emilienne slept most of that day. The next, they started in to work, in their varying capacities. The first thing Marie did was to spend a day, bribing lorry drivers and cajoling officers, to get back to Laventie and see what was left. The beetroot had been sold, the potatoes had gone with the horse and cart to Aunt Delobeau's near Bailleul, because for some time Marie had been unable to keep a man on the farm, and had worked it with such village women as had been stranded like herself by general mobilization, the Government being only too glad to leave them there, to cultivate almost under machine-gun fire, as long as they would. But since the fatal night, the gendarmerie had become nervous of the place, though the actual shelling had ceased. They would not allow her to sow the ground, and were moving the powers that watch over France to obtain an order of general evacuation of the commune, which they no longer desired to patrol. With difficulty she obtained permission to fetch away the seed and one or two agricultural implements. The dwelling-house had burnt out, for the split stove had flung its flaming coals on thatch and beams. She was spared the spectacle of inevitable looting by Allies, and on returning to the Spanish Farm, settled down into the position she had left, in 1910, to be married.

Outwardly, Madeleine acquiesced. Marie was the elder sister – eldest child, in fact – and had all the prestige of a married woman. She was also more purely peasant than Madeleine and easily jealous of her rights. Madeleine, since she had had Georges, had ceased to envy her sister. Now, losing Georges, she lost her secret comfort, and any satisfaction she may have drawn from being mistress of the house, brains of the farm. But Madeleine by long brooding on her secret fixed idea – Georges – had come to that point at which she accepted these outward superficial happenings, estimating their importance solely by the standard of that Fixed Idea. At first she was unable to see how the advent of Marie and Emilienne affected her reconquest of Georges.

\*

She was soon to learn.

Marie, for a few days preoccupied with herself, startled by what had happened, and rather grateful for home and shelter, soon emerged from that numbed state which, medically the result of concussion, is one of the first universal symptoms of shell-shock. She began to be masterful and critical of Madeleine's former management. She had run two messes for the Engineers in her small Lys valley house, with far less scope than the Spanish Farm afforded. Madeleine pointed out that she had done all that, and would have continued but for movements of troops over which she had no control. Marie agreed, sighing for the busy days when she had cooked and done for three officers, and scores of hungry men, just out or just going into the trenches, to whom Emilienne had sold chocolate, cigarettes, writing paper and candles to great advantage. Perhaps also she was jealous of Madeleine, of the younger girl's smarter looks, less peasant-like and matronly than her own, of her untouched good luck during the long anxiety of the war, for, like all the world, Marie knew nothing of the secret about Georges. But things kept happening. Presently the right thing happened.

Podevin, who kept the 'Lion of Flanders' inn, on the Grand' Place of Hondebecq, gave up. He had made money, of course, especially latterly since Corps Head-quarters had been in the village, and had enabled him to open a dining-room for officers. But, like so many, he had lost his only son at Verdun, and, heart-broken, cared no longer even to amass wealth. The long, biscuit-coloured house, with its two storeys and old steep-tiled roof was for sale. Marie saw the notice and told Madeleine at once:

'There's your chance!'

Madeleine took her habitual half-minute of reflection, trying this new idea against her Fixed Idea. They suited marvellously. Why had she not thought of it before? (The true answer was that she was not sufficiently imaginative.) She saw now that in taking the 'Lion of Flanders' she would be placing herself exactly where Georges must come if his division were moved this way, which was sure to happen sooner or later. And the whole thing was so natural that he would never be able to make her the one reproach she feared so much – of running after him and making their liaison obvious.

The two women went to see Podevin together, before they told old Jerome. Podevin could only say, 'I've lost my son – let me alone!'

They fetched in Blanquart, as was usual in such cases. The

grizzled schoolmaster arranged it. Madeleine pretended to be shocked at the price, standing in Blanquart's little parlour, with the sound of the school classes grinding out the morning lesson like some gigantic gramophone gone mad, just through the wall. But secretly she nudged Marie. The worst was over. The price was well within what she kept about her in the house in notes. She would not have to draw on the savings bank at Hazebrouck. That made all the difference in tackling her father. But when the two daughter broached the subject that evening, he acquiesced. It would be a good business, he said. Madeleine, who had never forgotten how he had, all unasked, fetched Lieutenant Skene to help her on the day of the visit to the hospital, wondered how much her father guessed of her secret. Something, surely. But it was just the sort of subject on which neither of them could speak to each other. So all she said was, 'You know, you're a good father!'

\*

The War, that had wounded her so deeply where she was most vulnerable, was kind to her in little things. No sooner was she installed in the 'Lion of Flanders', and had got together some three or four village women who had young families or other domestic ties that had made them anxious to get any work they could within a hundred yards of their doors, while forbidding them to go out for the day to the farms that needed them, than Corps Head-quarters arranged a Horse Show, a form of amusement that became very fashionable in the B.E.F. as the years went on. Officially, it was inaugurated to keep drivers and orderlies up to their work. Subconsciously it indulged that national failing, love of horses and open air, so curious in a town-bred nation. Madeleine, of course, paid no more heed to this than she did to any other of the curious foibles of these incomprehensible English, until she found that most of the officers of three divisions would be in the village nearly all day for this function, many of them ten miles from their own messes, and glad enough to find a decent meal. She laid her plans and purchased wisely and well. Then, only two days before the festival,

Sir Montague offered to take her to the show. She thought for half a minute, and accepted, almost jubilantly.

\*

She was feeling the long strain, however much she concealed it with silent composure. And, as with all women in her particular 'irregular' position, she had begun to hug the golden illusion that goes with it, and makes it for some so possible to bear. She had lost Georges; he was gone from her side, in spite of her, pulled away by something he held dearer. He had not come back, not written. She could not, dare not if she could, go or write to him. But she still believed, as all such women do, 'Oh, if I could only see him!' She still nourished that pathetic faith, still believed that if only she could stand face to face with him, things would be again as they had been. There was, however, that terrible danger haunting the attempt to get face to face with him. He might think or feel she was following him. That, she knew, would be fatal. In Sir Montague, therefore, she saw a heaven-sent angel. Too old, too cranky, too well known (as she had soon discovered) to be the object of scandal regarding her, he would take her under his wing and she would be at the Horse Show, to be seen. Georges, if he were there, would see her. That was the safest. Once he saw her she had perfect confidence in herself. She would know instinctively, would not look, not she. But she would will it, and he would have to come. She recognized clearly enough now, how simply, passively, unconsciously she had made their first hour alone together, when she had given herself, in the shelter of the Kruysabel. She had only to do it again. This also comforted her, for she was not original. She accepted Sir Montague's invitation graciously, and took care to look her best on the day.

\*

The day came, and she was ready. Radiant with health, wishing to be dressed in her own way, in a mixture of country primness and the English style she secretly admired (coat and skirt and all-weather hat), she had compromised at the skirt of her pigeon-grey saxony costume, a cream-coloured blouse that left her elbows and neck bare, with nothing on her head but her own crisp dark hair. Thus adorned, she esteemed herself as nearly a lady (i.e. a person who does not work) as she had any need to be, while not too far removed from the mistress of the 'Lion of Flanders'.

Before Sir Montague came to fetch her, as she was perfecting her arrangements at her restaurant, Lieutenant Skene appeared with a gunner officer she did not like, who was obviously joking about her. She greeted her friend kindly, in English, and ignored the other. She was flattered to see that the lieutenant was evidently taking her part, trying to make the other behave, looking very sheepish and funny as he clumsily concealed his obvious feeling for her. They reserved a table and went away. Sir Montague was punctual and she stepped up into the gig with the ease of one who has always had to use her limbs. She was elated. Men looked after her. The sun shone. In the queer gauche Flemish springtime, buds and shoots hung stiffly in the still air like heraldic emblems. A band was playing, people were moving about. Everything whipped her excitement. They drove on to Verbaere's big pasture, behind the mill, and put the gig with the other vehicles, all parked and stewarded as on an English racecourse. Sir Montague had a way of arching his elbow, twirling his whip, and fetching a great circle before he brought his conveyance to a standstill that caused, she noticed, much laughter, and the beginnings of a cheer.

He handed her into a rough enclosure, where English nurses in grey and red and white coifs, Canadian nurses in blue and scarlet, Australian sisters in grey-brown, fine big girls in their mannish hats, mixed with a sprinkling of the wives of local maires and notaries, small French officialdom and business circles. Some of these ignored Madeleine, perhaps did not know her, but the brewer's wife from the next village, invited by the A.S.C. colonel billeted on her, gave a cheery 'Good day, Madeleine,' that would have put anyone at ease. But Madeleine was already at her ease. She saw she was getting more attention than any other woman on the ground. She had dressed just right, awakened none of the submerged sensibilities of those queer

English. That and a glance at the lovely horses, shining, prancing, bobbing head and floating tail – for she loved fine animals – was all she cared to notice before she settled herself, eyes straight to the front, and put out all her feelers for the one purpose for which she had come. Poor Madeleine, no one had bothered to tell her that there were already over fifty English divisions in France, and among the men before her she stood one chance in seventeen of finding Georges. They passed about her, Easthamptons, Lincolns, Norfolks, A.S.C., R.A.M.C., R.A.F., gunners, Engineers, French Mission in blue and strawberry, wonderful staff people, in khaki and leather so perfect that it outshone all the bright colours of the French. She took it all in, tried to sort it out, mused over it, especially the name 'Lincoln', which, like all French people, she was incapable of pronouncing. She could form no idea of which group was the likeliest to be Georges', glanced over the face and figures of the French Mission officers. More than any close examination, her instinct told her, Georges was not there. A sort of numbness came over her, she felt it almost like a physical sensation. It seemed to be in her legs. She fought against it, would not give in to it. Then, all of a sudden, too suddenly for her strong, resolute, unimaginative nature, she did give in.

The corps officials had hardly begun judging the riding-horses when she slipped from her place, round behind the stand, out between the wagon-teams, waiting their turn, with cunning drivers of all arms surreptitiously dabbing metal and leather with handkerchiefs, looking stolidly over the exhibits they belonged to, speaking gently to them in low voices. She found a well-known gap in the hedge and got through into the back lane that ran towards Verbaere's mill. Up this, picking her way in the mud to save her best boots, she came into the village by the yard of the 'Lion of Flanders'. The numbness was gone from her legs. Instead, her pulse beat in her temples so loud that she hardly heard the band playing 'Watch your Step', and the cheering as the riding-horses, classed by the judges, filed round the ring, and out.

\*

She let herself into the 'Lion of Flanders' by the back door, which she shut with a clang. She looked magnificent and just a bit desperate, so that, of her waiting-women, one said to another, 'She's in fine fettle this morning, our young patronne!' But she was not the woman to do the more ordinary desperate things. No – yes. A stitch of her close-sewn self-control had parted. She was not going to stand it. Her mental attitude contained nothing of an English suffragette's logical, theoretical stand upon 'rights'. Her pride was hurt. Georges was Georges, dearer than life, but there now glimmered behind him something dearer than that – her dignity, what was due to her – Herself, of course, in reality.

She swept a glance round the neat, well-laid tables, sniffed the redolent preparation of the kitchen. She – dragged about behind a man's shadow that ever eluded her! Of course, her feeling was incoherent, ill-defined, just a sense of resentment against something she did not trouble to identify, but it was there. Reckless, she went down the stone steps into the cellar. Among the casks of weak beer and carefully 'lengthened' wine she had taken over from Podevin, was a bottle marked 'Chambertin', which she recognized as an oversight. It was good stuff. She had hidden it with the English Expeditionary Force canteen whisky and the rum she had got out of Sir Montague. Now her thought was, 'They shan't have it, those English!' She took it up, glanced at the coating of the bottle neck, and mounted the stairs with it.

'Berthe,' she cried – she had borrowed the girl from the farm for the day – 'four glasses and some bread!'

Putting on her black alpaca apron, she pulled the cork, holding the bottle steady with a firm wrist, and poured out. Raising her glass, she said to them: 'I give you that!' and drank amid a murmur of 'Thank you, Madeleine.' Outside the services of the Church, the only ceremonial she had ever been taught to observe was connected with good wine. The Chambertin lived up to her gesture, with its broad, almost coarse flavour, a legend among the frugal Flemish at their rare feasts. Outwardly, what she did was just a bit of unexpected generosity towards four employees who could do with a heartening for the twelve hours' hard work that lay ahead of them, from which she intended to draw handsome profit. Within her heart it was, unconsciously, perhaps, almost a sacramental act, the opening of a new life. The blood in her was beating out the time, 'I won't stand it any longer!'

*

The square-footed beakers, of the sort which would be called 'rummers' in England, were empty, the substantial finger-pieces munched and swallowed, before there came the sound of spurred boots on the cobbles and the clients began to arrive. First two Canadian majors with the Maire came to claim the table they had reserved, and found it kept for them, the coarse napkins starched, the heavy cutlery and glass in place, and Madeleine with her best smile and hardly a trace of accent asking: 'What would you like for lunch?' at which the Maire stared. Behind them trooped others. The room was soon full, the glass windows clouded with steam, the noise of conversation and table-ware deafening.

Imperturbable, Madeleine moved among it. The waiting may have been amateur. The cooking was thorough in the solid Flemish fashion. At least, no one was left staring at an empty plate or glass. Madeleine, a smile for every one, and a glib English explanation for every difficulty, used the mental arithmetic she had learnt at the market, in calculating bills. Her clients went off with heightened colour and laughing voices, amid trails of tobacco smoke. Manfully, Madeleine and her staff cleared the place, fed themselves and washed up. They had only got the tables reset before that extraordinary meal 'afternoon tea' was demanded of them. Madeleine was equal to the occasion. It might be a foolish custom, but it paid. And this merged into dinner, long and heavy as is the Flemish custom. Younger officers, and especially those down from the line, were getting boisterous, rude. She had to put up with many a clumsy joke, many a suggestion. She was too busy and too utterly unafraid to care. One thing did rather amuse her. At the table he had reserved for his party, the Lieutenant Skene was following her with his eyes and ears, and getting so cross at the treatment she was receiving. At length, just as it was all becoming too boisterous, and the younger officers were getting out of hand, suddenly, from the little private room that had been reserved for Brigadier-General Devlin and his friends, came the sound of a piano – the good piano she had got from the château. Not musical, and unwilling to spend time over such trifles, she was forced to stop and listen. It was Chopin, some one said. It had the most extraordinary effect. General Devlin and the officer who had been playing went away. The rest of the crowd in the big room went also, the rowdiness gone from them, subdued, seduced from their daily selves by the music. On Madeleine the effect was strongest. Wrought up by the events of the day and by sheer fatigue (she had been on her feet twelve hours), the lovely stuff, that could not act on her unreceptive spirit, antipathetic to it, merely saddened her. After another laborious wash up, she dismissed her helpers, locked the house and started for home. It was past midnight, and the day that had been so fine left a dark windy night, promising rain before morning. As she trod the pavé of the grand'route and the earth of the farm road, she felt miserable and beaten. It was easy enough to say, 'I won't stand it!' Like so many other people, she found it so difficult to do. How not to stand and what not to stand? Forget Georges? Could she? Would she if she could? Go and find him, and thus make him forget her? Which?

\*

The corps did not have a horse show every day, but the one just passed had been a good advertisement for the 'Lion of Flanders', and Madeleine began to do a quiet, regular business in luncheons and teas for the officers that incessantly circled round and about Corps Head-quarters. To be busy soothed her feeling of helplessness, and the necessity for this soothing kept her polite, skilful, attentive. Some weeks passed, and then again, far away, and high up, undreamed of by her, things began to happen.

The English offensive in the Somme, heralded as a great victory, had in reality made infinitesimal gains at the cost of enormous loss. The British Great Head-quarters, then still functioning in complete disunity with Great Head-quarters of France, and often in good-humoured disregard of the advice given it, went on butting, like an obstinate ram, at the same place. This, though it surprised the Germans more than the most subtle strategy would have done, cost the lives of many a thousand English soldiers. It was necessary to economize and economize again. The reserve corps would have to disappear, the line northward be more sparsely held. Here the long chain of action and reaction touched Madeleine.

For two days she was feverishly busy, officers wanting meals at all hours in great numbers. On the third morning, as she came down in the blaze of July seven-o'clock weather, she found a long string of lorries, grinding and jolting, behind them officers' servants with led horses, mess-carts, police. They went. A silence as of peace-time settled on the remote Flemish village, lost in the undulating fertile plateau between Dunkirk and Lille. Twenty kilometres eastward was the line, full of troops. Twenty kilometres west were the great manoeuvre areas where men learned to kill and not be killed more and more scientifically. At Hondebecq, nothing. It took nearly a week to convince Madeleine, who was not interested in the more general aspects of the War. She was not really convinced until the Baron walked into her empty dining-room.

'Good day, Madeleine, you have lost all your clients.'

Looking up from her knitting, she said gravely:

'It seems so!' But secretly she now believed it. If it were not true he would not have come. He disliked the crowd of junior officers who joked about his beard.

What was to be done? Not retain an empty restaurant where no one ever came. She saw enough at home in the evenings to know that Marie was firmly settled in, and didn't want her. The situation was beyond her. Her practical mind focused on the immediate was baffled. But things went on happening and once again the long arm of chance touched her.

It was about a fortnight after Hondebecq had been plunged in its unnatural silence. She was going home in the long July twilight. She no longer waited to serve late dinners, her only customers being occasional passing troops during the day. No local people used the 'Lion of Flanders', it was essentially an English restaurant. She was stopped at the level-crossing by the evening train from Calais going southward. As the smoke and noise faded away, she ran into Blanquart, the schoolmaster and communal secretary, stumbling over the platform-edging, wiping his eyes. The sight of that familiar figure in tears gave her pause.

'Why, Monsieur Blanquart, what is it?'

'It is my little Cécile!'

'What has she got, Cécile?'

Monsieur Blanquart blew his nose and said: 'I ought not to complain. She was a good girl. Naturally she has got a good job.'

'What job has she got? Where has she gone, then?'

'But to Amiens! You haven't seen the discourse of M. Paul Deschanel on the Recruitment of Women? It is hanging in the Mairie if that gives you any pleasure.'

Madeleine, grey-eyed, her mouth a straight line, her hands crossed over the little bag that contained the day's takings, stared at him between the eyes a full half-minute. Then she said:

'Ah, I sympathize with you. Good evening, Monsieur Blanquart.'

She went away thinking, and thought to some effect.

\*

First, a refugee Belgian family was installed in the derelict 'Lion of Flanders', where they all lived in the dining-room round the stove, boarded up the big windows, and got jobs in the village. Then Madeleine was seen in earnest consultation with Blanquart. Finally it was known that she had got a job in a Government office at Amiens, from which the men had just been combed out.

'Tiens!' said the gossips. 'Cécile Blanquart first, now Madeleine Vanderlynden. Who next?'

The formalities took a week. Then Madeleine emerged with

the papers of her appointment in her hands. She went first to the 'Lion of Flanders' and told the refugee family in no equivocal terms, how, when and where to pay their rent to Marie. Leaving them in a state of guttural exclamation, half gratefulness, half apprehension, she turned for a moment into the church, and stood by the high-backed prie-Dieu that bore the initials V.D. – Vanderlynden-Delplace – staring at the gimcrack ornaments of the altar, the eternal childish innocence of the Catholic Church decoration. Old Justine Schact was fidgeting about her verger's duties. Birds scuffled in the belfry as the chimes played their verse and a half of hymn tune that marked the quarter hour.

Madeleine's lips, set by habit to utter a prayer in those surroundings, formed something like this: 'Saint Madeleine, out of your divine pity, grant me that I may see him, then it will be all right!' Her lips ceased to move. In her unbowed head, her steady eyes took on the gleam of frosted marsh-pools. She squared her fine shoulders and clasped her large, capable hands on the chair-back. She might have been an allegory of indomitable Flanders. There was no mistaking the glance she bent on the altar. It said, 'Saint Madeleine, if you don't...' But the threat was never articulated. She turned and walked out, erect and sure-footed. At the farm she told her father what time to put the horse in, and when it came, appeared from her room, her canvas-covered wooden box locked and corded. She made her adieu thus shortly:

'Good-bye, Marie, what luck you came. I can go with a tranquil heart. Berthe will help you well. Good-bye, Berthe. Good-bye, Emilienne, I will send you a pretty postcard!' To the old house in which she and her father, and no one knows how many ancestors had been born, in which her mother had died, not a look. Either it was too familiar, or simply did not appeal to her. To the Kruysabel where she had known her brief hours of bliss – not a look. She was going to something better. Or perhaps, in her narrow personal way, she felt that these things were part of her, and that, so far as they existed, they went with her.

At the station, standing beside her box as the train came in, she turned with real affection to her father, probably the one being in the world she thoroughly understood and sympathized with. But she only said, 'Au revoir, Father,' and he only replied, 'Au revoir, my girl.' Then with a hoist of strong arms and legs, she was into the train, after which the old man stood a moment, staring. But she was already settling herself in her place, taking stock of her neighbours, girding herself for her new campaign.

# Part Two
## 'ON LES AURA'

*Part Two*

# 'On les aura'

Madeleine went to Amiens, but it hardly describes what happened to say that she went by herself without other companion than chance fellow-travellers, for, in her, there entered the capital of Northern France more than a single Flemish girl. She took up with her, all about her, an atmosphere of the frontier, of staunch Flanders, of the Spanish Farm. Countrified she might be, certainly a stranger, but there was nothing callow or helpless about her. She showed that maturity that connoisseurs of wine mean when they speak of 'body'. Generations, a whole race, living in one way, confronted century after century with much the same environments, had prepared that quality in her, which led no one to wonder at or pity her. Had there been any Society for the Protection of Young Girls at the station at Amiens, it would not have considered her a 'case', as she swung down on to the platform, produced her ticket and papers, and bargained with an old man with a barrow to take her box – a bargain she struck much to her advantage by shouldering the said box and starting to carry it herself.

The Amiens to which Madeleine went was the Amiens of mid-war – that is to say, a general manufacturing town of eighty thousand people, provincial, antiquated as such towns can be only in France – which town, plunged into European war, had seen the Germans march through its streets. It was now reserve railhead, camping-ground, last-civilized-spot for the avalanches of reinforcements the English were pouring into the line. Most of the French who fought beside them in that northern sector had to pass through it. Madeleine had not been able to calculate with any nicety how her move had increased her chances of meeting Georges, but she got as far as beginning to understand what the Baron had meant by the 'English effort', the immensity of that Volunteer Army, the constant watching and waiting that would be necessary to find Georges among the hundreds of French Mission officers that went with it. But like all vague steps, the one that she had taken was comforting because of its novelty, its unplumbed depths of possibility. Once cut adrift from home, and having suppressed a tiny shyness, rising in the throat, she flung herself into the new life with gusto. She was not wholly ignorant of towns, had been to Hazebrouck and St Omer, to Dunkirk even, once, and was ready as any country-grown girl to fall under the spell of town life and strive desperately to look as if she had always lived it.

\*

Her job was in one of those Government Departments, whose staff, depleted by general mobilization, and further by repeated 'combing-out', hardly sufficed to keep going that multiplicity of printed forms by which France is governed. She wrote a good hand, having acquired that art at a convent school where it, at least, was not reckoned among the subversive sciences. Perhaps she dimly saw in the power to write and read one of the advantages that such as she possessed over the less lucky. Handwriting, at any rate, was no difficulty. Figures she handled with respect, almost with appetite. As the first newness of the life thawed and broke before her, she began to prepare herself to take the lead in the office, as she had taken it at the farm. By the time August was turning into September, she almost smiled as she took her week's money. She would not have paid Berthe so much for doing such a job. Eight to twelve and two to six seemed to her a ridiculously light day. The heat of the town was sometimes oppressive, but the office, about the ill-kept state of which she grimaced to herself, was on the north side of one of those rococo barrack-like buildings that link the architecture of the chef-lieux of Northern France to that of Mediterreanean civilization. That is, it had the dank chill of a tomb. She survived. As for the life in general, her iron health stood it well. She missed the air and exercise, but her diet was not full enough to allow her to fatten. She had been welcomed, of course, by

Cécile Blanquart, and taken, not without a shade of kindly patronage, to lodge with the aunt who sheltered Cécile. The aunt was one of those widows of the small official class who seemed to have disappeared from England since Dickens. She was poorer, prouder, more impossibly ugly and mean than anything surviving to us. She would have housed Madeleine, had not each of her tiny rooms already contained two people at least. Clinging to any ha'pence that were to be had, she arranged that the new-comer should dine at the frugal common table she kept, and sleep a few streets away in the third-floor attic over the pork butcher's. Madeleine appeared to her what is called in France 'sérieuse'. To Madeleine, the arrangement appeared nothing short of heaven sent.

She had applied herself to her job. She had put out all her most feminine sensibilities to catch the right note in dress and looks, for she was nothing if not conventional. But in her heart she was simply passing the days and waiting her chance to find Georges. As she did her work, altered and supplemented her clothes, took little evening walks, or visited the cinema with the other girls, to all appearance just a strapping country cousin fitting herself into new surroundings, she was, all the time, vigilant, relentless. She drew the others down to the station on the pretext of buying a paper at the hour the troop trains passed or stopped. She preferred for her small needs the shops that fronted the well-known officers' restaurant, for Georges, she knew, would do himself well if he had the chance. As to what exactly she would say or do if she saw him she was not the girl to wonder. She had perfect faith in her illusion – just to see him face to face, anyhow, anywhere.

\*

Her companions with whom she worked, ate, and spent her evenings, did not annoy her. That is as much as she felt about them. Although only a year or so her juniors, there was nothing about them to excite her jealousy or even her respect. As she listened to them, making little muddles over their jobs, giving way to small passions and routine indispositions, chattering with affected solemnity or secrecy of their opinions, hopes, fears – above all of their love affairs – she almost smiled. She put more of herself into even the purchase of hairpins than they did into their liaisons. Not that she was more generous or less acquisitive than they, but simply because there was more of her. She had known real work, hard bargains, the utter depth of passion – things undreamed of in their little world of petty officialdom and shop-assistantship. Even the country girls like Cécile stood mentally where she, Madeleine, had not done since her mother died. Probably her principal minor preoccupation (as distinct from her one great secret preoccupation) was the size of her body. She was half a head taller and much more substantial than most of them. She knew she was dressing herself right, sombre colours, good material and cut, little or no ornament – but her hands and feet gave her some anxious moments, they seemed so big. She gave considerable attention to her hands, using every means she could hear of to whiten them, and manicuring them elaborately, bringing to the work much patience and sense and no imagination. For her feet, she simply bought the best she could afford, not attempting to pinch them, relying on her strong ankles, straight back and developed hips to keep her extremities in proportion. She was right. Men turned to look at her often enough and never with the superior, amused eye that she saw bent on her companions. She did not consciously care whether men looked or not, but there was just that comfort in it that she could tell that she was interpreting this strange new world rightly. Had she but known, she possessed two of the greatest advantages over most of the women in those surroundings – radiant health, that brightened her glance, polished her skin, burnished her hair – and, in spite of her quiet clothes and steady eyes, an air of independence of which she was probably unconscious, but which was far more attractive than the air of facile complicity with male patronage that many girls wore. Like all advantages, these carried with them their own inconvenience, as she soon discovered.

\*

Among Aunt Blanquart's lodgers were men, too weedy or too

## 'ON LES AURA'

well protected to have been mobilized. They functioned on the railway, or some other public service, she did not care what, with coloured brassards on their arms. She had paid no heed to them, secure in the fatal confidence of a strong nature, merely getting out of them anything they knew about the movements of troops, feigning the fatuous gossiping curiosity that was common enough. She was so immersed in her Fixed Idea that she was astonished when the more pimply of them slipped past Aunt Blanquart's semi-official vigilance, as she was going home to her room, and following her, proposed, 'Suppose we take a little walk, as the English say!'

Madeleine turned on him a freezing stare:

'What for?' she demanded, standing her ground.

The pimply-faced one faded back into the house, muttering excuses, only to confide in his friends later that Madeleine was a 'rosse', 'an awkward beast', as one should say.

Then again, when the skull-capped old gentleman who controlled her room went sick, the worried head of the department came across to Madeleine naturally with: 'Give out the work to the room, while this old Do-nothing is away, will you?'

She did the distribution of the endless schedules, minutes and circulars deftly enough, and corrected the errors with a firm hand. It took far less thought than most of her days at the farm. When the 'old Do-nothing' returned, skull-capped, pallid, smelling of lozenges, she met him with: 'I have done' so and so, and 'you will find this' there and that 'under the paper weight!' etc., going quietly back to her desk. At night he lingered, and was left alone with her, because she was never in such a hurry as the others to crowd downstairs, squabble in the lobby over the inadequate space allowed for dressing oneself for the walk home. She turned and stared as he asked her to dine with him.

An idea – one of her rare, slowly born ideas – had come to being in her head. In her seriousness she hardly noticed that he had taken it for granted that she would go with him. But she almost smiled when he began to detail his little plan. She, who had known not merely trials of cunning with Belgian horse dealers and hop merchants, but desperate evasion and deceit to meet Georges in the Kruysabel, agreed to pretend to Aunt

THE SPANISH FARM

Blanquart that she had a headache, and to meet this old man at the corner of the street. Fortunately it was dark at the hour named – dark with that war-time darkness of a town within the bombing area. She had a difficulty to recognize him in the crowd – and a great temptation to help his shuffling steps. She felt a sort of charity towards him, an inclination to take his arm and help him – a feeling which increased as she saw what careful plans he had laid. He did not take her to a restaurant, where the unequal couple they made would certainly have been the object of more or less concealed amusement, but to the back sitting-room of an old servant of his, who was now caretaker at a big shop. It was discreet, cosy. The cooking was good, the dinner ample, chosen from the more easily digested dishes. She was so touched by his evident enjoyment – though she had her own quiet confidence in her desirability – and by his desire to give her a good time – and things had been rather thin since mobilization – that the only tyranny she practised on him was to make him send out for a bottle of Burgundy; the pale sweet wines he offered seemed to her below the occasion.

There was no awkwardness during the meal, for she asked prudent, calculated questions – who really moved, housed and regulated the flow of troops – did he know the numbers or composition of the English divisions – all the small details most Frenchwomen – utterly innocent of spying – asked eternally out of sheer curiosity and interferingness. And when they had done eating she had to put up with the demonstrations that men make, who have either not had their fill in middle life, or who have come to regard it as a necessity not to be foregone. She had found that he did possess information and perhaps connections that might be useful to her Fixed Idea, and tolerated his attempts to solace his waning instincts, until, hearing the hour chime, she shook herself free, put herself tidy, and left him to find his way home – only, because he might be useful and sounded disappointed, she murmured, 'Another time,' at the door. Once in the street, she stepped briskly home, arrived at the door of her lodging about the usual hour of her return from Aunt Blanquart's and went up to bed. She was plotting and scheming

'ON LES AURA'

busily and had already forgotten her entertainer as though he had never existed.

*

Indeed, he might have saved himself that trouble. In that last week of September, just as she was beginning to feel no more strange as a government clerk in Amiens than she had felt as a farmer's daughter in Hondebecq, there spread through the minor French circles the news of a further English offensive. From what source it came and how it took shape no one will ever know, but the perpetual hungry curiosity of the sort of people among whom Madeleine now lived, was suddenly glutted with the news that there was to be an offensive, and that the Prince of Wales was taking part. This set flame to the French imagination, among whose republican embers a royalist spark has ever glowed.

To Madeleine, whose restricted imagination conjured up some long defile of troops through the cobbled streets, led by a fair-haired English boy, the news seemed of great promise. Georges was certain to be there. She saw him, accurately enough, in the blue and strawberry of the French Mission, riding in the cavalcade. She got a day off – her old man was 'complaisant', as the French say, and she found herself with a whole day on her hands, an equinoctial day of chill draughts and paling sunshine, of fluttering leaves and a stir in the blood.

She had tried to get some idea as to when and where the troops would pass, but all that she could gather was that the English police had been doubled. This only endorsed her preconceived notion of a parade through the town. She rose in good time and dressed herself carefully – in sombre colours, in coat and skirt, inclining rather to the English model, implacably neat, well-buttoned, without a spot of bright colour or a trace of expression on her face. She went out and down to the station, bought a paper, lingered about, tried to feel what was going on. The streets were crowded, and as she was seldom about at this hour she drew comfort from the fact. It was of course the usual crowd of the nearest town behind the line of an offensive, men

81

of all ranks going and coming on leave, base and line-of-communication people, young officers with a day off, grizzled officers' servants sent in from the innumerable camps for shopping. There were English, of north country and south country, London and Liverpool, Welsh, Scotch, Irish, Channel Isles. There were Canadians talking Yankee, Anglo-Indians, in wonderful blouses with mailed shoulder-straps, tall gaunt Australians, fresh-faced New Zealanders, swarthy or tanned English South Americans, South Africans and Naval details. More than once she was stared at, twice spoken to, once followed. If the Prince of Wales did pass down that street, it was in one of those fleet Vauxhall cars, with red-capped staff officers. There was no cheering, no procession, nothing of the crude, out-of-date spectacle that would have delighted and encouraged her. By one o'clock she was desperately hungry and tired, and burning with a sort of spiritual fever.

She did not give up, however. Partly faithful, partly merely obstinate, she stuck to her furtive prowling, keeping ever closer to the well-known Restaurant 'à la Paysanne Flamande'. She knew her Georges. A thousand accidents might take him into this or that street, by rail or car, on horseback or on foot, but, between noon and two o'clock, there was no possible error, Georges would be sitting before the best-laid table he could find, napkin tucked into his buttonhole, saying he had the hunger of a wolf, making caustic fun of the bill of fare, and standing no nonsense with the waiter. The celebrated restaurant, entirely a creation of the War, before which it had led a struggling existence dependent on a billiard-table and a mixed clientèle, presented a glass swing-door between two large plate-glass windows, protected by round iron tables and chairs set among desolate shrubs in boxes. The door opened into a little-used café-lounge; the eating-room had replaced the billiard-table on the raised portion of the floor up four steps at the back. Thus the public in the street could see the legs and half the bodies of the diners, but not their faces. Outside, a great sign-board, swung English-fashion on a bracket, depicted an alleged Flemish peasant-woman, in national costume, with international

'ON LES AURA'

features, and the immemorial vulgarity of such efforts. Madeleine never even guessed that the square of brilliant paint was an allegorical representation of herself, and would have been much astonished to have been told so.

Two o'clock struck, and half past, and suddenly she had a physical qualm. What was it? She realized she was faint with hunger. Together with the bodily emptiness and dizziness, there rose in her a bitter wave of disgust and disillusionment. For the second time she set her teeth. She would not stand it. Careless of the fact that she was doing what was only done by women of a sort she despised, because she considered they were driving a dangerously, badly paid trade, she pushed open the door, walked steadily into the café, and sat down just as the tables were beginning to go round. It was partly want of food, as she told herself, but partly, if she had admitted it, the moisture of desperate vexation in her eyes. She ordered a café crême off an unwilling waiter, who did not want French people there, in such a way that he brought it, at once, and properly done. The scalding sips soon revived her. She began to think, if thinking it can be called. Rather she just sat and felt. She felt the French equivalents of 'I'm fed up with this' – 'I'm going to put an end to it' – whatever It exactly was. Then less articulately she just felt sore. It was not in her to feel passively sore, but how to express her feeling by activity she could not see, at the moment.

\*

The souls of women come, perhaps rather more often than those of men, to steep places down which the least touch will cause them to hurl themselves. Madeleine had been hanging on some such edge ever since the day of the Horse Show. It needed but the stroke of a feather to send her over.

Her trance was broken by the sound of field-boots on the steps that led down from the dining-room. Two officers were passing to the door, middle-aged junior officers of infantry or artillery, with cleaned-up, discoloured uniforms, and faces and voices of those who had been 'through it', and had a good deal more to go through before they would have done with 'it' – 'it' being the War. Madeleine had seen hundreds such, going up to the line, coming down from the line, sitting round her father's table, taking charge of parties of men, with shy resolution. Little given to guessing, she could have told almost of what they were talking – of what they had done on leave, what sort of 'show' they were going to be involved in, possibly of the very inn of the 'Lion of Flanders' where they might have snatched a comfortable meal in the intervals of sleeping in their clothes and eating out of their hands. They passed beside her and she smiled involuntarily. Her long vigil had not been in vain. All the English divisions were bound to pass into the Somme offensive sooner or later, and there was nothing wonderful in her meeting two officers whom she had seen before. Nor was it because she was feeling the home-sickness or the loneliness of the acutely sensitive. But just because the starvation of her Fixed Idea had wrought her up to a point culminating at that moment, she smiled.

The shorter, fairer of the two, whose mere name she remembered (for she had that sort of memory, very useful for checking billeting returns), recognized her and spoke to his companion. The other turned. It was Lieutenant Skene, whom she had not seen, or indeed thought of, since the Horse Show. He turned, and their glances met. She saw in a moment that it mattered intensely to both of them what she did, how or why she could not see, but she knew that it mattered. She kept perfectly still, her face moulded in a smile. The door clicked. They were alone. Skene sat before her. What had she done? Nothing. By doing nothing she had placed him there.

He began questioning her: what was she doing in Amiens? and she replied briefly, not thinking of the words. She pushed aside her cup and rested one elbow on the table, her chin in her hand. She stared into his eyes, grey-brown, dilated by shell-fire, and reddened at the rims by gas, but full of feeling which she recognized at a glance as genuine. That feeling was concern for her welfare. She did not admit to herself, still less to him, that there was anything to be concerned about. But it warmed her in the depths of her heart, just as the liqueur he had ordered for her (with sweet cakes, and the way in which he did it showed his solicitude) warmed her stomach. It was true he was talking about himself. She knew in a moment that this was not egotism but English shyness. She answered him in a dream, rocking her body ever so slightly on her chair, as if she were nursing something. Indeed, she was – nursing some part of her spirit, bruised just as violently as her knees had been when the old horse fell down and threw her on to the pavé of the Lille road – for she had just been thrown out of her closed self-control, that hid unwelcome Truth even from herself, on to the bare realization of the long fast of two years, the sharp starvation of two months.

Now he was talking about *her*, with the polite candour which had made her say, the first time she saw him, that he was 'well brought up' and 'willing'. More, he was inquiring about Georges. She was not surprised; that was all part of it. She heard herself, as another person, replying coolly: 'He is dead!' and when pressed further: 'He is dead for me.' She could have laughed aloud at the same time, not for joy, but from the steady mounting beat of her own heart. His concern was trebled. Her heart beat faster, not feverishly, steadily. She had thought of her trouble: 'I'll put an end to this!' She was putting an end to it!

Then he actually touched her, and made sympathetic remarks. He was advising her not to frequent officers' restaurants, and she replied she did not care. It was true. She cared for nothing at the moment, had never felt more light-hearted. He asked what she was going to do next. She wanted to laugh more than ever as she said, 'Nothing!' He proposed a cinema. She assented delightedly, feeling as though she would have proposed it herself in a moment, it was so inevitable. She made a quick calculation. Cécile Blanquart and the other girls were at the office. Aunt Blanquart and the pork butcher's wife, at whose house she lodged, would not be shopping in the main streets, rendered expensive by English custom. It was safe enough.

Out in the street she stepped beside him with a pride which, she suddenly realized, she had never known. There are inconveniences about clandestine liaisons. She almost enjoyed the publicity. Fortified by coffee, cakes and brandy, as tall as he was to an inch or so, she seemed to float along on the wings of new-found comfort, effortless, smiling.

The cinema was full. He was nonplussed, she could see, did not know what to do next – knew what he wanted (as she did, and hugged herself), but, being English, had a difficulty in saying it. He wanted her. That was natural enough. She knew herself to be desirable. It amused her to hear him proposing to see her home to her 'Aunt's' – for thus she had described her lodging. She let him. It seemed now she had only to go on letting him, and the riddle of life was solved. She had not known an hour before that there was a riddle. Now she only knew she was approaching a solution.

They arrived in the narrow by-street near the cathedral as the clocks chimed four. At that hour the place was deserted. Their footsteps echoed, they might have been treading a world of their own. Madeleine felt it, but noticed that he was feeling something stronger. He had almost shed his English reserve – was talking volubly, about himself – how he had been twice in hospital, and must now go back to the fighting – how men like himself wanted a little comfort before they died. He spoke in English, but she understood most of the words and all the drift. His feelings coincided with hers and saved her the trouble of expressing them, to which she was unused and averse. At the door of her lodging they both stopped, she with her key in the lock, he looking at her with eyes that he immediately averted, and which pivoted round, in spite of him, to her. As she turned the key and opened the door, she said, with the feeling of turning something in her heart and opening it: 'Here we are!' Inevitably, as if she had taught him the words, he was saying: 'Don't send me away, let me stay!' and with a great sigh of happiness such as she had felt once before in her life – another life, surely – she retreated into the dark entry before him with: 'Well then, my poor friend!'

\*

When Madeleine next had attention to spare for such matters, the chimes were telling six o'clock, and through the glass of the

## 'ON LES AURA'

skylight-window a little star twinkled. She became conscious that he was slowly awakening from the stupor in which they had plunged each other, and was lying, open-eyed, waiting for her to move (just like him). Her mind sprang at once to the practical:

'What time is your train?'

'Gone this half-hour!'

She sat up in alarm: 'You will have trouble!'

'They can't tell to a few hours when I left camp!'

Reassured, she passed on to the next thing.

'You are hungry!'

'Yes!'

She was fully alive to the situation. The pork butcher's wife downstairs had opened, like every one in Amiens who could manage it, an eating-room. The particular public for which it catered were English and French N.C.O.s of garrison formations, not a field for high profit, but respectable and regular. There was a back room. It was better than courting trouble by going outside. She explained this to Skene as she sat up, shivered slightly at the contact of the air, lit the candle, and tidied herself. She was not ill at ease before him. Thorough in everything, when she gave she knew no stint. She did not boggle over the irregularity of their situation, any more than over her semi-nudity. Why should she? She had perfect confidence in what she had done, just as in her things, which were clean and good in quality, and in her body, which was firm and fresh with health. Of course, out in the street the conventions constrained one to dissemble, to conceal what one did, and only to show as much of one's skin as fashion allowed for the moment. But with Skene she was as frank as she had been with herself, poured him out clean water, and explained that with a small gratuity and a generous order, Madame would make no scruple of their having the best time they could. There were the French police to bribe, possibly, and worse still, the English, but it could be managed.

She was proud of Skene when they interviewed Madame. He spoke French with some fluency, and knew just how to flatter the old lady's sensibility and appeal to her greed. When they sat opposite each other in the little back room, he turned on her eyes still bemused, and looked at his watch with frank pleasure: 'No train till six-thirty. Still nearly twelve hours!' he said. Under the table she rubbed his ankle with her slippered foot. Their little dinner ended, as, alas! all dinners must. The pork butcher's wife, overpaid and adroitly flattered, rallied them, almost blessed them, as, his arm round her waist, her arm round his neck, they mounted slowly the dark, narrow stairs.

Hardly a breath of disillusionment spoiled their few hours together. He took what life could give him – life that was likely to end for him so soon and so abruptly. She, woman-like, put into it something almost sacramental, as though she were devoting to flames some cherished possession, and devoting it willingly. There was nothing Skene could have asked her for that she would not have given him, from money to her heart's blood. He asked simply to be loved – comforted, more exactly, in his starved, war-worn body. That was easy. She gloried in it, even went so far outside her usual self as to point out the bare cleanliness and order of her little room. That was just about the length of her knowledge of English character. A clean room would appeal to him. She never even stopped to wonder that she should be so anxious to please this chance acquaintance – this man of different race, religion, and language. She had never read a novel and was innocent of the romantic theories of love at first sight. She acted as she did from one of her slow-moving, undemonstrative impulses – just then so strong that it amounted to a feeling of almost physical well-being in her limbs – traceable, possibly, if she had been the sort to theorize about origins of feeling, to starved maternal instinct. She missed something – petulance, perversity – the whims of a spoiled child that she would have loved to gratify, as she had, long before, in the secrecy of the hut in the Kruysabel. But she did not miss her spoiled child much, for she had instead this good child – this man of quiet good manners, whose behaviour she had noted the first time she saw him, and who now accepted her suggestions without a murmur. So she invited him gently to see how she had moved the few articles of furniture, scrubbed the floor, cleaned the skylight, pasted paper on the damp-stained walls, hung her few dresses on hooks beneath a curtain, and put a rose-coloured paper shade round her candle. She was gratified to see how pleased he was, little suspecting that she had laid her finger on the very deepest desire in him. He had told her that he was no soldier, but a member of a profession that he had practised for twenty years before volunteering in August, 1914. Yet she was very far from forming any conception of the decent orderliness of the life he had left, the life of an assistant diocesan architect in a provincial English town, with its rooted habit of cleanly comfort and moderate happiness, that the war had hurt so horribly; and she never guessed what dim echoes her own Flemish domestic virtues aroused, of all he had ever felt to be the necessities of existence.

She was even farther away from him when his self-consciousness, awakening with the small hours, drew him to think of the future – of his and of hers. Like many another man in those years, his courage ebbed at the false dawn, and he questioned Fate aloud as to whether he would see another – whether he would ever again know the comfort of her. The simple cunning of her kind led her to propose arrangements to meet him again. This in turn led to the question of where she was to be found. This drew from him anxious questions, that flattered her immensely by the importance he attached to her welfare, but brought back unpleasantly into prominence that other whom she was trying so hard, so unconsciously, to forget. She burst out with a few fierce words, stamping and stamping on that dead image of love to make it disappear from view. It was when she did this, brutally dismissing from memory that spoiled child of her affections, that her new, good, well-behaved child gave her the first taste of his imperfections. He was solicitous, punctilious to a degree, questioned if he ought to take what was Georges'. She would have been angry with him in another moment had not a stronger, surer, more positive instinct prevailed. They had such a little time, might never have another. She wound her bare arms round his head and stifled his questions and doubts against the present reality of her tangible self. And surely she was right. In all those years of loss and waste it occurred to her naturally to build and replace what she could, and all the love and care she could not give to the children she might not bear, she gave to this grown-up child, who needed it, and took it willingly enough, once he ceased to think.

\*

In the grey dawn she was up and about, making coffee, heating water for him to shave, helping clean his endless buckles and straps. She let him out in good time for his train, and sweetened her kiss with the eternal hopefulness of that 'à bientôt', 'until soon', that is the happiest thing in French farewells. Then slowly, carefully she made herself ready for the day at the office, proud of the dark touches under her eyes, of the mat-pallor of her skin, of the little smiles that curled the corners of her mouth. And many a man, seeing her, wished he had been the source of the deep secret satisfaction she seemed to give herself that day.

All that week she retained the feeling of having done a good action – or, as she would have expressed it, had she expressed it at all – driven a good bargain with Fate. At the end of the week 'Papa', as the girls in the office called the head of the room, waited for her and asked her to spend the Sunday afternoon with him. It was his birthday, and he and she would celebrate it with a little Festivity. She did not look at him for fear she should laugh, for, taller than he by inches, she caught the sparkle of the electric light reflected on the top of his bald head. She asked, with averted face, 'Will there be many invitations?'

'But no – you and I alone, naturally!'

She shook her head slowly from side to side as she hooked her fur under her chin and surveyed herself in the little glass that hung on the door of the girls' lobby.

'But you promised last time that there should be other times – ' His voice had risen, his eyes darkened. It was wonderful what malignity could still reside in a little old man. Something stronger still inhabited Madeleine, since those few hours she had spent with Skene. Once again the blood in her veins had run like molten honey, and she, no spendthrift of herself, had felt in every limb as she gave herself up utterly: 'This is right – right – right!'

She was in no mood for senile trifling, and turned on him with the arrogance of youth, blazing, magnificent: 'And now I promise you there will not!' and left him, breathless and a little afraid.

\*

Another week passed. Madeleine became uneasy. The strongest emotional impression will not last. The time she had had with Skene began to fade into the background. It had been such a minute. It had no result. Instead of feeling perversely resentful against Georges, she now felt so against both of them. Skene neither wrote nor made any sign. He did not even give her the dubious satisfaction of obliterating the shame she felt at Georges' neglect. All this lay, a dumb ache, in her uncritical soul. But she had more immediate cause for annoyance. She became conscious that she was being looked at, whispered about. It did nothing more than ruffle the surface of her self-confidence, but when she and Cécile Blanquart went to the cinema together – she hardly noticed a half-unwillingness on Cécile's part, and that the other girls who often accompanied them had made excuses – she was brought face to face with the matter. Cécile said shyly, in the melodious darkness of the one-franc seats, where one had to keep one's hands in one's lap, because so many soldiers were lonely:

'You know what they are saying about you at the office?'

'No – what?'

'Oh – I daren't tell you!'

Madeleine did not press her. There is only one thing said by girls who cannot mind their own business – having, indeed, no business to mind. Madeleine had never spread nor listened with interest to rumours about other girls, simply because she minded her own business, having always had business to mind. But she knew well enough what the village gossip of Hondebecq was, and had found out that an office in a provincial town is only a village without elbow-room. She pondered a little over the matter, which grew increasingly serious as she did so. She did not bother greatly as to the source of any rumour about her. Spite on the part of 'Papa', love of scandal in the heart of the pork butcher's wife of her lodging – mere empty interest on the part of some person or persons who had seen her with Skene or with 'Papa', it might be! The point that disturbed her was the possible effect on her freedom of action. It might make it more difficult for her to profit by the next opportunity of seeing Skene–Georges – for the two were slowly merging into one at the back of her mind. This roused her. She began to think seriously, but in her slow way.

\*

Then came a letter from home – from Marie.

She read it several times, by candle-light, lying on her back in her narrow iron bed, one hand holding the pages of British Expeditionary Force canteen block note-paper, which Marie used because it cost nothing, covered with Marie's sloping convent-school writing – the other hand below her head, on which a handkerchief protected the long plaits of her hair, that she had never bobbed at the command of fashion. Gradually she mastered it. Marie was no correspondent; none of the sort that she belonged to, cultivated letter-writing or exceeded what was strictly necessary. The motive of the letter was baldly stated: 'Father demands to know how goes his daughter.' There followed a brief résumé of village news. Victor Dequidt was reported missing. Other persons had been married. There had been more bombing near St Omer. There was no news of brother Marcel; they feared the worst. Then followed the words: 'Father has seen Monsieur le Baron lately. He was furious. It seems that his son Georges has left the French Mission, where he was in safety, and has gone to make his training for an aviator in Paris. Madame is desolated'; and then commonplaces to the end. 'His son Georges' was a way of speaking Marie had picked up from living in the Lys valley, in the influence of Lille. It was not how they spoke in Hondebecq. This displeased Madeleine an instant. Then the real meaning of the letter dawned on her. Her father had shown by his conduct on the day of their visit to the hospital how thoroughly he understood what was between Georges and herself. He had made Marie write – Marie who knew and suspected nothing. Madeleine – the youngest, the one who had lived longest with him, who had replaced her mother in the house – responded to the old man's partiality for her. Unspoken, never visible, there was a stronger link between them than existed with the others of the family. She thought of him with affection. Her mind moved on. She could see the Baron, stumping up and down the earth roads, with 'Merde!' and 'Name of a name!' at every step; and the dining-room at the château, into which she had been allowed to peep, when running errands from the farm. She could hear Placide's nasal chant announcing dinner: 'Madame la Baronne is served!' and the Baron, still 'Merde'-ing and 'Name of a name'-ing, and the Baronne's tearful but dignified 'Voyons, Charles!' Paris, Georges was in Paris! Although affectionate in her way, she hardly paused to think of her brother Marcel, giving no sign from his German prison.

*

Then she had one of her intuitions. The very thing. She would teach the gossips of Amiens to tell tales about her – and give them something to tell of, all in one blow. The very economy of the idea appealed to her. There were always vacancies in the big Ministries in Paris, she had heard 'Papa' say. 'Papa!' she almost laughed. He would have his Festivity, after all. He should be made to work it. The idea was so new and beautiful that it actually kept her awake for half an hour after she had blown out her candle – a rare thing for a girl of her habits and physique.

The first person who was astonished at the turn of affairs was 'Papa'. He became aware, as he snuffled with rage and ill-health at his desk behind the screen by the stove, of kind looks and lingerings. His resentment and small suspicions soon melted. He ventured half-apologetic remarks, was not rebuffed. Nor did she hurry away with the other girls, as she had done all the week since his last propositions. Eventually he timidly complained that he had not had his little Festivity, that his birthday had passed unhonoured.

Madeleine felt something, almost compunction, but her Fixed Idea soon resumed its empire over her mind. She listened to him.

On the following Sunday, having drunk her coffee and eaten her roll, she replied to Marie's letter. She expressed her sympathy with all those in the village who had suffered bereavement, sent her congratulations to all those who had bettered their state of life. She asked to hear further of Marcel. She mentioned the Baron and the Baronne in the former category, also the Dequidts. She sent her father much affection and promised to come and see him soon. This was a mere convention. He would have been astonished had she carried it into effect, but it was testimony of her gratitude to him for having guessed her Fixed Idea, and having so astutely helped her. The letter, evidence of an orderly, unimaginative mind, wound up with sisterly affection for Marie – also a convention – for the two girls, realists to the core, knew well enough that they were friendly so long as they remained apart – and kisses for Emilienne. Having completed this, and posted it, she went to second mass at the cathedral. There, when it was over, she sat in the dimness of the sand-bagged windows and the ancient stones. She had never read Mr Ruskin, never glanced at the moral carvings of the west front, the historical carvings of the ambulatory – sand-bagged as were the first, and removed as were the second now – and would probably have made very little of them, save that they were the sort of carvings one saw in churches. Of all the long romance of that storied pile, from Robert de Luzarches to the German occupation of 1870, she knew and cared nothing – neither for its tons of masonry, glass and wood, nor for the million prayers that drifted on its stagnant air. Nor did she sit there alone from any religious motive. She was not truly religious – too sure of herself, too incurious, she kept of the faith of her fathers nothing but some habits, and some rags of superstition. She left, at one o'clock, when all the English officers were in their messes, and all French homes had that air of preoccupation which accompanies the most important meal of the week. The streets were empty. She passed rapidly to the big shop at which 'Papa's' servant was caretaker, and found the side door unlocked. In the back sitting-room Papa was waiting for her, skull-cap, clean collar, eyes watering with pleasure. There, amid solid furniture, marble-topped chiffoniers and chests of drawers, hermetically sealed, chairs and settees upholstered as if for ever, they held 'Papa's Festivity'. Once again Madeleine was touched when she saw he had ordered red wine to please her. But after the table had been cleared and his senile familiarities began, she hardened her heart. She questioned him straightly and searchingly, making him buy, with information, every liberty she allowed him. She knew well enough how quickly men changed, once they were satisfied, and chose the very moment before he lay back on the plush settee, exhausted by the violence of his emotions, to extract a promise that he would get her transferred to Paris, and a second promise of secrecy – because, she told him, there were so many spiteful tongues. She looked him full in the eyes as she said this, but he was at the stage at which he could only say, 'Yes, yes!' intent on gratifying his momentary needs. After this she poured him out some wine, and kissing him on his bald head – for his skull-cap had slipped off – she left him to reflect. She went to an appointment with Cécile Blanquart, whose father was visiting her for the day and chatted to him of village affairs. Her crude psychology was not at fault. For a day or two 'Papa' left her alone, but before a week was out he was pestering her again. She took it as a right, believing that men who had once desired her must do so again. In fact, it was this point at which Georges' neglect had so hurt her. But she had made her terms and stuck to them. She reminded 'Papa' of his promises, and he demurred, temporized. She cut him severely for two days and brought him to heel. He was not likely to find many women who would have patience with him, feeble and mean about money as he was, in face of the chances of a good time with some English officer. He did as he was told. She had to interview the Controller of the Service, but fortunately Paris was always calling for more and more help to fill the places of men combed out, and she got her transfer, and all the accompanying papers, complete. She was to go the following Sunday. She knew enough of the working of things by now to see that she was already out of the power of 'Papa'. With this, all compunction left her. She promised gaily to dine with him, and he little suspected the real source of her pleasure: the feeling that at last she would be near Georges, easily able to meet him face to face as she desired, and that, once met, she would work on him her charm, in which she had such implicit trust.

She arranged to meet 'Papa' at the station, because, she said, she wanted information about her train on the morrow. The information she really required was about that evening's train, the 18.05 for Paris. He drew her into the buffet, anxious to prime himself for his evening's enjoyment, and she went willingly, careless of appearances now. He ordered two of those compounds known as Quinine Tonics. She gulped hers down as the Boulogne–Paris train thundered in, bent forward to kiss him, and crying, 'Au revoir, mind you are decent to the girls!' swung out of the door, across the waiting-hall, and through the wicket, where he could not follow, as he had no permit. In fact, he did not try. He was first so astonished, then so enraged, that he choked over his drink, and dropped his glass, for the breakage of which a callous waitress charged him forty centimes. Alas, that a long career of getting the most out of women, and giving the least, should descend to this!

\*

Although so short a time had elapsed, the Madeleine who travelled from Amiens to Paris was a very different girl from the Madeleine who had left Hondebecq three months earlier. The very manner of her shaking off 'Papa' showed it. The habit of the village in which she had grown up, regarding railways, consisted in going to the station, hearing when the next train went to the required destination, and waiting for it. To possess and understand a time-table – more, to have mastered the complicated regulations of a militarized station in war-time, was the measure of how far Madeleine had advanced.

She found herself in a Paris that had an air of forced cheerfulness and dumb expectancy. True, the panic of the day of mobilization, growing right up to the Aisne battle, was over; the

'ON LES AURA'

alarums of 1918 were not yet in sight. But it was a Paris bereft of men, many a shutter closed; a Paris as yet unhaunted by Americans, but beginning to be desperate in its pleasures. What its best historians, its great lovers, Murger or Victor Hugo, would have thought of it, cannot be conjectured. Its fabled gaiety was gone for good. Its heroism had that poisoned quality that makes women cover broken hearts with cheap finery.

Madeleine, who had never imagined a town of the size before, spent the first month very quietly taking it all in. She had the sense to see that she must start all over again. She did her work with zest – it suited her. That suited her Controller, who put her to lodge with relatives – retired people of official class, who lived in an 'apartment', a tiny flat in a huge block of buildings situated just where the scholarly Pantheon district trails off into the poverty of St Étienne du Mont. No one could be more self-effacing than Madeleine when she wished to. During her first weeks in Paris she attended to her work, lived quietly with Monsieur and Madame Petit, dressed soberly, glanced at no one in the street, or in the great office where her duties lay. She made herself amiable and useful in the small precise household, left it in time to catch her bus, that landed her opposite the bridge, across which towered the world-famous gallery in which the Ministry to which she was attached was housed. She made herself agreeable to the girls with whom she worked. Some were country girls, shy or inefficient, but there was not a Fleming amongst them, and she concealed her opinion that she knew better than they about most things. As for the native Parisiennes, of whom all sorts and conditions were gathered into that great harbour of steady work and sure pay, she admired their ferocious femininity and put up with their moods – even when they called her 'Boche du Nord' – the equivalent of calling a Worcestershire girl a Welshwoman – which they did at times, out of sheer dislike of her demure capacity. To have seen her, no one would have suspected that she was gleaning every scrap of information she could with regard to the Flying Corps units that formed the Air defence of Paris. And she had better opportunity now. Paris was by no means the town-just-behind-

97

## THE SPANISH FARM

the-line that Madeleine was used to. Information was to be had, people got to know things and talked of them. Her Ministry, engaged in rationing one of the necessities of life, rationed Flying Corps troops among other people. She missed nothing. At last she found what she was looking for.

*

In one of those innumerable lists of men that were being produced by Government Departments all over the world, as well as in her particular Ministry, she saw the name Georges d'Archeville. It was a list of those young men designated, with the picturesque appropriateness of the French language, as 'aspiring aviators' who were 'directed towards the Front', that is, being sent into the line of battle. Madeleine and another girl were crossing them off the lists of the garrison of Paris. She stared so long and heavily that her companion bent over her: 'What! You can't find it – but there it is!'

Madeleine ticked the beloved name and went on, as in a stupor. This was really a blow. To come to Paris had seemed to her, somehow, the satisfactory culmination of her long vigil. She felt sure she would be successful in finding him. She had found him indeed. What now! The Paris garrison was not concerned with the fate of 'aspiring aviators' once they were struck off its rolls. Their fate was not indeed in much doubt, but there remained the horrible uncertainty as to which of the graveyards behind the four hundred miles of Front would hold his grave. At this point her common-sense and practical knowledge of affairs deserted her. She just wanted him, that was all. Feigning a headache, she excused herself and got leave to go home; but instead of going, she lingered about the quays and bridges, never lovelier than in winter twilight, with golden wraiths of leaves spinning in the bitter wind along the severe, well-proportioned grey lines of masonry. The fresh air calmed her; hunger at length drove her back to the Petits' apartment. She did not notice at first anything in the manner of her hosts. The only thing that she noticed was that M. Petit, as he handed her a letter, used the phrase:

'It came about four o'clock!'

That was the hour at which her eye had caught the name in the fatal list. All the threads and tatters of superstition that clung to her Flemish soul took life and substance at this. She muttered the words, 'Ah, yes! I expected it. It is a word from home!' She passed, quiet and self-possessed, to her little bedroom, one of those little rooms which lead one to ask if they were intended by the architect for anything, or whether they might not be an inadvertence. Lighting her candle, she sat on the thin coverlet of her bed, that reached from the tall window to the door, and resting her feet on the lower shelf of the washstand, thrust her thumb into the envelope and burst it open. It was from Skene. It was what is called in those English romances Madeline had never read or imagined, a 'love letter'. It asked her to spend his week's leave with him. That much she saw, and then put it down and buried her face in her hands. She had expected it to contain news of the death of Georges. Why or how she thought anyone should write to her on such a subject is one of those mysteries that hang about the most clear-minded, least bemused of people. She had felt it rather than thought it, and the revulsion was for the moment too much for her. She was roused by the clatter of plates, and the acrid voice of Madame Petit, keeping the supper within the smallest possible bounds. She changed her blouse, washed and did her hair, and hurried out to help Madame.

During a meal whose frugality would have driven a monk from his vows, she heard M. Petit say, 'Well, have you good news from home!' and herself replying: 'Yes. My brother writes to say he has leave, and asks me to go home to see him!'

She afterwards reflected that she could not have invented a better answer. The envelope was stamped with the British military postmark. The old man was inquisitive, and there was no knowing what use he might not make of any conclusion he drew. To have a brother in the English area was the one feasible explanation.

\*

These considerations did not weigh heavily with her, however. She slipped away as soon as she could, and read her letter through again and then again. There was much in it that she did not come within a long way of understanding – descriptions of the life of decent civilized men in camp and billet, not to mention trench and dug-out. These simply conveyed nothing and did not interest her. Then there was an involved scrupulousness that she had no means of sharing. But the main motive that had caused the writing of those four sheets was clear enough – Skene really wanted her. And if she did not admit it to herself, she wanted to be wanted. She did not reply to the letter, but put it away in a safe place, a little lock-up box in which she kept her immediate savings and a trinket or two, and went to her work in the morning, a changed woman. She had regained in a breath her old sureness. She now saw herself again the woman she desired to be. 'If I can only see him face to face' still ran in her mind, but this time it was Skene whom she hoped to see. Insensibly the symbol had changed, the emotions remained. She thought the matter over in her cautious way. He had supposed her still to be in Amiens and had written there. By good luck she had sent a card (one of those war postcards, all khaki and azure and sentiment) to Cécile Blanquart, having it in her mind that Cécile would describe to the full, in her next letter home (for Cécile was the sort that wrote once a week), anything that she, Madeleine, did. It had been an act of petty pride. It now seemed like the work of Providence – Cécile had redirected the letter, and here it was. Madeleine did not mistake what it meant. He wanted a week, like the few hours he had had, in Amiens. That was natural enough; she saw nothing in it. In her experience men were like that, and she secretly approved. For a week, at least, she would have some one belonging to her; beyond that she did not look.

After twenty-four hours' consideration she took the letter from its hiding-place, replied to it in most measured terms – judging to a nicety, by some instinct, what would make him say a little more and say it a little plainer, without committing her in any way. A week passed, and back came a further letter. It

## 'ON LES AURA'

filled her with a sort of steady glow. There was no mistaking it. He had written for a room in an hotel he knew of at the other end of the city, on the steep hill that leads from behind the big stations to Montmartre. She did not reply until old M. Petit, looking at her over his spectacles, asked her: 'Well, and your brother?'

She gathered herself together mentally. Of course, she had to fend off all that sort of thing. She replied briefly: 'I am going home for a week!'

That evening she sent Skene a card on which Union Jack and Tricolour were entwined. She wrote with a sort of exultation: 'I wish to be all yours.' Such an outburst must have been caused by something deeper than the paltry bickering of a little old man, or the prospect of meeting a young one with whom she had once passed a few hours of intimacy under the stress of strong emotion.

\*

The day came. She got her week's leave. It is one of the victories of women's entry into ordinary commercial activities of business houses and Government offices, that they have forced some humanity and reason into the mechanical discipline of such places. Having made no plans, she had put her few belongings into one of those black hold-alls that make all French travellers seem countrified, and stood on the platform of the Gare du Nord, waiting. She had dressed herself carefully – more carefully than usual, with hardly a spot of colour, and was conscious that every inch of her that was covered showed the finest possible value for the money. Her hands, neck and face had lost nothing of their firmness and pallor. The figure she cut seemed to culminate in the little leather satchel clasped against her fur – as if she were holding her heart in reserve, and defending it at the same time. The train roared into the station, and after a moment's confusion, she saw Skene coming towards her. She had been wondering fearfully for a moment if he would come, if she would recognize him, if any unforeseen obstacle would arise. When he reached her, she turned up her face and gave him her rare smile. When he slid his hand under her arm and hurried her down the platform to catch one of the few taxis, she pressed ever so little against him. Never in her life had she been happier than in hearing those heavy boots clanking beside her. Now that he had come she knew she was right. Skene was neither exceptionally handsome, brave nor rich – and she would have thought nothing the more of him if he had been. She neither knew nor cared for heroes of fiction, but admired the clean, athletic type of young man just then beginning to be popularized by the cinema. Skene had the looks and bearing of what he was – an average Englishman of the professional classes, who had passed through the successive stages of discomfort, danger, all but death. He had the sure movements, straight glance, and agreeable carelessness begotten of this, grafted on to middle-class standards of manners. Superficially, at any rate, he was more considerate than his nearest French equivalent would have been.

All this, which would have disappointed or amused many a Frenchwoman, captivated Madeleine, and in the taxi she gave up her lips to him with rich joy at the unmistakable warmth of his feelings. The moment, however, the taxi stopped at the restaurant she had indicated, she made herself prim and aloof. She had not wasted her time since she had been in Paris, and knew her way about. The restaurant dated from the period of those great Exhibitions that had served to rehabilitate Paris after 1870. Originally the home of the sort of people who gave some shadowy substance to Murger's bohemian Paris, it had long become the classic rendezvous of English and American visitors and of Frenchmen who wanted to sacrifice style to price. It still had the red-plush benches and gaily frescoed walls of romance, but the service and cooking were what Frenchmen call 'serious'. The place had just been worth preserving on a commercial basis in the commercial era, and consequently had been preserved.

Madeleine had lost nothing of her idea of celebrating an occasion. She ate heartily and did not refuse to drink with Skene. He was, of course, ravenous, and in the state in which drink had no effect on him. She smiled demurely across the table at him, more at home every moment. He was also amused at something. He had only known Paris fifteen years earlier, as a young architect half-way through his A.R.I.B.A., and was marvelling at the change – at the figure she cut in those surroundings that had for him such different associations: she almost bourgeois – he in the fancy dress of his uniform. Her manner with the waiter was perfect, and perfect her assumption of respectability. He loved it, felt almost at home, too. For in their secret hearts both of them were domesticated, conventional to the core. Both of them loathed the War and all it had brought. It was the queerest of contradictions that forced them to comfort their ultra-respectable aspirations in such a place and such a manner, both spoken of even in war-time, by many people, as 'irregular'.

\*

The meal at an end, they went, as a matter of course, to a cinema. One did, in war-time. Skene, who at home would hardly have walked to the end of the street with such an object – Madeleine, who had hardly heard of such a thing before she went to Amiens – went to the nearest cinema because it was war-time and no one wanted to think. Walking in the brisk air of a Parisian winter evening, good meat and drink within them, they enjoyed themselves prodigiously, Skene because he had existed in dubious snatches of comfort for a long time, and was likely to so exist for an indefinite period – Madeleine because of the reality of a man at her side. He was making jokes about the Place Clichy being the Place Cliché! She did not understand in the least, but laughed because he was happy beside her. And so on to the gaping portico of one of those establishments which advertise what is known in France as 'spectacle de famille'. This last was being loudly cried by a person, paid to do so, at the door – who added in stentorian tones that soldiers went in free, and nursemaids half-price. It was typical of Skene that he paid for two of the most expensive seats, and placed Madeleine in the one that gave him the best view of her profile. The film, unfortunately, was a French one, not an American. That is to say, instead of being confronted with the improbable adventures of a man looking somewhat like Skene, Madeleine realized with a start that she was watching a love story in which the principal character was a tolerable travesty of Georges d'Archeville, and behaved with just his perverse petulance. She turned her head, smiled at Skene, played with her programme, smoothed her gloves, and arranged herself with a minute care for her costume and the possible effect of the seat on it. It was no good. Cinema screens are insistent. It is difficult to avoid that great glare of white, with its intriguing figures in motion. It revealed to her what she would never have invented for herself – the idea that, like the hero of the film, Georges neglected her because he was engrossed by some other woman. She could not dismiss the idea; did not try, perhaps. She felt suddenly more wounded than she had ever felt since August 1914. That Georges might be hurt at her sharing an English officer's week of Leave never occurred to her. To her practical soul, with its incapacity for flights of imagination, things seemed all too readily what they appeared to the eye. Suddenly she rose.

'This representation is rasant,' she said to Skene, and marvelled a moment, as they threaded their way out, at his docile good temper. Not a grumble, not a protest. He just followed her and snapped up a taxi. In it he was more solicitous than ever, gentle, kind, with a Mid-Victorian kindness she had never known – the manners of one whose boyhood has been unspoiled by bitter thoughts about money.

They reached the little hotel at which they had dropped their baggage, and he handed her in. By this time his way with her was having the queerest effect. Had he been thoughtless, brutal, she would easily have braced herself to meet it. As it was, she felt something slowly dissolving in her. She held herself in yet a little, approving the place he had chosen, clean and reasonable in price. But when the door of their little room was bolted and she stood in front of the mirror by the rose-coloured curtains, unpinning her hat, he came gently behind her and slipped his hands under her arms. It was just Georges' way. She burst into tears. The moment the first sob had shaken itself free – for she did nothing by halves, and when, rarely, she cried, she cried bitterly – she knew she would feel better. Skene let her droop on to the bed and sat beside her, one arm round her, making very small comforting remarks in French and English alternately, but no inquiries. She kept her handkerchief tight pressed upon her eyes with both hands, but her sobs were lessening, and with every moment the agonizing vision of Georges with some one else grew smaller and fainter. She leaned ever so gently against Skene, who tended her as a woman might a child, did every little service for her, amazing her, who had never been so treated since she was four years old. Gradually she slipped down into the comfort of those hard hands, whose fingers kept something of the skill and discrimination of such as have been used for wise, gentle occupations. But only when she was at ease, with dry bright eyes and braided hair, did he seem to think of himself, and then only to ask so humbly for what he wanted. She gave him all herself, fiercely, as if for ever to prevent any of her from escaping again in those other hands that had neglected her so. More, when they two swam slowly back to the surface of normal existence again, in the quiet of the night only broken by the discreet bubbling of the calorifère in the corner, she told him the stark truth of herself and Georges, with a bareness of exposure of her very soul she had never before permitted, of which, perhaps, she had never before been capable. And when at last they slept, in each other's arms, it was the deep sleep of emotional reaction, for no less than she, Skene had looked for years past on utter shipwreck – obliteration of his individuality in the dark mud of Flemish trenches – and knew from a different point of view all she suffered, and what comfort she clutched at.

\*

The next day passed in that atmosphere known to English honeymooners. Not a trace remained of the emotions of the evening before – nothing but two healthy young people out for a holiday, both in the most incurious state of mind, and easily amused. The things they missed seeing far out-numbered those they noticed, as is the case with honeymooners.

Madeleine was so used to the English that she hardly smiled when he turned the little hotel upside down in order to have a hot bath and an egg for breakfast. The establishment, at length conceding these recondite advantages, ceased to interest them. They went out into the busy streets, in the frosty air, Skene's hands in the pockets of his 'British warm', Madeleine with one hand tucked into his arm, the other holding her fur tippet closed across her throat, as she saw other girls doing. To Skene, a free morning in Paris could only, by habit and association, mean one thing: – pictures. To Madeleine it could only mean another: – shops. As they descended into the roaring heart of the city, never busier than in mid-war, they found some of the galleries were still open, and Skene took her from room to room, pointing out old favourites, lamenting new gaps left by careful storage of some of the more valuable masterpieces. She moved beside him, confused, uncertain whether to blush or look away in front of many a splendid nudity, but drawn by the spirit that was on both, to squeeze his arm a little. In the mood of the moment she unconsciously identified herself with all feminine beauty, and he acquiesced. But he was not less in holiday mind than she, stood patiently for half an hour at a time in big shops, watching her wringing out to the uttermost centime the best value from scowling shop-girls. Skene begged to give her what she wanted – he had managed to visit three field cashiers and get francs from each – he had a pocket full of money. She accepted, loyally keeping herself within limits and wasting nothing. Both of them had their shocks. In one of the turnings off the rue de Rivoli they met a tall fresh-cheeked young man, scented and glittering, in a grey-green uniform Skene identified as Russian. Skene fell into a growling condemnation of all 'Base Pups', 'Head-quarter people', etc., etc., incomprehensible to her, save its long-stored ill-humour. But she was after all only saying the same thing in French, when a frail, fair, over-arranged lady kept her waiting in the glove department of the Bon Marché, when Skene heard her grind her white teeth, with: 'That sort of animal doesn't know what time's worth!'

\*

The next day was still queerer. Skene wanted what he called 'a day in the country'. Madeleine had no idea what he might mean, her notions of a holiday being confined to Church Festivals. She went with him, however, down the Seine Valley, as far as the regulations permitted. She gathered he once had regular haunts here, had gone by steamer with companions. She taunted him laughingly with having been one to 'rigoler' in his youth. She began to suspect that he was much richer than his worn khaki and careful trench habits made apparent. He took her to a well-known beauty spot, all shuttered and sad with war and winter, roused the proprietor and persuaded him to give them food and drink in the mournfulness of the dismantled salle à manger. The proprietor, like so many others, had lost an only son. It took a lot of gentleness and some of Skene's Expeditionary Force canteen cigarettes to thaw him. But gradually he expanded into the graveyard interest of his kind. What were the trenches like? Were the dead buried properly? Would one find their graves? Skene told all he could, painted a true picture as far as he could, exaggerating no horror, slurring over none of the stark facts. The old man was appeased. He liked to know. So his son was lying like that, was he, amid the Meuse hillocks!

Madeleine took no part in the conversation, but sat looking at Skene, totally uninterested in what he was saying, enjoying the masculinity of his movements and gestures. She was beginning to be curious about the one thing that ever aroused her speculation. What was this man's position in life? The men talked on into the winter dusk, the 'patron' offering liqueurs and cigars. She and Skene missed their train back and had to walk to a neighbouring depot, and get seats on an army lorry. Skene tipped the driver and Madeleine saw the man's face. That night, as they lay side by side in the sober companionship that both of them felt so right and justifiable, she asked him of his home. She was somewhat astonished at the result. He talked for twenty minutes, and was all the time incomprehensible to her. The old house in the Cathedral Close, the hereditary sinecure descending in the one family – the semi-public school, wholly leisured-class prejudices and scruples – the circle of maiden aunts living on railway dividends – the pet animals – the social functions – made her pucker her smooth, regular forehead with complete mystification. She could make nothing of it except that every one in England was rolling in money.

\*

Another day followed, and another. The end of the week was at hand. As it approached, they both regarded the impending separation calmly. The emotions that had brought them together were of the sort that will not keep. Neither of them were bohemians of the true water. The life of the little hotel where they slept and the restaurants where they fed was soon drained of its attractiveness. If Skene really wanted anything, it was to be back at his job in England. If Madeleine ever asked herself what she found lacking in those brief days, the answer would have been a farm of her own, a settled place in some village community, and, perhaps, children. But she did not ask herself such questions, nor did Skene admit for a moment that there was anything to desire other than what they shared. But there fell long silences between them. The tittle-tattle about topical events interested neither of them. The little news they could tell each other was told. They could not talk of Georges. Their only common memories were of the farm and the Easter Horse Show of the divisions. Both subjects were stale. The small attempt Madeleine made to understand Skene had led her into perplexity. Skene had let her more intimate self alone, having neat provincial notions of chivalry. The excursions of peace-time Paris no longer existed. The cinema and most theatres bored Skene. Madeleine could not sit out concerts. The day before the last, they went at Skene's suggestion to the Sorbonne. He wanted to feast his eyes, that must so soon look at decauville railways and trench-mortar ammunition, on the Fresco, by Puvis de Chavannes, which decorates the lecture hall of that institution.

He had first seen it as a young man, and the impression it had made was undimmed. He loved that blue-green twilight in which statuesque people stood in attitudes among Greek pillars and poplar trees. He loved it with an English love of things as they are not. Madeleine gazed at the great lecture hall. At last she said, 'It is not then a church!' No fool, she had grasped the speculative, investigating atmosphere.

'No,' Skene replied, 'it is a higher grade school!'

'As school decoration, it is not ver' useful!'

Skene had nothing to say.

Later, as Skene wished to dawdle over some architectural drawings in the Cluny Museum, she said frankly she would look at the shops. Their time was drawing to a close. The next day was the last. Skene did not know how to say that he hoped to meet her again. Did he?

*

For Madeleine it was easier. She simply went on behaving beautifully. The week had not been spoiled by one cross word. To the end, she found no fault with Skene, herself, or Fate. Such tenderness as life had not already rubbed out of her, showed itself in her solicitude as to his sandwiches and half-bottle of wine. It would be cold, she warned him, as they paced the platform of the Gare du Nord. If he passed by the farm he would say a word to her father and Marie. He promised, stoical as she, and habituated to War-time farewells. He did not allude to the future. She kept herself wrapped in uncritical passivity. The train was made up. She saw his out-of-shape cap, khaki back, and tightly clothed legs disappear successively in the doorway of the carriage. He came out again, having secured his corner, and they paced the asphalt of the station for yet a few minutes, in silence. Then at shoutings and whistlings and blowings of tin trumpets, without which no French train can start, he disappeared again, but, the door closed, hung out of the window. The train was full of French leave-men, many drunk. One in particular, who was wearing a bowler hat on his uniform, noticed Skene and Madeleine just as the train began to move, and shouted, 'I know what you've been doing, English officer and little lady!' Skene waved and was gone. Madeleine turned and went. 'Know what you've been doing' rang in her ears. A smile curled the corners of her mouth. Men looked after her again now that she was alone. She walked, taking pleasure in exercise and the keen air, to the little hotel in the stony street, paid the bill, with the money Skene had given her, reclaimed her hold-all, strained to bursting with the things he had bought for her. Then she demanded a taxi, which she dismissed in front of the Pantheon, and walked on foot to Monsieur and Madame Petit's. She ascended the stone stairs, cold and bare as penury, and knocked.

Monsieur opened to her with a short piece of candle, carefully screened in his hand. He closed the door and led her into the fireless dining-room, from which her room opened. He peered at her.

'Well, this war, how goes it?'

'But gently!' she replied, not guessing what he was driving at.

'Come, your brother told you nothing?'

In a moment it came back to her, that she had been spending a week's 'leave' with her 'brother'. She faced the peering old eyes.

'You know that the men in the trenches never say anything!'

He was rebuffed, but tried again.

'The Boulogne train must have been very late!'

But she was on her guard now, and replied readily enough:

'Very late. The Bosche were bombing Amiens!'

The old man grunted and left her. In her own room she smiled at her reflection in the glass. She was looking magnificent, feeling magnificent. To come from at least some degree of luxury, if not from home and love, at least from entertainment and admiration, to the bleak realities of her daily life, did not daunt her Flemish heart. She unpacked and undressed methodically, passed her hands over that flesh that had been so generously caressed, and seemed rounded and fortified by it, and wrapped herself in the hard-worn bedclothes, warming them with her vitality. Could Skene, buttoned up in his 'British warm', miles away on the northern railway, have seen her, he might have been attracted, he would not have been harrowed or flattered. She had rubbed off the contact with him by the passage of her hands over herself. She rubbed him off her soul no less easily. She was at her place in the Ministry on the morrow, and save that her appearance of well-being excited desire or envy, created no sensation.

Then as the days passed, very slowly, and all the more surely, reaction began to set in. She did not analyse it or express it, but it was there. The old feeling of having been done, cheated! There was the old void – and Skene, against whom she bore no malice – she was partial to him, rather – had tried to fill it and failed. It was not in him. Too well behaved, too incomprehensible, too English, he had, in fact, not asked enough of her. She would have felt more at home with him had he been subject to those moods of feverish desire and cold disgust that she associated with all that was most admirable in men. For that male perversity by which, when it existed in her father and the Baron, in 'Papa', and Monsieur Blanquart, in fact in all men, was the very thing by which war had been brought about, and caused her separation from Georges – when it appeared in that Georges himself, became simply one of his attributes. Her 'good child' bored her. Her spoiled, imperious one was what she needed.

*

The evenings lengthened. February came, and the Bosche retreat. Marie wrote that she was trying to get back to Laventie, where things were in a pitiable state, but good land must not be allowed to lie waste. They despaired of Marcel. Madeleine did not reply to this letter. The farm and all it contained seemed very remote. Yet the letter was a comfort; it brought no bad news, and no news was good. Already, she thought again of nothing but Georges. As for any practical plan to find him, she had long come to the end of expedients that her not very strong imagination could devise. She just wanted, and waited.

The chief of her department in the Ministry was one of those politicians who found the War dull. Its concentration upon the one great effort to beat the Bosche, and preserve the French nation alive, robbed such a politician of his living. There was little scope for anything but messing with contracts, trying and necessarily unspectacular. This one among the party-bosses of the French Chamber hit upon a plan which would advertise him, and at the same time give a sort of rallying-cry and style for the next political stunt. He saw shrewdly enough that Peace would one day burst upon an astonished world, and that those who were unprepared for it would be badly left. And what would be the best starting-place in the new Peace atmosphere? Why, obviously, to be hailed in a million farms, a million small shops, as 'That brave Monsieur Dantrigues – he was good to our poor boys in the hospitals, during the War!' It could be used as common ground for the Action Française on the one hand, and the extreme socialists on the other. And no one dared raise hand or word against it. The quickest, cheapest and best way to set it afoot was, of course, to make use of the organizing power of his immense department, the ocean of needy vanity in which the hundreds of temporary typists and girl war-clerks swam; the comic papers could be got to blaze it about – they were invariably hard up.

So it was that Madeleine, in common with all her companions, found herself invited to take part in a gigantic Charitable Fête. They were given little cards with the particulars – certain elements of costume were to be uniform, also an electric lamp in the hair, and a basket of gifts. They were to meet in the Tuileries, at certain spots indicated by numbers, from which decorated lorries would take them to the various hospitals of the metropolitan area, to distribute an Easter gift to every sick or wounded soldier. Monsieur Dantrigues was smart enough to see that this was much more effective than the same thing carried out near the Front. For if a man has incurred a gumboil guarding a railway in the Seine Valley, he likes just as well to be treated as a 'brave wounded', and is just as likely to vote subsequently for the man who organized people to think him so. On the other hand, the real fighting soldiers, nearer the Front, would mostly be killed and never vote at all.

The idea caught on. Generals, clerics, ladies old and young, blessed it and gave funds for costumes and presents.

\*

## 'ON LES AURA'

Never did a government department function so ill as that which contained Madeleine, as the ten thousand charitable maidens prepared themselves for the fray. Madeleine entered into the affair rather than make herself conspicuous. She had no sentiment about other people's soldiers, no anxiety to please men who did not interest her. But she went, took her number, arranged herself with sense and taste, and found a little comfort from looking nice. She managed to get a double supply of gifts and send one lot to her brother Marcel, hoping that it might bring a sign from him in his German prison.

The day came. Released at an early hour, the girls dispersed to costume themselves. The short-sleeved tunic of thin white material, with its girdle of artificial ivy leaves, suited Madeleine. Even Monsieur and Madame Petit, never prodigal of praise, admitted that she looked well. When she arrived at the rendezvous, she created some sensation. The uniform dress brought out precisely her better proportions and carriage, all her good looks that depended on health and hard work. As the lorries that were to take them to their places swung alongside the pavement, one of the girls said of her, 'That great Flanders mare ought to have two seats allowed her!' but the very spite in the speech was a compliment to Madeleine. They were set down on the steps of one of those great palaces of stone, common in Paris, that had been aroused from centuries of slumber by the War, and now sheltered hundreds of narrow white beds. Among these, up and down great vistas of ward and corridor, the girls processed, music in front, bearers of lighted candles behind. The fête, designed by a lady of cosmopolitan education, just then very intimate with Dantrigues, had elements of English carol-singing and German Christmas-tree effect, mixed with French delight in spectacle and uniform. Then the girls were divided into pairs, and given so many beds each for the distribution of gifts.

Madeleine was frankly bored with the whole thing. She hardly bothered to make herself agreeable to the men in her section of beds – passing them with a word or two of conventional good wishes, holding her clean, fair-skinned, smiling, slightly obtuse profile high above them, stepping easily, unencumbered by the basket on her hip. At the end of her bit were several empty beds, the nursing sister on duty explaining that the occupants were more or less convalescent, and had leave. She did not trouble to hurry off elsewhere, nor to obtain a fresh supply of gifts. The more or less innocent flirtations, which the other girls saw as one of the chief attractions of the business, did not excite her. The electric globe in her hair, which annoyed her, went out, and seeing a glass door leading on to a verandah, all dark and quiet, she slipped through unseen. She had hardly drawn the door to behind her than she had a peculiar sensation. She had stepped into a mild, humid spring night, the stars of which shone above the garden plantation of the place, beyond the stone pillars of the balcony on which she stood. But in her own mind she had stepped through the separation of over two years, as one puts one's foot through a paper screen. Georges was near her, she knew. The back of the balcony, against the glazed windows of the ward, was lined with a kind of fixed garden seat used by the convalescent. One of these convalescents was seated, lying there rather, his attitude expressive more of exasperation than of physical weakness. Before she could analyse or act upon her queer feeling of nearness of Georges, his voice arose from that recumbent figure, in the quakerish simplicity of French intimacy: 'It is thou!' was all he said.

She flung down her basket and sunk on the seat beside him. Galvanized into sudden life, he heaved himself up, clutched her in his arms, bent down her face to his. For some time, who can tell how long, neither of them thought of anything, content just to feel the emotions of the moment. Amid these arose the jangle of a bell. It brought Madeleine to her senses at once. It was the arranged signal – five minutes' warning before the charitable maidens rejoined their lorries. M. Dantrigues' lady friend had thoughtfully suggested that some of the young women might want to put themselves tidy. Madeleine stood up, telling Georges briefly what was intended. He replied with an army word, intimating how much he cared. She was tender, docile, careful with him, spoiling him every minute.

'Yes, yes, my little one. I know. But it is worth more to arrange where we can meet. Your Mado will wait for you wherever you say!'

It was the pet name he had for her those ages ago in the Kruysabel. At the sound of it, spoken as she spoke, all that lost Peace-time ease arose ghostly before them. He vented his indignation against Fate by picking up her basket and flinging it into the night, where it crashed softly among earth and leaves. The gesture delighted her. It was the old Georges, the real 'young master' of first love. She had been terribly frightened by his first greeting, that meek 'It is thou!' so unlike him, that he had uttered. He pleased her still more when he went on:

'If that's your bell, you'd better go. Don't get caught in this sacred box, whatever you do!'

'Tell me where,' she whispered.

'I'll find a place and let you know. I must get out of here. If not, I'll burst myself as I have bursted so many Bosches. Where do you live?'

She told him, pressed a kiss on his lips, and was gone in a flash, quiet, confident, alert. She was herself again.

The journey back to the rendezvous in the lorry was noisy and amusing. A score or two of young women, mainly at the minx stage of unattachment, chattered and squabbled, mimicked and raved. Madeleine sat in a corner unheeding. From the rendezvous home she took no account of time, nor place, could not have said by which street she passed, or at what hour she sat down to the Petits' supper. They were rather nicer than usual to her that night, feeling perhaps that she was a credit to them — for the charitable fête had been discussed from every possible point of view in that quarter of shabby gentility, and every one in the block of flats knew that the Petit's lodger had taken part. Madame Petit had seen to that. But Madeleine was not responsive — wrapped herself in a brown study — or was it a golden dream? — and retired early to her room.

*

The next day she was the same — quiet, polite, but detached, went to the office as usual, returned at the same hour, replied to questions in monosyllables, went to bed early. Monsieur Petit began to have his suspicions – could it be that the young woman had fallen in love ('made a friend' was the expression he used to his wife) at the fête?

The next morning, as they sipped coffee in their several déshabillés, there came a knock on the door. A message! Monsieur Petit, who took it in, handed it to Madeleine through the two inches that she opened her door. He dressed hurriedly, agog with excitement. The hour at which she usually left for the office passed, and she did not appear. Finally, she did leave her room, at nearly ten o'clock, dressed in her best, carrying her holdall and hat-box.

'Good-bye,' she said. 'I have left everything in order and the week's money on the dressing-table.'

Monsieur Petit stammered, 'But why?'

Madeleine's eyes gleamed in such a way that he stood aside to let her pass. 'Because I am leaving,' she said. 'Make my adieux to Madame. She is occupied, I know!'

And the old man stamped with rage as he heard her firm footfall descending the stone stairs. She was going, taking away a secret with her. Almost as well have taken one of the bronze figures of saints or knights on horseback from the dining-room – that would have been no more a robbery than to take away a secret from that little home where bronze statuettes and curiosity about other people's affairs were the only luxuries.

At the foot of the stairs Madeleine hailed a taxi and gave an address in the north-western quarter of the city, from the paper in her hand. Then she folded the paper carefully, and replaced it in her hand-bag with her money and little mirror, as the vehicle bounded down the Boulevard St Michel. Poor Monsieur Petit was not to be allowed to forget her departure. Three days later the postman brought a letter for Madeleine. Monsieur Petit turned it over and over, his fingers itched. Then something in his memory of superannuated government service stirred. He knew what it was, and told his wife, nodding and glaring malignantly.

'I have sent hundreds in my time. It is the dismissal!'

## 'ON LES AURA'

It appeased him somewhat, for naturally he could imagine nothing more fatal than to be dismissed from the service of the government he had served for fifty years, and which paid him his pension in consequence. Retribution indeed had fallen on Madeleine, in Monsieur Petit's eyes.

*

Could Monsieur Petit have divined whither Madeleine had flown, could he have followed her, confronted her as he longed to, crying, 'See, abandoned girl, cheater of my curiosity, how Fate has overtaken you!' it is doubtful if Madeleine would have bothered even to laugh at him. She sat perfectly upright, swaying with the rocking vehicle, staring at the chauffeur's back, as she was carried down steep crowded streets, across wide vistas of bridge and quay, square and avenue, up into quiet, almost sinister-quiet, respectable streets. Dismissing and paying her taxi, and watching him out of sight, she shouldered her baggage and found her way along by sign and number to a tall block of small flats, like a hundred other such. She waited a moment, hesitating between dislike of the concierge and equal dislike of becoming conspicuous by standing in the road. Finally, she walked boldly in, disregarding the gaping eyes and mouth that followed her from the basement, mounted to the floor she required, and knocked. She had to repeat her knock more than once before it was answered and the door was left unlocked for her to push open. There was no one in the little vestibule. She dropped her things, and, guided by Georges' voice, found the bedroom, where Georges, who had pulled the clothes over him again, was cursing the cold floor he had had to tread. That was the real Georges, the man who wanted her without bothering to get up to open the door for her, the man for whom she would have died. She put her arms round his neck, and bent down to him, so that he could have her.

*

He was very much real Georges that day. He lay in bed until hunger forced him to rise, and then would neither dress nor shave. He was not of that type that lives on the interest of the past, nor hurriedly discounts the future. Nor can it be said that the thought of Lieutenant Skene crossed Madeleine's mind. Had it done so, she might have reflected how much more she loved this, her spoiled child, than that, her good one. But she, too, was absorbed in the present. She did not even remember the Ministry, whose service she had so peremptorily abandoned.

When the first gladness of reunion was slowing down into the assurance that she really had got him back, and had now only to devise how to keep him – a task she did not feel very difficult – she began to question him, very gently and indirectly, as to his plans. She remonstrated with him on the folly of their being there together, an object of interest to the concierge, still more on his insistence that she should stay there. But he only shouted that he would 'burst up' all the concierges, and she had to humour him and promise to stay for the present at least. Not that he threatened to leave her, but that she would not and could not threaten to leave him. At length, in the evening, as he sat in gown and slippers before the fire she had made, at the supper she had fetched and set, while she tidied the room strewn with his things, he began to think of her, asked for her father. He only asked one or two brief questions, not being the man to take deep interest in anything outside his own comfort. When she had answered, he just said: 'This sacred war!' Nothing else. But Madeleine knew what he meant. There it was, all round and over them, enveloping, threatening, thwarting. No less than he, she rebelled against it, in her decorous woman's way. But for him she rebelled against it twice over, hated it, made it responsible for his loss of health that was new, and his violence that was habitual – forgave him, on account of it, his carelessness of her – this way in which he wanted to live – the obvious fact that he had had other women in this room. She did not reflect upon her own record, then. But she coaxed him to take supper – she had bought the war-products that were nearest to the hare-paté and spicebread and confiture of old times – gave him a bowl of hot wine and water, as she had many a time that he had found her, he, glowing and triumphant, with a dog at his heels. And sure enough, under the spell of her magic, in that firelit bed-sitting room of the little flat in Paris, there came back gradually but surely, the Georges of old days. His worn cheeks filled out, his eyes were less sunken, his hand less thin and shaky. He began to hold up his head and hum a tune. She hung near him, watching him, foreseeing not only every need, but every whim. He became almost liberal, expansive. He had fourteen days' 'convalo' – a visit every day to the hospital, which institution would not otherwise bother about him. At the end of that time he would either go back to hospital, or up to the front. He did not care which, he said, smiling. For the first time since she had rediscovered him, he did not call anything sacred, wish to 'burst' anyone, or use the expressive, untranslatable verb 'foutre'. She cleared away and tidied up and prepared herself for the night, as he sat glancing through the newspapers humming to himself, content, asking nothing. When he felt tired, he just turned out the light, and rolled into the place she had made warm for him.

\*

Days so spent soon pass, nor is there anything more tragic than physical satiety, with its wiping out of what has gone before. Madeleine, not naturally apprehensive, would have gone on had not hard facts pulled her up. Georges had spent his pocket-money on paying the quarter's rent of their retreat. She had spent hers on food for him and herself. No bohemian, she began to take counsel with herself as to how to obtain fresh supplies. One source of funds she dismissed at once. She would not ask Georges for a penny. That would have seemed outrageous to her. She did not attempt it. She had a handsome sum in the Savings Bank at Hazebrouck. But how get it? She did not want to write to Monsieur Blanquart or to Marie. Even if they could have withdrawn it for her (and the difficulties of such a step she did not clearly foresee), they would both of them have found out sooner or later something about Georges. And that she would not have for all the world. Her father she could trust, but she also knew his ingrained habits regarding money, his incapacity for reading and writing. A letter would simply stupefy him. If he got some one to read it to him, he would simply be stupefied the more. His Madeleine spending her savings? Never! He would do nothing. Should she, then, go by train and get the money? There would be endless difficulties in getting authority to journey into the British Military Zone – but the great difficulty to her mind, the insurmountable one, was to leave Georges for two days. She was nonplussed.

Just then it happened that Georges, turning towards her in one of his more expansive moments, said, in his spoiled way: 'My God, how I want you!'

Occupied fully with him at the moment, her mind retained the words, her memory searching for the last occasion on which she had heard them. Georges went out to his club that morning, leaving her sewing, washing, doing a hundred and one jobs in her thorough housekeeper's way. She sat brooding, almost waiting for some stroke of luck to help her with her difficulty. Suddenly she remembered who it was that last used that phrase – Lieutenant Skene. She sat down at once and wrote to him. She had no scruples. All the English were rich. This one had no outlet for his money. She had been worth it. The reply came in three days, to the post-office address she had given. It brought a hundred francs. They lasted a week, and few people could have made them last more, save that Georges only came in to supper now. He was getting restless, smelled of drink. She wrote again to Skene. No reply came. Instead there came the end of the fortnight of Georges' 'convalo'. That day she sat alone waiting for two things, a letter bringing money, or Georges bringing fatal news. Either he was not well enough to go back to the front, so that his state must indeed be serious, or he was well enough, which was even worse. She dared not ask him; he vouchsafed nothing, seemed well enough, but restless. She, meanwhile, for the first time in her life was feeling really ill. She had never met before with this particular cruelty of Fate, resented it, but only felt worse. Perhaps the town life had sapped her vitality. Perhaps Georges had brought home from his hospital, on his clothes, in his breath, the germ of some war

## 'ON LES AURA'

fever. The following day Georges was excited, and talked loud and long when he came back from the club. Her head felt so strange she did not understand.

\*

Perhaps it was as well she did not. Georges had been granted another fortnight's 'convalo', but it was not that. It was the news of the battle of Vimy that excited him. The English, of whom he was good-humouredly jealous, had taken that battered ridge, disputed for years. There was talk of eleven thousand prisoners and a quantity of guns. He had missed being 'in it'. But with the news came rumour more important still. The French were preparing a great offensive in Champagne. He would not miss that one, sacred name, not he! The spirit of that period of the war, the spirit of 'On Les Aura' burned in his veins like fire. As he strode and shouted about the room, cursing his 'convalo' that, a week ago, was all he desired, because now it prevented his being in the show.

Madeleine had the queerest feeling of all her life up to that day, for she was not a girl to faint – a sinking feeling, not painful, rather comforting. Then nothing. Then a reawakening, not so comfortable, dismay, weakness. Georges, who did nothing by halves, became, for the nonce, generous to the utmost limit of the nature of a man born with a silver spoon in his mouth and a cheque-book in the pocket of his first suit. Probably it never crossed his mind that she had taken infection from some carelessness of his. But he did better. He promptly called a young doctor of his set, who, having been badly wounded, was now permanently attached to the Paris garrison. Between affection for Georges and a handsome bribe – for the proceeding was thoroughly irregular – flat contrary to every by-law of the town and every order of the Medical Service – this young man took Madeleine in hand, visited her daily, did what was necessary in the way of prescribing, got a discreet sister of charity to nurse her. Being a man of the world, he further suggested to her, as soon as she was well enough to make inquiries, that she would not care for Georges to see her in her present state. That kept

121

her quiet during the weeks of recovery. But there came a fine June day when she was well enough to walk out a little in a Paris ever more feverish and deserted. Then the young doctor, as thorough as Georges or herself, told her the truth. Georges' thoroughness had taken the form of borrowing the identity disc and paybook of a hospital casualty whom he resembled in height and complexion. The young doctor had connived at the fraud, with the cynicism of Georges himself and all his set. Thus furnished, Georges had gone straight into the heart of that ghastly failure of the French in Champagne, during May 1917. The hurried scrutiny of his credentials had not found him out, he was in the line and fighting when his half-recovered health broke down once more, and fatally. He was buried in a huge, ever-growing cemetery, near the Aerodrome, at Avenant-le-Petit.

*

When Madeleine realized it, she sat still, looking at nothing, gathering within her all her physical vitality to meet this blow to the spirit. On her face, refined by illness, was something of the look that horses have under heavy shell-fire, bewildered resistance to the unknown. The young doctor let her alone for twenty-four hours, and then very gently led her mind back to practical considerations. The period for which Georges had hired the flat was expiring shortly. Had she money, or the means of getting some? It did not take her long to run over the alternatives – an attempt to get back into some sort of office – or a begging letter to Skene? She avoided both, not from any sense of shame, but simply because now Paris and its life had no meaning for her. She had wanted Georges. She had said, 'If I could only see him!' She had seen him. Now she would never see him again. Why bother?

The young doctor then suggested that he could obtain her a permission to travel by train to Hazebrouck. This brought to her mind the almost certain death of her brother, Marcel, in his German prison camp, and of Marie's return to Laventie. The mere name of the market town called up at once associations so potent, so much more real than all that had happened since. The farm understaffed, the old father being swindled out of billeting money! Those were realities. Those things appealed to her more than this tragic dream-life. She accepted gladly the young doctor's offer, and left him looking after her and muttering: 'What a type, all the same!' But she had no special contempt or dislike for him.

She left Paris in the same way as she left him. The old sacred towers, the new garish restaurants, the keen bitter energy, the feminine grace, of that metropolis of the world, that had once again had the enemy at its gates, and was yet to be bombarded by such engines as had never before been turned upon city of man – she turned her back upon it all, and, for her, it was not. On a grey July day she entered the train. As she travelled homewards, the day grew greyer and wetter. She passed, unheeding, through an immense bustle between Abbeville and Calais, and down to St Omer. Her train stopped frequently, and she glanced, uninterested, at the trains and trucks, materials and men, that choked rail and road. About her, people talked of the great offensive the English had begun, from Ypres to the sea. She looked at the crops and houses, thought of her father, whose very double, tall, old, dark-clothed, and bent, she saw in almost every teeming field of flax or hops, grain or roots, of that rich valley. Perhaps she had occasional bitter spasms of anger against this war, that had enslaved, and then destroyed Georges. But to her, facts were facts and she did not deny them.

*

Outside Hazebrouck the train stopped interminably. The guns had been audible, loud and angry for some time, but the long roll of them was punctuated now by a sharper nearer sound, that clubbed one about the ears at regular intervals – artillery practising, no doubt, she thought. After waiting in the motionless train as long as she considered reasonable, she got out, finding a perverse satisfaction in the use of her limbs, swinging down the steep side of the second-class carriage of the Nord Railway, and asking for her box and 'cardboard' (containing hats) to be handed down to her. Shouldering these, she marched along the asphalt with which the prodigal English had reinforced the embankment, showing no concern at the cries of 'They bombard!' shouted to her by her fellow-passengers. She passed the engine, from which the driver and fireman were peering ahead. The fields were very deserted, but she was hardly the sort to be frightened in daylight, or dark either. She passed the points where the Dunkirk line joined that from St Omer. Near by, stood a row of cottages, known as the 'Seven Chimneys', the first houses of Hazebrouck, on the station side. Her idea was to leave her trunk at the estaminet, for her father to fetch in the morning. To her astonishment, the whole row appeared deserted, empty, doors open, fires burning, food cooking. Somewhat nonplussed, she stopped a moment to get her breath, pushed her box behind the counter of the estaminet, where she was known, and then passed on, with her 'cardboard', keeping the path that separates the St Omer road from the railway. Where this reached its highest point, just at the entry to the town, she happened to glance across the rich, lonely, hedgeless fields towards the Aire road, and saw, on that side, every wall and alley black with people. She had no time to reflect on this peculiarity before she was deafened by such a roaring upheaval of earth as she had certainly never imagined. It took away her breath, wrenched her 'cardboard' out of her hands. For some seconds she could hear nothing, see nothing, but when her senses returned, the first thing she noticed was the patter of falling debris. The shell had fallen in the ditch of the railway embankment, and made a hole the size of the midden at home, and three times as deep. She picked herself up from her knees, dusted herself, recaptured her 'cardboard', and passed on, greeted by a long 'Ah – a – ah!' from scores of throats of the spectators, a quarter of a mile away. The incident annoyed her. They were bombarding, and no mistake. But it would take worse than that to prevent her from crossing the railway under the arch, and taking the Calais road. The rue de St Omer was empty, but undamaged. They were a jumpy lot, she thought; it revolted her to see all those good houses, left unlocked and open to all the ills that attack abandoned property. There was not

'ON LES AURA'

even another shell-hole nearer than the station, so far as she could see. She would have liked a cup of coffee and a slice of bread, but the town was empty as an eggshell. She heard another explosion behind her as she reached the Calais pavé. The persistence of those Bosches! But she was persistent too, and gathered her damp clothes and battered 'cardboard' to her, as she strode vigorously home. She was not sentimental – no one less so, but it may well have been that her blood quickened, and her rooted strength returned, as she found herself, once more, facing that salt wind, under those low grey skies, among which she had been bred and born.

At length she came to the earth road, the signpost, and the turning, and saw the farm, the fringe of dead wallflower stalks on the ridge of the thatch, the old 'shot' tower by the bridge over the moat. It was between six and seven when she passed the brick-pillared gate, noted a new bomb-hole, and signs of military occupation. Entering by the door, she found her father in the passage.

'It's our Madeleine,' he said quietly.

Madeleine kissed him and told him to fetch her box in the morning, from 'Seven Chimneys'.

He said, 'Thy room is empty,' and went into the kitchen, while she said a word to Berthe. It was true, her little room was just as she had left it a year before. She noted the fact with quiet satisfaction, but did not bother over the significance of it – over the fact that her father, who usually paid so little heed to anything that went on in the house, had kept her room untouched and empty for her. She quietly accepted the fact, conscious that he felt that neither the God to whom he muttered prayers on Sunday, nor the various temporal powers whom he obeyed, when he had to do, on weekdays, really understood him or cared for him as his younger daughter did. She sat down with him, in the dim kitchen, to the evening meal, by the light of the day that was dying in thin drizzle and incessant mutter of guns. Once some fearful counter-barrage made the old panes of the oriel window rattle, and the old man said:

'It's a swine of a war, all the same!'

Madeleine replied: 'It's something new for them to be bombarded in Hazebrouck!'

'I'm going to take the money out of the Savings Bank,' he commented. In his mind, unused to the facilities of book-keeping, and cradled in the cult of the worsted stocking for savings, he probably thought of his money as being held in notes or coin in the stoutly-barred vault behind the Mairie. After a long pause, during which he surveyed her hands, busy with household mending, somewhat neglected since Marie had relinquished it to Berthe, he spoke again:

'You are quite a fine lady of the town!'

'That will soon pass,' she answered, without ceasing to ply her needle.

Later he said: 'You know Marie has returned to Laventie?'

Madeleine nodded. The remark was not so stupid as it sounded. He knew she knew the fact. It was his way of appealing to her.

'Now you have come back, you will be just the Madeleine you used to be, and all will go on as before, won't it?'

Her nod was all the answer he asked.

Once again he spoke: 'You know Marcel is dead?'

Again she nodded. Again it was only his way of saying, 'Come what may, you will see me through, we shall not be worse off for the cruelties of Fate!' She understood and acquiesced. Nothing else passed until with 'Good night, father,' and 'Good night, my girl,' they parted.

Of her life during the past twelve months and all it had contained, not a word.

*Part Three*
# LA GALETTE

*Part Three*

# La Galette

The late summer of 1917, the summer of Haig's offensive from Ypres, was one of the wettest of the war, but the days following Madeleine's return opened fine.

She was up betimes, and soon made herself apparent in the life of the farm. Harvest must begin the moment things were dry enough, and before they became too dry, so that the cut grain would neither sprout as it lay, nor spill itself as it fell. Besides herself and her father, they had Berthe, and the family of Belgian refugees, two boys too young for service, and eight women of all ages. A thoughtful government had added two Territorial soldiers of the very oldest class, who could easily be spared from such military duty as they were fit for; and to this, a still more thoughtful Madeleine mentally added some amount of help that could be extracted, by one means or another, from English troops resting in the area. At the moment of her return there were no troops, but artillery came on the following day. There also came a platelayers' family from Hazebrouck, whose house was too near the big shells that had fallen. Madeleine drove a hard bargain with them, work in the fields as the price of a loft in the outhouses, until the latter should be required for potatoes. But these matters were not her first concern. She made a long and careful scrutiny of the billeting money that had been paid during her absence. Marie was too accustomed to the rough methods of those who live on the edge of the trenches, and knew little of the fine art of making the English pay.

Madeleine went to see Monsieur Blanquart in the morning recess of the school, and found him perceptibly greyer and more harassed, almost snowed under by the immense weight of paper, by which a government, in sore straits, discharged its expedients upon its humbler representatives. In addition to the correspondence and registration necessitated by general mobilization, and by the occupation of an allied army, there were now circulars and returns concerning food production, waste prevention, aircraft precautions, counter-espionage, and the surveillance of prices. In such circumstances, Blanquart probably wished her back in Paris, but she insisted. After bitter argument, he suddenly surveyed her with a gleam of interest.

'There, you aren't greatly changed; but what induced you to leave a good job in the Ministry?'

Madeleine realized that she was an object of admiring interest, with who-knows-what history invented for her by Cécile. She pushed it all aside. 'I had better things to do than to go mouldy in an office. Now, Monsieur Blanquart, for the month of March, there is only seventy-five francs marked down. How do you explain it?' and so on.

\*

She came back from the village across the fields, scrutinizing the crops, the workers, the new drains and telegraph wires the English were putting in everywhere. Already, in a few hours, her short assumption of town life and habit was dropping from her. She had put it away with the town hats Skene and Georges had bought for her, in the 'cardboard', on the half-tester of her bed. She went bareheaded, already stepping longer and holding her skirt, with both hands, up from the wetness of the knee-high root crops, and away from the waist-high grains. Her illness had squared and filled out her figure, deprived of its virginal severity, and now the refinement that indoor life, suffering, and impaired health had given to her features and skin, was yielding before fresh air, good food, vigorous action, and the habit of command. Only her straight glance, and erect carriage, that she had taken to town remained as the town was forgotten. The town could not take those from her, the country could only confirm them. Two officers' servants, who had let the chargers they were leading graze surreptitiously on the rich second cut of the water-meadows by the little stream that issued from the moat, hastily pulled up the horses' heads, and resumed the road.

## LA GALETTE

She had made herself known to the new unit that morning, already.

In the dark passage she ran into a dragoon-like figure, that even her accustomed eyes mistook for the moment for that of a soldier. Then she saw who it was, swallowed a lump in the throat, and said:

'Hold, it is you, Placide, enter then, and be seated!'

'Ah, it is you, Madeleine, returned. How do you go on?'

'But well! and you? You can surely take a cup of coffee!'

'I shall not say no! One wants something to give courage in these times that are passing!'

Madeleine was busy over the coffee-pot, and only said: 'Monsieur the Baron and Madame the Baronne have had a sad loss!'

Placide sighed like an eight-day clock running down, and then began. It took ten minutes for her to give her description of the reception of the news of Georges' death at the château – of Monsieur's fit of crying and swearing – of Madame's fainting and prayers. Madeleine stood before her, hands on hips, planted, resisting the sudden, unexpected agony of reviving grief. When Placide remembered what she had come for (eggs and anthracite) and had gone, accompanied by a Belgian with a barrow, Madeleine poured her untasted coffee carefully back into the pot, and slipped out by the back door and away over the fields.

In a few minutes she was mounting the steep sodden path to the Kruysabel. The sun was coming out, and all around the earth steamed. The hunting shelter, intact and not noticeably weathered, had yet an air of neglect. Grass grew where grass should not, the windows were dim with cobweb and fly-smut. The door stuck, and inside the air was warm and mouldy. The photos stared at her, the guardian spirit of the place, as she moved from room to room, tried handles, dusted, rubbed, and shook things. The seats invited her, the mirrors showed her active restlessness. At last she stood still, and some spasm of acute realization seemed to gather and descend on her, and she wrung her hands. 'What will become of it all?' she cried aloud. It, undefined, being the old happy easy life of pre-war. A great sob broke from her, and at its sound in that lonely place of memories, she pulled herself together, put away her things, and looked up. As she trod the reeking moss and gluey mud on the way home, she seemed to be treading something down into the earth, as, alas, many another was to do, like her, throwing in vain a little mould of forgetfulness on the face of recollection that, buried, yet refused to die.

\*

Day succeeded day, mostly wet, almost always noisy. The interminable offensive dragged to its sodden end. Unit succeeded unit, and then French succeeded English, and even the heroes of Verdun, Champagne, the Argonne had no good word to say of their new sector. Gas they knew, and shells and machine-gun fire, but to be drowned was the last refinement of a war that had already surpassed all notions of possible evil, all tales of Sedan, all histories of old-time carnage.

All this made little or no impression upon Madeleine. The old life had slipped back upon her like a glove. German bombs dropped in or about the pasture, spoiled her sleep, made her apprehensive of fire and damage. Otherwise she merely learned from the talk around the kitchen stove that the war was just what she had always felt it to be – a crowning imbecility of insupportable grown-up children. All that one wanted was to be left tranquil. There was always plenty to do, and, if one were only left alone, money to be made. Economics, politics, sociology were beyond her, and had they not been so, they would have weighed with her no more than they ever have done with agricultural, self-contained, home-keeping three-quarters of France. That Germany was anxious for her young industries, England for her old ones, France for her language and racial existence, that governments grow naturally corrupt as milk gets sour, by mere effluxion of time, that captains of industry must be ruthless or perish, all this did not sway her mind. All one wanted was to be left tranquil. Tranquillity being denied, she did the best she could.

The officers who hired the front rooms, the men and animals

billeted in the farm buildings, the N.C.O.s, orderlies, what-not, might be dispirited, jumpy, no longer the easy-going confident English of other years, but they still bought what she had to sell, and paid for what they had – more rather than less, as the conscripted civilian, craving the comforts from which he had been torn, replaced the regular soldier or early volunteer, who had never known or had disdained them. She got a good deal of help with the harvest. The English had all sorts of stores, appliances, above all, plenty of willing arms, that she wanted. The troops 'in rest' were glad enough for the most part, when off duty, to do any small job to take their minds off the world-wide calamity that enveloped them, or that gave the momentary illusion of peace-time ease and freedom. Owing to the submarine campaign they were rather encouraged than otherwise. The harvest, though not magnificent, was fair, and the ever-rising scale of officially fixed prices left always a larger margin of profit. Thus 'One does what one can!' was Madeleine's appropriate comment, when asked. Very little escaped her, as that murderous sodden autumn closed in.

\*

It was about Christmas time that the bombardment of all the back areas, especially Hazebrouck, recommenced in earnest. It was the period at which the Germans regained the initiative. Madeleine noticed a fact like that. She noticed also the extraordinary thinning out of the troops. They either went forward into the line or far back, into rest, beyond St Omer. But the headlines of the papers, the rumours her father brought home from the estaminet, moved her not one whit. The Russian revolution, the advent of America, the British and French manpower questions, Roumanian or Syrian affairs, all left her cold. She read of them in French and English impartially, with all the distrust of her sort for the printed word. It was not until she heard the Baron descant upon the situation, during a visit he paid her father, that she began to take any serious account of the way the war was trending. The Baron had been severely shaken by the death of his son. A view of life, which seldom went beyond personal comfort, had been vitally disconcerted by the final dispersal of one of its cherished comforts, the idea of a son to succeed to and prolong the enjoyment of life. He had the gloomiest forebodings, blamed Russians, Roumanians, English, Americans, Portuguese, Turks, Germans, in turn for the dark days certainly ahead. Madeleine listened with the tolerant submission proper from a chief tenant's daughter towards the master. When the Baron spoke of 'my son', her just appreciation was never misled into thinking that he meant her lover. The two were distinct. She had her own bitter memories, black moods, tears even. That was her affair. The Baron's loss of his son was his, a different matter. She sympathized demurely. As for the news he brought, the probable German offensive in the spring, she made a rapid calculation and dismissed the matter. Not good at imagining, she could not conceive of anything the Germans might do that she would not outwit. The crops and animals, she reckoned, could be stored in safety, the money and valuables she could trust herself to take care of; the solid old house and furniture she could not picture as suffering much damage. Of any personal fear for herself she felt no qualm. Except for a few moments during her illness in Paris, she had known no physical terror since, an infant, she had ceased to be afraid of the dark, finding by experience that it did not touch her. She poured out the Baron's drink at her father's request, and let him talk.

Poor Baron, though Madeleine did not realize it, what else could he do? Born so that he was four years too young to take part in the war of 1870, he was now eight years too old to take part in that of 1914. He could only fight with his tongue, and that he did. But he was fundamentally unchanged, rallied Madeleine on the havoc her good looks must have wrought in Amiens and Paris. Madeleine smiled dutifully. To her he represented one of the guarantees of order and stability. Without an elaborate argument, she concluded that so long as there was a baron above her, and her father, there would be, at the other end of the social scale, labourers, refugees, all sorts of humble folk just as far beneath the level at which she and hers swam. It seemed just that those above and those below should be equally exploitable by the adroit farmer's daughter, anchored securely midway.

*

Spring came, the spring of 1918: surely the most tragically beautiful of all the springs the old world has seen! The frosts and darkness passed. Flowers came out in the Kruysabel. It was a busy time of mucking, ploughing, rolling, sowing. Nothing happened. Hazebrouck, too much bombarded, ceased to hold its market. Madeleine went to Cassel instead. The news of the great German break-through on the Somme did not even impress her, she was busy preparing to get the main-crop potatoes in, before Easter. Let them fight on the Somme, so she might sow Flanders.

But three weeks later there did occur at length something to impress her. On the unforgettable 11 April 1918, the guns were very loud. On the 12th there were hurried movements of troops. All sorts of odd rumours came floating back from all points between Ypres and La Bassée. The Germans had broken through! The Germans had not broken through, but had been thrown back! Estaires was on fire! Locre was taken and so on. Madeleine had occasion to go to the Mairie, to argue as to why her old Territorials should have been recalled from the farm, and found Monsieur Blanquart packing all his records into a great wooden case. He stopped and stared at her:

'What are you doing, Monsieur Blanquart?'

He raised his hands with unaccustomed nervousness.

'It is a formal order from the Government!'

He would not listen to her tale of billeting money unpaid, and government fertilizer not delivered: 'There are other things to do at this moment,' was all he would say. For once Madeleine did not get her way. That impressed her. The next day the horizon to the south and east was black with pillars of smoke. By night these became pillars of flame, biblical, ominous. The incessant sounds of battle changed in timbre. The heavy bombardment ceased. Nearer and nearer crept the rattle of machineguns. Madeleine had one or two errands, and returning by the village shortly afterwards, was astonished to find all the shops shut. Vanhove, the butcher, was loading his best brass bedstead and mattress on to – what of all conceivable vehicles? Madeleine stared before she took it in. It was the roller, the road roller. None other. The well-known road roller the English had installed. Built by Aveling & Porter at Rochester in the 'eighties, it had ground and panted its unwieldy frame northward through many a township and village of England, passing from hand to ever poorer hand, as it deteriorated, until finally the obscure and almost penniless Rural District Council of Marsham and Little Uttersfield, failing to sell it, had painted their name on its boiler and kept it. Unloaded, like so many other derelicts, into the arms of the British Expeditionary Force in the glad enthusiasm of 1915, it had served the turn of an intelligent English Engineer, who, early in the war, had discovered that roads and railways, food and patience alone could win in such a struggle. He had soon been shipped off to the East, lest he bring shame upon his betters, but his roller had remained for years now, on that section of the Joint Road Control of the Second English Army, with the French Ponts et Chaussées Authority, who divided acrimoniously between them the control of the Hazebrouck sub-area. The machine had become a portent in Hondebecq. The children had swung behind it, horses ceased to shy at it, and Madeleine herself had come, in time, to have something almost like affection for it, as a monument of the queer, wayward genius of the English. No such rollers ever rolled the roads of France, but Madeleine had found it useful for both rolling and traction. She had made friends with the two middle-aged, sooty-khakied Derbyshire men who lived with it and got them to do jobs for her. Now, she laid a hand gingerly on the warm shining rail of the 'cab' and asked of the driver.

'What are you doing!'

'Got to go, mamzelle, partee, you know!'

'You like a ride, miss? Get up and we'll take you as far as St Omer!' his mate added. 'Alleman's coming, you know!'

Something fierce prompted Madeleine to say: 'I'm not going to run away!' But Vanhove, having hoisted his bedstead into the tender, was persuading the men to drive on.

Madeleine saw the lever put over, and the ponderous machine of another generation roar away upon the cobbles, its single cylinder panting desperately. Then she felt indeed disturbed, as though she had been forced to part with a conviction.

*

As she went back to the farm through the fairy beauty of the evening – (were ever evenings so beautiful as those of the April retreat?) – her step was no less firm, her glance as calm as usual. Passing over the plank bridge, and entering the house by the back, she was confronted by the spectacle of Berthe in her best hat, with a bundle.

'I'm going!' said the apparition simply.

'What has come over you?'

'After you were gone, an English wagon came, all full of people from Armentières way. The secretary of Nieppe told the patron that the Bosche are in Laventie, and that Marie has left, so the Patron has taken the tumbril and gone after her potatoes!'

Madeleine was at no loss. She even approved the old man's determination. Only she considered that it would have been better for her to go.

'You stay here,' she said. 'I'm going up to the château to borrow the young Baron's bicycle!' She knew well enough that Georges' machine was stowed away in the coachhouse. On that she could catch her father, and send him back. But she had not reckoned up the situation.

'No,' said Berthe, 'I'm going!'

'Why, you're not frightened like that silly lot from Armentières?'

But the terror-stricken faces and bandaged heads of those civilians in the lorry, who had so narrowly escaped the battle, had broken Berthe's nerve – which was never the equal of Madeleine's. She shouldered her bundle.

'I'm going!' she said simply.

Madeleine was not accustomed to being disobeyed, and there

is no knowing what she might not have done had she not been in a hurry herself.

'Very well, go then! Tell the Picquart family to lock up the sheds. I'm going after the patron!'

'The Picquarts are gone, this half-hour, with their things in the wheelbarrow!'

Just then the breeze that stirs at dusk swung open the door, and there entered into the darkening passage with startling nearness the rat-tat-tat-tat-tat of German machine-guns. Madeleine flung away: 'Go and burst yourselves as quick as possible, heap of dirtiness!' she cried, and set off at a run for the château.

The village seemed even more ominous than before, now it was half dark, and not a light in the abandoned houses. Some English transport was crossing the square, however, with the patient sour look of men going 'into it' again – 'it', the battle. She turned into the steep silent alley that led through the iron grille, to the 'drive' of the château, and broke into a run again on the smooth gravel. She had not gone twenty yards before she jumped as if shot. A black figure had risen behind the trunk of a tree with a sharp 'Hish!' She fell sideways, clutching an elm sapling that bent with her, staring. The figure made two steps towards her, and she, petrified, could only maintain her balance and stare. Then with infinite relief she heard: 'Tiens, it's you, Madeleine! What do you want?'

'Why, Monsieur le Baron, I didn't know you!'

'Be quiet then. There is some one wandering round the château. It may be the Bosche!'

'What, are they here?'

'The village has been formally evacuated. One expects them from one moment to another!'

At that instant steps and voices could be heard on the terrace surrounding the house, which, on account of the winding of the drive by way of the old moat, was just above the level of their eyes. The Baron, quivering all over, not with fear, but with sporting instinct, brought his spiked camp stool to the charge, and tiptoed noiselessly up the bank. Madeleine, clutching her skirt with one hand, swinging herself up by the undergrowth with the other, arrived beside him just in time to see two familiar Australian figures looming leisurely in the darkness. In another instant the Baron would have sprung, with no one knows what results. Madeleine pushed past him, stepped over the flower-bed that bordered the terrace, and walked up to the visitors, addressing them in their own inimitable language, learned from their own lips in the kitchen of the Spanish Farm:

'Hello, Digger, what you want?'

The tall lean men turned without surprise:

'To get in,' replied the nearer.

Madeleine hastily translated. The Baron, after staring a moment, led the way to the back.

The château possessed, of course, no bell or knocker, as Leon, the concierge, or his wife, were always to be found near the gate, to steer front-door visitors round to their appropriate entrance, and open for them. Lesser mortals came to the kitchen door, where Placide dealt with them as St Peter is reported to deal with ambitious souls in another place. Since the war, and more especially since the concierge and all his family had been evacuated, the whole of the windows and doors were closed, bolted and shuttered.

The first object that met the gaze of the little party, as they rounded the corner of the building, was Leon's garden ladder, reared against the window of the Baron's dressing-room, in the eastern wing, from which protruded the hind-quarters and legs of a man, in stout service riding breeches and dirty boots.

'Thunder of God,' cried the Baron, seizing the ladder and shaking it violently, 'come down, or I'll bring you!'

An Australian added quietly, 'You'd best come down, Mercadet, and tell Jim!'

A few hurried calls in Franco-English and laconic Australian replies, and a French interpreter climbed, an Australian soldier slid, down the ladder.

'Well, sir,' demanded the Baron of the former, 'you have large views of your duties!'

'Sir,' replied the interpreter, 'the place is officially evacuated. We have a right here. You have not!'

'I have said I will not budge,' replied the Baron, folding his arms, 'and budge I will not!'

'Monsieur le Baron,' interposed Madeleine, 'all these will be very useful if the Bosche come!'

The Baron strode to the heavy kitchen door and struck a succession of blows with his stick, shouting at the top of his voice, 'Placide, open then, you are as lazy as stupid!'

Very shortly a light glimmered and the bolts shot back. The door turned, and Placide barred the way, as an old-fashioned clothes-horse covers a blazing fire. It took her a moment or two to understand.

'Ah, it is you, Monsieur le Baron!'

'Did you think it was the devil?'

'I was upstairs seeing to the calorifère of Madame, who is in the chapel. I thought you were gone to the village!'

Her master pushed past. 'Here are officers come to billet. Are the rooms ready?'

He had, of course, assumed that none but officers would dream of coming to the château of Hondebecq.

Madeleine, by the light of Placide's candle, soon knew better. The Australian who had spoken was a Colonel, the other two and the French interpreter were privates. As they trooped into the passage, the Colonel called over his shoulder, 'Come on, boys!'

From the kitchen garden, where they had sat silent and unnoticed spectators of the scene, there emerged a Lewis-gun section and orderlies. Beyond them transport was dimly visible: mules silent as their drivers, standing as if cut in stone.

'Madeleine,' called the Baron, 'explain to these gentlemen that all my servants have run off, but that Placide will serve supper as soon as may be!'

The Colonel, however, was busy with his machine-gunners. The 'cubby hutch', as he called Leon's potting shed, half-way up the drive would do for one position well, but he wished to command the garden and meadow beyond, and the fields skirting

140

the village on that side. Madeleine understood perfectly. 'There is the cellar skylight, level with the ground.'

The Colonel went to look. 'It fits like the tail of Barnes' donkey!' was his only comment.

Before he would sit down to his meal he asked: 'Do I get the old man right, that his wife is here still?'

'She is praying for her son in the chapel!'

'Is he wounded?'

'He is dead.'

'He'll be just as happy if she keeps alive. I've got a limber going back St Omer way. She'd better go in that! Tell 'em!'

Madeleine explained the offer to the Baron, who thanked the Colonel profusely, saying that it was worthy of one gentleman to another.

The Colonel not understanding, when his mouth was empty, bowed as one unaccustomed and inquired: 'It is his wife, isn't it, all correct?'

Madeleine confirmed that the Baroness was 'all correct'.

But the Baroness was an obstacle. First Placide, then the Baron himself went up to see her. She would only moan: 'No, let them kill me, I shall see him again all the sooner. Besides, it is too late, and I am at least warm with the calorifère!'

Then Madeleine went up. There was nothing dramatic in the meeting between those two, the mother and the mistress of a dead man. Madeleine said steadily: 'Madame, Monsieur Georges would prefer you to go!'

'You think so?'

'I am sure, madame!'

'In that case, I will!'

Madeleine helped her. But no one, unless it was the French interpreter, realized the pathos of the moment. The limber had been furnished with cushions, a small trunk, and a wooden box of Placide's. The driver had announced that he was 'going by the dirt roads, it's easier for wimmen.' Then that faded lady kissed the man whom she had married because the Second Empire told her to, and replied to his 'Courage, Eugènie,' simply: 'I think I shall not catch cold!' and went away in an army limber, with Placide stalking behind.

*

Madeleine watched them go. Alone of all those present she, perhaps, noticed the change which seemed to settle down on the house, almost at once. It was not yet abandoned, but its women, its natural guardians, had gone from it.

The orderly, ration 'fag' in mouth, cleared the table with a clatter, spilling grease on the floor. The marble overmantel, between the vases a former D'Archeville had brought from the sack of Pekin, and the Sèvres clock, became, as though by magic, littered with pipes, ashes, revolver ammunition, maps, indelible pencils – all the flotsam of men campaigning far from the decencies of property and housewifery. She tried to get the Baron on one side, having not for a moment forgotten her business at the château, but he was busy giving the Colonel, and a young officer who had come quietly in, as if by chance, some detail of the district. Before she could make her wants known, the Colonel, who had swept back the cloth, silver salts, plates, flower vases, all at one sweep, planted his 1 in 40,000 army map, and had his finger on the square pasture, and centreless E of building labelled 'Ferme l'espagnole' – the Spanish Farm.

'That belongs to mademoiselle,' the interpreter interposed, prompted by the Baron, indicating her.

'Arthur,' said the Colonel to the young officer, 'your platoon can make a "strong point" there, where the roads join, and sleep in the house, while it's worth it!'

In an instant, Madeleine relinquished all thoughts of pursuing her father on the Baron's bicycle. It was not merely that if she had had to choose between loyalty to her father and loyalty to the home, she would have chosen the latter. It was also that, had her father been there to counsel her, he would certainly have said, 'Gardez la maison, ma fille!' 'Stick to the house, my girl.'

'I'll go with you,' she told the lieutenant, and went out into the darkness with him.

## LA GALETTE

The horizon, from beyond Ypres, to the north-east, right round to near Béthune to the south, was ablaze. Over captured Merville, Estaires, Armentières, hung floating lights. The bombardment had ceased, the Bosche being too fearful of hitting their own advanced parties. The machine-gun clamour was subsiding, both sides no longer knowing in the darkness where their bullets went. The farm Madeleine found already occupied. Tall lean figures, magnified in the candle-light, had stripped lengths of fabric from an aeroplane that had come down in the pasture, and lay half buried, grotesquely mangled, a putrefying mass of charred human flesh, wood and delicate machinery in the middle. They were covering every crevice in the kitchen windows. They made shelters, and gun-pits, and loopholes. By midnight the house was no longer a farm, it was a tactical 'strong point'. Madeleine had too much sense to protest, and declined firmly to be evacuated. Calling the officer and sergeant together, she pointed to her door:

'This my room. I lock the door. See, diggers?'

'All serene, missy, sleep well,' was the reply.

Madeleine did so. Like all those strong enough to stand it, she felt a kind of exaltation rising above any fear. Many a man felt like her that night. The long-distance bombardment, under which a human being was matched against a lump of steel as large and many times harder than himself, was over. To it succeeded the direct struggle of man against man, with machine-gun, rifle and grenade. The Bosche were no longer awe-inspiring once they got beyond the range of their big guns. Let them come, the sooner the better. The great offensive had been threatened for months. It was here. Some would survive it. Meantime the chances were even. Madeleine slept.

\*

No one knows, to this day, why the Bosche never got to Hondebecq, but they halted a mile short of it. Nothing happened. Anticlimax ruled. War moods of exaltation, begotten of danger, and the vitality that rises to meet it, cannot last. The battle of Bailleul dwindled out in grey, cold spring weather. The trench line stiffened and became as fixed as the old line from the Ypres salient to La Bassée had been, before Messines and Paschendaele. The Bosche tried again and again farther south with no more effect. In the north the reorganized English line held good. The mood which came with this new state of things began to show itself, in civilians and soldiers alike, to be one of steady exasperation. For what did all this endless effort amount to? One lived in a state not comparable to that of Peace, as regards comfort, business, or personal liberty. One side or the other made an offensive. The discomfort increased, the hectic war-time business was dislocated, personal liberty disappeared. But one thing remained – War. Enormously expensive, omnipresent, exasperating. Civilians and soldiers, the latter nearly all unwilling civilians now, felt its exasperation. Madeleine felt it. The Baron felt it. The troops billeted in the château and the farm felt it. The Baron, relieved from his wife's querulous exactions, Madeleine, set free from dutiful if doubtful belief in her father's methods of business, found the first Australian troops, if not charming visitors, at least good companions for the work in hand.

When it became certain that the enemy could get no farther, they were relieved, first by French troops, then by a Clydeside labour battalion. The Baron found his salle-à-manger filled with officers, who, though not actively ill-behaved, and probably well-meaning, he could see, whether he spoke their language or not, came of no particular family.

Madeleine found herself confronted with a set of cooks and quartermasters as businesslike as herself, far more akin to her methods and outlook than had ever been the original volunteer army of England – who had paid what she asked with shy good humour. The neat walks and formal 'bosquets' of the château garden, box-hedged, and decorated with plaster figures of nymphs and cupids, situate amid greenish pools, became pitted with latrines, and scarred with dug-outs.

The village was beyond bullet range, but a 5.9 shell crashed in the top of the 'shot' tower in the yard of the Spanish Farm. But worse than these evils were the continual thefts from the cellar of the château of wine, coal, and mattresses (for half the village had readily obtained leave to store their possessions there). At the farm, Madeleine was amazed to find herself forced to sell beer and butter, at less than cost price, by well-organized 'strikes' that threatened to leave her merchandise on her hands.

The Baron, moreover, like so many of his age and nation at that time, had his private sorrow. Sharing his meals with the ever-changing messes of officers that filled his salle-à-manger (for the village being evacuated, there were no shops, and he was glad enough to trade away the accommodation he could to provide for food), he would stare round the youthful, unwarlike faces about him, faces of professional or business men, farmers or engineers from all corners of Great Britain or the Colonies, and would mutter, 'I have no longer my son!'

Madeleine, more self-controlled, wore black. No funeral service had been said for Jerome Vanderlynden. He had 'disappeared' in the trite phrase of the Casualty Lists. The old church in the 'place' of Hondebecq had three gaping shell-holes in the roof. The doors were closed, and it was declared in brief official notice 'Unsafe'. She did not even know if her numerous cousins and relations by marriage, scattered by the evacuation all across France from Evreux to Bordeaux, had heard what had happened to him. Nor did the thought of them greatly trouble her, accustomed to think and act for herself. She was doing what she knew so well her father was expecting of her. She was looking after the farm. The crops were sown. Such beasts as remained were tended. Jerome Vanderlynden had disappeared! That could not be helped, any more than the thefts of all the fowls from the yard. Madeleine just went on.

*

The days went by, and the two civilians left in Hondebecq hardly noticed a change that came over things in the last week of July 1918. That war, continuing year in and year out, could not be measured according to its 'victories' of one side or the other, by people so intensely intimate with it, because they lived on the edge of the trenches. The most perhaps that they noticed was the gradual cessation of the shelling. It was no longer necessary to run to dug-outs from one's bed at dawn, or from one's evening meal. Yet at last, something really had happened. Madeleine was dimly conscious of a new atmosphere in the shuttered and sand-bagged salle-à-manger, when she went up on one of her usual errands to the château. The old interpreter, Mercadet, attached to the area, was sticking flags in the map of the Western Front, with his melancholy precision. 'One has still some force left!' he announced, and Madeleine saw without heeding that he was *moving the flags forward, instead of back.* It was, of course, Mangin's flank attack of July, the turning-point of the war. She paid more attention, however, a week or two later, when the troops in the farm began to move. The Bosche were gone from Kemmel Hill, was all they said. She lost touch with the war at this point, having no one to give her news.

She contrived to secure a couple of mules she found wandering about, and being handy with animals, shut them up and fed them sparingly. Probably nothing in the whole war frightened her so much as those weeks of the month of September, when she was quite alone. Even the dog had been killed by the shell on the 'shot' tower. Then, as the troops abandoned the château she found there a couple of aged veterans, left as billet wardens, and induced them, by pointing out truthfully how much better they would fare with her than in the Baron's company in the lonely château, to move to the farm. These two old casual labourers, who had enlisted in 1914 when drunk or workless, and had ever since been living better than before the war, made no difficulties. But it was no object to her to make hardships for the Baron, once she had gained her point, and secured potential guardians and labourers for the farm. She invited him to take his meals with her, and neither laughed nor chided as he stumped off, cigar glowing in the dark, to sleep on the motheaten rugs in his gun-room, revolver beside him, lest the château should be robbed – though what indeed there remained to steal in the darkened rooms, save the heavy furniture, no one could have said – wine, food, bedding, small objects had gone one by one, for use, or as souvenirs. The silver had been buried by Mercadet in the garden. But the Baron slept in the empty château, by instinct.

He was not alone long.

There was an almost dramatic fitness about the Army's choice of his one companion. A red-headed Welshman, answering to the name of Jacobs, was posted there, as District Sanitary Engineer. The glamour and intensity was gone from the war, and the situation was now one for Municipal Health Officers. The appointment was additionally fitting. For though adorned by the title of 'doctor', and adorning the rank of Captain, Jacobs was by profession a Borough Sanitary Engineer, one of those species peculiar to Great Britain. In its dying stages, those who ran the war were at last learning to put men to the job they could do best.

\*

Such was the situation of what the French staff aptly called the 'open town' of Hondebecq in the last weeks of the war. By daylight, the Spanish Farm was at work, Madeleine and her two veterans, with the two mules, getting in all the undamaged crops – for nearly a quarter of the total acreage of the farm was lost in trench and wire, dug-out and shell-hole. Hardly a day passed but had its hair-breadth escape from buried 'duds' or unexploded shell, or caved-in gun-pit. Madeleine worked because it was natural to her – because she had nothing else to do, possibly with some unconscious idea of dedication to her father's memory. At dusk, Jacobs and the Baron would arrive, on bicycles, the one having toured his area, which stretched from the line of evacuation that ran from the Belgian border, through Hazebrouck down to Aire – away to the maze of desultory trenches from which the English troops were slowly pushing the last German machine-gunners. The Baron usually acted as his guide, and in Jacobs' company avoided otherwise certain arrest. Madeleine would just be finishing her evening meal with the veterans. Jacobs would produce a field message book in which he had noted the map reference of any unburied offence, human or otherwise, and at his order the old men would jog off with one of the tireless mules in a salvaged limber, two shovels, a tin of disinfectant, and a lantern clattering in the springless vehicle. Madeleine cleared the table and served dinner to Jacobs and the Baron, who would sit over it, drinking canteen whisky and discussing in English–French and French–English the submarine menace and surface drainage, by means of any daily papers they had gleaned during the day's wandering, and with the help of Madeleine's translation. By the time both were ready to return to their never-made 'beds' in the château, the veterans would come clattering back, the mules going at an unearthly amble in the darkness, and all was ready for the morrow.

\*

The War had been full of surprises – had been one great catastrophic surprise, since its declaration, and had kept up its pyrotechnic suddenness of change through all its four years. But the change that extinguished it outdid all else in strangeness. Late in October, the inhabitants of the château and the farm had heard the familiar sound of twelve-inch shells falling in Dunkirk, and never dreamed that they were never to hear that sound again. All day the roads and rail had been busy with French and English troops. They had halted in and around Hondebecq and passed on. The inhabitants of the farm and the château little dreamed that no more were to pass that way. The days and nights became quieter and ever more strangely quiet. There was a continual tension of the ear to catch that familiar rat-tat-tat, swish, boom. No sound came. Then, early in grey November, Jacobs and the Baron returned earlier than usual from their eternal cycling tour. In all the cellars of Hazebrouck, in all the hastily contrived, already-forgotten 'strong points' in the area, they had not found one unburied mule, one neglected latrine. Or Jacobs had forgotten to take map references, for both were excited. Instead, they bent over a day-old English paper, that pretended to have the terms of the Armistice.

At first it was mere meaningless words. Nothing happened.

## LA GALETTE

The daily life of Hondebecq did not change. But soon a phenomenon was observed. Up the solid grey pavé road that Napoleon built from Lille to Dunkirk, along which the victorious armies of mid-October had advanced, there flowed, in the opposite direction, another human stream. No army this, and nothing victorious about it, though here and there a dirty old hat, or wonderfully made, decrepit wheelbarrow was decorated with the flags of the Allies, bought from Germans who had been selling them during their last weeks in the French industrial area. By one and two, here a family, there an individual with a dog, all those civilians who had been swept within the German lines in the offensives of 1914 or 1918, were walking home. Such a home-coming surely never was since misery began. Doré used to picture such events in his illustrations to the Bible, but no one has even seen the like in reality. For censors had been strict, and the line of trenches where the Allies had fronted the Germans unpassable. Many a man of the Flemish border, or the Somme downs, had hoped to find his house or his field spared, and had to go to look himself in order to be finally disillusioned. Madeleine, superintending the cleaning of the fields, the weed burning, and autumn ploughing, saw them come incuriously, not able to realize that even she, who had seen the whole War through, with the trenches only just beyond the sight of her eyes and never out of her hearing, had only now to begin to learn what it really had been.

She left the veterans and the mules, busy in the fields, and stood, for a few moments, on the edge of the pavé, where the by-road to the farm left it, watching the melancholy procession. True, some were laughing, or greeted her with a cheer, but the general impression of those pinched faces and anxious eyes, above worn and filthy clothes, gave a better idea than any historian will ever do, of the rigours of the blockade. Madeleine gained from the sight just her first inkling of the irreparable LOSS, that was to weigh upon the lifetime of her generation. War, the Leviathan, was giving up that which it had swallowed, but there was no biblical jubilation in them, none of those sharp terrors that, in scripture, foretell everlasting joy. Madeleine, better than any Bible-reading Protestant, comprehended. These poor souls (as she called them to herself, pityingly, for they had been 'caught out', a defect she did not admit) had now got to work to catch up the wastage. A bright chance for most of them!

She returned to the farm, and now, finally convinced of the Armistice, yoked the mules to the strongest tackle she could find amid the abandoned and salvaged engineer .stores that Jacobs had gathered, and began to pull away the barbed wire that laced the farm about, fifty yards at a time.

\*

She worked thus with the veterans, beating, shouting at, jerking the mouths of the mules, tugging, cutting, coiling the rusted venomous strands, piling the stout pickets on one side for further use, until it was nearly dark. Hastening home to prepare supper she noticed a dark bent figure standing irresolutely in the courtyard. She was walking over the slippery furrows by aid of a half pick-handle, but, though thus armed, was unafraid, and found something unaccountably familiar in that listless bent-shouldered form. Coming up to it, she gave a cry. It was the ghost of Jerome Vanderlynden. She took him by the hand, called him 'Father', told him with a choke in her voice that she was glad to see him back. He just stared at her, but when spoken to with decision, sat in the settle by the stove, and smiled at the warmth and the smell of food. Other sign of animation he would not give, nor could she elicit what he thought, or how he had found his way home. When her veterans came in from the stable, she introduced him, and they displayed all the kindliness of their sort, seemed to understand at a glance the nature of the case, called him 'Poor old gentleman' and offered him a ration cigarette, which he took, and immediately laid aside, as if he did not know its use. He appeared better for the food and rest, and was willing to be led to the bare tiled bedroom in which he had always occupied the crazy old double bed, where his children had been born and his wife had died, and which, with the big old press, two pegs, and two photos of the children, constituted

## LA GALETTE

the whole furniture. He allowed Madeleine to help him off with his sodden, shapeless boots, rolled on the bed, and slept. Madeleine covered him and left him. In the morning he appeared, awakened apparently by habit, or the smell of food, but replied only by vacant looks to his daughter's questions – pertinently designed as they were – 'What has happened to the horse and tumbril?' 'Where have you been?' 'Do you remember me?'

To the blandishments of the veterans (well-meant attempts to cheer him up), he paid no regard. It was not Jerome Vanderlynden who had returned. It was his ghost, something that having lost its human mortal life, could not quite die, but must wander about the scenes to which it was accustomed, handle the objects it had used, but nothing more.

\*

The condition of her father might have weighed heavily on Madeleine's mind had it been her only preoccupation, but fortunately it was not. First of all there was work. She was working harder than anybody ever works in England. From before the grey wet winter dawn, until long after the solitary army candle had been lighted in the kitchen, making grotesque shadows in the broken glass of the oriel window, her hands were never still, tugging, smoothing, shifting earth, timber, wire, weeds, produce; housework, cooking, mending, were relaxations. Her mind and voice, thinking for and directing the veterans, the mules, presently the four bullocks and two milch cows, she contrived to obtain from those wandering loose after the break-up of the trench lines, were never still except during the six or so hours that she slept. She regarded the Armistice as a piece of personal good luck. She would get the ground into some sort of order before the spring sowing. There would be manure, too, now that she had beasts, and with manure at hand, no Fleming ever quite loses heart. But besides work, the Peace that had so suddenly descended upon earth (without, alas, bringing that Goodwill supposed for centuries to accompany it) proved itself more inexorable than War.

Things began to move, released from the numbing strangulation of four and a quarter years. Jacobs and the veterans got orders to proceed to Courtrai, and continue the good work of cleansing the ornamental waters of that town from the use to which the German officers had put them. This disturbance of her source of labour gave Madeleine some moments' thought, but the sight of the Dequidt family, trudging back to their farm on foot, having been returned from evacuation in the Cherbourg district, opened up a new means of dealing with the problem. Her farm was nearly in order, her house more or less intact, her larder stocked with the good tinned stuff of the British Expeditionary Force Canteen. Theirs would not be so. She would give of her ample store, in return for work. There was one duty with which, however, she preferred to trust the two veterans, rather than any of her neighbours. Now that they were going, she thought of them in the terms in which she had once thought of a lieutenant called Skene. They were willing and well behaved. Moreover, they were going back to England (indicated by their saying to her, 'What Ho, for Blighty,' many times a day), so that they were safe. With smiles and encouraging words she led them to the foot of the shot tower. It was badly cracked by the shell that had hit the top, and great lumps of brickwork, a yard cube, had fallen, blocking the door; elm beams a foot square lay jammed across the broken floor. It took three hours' hard work to effect an entrance. Then Madeleine kneeled down, put her arms through the broken boards, and fished up a length of stout iron chain. 'Pull,' she commanded, handing it over. The veterans, spitting on their hands, and setting their heels against the cobbles, called 'Heave-ho!' as the chain emerged link by link. Finally, with a clatter and smash, a great iron box was retrieved. Madeleine unhooked it from the chain and bade them carry it to the house.

Once she had it on the kitchen table, having wiped the worst of the muddy water from it, and assured herself it was intact, she gave a sigh of relief. It was the savings of her father's lifetime, that had been withdrawn from the Savings Bank when Hazebrouck was first bombarded, and hidden thus by her. Seeing it before her, Madeleine made what the French call a 'gesture' – one of those actions prompted by emotions deeper than reason – in this case by the only genuine feeling at the base of the otherwise politician-manufactured Entente Cordiale. She had found the English friends in need, not too exacting, fairly ready to pay for what they wanted. They had been a comfort at the beginning of, through the long length of, and now at the daily growing aftermath of disillusionment with, the War. She took two notes, 20 francs each, from her purse, and distributed them to the veterans. Those members of England's Last Hope pocketed the money, exclaiming with one voice, 'Thank you, Maddam,' winking solemnly at each other.

That evening Jacobs took his leave, and she charged him for exactly what he had had. He departed into the darkness, to catch the newly established train service over the hastily repaired line, the veterans wheeling his valise and their own packs on a salved Lewis-gun hand cart.

\*

With the departure of that party the British Army in Flanders finally left the Spanish Farm, after four years. The longed-for golden reign of Peace was re-established. And anything less golden cannot be imagined. Madeleine lost no time in getting into touch with the evacuated neighbours now returning to their farms. They were nearly all women, and though they were willing enough to work, they had neither the dexterity nor the resources of the British Army. Madeleine wished indeed, before many weeks were over, that the War had lasted longer. There was the big kitchen window, not to mention sundry other panes broken by carelessness, or by concussion of bombing and shelling, to be reglazed. There were leaks in the roof to mend, there was the shot tower to rebuild – unless indeed she built some other stowage room for all the things it used to hold – sacks, 'fertilizer', tools, roots, grain, hops, spare cart covers, timber. There were nineteen gates missing, endless lengths of hedge and ditch practically to be made over again. The hurdles were all gone, and worst of all, the great fifteen-feet hop-poles and stout wire. As was usual throughout French Flanders, the British

Army had burned every piece of wood upon the farm. Madeleine did not blame them. A French or any other army would have done the same. There was, however, one good job that the War had done: the tall elms round the pasture had been completely barked by the numerous mounted units that had succeeded each other. They would die, and the proprietor (the Baron to wit) would do well to sell them at once, while the price was so high. The ground would be disencumbered, more grass would grow and the great roots would no longer suck up all the manure one put down. The only loser would be the Baron. It was his affair.

\*

For already Peace had brought that endless attempt to go one better than one's neighbour, which, for four years, had been hidden under the more immediate necessity to go one better than the Bosche. Thus Madeleine, perceiving that whatever the eventual scheme of compensation, she must pay, in the first instance, nearly all the loss occasioned, began actually to grudge the English their demobilization. Had they (and their dumps of material) remained in the neighbourhood, she would have got them to do plumbing and glazing, ditching and joinery, and to give her good telephone wire, aeroplane canvas, oil, paint and nails. Instead of which, every day that she went as far as the Lille road, she saw trainloads of useful English, singing and cheering on their way to Dunkirk, where they were being demobbed by thousands a day. So she grew bitter, and having no one else to blame (for who could blame old Jerome, wandering helpless like a worn-out horse) she began to blame the English for going away. Madame la Baronne had returned to the château. Placide was once more functioning, and the Baron was only seen at the farm on his walks, as before the offensive of 1918. So that there was absolutely no one but the English to blame for having departed so inopportunely. There was nothing exceptional in Madeleine's case. It was, indeed, the common feeling in all those French and Flemish farms on the border of what had been the trenches (the frontiers of civilization) and was now the Devastated Area (something no one wanted, and everybody was tired of hearing about). This being so, the Government, depending upon votes, saw that something must be done to retain those sources of its power and emoluments, lest they be filched by Bolsheviks, Germans, Socialists or other enemies – in fact by persons who might come to wield the power, and enjoy the resulting advantages, which every government looks upon as the permanent reward of the endless corruption by which it has maintained itself.

Thus, about this time, Madeleine began to hear of things called 'Reparations', that the Germans were going to be made to pay. She was invited to inscribe at the Mairie the list of damage done by the War to the farm. She went to see Monsieur Blanquart, and furnished him with a list that totalled 131,415 francs 41 centimes (the total market value of the farm in 1914 being about 120,000 francs). Monsieur Blanquart inscribed the lot. He did more. Like every one else, he felt that he had had an atrocious time for many years, and that nothing was too good for him. Keeping in close touch with his daughter Cécile, at Amiens, he had been quite sharp enough to see how things were shaping. He had hung in the windows of his little parlour, and all round the mayoral office at the Estaminet de la Mairie, in place of the patriotic appeals by M. Deschanel to fortitude and patience, in place of lists of conscripts, and of ever-mounting food prices, little cards incribed 'Blanquart, financial agent'; 'Blanquart, bonds, shares, assurances'. He unfolded golden schemes to Madeleine, who, listened with her special 'stupid peasant' expression that she kept for the occasions when she was thinking hard. Her list of war damages was based not so much on facts and figures as on her one idea of any monetary transaction – namely, to ask twice as much as a thing is worth, in the certainty that you will be beaten down by at least a quarter. She was no more deceived by the talk in the papers than by Blanquart's 'financial operations'. She knew how difficult it was for her to part with money or money's worth, and judged the Germans, and Blanquart's stocks and shares, by her own standards. Pay! Not likely, Germans or Royal Dutch, not if they could help it. But standing hatless and vacant-faced before Blanquart, she was working out in her mind one of her slowly conceived plans, so much less simple than one would have supposed from her appearance. She had enough cash in the iron box to buy two horses and get along until harvest.

'Look here, Monsieur Blanquart, I'll take 50,000 francs' worth of your bonds, and pay you when I get my "Reparations".'

But Blanquart had not lived in the village all those years for nothing. 'You comprehend,' he replied, 'your reparations are subject to discussion!'

'No doubt; but I suppose one will pay us something!'

'Undoubtedly, but how much? – that's the point!'

Madeleine got up and moved towards the door. 'Oh, well, it's a pity!' she said.

Blanquart hated to see her go. She was one of the richest 'heiresses' in the village (as heiresses go in France), and there was only Marie to divide it with her when old Jerome died. Moreover, she had quite a reputation for the part she had played in the last phases of the War, and it would be a great help to be able to say to the others: 'Madeleine Vanderlynden has taken 50,000.' He offered: 'Look here, I'll buy your reparations for 40,000!'

'No, nothing to be done,' was the answer, hand on the latch.

In his heart Monsieur Blanquart pested the sacred peasants. But something must be arranged. 'Very well, I sell you 40,000 worth of securities, and you can pay me when you get your "Reparations"!'

Madeleine left the doorway and came back to the table. Looking through his stocked portfolio she chose only bearer bonds (coupons appealed to her; the less tangible dividend warrant of inscribed or registered stock did not), some national, some industrial, some lottery. Thus armed, she returned to the farm.

\*

Thus came what Politicians called 'Peace', but mostly French people, realists in a sense that the English public never is, spoke of it as the 'era of La Galette' – the cake which one could eat

## LA GALETTE

and yet have again, the pie in which every one's finger might be – the lucky-bag into which all might dip.

Upon the mentality of France, with its dominant peasant outlook, only one deep impression was made. The Germans were beaten. Therefore their money could be got at. Anyone who did not get at it was a fool, simply. This was not piracy. The Germans had invited a contest, and lost. The loser pays – that is logic as well as human nature. When the first hints were dropped that there might be delays, even a dwindling of the golden stream that was to flow from Berlin – public feeling became so strong that Government had hastily to vote sums 'on account of' the Reparations to be exacted. In every village, men, and more often women, asked each other: 'What have you estimated your damages at?' 'What have you received on account?' In place of the War-time watchwords 'La Patrie est en danger' and 'On les aura', there might very reasonably have been displayed another: 'La Galette' – The Cake that every one might take. 'L'assiette au beurre' – The butter-dish to grease every itching palm. 'Le pot au vin' – The loving-cup that was ever full.

\*

Before she could put the War finally away from her, Madeleine had to go through a process which might be called in English, the laying of ghosts. Without active belief in the supernatural, and prone to laughter at those who dared not pass the Kruysabel, after dusk, without crossing themselves (this superstition was one of the safeguards that had kept her meetings with Georges secure), she preserved to the full the clear feeling of all primitives, that the Living are connected with, influenced by, the Departed. The most immediate case was that of her father. Jerome Vanderlynden had never recovered his reason, but had recaptured a few words, and most of his bodily functions. What had been done, or not done, to him, during his eight months behind the German lines, will never be known. A neighbour, also swallowed up by the swift invasion of April 1918, had seen him, near Lille, working in a field, under German direction, but had not been recognized. At that date, even, the old man had lost his senses. He bore no particular signs of ill-usage, other than the common starvation caused by blockade, and, after weeks of loving care, Madeleine, nearest to him, most like him of all people on earth, managed to make out what he mumbled to himself, with that scared look, when his food was set before him: 'There's nothing left to eat!' he whispered, with a frightened glance around. Then, when coaxed, he would eat, rapidly, defensively.

Madeleine, no theorist, came to the conclusion that the fact that he had been interrupted in the middle of sowing his potatoes, and had then found the stock of food at Marie's farm destroyed or taken, had unhinged his mind. At that she had to leave it, and although the old man's iron health did not vary, she had sorrowfully to admit that, as father and parent, as companion and guide, he was gone from her, just as effectively as though she had buried him in the churchyard, beneath the battered, spireless old church, that filled all one side of the grande place of the village. So strongly did she feel this, that she refused to let the curé worry him about his soul.

Thus was one ghost laid.

\*

There was another ghost, one that haunted her with no material presence, did not inhabit the farm, but hovered, a dim grey figure at the back of her mind.

About Christmas 1918, in the dead slack of the year, when most of the clearing of the land was done, when the autumn sowing was over and it was too early for the spring one, she had leisure to go up to the Kruysabel. She had neglected this ceremony since the invasion of 1918, chiefly because the disappearance of her father had left the whole weight of the farm on her shoulders, partly because, steadfast as she was, she changed as must every living thing, and Georges was receding from her, with the past. She knew that the place had been fortified into a 'strong point', and had she not known, she would have guessed from the fact that the wooden-gate was gone, and the alley that led up the hill, beaten into pulp by military traffic. She

## LA GALETTE

scrambled up among the undergrowth, untouched save for shell-holes, and a few places where the vegetation had fired, or hung grey and sickly, reeking of gas. This made her frown and put on her expression as of one about to smack a naughty child. At the top, treading some barbed wire, she came out into the little clearing, leapt a half-decayed trench, and stood by the hunting shelter. Outwardly it was not much changed. A woman, looking at it with the eyes of Madeleine, could see that it was no longer the same place, although its greeny-grey woodland colour, and shape that blurred into the surrounding undergrowth, had been carefully preserved, so that it was probably imperceptible to the best glasses a few hundred yards away. The door was undone, and she pushed it open, stood and gasped. Nothing in the previous four years and a half had quite prepared her for what she found. The place had been skilfully gutted. Not only the glass from the windows, the whole of the rugs, cushions, seats, and fittings were gone, but the actual partitions had been removed, leaving the brick chimney-piece alone supporting an empty shell. The trap of the cellar had been forced, and in the aperture left was a steel and concrete 'pill-box', its machine-gun embrasures level with the window-sills. At the opposite end, just where there had stood the divan on which she had held Georges in her arms, the floor had been torn up, the earth dug away, to make room for a similar erection. The only recognizable remains of the furniture were some of the animal heads and photographs of hunting groups, all adorned with moustaches or other attributes, obscene or merely grotesque, in army indelible pencil, or fastened with field-telephone wire. It took Madeleine's plodding mind a moment to size it all up, from the gas-gong hanging from a nail, to the painted wooden notice-board, in English: 'Any person found using this Strong Point as a latrine will be severely dealt with. C.R.E. Defence lines.'

Then she let the door swing to, turned her back on the place, and walked away. It was not in her to philosophize. What had been done, she felt like a personal injury. If the place had merely been dirtied and damaged by billeting or shell-fire, she would have shrugged her shoulders and put it straight. But this systematic conversion struck deep at her sense of personal possession. They had challenged her right to something she felt to be most deeply her own. For once she was at a loss, was done, beaten, did not know how to adjust herself, hit back. Georges seemed smaller, further off, than she had ever felt him. Her love for him now seemed almost ridiculous, temporary, and for ever done with. She was aroused from her reverie by the thick undergrowth that barred her steps, and realized that she was walking down the north-eastern slope of the wood, with her back to the farm. That recalled her to herself. She retraced her steps, skirted the clearing, dodged the trenches and wire, and descended the hill towards home, head up, face impenetrable, mistress of herself. But in her heart she was banking up the slow burning fires of resentment. The less easy it was to find legitimate fuel for them, the more she fed them with the first thing or person that came to hand, feeling herself wronged and slighted by all the world.

\*

There remained one more ghost to be laid, one thin wraith that Madeleine hardly noticed, hovering at the back of her war-memories. She did not call up this last apparition, it came to her.

As grey January slid into February, she became aware, amid her engrossing preoccupation with the farm, that a Labour Corps battalion was working on the clearance of the neighbouring trench-lines. They were composed of German prisoners and Chinese, officered by a few English. Presently an orderly called, a German orderly, sent to buy eggs. She sent him about his business, curtly. This brought an officer, fair, bald, thickset, speaking little French. He smiled at her with an irritating cocksureness, and inquired for her father. Then she recognized him. It was the Lieutenant Millgate who had come to the farm late one night in 1915 with Lieutenant Skene, to join the Easthamptons. She found him some eggs for old times' sake, charged him a pre-war price and forgot him again. He was no ghost; he was an insignificant fact, and did not haunt her.

## LA GALETTE

But there came a grey day when he reappeared, and not alone. Another officer in khaki, taller but slighter, was riding behind him, and tried to greet old Jerome, who ignored the greeting. Before she knew what had happened, Geoffrey Skene stood before her. Almost mechanically, for she could not say what she felt, she bade him enter and sit down. Once he was seated, following her with his eyes, all her vindictiveness found vent in the words:

'Will you have some coffee? The Allies stole all our wine!' Then she softened again, and gave him good coffee, because, like all women, she had a tender spot somewhere for a man who had once desired her. But it was only for a moment. He sat there, unaltered, just as he had sat when she had sent him to deliver a message to Georges. And the thought that Georges had gone out of her life, and that this lesser man of hers was on his way to England, to go out of her life just as effectually, hurt her possessive and domineering instincts. She said bitterly, 'I lost my fiancé, after all!' and as he murmured some condolence her spleen overcame her, and she lashed out with her tongue at all the damage done to the farm and to her father, the destruction of her brothers and Georges, at the work there was to do, and no one to do it.

She saw Millgate fidget, heard him say in English, 'Come on!' Then she saw Skene rise, bid her good-bye, and go. She moved to the door, but for the life of her she could not say if she wanted him to go or stay.

Then, as he swung his leg, in its soiled army clothes, over his horse's back, straightened up, and clattered away, she knew. She did not want him, had never wanted him, nor any Englishman, nor anything English. He was just one of the things the War, the cursed War, had brought on her, and now it, and they, were going. Good riddance. Nor was her feeling unreasonable. The only thing she and Skene had in common, was the War. The War removed, they had absolutely no means of contact. Their case was not isolated. It was national.

*

So Madeleine remained in the Spanish Farm, and saw no more English, for the Labour Corps soon broke up and went, and she did not care. She was engrossed in one thing only: to get back, sou by sou, everything that had been lost or destroyed, plundered or shattered, by friend or foe, and pay herself for everything she had suffered and dared. And as there was a Madeleine more or less, widowed and childless, bereaved and soured, in every farm in north-eastern France, she became a portent. Statesmen feared or wondered at her, schemers and the new business men served her and themselves through her, while philosophers shuddered. For she was the Spanish Farm, the implacable spirit of that borderland so often fought over, never really conquered. She was that spirit that forgets nothing and forgives nothing, but maintains itself, amid all disasters, and necessarily. For she was perhaps the most concrete expression of humanity's instinctive survival in spite of its own perversity and ignorance. There must she stand, slow-burning revenge incarnate, until a better, gentler time.

# D'Archeville : A Portrait

# D'Archeville: A Portrait

I

A wet greyness – such as only comes to perfection round the shores of the North Sea. A heavily-paved, rather narrow street between substantial houses, none very new. An atmosphere of pretty good cookery and pretty bad drains. It is morning – Spring – for the steady wind is stronger than the fitful sun. Something in the picture wants to say French, but can't quite say it. This North Sea greyness forbids us to think of Switzerland, so it must be Belgium. Certainly Belgium in this rather heavily-furnished room – and a queer feeling of spring-cleaning – no, a more catastrophic upset than that – furniture pushed about. Maps, pencils, chits, revolver ammunition on the mantelpiece. A shame-faced, necessitous communism about the bottles and etceteras on the sideboard. We should not be so ready to share, did we not fear that tomorrow we ourselves may be in dire want. By the way, the upper panes of the window have been broken and mended with flattened-out biscuit tins. Ah! that's it! War! It is war time.

It is not wholly a disadvantage that he appears to me against a background of war. To anyone interested in national characteristics it is perhaps an advantage, for these never stand out more clearly than when outlined by uniform and conditioned by the drastic expediency of a campaign. The very figures grouped about him, help him to be most French of the Frenchmen who were in their 'floreat' – their twenties, between 1914 and 1918.

Let me touch those other figures in first, for they need but a stroke or two. They composed the 'C' Mess of the Nth Infantry Division of the British Army at Poperinghe in March 1916. There is not a word in that sentence that is unnecessary to an appreciation of him. March 1916 was the moment at which the

New, or Kitchener Armies had recovered from Loos and not succumbed to the Somme; Poperinghe was the railhead for that essentially English battlefield, the Ypres Salient. The fact that our divisions already ran to Nth in number, shows that there were more unmilitary civilians in that army than there have been in any British Army since the civil wars of the seventeenth century. The 'C' Mess was the one in which the middle-class professional man lodged, the few remaining regulars being in 'A' with the General, or 'B' with the chief Veterinary. Now regular officers of any nation are just soldiers. The technical specialists of 'C' Mess – Padre, Assistant-Director of Medical Services, Dados, Signals, Supplies, myself, were English all the time, soldiers by momentary accident. Hence our importance.

Against us, as against no group of real soldiers, Georges d'Archeville is silhouetted. Truly, some one had said, 'I hear this new French liaison officer is messing with us!' but the news only elicited that sort of grunt that greeted the news of those days, confined as it was to so-and-so having been killed and some one else sent to replace him. It made no impression, but when a high, rather throaty voice was heard in the passage: 'This "C" Mess? Is the Mess President about?' I became aware of d'Archeville. I shall never forget him until I die. I should like some one to remember him even after that. That first lunch together told us but little, probably he was trying his hardest to be elaborately English, certainly he was taking his duties as liaison officer very, very seriously all the time. He was wonderfully successful – spoke our island tongue with glib fluency – chose subjects which he might be supposed to think we preferred – drank whisky – then lit his pipe, and went about his liaisoning with a: 'I must be off. So long!' which was very nearly perfect. But not quite.

As I went about that afternoon, preventing mules in wet meadows from eating the bark of Holland elms, sending parties of khaki-coloured men away down paved roads, I got him into better proportion. His hair and eyes were darker, his skin more olive, his uniform more sky-blue and strawberry than any English officer's ever were or will be. His voice was too excitable, his affability too obvious, his talk about polo, which he must have imagined to be the popular game of people like ourselves, as it is of regular soldiers, too offhand to be convincing. With us the public-school-taught tradition of the British Army still hovered. None of us talked 'in the mess' either loud or long. While I do not suppose that any of us (except, perhaps, the Padre) could boast of an education more expensive than that of a county-town grammar school, we were whole-heartedly English in our snobbery, and carefully avoided 'shop' or any topic upon which anyone had any special knowledge. It was 'not done'.

Now d'Archeville, I felt, was the other thing that Western Europe contains. He was the man from the Mediterranean, who, extending his culture to the Atlantic or even the Channel, had no real foothold on the North Sea. He was the man to whom things were black or white, to whom it was either day or night, to whom our eternal compromise with the supposed standards of a non-existent aristocracy would be quite incomprehensible.

In this frame of mind, that night, as our tinned and chlorinated meal ended, I heard d'Archeville proposing a toast. I took a swift look round that circle of blunt, fresh-coloured English faces. They were all blinking and trying not to look at each other or at d'Archeville. To drink 'the King' was usual, because, although most of us were what is called in England 'practically teetotallers' – men too busy to take anything in the middle of the day, but who kept a bottle of whisky in the house, sometimes drank some, and treated our wives to a bottle of Beaune after golf on Saturdays – yet once we became officers we felt obliged to keep up Army ritual. But beyond that – no! What was this foreign fellow with the vivid face saying? 'Entente Cordiale' – I, because I liked d'Archeville, the Padre, because he loved his neighbour as himself, raised our glasses. There was a general grunt and a gurgling noise, and every one began talking. But the Supply Officer, a heavily-built exciseman, kept eyeing d'Archeville, as if to catch him out evading the regulations.

He had thus established himself on our consciousness, when the Division went out to 'rest'. Blessed word! We, the division-of-all-work, the Cinderella of the Salient, were going out right

## D'ARCHEVILLE

behind Hazebrouck for a month. Few of us saw that metropolis more than twice a year. Incidentally, the tension being relaxed, we had much more leisure to observe each other and ourselves. After the first week, the glamour was all gone. Away from the line, the War lost even the feeble reasonableness that Death lent it. We began asking ourselves how long it would be possible to live with six other individuals with whom each one of us had no common bond but that of having got mixed up in this affair – to exist in this bankrupt-boarding-house state of existence, whose very leisure only made us want more fervently to go home. In such circumstances d'Archeville was invaluable. He could and did suggest and carry out almost a revolution in our food – bullied or cajoled farmers' wives to selling to us and cooking for us, things we had never heard of. He had a French view of the importance of the stomach – much more helpful than the English careworn avoidance of the subject.

His voluble cheerfulness was punctuated with tiny slips of grammar and of our suburban 'good taste' – and behind it all lay the continuous interest in what the fellow would do next. There was not so much insular prejudice in this latter sentiment as might be supposed. During the heart-rending leisures of 'rest', another of d'Archeville's qualities – perhaps his main – quality had come out. We others were severally a clergyman, doctor, architect, exciseman, polytechnic lecturer and shipping clerk, who had become temporary soldiers, and didn't care how soon they returned to their proper avocations. D'Archeville, on the contrary, was – Nothing. Not even a soldier. Apparently, the War once over, he would go back to Nothing. Born of the small nobility (his father was a baron, title so incomprehensible as to verge on the ludicrous), he had been taught as accomplishments to ride, shoot, dance, speak English and to sing. He appeared to live in a small château of sorts with his father and mother who owned some farms, and some land on which were vineyards or houses, but when there was no shooting, and when he had, for the nonce, finished calling on all the neighbours, he appeared to live in Paris, and have a 'high old time'. The expression is his own and does great credit to his knowledge of our language. I suppose there were people like him in England in Georgian days. There are none now.

Imagine, therefore, how interesting he was to watch. Not that he held himself out to be in any way representative of his nation except in his official position of Liaison Officer between the Division and the local French people, and French civil and military authorities, and even troops, where we touched them. He was even good enough to point out that his formation was recruited from the most incongruous elements. He said: 'In my corps, we have all the fellows of good family and all the *maîtres d'hôtel*.' Ah! but we had not grasped, yet, of what aspect of the French nature he was deeply typical. Certainly he was not industrial nor agricultural, learned or official, as I suppose most Frenchmen must be. He was something far deeper – all the more, because, in our hard-working, middle-aged, married professional-class mess, he was peculiarly Nothing – a man of empty life. A mere Frenchman, and that was all.

Another thing that came out under the influence of 'rest' was the question of morals – or, to be more exact, of Sunday. I suppose English and French views of that day are fixed, apart, and never will meet until the League of Nations educates us to an incredible degree of cosmopolitanism. We others considered ourselves modern business men, enfranchised from the puritan shibboleths of our forefathers. But were we? Did we not drift into the habit of doing nothing on a Sunday afternoon? Did we not, one after another, when we thought the others were not attending, apologize to the Padre for our non-appearance at the service which he, in spite of the most withering indifference, managed to hold in some barn or stable? Did we not, after lunch, get away into any corner where we could keep our feet warm, or even sit down brazenly in the 'Mess' (dismantled *salle-à-manger* of some small *rentier*) with canteen block-note pad, to write home to mother, wife or child? Did we not, after tea, go off, two by two, for a walk around those Flemish meadows, with all an Englishman's instinctive, sentimental regard for the first bud and the bird's last call. Of what were we thinking? Of our dear English Sunday, which began, if we were lucky, on

Friday night, or at worst, by Saturday noon, when we said to our wives: 'My dear, if you'll hurry up, we can get in a round (or two rounds) of golf!' Of English Sunday morning, lying late, of tea and a real white enamelled bath, of breakfasting heavily before morning service (I hope!); of English Sunday midday dinner (roast beef and apple tart); of the sedate walk round the Park with the children (because the golf-course was closed), and Sunday evening with its: 'No, my dear, I didn't think of going to evening service. I rather thought we might talk of our spending next week at — if we could get Aunt Jessie to come and mind the children.' O! golden English Sunday, oh! Peace on Earth and Goodwill!

D'Archeville, I think, would have found the whole thing totally incomprehensible and utterly boring. He did not share our dreams. He went to Mass early in the morning, and later would be found getting into a borrowed car, or even on horseback, bound for a destination which he never divulged, but which instead of appearing golden was rather redolent of purple and heliotrope. The Supply Officer, always the least sympathetic, would not fail to remark: 'He's up to some game!' the inference having obviously a feminine direction. I believe he was right, but always disliked the queer note of grudging envy!

Was d'Archeville immoral? Gentles, let us face the truth; d'Archeville was immoral, just as immoral as it may be to be born in the Artois instead of in Norfolk, and no more. He was a man who, geographically, climatically, racially, found it comic that six men of thirty years of age or a little over, were married, had children, and had dismissed sex from their minds. He regarded sex as a matter for adequate catering as he regarded the stomach. He was probably very selfish as regards women, and easily became brutal. Was he immoral? Were we immoral? Let us face the truth; we were just as immoral in our own island way. Practically teetotallers, we found, under the stress of war, that a good stiff whisky helped us to sleep without thinking of the Cosmic stupidity in which we were involved. Insensibly that whisky became two or three, invaded lunch, established itself in the middle of the morning. The fault, if any, lies with

Society, the civilized society of Western Europe, which could neither foresee, prevent, nor control such a war. Some of us, since, replanted in our right environment among wife and children, and steady engrossing business, have thrown off the habit. Men of a certain age or temperament have not.

Were we more or less immoral than d'Archeville? We were, under pressure, just the same self-indulgent humanity whose outlet was different, the difference dictated by accident of climate and race, for d'Archeville could not drink three whiskies running, and, I believe, disliked the taste of it! Not there is the striking point of his portrait, but in another downrightness of his, that none of us could emulate or understand.

Our month's 'rest' came to an end!

None too soon for d'Archeville. The 'news' of those days consisted in the bi-weekly attacks of the German Army upon Verdun, with their accompanying twenty thousand or so prisoners and casualties to the French. D'Archeville became sombre. At length, just as we were about to move, he burst out: 'It is time! When are you going to do something, you others?' We took it very well. We did not feel that we had been having much of a picnic all the winter, and the rumour of the Somme preparations were already leaking through. Nevertheless, after d'Archeville had gone up to Army Head-quarters to see his chief, the Supply Officer said:

'That fellow's a spy!'

'What?' Everyone was incredulous.

'Of course he is. He speaks German too well!'

I felt it to be absurd, and replied warmly: 'I wish you or I spoke French half as well.'

The Supply Officer waved all that aside. 'You heard what he said. Dam'd insulting.'

'My dear fellow' (I liked the Padre, with his sweet reasonableness), 'he probably feels that French culture is at stake. If Verdun falls – and it is not easy to see how it can be saved – we shall be able to get back to the Channel – but the French – ?'

Certainly we did not see our friend for a day or so. In the upset of changing quarters, no one remarked upon it, except the

Supply Officer, who said: 'I told you so, he's cleared off!' When he did reappear he was more vivid than ever, his voice higher, his cordiality more obtrusive.

'No, I'm not "dining in,"' he was saying; 'in fact, I've come to say good-bye!'

'Got a promotion?'

'No, I'm going to begin all over again; I am going into the French Flying Corps!'

'Whew!'

'Well, we are losing too many men, and I am of the right age! So long, all!'

He went, leaving an uncomfortable silence behind him. True, all of us had been infantry officers, if not infantry privates, in the line. None of us had got our jobs by favouritism, but by the possession of various sorts of technical knowledge that the army wanted, and had sent urgent messages around all its civilian-filled battalions to obtain. We had long fathomed the utter futility of trench-fighting – the impossibility of one man, more or less, making any difference with his individual rifle or bomb – so that we worked away at our jobs with clear consciences. And yet – and yet – now that this Frenchman had gone and thrown up his comfortable job at Divisional Head-quarters, and had deliberately volunteered for a corps where the average 'life' of an officer was about six weeks! We all felt a twinge. No one said: 'That's the stuff to give 'em!' (an expression just coming into vogue) because some one else might have said: 'Then, why don't you or I give it 'em? If d'Archeville can, so can we!' No one remarked on the matter, we stuck to our none too comfortable jobs, and day by day the War got worse and worse, and every day the human wastage grew greater, and every day the quantity of machinery and the piles of paper that compassed the slaughter mounted higher and higher above the head of Hope.

I forgot d'Archeville, and it must have been nearly eighteen months before I saw him again. Coincidence? Not a bit of it. The offensive from Ypres to the sea, of July 1917, was so fantastically expensive that every one was bound to be in it sooner or later. In some Flemish village to which I had gone to enforce some order obsolete as soon as it was issued, I stopped for an omelette and white wine, and found myself among French Flying Corps officers: 'Aspiring Aviators' in the perfect fitness of the French language. There, almost unrecognizable, so thin, so morose had he grown, was d'Archeville. His eyes had yellowed and dwindled. Gone was his azure and strawberry uniform, gone his egregious friendliness. He was making no liaison now, with English or any other men. I have often thought I could tell those who knew that they were going to be killed, and I was sure that he knew. I doubt if he would have come across to my table, had I not gone to him, so unimportant had I, or any other living creature become. I offered him my flask, for he was drinking hot wine and water, but he refused it, saying something indistinctly about *sacrée colique*. He only added in response to my clumsy attempts at cheerfulness a muttered *sacrée guerre*, *sacrée vie*, and left with his comrades. I never saw him again. Is that true? No, I see him now, I shall see him always, I am trying to see him clearer and clearer, but however clear, alas, he is but a portrait, life-like, I hope, but flat upon the canvas, greyed with memory. Some one told me he was killed, but I knew it. And now, haunted by his eyes, before I can hold out my hand in greeting, I must raise it in salute. I am English, he was French. He *meant* his war.

# Sixty-Four, Ninety-Four!

*'Sixty-four, ninety-four –
He'll never go sick no more,
The poor beggar's dead.'*

# Preface

Books about the war of 1914-1918 are supposed to require an apology. This one has only a reason. That war is only tolerable, as a memory, when one can feel that some one learned something from it. Otherwise it becomes a mere nightmare of Waste. How learn, except from books? – and books there are! Histories, necessarily official, memoirs, necessarily personal, novels, necessarily fiction ... something of all, and yet something more than these is wanted.

And it seems as well for all of us whose experience of the War was not confined to one unit or place, to set down what can be remembered, before it becomes too dim – to set it down with the least official, personal, or imaginative bias, so that perchance the record each makes may contain some of the Truth. In this way, before the generation of the War has passed, there may arise a real Cenotaph, a true War Memorial – a record, at which gazing, our children may be able to imagine a way of settling disputes more intelligent than maintaining, during years, a population as large as that of London, on an area as large as that of Wales, for the sole purpose of wholesale slaughter by machinery.

If we cannot provide the information which will make it possible to avoid this, and if those children of ours cannot use it, then indeed the Nightmare of Waste will visit us – more than a Nightmare, a reality in which our children, and with them the white civilization of Western Europe, may well disappear. And deservedly, for we shall have betrayed all those dead comrades of ours, rendered their willing sacrifice a ridiculous futility, and, by comparison with us, Judas will be shining white.

For this reason, this book had to be written.

One word as to the persons and scenes of this book and its

## PREFACE

predecessor, 'The Spanish Farm'. There were hundreds of Skenes and Earnshaws and Madeleines, dozens of farms called 'L'Espagnole', fifty divisions known at Nth, fourteen 'Umpteenth' Corps. If there lives today a man whose regimental number was 6494, I apologize to him. He is not intended. The sick call was variously blown and all sorts of words went to it. I hope he will let me use his number on this understanding. There was no appointment called 'Clearance Officer', but the many men who did the job may substitute what name they like. In short, there is no futile impertinent pen-photograph of anybody. There is, in the words of the writer of the preface to 'The Spanish Farm', many a 'composite portrait', good or bad, but always composite.

1925

## Chapter 1
# Sixty-Four, Ninety-Four!

In the fine autumn weather that succeeded the Battle of Loos, the tenth battalion – a 'Kitchener' or 'New Army' battalion as it was then called – of a well-known English line regiment found itself in and around one of those big, four-sided farmhouses that the Spaniards used to build to protect their Netherland territory from the French. It stood just where the chalk downs of the Pas de Calais slope towards the Flemish plain. Its inhabitants spoke French or Flemish indiscriminately and were beginning to pick up a good bit of English.

The battalion, reduced to below two-thirds of its normal strength, was still large enough to fill the premises, the officers in the ground-floor living-rooms that looked out on the manure heap, two companies in the great barns and stables that spread at right-angles to the house; beyond the remains of the moat, an oblong duckpond filling the fourth side of the square, stretched a further yard, with cartsheds and hop-presses. Another company and a half were close by. Spanning the moat was a red-brick bridge commanded by an old loop-holed 'shot' tower, now granary and pigeon-loft in its successive storeys. Against it stood the dome-shaped kennel of the old yard dog. The ridge of the thatched roof of the dwelling-house was tasselled with wallflowers in a brown fringe. The mellowed brickwork of the front, between the low eaves and the wide-spreading, bluish-green shutters, was bolted by old iron bolts, whose heads were worked into the date 1610. Before the house was a ten-acre pasture, surrounded by a double row of Holland elms, with an avenue that led to the road. Behind was a smaller pasture. Westward against the skyline were the downs beyond St Omer, and northward the gravelly hillocks that connect them with rolling country between Ypres and Courtrai. The enemy were twenty kilometres east by south away down the Lys valley towards Lille and the Béthune coalfields. Over all hung the heavy, moist, fertile beauty of a Flemish autumn; root-crops knee-deep, hopfields turning russet. When the sentry on the gate was changed at six, the close mist still clung between the trees of the avenue, about the buildings, and above the moat. 'Revelly' seemed to dissipate the thickness of the atmosphere, but what it really did was to make the emptiness of the meadows alive with khaki figures – little strings of men going, section by section, through roll-call and kit inspection, while the Adjutant, a small wiry infantry officer, once the familiar figure in all photos of a celebrated polo team, passed between the groups with the Regimental Sergeant-major, trying to gauge how far the loss and disorganization of Loos had gone. A keen man, this Captain Hunter, the Adjutant. He had retired a year or two before 1914 from a profession by which he set more store than was supposed by many people, who mistook him for a mere idle polo-player. He had rejoined at once and become the only ex-regular officer of one of the New Army battalions. It was clothed in blue serge and unarmed, and commanded by a motherly old ex-Territorial Colonel, who had recruited it; but it was composed, as his instinct soon told him, of material such as regular English officers only know in dreams, if ever they have any. Working on this material with the military knowledge gained in South Africa, and a good deal of practical skill and tact, he had brought them to a very fair state by the time they had been ordered to France and involved in Loos. Emerging from that somewhat catastrophic experience, Captain Hunter, never theoretic or abstract, had grasped at once the immediate necessity – reorganize – refit – retrain even, and – have another go. Moving among the busy groups on the extemporized parade-ground of the home pasture, throwing questions at the Sergeant-major, he did not forget to look at the weather, the country, the farmhouse; or listen to the distant rumble of gunfire along the front, the hum of a threshing machine and the 'Hue!' of old Vanderlynden the farmer, beyond the hedge ploughing with a white jennet and a great Boulonnais horse, harnessed to what

## SIXTY-FOUR, NINETY-FOUR!

looked like a garden hoe fastened to the chassis of a perambulator. 'Extraordinary people,' thought Captain Hunter, 'can't leave the stubble alone five minutes. No wonder they've no sport!'

Having seen enough to make him ponder, he dismissed the Sergeant-major with the necessary orders, and went back towards the house. The brisk Doctor was standing there 'at gaze', with his orderly, a heavily-built chemist's assistant, 'pointing' beside his officer like a well-bred dog.

'Mornin', Doctor!'

'Mornin'. Can I have a fatigue of ten men?'

The Adjutant winced. 'You'll have to have it if you must, Doctor, though the Colonel . . .'

'Must is the word! Do you know what a sick parade I've got? Eighty! Yes, I have. It's trench fever – insides all inside-out and temperature like – well, some'll have to go down to base. Meanwhile I want to isolate the others and try and pull 'em through. I want that shed and I want it empty.'

The Doctor pointed to a long low extension of the farm buildings that ran out from the back of the dwelling-house to the grassy dip of the dry moat. The door was barred and padlocked.

'*"Privée – entrée interdite."* Does that mean we mustn't go in?'

'That's it!' (the Adjutant was guessing) 'It's full of marsh hay, isn't it?' He peeped through a chink.

'Flax, man, flax! I'll use it for bedding when it's spread, then we shan't need to ask for straw and be told we can't have it.'

Having sent the necessary instructions by the orderly, the two entered the house from the back, past pig-swill carried in pails and a separator humming like an aeroplane. Coming round the corner of a high oak partition, they entered the mess extemporized in the front parlour, and were greeted by that national password, 'Morning'.' It came from Colonel Gilford, their commanding officer, who was seated before that plate of eggs and bacon which it would have taken more than a German Army to prevent his servant from providing, done to a turn, and served fresh and hot. Born in and bred up for the Army, inheri-

181

## SIXTY-FOUR, NINETY-FOUR!

ting just enough gentility of blood and security of income to be unconscious of either, of Art, Religion, Science, Business and Politics, Colonel Gilford knew nothing and cared less. During twenty-two years' service he had seen six weeks of actual fighting, all of it against black men or Asiatics; there was not a sport at which he did not excel; and his physical courage – at once an instinct and a creed, and his belief in himself – as complete as most men's in God – were masked by an expressionless good-fellowship towards the few people he considered his fellows. He had been ordered to command and take to France a battalion of the New Armies, in which Captain Hunter and one or two N.C.O.s were the only regular soldiers. Face to face with an enemy of whose language he did not understand a word, and whose theory of International Relationships, military training and general conduct would have been quite beyond his comprehension, his bearing did him and his kind every credit. He went into the Battle of Loos, ostensibly an experienced veteran, really as strange to the new conditions as the mechanics, clerks and labourers of which his battalion was composed. The Kotal campaign of 1900 gave him no hint of what to do in the face of machine-gun and heavy artillery fire, such as he had never conceived possible. In spite of all this, through three days and nights, sleepless and practically foodless, he had carried out such orders as had reached him, held on in the absence of orders, and when finally relieved by the arrival of another unit, had gathered together what remained of his men, whole platoons of whom were missing, withdrawn them, entrained them, and established them in an entirely new sector. And now he was billeted in a farmhouse whose inhabitants spoke a tongue which the Adjutant thought was Cape Dutch.

He had slept soundly, awakened fresh; had bathed, shaved and appeared at breakfast among the remaining officers of his battalion. In those early days Colonel Gilford still maintained the peace-time taboo of 'No shop in the Mess.' The conversation was therefore restricted to the weather. It was impossible to discuss the English papers, which contained accounts of the 'victory' of Loos, from which the battalion had with such difficulty emerged. In the silence, only broken by the sound of hearty eating, the noise of a dispute, carried on outside the window, forced itself on every one's attention. Colonel Gilford, who expected his marmalade to be allowed to subside in peace, before he drifted on in decency and comfort to the necessary business of the day, raised his eyebrows. Whereon the Adjutant rose from his seat and passed outside.

The argument was between old Jerome Vanderlynden, the farmer, and Adams, the Quartermaster, the one slightly bowed in deprecation and clasping his cap to his stomach, the other stiff and square in worn khaki with the long-service ribbon at the breast.

The one was speaking Flemish and the other Lancashire.

'They have burnt my hop-poles for kindling, they have grazed their horses in my pasture, and now they turn my agricultural implements out of my shed, to leave them in the open air all night, so that they rust . . .'

'Get out, you dirty native! I've twenty years' service to my name; I can't understand a word you say; it's no business of mine; go and talk to the Adjutant, Transport Officer, Chaplain, Brigade Interpreter. I gave you sugar and butter in exchange for the coffee . . .'

The Adjutant broke in. 'What is it, Adams? Grousing again? *Qu'est que c'est*, Mossoo? Devil take their jargon!' He went back into the Mess. 'Does anyone speak French? Oh, good. You do! Well, when you've finished your breakfast, you might see what he wants.'

The officer addressed rose from the lower end of the table and went out to where Vanderlynden, the farmer, relinquished by old Adams, was still turning over and over in his hands that high-crowned cap with glazed peak, so much more Dutch than French.

This young officer, by name Geoffrey Skene, had not been with the battalion twelve hours, and regarded himself as one of the most fortunate men on earth. A few hours ago he had been prey to a dreadful fear – lest the victory of Loos should end the War, without his ever having fired a shot . . . And suddenly his orders had come, and with a beating heart he had left the reinforcement camp at Étaples, to join a battalion he had never seen. By chance in the only other occupant of his railway carriage he had found a man called Earnshaw he had known slightly in England. They were both bound for the same unit – perhaps the first of the depleted regiments to be hauled out of the line and given a chance to fill up; and there sprang up between them one of those quick intimacies of the early days, before everyone became bored and bewildered. Skene and this Earnshaw had seemed to have much in common: both of them had gone in the first rush of Kitchener recruits to those public meetings at which men shoved and fought for attestation papers, which often could not be supplied for days. To Skene this had happened in the county-market-cathedral-garrison town where he had lived nearly all his life. To Earnshaw it had happened in the dark busy heart of Manchester, where he was staying in the Imperial, just home, 'fed up' with Canada. Their experiences had been almost identical. With incredible difficulty they had succeeded in becoming members of that herd of men, tens of thousands, inhabiting the wooden town of Shoreham, the vast camp of Black Down, or scores of similar places. There, dressed in blue, unarmed but very healthy, all through the winter of 1914 they had drilled and drilled, with dummy rifles, without rifles, heard lectures, laughed at the Army routine, been happy because they were 'learning to fight'. They wished to fight – Skene because he saw in some confused way the Belfry of Bruges, the iron clock of Malines, the streets of Louvain, battered or burning, with a generous feeling in his heart of: 'Look here, you know, this must be stopped'; Earnshaw because all over the world he had found 'dam' Germans. Exactly why or how they were 'dam' he could not have explained, but he was just clear that the chance of a lifetime had come to 'larn' them. The will to fight, and the business of learning how, had filled the winter nicely. At times Earnshaw was rebellious. He had half-a-dozen shot-guns and sporting rifles at home, and laughed at the old long Lee-Enfield; he was appeased by being put into the transport section, where he groomed riding horses and was promised mules later. He had 'used' mules (no one ever spoke of 'riding' or 'driving' mules, but always of 'using' them) in two continents, and the thought cheered him. It was something he could *do*. Skene, an architect, fancied that he knew something about plans, that trenches were not unlike the foundations of houses, that he had experience of cements and ways of reveting that might be useful. He was appeased by being put to dig mile after mile of trenches that were only holes in the earth. Both earned their third stripe by Christmas.

Spring had come – Neuve Chapelle – Festubert – the Dardanelles – the fear of not getting out – of not being 'in it' – became a panic. Skene and Earnshaw, amid thousands of their kind and age, were up against the old 'dug-out' Colonels, who would not grant commissions to their 'men' for fear of spoiling a smart company, from a belief that the private soldiers of the New Armies and the 'Tommies' of Indian and South African wars must be alike, or from who knows what prejudice or paralysis of brain. But circumstances fought for Skene and Earnshaw. Losses in France were too heavy, especially among Infantry officers; commissions had to be granted. Earnshaw had applied for Artillery or Horse Transport. Skene had applied for Engineers or Intelligence; thousands of others had applied for special branches, stating qualifications that ranged through every useful branch of knowledge. All – all, except the few who commanded influence in high places, were sent into the Infantry.

Skene and Earnshaw had gone to the Second Reserve Battalion of a county regiment on the East Coast. The earlier 'K' formations were already filled from Universities, and county families and public school O.T.C.s; and the Second Reserve were accumulating messes of 100 to 150 officers and battalions of 1,500 to 1,700 men.

Skene, Earnshaw, and many others, men whose thirtieth birthday was passed, were 'fallen in' and addressed as 'young officers' by Adjutants who had never been out of England, or put through their 'setting up' drill by Marine Sergeants whose greatest experience of war was the Boxer Rising of 1900. How they existed through that summer many never knew. Some got away by influence or chicane to other jobs, some were mildly mutinous, or thoroughly dissipated. The majority had 'stuck it', taking 'courses' of machine-gunning, going route-marches with that bloated battalion that looked like a brigade, taking leave, granted or ungranted, listening greedily to anything wounded officers from France would tell them, or to the tales of the many Colonials among themselves. At last, with the shadow of Loos looming near, some bright intellect at Whitehall – some younger man who had perhaps been as far as St Omer – asked: 'Look here, why not have some reserves handy? We're bound to have casualties.' The logic was irrefutable. The dispersal of those reserve battalions began: some went to the Dardanelles, but most to France. Many were middle-aged, some grey or bald, three-quarters were townsmen, as perforce any collection of Englishmen must be; some were Colonial, British South American, or Indian born. Skene was bidden to report to Embarkation, Folkestone. Excited, half-dressed, he rushed into the hut, where a tea-planter, a ship's steward, and the biggest cash-draper in Durlam were also dressing. 'I've got my orders! Come and have a drink before mess.' There was a moment's silence. Then: 'Why should we drink with you? Why should you have your orders? You're not senior. It's influence, that's what it is!'

He spent a miserable week hanging about the base camp at Étaples, then a mere suggestion of what it afterwards became. Officers lived in little wooden messes, on their rations. There were no clubs; the one or two restaurants that provided meals were crowded out by 6 p.m. Skene, who knew the town through having stayed there one holiday to attend an art school, wandered across into the stucco flimsiness and shuttered desolation of Paris Plage. He knew a battle was going on – how was he going to get to it? Then his orders came.

He and Earnshaw found the battalion, not too easily, that night – and were astonished at the warmness of their welcome, until they dimly realized that the ten officers round the newspaper-covered table in that Flemish parlour, waiting so anxiously for some warm food, were the survivors of a full battalion mess of thirty.

## SIXTY-FOUR, NINETY-FOUR!

In the morning Skene and Earnshaw were up early – too early – they wandered about for an hour before they could get any breakfast. They looked at the transport lines, and the early parade – astonished at the weak and lop-sided look of many platoons, the queer appearance of men without arms or equipment, who slunk into their places, looking dazed. They heard the bugles go 'Sick parade'. One of the cooks by the field kitchens sang the words:

> 'Sixty-four, Ninety-four,
> He'll never go sick no more,
> The poor beggar's dead!'

Skene was struck with horror ... there, in face of the enemy, men sick, useless, clogging the wheels of the fighting machine! Somehow he never got over that feeling.

It was the first rude blow at the idea so prevalent among the enthusiastic volunteers of the New Armies, of going out to 'fight', of pushing some such business as Loos on and on right into Berlin. It was a shock to find that the fighting depended on a large stationary military population, as vulnerable to illness or accident as the population of London. He went to breakfast hurriedly readjusting his mind. At the words, 'Does anyone speak French?' he had almost leapt to his feet. Here was something he could *do*.

As he passed out to where old Vanderlynden stood, the Colonel asked: 'Who's that officer?' and the Adjutant replied: 'New reinforcement officer; came after you turned in last night, sir.'

From the extemporized mess to the farmer's part of the house, was like stepping from modern war into a Yorkshire farmhouse of the eighteenth century. On the long, smooth-worn bench under the window in the kitchen Skene sat with a cup of impeccable black coffee, and a wineglass of unpurchaseable brandy. Across the table, old Vanderlynden, who had resumed his cap, was propped in the one chair that could be described as easy, with his feet towards the closed Flemish stove, on the clean tiled floor. 'Leinsche!' he called ... 'Madeleinesche!' ('little Madeleine'). From one of the inner rooms there came out one of those women who do not exist in England ... whose dress was that of a woman of thirty, but whose clear, unlined skin and easy movements belonged to a girl in her teens; whose figure and manners might have earned her good wages in a big shop, but whose hands were developed by continuous use of the spade in youth ... who served Skene without looking at him, but who, at the bidding of her old father, sat down opposite the Englishman, and looking him straight in the eyes, began, in a pleasant contralto voice, to expose in convent-taught French what was in the old man's mind.

The young woman was terse. Skene took down the items; hop-poles stolen, horses grazing, a shed used for some purpose he could not quite understand. He made the whole into a report in his Field Message book, like a well-trained young officer of the New Armies, and went outside to see the damage. It was quite evident. The great hop-poles were in the transport lines, with mules and 'riders' tied up to them, stamping and feeding. Other horses, 'a bit poor' with the journey, had been cast loose and were grazing; but it was the shed at the back of the dwellinghouse that was the real trouble.

Here, in stretchers or in blankets on the grass, lay some eighty of the battalion, all with the new disease, called everything from 'para-typhoid' to 'cold-feet'; known not by its symptoms but by its causes – standing up to the waist in filthy water without food or sleep, or 'resting' in cattle trucks or barns, still wet. Nothing to be done – part of the enormous waste of war! It was the first real lesson on war's nature that Skene was taught.

He put it all down in his Field Message book. He further put down exactly what it was that Mademoiselle Vanderlynden said her father complained of. 'You must not suppose that we are against the English. We know that we should have been beaten without our Allies.' (No trace of cajolery there!) 'It is a pleasure as well as a duty to have the troops billeted in the farm. We know quite well that the men must live, that their rations are never sufficient. We have men of the family mobilized, who would tell us all this if we did not know. But the Government force us to grow corn and keep cows, and we cannot do this if

# SIXTY-FOUR, NINETY-FOUR!

you take our pasture and spoil our reaping machine without paying for the damage, not to mention the hop-poles you have destroyed or burnt – or at least give us a requisition paper.' Satisfied that she had made Skene understand, she appeared to take no further interest in him, until he had finished writing his report. Then she said: 'You are going to see to it at once?'

'At once, Mademoiselle.'

'A thousand thanks!'

'What a woman of business!' thought Skene and went to the orderly room.

He had to wait some minutes before the Adjutant, busy with a pad of wires, a map and some typewritten orders, noticed him.

'Well, Skene, what is it? Oh yes, what did old Kruger want? Oh! I see! Well, go back and offer him forty francs, as you suggest, and tell him he can have his barns and out-houses and any dam' thing he pleases. I can't say about the hop-poles – tell him to make a complaint. We move in the morning up to the Line. You'd better cut along and see – oh, yes – see Thomas, D Company. That's all.'

'Yessir. Do you want this, sir?' Skene was still holding his report.

'No. Tear it up. Done with.'

And Skene went off to settle old Vanderlynden and then to find Thomas, having learned another lesson in the art of that war worth more than musketry or marching, drill or discipline; to keep abreast, not of the actual situation, but of the next but one; so rapidly did changes come and the necessities of the moment outrun the provisions of the past.

Who would be Sixty-four, ninety-four next?

*Chapter 2*

# Up to the Line

Next morning the battalion moved off. Skene had been posted to No 13 Platoon, which gave him the best possible view of the hindquarters of the charger ridden by the Commander of D Company. This did not seem amiss. Nothing did on these fine October mornings when the New Army, undaunted and high of hope, started on those first marches in which the physical comfort of motion was still combined with the illusion of really going somewhere. The tedious unreality of training was over. Loos was a brief bad dream. They were going to fight. That was what he had enlisted for.

An hour passed and the first halt was called. On moving off again, the Company Commander, a tall fair lad of eighteen, got down and walked with Skene, giving him his first true insight into that 'great British victory', as the papers called it, the Battle of Loos. 'Never saw such a show; weeks and weeks of marching, full of beans; then up a road to a place called Vermelles; everything chock-a-block; mules and men and guns all mixed up. Then they took us out over the open; bare ground all cut up with shell-holes, old trenches; then it began to rain. When we took up our line, everything was soaked, no one knew anything; no grub, no water, no ammunition; and when at last some one found us, after the Bosche had blown hell out of us for two or three days, some fool on our left had given way and the only order we got was to go back. My word! you should have seen us! ... The men have picked up wonderfully these few days, but there's heaps of sickness besides the casualties.'

The speaker, by rank and name Captain Thomas, more than ten years Skene's junior, had obtained a Special Reserve commission straight from that University in which, at the outbreak of war, he had been learning what bad form it was to know anything. The narrative of his experiences at Loos was given in the disjointed sentences of one who knew that description was not his business. It conveyed little to Skene, not because it was bald and disjointed, but because Skene, like all the New Army reinforcements, was thinking: 'Ah yes, my boy, that's what happened to you, but wait until I get there!' The warnings that should have surmounted even the scrupulous understatement of Thomas were lost on Skene, who was admiring the roofs and spires of the rail-head town they were approaching. Not Bruges, by a long way, still less the Italian cities of Skene's education, but it had tall towers with belfries, long regular whitewashed buildings, barracks or convents, with steep roofs, weather vanes, and many trees.

They halted; a rumour came down to D Company that the town was under long-range bombardment.

Ahead, the Adjutant was consulting a military policeman as to an alternative route. Having seen his men fall out correctly, Skene joined a group of officers to watch. Then, for the first time in his life, he heard an unforgettable sound, as though the heavens, made of cheap calico, were being torn to lengths by some demoniac draper. The bump of the shell followed and a crashing explosion, with the roar of falling bricks, and a shriek of scattering humanity – then a pink cloud of brickdust rose and bellied out over the cobbled streets of the Flemish town. The men cheered, groaned, made bets on the next shot; the officers grinned in sympathy.

It was dusk before the battalion passed beyond cultivation to the desolation that bordered the trenches, and found, at a battered and deserted level crossing, four mud-plastered guides.

This was before the day of regular trains, and the battalion passed the zone of the heavy guns and forward dumps on foot, breaking up first into companies, then into platoons, and marching in silence. The night was fine and dry, the deepening silence was punctuated by a noise, that was to become as much a part of life as the ticking of a clock in the midnight silence of home – a noise as of some insane woodpecker; the rat-tat-tat of the indefatigable Bosche machine-guns. On a crest that rose slightly above the dead level of the plain, a greenish glare soared up, hung a moment, and wasted out. Then another soared further to the right, amid the gaunt skeletons, crowned fan-shaped with splinters, of a row of trees. By this light Skene saw that the soft mush in which he was treading was the self-sown, unharvested corn of a once tilled field.

Among the ruins of a cottage – a murdered handful of battered brick and mortar – they entered the communication trench.

Such trenches, afterwards developed to perfection and complexity, were then nothing more than waist or breast-deep excavations, with slipping walls and floored with deep and noisome ooze. They were, moreover, so few and well known to the enemy and so regularly shelled or enfiladed by machine-guns, that the older hands preferred risking the open.

The first few bullets whistled overhead, too high. But soon came the tearing shriek, the crash and scatter of shrapnel, the ducking and bunching of startled men, and that first hearing of the cry, never quite to be forgotten: 'Stretcher-bearer!'

Details of the next three hours are merely tedious and incomprehensible to those who have not been 'there', tedious and only too comprehensible to those who have. Skene found the rear of his platoon held up by the stretcher party, and then his passage blocked by other units. His guide tried a short cut which led into mud and wire and on into the lines of a brigade that was not his. Back, in mud and wire, over drains and trenches, bodies and ruins, in and out of latrines and shell-holes, lying flat for minutes together while machine-gun fire swept over them, Skene entered at last, from the spoil-pit at the back, the trench he was to hold, two hours overdue. He found a weary subaltern with sarcasm on his lips and a crumpled list of trench stores in his hand. 'Sign! I don't want to be caught in here in daylight.'

Skene signed. The subaltern and his men moved off, and the last he heard was:

'What's yon relief?'

'Noo armies!'

'That means comin' back tomorrer night t'take these trenches back again, sure enough!'

Skene, bitterly insulted, bit his lips and kept silence.

The dawn broke in a fierce crackle of musketry. Skene rested his head against the parapet, the only dry firm place he could find. He had thoroughly surveyed his ground. His men were all 'standing-to'.

They were in a section of fire-trench fifty yards long, blocked at each end and fed from a communication trench half cemetery and half latrine.

They had two and a half boxes of ammunition, two boxes of bombs, and some Verey lights. There were some noisome holes for dug-outs into which none of his men had been as yet fatigued enough to crawl.

What would happen if the enemy attacked, or if he himself were ordered to attack, he did not even consider. He was thinking, with a sense of almost tragic finality, that this was the end of the journey. The recruiting room, the training camp, the O.T.C., the base camp, the railhead town, all led to – this. There, a few yards away, were the Germans. And he, who a few months ago had never thought of being a soldier, much less an officer, least of all a combatant in the front line of a European War, was, on his own and only responsibility, standing to hold No 13 Section of the 'Z' lines of the British Expeditionary Force, against the enemy. The hierarchy on which he had been trained to depend had suddenly disappeared. Brigade, even battalion head-quarters, were miles away. Thomas, with the remainder of the company, was four hundred yards back, only accessible by a field telephone that had already been twice cut by shell-fire, and could not be repaired in daylight. Training had hardly covered these possibilities.

In the twilight chequered by the greenish German flares, listening to the ceaseless tapping of the Bosche machine-guns, and the continual swish, crash and clatter of shells, over nearly a hundred miles of French or Flemish soil, Englishmen like him were doing as he was – in the Line.

*Chapter* 3
# Relief

'SOMEWHERE IN FRANCE
'*November* 1915.
'Dear Uncle,
'I duly received your letter, together with the books, cigarettes, woolly cap and socks. Thank you all very much, the parcel was most acceptable. The post here is wonderfully regular, and we get a delivery once a day, bar accidents.

'You ask me what it is like, but I fear I can't give you much idea. You see the address from which I write – well, that secrecy runs through the whole business. We are as anonymous and invisible as possible. We are told that if information as to the names or positions of units is put on paper, it is likely to leak out, and we shall be spotted and shelled. That is dangerous, of course, and above all uncomfortable. Here am I, with all my clothes and equipment on me, lying in a wooden box like a coffin with the end knocked out, buried in a beetfield. The space where my notebook lies is the only dry bit on the floor of my dug-out, but I am protected from the rain by the roof. Now, if we are shelled with any accuracy, these small comforts will all disappear, and we shall all have to wallow in the mud in the rain until we can burrow out some more holes. So you see there is some point in all this secrecy.'

Here Skene's elbow, on which he was leaning, hurt him so much, that he had to give up and rest.

He was writing to his uncle, who had asked for some idea of what the life was like and how he was getting on, as relatives did in those days, when to have a nephew, son or cousin 'fighting in the trenches' was still new. The Bosche then had what used to be called 'command of the air', and to be seen by their planes meant a length of trench shelled to bits, somebody killed, and the rest left shelterless in the Flemish winter; so the 'fighting' that went on 'in the trenches' consisted in keeping out of sight. Skene had, therefore, ample time and tried to set down things about him as he saw them. He went on:

'During daylight we have to be very careful to keep under cover. I can put my head out, or even stand up, if I am careful, but I can see nothing except what appears to be miles and miles of sewage farm, upturned earth, broken posts and wire, decay, stench and desolation, with here and there a mound of splintered brick or a length of granite-paved road, to show that it was once a stretch of goodish agricultural land, not unlike some of the Peterborough flats below Wansford. There is some high ground, gravelly and wooded, to the south and west, but north is the sea-level marsh, and the Bosche sit all round us on a ridge that rings us into it. However we've managed to hang on here beats imagining.'

At this point, perceiving that he had written what would not pass the Censor, he tore it up.

He next began: 'One gets rid of many preconceived notions. For instance, Baptism of Fire, as it used to be called, is not panicky in the least, but rather exhilarating. The first shelling near us made the men cheer and I wanted to join them. The first bullets made them mock and I even smiled, the first dead man was not pretty, but after a curious feeling of "where are the police? something ought to be done about this", one gets used to it. Of course one's first impulse when a man stumbles and drops is to tell him to get up. But there are many one does not see. The Bosche knocked down a house on to eight of my men the other day. We dug the ruins over but only found two bodies. The shell fell directly on the others, I suppose. They are reported "missing". It looked simply like a bad accident in a brickworks.'

When he got to this point, Skene read what he had written. 'Oh, Lord,' he thought, 'I shall give them the horrors!' and he tore it up.

He began again:

'At dusk, directly the light is too dim to see movement from one trench to another, there's a most extraordinary scene. Do you remember the old Doré pictures of the Resurrection? Well, just like that. Men that have lain hidden in or just behind the lines suddenly appear out of their holes. From further back come parties to dig, bring rations or ammunition, by hand, or by limbers drawn by mules.

'What has been all day a solitude, baleful and ominous, suddenly becomes as busy as a market-place, and the Bosche never leave off their incessant machine-gunning. Darkness makes no difference to them, because their theory is, not to aim at a man and hit him with a bullet, but to cover any interesting point on the map – crossroads, copse or bridge – with a sheet of lead that anything moving must walk into. We say the Bosche is nervous, is afraid of us, and nearly beaten. Certainly he makes more fuss. The everlasting flare-lights, the continual shooting, the immense care in screening his men, are symptoms of it. We think that once the winter is over and we get a move on, we shall crumple him up.

'Personally I shall be glad. I think it will be a relief. This living in the Line in the face of machine-gunning that is always superior to ours, and artillery and aircraft that generally are, takes it out of a man. But what a splendid lot! My best men are a poacher and a Salvationist preacher. Then come the young football-playing clerks, to whom sniping and bombing are still exciting; the older men, mechanics, artisans, shopkeepers, are wonderfully sensible and handy. At first they were nonplussed, as everybody is, by the casualties and the primeval conditions. But they soon set to work to make the best of it. Most of them are quite handy at getting a good fire to cook food and dry oneself by – which I now see to be the first cardinal point, and very nearly the whole art of soldiering. The actual shooting and bombing don't take up much time. There is no bayonet work. The agricultural labourers we keep for digging and sanitary fatigue. They have so little spirit, I don't feel sure how they would behave if rushed, and their health is so poor. The great thing about them is that they don't care what they do, making graves or emptying latrines!'

Skene read it through, then tore it up. He rested his head on his hands. He did not know what to write. Eventually he put down:

'Dear Uncle,

'Thanks for the woolly cap and the cigarettes and chocolate. They were most welcome and it is jolly good of you. The weather is not too bad for the time of year. Give my kind regards to every one at the office and tell them we are winning fast, and I shall soon be home.

'Ever yours,
'Geoffrey.'

At the end of a wet week, after many false rumours, a message came that the battalion was to be relieved. It was brought to him from Company Head-quarters by an orderly who reached him just before daybreak. He spent the daylight hours, during which no one could move, in making a report on the state of the section of the line held by his platoon. At last, the early dusk came down, opaque and humid, and the first star-shells began to rise from the German lines; he set out with his orderly along the parapet of a water-logged trench for Company Head-quarters, the only possible path, to take his orders for the move. Good Lord! Those rehearsals of that movement during training in England! The scenery had been lacking a bit! But Skene was engrossed in his carefully written report on the state of the trenches, with illustrations.

Even that persistent race, the German machine-gunners, were less active in the autumn damp and darkness. Few bullets hissed about his ears, or thumped the greasy embankments beneath his feet; above the moderated clamour he could hear a sound of wading in the glutinous sludge between the trenches, and the lively whistling of a music-hall tune. The whistler was little Mansfield, the machine-gun officer, a brown-eyed, under-sized imp of eighteen, just let loose from a public school, who, after the shortened course at Sandhurst, had come out to France that summer without passing through the ranks. A more perfect temperament for trench warfare than that of little Mansfield could not have been invented. Still a child, completely irresponsible, with nothing in his past to ponder over, and no inclination or capacity for thought about the future, with fox-hunting ancestors, and a public school training, he was the very plum of perfect health and physical condition: the desolation in which he lived didn't even touch his insensitive little spirit, and his English humour, often called today 'the modern love for ragging', as if there were something new about it, found plenty of time for expression. He was given to 'ragging' Skene and Earnshaw. They seemed to him, no doubt, to deviate from that exact good form to which he had been brought up. Skene had a knowledge of drainage and draughtsmanship, had been heard discussing Home Rule without violence – very middle class. One didn't ostracize a brother officer, of course, one merely 'ragged' him for his good. Besides Skene was bigger than himself, so that sarcasm was all Mansfield's sense of fair play permitted him to use.

With Earnshaw, Mansfield was more cautious. The Lancashire man had travelled, and was less tolerant than Skene. He said openly that he had 'no use for school kids'; and refused to loan a limber to the machine-gunner, saying he would only 'mess my mules about. He's not old enough to be trusted!'

But Mansfield was irrepressible, no snub ever affected him for long. 'Hallo!' he chirrupped at Skene. 'How are you enjoying the War? I know I shall have a cold. Mother said I wasn't to play in these nasty trenches. Hurry up, Skene, you'll be late for the office!'

They splashed and slid together in the dark foul waters of the second-line trench, to the one-time cellar of an estaminet that had stood by a paved road. In those Company Head-quarters, Long Thomas, the Captain, Earnshaw, Skene and Mansfield (the company was always two officers short) were just able to wedge themselves between the grimy sweating walls and a Second Empire lacquer and brass-bound drawing-room table, brought from a neighbouring château, which occupied the whole floor space. With heads against the raftered ceiling, and feet propped on sandbags out of the six inches of water on the floor, there was just room to use map, message book and pencil. Stuck in a bottle was a candle which smoked the studies of the nude from

'La Vie Parisienne', nailed on the boarding by hands now folded probably beneath the sodden clay of spoil-pit graves.

Long Thomas detailed the instructions for handing over their trench to the incoming battalion, and gave them a rendezvous for marching back to rest camp. Skene diffidently brought forward his report, with its suggestion that bits of the line should be held by patrols of machine-gunners, and the rest of the men saved for emergency. He was heard in gloomy silence. Thomas put the serious obstacle: 'You see, we're weaker than the Bosche in artillery and machine-guns, and if once we let go of a bit of line, goodness knows how we should ever get it back, and the effect on the men would be very bad.'

'The effect on the men is bad as it is,' persisted Skene; 'they've neither shelter from the weather nor cover from fire; I've lost eight by wounds and seven by sickness, doing absolutely nothing!'

Mansfield's voice rose in broken squeaky imitation of the battalion's venerable Major left behind at Brigade Head-quarters: 'That's what you're here for, sir! What d'you think I brought you all the way from England for, sir, except to be cannon fodder?'

Just then the Quartermaster-sergeant's Corporal appeared with his report: 'Rations up, and all correct, sir, and letters!' There was one for Skene, and one for Mansfield.

Skene's was from Madeleine Vanderlynden. The feel of the thin grey note-paper, covered with spidery sloping French script, gave him astonishing pleasure. 'I must be enjoying this life even less than I knew,' he thought.

The letter ran: 'Excuse the liberty I take in addressing you, but I do not know to whom to apply. You arranged so well that the soldiers of your regiment should respect the buildings and machinery necessary for our agriculture, and since your departure another regiment has come and taken all the barn, and has broken the fences of the pasture so that we have to pay a boy to keep the cows from straying. I regret troubling you, but I do not know to whom to apply.

'My father sends his respects and wishes he were with you.

'We have no news of my second brother Marcel.

'The regiment is the Cannock Chase Rangers.'

These everlasting civilians, couldn't they understand it was war-time? Perhaps it was just as well they couldn't!

The squeal of Mansfield, who had long read his letter, a tailor's bill, and who had been turning over Skene's neatly written and sketched pages, broke the silence: 'Report on the state of the front line, section Z13. Look here, Thomas, this fellow Skene's written a book about the War. What's an outfall? Is that where you fall out!' Thomas scanned again the closely written sheets and plans.

'I think I'd better not forward this report of yours, Skene; it won't do you any good with the General!'

Skene agreed (no one disagreed with Thomas), called his orderly, and set out for his platoon.

\*

The 'relief' of the battalion by that which took its place was dragged out for hours. Skene's platoon was not relieved until nearly eight o'clock. Skene let his men squeeze out and get on their way with his Sergeant, keeping only his servant with him.

He found himself faced by a dejected young officer whose first remark was, 'You 13 Platoon, what a mess you've let the place get into!'

Skene explained that in the absence of any comprehensive drainage system all they could do was to shift the omnipresent flood from one small section into the next and back: he handed over the meagre trench stores, and recorded his opinion that the front line was only fit to be held in parts by moving patrols, and not fit for habitation. At which the other shrugged his shoulders and replied: 'I suppose we shall get on somehow. Where are those d—d rations?' It was the attitude, at that period, of the whole B.E.F.

Scrambling back through shell-hole and over broken posts and wire, Skene and his servant got as far as the second line, where in the communication trench they met the ration party of the incoming battalion huddled under a crumbling parapet.

'We've just had one over, sir, and Fritz always send two!'

Sure enough, in a few seconds came the second shrapnel shell, falling short with a great splashing of muddy water and whizzing of jagged bits. Skene pushed on, overtook his own platoon, and heard his Sergeant's report of the slow progress. 'First we was stopped in the trench and had to get out into the open, sir; then we found a lot of wire and had to go round it; then, afore we could get back into the trench, young Lewis was hit by a stray – bad he was – and we had to send him off.'

They struck out on to what remained of the Courtrai road, let the returning transport by, with its shrapnel-inviting clatter, and plunged wearily down, through shell-holes and past remains of mules, farm carts, hedges and trees, till, under the welcome shelter of the canal bank, Skene gave the word: 'You may smoke!'

When, leaving the canal bank, they made for the ploughed-up and deserted railway crossing, it was now nearly eleven by Skene's wrist-watch: the men's fatigue and the bad condition of their feet had reduced the pace to a crawl. They passed D Company stragglers; the weary, cheerful voice of Thomas hailed them. They had rejoined the company, sagging and plodding towards the camp in the wood. Skene remembered counting his men in like sheep, including one on his hands and knees to save his raw feet, and two left at a wayside dressing station. How he got to his hut and fell asleep he did not remember. It was not necessary. The battalion was relieved.

*Chapter 4*

# The Natives

Who will ever forget the first hours of 'Divisional Reserve' after the trenches? The camp in the woods was only three miles from the line, long-distance shots at railhead went clean over it; it was at best a swampy clearing, cluttered up with tree stumps; furnished with two or three huts for 'messing', a score of shelters for sleeping, horse lines, and the remains of the yellow-flagged urinals of an Indian division. But you could walk about, bolt upright, without ducking your head, you could whistle and sing, sit at a trestle table to feed, meet the other companies of your battalion; and, best of all, you were 'fallen in' and marched, with halts if there were much shelling, to the old brewery at railhead, where the men had the great vats and the officers the mash-tubs, for a bath. There were still shops open here, a market-place, civilians afoot, and you could wander about a bit. At a restaurant in the side street you could engage a table in the hopes that you might come in to dinner one night and even go to the cinema. Never was there enjoyment like it. Old London days and nights seemed tame.

And the men! It took little more than twenty-fours hours for these sodden and disconsolate scarecrows to become, by aid of sleep, baths, parades and the last autumn flicker of the sun, the same light-hearted crowd of overgrown boys that had marched out from the Spanish Farm, ten days before.

On the second morning after being relieved, Skene woke in the pinewoods with a light heart, and a body at ease. Long Thomas had promised him the loan of his 'charger' to ride over to the Spanish Farm; Earnshaw, on a mount borrowed from the transport Sergeant, would ride with him as far as railhead, to get money from the field cashier.

It had happened that, coming back from bathing parade,

## THE NATIVES

Skene had been sent for by the Adjutant, who handed him a file of papers. 'Can you remember about this?'

Skene turned it over. 'Passed to you, please,' from battalion to brigade, from brigade to division, from division to some authority at Boulogne of whom Skene had never heard. At the very bottom was a blue French printed form, headed 'Claim for damage to Civilian Property, in view of law article' covered with R.F.s and the stamp of the Mairie of the Commune. Here, duly set out and supported by *procès verbal* made by Valliant, Marius (gendarme, on duty), Skene read how Mr Vanderlynden, Jerome, a cultivator, made the following complaint of hop-poles taken, grazing, and deterioration of agricultural machines.

'What does it amount to?' said the Adjutant.

Skene began to tell him.

'Oh, yes, and all the rest of it. I suppose we did it?'

'Part of it, there's no doubt, sir! The rest has been done since!'

'Can you settle it for another twenty francs?'

'I'll try, sir!'

'Here you are then. That's all brigade have sent!'

It was a fresh late October morning; the last clusters were brilliant in the hop fields, and over the broad leaves of the sugar beet was spread a steel blue sheen. Long Tom's charger, black with a white blaze, took the lead of Earnshaw's Argentine-bred beast, which had the belly and ears of a mouse, the neck of a giraffe, the mouth of a wooden horse on the roundabouts, and paced with that disillusioned air peculiar to the animals of Infantry transport.

'What a country!' thought Skene, to whom the little squares of haricot, roots, and stubble already ploughed were like an immense tapestry unrolled. 'These people must work dashed hard for precious little money,' said Earnshaw. 'What are you going back to the old billet for?'

'Row on about troops interfering with their agriculture. Going to see if I can interpret.'

' 'Myes, there's a girl there, isn't there?'

'I don't know and I don't care.'

'Oh well, so long,' said Earnshaw, as Skene turned off west, 'I'm going to lunch in the town; meet you here at four.'

Under the high-pitched roof and the old brick tower of the farm, Skene could see no sign of life. He had led his horse all round the outer yard and across the bridge, before he saw old Vanderlynden, bent and black, coming towards him between the currant bushes and the spirals of myriad flies gleaming in the sunlight. The old man took Skene's horse, silenced the clamorous dog, and ushered his visitor with much deference into the kitchen.

Yes, he had made his daughter write, because really there was no making oneself understood, but now the troops had moved on and they were left in peace. He regretted having deranged the officer.

For the second time, Skene absorbed that great lesson of the War: 'Never obey an order you have received. It is already too late. Obey the order for the time after next!'

Pulling out the old Fleming's 'Claim for damage to Civilian Property', he said:

'Then this is useless. You renounce it?'

The old man shook his head.

'No. I claim what is due to me by law!'

'Yes – yes – but how can I tell how much was done by my regiment, and how much by the next?'

'If the officer will only give himself the trouble to step into my pasture and look!'

They passed through the low dark old doors – through the varying layers of smell and mess to the old shed where the sick men had lain. There the flax was stacked at one end, the reaper-and-binder and cultivator parked at the other. In the rafters lay the heavy poles to which Earnshaw had tied his horses. They returned to the kitchen.

'Listen, Monsieur Vanderlynden,' said Skene: 'your hop-poles want a coat of tar; your machines a squirt of oil. Your pasture is all the better for the manure. Ten francs will cover the damage since I last settled with you!'

The old man heaved a sigh.

'I do not share your opinion!'

Skene took from his pocket two of the five-franc notes the Adjutant had given him.

'Will you take ten francs, or not?'

The old man grinned.

'There is no getting round you, my Lieutenant. Ten francs let it be. And now let us have something to take!'

Skene sat down in pleasant lassitude. How comforting to the eye were the greenery and sunlight, the clean tiles, black oak and shining pewter after the ugly miseries of the past fortnight! The old dog sprawling underneath the coffin-shaped stove blinked at him. In the dairy a separator was humming; there was a smell of coffee, hops, burnt wood and drying clothes. And the door was opened – by Mademoiselle Vanderlynden.

She seemed to have grown since Skene's last visit. Her carriage, dress, doing of her hair, well-buttoned boots, and clear colour were the same, but she seemed years older. She greeted Skene with formal politeness, and went, at the old man's request, to fetch a bottle of that special Burgundy which, apparently, he had bought from time to time to mark the progress of his tranquil and laborious existence, his marriage with Madeleine's mother, their succession to the farm, the birth of their children, the prizes gained by his stock. 'And this,' he said, 'is the dozen of my son Marcel, of which we will drink a bottle because we have again news of him.' He nodded to an enlarged photograph on the wall, of a young man whose chasseur's bonnet and tight collar, with bugle and numeral on the lapel, faintly disguised the bullet head and round shoulders of a Vanderlynden and a farmer. Smacking his lips, he added: 'Good! Good stuff! What do you say?'

It was. Never had Skene felt so well, never was old kitchen so picturesque, garrulous old man so interesting, or girl so well worth looking at, though she never spoke a word. Skene accepted their invitation to the midday meal. And when the old man went off to see to his men, he stayed watching Madeleine interrupt her cooking to fill his glass. No, she was not exactly a pretty girl, and she was dressed for work rather than for show.

## SIXTY-FOUR, NINETY-FOUR!

But she was a person – not a chattel or a clothes-prop. She was like one of those women the old Flemings used to paint – quaint rather than beautiful – trim enough in figure and complexion – but real people, who ruled houses and probably husbands, and who made up in vitality and character for what they lost by not being fair and frail. When the silence irked him, he broke it with a commonplace, and she answered:

'Ah Monsieur, this War, when will it end?'

'Quite soon, I should say, Mam'selle; we are going to—'

'I know – I have heard it all before –'

'Indeed – when?'

'Oh – how long ago – twelve months – the first time we saw the English –'

'And what did you think of us?'

'One was not in a state to think – the Germans had come as far as the crossroads – one heard the machine-guns – I was alone here with my father, for my brothers, of course, were gone – Then, all at once, I saw men in flat caps in the yard!'

'What did they say?'

'Ah! funny things – an officer - a quite young boy, spoke to papa – with some trouble we found he was talking French.'

'Did you get on with them?'

'Oh, yes. They were nice to deal with – better than our poor old territorials – and so frank. The officer told papa – "We are going straight between Douai and Lille!"'

Skene could not help smiling. He could see so clearly the well-dressed, brave, ignorant youth who was going 'between Douai and Lille'.

Mademoiselle Vanderlynden went on:

'That was a year ago – they have not yet gone between Douai and Lille, and I sometimes think –'

'Courage, Mademoiselle, we are not beaten yet – on the whole we are winning.'

'Oh yes, we are winning – but – do you know what I think, Mister Officer?'

'What do you think?'

'I think the War will end up here, in these fields!'

Skene laughed. 'What, no march to Berlin?'

'Never – Brussels hardly – Lille perhaps and Strasburg if there are any left to march!'

'What, out of all the English, French and Russians?'

Watching her gaze at the flat Flemish landscape, woolly with slanting sunshine and moisture, Skene did not know what to say. There was an uncanny note of prophecy in her voice. Then she came and sat opposite to him, paler than usual, with eyes shining and red lips pressed out into a straight line.

'Listen! You have French troops near your trenches?'

'Yes!' said Skene guardedly, 'somewhere near!'

'You would not do me a little service?'

'Why, of course, anything in reason!'

'It is this. The regiment of my fiancé is there. You would not go and see if there is news of him?'

'Why not? It might take a little time. One doesn't go into the lines of another army too easily.'

'Of course, of course! If you would just go and ask?'

'Go and ask! Why, I'll go and find him, and take him out to dinner if I can get the evening off.'

'No, no, I only want news of him.'

The rosy clouds of Burgundy were suddenly pierced by the grey light of reality. 'You mean you're afraid that something may have happened to him?'

She stood up to attend to a casserole which was just coming to the boil. 'I suppose so.'

Skene could think of nothing to say. She pushed the boiling pot aside and knelt – a pleasure to watch – by the lower cupboard door of an old press, gaily painted, polished with use, crowded with wedding crowns, pewter jugs, gaudy Flemish china, and cap-badges of British regiments that had been billeted at the farm. Madeleine unlocked a small drawer in the lower portion. 'I'll write you the name, but it is not to be shown to your friends, please. I trust you because you are *gentil*.'

She wrote out and handed him the name: D'Archeville – 53rd régiment de Cavalerie!

So that was her young man? 'But, my good girl, he's never

going to marry you,' he thought, and as though she could read that thought, she said:

'He is my *ami* – one calls it fiancé to English people – you will try to hear of him, won't you?' And Skene promised.

A cloth was laid at the head of the table for the family and their visitor, while the men and women sat at the other end. The long heavy Flemish dinner, with its roast and boiled, gooseberry jam and gingerbread, wine and beer, spirits and coffee, dragged on into the autumn afternoon. Madeleine was entirely absorbed in serving her father and guest, and in passing their portions to the labourers. Skene was nothing loth to mount his horse, the farmer's good cheer, heavy and solid, like the men, the houses, the beasts, the earth, even the thick, woolly sky of that country, had made him drowsy to the point of sleep.

Long Thomas's charger, properly watered and fed, was lively enough to rouse him before he got to the crossroads where he was to meet Earnshaw. He got down, lit his pipe and looked back through the elm-shadowed pastures and chequered arable at the Spanish Farm. There it stood, under the gravelly hillocks which continue the blue chalk downs of the Pas de Calais, across the Flemish plain into Belgium. Past the trees he could just see the weather vane on the shot tower and the wallflowered peak of the thatched gable from which he had come. From the hillocks to the north, and far down to the slag-heaps of the Lens coal-fields on the south horizon, was a land of unexampled fertility, of that satisfying beauty which exists only where form and colour are the clothing for home and plenty. And clean across it lay the chain of those old Spanish farms, from the Artois to West Flanders, memorials of the time, not four centuries ago, when men had fought for that rich land. Generation after generation, fighting and grabbing and snatching – Romans and Franks, Spanish and French and Huns, and nature covered it up, and went on producing more than ever was destroyed. 'Yes,' thought Skene, 'but we die of the process – we others.'

And just then Earnshaw arrived, and remarked that it was a fine evening and a wonderful year for hops; he had had a deuce

## THE NATIVES

of a job to find the cashier and a long time to wait to get his money; and a dam' good lunch, rather expensive, and they'd have to trot home most of the way to get through that beastly wood in daylight. Having told all his news, he asked: 'How did you get on with the natives?'

*Chapter 5*

# The Chance

Such Englishmen as Skene and Earnshaw, who towards the end of 1915 were swamping the professional element in the British Expeditionary Force, had been picked, by a very rough sort of natural selection, from the million enlistments of the 'Kitchener' armies; and they had under their orders the mass who had not the education, initiative, or will to rise out of the ranks. Above them, the small groups of regulars had, almost to a man, been of necessity pushed into staff appointments. Around them were a hundred thousand like themselves, company or battery officers of fighting units or services. They were drawn from the two main streams of English middle-class life – for the public-school men of military ages were either in, or as near as they could get to, the regular army, and the manual worker, however skilled, seldom rose to be an officer. One stream came, like Skene, from the professional and cultured circles – the other, like Earnshaw, from the business and speculating crowd.

The New Army of England contrasted sharply with the other armies of the world. Those who composed it were indubitably less soldierly, less trained, less officer-like than men of other nationalities, bred up in the close caste of conscriptive tradition. They were not so much officers of a national army, as prominent members of a gigantic football team – transmitting orders and taking initiative from a good-humoured agreement that – well – some one had to.

On the other hand, they possessed an immense advantage in their endless adaptability. From the early days, when recruiting posters portrayed them, with the query, 'He's happy, are you?' to the petering out of that grim jest about 'enjoying the War', there hung over them a preposterous air of riding a hobby. They learned to kill with a detachment as of learning fretwork.

Even the serious Skene was interested in the upkeep of a trench, not because it was an order, but because he liked experimenting with earth and sandbags and water, bombs, and telephone wire. The proudest day of Earnshaw's life was that on which he was appointed Transport Officer. They mostly carried the 'pack' like their men, and French officers were just beginning to envy them.

In the rough draughty 'mess' hut of the camp in the wood, during their four days' respite, there was little brooding over the morrow, or the fate before most of them. When the Colonel had withdrawn to his bunk, the Adjutant to his 'office', and old Adams to his store, the rest played bridge or poker, yarned, smoked and sky-larked. Any one glumly complaining of a black eye from falling into a shell-hole, or of the rats in his dug-out, was recommended to 'take more water with it'. That year-long grapple with death was perforce to be looked on as an entertaining experience that no one ought to miss, in spite of the obvious gaps at the table, and the narrow forty-eight hours of safety that remained. Will there ever be again such 'messes' as those of 1915?

The mail-bag was enormous, far larger than any regular soldiers would have had. For all these 'young officers' (so recruiting authorities spoke of that unique gang of men whose average age was over thirty) had folk belonging to them far more fussy and articulate than the relatives of the 'regulars'. But if, into one of those messes, some one came with a rumour, 'I hear there's to be a stunt at ... next week,' or 'We are taking part in the 579th Brigade attack on the 20th,' then all the indelible pencils and writing blocks would be neglected. To attack, beat the enemy, and get finished with the War was the primary desire of an army that wanted to get back to its proper job. Shell-fire, gas, and bullet wounds – horrible, of course, ghastly – but it didn't do to say so, not even to feel so. Carry on!

As Skene and Earnshaw led their horses back through the wood to the camp, Skene said:

'You needn't make a song in the mess about my going to the Spanish Farm billet. I went to oblige the Adjutant.'

'You may have. But most fellows will think you went to see that girl!'

'Girl's nothing to me. She's got a young man of sorts in the French Army!'

'You know all the family history.'

'What do you mean?'

'I think you're a silly ass!'

Just then the sentry on camp guard challenged, and they passed over to the transport lines in silence. Wading in the mud Earnshaw grunted: 'I'll have this sort of thing altered. Ruining all the horses!' This was an *amende honorable*, for not at the point of the bayonet would he have said a word that might make a 'mess' joke of Skene's visit to the Spanish Farm. He was as English as Skene, even more so.

Skene had hardly finished washing down the coarse, ample food, with whisky and water, when he was told an orderly was asking for him.

'What is it?'

'Wanted at Brigade Head-quarters!'

'Aha!' chirruped little Mansfield. 'I thought as much. Wanted for espionage. I shouldn't wonder, receiving letters from French civilians, as you do.'

'Hope they're not going to give you a job, Skene,' said Thomas. 'We're short enough as it is.'

'Bad company, bad company,' Mansfield's voice pursued them. 'Give my love to Uncle Charlie!'

At that period of the War, the ordinary company officer like Skene regarded Brigade Head-quarters as akin to the throne of the Almighty. Divisional Head-quarters was an unknown seventh heaven that never came much nearer to the line than railhead. As for Corps and Armies, they were outside this universe. With excitement and awe, then, Skene knocked at the newly painted door of a very new hut which an ambitious Royal Engineer had taken pains to surround with a white-painted railing. Bidden to come in, Skene came to attention in the small office, almost entirely papered with maps of the sector and nearly filled by a new pinewood table.

# THE CHANCE

'Lieutenant Skene, sir, 10th Easthamptonshire Regiment.'

'Quite so, wait a minute!'

Skene stood and stared.

Standing by the table was the best type of the pre-War army. Captain Castle, having fought through the bitter months of '14 and '15 as a company officer, had been made Brigade Major while under thirty, and had only remained so out of loyalty to a selfish Brigadier. Well-born, well-made, faultlessly brave, as indeed were all those old regulars, he was also thoughtful and well read, loved by his equals and adored by his men. Before the War he had mastered his job in double quick time, and had been thought none the worse of for excursions into Asiatic gendarmerie and colonial militia. After twelve months of War, he was thinking far into the second and third years to come. He had never laughed at Territorials nor snubbed the New Armies. He was a skilled pianist, had abundant good-humour, and was already on the brink of those large opportunities he subsequently used so fully. Standing between Colonel Gilford and a French interpreter, and so tall that he had to stoop, he had his finger and his keen eyes on a trench map, and his right ear cocked, as it were, towards the blanket-curtained door to the little mess-room where the General, a red-faced, white-haired cavalryman, Devlin by name, and known as 'The Devil Himself', was leading the discussion with his habitual snarl.

'They tell us that you speak French?' said Captain Castle.

'Yes, sir!'

'Are you sure?' came the bitter query from beyond the curtain.

'I think there's no doubt, sir; I hear that he has already been useful in that way.'

The snarl continued:

'What is he in civil life?'

'What are you?' asked Captain Castle.

'Architect and surveyor, sir!'

From behind the curtain came a muttered 'Good God!' The Brigade Major covered it with, 'Maps no difficulty to you?'

'None at all, sir.'

# SIXTY-FOUR, NINETY-FOUR!

'Very well, Colonel Gilford and the interpreter will take you by car to the Head-quarters of the French division next us. Yours is the flank platoon on our left. It is most important you should be in close liaison with the French. Have you got it?'

'Yes, sir.'

'Have you anything else for Skene, sir?'

'No.'

'Very well, good night, Skene!'

Out went the Colonel and Skene and the interpreter along the white paling to the car. The night was fine, the moonlight of amazing brilliance. Up the pavé and over the bridge, they passed through a village under a belfry whose chimes swelled to meet them and died away behind; then, still on the pavé road, along the bank of a canal lined with French poplars, over another bridge into another village whose belfry chimes were marking the next quarter. They seemed to be going round and round in some moonlit dream and the numbing cold of the October midnight. Skene tried to break the spell by listening to his companions' monosyllables, but the dream went on, of shining sky, black poplars, gleaming canal.

They passed the sentry box of a British military policeman doubled by a blue-cloaked, helmeted gendarme; turned down a drive between two Noah's Ark trees to a doll's house of a bargeman's cottage, where, flapping in the moonlight, the tricolour swung above the porch. The car stopped with a crunch, they unbent their stiffened limbs and got down. A plane buzzed over them high up in the greenish silver sky, on some bombing raid.

Inside the cottage, in a well-shuttered room, some lean, autocratic gentlemen, with high, closed collars, white cuffs, and no belts or impedimenta, were engaged round files and maps and telephones on white deal tables. Skene reflected that never would any of his own polo-playing, pheasant-shooting superiors be so dry, so old, so competent as these sportless Continental theorists! Presented by the interpreter, welcomed with conventional effusion, complimented on his French, Skene was left to wait in a mess-room, and chat with a charming, sleek-haired, scented boy in pale blue, crimson and silver, over a glass of sweet 'Malaga' and a harsh cigarette. This was his chance to ask for Madeleine's friend.

'D'Archeville,' repeated the rainbow youth, 'no officer that I know of that name is with the division, but we change so fast. You do not know the regiment? The 53rd Cuirassiers. But we are an infantry division. Well, well, he may be with the machine-gunners, as a private soldier. Many sons of good families prefer to remain in the ranks among their own sort. One is more at home. Does not that also occur with you?' And he lifted his pretty eyes, dark-circled with fatigue.

Skene thought not.

'Indeed!' replied the boy. 'Do you know D'Archeville?'

Skene was forced to admit that he didn't.

'Well, then, my friend, I don't know what interest you have in him, but if you really want to see him there is nothing for it but to go up to the front line, which is particularly bad on our front, and in this there would be some difficulty, on account of your uniform. But I could send a message for you if it is urgent?'

'No, not at all.'

'In that case, my friend, if it is merely for the pleasure of seeing the face of someone you do not know, I should wait, I think, until circumstances are more favourable.' And having thus delicately conveyed that he thought Skene mad or a liar, he filled up his glass and laughed. A gunner officer appeared with a bundle of papers, and led out into the moonlight. He spoke in fair English to Colonel Gilford. 'When you begin, we will let loose the forty thousand devils.' Skene stared. The gunner was replying to Colonel Gilford, and led beyond the canal bank, into the mouth of a communication trench. 'Think you can find this again, if necessary?' Skene thought so. 'Now, look here...' and comparing his map with Skene's he explained certain details. Skene noted them with nervous care and took his leave. An attack! The icy shock of the thought! Back in the car, scudding along the moonlit pavé, Skene revolved the problem – what, where, how on earth would they attack? The interpreter was speaking. Only by pressing his cheek close against the humid

## SIXTY-FOUR, NINETY-FOUR!

grey moustache could he make out the words, 'What is it you want with D'Archeville?' Skene had forgotten all that in his new excitement. Madeleine and the Spanish Farm seemed worlds away. 'A friend of a friend of mine ... I should have liked to have shaken hands with him.'

'You will find it difficult, he is a very particular young gentleman. I, for one, could not help you. He is a member of what they call the New France – all that there is of conservative and behind the times.'

To Skene, who knew something of French politics, and that the interpreter was an agnostic paper manufacturer from Lyons, this cast little light on Madeleine's mysterious *ami*.

Dawn broke, it was near sunrise when they reached the level crossing, and Skene was dismissed to rejoin his company.

Back across fields and through deserted farms to the battalion, which had moved up during the night to a line of dug-outs in the embankment of a canal, Skene went to see Long Thomas and found that they would not move till dusk. Rolling himself in a blanket he lay down, tired out, on the wet earth. Through the opening of his dug-out, he could just see the dark canal, the row of poplars, with leaves glowing straw-yellow in the autumn sun, and beyond them again a little whitewashed lock-keeper's house, whose gaping windows and torn thatch let in the pale Flemish sky. And that small point of domesticity amid all that was so warlike brought his mind back to Madeleine and her lover. Hang the fellow! What was he to do? Write to him? See him? On what imaginable grounds, with what imaginable result? The wet came soaking through his blanket. 'This time tomorrow,' he thought, 'I mayn't be here. There may be no me, no him – nothing!' And, rolling over on to what seemed a drier patch, he fell asleep. He had had his chance.

*Chapter 6*

# A Brigade Affair

His orderly was not to wake him till tea-time, but the sun had just set when Long Thomas stirred him up with one of those broomsticks then in vogue among officers for sounding the impossibilities of the trenches they were supposed to use, and invited him to come and have a look at the scene of the night's operations. Crossing the canal by a pontoon bridge to the rear, they climbed the left wall of the lock-keeper's ruined cottage, and, lying flat on charred rafters, peered out through the shell-torn thatch. At their feet was the canal; beyond its further bank an ever-increasing desolation, where communication trenches ran out among the weeds and self-sewn crops of fifteen months' desertion, the mud lagoons of undrained ponds, the gaunt scarecrows of splintered trees and ruined fragments of walls and gateways gleaming like bleaching bones in the dying light. Right on the sloe-coloured horizon, always on the highest visible ground, the first star-shells of the evening vaguely marked the enemy entrenchments. To Skene it seemed flatly impossible that human beings should make their way in darkness across so many sloughs and pitfalls, but the cheery voice of Long Thomas giving him his orders, precisely in the tone in which he would have told him to go in first wicket and hit the bowling, was incredibly reassuring. 'Two trees, and some brickwork, just there,' and Thomas pointed; 'you're second wave! If you're stuck, you stay there!' Skene said: 'Yes, I see!'

Climbing down, they went to the dug-out which served for mess-room and Company Head-quarters, where Thomas was to meet the other officers of his and the adjacent companies, for a last word. Years after, Skene used to shudder when he remembered that moment. The amateurishness of it all, that tiny concentration in plain sight of the Bosche, the utter lack of preparation or reserves – the, afterwards, patent fact that General Devlin, scornful of others' failures, was just experimenting, with a view to the command of a division. On the sweating walls of the candle-lighted den hung belts and rainproofs, between posted-up cartoons from 'Le Rire', showing the Kaiser with a withered arm; its improvised table was covered with maps and signal forms, little pools of wine, little smears of grease and cigarette ends. Outside, the N.C.O.s were 'falling-in' the men under shelter of the embankment, in the gathering dusk. Within, one heard: 'I see . . . here and then here . . . good enough . . . I suppose we shall – what's your watch!' and then an awkward silence, as if they were wondering.

From without came a North-country voice growling: 'If Aaa catches 'em a'll slog 'em, bah gom!' and a Cockney: 'Mind the barrow, please! The Sergeant said I was to have my little spade, but 'e won't let me take me little pail, no'ow, Gawd 'elp 'em!'

And Skene prayed from the bottom of his heart: 'Pray God, don't smash me up this time. I didn't start this silly show. It's not fair I should be killed!'

A tall high-shouldered form came splashing along the slippery pathway and stopped beside him. It was Captain Castle.

'Hallo, Skene! Thomas in? Let's see him!' Bending nearly double under the low opening he passed into the dug-out, with a word for everyone, a fixed time here, a definite place there, making sure that everybody knew where to look for him, and which way the walking wounded were to come. Skene ceased to pray. To trust in Castle seemed more effectual.

That fine day had ended in a clear sunset, but with darkness a light rain began to fall. Skene, with his Sergeant, passed slowly up the line of his platoon, feeling for himself that the extra shovels, bombs, and bundles of sandbags were in place; then, glancing at the luminous dial of his watch, he led his party along the steep embankment to the bridge. At the top, two tall figures stood, motionless, and as Skene passed, the Colonel's voice said: 'All right, Skene?'

'All right, sir.'

'Good luck to you.'

## A BRIGADE AFFAIR

Then began the slow and tiring journey to where they would 'jump-off'. The rain fell steadily; the mud rose above their ankles; there was constant hesitation in the pitchy quagmire to make sure of the right trench, constant halts to let those in front draw ahead, or close up the tailing-out which no amount of discipline or forethought ever entirely prevented among men marching in file. Of the enemy no sign save an occasional greenish star-shell that soared up into the downpour, hung glaring for a moment and went out; a few rifle-shots and a couple of long-distance shrapnel bursting far back over the transport routes. Then, before they had reached their shelter trench, the western horizon suddenly flared brick red, and, with a nerve-racking hiss, the first English shells passed over their heads and burst with dry crashes amid the darkness of the enemy trenches. From their left came a sudden, rapid, continuous, almost purring roll of gunfire. It was Skene's French friend letting loose 'the forty thousand devils'. By the time they had reached the jumping-off place, where the water rose halfway to their thighs, the bombardment was continuous. Skene leant against the low parapet in front of him. His head was singing and drowsy with the uproar – he squeezed down the line of his men to make sure they had each found proper foothold. Before he reached the end of his line, he was stopped in the narrow trench by some one coming from the opposite direction. It was Long Thomas.

'All right, Skene?'

'All right, Thomas.'

'They aren't half getting hell, are they?'

'It sounds like it.'

'It's nothing to what we'll give them presently.'

'Rath-er!'

'Cheerio! I'll come and see you as soon as you're settled in.' He passed, and Skene thought: 'Will you? I wonder.' At last his watch marked the minute, and he gave the signal. Everyone scrambled or hauled himself on to the parapet. In an instant the lucky and sure-footed were yards ahead of those whose foothold had slipped in the dissolving mud, or, too eagerly, had slid forward on to their faces. Skene, in an incredibly puny voice, as it seemed to him, kept shouting: 'Keep together – keep together!' Then he was walking on nothing, immersed in evil-smelling mud. A crash that seemed inside his head deafened and bewildered him. Struggling to his feet he ran his knees into a kneeling figure.

'There's a man hit, sir!'

'Never mind, go on!' And on they slid and stumbled together.

The uproar was now continuous, behind, above, before them; and beneath them the marsh quaked. Mud and iron flew through the air in what seemed solid masses; it had become as light as day. Skene could only think of one thing, to keep on cawing hoarsely, 'Go on, go on!' The Cockney catchword he had heard in the dusk had caught on, and all about him, shopmen and clerks, labourers, mill hands, miners were bellowing at the top of their voices, 'Mind the barrow, please!' as they skidded and waded, fell and died.

With a sort of dismay he was brought up sharp by the inky line of a trench. The voice of the Sergeant-major shouted to him from the darkness: 'Half left, sir, half left. There's a plank across, and keep half left, sir. You're too far to the right!' He realized then that he was crossing their own front-line trench.

When he was over it he seemed to have before him a field of oats, 'All a-blowing, all a-growing,' but it was a thick bank of wire and they must grope their way to the opening. With demon hands scratching his face, tending his clothes, tearing his water bottle from his hip, his cap from his head, he plunged through that devil's garden, and blundered at last into a group of men, digging, grubbing, tugging asunder the tortured soil. They were the next platoon. Thrusting before him to the left such of his own men as he could find, he reached the mound of splintered brick and the two elm stumps, with their ragged fans of bough allotted as his position. The German trench was beyond, but shells were still falling into it, making of it a quaking line of light, a continuous eruption. Of the first wave, no sign. By chance, the right thought was uppermost in his mind, 'Dig. Get cover.' He passed from man to man, speaking a word here, giving a hand there, and praying in vain that the third wave would bring the reels of wire that alone could make them safe. The filthy mud splashed back in clods into the miserable gully that was beginning to appear, the air was alive with hurtling metal; the score or so of men were dropping one by one; a sort of dull frenzy settled down on Skene. He could hear a small voice calling, 'Is that you, sir! Is that you?' 'The fool!' he thought, crawling backwards and forwards amongst his men, 'Who does he think it is!' Some one was pulling at his arms, a Cockney voice said: 'I've brought Mr Mansfield, sir.' Suddenly around him appeared his own Sergeant, Mansfield's Sergeant nursing a Maxim gun, another of Mansfield's men with a tripod over his shoulder, and then a shrill mocking voice, as of some parrot from the underworld, said: 'I say, Skene, do tell the band to stop! I want to reverse,' and out skipped Mansfield's little figure in a smeary raincoat, mud-clotted from head to foot. The enemy's fire had slackened, and his voice chirrupped above it: 'Where have you been? I've been looking for you all over the infernal room. And here you are, sitting out by yourself – you know the next is ours!'

In the Operation Orders had occurred the sentence, 'Immediate provision will be made for adequate machine-gun protection against counter-attack.' Skene began to laugh. He held his head in his hands and a sort of dizziness overcame him. He sat down in a puddle. His Sergeant, kneeling beside him, was telling him how the rear section had got separated by a patch of impassable wire; they had been picked up by Mansfield and brought on to the old German trench which had been the first wave's objective. 'But there's nothing to be done with that, sir, it's all to bits. There's no one in front, and nothing has come up from support. And what shall we do with these wounded, sir?'

What, indeed!

After setting up his gun, Mansfield passed with a jest, making his way further along. By the first glimmer of a feeble dawn Skene could see that they had scratched out some dozen yards of trench waist-deep behind the two tree stumps. Then the hurricane burst out afresh. Some one shouted: 'Here they come!' Mansfield's machine-gun set up an unceasing gibber. Skene saw that his Sergeant was passing up and down behind his men, tearing open boxes of small arms ammunition. There was no need to order a rapid fire. With one long yell, 'a-a-a-a', the men were beginning to work the bolts of their rifles as if frantic. Nothing else to be done! It was instinctive, the one poor outlet for what all had been feeling. The men were behaving well, after what they'd been through! Pulling himself up behind a jutting ledge of brickwork, Skene stared into the greenish-white vapour, where the British barrage was bursting, and into which his men were emptying their rifles. For several minutes, it seemed, he watched. Nothing emerged from that belt of vapour. The firing slackened. The counter-attack was not maturing.

Instead, as the sullen November day came up, Skene found himself chained by a network of machine-gun fire. Two of his men were hit at once, he told the others to lie close. He himself peered out from time to time. Nothing to be seen but vapour – freshly torn earth – broken pickets – shredded wire – bodies and water – and all visible surface whipped with vicious bullets. No message could reach him, no ammunition, no medical aid.

About midday he let his men eat what they had on them. There was no hope of cooking anything. By two o'clock the enemy were enfilading the little trench. Skene crawled along, literally over his men, some sleeping the sleep of exhaustion, some grim and pale, shivering as they clutched their rifles. The wounded were quiet, very white, either dead or collapsed. At the end of the line, Skene found his Sergeant lying on his back, his cap over his face. Skene pulled him by the arm, but the arm came away in his hands. The Sergeant was cut limb from limb by a shell that had landed beneath him.

Next, a long-distance bombardment was opened on them. Their machine-gun, the brickwork and the tree stumps were first smashed piecemeal and finally blown away. But the Flemish winter day is short, and with dusk came a runner, worming his way in on his stomach, with a written order from Thomas, 'Bring in your men.'

Under cover of darkness, twenty-three men, dragging and carrying two wounded, who still appeared alive, all of them

## A BRIGADE AFFAIR

soaked and starved, scratched, torn and plastered with mud, made their way back in darkness to the old front line.

Skene went to see Thomas. The companies were all mixed up. The first wave had been held up by uncut wire and blotted out, leaving Skene's party uncovered. It was not even possible to know how far the artillery had helped or hindered.

So ended that Brigade affair. Skene had lost half his men, had not seen a German, and had come back to his starting-point.

## Chapter 7

# One Game and Another

The battalion had been at rest for some days in a convent of a railway town. They were no longer recognizable for the same men that Skene had helped to march back from the line.

Reclothed, roughly but well fed, shaved and no longer starved of sleep, they were laughing and singing about the field kitchen in the courtyard under the giant chestnut trees. It was a fine November day, and the blue smoke curled up quietly through the rust-coloured leaves into the pale Flemish sky. They had got over the exhaustion of the attack, the despair of failure, the jealousy of the kilted battalion of regulars, who, helped by a bombardment of three days instead of three hours, had eventually straightened the line.

They had got over the bitter nights and mornings of torrential rain, and those first frosts, when every semblance of a trench fell in, and the battalion after being relieved, instead of coming out from the line, had been kept on the canal bank and sent up every night to dig. Here in the town they could walk about on the firm paved road, where the mud was seldom above their ankles, where there were still a few shops, restaurants, and actually a cinema. The third week of November had turned mild and fine, and with the sun and rest, the old jaunty spirit had come back. Skene shouted for his breakfast and hurried the N.C.O.s through the necessary parade and company business. Thomas had gone to Brigade Head-quarters, Skene commanded the company, and they were to play the semi-final of the Brigade Football Tournament that afternoon on the archery meadow behind the church.

Free of his duties, Skene set out for the field behind the church. It was market day, and crossing the square, he wondered if he would see Madeleine or her father. Here, amid rows of black-hooded gigs, and the low stalls stacked with butter, eggs, chickens and cheese, people were haggling and bartering – old men in black broadcloth with black glazed peaks to their Dutch caps, old ladies of astonishing circumference and garrulity, bareheaded young girls with their hair carefully dressed, and wonderfully neat stockings and boots, rough skirts, cotton blouses, and strong hardworking bodies. One or two of them offered their wares to Skene, but the majority were content to examine him with leisurely curiosity. He could see neither Madeleine nor her father, and, having made sure that the football ground was in order, went back to the billet. In the afternoon he lounged peacefully smoking around the pasture where the match was played, trying to explain to the Brigade interpreter why it was fitting that officers should turn out in shorts and referee, and treat respectfully the captain of the side, although he was the Sergeant-major's servant. Under a mild sky, in that damp rich meadow rose the old familiar shouts, the drub-drub of the ball, the rustle of feet, the piercing whistle of the referee. It was England, simply a piece of English life cut neatly out and pasted on the map of Flanders. Behind the spectators – men and officers, astonished natives and a few derisive French soldiers home on leave – Brigadier-General Devlin strolled with Colonel Gilford, smoking and watching the play. Skene caught these words:

'Have you got accustomed to these middle-aged subalterns?'

'Yes, pretty well. That bald-headed officer over there gives his age as thirty-five, and none the worse for that. On the contrary, all work and no raggin'!'

And just then Skene saw old Vanderlynden in a high cart behind an old white horse plodding slowly along the pavé bordering the pasture without much guidance from the reins. He slipped through the hedge and put his hand on the shaft. Old Vanderlynden raised his cap. 'Good-day, my good sir! We have had bad news. My young lady's young man is in hospital!'

Skene expressed his sympathy: the old man, elbows on knees, looked at the flies on the horse's back.

'We have been to the hospital, but he is not to be seen!'

'How is that?'

Here the old man became strangely garrulous. 'My good sir, it was like this. We got the news that he lay in hospital at five o'clock of the evening. Too late then. We went to bed; she slept little, I think. In the morning, we got out the cart and started. At the station we found a notice. In case of necessity, relatives of wounded can have half-fare ticket. We ask, but it is not granted without the written request stamped with the stamp of the Mairie. So we went back, to write our request and get it stamped. Blanquart, the Secretary, is not at home, but at the end we find him and it is done. We catch the train and arrive at the hospital and show our papers. He is not there!'

'Do you mean they have evacuated him?'

'They do not say: they only say, in French, he is not there!'

Skene looked at the round eyes, the roughly shaven chin, the horny outstretched hand. He saw so plainly that utter incapacity to spend three francs too much even to cheat Death, the dumb acquiescence in some orderly-corporal's 'Pas ici!'

'Well, what are you going to do now?'

'It is just that, my Lieutenant, for which I have come to speak to you. My daughter thinks you might help her...' ('Oh, yes, I daresay,' thought Skene.) 'It seems, since it was an English hospital to which he was taken, he will go to an English base. We, as civilians, may not use the telephone, and I do not know if they would answer us, at the hospital – but they would answer you!'

'You want me to telephone, do you?'

'My little girl waits always at the station to see if you will not, my Lieutenant! You have only to get up here beside me, and come and speak to her!' He spoke to the old horse in Flemish.

Colonel Gilford, on his way from the football field to a conference at Divisional Head-quarters, heard – above the cheering and the raucous: 'Come on, you Clyde-strikers!' 'Right, we will so!' – the clop-clop of the heavy-footed old white horse, and saw one of his officers being driven down the street by a 'native', in a black gig. It confirmed his saddest suspicions of the New Armies.

The station was a stucco building with a portico and arcade, cluttered up with military offices, and almost lost among sandbags, waiting lorries, and fidgeting mules in limbers.

In the dark waiting-room sat Madeleine Vanderlynden, between a swine-fever notice and an appeal of the new War Loan. She had left off for the occasion the clothes of her daily life, and was dressed in a dove-grey tailor-made costume, and what Skene would have described as a 'decent' hat. She was sitting perfectly still, holding her gloves and her little bag. Skene thought that except for her boots, too high and pointed in the toe, she might have passed as 'nice' in Easthampton suburbs. She rose, held out her hand, and said: 'Monsieur, you would do me a great service if you would telephone!'

Skene pushed into the R.T.O.s office, told off the Corporal in charge, and called up the Clearing Station. He got through to the orderly officer and put his question. The officer didn't know. He was a busy man, and relatives were a plague. Casualties were notified through the proper channels in due course. As for French casualties in an English hospital, they were a nuisance, like their relatives. Their nominal roll was kept separately and could not be found. Anyhow they had gone. Skene went back to Madeleine, who was sitting just as he had left her. The old man stood by her, gazing at the floor, with his hands hanging at his sides. In that case, she asked, would he not get her a lift in a car to the base? Skene couldn't do that. He fidgeted, and looked at his feet. Madeleine stifled a sob, while the old man spat carefully in a corner. 'Perhaps he's been transferred to another sector,' said Skene. She answered bitterly: 'I want to see him!' It dawned on Skene that she didn't understand, and didn't want to understand, even the most necessary and elementary Army Routine. He felt helpless, and cast about for some phrase to express his feeling that what was done was done, the dead were dead, and here was he alive, today, and possibly dead tomorrow, and the least bit tired of being a disinterested third party. But he only inquired what troops were now billeted on the farm. Madeleine sprang to her feet then, with a dab at her eyes, and a brusque 'Yes, it's time we were getting home.' And as the old black gig trailed across the cobbles of the square behind the old white horse, she turned her head to say: 'You must come and see us again soon.' That was the only thanks Skene got.

## Chapter 8
# The Day of Rest

The company was in Brigade Reserve – not even so far back as the camp in the wood. They were to be quartered in Dead Dog Farm, just out of bullet range, but within that of field-guns, and were advised not to walk about in daylight. There was no fear of that – they would go up at four-thirty every afternoon to dig; besides, the artillery dug-outs in the cellar had several feet of brick rubble over them, which meant that they hadn't been abandoned without good reason.

On the first night, at ten o'clock, the company tumbled in from the relief which had been taking place since five. By the help of two candle stumps the officers saw the men under shelter. Their swelling chorus of songs, oaths, thumps and clatter of rifles and equipment, while they got their hot tea from the cooker in the yard, died away into snores. There was no digging that night.

The morning dawned grey and thick with fog. Skene and Thomas went round the place to see what could be done with it as a billet.

It reminded Skene of Spanish Farm. It was, in fact, another of that chain of farm-fortresses left by Alva, three hundred years ago. On three sides of an enormous midden, the red brick buildings towered up, solid as when built – badly holed by the Bosche, but hanging together still. On the fourth side stood a shot tower thirty feet high, and so solid that a 4-in howitzer shell had not destroyed the whole of it. They were just returning, when a mounted officer clattered under the arch of the gateway and dismounted beside them.

Was it credible that there could exist anything so clean and bright as that officer? Cap, well-shaven face, raincoat, field-boots, shining spurs, black metal cross – ah! the Padre from

Brigade. Thomas, the public schoolboy, covered his astonishment, called a man to take the horse, and asked the Padre to breakfast as if he had been expecting him for months. 'Why, of course,' thought Skene, 'it's Sunday!'

For so long, Sunday had meant nothing more than any other day. An hour later the four platoons filed along the cobbles to the big barn.

The fog was dense, the front quiet. There was nothing to fear from observation. Thomas and Skene considered the danger of having so many men together in a confined space, but agreed to risk it. The only light came through the upper half of the great doors – the light of a wet Flemish winter – and fell on shaven heads and newly brushed khaki, freshly shined leather and brass. The Sergeants distributed little paper hymn-books. The Padre produced a surplice from his haversack and put it on in a corner, and Skene was perversely reminded of a girl he had known, years before, who, after hours of shining nudity, would suddenly get up, turn her back, and slip on a nothing of linen and lace with just such an action.

The hymns the Padre had chosen were good and old. Skene amused himself by picking out from amongst the men the well-trained little village choir boys. The singing ceased. The young Padre was speaking; what he said appeared simple, sincere, sensible. The men, heartened by having opened their chests in singing, were listening, absolutely still. Skene's mind wandered. That young Corporal by the door, with the light on his clean features and cropped head, the healthy sheen of his flesh against the deep brown of the barn, might be out of a Flemish picture – a Van Dyck. Somewhere a man snored – and with the sound the picture changed to a Hals or Jordaens.

Did those old painters, who lived in the midst of wars as brutal as this one, draw inspiration from the tremendous emotions of their time? And should we see, in our generation, art rise to equal heights? Or was fine art sent wandering from heaven, like the wind, to descend only on the unconscious!

But everybody was bending head and shoulders. The young Padre was praying now. Direct and simple, asking that they might keep before them the high purpose which had brought them together to do their duty in a strange land, whatever might be the consequences. But Skene thought of young Murdon and Bolton, the boy-Corporal, and suddenly felt he wanted to cry. The young Padre started another hymn, and gave them benediction. The men filed out.

Divested of his surplice the Padre was cheerful, obviously hungry. He would stay to lunch. Thomas went over to Brigade. Skene entertained the guest. The mess orderly had got pork chops from goodness knew where, a tin of beans from the canteen, a bottle of French beer, there was ration cheese and shamrock 'butter'. And the Padre produced a flask of canteen port.

After lunch, Skene, and the young Padre who volunteered his help, sat smoking in that ancient basement, smelling of pigeons and rats and old age, and turning over on the greasy 'table' the letters home of nearly two hundred men, which had to be censored and sent down that night.

Such letters home – letters to parents mostly! Some to children – the longest of course to sweethearts – some well written – nearly all affectionate – some obscene like the simple classic, 'Dear Mother, This war is a b... Tell Auntie!' About them all was the curious anonymity of letters whose writers are forbidden to say where they are, what doing. Skene looked for the crude pothooks of his own servant, fearing that the fellow's loquacity, fortified by the extra leisure and liquor of officers' servants, might have prompted some effusion that would get him into trouble. What he found, however, was this, with the spelling corrected:

'DEAR WIFE,
  'Hope you are well and keeping your heart up. Give my love to the kiddies. And do keep your heart up. That's a rum 'un, old Mrs ... being dead. Mind you ask her girl Alice for some of the potatoes if they are not going to keep them. And keep your heart up. Now I must close. Your loving husband,
                                                        'JERRY.
                                                  'Somewhere in France.
  'Love to my kiddies.'

## THE DAY OF REST

Slowly the pile of cheap envelopes diminished. Presently they were gone. Skene and the young Padre faced each other in the candle-lit dusk. The latter was flushed. 'The men are splendid!' he said. But on Skene had already descended the irritable mood which used to come to the most hardened, when about to leave such meagre comfort and safety as they had in billets, for the misery and danger of the trenches.

'We get used to it,' he said.

'One is glad the spiritual fires are burning so brightly, a good augury for after the War!'

On the tip of Skene's tongue was the retort he had made the week before to an Engineer officer about the siting of some dug-outs. 'You may know a lot about trenches, but we have to live in them!' But he looked at the young Padre's clean pink face. 'After all,' he thought, 'he might easily have stayed at home!' and said instead: 'There won't be many left for after the War – at our present rate of going on it's rather an expensive education, isn't it?'

'I fear so, I fear so! At any rate those who fall have satisfaction of knowing that they have done their duty!'

An eternity of satisfaction! Skene replied: 'Let's hope so!'

'Well, now I must be going. I shall have tea at Brigade. Is there anything I can send you?'

'The men are always grateful for novels and cigarettes.'

'Comforts them – what?'

'Prevents them thinking. Good night.'

The Padre clattered out into the dusk. 'Tea, sir!' said Jerry the servant at his elbow. He drank it, reading 'Tristram Shandy'. He was roused by his Sergeant-major: 'Company ready to move off, sir!'

Pulling on his gear he sallied from the farm at the head of that procession.

That night he lost four men from shrapnel and two from machine-gun fire. Sunday!

*Chapter 9*
# Stands England where she did?

Who that ever had such a thing can forget his first English leave? That leave, which came after months of waiting, and was often despaired of – for it was not then the usual thing it afterwards became – those eight days which seemed to promise an eternity of leisured comfort. Towards such bliss, Skene, like everyone else, travelled slowly and with difficulty. Relieved from his command in the support line, he had a mile or so to walk across the open, past the dump, and along the shell-swept road, until, near the bank of the canal, he was lucky enough to find some regimental transport, returning to the horse-lines. He took the Sergeant's horse and, pushing ahead, found old Adams in his 'Armstrong' hut, and shared the old man's nightcap whisky, under the Bosche midnight salvo flying over their heads. Then, buttoning close his British-warm, and commending his valise to the old soldier's care, he stumbled through the darkness, down the remaining mile and a half of camp-surrounded pavé to the station. This was before the days of rest-houses and officers' clubs, and he slept sitting on his pack, against the sandbags of the R.T.O.'s office, until a freak train, made up with Belgian, French and English carriages, rolled dissolutely in. Flinging himself into the nearest first-class compartment, he slept until the bitter morning rain, blowing through a broken window, awoke him between Calais and Boulogne. Around him on the seats and floor lay half-a-dozen other officers, whom he had never seen before. His grumble at the length and slowness of the journey was answered: 'Ever been by Havre? No? By Golly, you should go by Havre!' Luckily Skene had biscuits and chocolate and some one had some coffee and rum in a Thermos, for it was eleven o'clock of a grey, drizzling morning when they stretched their stiffened limbs on the platform at Boulogne, and were promptly captured by a Military Landing Officer who took their warrants and gave them 'duty' tickets for the boat. Too green, then, to 'dodge' obligations of this kind, too keen, perhaps, to wish to, and much in awe of the limping captain with the D.S.O. who gave the orders – 'base-port people' had not yet become an alien and hated race – Skene spent the two hours crossing in charge of the port side of the main deck, and did not really feel free until he emerged through the portals of Victoria Station. He had travelled up with two homeless Englishmen who had hurried from the West Indies to enlist. They were going to dine at a restaurant and see if they couldn't 'pick something up' at a music-hall. Skene sent a telegram and took a taxi to a northern terminus and caught the night train to his home. He slept the whole four hours. Clouds were racing over the bright moon till the very Cathedral spire seemed in motion, when he let himself into the Cathedral close and put his key into the latch of his uncle's house. They had remained faithful to him then – all these familiar things! He switched on the light in the low, wide, polished old hall – and instantly felt for his revolver – coming to meet him was a red-eyed, shorn fellow in a greasy collar and British-warm, nondescript cap and sodden puttees. It was his own reflection in the mirror – what a brute he looked – red, coarsened, broadened! The old mirror, that had reflected him a thousand times, told him the truth as no human being would have done; and stuck in it was a note: 'Dear Geoffrey, I have gone to bed. There is some hot milk in the Thermos. Uncle.' . . . Milk!

Morning! O taste of the first cup of English-made tea. O first bath in a real white enamelled bath with unlimited hot and cold water. Having shaved at leisure, and breakfasted bloatedly under the admiring eyes of housemaid and housekeeper, Skene sauntered out. He first met one Sharply, in the local bank, who had not enlisted, and kept him talking, till the reluctant wretch, who was perfectly fit, and of military age, but who wanted to 'get on', stammered: 'Of course, I can't go, we're so short-handed!' He next met the stumping Captain Bittern, who had left a leg at Mons, and was greeted as a brother officer, before all the world. Then came a glass of sherry with Griggs the wine merchant, who had known him 'as a leetle, totty boy – and now look at ye', then a tearful blessing from an unknown old lady, who *would* shake his hand because she had lost 'her boy' in the trenches. It was nearly midday before he turned the corner of the Chapter House and stood before his uncle's office, with its brass plate, 'Diocesan Architect and Surveyor'. There was the bald head and toothless mouth of old Hanson, his uncle's clerk, quavering out: 'Well, if it isn't Master Geoffrey come back from the War – what will the Gov'nor say?' as if he had stepped out of the pages of Anthony Trollope or Bulwer Lytton.

And here was his uncle – that genial, decorous person, who had been father and mother and tutor to him, with the beautiful white hair and rosy cheeks, in the leisured tidiness of that office, where the architectural drawings gleamed out from the neutral-tinted lincrusta – was it all a sort of a play?

War had not touched the people at home. Lighting regulations, recruiting, daily casualty lists – it hadn't really touched them. And if it hadn't, what would? 'Well, Geoffrey, my boy!' And then a tale of who had been born, married or died during his absence within the little friendly circle of The Close. 'So-and-so has done so-and-so – ah! but you wouldn't know him, he's in the town ... Mrs Someone's son Lionel has got a commission, and went to France on the 14th; I don't know if you met him!'

'I can't say I have, Uncle; you see, there are over a million and a half of us there!'

'Just so, just so! And now, my dear boy, do tell me what it is like, your letters don't give us much ... data!'

'No, you see we have strict censorship!'

'Quite! Quite! I suppose it is very terrible.'

'It's like – like – ' How could he find words, in that quiet room, for the barren maze of putrid water and ragged wire – for the formless misery and roystering leisure of billets! 'It's like the end of the world!'

'My dear Geoffrey! Well, I suppose so!'

His uncle demanded no further explanation. He had more engrossing things on his mind. They walked home to lunch.

There were cutlets and stewed rhubarb. No cream: 'War-time, Geoffrey. We all feel it.'

The days passed. They passed in visits to his tailor, his old school, his uncle's friends. His own friends were either gone, or, as he now felt, worse than gone. He did not want to see those who had stayed behind. He felt uncertain as to whether he made them feel awkward, but certain that they made him feel so; the seventh day came. He had to go up to town in the afternoon, to be in time for the boat train, judiciously arranged so as to start at an hour at which all men are sober. His uncle sitting opposite him at lunch (roast beef and apple tart) ventured: 'Well, my dear boy, the sooner it's over the better. I shall want you when we get really busy with the memorials – there'll be a lot!'

Skene agreed. They parted at the station with a handshake. What his uncle thought none can tell.

In town, he had a hot bath and a good dinner, not knowing when he would have either again, and strolled into a music-hall, having no one in London to see and nowhere else to go. In that unreal maze of mirrors, plush seats and gilding he felt curiously detached. The allurements of the place, the promiscuous pleasures, that lay ready enough to the hands of young officers on leave, did not allure him somehow. He was far from realizing as yet the bleak certainty of illness, breakdown, wounds, eventual death that lay before an Infantry officer. The crowd cheered him up. He felt that the country was putting up a good show for war-time. He felt a cheerful compassion for all these women, chased out of Belgian watering-places under circumstances he could well imagine. Two-thirds of the men were in uniform, and mostly junior to him – he sympathized with them no less. By the bar a young officer, trying to converse in broken French with an over-dressed elderly woman, cannoned against him and apologized. It was Wheather, the Signal Officer, just drunk enough. He hailed Skene with effusion. 'I tell her I will go up the golden stairs,' he pointed to the ornate stairway leading up from the bar, 'but she won't let me.'

The lady pounced on Skene as an ally; she was hardly less

drunk, but more used to it. What claim she made on Wheather – an introduction she had given him, or a room he had hired from her – Skene couldn't make out. Her French, he judged, was inferior to his own, and she would not accept his polite intimation that his friend was tired, and he was going to see him home. Instead she stuck to Wheather's arm, and impounded Skene's, who dare not withdraw it for fear that she should fall. And together the three gyrated, to the amusement of the world, but not to Skene's. A commissionaire said with a grin: 'Now, sir, we must clear, if you please!' In the crush that followed, Skene, separated from Wheather, was anchored on the stone kerb, by this elderly lady in loud clothes, dragging on his arm and stuttering in rapid, mutilated French, 'malade – malade à en crever – sick enough to bust myself.'

'Taxi, sir?' said the grinning commissionaire. Skene nodded.

The vehicle slid up, the old lady collapsed. 'All right, sir, shove her in; I know her!' said the driver. Skene shoved her in and got in behind, holding up the poor old bones and lolling head as best he could. The machine stopped with a whirr at the doorway of an establishment against which nothing could be said so far as appearances went. A porter in uniform called a maid from an upper flat; Skene delivered the old lady to them without remark and received no thanks. Returning to the taxi he drove to his hotel. On getting out he asked the driver: 'Who was that person?' 'Well, sir, we calls her "skinny Lizzie". She often goes home like that. Don't get enough to eat, they say, since the War!'

Skene went up to brush off the scent and powder.

Morning was breaking grey, in that grey place, Victoria Station, when he picked his way among men sleeping on the asphalt pavement, and women weeping against anything that gave them semblance of shelter. Dodging and pushing, he got his boat ticket, found the Pullman breakfast car, and cast his pack upon a seat.

Half-past six of a winter's morning strikes chilly on an empty stomach, however healthy. Skene stamped his feet, in the cold and sodden twilight that the shaded lamplight eked out into the dawn under the sooty girders. Around him, officers whose relatives had come to see them off were trying to look anywhere but at those women's faces, so brave, so white, so strained. Skene thanked his God that he had no one. Across on the platform where the rank and file were boarding their separate train, emotion was allowed fuller vent, the atmosphere was easier. There, stout buxom mothers, and pale neat mothers, trim or draggled sisters, sweethearts, wives, and some few who were none of these, were clinging and crying to their hearts' content – and the men, a few painfully sober and earnest, but most jolly, or just recovered from jollity, elbowed their way into the carriages and began to sing.

An eddying movement round the carriages of his own train, a closing of doors, caused Skene to seek his place. The train moved, gently, noiselessly. Strained faces turned away; a rustling of newspapers, in a dead silence – the men's train, and its 'Are we downhearted?' dropping behind in the grey suburbs. And, oddly, as the speed increased, and the last suburb yielded to the parklands of Kent, and the first gruff small talk of Englishmen ashamed of their emotions began, Skene felt his spirits rising.

Opposite to him an R.E. officer yawned and sat up, with ends of his hair straggling over his bleared eyes. It was Wheather.

Each of them said 'Hallo!' and sat silent.

Presently Wheather leant across the breakfast table and said: 'Lend me some money!'

Skene did so. 'Thanks,' said Wheather. 'Where the devil did I see you, Skene?' Skene reminded him. 'Hoh! It was a muddle. You see, before the War I used to know a little party in a shop, you know, in the West End. I wrote and told her to meet me on leave. She used to wear a decent black dress, an' a little hat, and looked just all right – looked like what she was. I used to take her to the Palace, and they never said a word. When she met me, on leave, my word, you should have seen her. The first evening cost me a little short of ten quid – why, we used to go to the pictures and have supper, and the whole go was about thirty bob! I was so tight I don't know how I got out of her flat. I had to go home, of course, and see my people that day, but I arranged to meet her again last night. She was a bigger swell

SIXTY-FOUR, NINETY-FOUR!

than ever. She'd had trouble with her landlord, and wanted to come to my hotel. But I said, "My dear girl, I've booked my room and that sort of thing isn't done." "Oh, I'll get a chaperone and take a room with her," she says, "and be your fiancée and sling the lead like anything with the office." So she produced the old girl as a chaperone, and by that time I was tight again, and she turned up rotten and went off. An' then I saw you, an' comin' out I got collared by another girl in a taxi, who swore I'd kept her waiting.'

The waiter passed. 'Here, get me some more coffee – hot – an' never mind the sugar.'

'I got so fearfully mixed up I didn't know where I was. Another girl, another flat. Everything else the same. She got me up at half-past five, gave me some sort of breakfast, and pushed me out like a good 'un. I got here somehow. But one of them had been through my pockets. My case was gone and the return half of my leave warrant stuck in here – breast pocket – loose!'

Skene laughed and thought: 'What a beastly mess!' And everything seemed false and artificial – his guardian's offices – these ladies and their flats! Well, he was going back to something – real!

Folkestone! The train slid down to the quay. The sharp air stung his nostrils. Thank God the flood was at full – no waiting. Outside the pier the wave-caps were white and the destroyer convoy circled sharply black against the grey. Tramp and bustle as the leave boats swung at their moorings, flapping of ropes and gulls' wings, roar of steam cranes and shouting.

Skene pushed his way well forward. He suddenly realized that he was glad, actually glad to be going back. He felt as if he were going home, leaving behind a certain comfort of body and leisure of mind, but leaving, too, something that he felt to be false – the complacency of that Cathedral town – the silly waste of the night in London. He was going back to discomfort, hardship, danger, death perhaps, but he was going – he felt – to where anyone with a spark of manhood ought to be, fighting this war to an end, cutting a clean line with the past, and making a fresh start possible, to a better future.

238

*Chapter 10*

# The Waging of War

The year 1915 closed, dark and wet, and 1916 opened, dark and wetter still. For six weeks the battalion was never completely out of the line, the digging and carrying was incessant. An attack of trench fever took Skene to the casualty clearing station for a fortnight. He returned to his battalion in mid-March just as snow was beginning to fall. The officers were billeted just then in a half-demolished windmill, while the men were in the outbuildings. Skene sat there one bleak afternoon, writing in his Field Message book letter after letter. They were all the same. There were so many that he used his carbon sheet to duplicate them.

'In the field. March, 1916.
'Dear
                                                                                   (son)
'I very much regret to inform you that your (husband) was
                                                                                   (brother)
(killed)
(missing) in action on the ....... He was very popular with his comrades, who will feel his loss severely. He was a good soldier and liked by his officers. As soon as possible a cross will be erected, bearing his name, etc., on the spot where he laid down his life for his country.

'Yours faithfully,
'G. Skene, Lt.'

After filling in the names, he addressed the envelopes, some to sooty streets of the northern mining and industrial towns – some to the big estates and farms of the southern side of the county – some to the salt-smelling alleys or villa rows of the east-coast ports and watering-places. It was considered a duty in

## SIXTY-FOUR, NINETY-FOUR!

the battalion to write to next-of-kin, so that the bald official announcement was not the only last message they received. But it was becoming difficult to keep up with the ever-increasing list. Sometimes the platoon officer and N.C.O. both figured in it, and the rest of the company did what they could. Often, no trace could be found of men who perished in direct hits by big shell. Skene regarded it as the only tribute he could pay to men who shared the life with him, but had not his luck. He was only responsible for his own platoon, at most for his company. But the casualties did not end there. The Colonel had been killed by so many machine-gun bullets that his head was demolished. A bad business! Skene remembered how in his trench he had heard the Colonel's firm step, splashing along, on coming his round, his heavy breathing as he climbed over a smashed-in traverse – the deep voice:

'Mornin', Skene!'

'Good morning, sir!'

'All right?'

'Two men hit, on rations, sir!'

'Ah! Be glad when we can get some of our own back?'

'Yes, sir!'

'Anything special?'

'No, sir.'

'I'm going along to see Andrews. Straight ahead?'

'Yes, sir, but turn to the right down the "S" lines: the way to the left is all broken up and it's enfiladed. Shall I send a guide?'

'Not necessary. Good day!'

'Good day, sir!'

He had passed on, tall, long-striding, followed by his orderly. And the grey morning had broken with the usual crescendo of enemy machine-gun fire. Skene sent a Corporal to see that all his men were standing-to and getting the fires in the braziers past the smoky stage before the Bosche could see the smoke. He was in good spirits, because the end of his watch was near, and Jerry, his servant, was preparing his steaming tin of porridge (Mansfield insisted on porridge, in the trenches: 'It makes a sort of buffer on the tummy, and when one falls flat, to avoid fire, one falls soft') – he would swallow it, soused in condensed milk and rum, then crawl into a filthy hole and sleep, while the bullets thumped the parapet. And suddenly the Colonel's orderly had appeared before him, shaking and saying: 'Oh, sir! Oh, sir!'

Skene went with him to look, keeping well down at the broken parapet where the 'S' lines branched off. There lay Colonel Gilford, full length, his feet sticking up stiffly, his head unrecognizable. All the orderly could say was, 'I told 'im, sir, I told 'im!' Skene quite understood. The Colonel was known to be obtusely brave. He could not easily read a map and was stubborn before suggestions. It took hours to work a stretcher to where he lay, and another twenty-four hours before his long form could be carried out and buried, near Brigade Headquarters, more than a mile back. So perished Colonel Gilford – and his iron imperturbability.

The next officer to go had been young Murdon. That was another sort of story. Young Murdon – Skene could never help being rather nice to him because it was so obvious that the Major and Thomas and the others regarded him with suspicion. For instance, in arranging the tours of duty in the company (always under-officered) Thomas would always give the easy ones to Murdon – taking the harder and more dangerous for himself, Skene or Earnshaw. The latter spoke out to Skene when they were alone. The kid was no good, just an ordinary funk! Not long after that they were in brigade reserve – a mile or two back from the trenches, going up every night to dig or carry, as now. Murdon simply couldn't be missed out of that. Thomas went the first night, Earnshaw the next, and Skene the next. The fourth night Skene, crossing the yard of the warehouse where they were billeted, in a shelled-out village, saw the party paraded under the N.C.O., the men standing as they do when they know their time is being wasted, and the N.C.O.s talking together in a group. He went into the mess-room and met Thomas's eye.

'Very late getting off, aren't they?'

'Pretty late!' said Skene. The murmur of talk and the fidgety stamping of the men increased.

Thomas looked at his watch. 'Where's Murdon?' he said.

'I'll go and see!' Skene went to the hop-press where the officers' valises lay side by side. He had to strike a light. There was Murdon sure enough, his head in his hands, queer sounds in his breathing.

'Aren't you well? – your party's waiting.'

'Oh, Skene, don't let them send me – I shall be killed, I know I shall, I dream about it!'

Skene pulled on his boots and goatskin, mackintosh and equipment with the speed taught by many a cramped awakening in the dark. 'You lie still!' he called over his shoulder, and ran across the yard, shoving his torch and revolver into place.

'All present, Sergeant Evans? Right-in-file; lead out on to the road!' He put his head into the mess: 'Murdon isn't feeling well; I'll take his lot tonight!'

Thomas grunted. This sort of thing couldn't go on long. It didn't. The battalion had four days' divisional rest at railhead. Murdon seemed happy, took Skene out to dinner and to the Follies, where the red-nosed comedian used to interrupt the serious songs with, 'Did you want to buy a dug-out?' and eight hundred officers and men sang the chorus, 'There's something in the seaside air!'

Now, it was that period of the war when white-moustached old gentlemen used to say, 'The men are getting soft, sir!' or 'The Bosche want gingering up, they're laughing at us!' To remedy these evils, some one who didn't live in the trenches invented trench mortars and trench raids. Those who lived in the Line – still keen, as many were, on an offensive, still dreaming of the rush that was only to stop at Berlin – knew that the only possible policy for the side weaker in artillery and machine-guns was to keep quiet until a real offensive might have some effect. But the London papers, the political situation, and the professional soldiers who had never fought, had it their own way. Curious little brass instruments (it was before Stokes invented his simple and sufficient mortar) were carried up to the Line and allowed to have their shoot and depart. The Bosche simply blew the place where they had been to pieces, and the

Infantry who lived there lost their sleep and food and many of their lives. The raids were more successful. The pugnacity of the individual Briton and his exasperation found their vent. Twice Skene took out three or four men, exchanged rifle-shot and bomb with the Bosche, tried to take a prisoner or machine-gun. Each time wire, or swamp, or the instinct of his men, selected from the poachers, rat-catchers and horse-slaughterers of his company, to kill at sight or touch, had prematurely spoiled the game, and he had come back to his own lines, soaking wet and somewhat flustered, but more and more confident that the individual German was afraid of him. This time, when the battalion went back to the Line, Skene was told to take young Murdon and selected men and find out what the Bosche were building at C.29. (It subsequently turned out to be the first pill-box of concrete, but the idea was shelved during the Verdun offensive.)

Skene himself always felt shaky, until he had fairly started – and the look in young Murdon's eyes affected him so that he offered Thomas to go alone. 'No,' said Thomas, the Major (now commanding) had noticed young Murdon, and said he must get used to it. They went out in the old 'diamond' formation then in vogue, cut some wire, lay still while flares went up, and machine-guns rattled over their heads – then, Skene and a Lance-corporal, busy scraping and probing of the hump of earth they had to explore in the light of a flare, saw men with tin hats (the English had no steel helmets then) all round them. Instinctively he squeezed his heavy 'Colt' once – twice – thrice – ducked and slid off the parapet, while a rifle went off in his ear and another in his face. Shouts and running, silence and darkness. Surely some one still running behind him! His Corporal, on whom he had fallen, was making a gurgling noise – was he hit? No, spitting out liquid mud. The Bosche had given the alarm. The whole field of No-Man's-Land was laced and perforated with traversing machine-gun fire, and salvos of whizzbangs crashed and scattered over the trenches. Nothing to be done for minutes that seemed hours, but lie quite flat and still. Then, face to rank grass and stinking ooze, Skene and the Corporal found some of the party and turned them crawling homeward, to that slantwise gap in the wire where Thomas was waiting to take from his hand, as he slid into comparative safety, any weapon, accoutrement or other spoil, to be sent to 'Brigade' for inspection. Perhaps no exhilaration on earth will ever be again like that of crouching in a dug-out over hot black tea, gritty with sugar and stinging with rum. Between mouthfuls of an enormous bully sandwich, Skene, his eyelids nearly closing over shining eyes, told Thomas how the 'show' had fared. Thomas nodded.

'Well, you couldn't do any more. I'll put a report in. You sent young Murdon to Head-quarters?'

'No!'

'Where is he then?'

'He was rearmost; must have come in first!'

'Did you see him?'

'No, I was t'other end. Sent Sergeant Evans to tell him!'

'All right. You get a sleep. I'll go and see!'

'I say, Thomas, you don't think he's . . .?'

'I'll just go and make sure. So long'!

Skene rolled over and slept. He awoke with a start.

'Stand to!' Thomas was sitting beside him smoking, caked with mud from head to foot.

Skene squelched as he turned, shivering as men shivered nowhere as in Flanders. 'Hullo! You've been out!'

'Only as far as young Murdon!'

Amid all that cheerfully accepted horror, a fresh special horror grew on Skene's face, as Thomas told him. So far as could be made out, young Murdon had rushed back at the first shot, not obliquely, up the alley in the English wire, to safety, but straight on to the wire, and been caught in it, opposite the communication trench where the Bosche machine-guns sprayed all night and day.

'You know the big crump-hole, right in our ditch. Well, he was hit more than once, but one had paralysed him and he slipped in there. We were after him until dawn, he was moaning all the time and shrieking when we touched him. We tried all ways to get him out and fed him with stuff; he got quieter bit by bit!'

'Do you think he's snuffed it?'

'Can't say, couldn't stop to look. Had to come in when it got light. It was a miracle we lost no one, as it was. We'll try again tonight!'

'The Bosche will do him in before then.'

'Don't think they can see, if he keeps still and quiet!'

Skene passed a miserable day, and was over the parapet and down the wire the moment it was safe. Young Murdon was lying back, with outstretched arms, as if crucified. His open eyes, however, had not the orthodox expression. Skene was hardly sorry when, after hours of building a 'float' with pickets and boards, and gradually raising him in four men's arms, he died on the stretcher before he reached the dressing station. The men kept away from the place, during all that tour of duty. They never said why, but however carefully Thomas or Skene spaced them out, the two bays by the crump-hole at the mouth of the communication trench were always empty. No one would stay there.

And, as the Colonel and young Murdon had gone, so the men went, one by one. The irrepressible boy who played the mouth-organ was killed by a falling house – tons of masonry on his limber, fair-skinned body. They never got to him, Skene had to rely on what his comrades remembered for his next-of-kin. The hoarse-voiced Sergeant Strood, a fish-hawker, was killed outright by shrapnel, on a ration party. The Salvationist, who would sing hymns while wiring, got a 'stray' through the chest, and lay on the stretcher loudly exclaiming, 'Glory be to God, I'm dying, I know I am, Glory be to God!' New men came and disappeared – those on whom shells fell directly, so that no trace of them was ever found, were posted 'missing'. So was one who went mad and was found cooking for a railway section, miles back, harmless, and insisting he had been sent there. They passed so fast that Skene needed a list from which to write his letter to their next-of-kin, in the half-demolished mill, by the snow-glare on the ceiling. March it was now; he had not been 'out' six months, and half the battalion had changed . . .

He glanced up at a whirring sound, fearing a long-distance

shot. He was wrong. The low aperture through which he was looking out was filled by the bonnet and front wheels of a Staff car that had slid half round to its brakes on the greasy surface. Enter Captain Castle, huger than usual in furs, brisker and more tonic than ever, a personality that laughed at circumstance. At once the low brick vaulting rang with his cheery energy. Thousands of yards of white material were wanted to make shifts for the men out on patrol, in case the snow 'lay'. Skene was to go with the Ordnance Officer and interpreter to the nearest towns of any size beyond railhead and purchase every inch he could lay hands on. Three minutes later, Skene and the interpreter were being rushed through the keen air towards railhead. There they picked up the Deputy Assistant Director of Ordnance Stores, known to friends as D.A.D.O.S., of the Nth Division.

Their quest took them far afield. At dusk of the following day, they saw the first consignment of the white material unloaded at the Division Laundry, where in a dismantled brewery sempstresses would make it up into the smocks. It seemed a pity the job was over, it was a relief from the futureless monotony of company routine. Dados said:

'Well, you chaps have helped me no end, and I suppose I'm safe for the M.C. over this, so we'll have champagne.'

They had it, such as it was, with the gusto and in the quantity proper to men whose next drink may be poured out by Lazarus.

Out presently in the snow-lit dusk, watching the chauffeur laboriously start up the car, the champagne gave Skene an idea: why not go back by Spanish Farm? Dados was indifferent. Mercadet, the interpreter, smiled indulgently. They left the Calais–Béthune road and turned east, eight kilometres along the Courtrai road. With much barking of dogs and opening of heavy gates, they got the car into the yard. A light was shining from the kitchen. Madeleleine, standing by the stove, smiled.

Skene went straight across to her. He wished to be sympathetic, if her young man was dead, hopeful if he was alive.

'Ça ne va pas trop mal?' he began.

'I am always waiting; in a month or two I shall know, I suppose.'

And that was all Skene could get out of her. She and her married sister, a bigger, darker woman, who was a refugee, with her little daughter, made omelettes of the usual level excellence, one of the old bottles was brought out and a hare paté, garlicy and gamey, in an earthenware jar. Dados became excited, played with the child, calling himself 'cochon' when he meant 'cocher'; Mercadet's eyes ran with cold and wine; Skene drank and gazed at Madeleine. One might die tomorrow, meanwhile one would live.

The studded wheels ground over the frozen snow, the old house was left dimly outlined in the luminous night, and in the bright open doorway the family waved them adieu.

'And very nice, too,' said Dados. 'He does know where to find them, doesn't he, Mercadet!' From the depths of his wraps the Frenchman answered: 'Ah, Skene, you know, is one of those ones!'

The more Skene protested the more they laughed at him, till Dados, overcome by high living and low temperature, went to sleep with his head rolling in the high collar of his British-warm. Mercadet, nudging Skene, said: 'You have done him well, and amused him, my friend; now we shall never be short of stores in the brigade.'

Skene growled.

'I wish I hadn't amused him so much! Nice yarn he'll make of this!'

'Quite so, mon cher, and very much to your credit. They will say you are no end of a boy for the girls.'

'Look here, Mercadet, leave the beastly girl out of it!'

'Oh, no! Not at all beastly.'

'Good Lord, man! She's got a chap of her own.'

'Yes, yes, the one you inquired after so tenderly, when we went to the French Head-quarters.'

'I only tried to find out what had happened to him; haven't you any sympathy, you old sinner?'

'Yes, plenty of sympathy, but I have two sons older than you, and both dead. And I can tell you all you want to know about him.'

## SIXTY-FOUR, NINETY-FOUR!

'Mercadet, are you a liar, or merely a prophet?'

But Skene never found out. The car skidded under pressure of the brakes. Skene and Mercadet peered out. A square, stumpy figure, all British-warm and field-boots, was holding up a hand. 'Are you going near C.21?'

'Hullo, Earnshaw, what are you up to?' Earnshaw climbed in and squashed down between them. 'Let me introduce you. Lootenant Earnshaw – Dados. His real name is Mills. He's the man who grows grenades!'

'I've been buying bricks!' said the serious Earnshaw.

'What, to build a bridge over the Bosche?'

'For horse-standings! Do you fellows realize the quantity of animals we're losing?'

Skene was a townsman and had little to do with animals, but he was English, and had scruples about beasts.

'Bravo, Earnshaw, well done!'

Dados was not so sentimental. His professional dignity was hurt.

'What bricks? How did you pay?'

Earnshaw nodded. 'In that brick yard behind the pub. Gave the old chap a requisition, as soon as I'd seen them on to the lorries – empty ration lorries!'

'My word!' gasped Dados, 'you'll get yourself into trouble over this!'

'I don't think so. It's common sense. Horses and mules must have something firm, and reasonably hard and dry, under their feet. Divisional H.Q. ought to be grateful. I've told 'em twice, and now I've saved them the trouble!'

'You'd better send back your bricks, and recover and tear up your requisition, as you call it. You're not entitled to give it!'

'Well, the Field Pocket Book says I am – anyhow, the bricks are down in my horse-lines, and my section are cementing 'em in with plaster from the house at the railway!'

'You'd better get transferred in a hurry – ' Dados began.

'Oh, go to hell!'

'I wash my hands of it. Well, here we are! Good night, gentlemen!' The car had stopped by Brigade Head-quarters.

Half-melted snow still hung about the road and the yard of the mills, as Skene and Earnshaw stepped out into it, very cheerful. Skene had had a holiday – forty-eight hours, and was full of drink; Earnshaw had had an argument.

'These Divisional Head-quarters Wallahs don't know there's a war on.'

'No,' said Skene; 'I tried to tell 'em about the trenches!'

'This is plain common sense. I should like to see 'em object!'

They stumbled over Thomas's legs in the loft where their valises were spread. He said sleepily, 'Hope you've enjoyed yourselves!'

Skene loosened his collar, kicked off wet boots, and wound his watch – his toilet for the night. 'Ungrateful brute,' he said; 'I've been working hard to save you from being shot as a dark moving object on white snow!'

'Oh, well, we shall be dark, moving objects at six Ack Emma; the Brigadier's coming to address us on harassing tactics.'

'He ought to know, the blighter!' grunted Earnshaw, folding his overcoat to make a pillow.

Skene sat up suddenly among his blankets; something had crunched in his pocket as he burrowed. He felt and found the letters to the next-of-kin, that ought to have been posted two days before.

'Oh well!' he thought, rolled over, and slept.

## Chapter 11
# The Divisional Show

At last the division went out of the Line to rest. Rest – what that word used to mean! It was a fine dry April, and even Flanders, whose colour and shapes are generally woolly and gawky and wet, had for a few days the clear joyfulness of Italy. The division trailed back – in those days divisions moved as a whole – not merely to railhead and its adjacent camps, but far into an unknown hinterland. It passed among budding trees and flowering bushes beautiful with that queer stiffness, as of heraldic symbols, peculiar to spring. Each morning, with steadily rising spirits, the battalion set out, clean, fresh and properly fed, from billets showing less and less the wear and tear of war; each evening it settled down in lengthening twilight among peaceful farms and villages, where the glass was still in the windows, and the towers on the churches. After about a week they halted at Hondebecq, just where the Pas de Calais slopes down to the Flanders flats. A typical village through which the paved Rue Nationale from Paris to Dunkirk ran from south to north, the equally important road from Béthune and St Omer to Lille crossed from west to east. The crossroads made the Place, whose whole north-east corner was filled by the high-shouldered hump-backed church, chiming a hymn tune every quarter of an hour, and whose south-west corner was filled by the stone-fronted, round-gabled inn 'Lion of Flanders'. In peace-time it was the weekly meeting-place of Belgian horse-jobbers, and hop and flax merchants; now, with the War only twenty kilometres to the east, it had become the nearest available restaurant for officers of the resting battalions.

Before this estaminet, that fine Easter Sunday morning, Skene, with a gunner officer called Wellin, gave their horses to a small boy. They had ridden in to enter their respective units' teams

## THE DIVISIONAL SHOW

for the Divisional Horse Show. From the opened west doors of the church, to the music of the organ, came a procession of little girls in white, and of little boys in blue suits with peaked caps, carrying sprays of the first flowering bushes and followed by priest and beadle, mayor and schoolmaster, and members of the societies for good works that abound in the devout and wealthy parishes of the north.

Skene was trying to drive some comprehension of all this into the bullet head of Wellin, when a voice said in his ear:

'Good morning, Mister Skene.' It was Madeleine Vanderlynden.

During all these months of dangerous duty the thought of Madeleine had always been remotely comforting to Skene, reminiscent of ease and rest, a change of scene and diet, a spot of pleasant colour and an echo of civilized conversation. Now he felt almost proprietary – confronted by this carefully dressed, well-looking Madeleine, explaining in more or less fluent English that she had taken over the restaurant of the 'Lion of Flanders'. He hated Wellin's prominent eyes surveying her from top to toe.

'What about having a little grub here, Skene, after the horse show tomorrow?' Wellin was saying.

'I shall be getting back.'

'Well I'm going to, anyhow!'

'All right, then, I'll come.'

They arranged to take a table for four and make up a party. Wellin proposed Wheather, the signaller, and Skene old Mercadet. Au revoired, in Madeleine's best English, they went across to Head-quarters. Riding back to their respective billets, between brown tilth where, as yet, no green was showing, Wellin said:

'I go off here. See you tomorrow! She ought to be easy fruit, that girl at the pub!'

With a guarded 'Looks like it,' Skene spurred his horse and cantered away down the green border of the by-road, to the discomfiture of an old woman feeding a rabbit and a goat.

Next day, the big pasture where the Lys skirts Hondebecq looked something like an English country race-course. Round the white-palinged track ambled English Yeomanry officers, Masters of Hounds, some of them; grooms from regular Infantry battalions accustomed to playing polo in India; gunner N.C.O.s on mounts groomed to the nines, with their Artillery air of 'We're as good as the Cavalry any day!'; here and there a perplexed guest – some big local farmer or wine merchant, trying to understand why English Infantry officers ride so indecently well, or where on earth all the transport came from, and how the A.S.C. Captain, driving that swell car, could be only a Captain, and not either a chauffeur or a Major-General.

Then there were ambulances with Nursing Sisters – English in grey and scarlet, Canadians in scarlet and blue, French and Belgians in white. There was a naval officer doing liaison with the Corps Artillery; and, last not least, a grey-whiskered baronet, Lord Lieutenant of his county, who, having insisted (some said to keep up his reputation for eccentricity) on coming out to France as a private in the R.A.M.C,. had been appointed Salvage Officer to stop his plying convalescents with illicit drink.

He appeared on the course heralded by cheers and laugher, driving a smart chestnut cob between the shafts of Vanderlynden's old cart, with all the whip-flourish and elbow-arching of Sam Weller, senior, and beside him, not a hair out of place, not a wrinkle in her gloves, in her lightest colours and with her brightest smile, sat Madeleine herself. The police smiled and made way, the A.P.M. frowned, and grinned, the French officers stared and murmured. The old man made a circuit of the course, drew up by the enclosure, got down, gave his hand to the lady and conducted her to a seat near the English Nursing Sisters.

Skene muttered:

'Curse his cheek! what does he want to make a show of the girl for?' Cooler reflection followed. Far better old Fryern – a licensed 'character' – whom every one knew and liked, sixty years old and not likely to do any damage, or even to remember the week after next – far better than some Staff pup, rich and young and lazy, who would spoil her if no worse. Then followed reflection cooler still: what on earth had it all to do with him – Skene?

A yeomanry Major led the parade, in which old Mercadet, brilliant in the blue and strawberry of the French Mission, was putting his horse through the antics of the Haute École.

After the riders came the wagon teams, Engineers and Medical Corps, Artillery, A.S.C. and Infantry, all to the sort of music that appeals to horses. Then came the jumping, and boxing, and various competitions, until at last in the spring twilight Skene led old Mercadet to the 'Lion of Flanders', where their table was set ready in a corner. The place was packed with officers, humming with talk and the chink of glasses, thick with cigarette smoke.

Madeleine, in black, was threading in and out among the tables. To Skene she seemed years older again these few months. She had eyes and ears for everything, answered questions and gave orders all at once, turned aside the sharp puns in French and clumsier slang in English, and, with the same frigid indulgence, disengaged the fingers which, even at that early hour of the evening, were inclined to pinch her wrists or elbows, and made the appropriate remark to each fresh arrival, as though he were the one looked-for guest. For Skene, even, she had the right thing to say: 'You have not seen my new piano, the one which used to be in the château. It is there in the little salon.' And she nodded back over her shoulder, 'Will you not play?'

Skene would not, devoting himself to his excellent dinner, and trying to think of nothing else. Wheather was recounting an adventure in his deliberately boobyish manner; to Skene it sounded like the buzzing of horseflies over a muck-heap:

'And so, I said to her ... And so ... she said to me ... and then she went ...'

And so on, through two courses, with oafish laughter and pigeon French. It took Skene his third glass of champagne to wash the taste from his mouth. Old Mercadet, old enough to be the father of the other two, was giving them addresses in Paris. The crowd was thinning now, but the heat had frosted the windows. Skene, sitting back to the wall, had a clear view of

Madeleine passing in and out among the tables and disappearing to the kitchen or the cellar, or under the curtain to the little salon where, as she informed Wellin to check his guffaws, she had the Brigadier to dinner.

Wheather, to live up to his reputation as a funny man, had taken to calling for her, and asking her some stupid question in pigeon French, to which she invariably answered with a curt smile. Skene said sharply:

'Let the girl alone! She has quite enough to do to run her show without your foolery.'

He spoke almost with the rasp in which he gave orders, and caught Mercadet's quizzical eye instantly on him, as if to say, 'Ah, my young friend! That fetches you.' The effect on Wheather was even more disastrous. He sprang to his feet in imitation of a Tommy coming to attention, while his chair fell backward with a clatter.

'Sit down, you fool, you're drunk!' But Wheather stood his ground.

'On parade's on parade, and off parade's off parade.' This old tag of the Regimental Sergeant-major brought laughter and applause, while Madeleine stepped forward and picked up the fallen chair. Imitating the well-known gesture of Charlie Chaplin and the statue, Wheather kissed the chair-back where her fingers had grasped it.

Luckily for Skene, at that moment, from behind the curtain came the opening bars of a Chopin Nocturne. Every one started, so strange in that place was the feeling of the music. Skene knew it by heart, fairy cobwebs on moonlit lawns over the footmarks of lovers on the grass; not wonderful for him to sit and listen. Far more strange was the effect on others, who could not even have named the composer. Wheather sat heavily in his chair, Wellin's jaw dropped, Mercadet began crossing his fingers, and his eyes shone. Laughter everywhere was stilled, glasses ceased to clink and feet to shuffle. Madeleine softly closed the door to the kitchen and stood with one hand on it, and lips just parted.

In Skene something seemed to sink, some cool draught of

unearthly succour, down and down through the fumes of champagne and chartreuse, lengthening and clarifying his vision. He saw all those fellows not as the brutes he had thought them a moment ago, but as pitiful child comrades bent on an escapade of which no one of them could see the fateful issue, overhung by the shadow of death.

The music ceased. Wheather got up and butted his way out. Wellin followed. 'He's very white . . . expect he's going to throw up his drink. I'll go and see he doesn't fall on the pavé!'

As they passed along in the twilight the side door of the little salon opened. Captain Castle could be seen drawing on his gloves, and waiting for the Brigadier.

*Chapter 12*
# The Somme

The division moved to a manoeuvre area; the training for open warfare was begun. The weather was fine and hope ran high, rumours of the colossal struggle at Verdun were as yet vague and little appreciated in their reality by the New Armies that did not remember 1914, though they made old Mercadet very grave. There was quite another rumour, too, newer and more personal, having all the advantage of untarnished hope over grimed reality. Gough was supposed to be gathering a great English army for one decisive blow, and the division to which the Easthamptons belonged was to form part of it. In the lengthening evenings men and officers grew more and more cheerful. The horrors of the Flanders winter receded. They were encouraged, too, by the issue of steel helmets and box respirators, and by the obvious turn of the tide in the matter of heavy artillery and the air.

Then one day all was bustle and excitement. The orders had come. The division was to move south, for the Great Offensive. Queer today to recall the keen anticipation caused by that news. Some merely realized, perhaps, that they were sick of trench warfare, and that, as Ludendorff was to admit years after, attack was easier than defence – a few perhaps, that the hectic excitement in which they lived must burn itself out, and that whatever they had to do in the strength of its flame must be done at once. None realized what an artillery-prepared offensive on the then new scale would be. In the main, the feeling was probably simply a craving for something fresh, a refuge from trenches or drill. Besides, the reinforcements that reached them now did really bring the companies up to strength, and were not cancelled by casualties the same day.

Skene was walking up and down the little yard of a small

pork-butchering establishment, at kit inspection, dismissing his platoon by sections. He hated keeping men standing about uselessly and believed it did nothing but harm.

'Cap'n Thomas wants you, sir!'

In the front room of a little shop, where the backs of the words *'Quincaillerie – machines à coudre'* stared from the windows, Thomas was standing with Captain Castle.

'Division want you for a billeting stunt. Can you go?'

'If Thomas says so, sir!'

'Do you want to go?'

'I don't want to leave Thomas, or the men, sir!'

'I don't want to lose him, sir,' said Thomas.

'You shall have him back! Get into the car!'

'I thought as much!' grunted Thomas.

An aged closed Daimler grunted and whirred up across the Place.

'You are going with Major Fryern to get our billets ready in our new area. Remember to treat people properly: there's a lot of bad blood between us and the French. You can make them understand, and old Fryern will do the tactful with any swells you meet. I'm too busy to come and I want Mercadet here. For God's sake get us a Brigade Head-quarter billet where the General can sleep!'

'I'll try, sir!'

'If you do, you may go far!'

Reporting at the château where Divisional Head-quarters were installed, Skene was sent to a disused lodge looking out on the Calais road; his knock on the door not being heeded, he stood admiring three horses – a taper-legged, full-shouldered, dark roan, so bright and quick that it could never have seen a remount camp; a big-boned, useful grey, one of those that always do better than they look; and the chestnut that had been driven at the horse show.

One of the grooms said to him, 'I should go in, sir; he'll never hear you!'

Skene went in. In the small paved and plastered interior, intended for a gamekeeper, stood that aged baronet who had broken every regulation from age-limit to kit-restrictions. No one could possibly call 'old Fryern' to book – no one that was anybody, because he knew every one of that sort – whiskered half-way down his face, cigar in mouth, Sam Browne undone, directing a chauffeur and two servants, who were packing shot-guns, fishing rods and cameras. He stared at Skene, and told him to fetch his kit and servant and be at the crossroads in an hour.

Outside the gate he found an old red Panhard driven by a Belgian; got into it, and was taken back to his billet.

The Baronet was punctually at the rendezvous, with his almost regal state reduced to one chauffeur and one servant. The old car went well, and it was yet early when they passed through the medieval gates of Cassel under the old brazen weather vane with the motto:

> 'Quand ce coq chantera
> Le Roi dans Cassel entrera!'

Far to the north were the twin towers of Dunkirk, and the tree-bordered Napoleonic route nationale running on towards them. East, beyond the dry bones of Ypres, ghastly white in the sunshine, the noise and vapour of the Canadians engaged in the third battle, that desperate fatal skirmish of Maple Copse that no one ever knew about, so overshadowed it was by Verdun and the Somme. Westward were the towers of St Omer at the foot of the chalk downs, where the home road wound to Boulogne. But the old Panhard slid south towards the slag-heaps by the coalfields and the Amiens road. Through merry Hazebrouck, that had seen Belgian and Bosche and finally English Head-quarters in its square; through St Venant and Aire – Flanders was left behind. They were passing now through little rows of stumpy, sooty, miners' cottages. At that period of the War, when troops lived in the line and never went far back, it was usual for a 'young' officer to know nothing outside his sector; Skene missed the Spanish towers, the elm-bordered pastures, the teeming fields of rich moist Flanders. Then they came to a more open road, and began to climb the first of the great chalk downs. They dipped into valleys where the streams actually gurgled, and the villages were clusters of one-storied, wattle-and-daub thatched buildings, beneath great stone châteaux surrounded by trees.

They came to villages where the flat cap, the innumerable transport, and indomitable good-humour of the English were replaced by coffee-coloured men, with red fez-caps, or blue-coated, blue-helmeted machine-gunners – the French zone. It was now nearly two o'clock. Near a tiny village by a stone bridge, the Baronet said, 'Lunch, Jevons,' and got down, unfolding his long bones section by section like a human foot-rule. 'Let's come down and look at the big trout.'

Skene was completely mystified. He followed the languid old gentleman down to the bridge, where they lay flat and peered at the dark shadow under the arch, depth uncertain. 'Not at home today,' and they retraced their steps.

A cloth – a real cloth – had been spread on the grass under a dog-rose in flower – the car removed to a convenient distance – sandwiches, cheese biscuits, and moselle stood among the daisies and dandelions. The Baronet murmured amiably along, not unlike the sound of the stream below the bridge – larks rose from the high bare downside into the pale high sky – the stunted oak, may-bushes and grass were all aswing in the westerly breeze that had come no great distance from the sea. It might have been Sussex. The Baronet's conversation glided from trout (he was so sorry Skene had not been able to see the big fellow below the bridge) to woodcock (he would try and get Skene invited for the shootin') with the easy assurance of one who never has to bother whether what he has to say will be listened to or not. He knew everybody and talked gently about everything, smoking his special cigars; Skene puffed at a pipe and listened.

They rejoined the car and continued threading the width of two and a half armies as far again as in the morning. If the trenches were the slums of that great city of two million English-speaking men, stretching across eighty miles of France, the road from Frevent through Doullens was the residential suburb.

Sentries and military police gazed uncertainly at the French car in which English officers were driven by a Belgian chauffeur. They came to the hill-top village inhabited by their new corps at the sacred hour of tea.

In the middle of the old stone square, surrounded by houses of French rentiers who had gone to Brittany or Nice while their sons went to Verdun or Champagne, the car stopped before the inscription 'B Mess' on a red and white Corps placard. A pleasant, high-pitched voice came through the open window, 'What are you doing here?'

'Looking for you!' The Baronet unfolded himself. 'May I bring my little boy?' And Skene was presently drinking tea among gentlemen wearing red tabs in a Picard parlour, and the atmosphere of a London Club – tea, cigarettes, conversation all belonged to people used to the very best, who were not going to alter their habits for a mere war.

He was taken to his billet by an A.D.C. whose perfection made him feel ashamed of his puttees, his trench-worn tunic, with leather cuffs, and the bullet hole in his cap. He did not dine with the Baronet, but with this lovely creature and half a dozen other young sparks who played poker after dinner. Skene could not afford it, so he smoked his pipe and presently went out for a walk. It was still early in the War. Specialists had not yet invaded Corps Staffs ... No one would let him look at the job he had come to do between tea and tomorrow's breakfast. He slept well in the good Somme air.

After breakfast at nine-thirty, he and the Baronet started out in the car with a map and references. Skene wanted to work hard, to shrive his soul of that atmosphere of Corps Head-quarters, where those tall, well-bred gentlemen seemed to live so well and never outraged good form by mentioning the War. He wanted to see every billet on his list, but the Baronet did not. They could see the Brigade Head-quarters (Infantry and Artillery), and have a glance at the A.S.C., Engineers and Medicals. When Skene criticized billets that were either open fields or already crowded, the Baronet said it was up to the troops to get in where they were told. When Skene began measuring spaces

## THE SOMME

for infantry transport, the Baronet left him, and had tea with a friend who told him the name of our new ambassador and what they were doing in London about butter.

Finally he motored Skene to within a few miles of the detraining place of his brigade, where they met the dark roan and the grey being ridden, and the chestnut being driven in the spring cart piled with what Skene knew to be guns and fishing rods. Here the Baronet bade him a genuinely kind farewell, hoping to see his 'little boy' or 'young feller' again. 'Take care of yourself, and I'll get you some shootin' in the autumn!'

\*

At that time the Somme country was still beautiful. The French, who originally held this part of the Line, had never fought any great engagement there. The English troops that filtered into it up to June 1916 found wild flowers – poppy, cornflower, campion, and a climate as different from that of Flanders as the climate of Sussex is from that of London.

They were in high hope, too. To have got away from the Salient, or La Bassée, was much! The tragic bungle of Loos was quite forgotten. Besides, the news was not so bad. The failures of Kut and the Dardanelles were over and done with. The French, left alone to stem the tide at Verdun, might say that an offensive between the Somme ridges was folly, but who believed them?

The Russians were astir. The Navy had fought another inconclusive 'victory'. The weather was glorious. A mournful splendour shines over the memory of the preparations for that adventure of the Somme, that ended in the mud of Beaumont Hamel and the swamps of the Ancre; a splendour that never gilded the sodden atrocities of 1917. It was still a voluntary – probably the greatest voluntary army of history that went cheerfully to victory! Skene, rejoining his division when it detrained behind Albert, felt like a happy schoolboy, after the Easter holidays going back, not so much to school, as to cricket.

It was in the light dusk of a June evening that beneath chalky downs arching purple to where the last sunset colour gave place to the first stars, he followed a white road beside such water and slim poplars as Skene at least associated with the frescoes of Puvis de Chavannes. Far behind him was the winter in the Flemish flats; here on a dry and powdery soil that looked as if it never could become mud, he saw himself heroical, as in those high visions of 1914, which had claimed him and many others for the ranks of that goodly company, setting out on a splendid and, incidentally, successful crusade. The smoke rose blue and straight from the field kitchens, the mules squawked and fidgeted in their odorous lines, small children ran out from whitewashed thatched cottages with flowers and postcards and chocolate, and all along the road, through gunners and sappers until he came to the Infantry, it was one long greeting – here Wellin and his guns, there Wheather talking to young Calthorp, and finally where the young moon silvered the tents and bivouacs, Long Thomas and Earnshaw welcoming him back, and little Mansfield twittering round like an overgrown canary.

'Hallo, our own sleepless man – been awake eight days and nights. No good your coming here like this, with the milk in the morning! – better have stopped away.'

'Don't you believe him, jolly glad to see you back – we move in an hour,' Thomas interposed.

'Skene, you're trying to get on in the army – hanging round Castle and doing his jobs – disgusting, I call it! . . .'

'Earnshaw's got the map – now look here!'

In Thomas's tent, eating gingerbread, smoking, poring over the route map, they squatted, and all around them the moonlit chill of the chalky bottom seemed to freeze everything but the ground-base of the thundering bombardment.

A week or two later the division went into one of the mid-July attacks. They threaded their way through such a labyrinth of transport, dumps, light railway tracks and guns as had never been dreamed of. The attack had been carefully prepared, discipline was strict, they went into action without a sound.

They reached the sunken road which was their jumping-off place, a little after midnight of a close summer day, vibrating with gunfire. They stood waiting, still and silent, and yet with the sense of a great busy crowd about them; for they were only one of a dozen divisions waiting down miles of line for zero moment. It came. Skene gave the word to his platoon. Strung-up to intense excitement, it seemed hardly strange to him that, after leaping out of the sunken road with the others, he had not really moved but was lying on his back, his hands full of small round lumps of chalk. He had a vague idea that he ought to be going on with the company, but it seemed difficult to move, and, instead, he went, surely, to sleep. He woke up in darkness and a great noise, not the noise of the battlefield, but of a railway station. He was lying in the corner of what was, so far as he could see, a dingy and minute *salle d'attente*; his head ached with such pain as he had never felt before, and he had a strong desire to vomit. The noise that had awakened him was the jangle of a line of small cattle trucks running one upon the other; a miniature engine slid past the door within a yard or so of his face and stopped. Shouts, noise of steam, of iron rattling, the tramp of army boots, the passing of shaded lanterns – then dark forms bent over him, picked up the stretcher on which he was lying, moved him under a strip of sky, and then into the blackness of a cattle truck. He vomited with incredible pain and discomfort, then lay still on his back, not daring to move for pain and helplessness, watching the paling stairs through a shrapnel hole in the roof.

For hours, it seemed, he lay, while the bass of a now distant bombardment was punctuated from the stretcher placed beside him by the refrain:

'Orderly! Isn't he ever coming? Aren't there any blank orderlies on these dashed trains?'

The little train was rattling at walking pace along the side of a bare down whose outline, seen through the doorway, became distinct against the grey, the silver, and at last the lemon-coloured light, and there swept suddenly into that little prisoning box on wheels, unmistakable, unforgettable, the smell of summer dawn, as though the flowers in resurrection, and the ghosts of scent and colour, summoned by Catastrophe, were walking.

It gave Skene the utmost delight. He realized without shame that, more than anything in the world, he wanted to cry. Beside him the voice rose above the rattle of the train: 'Orderly! I want an orderly.'

'What's up?' asked Skene in a voice he did not know. He could hear the other grunting with the effort of turning his head.

'It's my infernal shoulder. They've put me in so that it jars. Can you help me to turn a bit?' Skene did not think he could, but trying gingerly he found his left arm would move, and stretched it out. 'Here,' he said.

He could hear the other breathing hard, fighting the few inches between their grip. Then his hand was clasped and his wrist tugged with a groan that was a cry. Then there was silence, but for hard breathing, and then:

'That's damned good of you! I say, who are you?' Skene gave his name, rank and regiment.

'What have you got?'

'Don't know, except that I can't move and my belly's empty, and I wish I was dead.'

'Well, you are, very nearly. I should think you're the only one left of your lot.'

'Why do you think so?'

'Well, I'm Staff Captain, 506 Brigade. We were supposed to be on your left, but you weren't there, and when I came through the dressing station it was bung-full of your chaps.'

'Which day was that?'

'Day before yesterday or day before that. Hell! I don't know. I was hit at eleven o'clock in the morning, and when I got to an ambulance, I saw one of your lot – Hunter, used to know him in India – '

'Yes, he was Adjutant.'

'Oh well, he isn't now. He was hit in the neck, and when we got to the station, he'd slipped out of his stretcher, I suppose, at that infernal hairpin bend at what d'you call 'em. Anyhow he'd bled to death. My God! I am thirsty. Isn't there an orderly on this train?'

And Skene thought: 'Soon I shall be dead, and I shall lie on the floor of hell, shouting for an orderly that never comes.'

He must either have swooned or gone to sleep, for his next sensation was of falling down, down, down through nothing. The train had stopped, he noticed that it was a bright summer noon. The usual station noises were speeded up suddenly by a bugle call, whistles, shouts and scampering. They were whipped out of the truck, he heard his companion cry out with pain, had an instant's glimpse of a busy station yard, and found himself in a white-painted ambulance, whose whirr and pulsation were echoed, as it were, by another whirr, as of aeroplanes, and the single drum-tap of machine-gun fire.

'Air raid,' thought Skene. 'This'll finish us probably.'

The noises swooped up in a crescendo to a crash, shrieks and the tinkle of broken glass, but the ambulance still went on and Skene had just energy enough to think: 'Missed it again, by George!'

At sunset of that evening he lay, washed and cared for, in a ward with only two other cases, waiting for the Doctor's evening round. By great good luck he had been taken to a hospital installed in the château of a French lady with English connections, who had lent it as it stood. Skene could pass his gaze from white panels and shining floors to the laughing Cupids and gay garlands of Louis XVI.

Gingerly turning himself about and about with pain and difficulty, he could not discover the smallest abrasion of his skin. But for a grinding headache and the fact that nothing would stay on his stomach, he would not have been too ill at ease so long as he kept still. When the Doctor asked him: 'What's the matter with you?' he answered faithfully: 'I don't know.' Two sets of stubby fingers passed all over him. 'You don't remember what happened?'

'No, Doctor.'

'Not sitting on a dump and throwing away matches carelessly?'

'No, Doctor.'

The Doctor gave him a little shaving mirror. He saw his head and face with one side bald, and the skin either feathery white or angry red.

'Well, you've had a very lucky escape.' And with that he was left. Through the great windows, wide open and covered with gauze against the flies, Skene could see the sunset over the beech-groves and bird-haunted lawns of the park, like a pattern worked in luminous silks.

With dusk he fell into that half-waking state which an unspoiled constitution opposes to overstrain and shock; into a repose just spoiled by phantoms. His heart drummed in his ears. He could hear the far-away bombardment, and fresh convoys arriving below. In the faint light that came in from the corridor crowded images kept chasing. He was trying to find billets for interminable streams of men and mules in a sunken road where the enemy's fire beat them down as the hailstorm beats down corn. He went to Castle for leave to get them out of it, and Castle changed to Hunter, and Hunter bled to death, and when he fetched a cattle truck to take him away, there was old Mercadet laughing at him. And the laughter changed to tears, the face to Madeleine's. All that she would say was:

> 'He'll never go sick no more,
> The poor beggar's dead.

He woke. The summer dawn had come, and far away, ethereal as feathers from an angel's wing, the faint notes of the bugle that woke him, woke many for the last time.

\*

They kept Skene on milk for ten days, and he began to be able to hold his food and to move without too much difficulty. His head and ribs were bandaged, his eyes protected by yellow-tinted glasses. Presently he could creep with increasing ease about those high white passages, those festooned corridors with mirroring floors, and the straight alleys of the garden. But he was not right yet. At sunset especially, he was fearfully sorry for himself. This was a symptom indeed that became chronic with Infantry officers as the War reached what proved to be the half of its course. It was so obvious that one had only to go up to the Line often enough and death was certain. And this thought, not yet deep enough in Skene or his kind to overcome what had been the main impulse that called the New Armies into being, and is best expressed by the tag, 'beating the Bosche', was yet strong enough to set recurring in the minds of the more imaginative the longing to 'live' before they died.

On the day Skene was pronounced fit to return to his regiment, he sat down in an arbour covered by dusty and untrimmed roses, and wrote to Madeleine. But he only inquired after her health and her father's, and asked whether she had news of her fiancé. He disliked posting the letter, feeling as though he were making a fool of himself, and finally destroyed it, when, two days later, he and his valise were deposited by the light railway amid a sea of tents on the western side of a bare hill, where with incredible difficulty he got himself at length directed to his battalion. He first fell in with the Quartermaster, old Adams, on his unhurried bandy-legged way towards the transport lines.

'Hallo, Skene, you've come back, 'ave you? That's more than most of them'll do. Oh yes, the Major's there, what's left of him. Barring me and him, there's hardly a soul you know. Come over to my tent and let's have a snappy one! Plenty of time for reporting after lunch!'

Nothing loth, Skene followed the squat figure; and, sitting on the end of a stolen stretcher which the veteran conveyed with him, all over France, he listened:

'Never seen such a job in my life – fourteen officers gone, including the Adjutant. In D Company, Thomas is wounded; Earnshaw is wounded. They sent back for young Vickers, who was doing transport, and he went into the next show, commanding a company. But neither him nor the company has been heard of since. Reinforcements? Well, I've been doing transport and giving an eye to the orderly room, besides my own job, and I ought to know. Seven hundred men while you've been away, and even now we're not up to strength!'

What he saw when they went over to lunch dispelled Skene's

remaining doubts. The Major, perceptibly greyer and slower, was almost cordial in his welcome. Round the trestle table were a score of fresh faces, subalterns straight from the big reserve battalions in England with the gloss of home training shining all over them, and older men, obviously recalled from jobs of all sorts and reduced from home-given captaincy – one and all staring at Skene with that half-resentful respect which those who had still to go 'through it' used to show to those who had already been 'through it'.

Skene found himself in command of a company and spent the afternoon in making the acquaintance of the officers and N.C.O.s.

'All they want,' the Major had said, 'is a little experience!' Skene, who had observed that in this War, contrary to all others, experience rendered one less, and not more, fit to carry out one's duties, was cheered all the same by their unsuspecting good spirits, willingness, and that delightful gust of the old 'Beat the Bosche' tradition straight from England.

Shortly after that, he was marching his company up through the interminable layers of transport and dump, artillery and trench tramway. Helmets and respirators, bombs and artillery, everything was improved, and the spirit of the hour was that of victory. The French had hung on at Verdun, the Russians were attacking; our offensive, if not a complete success, had strained the enemy to the point of putting dismounted cavalry into the Line. Then there was our new method of attack, and Skene plunged along in the rear of a tank. Shuffling and stumbling, and trying to keep his men together in the fearful medley of noise and vaporous dusty murk, he kept saying to himself: 'This is it – this is really it. At last! A real attack! A real victory!' and shouting: 'Keep up, keep up!' The tank disappeared in mounds of broken bricks, iron posts, and wire. 'Now for the Bosche!' he thought, loosening his revolver. The next moment, the barrage descended on him. Stunned breathless, crouching in a hole, he waited. Suddenly the clamour dwindled and passed.

He sat among the powdered ruins of a village from which the early morning sun was drawing the stench of decay and chemicals. The next wave carried the roar of the battle further on. He wrote home a cheery postcard in the intervals of collecting his men and awaiting relief, but no relief came, and no rations. He sent back runners, but by the time a reply came, his head had begun to go round and something had drawn up his stomach as a bootlace draws up a leather purse. By the time his servant had made some sort of tea and he knew where his rendezvous was, his knees had folded up under him and his eyes were closing. He reached the camp – four tents in a patch of star-fissured mud – leaning on his servant, deadly sick – ill, in the midst of all that. When he came to, a Doctor was bending over him, and talking to another.

They said 'operation'. They might have said 'operations' – sleepless nights and foodless days and the everlasting punch, punch, punch of earth-shaking explosions on ears and brain, on backbone and stomach, had reduced his resistance, and the most commonplace civilian ailment easily had him down.

At the last halt, whence they had fetched him in, he had, in the course of 'cleaning up', unearthed three unwounded Bosches in a cellar – seeing only Skene's bayonet man, walking alone, the first Bosche put his hands up, the second fired a Mauser automatic, and the bayonet man dropped. Skene squeezed his heavy Colt instinctively, and the Bosche rolled into a shell-hole: the left side of his face was gone, but his glazed right eye stared fixedly at Skene, who had then sat for who knows how long, staring back and saying aloud, 'Well, you shouldn't have done it!' as his senses and self-control steadily left him.

He wanted so badly to explain to the Doctors that he was suffering from 'evil eye'. They sent him home to England.

*Chapter 13*

# Interlude

Skene's second bout of hospital life was passed in a big hotel at a semi-deserted south-coast watering place. A German destroyer had fired one shell into it, and a Zeppelin had bombed its outskirts. The lighting, the trams, and the usual places of amusement, were therefore absent, and two depots of county regiments were present; the result was an atmosphere in which it was simply impossible not to get well. There was nothing to do but eat, walk, sleep, play games, and read. Away from irregular meals and rest, from bullets and shrapnel, from the everlasting concussion – the punch, punch, punch of continual explosions on the nerve centres, the healthy, unbrooding youth of England recovered fast.

Getting out and about in the summer sunshine, Skene had the sensations that a fly has perhaps on a window-pane – a curious little dizziness, from being upright, and at right angles to the ground; he had, too, a lively appetite, weak knees, and a great faculty for sleep. The neat little place that had been cut in his side, to take out something that was turning black, healed gradually.

From that moribund atmosphere he got no very clear notion of how England was progressing, in the third year of the War. But being pronounced cured, he was given a week's leave before rejoining, and went home.

A changed home! While still on his back, a black-edged letter had brought him news of his uncle's death. 'You remember how he used to complain of his breathing.' (Skene had forgotten.) 'It seems that his heart was weak. He took a chill at the bazaar for the relatives of the wounded. Pneumonia supervened, and he died in two days. The only explanation the doctor can suggest is that the War excited him, in some way he did not show!' No, truly! thought Skene, but he was genuinely grieved, and even more surprised – not so much at his uncle's death, as at the nature of his own feeling about it. Grieved, yes – but somehow this death, of his nearest relative, did not affect him greatly. It was like the death of some one in a very good story or play – moving, but not vital quite. Was it that he had seen too much death? No, deeper than that! He was changed. The old quiet life of the office in the Close was like another existence – an existence in fiction – good fiction, life-like, but not real.

Skene went to an aunt's – to a new, hygienic, scrupulously neat house, in a new healthy suburb on the hill, a mile from the Close and the old town. He was greeted warmly and taken good care of. The life was simple to frugality. He gardened and grew fit; when the day came to rejoin, he was annoyed with himself that he was not sorry to go. It seemed ungracious. His aunt had taxed her little establishment to its limit, let him smoke in her living-room, and come down late to breakfast! But he could not help it. His place was in France, in the B.E.F. He didn't want exactly to go back, but he didn't want to stay.

He returned during September to be one of the seething crowd in the great Base Camp at Étaples, with, not merely the War, but the same battle still going on.

It was almost a year since he had passed that way. The first year of the War had changed him from a quietly happy, rather commonplace provincial architect, who might easily have slid into middle life without more excitement than influenza, moving house, or receiving a legacy, into a young officer of the New Armies, punctilious from over-training, callow from want of fighting experience, but very earnest in his one idea – to contribute his share to the overthrow of the enemy. Now another twelve months had almost passed and he was again at Étaples. But not the same Skene – not the same Étaples, not the same war.

He had now seen more actual continuous warfare than any pre-War officer had seen for a hundred years. He was stretched all over, in mind and body. His clothes failed to cover his wrists and meet round him. His skin was hardened and reddened, his voice coarsened from shouting in the open, and he coughed from time to time as only men do who have breathed gas. His mind was full of expedients, ways of obtaining food and drink, of avoiding toil and danger – it contained a new scale of values, as to who must be saluted and obeyed and who could be bluffed and ordered off.

The camp, which he remembered as an open sand-hill, dotted with tents and a few wooden mess huts and baths, had become an enormous enclosure containing probably a hundred thousand officers and men, streets of buildings, partly brick or concrete, railways, roads and drainage far ahead of most French provincial towns. No longer was it controlled by a few weary regulars, wounded at Mons or on the Marne, and filled with eager young or young middle-aged men like himself. A new type – the real base officer who did not go, and had never meant to go, within miles of the fighting – was functioning now in proper offices, with all the dignity and perversity of Aldershot or Chatham. And round them eddied the ceaseless tides of reinforcement officers and men.

Skene met Earnshaw in a queue of eighty odd, that were filing through a medical-inspection hut, before three doctors, who, beginning by examining men carefully, were being driven to mark them A or B and keeping the crowd moving. Skene exclaimed: 'Hullo! Thought you were dead!' and heard Earnshaw speaking the same words. They laughed and compared symptoms. Earnshaw had been hit in the thick of the leg; not hurt much, he said, but he had started 'going bad'. He added, 'It's left off discharging now and I reckon I'm all right!' But there was no volunteering spirit in his voice. They had both reached the point now of supposing they would have to 'go on with it'. They were both passed 'A', and posted to battalions they had never heard of. 'Conscription coming,' said Earnshaw.

The attitude of the great voluntary army which fought the battle of the Somme towards Conscription was definite. A man might have the best reasons for staying at home. He might be honest and right in deciding to do so. But he had cut himself off from the Voluntary New Army of the War. If he was forced in now he would never be one of them. Skene felt it. Earnshaw, the least imaginative man in the world, felt it. As to the Australians in the fighting line, even at the end of the resources of voluntary enlistment, they voted against forced service.

That Base Camp, in which Skene and Earnshaw spent the next few days, held tens of thousands of men – a wooden and canvas and concrete town on a bare sand-dune. On those light evenings, when the parades of the day were over, it was like a gigantic ant-heap. The men swarmed round the canteens, cinemas and concert halls, and the thousands still left sprawled on the warm sand, a few writing and reading, more smoking and talking, but the most playing or looking on at great childish gambling games, 'Crown and Anchor', 'Poker', 'Slippery Sam', the usual transparent race-course swindles, but most of all 'House'. And on the Picard beach, between the ragged firwoods and the never still railway, the place hummed in the long twilight to the tune of: 'Housey – housey! thirty-four – forty-five – legs-eleven – click-ety-clicks – top of the house! Come on, me lucky lads – who's for a card?'

Officers were rather better off. They had free access to what was becoming a very tolerable club, they could even get as far as Le Touquet or Paris Plage, bathe or play tennis, visit their friends in that little kingdom of hospitals, or have tea. No longer were they compelled to wait, as twelve months ago, in a queue by a small hut, where a voluntary canteen run by ladies provided a bathroom at which a tame donkey watched ablutions through the window, and a Scotch orderly stoked the tiny copper. Skene and Earnshaw were so unlike that they respected each other. Besides, they had gone into the War together at the start. As old, experienced soldiers they escaped much tedious duty, and could usually spend the afternoon at Paris Plage or dine at the club. Those were golden days of returning health and almost perfect idleness, and they passed too quickly.

Their orders to report arrived on the same day, and they went to Amiens together, arranging to meet at a well-known restaurant for lunch. They sat opposite each other there, and saw each other in innumerable mirrors. Skene drank Chambertin, and reflected that officers, whether in mirrors or not, were deucedly alike. Earnshaw drank whisky and probably thought of nothing. They had a dispute over a liqueur called Cordial Médoc which each imagined he had discovered.

As they were going out, Earnshaw grinned: 'There's a friend of yours!' And Skene, turning his head, saw in a corner Madeleine Vanderlynden sitting at a table on which stood a little bag and a café crème. He felt as if he had dropped clean through the earth. He heard Earnshaw chuckle, 'So long, old thing!' and a click of the closing door. Without any attempt to follow him, Skene started, with what he felt to be a jerk, to cover the ten yards that separated him from Madeleine. There was no reason in him at that moment.

It was not so much that he wanted her, as that he wanted to be cared for. The moment had been preparing during the whole of his year's service in France. The dangers he had faced, the rough out-of-door life, the fasting and feasting, his guardian's death, and his own growing perception of the inevitable fate before him; the nervous overstrain and shock, the convalescence and rest – all culminated in that instant with the fatal appropriateness called Providence.

Whether or not he showed her anything of this, she remained perfectly composed. She said she had lunched, but she accepted a liqueur, and then began to ask politely about Skene.

'So you have left the farm?'
'Yes. I have placed myself in a Government office!'
'Well, I've been to hospital twice since I last saw you!'
'Ah, but you are well now!'
'Yes! I'm going back to It tomorrow!'
'Ah!' She put into it the only feeling that was possible. Not commiseration, not ignorance, just simple understanding.
'And you, what are you doing here?'
'I am staying with my aunt!'
'For how long?'
'How should I know?'
Skene pushed on breathlessly:
'How is your father?'

'All right, I suppose. Why not?'

'And your fiancé?'

Madeleine turned her face, a pale oval, between her white hat and her white hands.

'He is dead.'

Skene dropped his hand on her forearm.

'When?'

'How should I know?' She looked away, but did not move her arm.

'Then are you sure?'

She turned to him again, her whole vital self shining in her eyes.

'He is dead, for me!'

Skene could only find to say:

'Believe me, I am sorry.'

Turning her face with its brimming eyes away, she shrugged her shoulders, but still did not move her arm.

A sense of futility enveloped Skene – futile the words he had said, futile to offer any kind of sympathy with the trouble before him.

It was the last moment he ever spent in his peculiar attitude of sympathetic friend.

'You know this is an officers' restaurant?'

'I know now.'

'I shouldn't advise you to come here, unless of course you wish to.'

'It's all the same to me.'

Skene thought: 'Oh, is it?' and put his glass down. So did she. After all they were empty. It was the vacant hour when lunch is being cleared away and the tables re-set in readiness for the English tea, just beginning to invade the English bases. The waiter was obviously wishing them gone; the very silence and emptiness robbed them of privacy.

'What shall we do now?' Skene asked her.

'But I have nothing to do.'

'It's too early for tea. What about the cinema?'

'I don't see any obstacle.'

Skene paid, and they went out into the street, full of the uniforms of half a dozen nations. Before the door of the cinema was a long queue controlled by military police. At the doorway they were met by a flat refusal – not a seat to be had. They turned away: Skene's heart was thumping. He managed to get out:

'There's nothing to be done but to take you back to your aunt's.'

'Nothing but that.'

In a quiet cobbled street near the cathedral a well-kept, unpretentious café was displaying the English legend:

EGGS, FISH, CHIPS, TEA

pasted on the glass of the windows.

The private house door was to the right. Madeleine turned to Skene with a simple 'Here we are!' In Skene, with every step from the cinema, the blood had run faster – the blood hammering out in his temples the fateful doggerel:

'He'll never go sick no more,
The poor beggar's dead.'

His voice changed in his throat to a voice he did not know, stammering, beseeching:

'Look here – I've got to go back to It again tomorrow . . . Let me stay . . . Don't send me away.'

And Madeleine, drawing back into the darkness of the entry, answered, 'Well then, my poor friend – !'

\*

Two hours later, they sat opposite each other at a little wooden table set for them in the private room of the café. The wooden panelling, painted stone-blue, was decorated with large and awe-inspiring photographs of the proprietor and his wife, and with certificates of the secular and religious instruction of their children. On the middle of the mantelpiece, under a glass bell, stood Madame's 'couronne de noces', flanked by picture postcards,

English and French, bearing the stamps of all the different theatres of war. Over the glass door that separated them from the steam and uproar of the bar was a spectacular representation of the last pilgrimage to Notre Dame de Lourdes. Over the black and odorous entry to the kitchen was the highly coloured advertisement of a firm of champagne-growers, representing an incredibly waisted damsel pouring foam from a bottle into a flat glass held by the now forgotten pre-War *piou* in his red breeches and *képi*. From one doorway or the other, Madame kept coming in, bringing with her own hands this dish or that bottle.

While Skene feasted, his eyes devoured Madeleine; there were puckers at the corners of her light silky eyebrows.

'Listen now,' she said. 'Since we are together like this, I do not wish to deceive you. Madame here is no aunt of mine.'

'What does it matter?'

'Only this – she may not want us here on account of the police – better give her something!'

When the Patronne swung her enormous circumference near them with the bill, Skene explained that it was now too late for him to rejoin his camp.

'Madame,' he said, 'has sons who are soldiers – she well understands that when one is young, one cannot always go back to camp.'

A lucky hit! For ten minutes they had to listen to the tale of Madame's sons – the one in the Infantry who was a priest in civil life; the one at Salonika; the one who had been killed at Verdun. Then Skene kissed the old lady good night, to her intense gratification, and as he and Madeleine mounted the narrow stair abreast, she called after them *'Bon amusement!'*

\*

Midnight had hardly ceased chiming on old bells before Skene began to think.

Lying on his back, his right arm crushed under a burden that had in a few hours become so suddenly and vitally precious, he turned his head from the sleepy smiling face at his shoulder, to the spotless cleanliness of the little room ('I put it a little in order myself,' she had said) lit by a candle flickering under a pink paper shade ('Because I like us to see one another'); he turned back again and framed the first question he had put for many hours: 'Tomorrow?'

Bare arms closed round his head so that he could neither speak, hear nor see.

'Tomorrow will be like that over again!'

'No, but listen. You know perfectly well what it is to be a soldier ... A few hours late, a day or two absent, and then endless trouble ...'

'There is always trouble, one way or another!'

'Better be sensible and arrange where we can meet when I can get leave.'

'I know that as well as you!' She was smiling no longer, wide awake and business-like as ever he had seen her in her father's kitchen or her restaurant.

With puckered brows, she stared at the ceiling. Outside a patrol passed in the echoing street, with a clank and a grumble of voices.

Skene went on: 'For you it's easy enough. You have my address, and wherever they send me my letter will follow – unless the censor's jealous – But for me – shall I write to the farm, or where?'

'That's just it. I don't know.'

'Have you sold the "Lion of Flanders"?'

'Yes. Sold it well, at a profit!'

'Why? Were you tired of it?'

'No!'

'Then why!'

'Because there is only one way from Verdun to the Somme, and he must come by it! It is the railway, here!'

'But you say he is dead!'

'One says those things!'

'But, Madeleine, what am I doing – here?'

'That's what your General will ask you – if he finds out!'

Skene was nonplussed.

She went on: 'I write and write to him. I know for certain he gets my letters . . . but at last, you know, there comes a point at which one says "I won't be served like this!"[2] And the same day I see you, and now I wish to be for you.'

'You don't wish to go home?'

'No, not that in any case.'

'Where then?'

'How should I know?'

'My poor Madeleine. What will you do?'

'Work, to be sure! I have already placed myself in an office!'

On that unromantic basis Skene had to leave it.

## Chapter 14

# The Functioning of G., A., and Q.

The convent that occupied all one side of the little village street of La Croix sur Flanche, in the Department of the Somme, was of stone, with a steep slate roof, between dormers on which an aged bright-coloured lichen had worked fairy patterns. Inside, the rooms, whitewashed, and furnished with unpainted wood, had long been evacuated, and were now inhabited by the staff of the Nth Division, pulled out of the line in a battered and decimated state, to fill and fatten up for another 'show'.

At that period, Division Staff was very much what pre-war organization had made it, though its personnel were already entirely changed. It was still a Council of Ten Red Hats, General, two Aides, three 'General' Staff Officers (who directed operations when there were any to direct), three officers representing the Adjutant-General and Quartermaster-General and the A.P.M. But with the perversity of that war, things were already getting upside-down. The General and Aides were obliged, by the complexity of the training, the maze of Intelligence Reports, to do what the G. side told them. A. & Q. were rapidly overshadowing G., as it became increasingly obvious that in years of maintaining a division in the field, there could only be some weeks of operations. Above A. & Q. were already towering the three technical specialists without whom nothing could be done – the Heads of the Medical, Transport and Ordnance Services, by whom alone it was possible to live, with the necessary food, ammunition and weapons. Still undreamed of, there loomed in the future, all those others, specialists in bombs, tramways, gas, forestry, roads, agriculture, claims, courts-martial, rats, incinerators.

In spite of their new and relatively comfortable surroundings. Divisional Head-quarters was not happy. The first series of

## THE FUNCTIONING OF G., A., AND Q.

attacks on the Somme in spite of the 'Victory' headlines in the English papers, and considerable drain on the resources of the enemy, had devastated the domestic arrangements of the B.E.F. So-and-So had been 'sacked', sent back to England with loss of rank and future prospects. 'Yes, really. So-and-So, by Gad!'

There had been consternation at conferences at G.H.Q. and various Army Head-quarters, from which saddened commanders of formations had returned and spoken seriously to their immediate subordinates. 'Either,' they said (they had it straight from G.H.Q.), 'there must be better staff work, or examples would be made!' Examples! Old So-and-So!

Thus consternation had filtered down to the actual working staff of the Nth Division, transmitted by their Commander, at a long conference, held at eight in the morning (summer time) to a properly shaved (but as yet unbreakfasted) roomful of officers, on whom it made a profound impression.

No one knew what was going to happen next. High up in the hierarchy of the B.E.F. well-known faces had disappeared, men no one had heard of were doing old jobs, more curious still, new men were doing new jobs that no one had heard of either. Roads, water, tramways, machine-guns, timber, were all being taken away from the jurisdiction of units of brigades, divisions, even corps, and made into separate 'services'. It was rumoured that even so exalted an authority as 'Corps' could not run a train or close a road without referring to the Deputy Administrator of Something or other.

As for a division – well!

Every one spoke of all this as a personal grievance. No one saw it as an inevitable step. No one had read General Ludendorff's Memoirs – they were not yet written – so that no one knew that the same thing had already been done by the Bosche.

G. branch, the strategic and tactical – or as they preferred to style it, 'fighting' side of the staff – came out of its monk-like retirement and consulted the Adjutant-General and Quartermaster-General's side – (commonly known as A. & Q. or more briefly, Q.) – as to what was to be done. United wisdom arrived at the conclusion that they must have more 'help'. You could not increase the establishment of the Divisional Head-quarters, but you could 'take some feller out of some crowd or other, and make him do something!' This was the idea of G. branch. G. took a high line all along. They were the real staff, precedent in the hierarchy – it was all the fault of Q.

'How,' asked G. of Q., 'can you expect us to function, when we order an operation and you don't give it the necessary supplies?'

Q. went white all over with excitement. Just like G. to talk like that! It was G.'s way to say, 'The division will now move to . . .' (so often misspelt) and leave it to overdriven Q. to find out how twenty thousand officers and men, and nearly ten thousand animals and vehicles and God knew (Q. didn't) what other clutter, were to get there. But Q. didn't say so. It had to keep its job. All its pre-war staff had long been gone here or there, and Q. was now filled up with mere junior regulars who had wounds, or uncles in England, and was getting along in this God-forsaken country by the light of such common sense as it possessed. What Q. did say, and quite respectfully was: 'Had G. heard of the new extra burdens imposed on Q. by trench warfare – trench boards, trench mortars, trench helmets, trench stores, all going up or down the same one-way road?' G. shrugged its shoulders. That was Q.'s business. Q. pointed out politely that it was not. On the contrary, it was not even A.'s business. No! to be precise, in a division, it was the A.P.M.'s.

This brought matters to a head. The Drama had its unities. It only remained to call in the A.P.M. and ask him more in sorrow than in anger, why the traffic on the strategic roads was not better controlled during operations.

The A.P.M. was (of course) a middle-aged cavalry officer, good at the game of polo, for which the division hoped to put in a good team, when next at 'rest'. He met the G.S.O.2. (second dignitary of G. branch) at lunch and wanted to know how the hell he was to superintend traffic when he couldn't get into his office for suspected spies and claims for damage to civilian property.

About this time it changed – on such slim threads did man's

destiny hang during the War – that Captain, now Colonel Castle, translated after a glorious apotheosis in the first Somme attacks, to the far-away heavens of 'Corps', heard of the difficulty, and said he would see what could be done.

'What we want,' said the division (and he had heard the same at eight other divisions in the Umpteenth Corps), 'is a feller who has some combatant experience – otherwise he won't know what's what – he must know something about roads, an' be able to read a map – he mustn't be a captain or we shall be told we are reducing the available number of company commanders – he mustn't be a boy – and – oh, very important – he must be able to speak French and – er – Belgian (for to the end, the Staff found it difficult to know exactly what to call Flemish – it sounded so like Yorkshire) and – er – Bosche if possible – then he'll be able to deal with – natives, and prisoners!'

Colonel Castle, gifted with that capacity for abstract ideas so rare in the army of his native land, had also a thorough knowledge of the actualities. No divisional staff could tell him anything about the horrors of rain-sodden darkness on shell-hole-pitted roads, when ammunition going up jammed ambulances coming back, and civilians evacuating farms got stuck in infantry relieving. He went to his hut and drafted his well-known report on 'the congested state of the traffic-arteries in forward areas, with a suggested remedy'. Peace settled down again on the Convent of La Croix sur Flanche. Castle had an idea. That was hopeful. And the idea of Colonel Castle grew and grew. Admired by his juniors, loved by his contemporaries, respected by his seniors, he had also, through relatives highly placed, and through school and regiment, that influence without which nothing could be done in the B.E.F. Above all, there was his personality, undimmed by two years of war, of which eighteen months had been spent never farther back than Brigade Headquarters – the personality of Colonel Castle who wanted to fight on and win, but thought that victory lay in economizing our men, while the enemy squandered his. And so in the fullness of time, there was issued a General Routine Order, instituting the appointment, by divisions, of an officer, to be known as 'Clear-

## SIXTY-FOUR, NINETY-FOUR!

ance Officer', possessing the following qualifications: (*a*) not less than one year's active service, (*b*) knowledge of foreign languages, and (*c*) proficiency in map reading, who, stationed at the most convenient spot in the divisional area, would, in liaison with Q., French Mission, and A.P.M., examine, classify, direct, and control all traffic whatsoever, military (personnel or stores), civil or prisoners of war, upon the forward traffic-arteries, and should receive additional duty pay at the rate of umpence a day.

\*

The Routine Order was duly read by the Staff of the Nth Division. They read many, every day, without enlightenment. And one day when Castle was present, inspecting, arranging, advising on a thousand and one things, some weary wanderer in the tangle said to him:

'The memorandum of yours. It sounds all right, but who on earth shall we get to do it – old Dakers?'

'Who's that – the old chap from the Canadians – has he any qualification?'

'No – but we usually give him any odd job, and he gets through it!'

'I see!' Castle's eyes twinkled. 'Yes, look here – give old Dakers the job and the pay, and attach young Skene to him, 10th Easthamptons – between them they'll help you a lot!'

'Stop a bit – let's write it down – who did you say – how do you spell it. Right-O. Thanks awfully!'

Thus, through the complexity of that great machine, with its millions of men, its mountains of material, its interweaving and reaction of thought and deed, a little thread spun itself out to Skene, and drew him into new paths.

It reached him, dejected and wet, on a soaking day amid the ruins of a Picard village. He had found his new battalion – but he could not feel the same towards – it – and no wonder. It was composed of people who for one reason or another had not come out sooner, and others who would never have come out at all but for the looming shadow of Conscription.

## THE FUNCTIONING OF G., A., AND Q.

They were determined and well trained; but for Skene it was like having to start all over again – he felt as a boy feels who has been put back, unjustly, to a form from which he has emerged a year before. The lot of them, good or bad, had now to learn all that he had learned in the twelve months passed.

Although he never had any doubt that England could not be beaten, he began to wonder, now, if the victory would be so complete as he had always assumed. He had always taken it for granted that he would eventually land in Brussels if not in Berlin, and then march home with the battalion.

He began to wonder now, listening to that familiar sound, the tap, tap of the German machine-guns, the same sound, the same guns and men, perhaps, as of the year before.

It was partly his experience of the expenditure of time and treasure and human life necessary to conquer a line of smashed-in burrows and rusty wire that meant nothing on the map. Partly a funny feeling in his inside. Partly new realization of the infinite comfort of a woman – partly a dawning doubt as to whether the staff work was all it might have been.

When Skene got orders to report at Divisional Head-quarters, he obeyed without elation but with a sort of curiosity.

By that war-method of travelling, known as 'lorry-jumping', that is, by waiting in an obscure Flemish or Picard lane, turned by fate into a traffic-artery, and boarding a lorry or ambulance, splashed to the neck, with all one's household goods on one's back – Skene arrived at La Croix sur Flanche, and saw the red and green lamps and the sentry at the Convent gate. In the Nuns' garden, he wrung out his cap, and wiped his boots. The doorway, in addition to its little crucifix and holy water-stoop with sprig of box, now bore the letters 'A. & Q.' roughly drawn on a bit of board and hung on a nail by a piece of string.

In the white-washed schoolroom he found a weary young man with that pale complexion that comes from the shock and the loss of blood, following a bad body wound, however well healed. He stated his business.

'O my God!' said the young man, and rummaged hurriedly among piles of papers. 'Here take this!' – an armful was thrust on Skene – 'you'll find your C.O. in the cubby-hutch by the gate!'

Relapsing into his papers, the young man called after Skene, 'Are you sure you can speak French, because he can't! Have you brought your servant? What do you say your name is?'

Skene traversed the soaking garden, where the odour of good green vegetables mingled with the stench of bad drains, and dived into the porter's lodge.

That little lodge was a dark stone-and-plaster cubicle against the high-tiled wall of the convent schools. Here old Jules Lemoineau, gate-keeper and gardener, had lived with his aged wife until the first shells fell. The old wooden bedstead behind the partition, the crucifix, family photographs, picture postcards, were still in their places on the white-washed walls. Vine leaves round the little barred window reduced light to a greenish twilight.

On the door was a little wooden placard, 'Divisional Clearance Officer'.

Inside, a venerable old gentleman, grey and bald, with Maple-leaf badges in his lapels, was reading through spectacles. Skene just refrained from saluting, catching sight of the three stars on his cuff. The old man looked up: 'Come in 'n' have a drink!'

No one ever resisted such an invitation on a wet day on the Somme. They sat over two ponies of whisky and water, produced from under his chair, while the shrewd old Colonial sized up and summarized the situation.

'They've too much to do!' he nodded his head in the direction of the Head-quarter Offices, 'and most of 'em never earned ten dollars – so we'll have to help 'em. I can't run, and I can't parlee, but you can' (he said 'Kearnt' and 'Kean'). 'We mess in "D" Mess, but I expect we'll get one of our own. You sleep here. Tell your servant!'

In this way Skene's life was saved.

*Chapter 15*

# Sheer Devotion

As a matter of fact, Skene was without a servant at the moment, and lost no time in seeing the Officer Commanding what was then known as an 'Employment Company', with a view to rectifying the omission. There followed the first of the busy nights, preparing for the division to take up a fresh sector. Skene had to go right up forward to take over, and returning about five in the morning, had slept through, as agreed with Captain Dakers, until lunch was on the table.

'Your new batman has come!' said the old Canadian; 'he's some cook!'

Skene looked at his plate, and thought hard. Pork chops and beans. Not half bad. Where had he tasted that savoury dish last? Rum omelette, by George. Red wine, instead of that everlasting whisky – Coffee.

'Like to see your new man? Don't mind me. I'd like to see him myself!'

'Yes, please!'

'Burnside, send Mr Skene's servant here!'

A squat figure with the ghost of pre-war regular soldier's 'smartness' about it filled the little doorway. Skene only took one glance, and threw his harshest rasp into his voice:

'What the devil do you mean by this?'

'Orders was to report to you, sir!'

'Go back to the kitchen. If you move, I'll have you put under arrest!'

'You seem hard on the man, Skene, what's up?'

'Tell you when I've spoken to that Employment Company!'

After a short conversation, Skene put down the field-telephone receiver. 'I'll have him back, if I may. You'll hear what he says, and if you still wish it, I'll keep him, but you must hear first. Jermyn!'

The square figure in well-brushed khaki reappeared.

'You've spoken the truth, I find! Why did you volunteer for the job directly you knew it was with me?'

'Wished to come back to you, sir!'

'If you do, you'll be on the strength of Captain Dakers' unit. If ever I have to "run" you for anything, he'll deal with you severely. Do you understand that?'

'Yessir!'

'You've got a perfectly clean conduct sheet?'

'Yessir!'

'Of course you have. You're an old soldier.'

'Yessir!'

'After the retreat you were found wandering about, and were arrested. Your regiment moved and you were at Base and got the job of storekeeper to the Quartermaster of the East-hamptons!'

'Yessir!'

'He had to get rid of you –'

'There was a little misunderstandin', sir!'

'A little missing, you mean. Then you took on as my batman because you thought it was a soft job. Was it?'

'No, sir!' A grin here.

'Where did I take you?'

'Front line – 'orrible dangerous places!'

'You'll go there again if you try any tricks!'

'I'll be no trouble, sir. I can cook!'

'You always could. Why did you leave me?'

'I – I don't like to say, sir!'

'No. You stole my trousers, and sold them to another officer's servant, and got drunk on the proceeds, in Boeschepe. You went to clink. Your second go, in the army. You'd been in clink in civil life. What was your job?'

'Light porter, sir!'

'Rot, you picked up odd jobs on racecourses!'

'I've 'ad misfortunes, sir!'

'That's nothing to what you'll have, if you touch anything that isn't yours, or get the worse for liquor here! Got it?'

## SHEER DEVOTION

'Yessir.'

'Right. Here's five francs to start with!'

'I 'ave money on me, sir. I'd rather bring you a list at the end of the week!'

'Good start. You're improving. That's all!'

Left alone, Captain Dakers smiled at Skene.

'You're mighty particular. Do you mean to say you worry what a man's been?'

'We don't like dishonesty or drink. Anyone who has to do with racing is generally afflicted with both. Anyone who's been to prison usually goes again. I shouldn't employ that man in civil life. But he can cook and I've a hold on him!'

'He seems to like you!'

'That sort like anyone who'll give them a sharp short order, and make them obey!'

'We take men as we find 'em, in Canada!'

'We don't!'

Captain Dakers' man was a Belfast schoolmaster called Burnside, whose eyes had been badly damaged by gas, and who had learned all that the army could teach him about cooking just as he would have learned and passed examinations in any other subject under the sun, but he lacked just that touch of imagination born of necessity which Jermyn (always known as Jerry) supplied out of the bitter experiences of a horrible past. This was not wonderful, for whereas cooking for and valeting an officer meant all that Jerry expected of life, an easy job diversified by three hearty meals – for Burnside it represented a slight alleviation of a state of things which was otherwise unbearable. It was not so much that he hated discipline, and rations, and wounds, and censorship – though he did hate them – as that he was constitutionally incapable of using so little of his brains as the life demanded of him. Hoping, as he did, to get away from teaching to a professorship of comparative philology, he put up with being Captain Dakers' servant because it allowed him more time for reading than any other job in the army. The rests that his eyes forced him to take, he devoted to Captain Dakers.

Burnside and Jerry made the queerest combination, for they did combine, which was perhaps queerest of all. Skene's theory was that they were so utterly unalike, so removed from all possible competition, that they respected each other. Anyhow, they did not quarrel, as most servants did. Burnside immediately appreciated Jerry's lick-my-thumb cookery, and left it to him. When the division lay at Acheux, and Jerry heard Burnside bargaining in fluent French with peasants and shopkeepers, he remarked: 'You can't 'arf parlee the bat!' and never again resorted to his pigeon English. Burnside was extremely anxious to learn from Jerry the racecourse 'tic-tac' code, which he believed to be associated with that obscure and ancient slang language, which the modern tramp inherits from the gipsy, who had it from – where? That was what Burnside wanted to know. In return for the knowledge, he allowed Jerry to win money from him at 'Slippery Sam', and even to play the concertina. Thus Skene, puzzling his head over the problem of two-way roads east of Albert, would be roused by the strains of:

> 'The roses round the door
> Make me love mother more,' etc., etc.

Hammering on the partition of the hut they now inhabited, he would shout:

'Stop that d—d noise!'

And the noise would stop, until he went out to his rounds, to see the dumps cleared, the roads policed, straggling units redirected, when behind him would arise in the night:

> 'Don't chase the pore sparrows away,
> You may be a sparrow some day,
> But spare them some crumbs
> From your ha'penny buns,' etc., etc.

through verse after verse of Christmas-card sentiment, as the concertina bleated and brayed.

'I can't think why your fellow puts up with it!' he complained to his Commanding Officer.

'Perhaps he likes it!' returned that veteran. 'I do!'

But Skene questioned Burnside and discovered the truth, and endeavoured to be more lenient in the interests of philology. He was equally mystified by Jerry's unaccustomed sobriety, amid the tangle of low back-area estaminets, until one night when he and the Captain had strolled out late to try and make up their minds as to the visibility of the dumps to aircraft. Returning to their billet, noiseless in gum-boots, they saw before them two figures, the square, squat one walking very wide, and depending on the tall gawky one's wooden stride. They heard Burnside's scholarly articulation:

'Now get in and lie still, you swill-pot, and sleep it off!'

'A'ri', lovee dearie, clean my bloke's belt for me!' which Burnside, whose keen head no drink could fluster, and whose puritan self-control enabled him to refuse drinks he didn't want, with a 'Dam' you' if necessary, forthwith did.

So that extraordinary partnership went on.

One day, when they both had to ride up to Corps Headquarters for detail, Captain Dakers, surveying their usually unlovely remounts, hoofs blackened, faultlessly groomed, saddlery glossy, remarked to Skene:

'This isn't Burnside. This is your chap, teaching him what!'

'They know when they're well off, both of them!' rejoined Skene, not without satisfaction, 'it's sheer devotion!'

*Chapter 16*

# Paris Leave

What heartfelt prayers Skene offered up during the ensuing six weeks! The division went into the last attacks of the Somme offensive. Skene's work was dangerous enough – out every night, now running a wooden tramway that carried trench-mortar ammunition – now shepherding down batches of draggled, dazed prisoners. But he slept during the day, got some food, and did not get drowned like many an infantry man. Then suddenly without warning, he found Head-quarters packing up, the usual signs, a junior officer of Q branch disappearing with the A.D.C. in a car – the Quartermaster-Sergeant burning returns, orders, schedules, and time-tables of the Corps they were leaving. The division was going out to rest.

The moment the attacks stopped, the rain stopped; some said it was the God of the Bosches, others that the gunfire brought the rain. Anyhow, the weather became crisp and fine, and down those poplar-lined roads the division filed out.

Skene's work changed. His Commanding Officer, known throughout the division as 'Uncle' on account of years and miscellaneous wisdom, had been given charge of some seventy men, unfits or technical specialists – not on any account to be called the 'H.Q.' Company, because there was no such unit in the list of Establishment issued from Whitehall – and the Americans had not yet shown the necessity for such a body. No, they were just 'attached' or 'employed', and rationed and paid as such. Uncle had been given the real job of Clearance Officer, on the lines embodied in Colonel Castle's memorandum, and was nominally responsible for half a hundred odd jobs that Head-quarters had no time, no inclination, and so Uncle said, no ability to do.

Skene did these while Uncle made himself invaluable to the

## PARIS LEAVE

Deputy Assistant Director of Veterinary Services, for he could circumvent the climate and the mules, he could build horse standings and ovens with nothing, and steal nothing to do it with, without being discovered. He was invaluable to the A.P.M. because he could handle Colonials who sometimes strayed into the divisional lines, and who could not understand and would not submit to English Police. Also he understood Massey Harris reaping machines, and helped local farmers, who in return might be induced to lend their fields for polo. So while the old man gave sage opinions, Skene, as a change from prisoners, and ammunition, and routes and gas alarms, did traffic and salvage, ushered units out of the Line and saw that they cleared up properly.

Day by day the War was changing. Instead of the old divisions still more or less like big families – men of one or two neighbouring counties often with their own traditions well known and observed – Skene now saw no cavalry, no cyclists – they had gone to Corps – no artillery, they had been left in the Line for the benefit of some one else's infantry, and the four regular battalions, the three territorials, and the five New Army ones, fitted out with Welsh engineers, the A.S.C. of a Scotch division, and Colonial field ambulances.

They squatted down in the valleys east of Doullens, and Uncle and Skene billeted near Head-quarters at Louches, in a château in a wood, on the top of the chalk cliff that overlooks the untouched medieval village bordering the stream. They had an office in the stone gatehouse that bridged the village street, and from thence Skene went, riding or cycling, every day – his job now was civilian claims for damage.

In those wattle and daub-built farms, the successive units had wrought a havoc greater probably than shell fire over the same period. The old English regular army idea of 'Barrack damage' had broken down. Who was to say which of fifty successive units caused the wall of a 300-year-old barn to collapse? This brought up the question of renting permanent sites, since every one now agreed the English armies would not be in Berlin this Christmas. And, to Skene, whose colloquial French was fair, all

## SIXTY-FOUR, NINETY-FOUR!

this was interesting – not merely because it occupied the mind and did not expose the body, as the work of an infantry company officer did, but because he could feel himself of some use, somehow. The peasants liked him because he understood them and took trouble. Head-quarters liked him because he took a load of half-understood bothersome detail off their hands. Uncle was a good master. The officers of the French Mission, the Maires of the villages were easy to get on with.

But there was a deeper reason than any of these for the glow in his heart.

As the War was changing day by day, it was changing everybody that came within its scope. Men over thirty grew so that they could not wear pre-war clothes; more frequent, more curious and more catastrophic were the cases of the men whose minds would never again fit their pre-war habits.

The education of war was profound – it attacked the middle-aged who changed as they had never dreamed of changing. A few weeks counted as years and left individuals unrecognizable. And it was permanent – there was no undoing it.

All this disturbance, psychological more than physical, demanded compensation. Habits, points of view – restraints had been destroyed. Simple enough for those who, unable ever again to become the citizens they had been, found in the swift death of the battlefield a halo that endeared them to a generation. But for others who lived on, through months – years – of shell fire and bombing, of Army orders and Censorship, not so simple! They had to alter if not to rebuild themselves. To a few men, soldiers by instinct like Colonel Castle, work, and more work, a little ambition, a spice of danger, but always more occupation, bridged the chasm. To many, that easy slip for Northern peoples – a little more strong drink sufficed. Uncle, who had always taken his whack, took a little more. Whisky deteriorated less perhaps than anything during those years of stress. Life was lived outdoor, food was not scarce – Uncle was never drunk, but just cheerful every night. What one would do with such a habit on returning to civil life, did not bother men. The chance seemed increasingly remote. Whisky best, other drink second, kept many going. There were other means of recuperation – such sport as could be got – polo, football, cards in the mess – expensive trips to the nearest town to see a lady. A few read, sketched, photographed if they dared, kept pets or diaries.

Skene's trouble was different. He was worn in body, but it was his feelings, the complex inherited and acquired habits of a comfortable provincial professional man that were so injured. Ought he ever to have volunteered? Should he not have waited and got one of the innumerable jobs where his draughtsmanship would have kept him busy and safe at Calais, St Omer, Abbeville, Amiens or Béthune, in one of the great departments now springing up. But here he was. Soldiering did not appeal to him, drink made him sick before it made him silly. Sports and hobbies did not go deep enough. The ordinary after-dinner jokes he let pass with a grin and a shrug. Promiscuous women did not tempt him. Madeleine did. To be cared for – to be wanted – to have some one looking for his letters – arranging to meet him – that staid, demure, yet physical responsiveness – that was the thing. He did not boast of his precious feeling, but hugged to himself the thought that although he was but a small screw in a great machine, he had his private, and special Heaven, where no one else could go. He felt perfectly secure. He knew enough of France to be sure that Madeleine was not making a business or a hobby of men. It was of course impossible for him to ask himself, critically and coolly, what she was making of him.

Few men possess that best of Guardian Angels, a candid friend. And to Skene, anyway, he would have been of doubtful benefit with his probable: 'You are an Englishman. There is only one way with a woman for you. Marry her or let her alone. In England you were born and educated, and are totally incapable of a liaison. You have no idea of what she means by marriage. You will only hurt yourself or her, or both. Let her alone!'

Skene had too good a reply: 'I am saturated with the daily stimulus of this war as if I were fed on alcohol. I have just escaped from the trenches, I am living and shall probably live for years more or less under shell fire. By the law of averages, it is unlikely I shall survive. I must have this woman or go mad.'

## SIXTY-FOUR, NINETY-FOUR!

Who could have gainsaid that?

But he had no frank mentor at his elbow; not even the grim cynical Earnshaw to laugh at him. The matter was never present in concrete form to his reason – it just made a little rosy cloud in the corner of his eye, sometimes spreading over his whole vision. Passing up and down those valleys between the chalk ridges, incredibly beautiful in the clear weather, where the small-wooded, dense French plantations made a bluish sheen on the downside, and the rushes in the beds of the clear, blue-and-white reflecting streams had scarlet stems, where the poplar leaves were spinning like so many gold sequins – all the time he had that glow in his heart. The War lost its hold on his attention. As he laboriously waded through the assessment and verification of great piles of claims for occupation of pasture or arable, for damage to plastering of barns, or pavement of courts, he was arranging in his mind the strategy for obtaining leave.

\*

He wrote to the address at Amiens, a letter beginning 'Chère Amie' and signed 'Geo'. – for it was of course nationally impossible for her to spell or pronounce 'Geoffrey'. He posted it by help of a French permissionaire in a civil post office. He waited a week, surprised at himself, slightly annoyed each time it was post time to find no reply – surprised at his perfect confidence that it would come. At last it was there, post-marked Paris, and opened by the censor.

The letter was calm and cool. She had got work in Paris. She was pleased that the War went so well. *Beaucoup de bons amitiés*. Skene was not disappointed. It was the very letter to pass the censor. He could get Paris leave. It was a new institution, invented to ease the traffic in the Channel boats. He saw Uncle and Head-quarters and got eight days' leave to Paris. He wrote to Madeleine to meet him. He got in reply a postcard with Union Jack and Tricolour entwined, inscribed '*A bientôt!*' Then, only three days before the appointed date, came a letter, beginning simply '*Chéri*'; it went on in her vigorous language:

'All men are bad devils except you. I wish to be yours altogether!' and promising to meet him on the Gare du Nord at the six o'clock train.

So with a beating heart and a blushing face caused by a firm idea that his Quartermaster-Sergeant had read all the postcards and guessed the contents of most of the letters, Skene got into the Ford tender that should take him to railhead, and prepared himself for a freezing eight hours in the train – through Abbeville and Amiens – down to comparatively civilian Creil. It was dark at Paris.

Madeleine was there on the platform; once again he thought her slightly and advantageously aged; thinner and paler, also to her advantage; better dressed than ever, and surely glad to see him.

In a moment the barriers of absence and strangeness were gone, and as they passed out through the dark street to catch the last taxi, he felt the warmth of the perceptible pressure of her arm, the bird-like lift of her dark and shining eyes in a face pallid between the fur of her collar and the brim of her hat. He had left the choice of restaurant to her, and soon they were in a garishly painted dining hall, which had, presumably, from its panels of naked goddesses and red plush and gold seats, begun by upholding the old 'how delightfully wicked' Montmartre traditions, but had relapsed, under the influence of that gradual commercialization of Paris, into catering for the steadier custom of the clerks and better-class business employees of the district surrounding the factories and goods stations of the northern arc of the city.

Delightful to see the figure she cut among these diners! She had drunk in Paris as if born there. A briskly pleasant, dictatorial manner with the waiter, which one felt ready at the least shortcoming to break into icy acerbity, the perfection of her gestures, her complexion and her voice, where the least touch of superior tone rested on a solid basis of assured sufficiency – all were perfect imitations of the girl earning a good living, and conducting a successful liaison with a praiseworthy young man towards a comfortable marriage or other permanent settlement. And as Skene got further and further away from the primeval masculinity of army life, from the freezing cold and bitter loneliness of his journey, and was more and more intimately warmed by her glance, and the dinner which, instead of being delivered to him as a ration was bestowed on him as a benediction, he thought with increasing amusement how much more of a true Bohemian he was than she.

It was the first time during the War (save for his rare spells of leave) that he had been in a big town entirely outside the zone of operations, where civilian atmosphere was the rule, not the exception. And in this new Paris, compared with the Paris he remembered fifteen years before, it was he who, dressed in the fancy dress of his uniform, after running risks of life and death, was snatching a few brief hours of happiness, careless of the morrow; and it was she who sat there, imperturbable and unimpeachable, with clothes on the sombre side of good taste, and a bearing on the stiff side of good breeding.

Because his dinner warmed him – because his mouth was full, because he had nothing to say that could be freely said in such a place, he was silent and made use of one of the innumerable mirrors with which they were surrounded to steep his eyes in her image, from the covering of her head ('a three-cornered affair of dark velvet – very quiet and nice') to the point of a glacé boot, set upon the iron of the table support. What was it about her that made her so compelling? No jewellery – just one ring, one brooch, solid, old-fashioned, unpretentious – no glaring colour – no trick of gesture, no pose of features or figure. Ashen-brown hair, dark grey eyes, shining a little, under lowered lids, even, rather pallid complexion, mantling the least bit as with suppressed excitement – expression imperturbable. Nothing to catch attention, and nothing to get tired of.

That was it perhaps – character – strength of will and sureness of own judgement – inherited from pure peasant stock and preserved and hardened in the undisturbed rusticity of Flanders. She had come out, expanded, in the atmosphere of the great city where she was making her way. A hardy plant from a stiffer soil. She showed to advantage beside the light more obviously 'attractive' women round her, with their Parisian tradition of

## PARIS LEAVE

doing their utmost to be attractive, and their inevitable Paris clothes and fallals.

The contrast between her effortless self-possession and the almost professional gaiety of the neighbouring tables moved him to convey to her what he was feeling, with one of Mercadet's jokes: 'They ought to call this the Place Cliché!' She smiled so vaguely that he wondered if she understood, or again if she disapproved; she paused a moment to survey the other diners – slightly curious, slightly antagonistic, wholly critical, and went on with her dinner.

The dinner came to an end, as even good things must. She sent back the bill to be corrected, and when he had paid it, preceded him, drawing on her gloves and glancing at the waiters and the other tables as though they did not exist.

Outside, in the clear-aired bustle of the Place Clichy, which even the War could not rob of an air of wearing its cap over one eye, she chose a cinema, and they took the best seats in one of the *'spectacles de famille'* sort. She was decorously amused until the drama achieved its usual pseudo-tragic separation between the male and female, when she rose and said. 'Listen, this representation is "*rasant*". I ask nothing better than to go.' Skene followed her into the street. He had taken a room in an old haunt of Mercadet's – a little private hotel in the Rue Biault. He asked anxiously: 'Would that do?' She replied: 'You deserve it!'

With the warming sense of possession that fades with frequency Skene handed her through the glass door with its English patent spring. The proprietor, a little grinning bear-like Alsatian, recognized him at once. In reply to inquiry after his health, he made the answer so often heard: '*My* good sir, I lost my son!' and wished Skene and his '*petite dame*' a very good night.

Madeleine, who had been standing a little apart drawing off her gloves, her feet at just the right angle to each other, her head at the right poise, turned and gave him the smirk a middle-aged bourgeoise would accord a necessary institution. Even on the stairs she did not abandon the attitude, saying over her shoulder:

'Well, my friend, you have a pretty taste in hotels – it is at least quiet and altogether clean!'

And upon this the door closed behind them.

In that clean little room with its rosy curtains and quilt, Skene sat on the edge of the bed to unlace his boots, marvelling at the grace of her raised arms as she unpinned her hat. Passing round the bed in his stockinged feet, he took her from behind to kiss her lips before the fresh chill of the streets was off her face.

It would not have astonished him if she had pulled away, but instead she shook all over, and the face he kissed was deluged with tears.

\*

It says much for Skene's middle-class upbringing, the most 'gentle' upbringing in the world, that he instinctively slipped from the hungry lover to the kind-hearted friend, and more slowly back again from drying her eyes and doing her little services to possession of her lips, and, so far as man can know, of her thoughts and senses.

It was hours before that sudden collapse of the spirit was entirely bridged, and they lay, side by side, at peace in the cosy stillness of that little room, talking in voices such as married couples use for the last few moments before they rise.

'My poor friend, I do plague you, don't I?'

And while Skene denied it softly, by word and deed, she showed more rancour than he had yet seen.

'But you well understand that it is not you, but him?'

'You have no bad news?'

'No, except that I always think he has gone with some one else. Ah, if he could only let me see him, it would be all right!'

Pathetic, an abandoned woman's undying belief in her power of attraction! 'Meantime, I love you much the more. You are more frank, and much more a man.'

To Skene, fresh from mud and cold, from the tremble and roar of great explosions and the mean loneliness of a Nissen hut, even this qualified vow, backed with the pressure of soft shoulders against his arm, was the very gate of heaven.

\*

He woke with that feeling of comfort which can only be realized by those who have slept in 'gum boots' for months at a time; he rose with the cheerful certainty of having all day to do just what he liked. Madeleine, too, was in excellent spirits, no trace left of her sombre collapse a few hours before, and finishing her deft toilet before he was half through with his, made fun of his hot bath, his difficulty in getting his belt and boots done to his liking, and his egg for breakfast. They passed out into a frosty Paris, sandbagged and darkened, but serene and busy, as yet not over-bombarded and still possessed of taxis.

\*

In infinite ease of mind and body Skene passed those few brief days of complete holiday – the completer because his companion left a whole province of his mind untouched.

Reaching him only through his less-educated senses, she led him, daylight long, from shop to shop in quest of stockings, a stole, or linen, which she consented to accept from him, and in the choice of which he could only respect her acumen and good taste. They would pass the Musée de Cluny, the Sainte Chapelle, the Place de la Concorde, places that had for Skene associations to warrant hours of dawdling reminiscence. Madeleine was simply unaware of them, she cared more for the use and appearance of a building than for its size, more for the style and management of a shop than for its name or its pretensions; she was interested in herself, but generous of herself, knowing how to make herself valued, liking to see and be seen, light-hearted, stoic – ideal for him and for the occasion.

He insisted on making the pilgrimage to the Lecture Hall of the Sorbonne, to see what was, to him, The Fresco.

She looked at it in silence. At last she said:

'It is not, then, a church?' The atmosphere of the place had penetrated her consciousness. He explained the uses of the Sorbonne, its place in her nation's life. 'No doubt it is necessary!' she admitted.

The week went like a flash.

To the last moment, she was perfect. Standing on the platform of the Gare du Nord, as the six-ten for Amiens began to move, Skene admired her, and saw how other people did the same. Restrained, attractive, mistress of herself and of the situation, her farewell was an unconscious masterpiece, a glimpse of perfection. Skene would have been miserable that journey, had he not slept like a log.

*Chapter 17*

# The Field of Arras

A week later, Skene was standing as close to an army stove of the 'Queen' type as he could get without burning his whole stock of clothes, which, indeed, he was wearing all at once. He was in a wooden hut which his Commanding Officer had 'wangled' from a Canadian Railway Company who had moved farther off.

The great cold of January 1917 had set in, and the ground was frozen, certainly inches, some said a yard deep. Shaving was difficult and keeping still was dangerous. Over the high plateaux of the Somme district, the wind cut like a knife. The trenches were enviable, comparatively dry and sheltered from the wind.

For Skene, the problem was whether to shiver near the fire or to walk the length of the little cabin and feel how desperately cold it was at the other end, three strides away. His C.O. wrapped in blankets, with nothing showing but a red nose and a ragged moustache, was snoring the thankful snore of one who has enough to drink only once a week.

From outside came the stamp and bellow of the mules, and from the men's cookhouse a cheerful roar of:

> 'Mademoiselle No Bon
> Après la guerre finie
> Umptity – Umptity – umptity – um
> Tous les Anglais partis.'

His week in Paris seemed years ago. So much had happened since. Far behind was the 'rest' in the old untouched villages behind the Somme. He had returned to a B.E.F. that was rapidly passing out of recognition and that was never unchanged, no, not even for two days.

## SIXTY-FOUR, NINETY-FOUR!

By the time that Christmas was over the developments that had drawn him out of the Line, to be a 'Clearance Officer', had gone much further. The root idea now was, to work everything by Corps. Uncle, Skene, their men and office were to be Corps troops. This marked the disappearance from the War of the last shred of individuality.

At the beginning there had been the personal appeal to enlist, the attractions of units, whose names or deeds called in one way or another upon local patriotism, or historical glory, or whose terms of enlistment, or the personality of whose commanders, were well known and appreciated. All this was lost to men's minds during the Somme. In the gigantic dimensions of that battle no one could remember what ground had been won by the Prince of Wales' Own Light Infantry (the Cardiff Buffs) or in what gallant circumstances the Duke of Glasgow's Carabiniers (dismounted) had been wiped out. Men learned to count not by battalions but by divisions, that did to some extent remain recognizable. Divisions, even though shorn of cavalry and cyclists, artillery and A.S.C., had been still, as to their infantry, London or Lancashire, Scotch or Colonial. But now even this was lost. Reinforcements came from anywhere or everywhere. The old badges, the old divisional signs, might still be found, but the spirit was gone. Often not even the badges and signs remained. News came of trouble, almost mutiny, because Birkenhead Irish were sent to reinforce Cumberland Light Infantry, that owned nor pipes, nor shamrock. The old proverb of the estaminet girls in the back areas, 'A Colonial private is worth a Highland lance-corporal, who is worth an English Second Loot,' became deceptive. The Colonial, the Highlander, and the Englishman all came from Liverpool.

Where Skene now lay, the width of the Doullens–Arras road separated him from a Canadian Corps. They were indistinguishable from other British Troops, except for the Maple Leaf and their accent. They were unrecognizable for the old Canadian Divisions of the salient who wore slouch hats, carried their flags into action, and would salute none but their own officers.

And in and around the British Troops were now dotted the immense and growing camps of the Labour Corps – African Negroes officered by Missionaries – West Indians and Egyptians that grinned and chattered in the damp, numbing cold. There were rumours of Chinese.

No longer did Uncle and Skene depend upon the small, harassed dignitaries of the division, local and, as it were, tribal gods. 'Corps' brought a larger if chillier atmosphere; it lived miles away and only communicated by wire or dispatch rider. The people that really had to be feared and propitiated were the new theology – or demonology – of Roads and Railways, of Labour of Transport or farther back, Forestry or Agriculture.

Those to whom life is bearable – and they are perforce a majority – are astonished when they examine the nature of the compensations that induce them to accept the inevitable. So with Skene. Just when it became impossible for him to feel any longer that it was *his* war, to be won by his own individual sacrifice, it became possible to feel that he need not sacrifice himself either immediately or continuously. Having so narrowly escaped death, he might now live a bit and not bother. To live was not so easy. Apart from getting bombed and shelled he had to find food, drink, housing and leave. Uncle was the finest possible tutor for a young man anxious to live. He taught the three arts of war, so much more necessary than musketry, field engineering or tactics. Or were they, perhaps, part of tactics? Wangling, Scrounging, and Winning.

Wangling was the art of obtaining one's just due by unfair means. For instance, every officer and man of the B.E.F. had his allotted daily rations, his camp or billet, his turn for leave. In practice, to get these necessities, it was well to know the man who provided them and do him some small service – a bottle of whisky, the loan of transport (if you had any) or of a fatigue party. Wangling extended to the lowest ranks. Men wangled from the N.C.O.s the better sorts of jam and extra turns off duty. The main stream of wangling flowed from the enormous and growing number of small units, like Uncle's, the apportionment of whose daily subsistence was at once a nuisance and an opportunity to the Supply Officers and the Railhead Panjandrums – for the bigger units, battalions, batteries, Headquarters had to be and could be more easily provided for. But Wangling was by no means confined to troops in the field. As the War grew and grew – the contracts for supplying steel helmets to Americans, the Command of smaller Allied Armies, the very sovereignty of nations all became subject to the Wangle, so remote had become the chances of justly obtaining bare justice.

To return to the unit in the fields, when its Wangle was completed, behold it housed, fed and allowed some leave. But life was still very hard – almost insupportable – to bear it, men, those fathers of invention, evolved the art of Scrounging.

Scrounging could be defined as obtaining that to which one had not a shadow of a claim by unfair means. It was more insidious than the Wangle, but just as necessary – men scrounged the best dug-outs off one another, or off neighbouring sections. N.C.O.s scrounged rum by keeping a thumb in the dipper while doling it out. Officers scrounged the best horselines from other units. Colonials scrounged telephone wire to snare rabbits. Nations scrounged territory or trade. It was simply done. You walked about whistling, with your hands in your pockets and a cigarette in your mouth, until you saw what you wanted, and then took it. The main stream of Scrounging was for wood. The armies were provided with coal and coke and presumably intended to ignite it by holding a match to it. In result, millions of men during the five winters of the War, burnt a colossal cubage of wood. It was easy to obtain. Vast quantities were being cut by an entire Forestry Corps that had rights over several Picard and Norman forests and did nothing else but provide the timber required for dug-outs, railways, roads and gun-pits. No great percentage ever reached its proper destination. A little was built into huts, horselines or billets. The bulk was burnt. From the timber dumps in the great cold of January 1917, whole stacks disappeared. If any high authority went into the matter, a dumb, putty-faced sentry was produced who had heard nothing, seen nothing, knew nothing. But even the enormous quantity taken from dumps was not enough. Farms, houses, public buildings were ransacked. Shelving, forms, ladders, carts, partitions disappeared. In the Belgian hop-fields the British Army alone is said to have destroyed 1,000,000 hop-poles. Who shall blame them? Shall a soldier die of cold as well as of other things?

Wangling is known in peace-time. It is a necessity of civilization, where violence is difficult and costly. Scrounging was a necessity of war, for men must live. There was another Art that was more truly an Art than either of these. For it did not rest upon necessity, but was an ornament, a superfluity, a creative effort of the mind. This was the Art of Winning. It may be defined as Stealing. More fully, it was the Art of obtaining that which one has no right to, for the sake of obtaining it, for the joy of possession.

Some say that it arose from taking millions of decent civilian people and planking them down upon battlefields from which the last sign of decency had disappeared, in a war so bloody and so endlessly long that the issue of it was beyond imagining. Some say it was simply the primeval joy of loot, ever present in man, and bursting out from time to time in Tudor or Elizabethan Filibuster, in Georgian Colonists, or Victorian Journalists.

As the War went on the contagion spread. Decent Flemish and Picard girls, with no particular tenderness for any one man, possessed glazed cases containing the badges of every unit in the B.E.F. Decent English boys conveyed or sent home, every sort of appliance, equipment, projectile, arm – not one of which they had obtained by personal combat, but which they had found lying about and appropriated.

As Skene stamped his feet and listened to the snoring of his C.O., he looked round on their joint handiwork. The Hut, the men's hut, the coal, the oil from the lamp, had been wangled from Q.M. stores, dump guards, area commandants, Town Majors. The wood for the fire, the sacking on the floor, the roofing of the horse-lines, the gum boots for officers and men had been scrounged, who knows where – or where not. The picture of the Virgin Mary, the fire extinguisher, the armchairs had been won. All up and down the great open-air town from Dunkirk to Basrah it was the same. And Skene, the law-abiding, decent professional man from a county town, was not ashamed.

These acts were not discussed in any abstract way by the officers and men who instinctively performed them. To any charge of moral obliquity, their defence might have run: 'England needed us; we came. England wasted us; we died or survived. England leaves us here for no one knows how many years to get along as best we can. Well! we are getting along!'

Skene turned all these things over in his mind, and was not discontented. He was 'in it'. From 'stand to' in the morning, when he staggered out in gum boots and a muffler to see the men were about and stirring, guards relieved, animals fed and groomed, to the present moment, while waiting to hear that the last of the evening ration traffic had passed, his life was full with guarding four dumps of different sorts of material and ammunition, regulating streams of traffic, collecting and classifying salvage. And behind and beneath the mechanical preoccupation of his daily existence, his real preoccupation was now – Madeleine, a warm spot against his heart. Two things went on, not interfering with each other – Madeleine and the War.

He listened a moment to a faint drumming noise. It sounded like planes. It faded. He thought: 'Damn this cold. I'm fed up. I must try next time Uncle's up at the Corps and see if I can wangle another Paris leave. If I can't I must win another stove from the R.E.'s and scounge coal at the railway!' Then he became conscious of another of the daily 'new' elements of the War.

The head of his Quartermaster-Sergeant appeared in the doorway. 'Bosche signalled over, sir!'

'Very good, have the gun teams standing to!'

Skene pulled down a knitted cap over the tips of his ears, wound his muffler twice round his neck and head, and shoving his hands into his pockets, went out into the piercing starlight.

Around him was a bustle of men covering the lights from fire or lamp, and 'standing to' around the two Lewis guns that stood slung on posts a few yards apart.

In front where the double line of trees that bordered the great road melted off into darkness, the bursting shrapnel of the new 13-pounder anti-aircraft guns was visible against the blue velvet of the night. Then that familiar sound – the rhythmic groan of the Bosche bomber's engine crept up, penetrating, immense, unforgettable – a nightmare in men's memories, as in the first reading of fairy stories the Giant's 'Fe, Faw, Fum' is to a nervous child.

For Skene this bombing was nothing new – billeted in railhead towns, halted in stations, sick in hospital, he had heard it going on around him. But tonight, the invisible bird kept circling above his head, and he could not fix the direction in which to fire. As usual, no instruction had been issued, save that the railway dump was to be guarded, and it only occurred to him after several minutes that the Bosche was probably flying on a photograph some days old, showing it full of stores, and swarming with personnel. Then came a curious shrieking whirr, the dead silence of a stopped engine; a boring as of some gigantic corkscrew into the solid earth; an explosion that seemed to tear the ground from under his feet, a rain of débris that lasted several seconds. His Sergeant beside him voiced his very thought: 'Big stuff, that!' He ordered fire-traversing above the dump. Flame leapt from the mouths of the two guns and their continuous rattle drowned the scuffling of the frightened mules in the transport lines. A second explosion followed farther off, then nothing more. One gun had jammed; Skene ordered the other to cease fire.

Having seen all clear, he dismissed, and went back into the hut. His C.O. had not moved a hair for the noise. Smiling, warm through, with his heart beating and his feet tapping, Skene almost wished he were back in the trenches, so infectious is Activity, so much more attractive than its pensive sister Reflection.

*Chapter 18*

# Another Paris

In the clear bright morning that followed the first raid on the Corps dumps a single Bosche flew over, and then retired. Apparently the enemy had gathered that he was wasting his time. The following night, though bright and clear, was quiet. Skene wrote a long letter to Madeleine, his Field Message Book on his knees, his feet on the stove until his boots scorched, while Uncle snored just out of the circle of lamplight, and outside the road was never quiet and the sentry stamped on the iron ground. Skene wrote fully and enthusiastically – not because he had much to say – she was probably not very interested in such details of his daily life as would pass the censor – but because it comforted him to write. He told her now much he loved her, how lonely he was, how he enjoyed staying with her. He explained that he could not get leave often even to Paris, though that was easier than English leave, but that he would try to get a couple of days off in February. He folded and franked the letter and put it in his pocket, to post it when he could do so unobserved.

In the morning 'Corps people' in blue caps and red caps, seated in motor-cars, were reported to him, as he wolfed his breakfast, his porridge, his bacon and eggs, his bread and marmalade. His servant who brought him the news, left him his well-brushed British warm and his going-on-leave cap on the bench. Uncle was still snoring and Skene hurried out 'clean and properly dressed' to see what these inhabitants of a higher firmament might require.

They were nice people; well shaven, well breakfasted too, one or two regular officers and several of the new 'Goods manager' type of highly placed civilian organizer, who was now flocking into uniform and getting into good positions by influence before

310

ANOTHER PARIS

conscription caught and made infantry privates of them. They wanted new dumps, more dumps and another railway. Skene ventured to suggest that the place was already 'spotted' and that the Bosche, suspicious of it, could watch and bomb it again if he saw any activity. And there was that nasty straight, tree-lined road that ran past it, shown on every map, visible in every photograph, visible even at night, so airmen said. Skene noticed that his remarks were not attended to and held his tongue, fearing he had been guilty of 'cheek'. It only occurred to him later that the nice gentlemen he was talking to simply did not understand him – did not realize what bombing meant, never having seen any. Two days later he found his half-finished letter to Madeleine. It seemed stale, inadequate. He tore it up.

So the dumps came and the railway was begun. Skene's work was doubled and trebled. The weather broke and covered him with mud. At the end of January as things were settling down, he wrote a letter to Madeleine. He read it through and ordered his horse, telling Uncle he was 'fed up' with dump guarding and was going up to Corps to wangle two days' leave.

'I hear what y'say!' was the only answer. The letter in Skene's pocket said the writer wished to be with her, and had a blank space for the exact date of his leave to be filled in.

It was just before eleven when he got to the château where Corps lived and got his horse held. 'Old Bill', as the men had christened that interesting experiment in Zoology, did not require much holding, having arrived at that time of life when to stand still in anything soft, nose down, occasionally taking a bite of any vegetation within his reach was all he desired. But, Skene, knowing this, was afraid for the Corps Commander's wattle mats.

Skene worked his way into the office of the Staff Captain whom he and Uncle saved most trouble, and was just beginning to talk about something quite unconnected with the object of his visit, after the approved manner in which wangling was camouflaged – when Colonel Castle, who was passing the door, looked in.

'Hullo, Skene, you'd better be getting back if you ever want to see Uncle and your fellow-criminals again!' (That was how the detachment was spoken of by those who used it.) 'The Bosche don't like your camp and they're knocking it over!'

Skene saluted, ran to 'Old Bill' behind the shrubbery, jerked him loose, jumped on and rode. From the wooden-jointed distance-devouring trot of the old and weary beast-of-all-trades he appeared to know that something was the matter. Or was it the common equine instinct for knowing when the nose is towards home? It brought Skene in less than an hour to the cross-roads where one of his men was diverting traffic. A little farther on his servant, seated on his valise, was smoking and surveying the scenery from an untilled field. Skene pushed up beside him among the dead vegetation, and caught sight of the camp and dumps. They were all lifeless and empty and dotted with big black holes and lumps of chalky earth. In the middle of the desolation Uncle was walking steadily up and down beside the collapsed card house of the mess and office. What casualties? Two of his own men killed, it appeared, for certain; two or three more not yet discovered, but might have run off. Among the dumps, numbers not known, but 'I got your things out, sir!'

At that moment, 'Old Bill' stiffened under Skene. There was a tearing grinding noise. A great column of black smoke, earth and debris flew up and hung towering over their heads, followed by that unforgettable roar and patter of falling bits. Uncle turned to look mechanically and resumed his walk. Skene gave 'Old Bill' to his man and scrambled down shouting, 'Come out of it or I'll come to you!' Uncle shouted back: 'The whisky came this morning! D'y' think I'd leave eleven and a half bottles to these hoboes?'

The business came to an end. Instead of dying heroically amid the debris of their camp, Uncle and Skene and their detachment spent the night gathering up fragments and moving themselves and the dumps.

It was days before life was even decent again. At last he had time to write another letter, to say how anxious he was to see her, but that he had difficulty in getting leave. He added that the

## ANOTHER PARIS

War was long, but that he would soon write and say when he was coming. His own words struck him with a chill compunction. He had been so busy, he had hardly thought of her. There were rumours of an early British offensive in connection with the French, which, added to the rearrangement of the dumps and camp had kept him at it night and day. He felt he must not post the letter until he could say he was asking for leave. Uncle was late for breakfast, Skene went across to the office they had rigged in the corner of a stable, roofed-in, watertight, with scrounged tarpaulin, for the N.C.O.s and stores.

As he called his man to get out one of the army bicycles, for he was going up to Corps – the field telephone jangled out. He put the receiver to his ear. It was the Staff Captain, Q. 'The Bosche has walked!'

'What!'

'The Bosche has gone, we haven't touched him for days. There's no one in his trenches. Pack up and be at (Map Square) by noon.'

Not that day either did Skene apply for Paris leave. His letter became soiled in his pocket. He tore it up. Then came the Bosche retreat of February 1917. The next letter he wrote was from near Arras, in full preparation for the impending battle. He wrote in unmeasured terms, explaining how he was prevented from joining her immediately. On re-reading it, it now appeared to him to have been written in an absent-minded moment. He read it and re-read it. The phrases were all he could ask, but something seemed to have dropped out of him, and there was no mention indeed of leave, much love and reflection on this terrible war – and no fourth page. He searched in vain for something to put on that fourth page, which he felt all such letters should have, but failed to find it. He never posted that letter either.

His Corps going out to rest, he hastily applied for two days' leave to Paris, but before it could be granted, the fine spell of mid-March had come, the bombing was incessant, the movement of troops by day and by night continuous, and to crown all, the Corps moved. Whether his application was lost or destroyed he never knew. Then one morning, he received a letter from her.

He opened it after a sleepless night and busy morning, during a spell of bright weather after snow, when it was too clear for troops to move, and he had some respite. He read it three or four times, then folded it up and pocketed it, and stared over his extinct pipe at the desolation about him, for within was a desolation greater still.

In spite of some slight attempt at concealment, in spite of cordial phrasing and hopes for a speedy meeting, this letter was simply a request for money.

Among Skene's faults there was never any meanness in such a matter; pulling out of his wallet the hundred-franc note he kept by him for emergencies, he thrust it into an envelope with a few lines on a sheet from his Field Message Book, stuck it down, addressed it, franked it and chucked it into a slotted biscuit tin, the pillar box to his unit.

The pale April sun sank behind the south-western downs and with it something bright and clear faded out of Skene's heart. The sum was nothing, he would have spent many times that on her in a single day's leave, enjoyed together. What hurt him was something deliberate and calculated that scraped his fastidiousness, robbed their liaison of all there was personal, intimate; degraded it, and covered it with the sticky dirt of 'relations mondaines' advertised on the last page of a comic paper. Thankful was Skene when his servant pushed a cropped head out of the hut door to snap 'Tea's on, sir!' Happier still when dusk awoke the bugles of 'Stand to!' and he could think no more.

Arras, that fierce bitter battle in the snow, in part, at least, a surprise to the enemy, dwindled out in hopeless attacks in mud and filth. More deadly and more hopeless than the Somme, it had not been heralded by such preparations and boasting, and more important, it had not lasted so long. There was magic in that. If only the War had lasted for two years; if only the War winters had been six weeks each – if only – if only!

The effect on the mind of the quantities of prisoners and guns – the considerable extent of ground gained, all coming after the

## ANOTHER PARIS

Bosche retreat, altered the whole tide of the men's feelings.

The exhaustion, the hopelessness, the failure of the winters after Loos and the Somme, the coming of conscription, the cold of January 1917, all had been driving the men's optimism down and down.

Now the tide rose again. In the Bosche retreat of February men saw tangible results from the Somme – a whole great corner of the Bosche line gone – even untouched villages with civilians in them – all that had not happened since the Aisne, two years and a half ago. And on the top of this came Vimy – Vimy, the Canadians' prize 'show', and men gasped – for years Vimy had been a legend in the armies. The French had said, 'Our black troops have it.' The English used to send over battalions, even brigades, against it. But, eventually, it always rested with the Bosche. Now the Canadians were far beyond it. And while that fighting dwindled out, came the news of America joining in the War.

Northward again – the drift of the War. All the troops that had streamed out of Flanders to Loos, and after Loos down to the Somme, were now streaming back, some tarrying at Arras to be put into the last convulsions of that struggle, but all in the end coming up, through Abbeville and the villages of the Picard downs, or up the St Pol-Frevent–Lillers road. The next 'victory' was to be further northward still, and incidentally Skene's Corps went out of the Line for a rest. He was not slow in seeing the Staff Captain who worked the leaves. He got eight days.

Somehow, Madeleine's face was dim. Something had come between them – the War, of course. He wrote twice hastily. He received no reply. He sent a last note with an appointment at the little hotel in the Rue Biault and set off for Paris.

Once set free from the daily round of responsibility, and preoccupation, it fared ill with Skene. All these busy months since Christmas he had hardly had time to think; he now began to ask himself questions.

Passing in the hot, fine weather through to Boulogne, Étaples, Abbeville, down to Amiens, he tried to recapture the thought that had possessed him, such few months before, making that same journey, thinking of the same woman – the woman who had written him those last two letters, the incomprehensible letter that said nothing in a few words, and the fatal letter that he could not bear to unfold, but kept close in the back of his wallet, the letter in which came the sentence:

'I know that you are generous, and life is so hard. I am so plagued for money, could you not help me?'

The old exploiting of the wealthy, silly young English officer by the fair but necessitous girl! He had heard of it, seen it happening so often, had told himself that he was above it, not to be entangled in such a mess and now ...

When he had reached a certain depth of despair, the other Skene in him, the Skene who had lived over thirty years in the world, and thirteen of them in ordinary business to earn a living, rebelled. 'Why not I – as much as any of the others? I've had my fun, and now I want it for nothing,' and on this conclusion, there would intervene the tag from 'Alice in Wonderland,' 'nothing for nothing and precious little for sixpence'.

With balance restored and sense of humour readjusted, he thought:

'All imagination. She's hard up – of course! Who isn't! I ought to feel flattered that she trusts me ... in any case I'm going as fast as I can to see what's the matter!' And on this, like a wall of fog would come her silence – the silence of the last weeks; and the miserable treadmill of rumination would begin again.

It was a changed Paris – bombardment or disillusionment at failure of the Champagne offensive had affected it. There were no taxis to be had; Skene cursed, trudging with his pack up the steep stifling streets to the little hotel.

The place had no glamour today! Perhaps it was the May daylight that robbed it, but deep within him, Skene had a sinister premonition. No longer was it a sheltered nest, quiet resting-place of the war-worn – but simply a clean but ordinary hotel, in a rather undesirable street, where officers and others took their young women. The little proprietor, in his glass cage, was better dressed, more independent. He fussed over having just one room left – it was lucky Skene had written. No, no one had called – was Skene expecting anyone? A lady – very good. She should be shown up.

The baize-aproned, bemedalled boots took Skene up to Room No 6 and left him to sit on the bed on the very coverlet of rose-coloured silk in the same room where he had watched her bare arms above her head. With a fatal sinking of the heart he washed and changed and waited.

It was long past eight when appetite rose out of the sea of his mournfulness, and forced him out of the brasserie in the Place Clichy to eat and above all to drink.

He was just beginning to tell himself that he did not care, when a thought pricked him to the heart – she had been detained at her office, and was now at the hotel waiting for him. Paying his bill, he left his change and ran.

The proprietor came out of his den.

No, no one had called. And Skene knew that in turning on his heel, he turned his back on an apish grin.

For hours he walked the streets, his world turned upside down. He kept flinging himself at the blackness that seemed before him, only to know that it was within him, behind his eyelids, not before his eyes.

Why could he not do without this woman, as she without him? As he without so many others? Where was the lightness of heart with which he had left her a few months before, probably as important to him then, as now – parted with her after a few days at the call of duty – where was the ease with which for thirteen years he had done without women – too busy, too happy in his job to notice them?

He thought, with detachment, of morality, as he had so often heard it expounded, of all the moral people in the world whose virtue was never to have wanted anything with their whole hearts, as he now wanted Madeleine, but the detachment did not last him long.

He wheeled briskly and started back for the hotel. Hope reconquered him on the doorstep. Passing the cage of the proprietor without a word, he leapt up the little stairs three at a time and wrenched the door wide.

A rustle set his heart beating in his head. It was the blind disturbed by the draught from the door. The beating of his heart almost ceased and he felt sick. He flung himself on the bed and remained still for hours.

*Chapter 19*
# A Matter of Business

Skene arrived back a day earlier than he need have done, and walked from railhead until he caught a lorry going towards his billet. He was expecting ridicule over his early return, but the little Uncle was busy and glad to see him. One of those big reshufflings that always preceded an offensive was in progress – the whole corps was going into the Line again, and every one must move.

After some days, Uncle and Skene found their appointed place in a small industrial town lying just inside the British trenches, one of those cotton-spinning and mining centres that make the country round Lille like a leisurely imitation of Lancashire.

Dangerous to hold on account of the number of casualties possible in the narrow streets, costly and difficult to attack, it was left alone by both sides as much as possible. The British allowed some hundreds of civilians to remain in the less-bombarded streets and work the one or two factories that were still being run.

At the western end of that town, touching the river bank, was the wreck of a miniature garden suburb. A quadrangular walled-in space giving northward on the river contained a house or two in the architectural style associated with housing reform, a model infant school, shrub-planted walks, and, most important, an asphalt tennis-court, dry and firm in all weather, and roofed in, making a splendid dump. Here in the cellar of a model house half-destroyed by shell fire – social reform murdered – they made their Head-quarters; and here towards the end of May they heard the bombardment that preceded Messines.

For Skene the War had become a regular business. At dusk

every evening he went out to visit his men on the four bridges and the six dumps for which he was responsible, to see that the ration traffic cleared itself, to settle disputes and evacuate casualties. He returned at midnight, and had a night-cap with Uncle. He was out at 'stand-to' in gum boots and a British-warm over pyjamas, to see that things did not get slack. There was salvage to be sorted, correspondence to deal with, orders to issue in the morning; if he had not a journey to settle some claim for damage to civilian property or to see Corps or other Head-quarters, he got the remainder of his sleep. In the afternoon there was nothing to be done but keep everybody under cover. Old soldiers like Skene and Uncle knew that to be seen meant long-range shelling and destruction of the happy home. As soon as the morning mist had cleared, nothing was to be seen of the little camp – no white posts, no brick pathways. The men on the bridge-guard were screened, and the horse-lines camouflaged. Yes, this phase of the War became mere business – even to the early morning cup of tea, and the Sunday afternoon off. Skene, alas, had leisure to think over and over what had happened to him. He became silent, brooding, dully mechanical. He received no letter. He no longer expected one. He had two hopes – the end of the War or the end of his life. He began to think.

He had plenty of time to think, going about on duty with his orderly or N.C.O., through the grass-grown streets of the three-parts deserted town, picking his way among shell-holes or fallen tiles by the light of the Bosche flares, or of the bombardments where the fighting at Messines was flickering out, and that at Paschendaele being prepared – or in broad daylight, when he followed those same streets, keeping under the lee of the houses, so that any odd shrapnel or tiles flying about should miss him.

Or when he set off riding, or in the box car, with or without Uncle, to Corps or Division, to argue with staff people about orders or returns; with farmers about horse-lines or barns destroyed; or even into the town at times to dine with passing units to whom he had been able, and was always willing, to do a kind turn. All the time he thought – stopping to speak to sentries by dumps or bridges, or to staff officers – stopping to watch files of men and limbers passing dangerous spots – stopping to watch games of bridge in cellars, to measure with his eyes how many posts, how much brickwork, what width of corrugated iron must be made or destroyed to allow English-speaking Tommies and mules from Lord knows where to live in French factories or barns or pastures or copses, until they were sent away to be killed.

He thought and thought and began to see so clearly how the whole thing had come about. He saw why Perfide Albion or Gott Strafe England had always been on the lips of other peoples, a curse at the extraordinary luck of the sea-girt country from which he came – where climate and temper, lack of foreign invasion, new paths of knowledge, and a world-wide Empire, obtained from discoverers by purchase or settlement, had all combined to give England, in a sort of triumph of lucky expediency, the lead of the industrial era – so many harbours, so much coal and iron, such a hardy, pushful people that the whole world spoke her language, borrowed her money, used her ships.

So extraordinary had been her luck that, when the world-war came, her children, like Skene, entered it with an ingrained romanticism possible only to those who live in comfortable leisure, with enough to eat and drink, no frontiers, and plenty of novels; presently to find as the struggle lengthened and lengthened, that they were fighting a war that their own luck had rendered inevitable perhaps – a war of life or death for their business and prestige, on other people's ground. Could any luck be more colossal than that?

Further than this he seldom went, and used to say – 'Well, I don't care, here I am, and must stick it!'

The thought of Madeleine was at first simply an everlasting ache. Skene, whose pleasures lay in the imagination, supported on a slight basis of reality, could find no comfort in the ordinary promiscuity of the base or railhead towns. If he could not have Madeleine, he must go without. He began to recognize that he was not dying of it; then to see that here too he was the Lucky Englishman. To have had her at all had been a lucky accident, a pleasant coincidence – nothing more! How could there be a permanent relationship between an Architect in an English county town and the daughter of a Flemish farm?

And the summer wore on, and hope in men's hearts began ebbing again. After all, it was only the hope of an early ending that was left.

The Bosche retreat, the capture of Vimy, the French Champagne offensive, had been but qualified successes when they were not ghastly failures.

And it was now patent that the great Ypres offensive was a failure. Begun too late, with the old obvious methods of gigantic concentrations of troops impossible to hide, and colossal bombardments that even the mules in the lines and the birds on the trees could not possibly mistake, it had almost alarmed the Bosches, who of course had made corresponding efforts to meet it.

By the end of August men were talking of another winter. The Russians were giving way. The Americans were not arriving. Skene, moving among the farms in the back area, would hear from 'reformed' soldiers, or men on leave from the French front: 'It's all very well – one more offensive – and we shall have no more men!' Some French troops were fighting between Ypres and the sea, beside the English, liking it as little as anyone else and making prodigious sacrifices to gain a few yards of unrecognizable 'ground'.

From the British front Skene heard no better news. In the offices at Corps Château, he would hear officers saying: 'I suppose we shall really go on fighting, if we don't get through this time!' – 'this time' being one of the weekly attacks made under the direction of an Army Commander, whose renown was enshrined in the doggerel:

> 'All Hell's Bells!
> Butt in anyhow,
> Kill all your Infantry,
> Get some more from some one else!'

The services, the bases, the camps in France or England were raked for men and still more men. Orders to re-examine ever more drastic came to Corps, and just missed Skene because he was too useful, Uncle because he was too old.

There was another change too in the nature of the War. The line of destruction could barely lengthen – it stretched from sea to sea – but it broadened and deepened to three or four times its old size. Not only where the quasi-successful offensives left miles of weed-growing, evil-smelling desolation, but in sectors like that held by Skene's Corps, on the back edge of the bigger battle, where the old trench warfare was still more or less in practice, the danger zone had greatly extended. In Skene's time, troops never came back farther than the outskirts of Ypres, or the mining villages east of Béthune; 'rest' in railhead towns like Poperinghe or even Albert, was rest indeed. Now towns twenty miles from the Line, and of course Paris and London, to say nothing of Amiens and St Omer and Calais, were bombarded with guns or aircraft of ever-increasing calibre. It seemed that there could never be any end to the War. Collapse of one side or the other, for want of men, money, material or courage wasn't working out. The nations were always willing to go one better under any demand made on them, and business boomed. The War seemed illimitable. From Karlsruhe and Cologne to Paris and London; from Vladivostok, over all Asia and Europe to New York and San Francisco; from Scapa to Cape Town and the Pacific Islands. And it had become a different army, a conscript army that carried on the War in France.

Superficially there was not much difference. The old volunteer army had been of all ages, and all degrees of fitness; those who succeeded them were much the same. The last classes to come out showed rather less spring and good-humour, perhaps, but on the other hand they never regarded the War in any sense as a picnic. Their one thought was to get it done. Apart from this they were the same hard-elbowed, music-hall song-singing lot. One night, watching a battalion coming out from the Line, just north of the river, where it became moderately safe, Skene seemed to see a ghost, with a ghost's voice and laugh, standing beside the muddy way.

'Good evening, sir!' he said, going up to it.

By the light of the Bosche flares, a drawn face was turned. But Skene was right. It was Thomas, now a major.

Skene took him to the garden suburb – a changed Thomas.

He seemed to have grown, but he had really only become extremely thin. He still had all the engaging qualities acquired at Public Schools. He was charming to the garrulous and fuddled Uncle (whom he must have thought an unqualified old reprobate), charming to Skene, and gave him news of the old battalion, of which he was laughingly proud to be, with the Regimental Quartermaster-Sergeant, the only survivor. He ticked them off on his fingers, from the Colonel to Mansfield. 'Earnshaw's still alive,' he said, 'and you! You're the lucky ones! And jolly glad you are, and here's your very good health, and yours, sir!'

The duty orderly put his head under the waterproof sheet.

'Horse transport with materials, sir, and can they put it on B dump?'

Thomas rose with Skene and they went out together. 'Back to our jobs! How queer we should feel without 'em!' was the last thing Skene heard him say.

He was killed, of course, at Cambrai, but the War went on.

A few days later Skene had another ghostly visitor.

It was a blustering morning, too much wind and flying cloud for aeroplane observation, and he had 'gingered' Uncle up to having a thorough sanitary inspection. Together they had tramped those grass-grown streets, visited every police post, spoken to every gendarme, chaffed the little Communal Secretary in his sand-bagged office. Uncle stopped to lunch with a mess of officers billeted in the town. Skene came home to the garden suburb to see that everything was smooth. He called for food, dived into the dug-out, and saw an officer sitting there.

It was Earnshaw – a little stouter, a little balder, but flushed and with blazing eyes, in the devil of a temper. He only said 'Hallo!' Skene answered with: 'Have a drink. There'll be some grub directly.'

Over two chipped enamel mugs of whisky and water, Skene

## A MATTER OF BUSINESS

went on: 'Well, old man, how are you and where are you, and all that sort of rot?'

Earnshaw replied: 'I want you to do me a favour!'

'Why, of course. What is it?'

'Put me under arrest!'

'Burnside,' shouted Skene, 'look sharp with lunch for two!'

Earnshaw stuck out his jaw.

'I mean what I say. Will you?'

'Anything you like, old man, but what for?'

'Do you remember, when we were with the battalion, that you were sent off to buy . . .'

'Don't I just – nightshirts – The whole brigade called us the Pyjama Fusiliers!'

'Do you remember picking me up in a car?'

'Very well. You'd been stealing bricks!'

Earnshaw thumped the table, and the two mugs jumped.

'Dammit, you're as bad as the rest. I'd been *buying* bricks to save my mules!'

'Of course, jolly good standings you made.'

'Well, they've raked that up.'

'What after – let's see, eighteen months?'

'Raked it up. The dam' Requisition Service, or whatever parcel of fools it may be, wouldn't pay on the chit I had given.'

'Red tape – awful – I know,' murmured Skene, who knew better than 'I told you so'.

'So I paid – paid out of my own pocket. I'm not complaining of that. I saved the mules!'

'You're a good sort, old Millgate!'

'Had to go through a Court of Inquiry, of course. Ever held one?'

'One or two.' Skene omitted to say that they were generally upon cases of theft, for fear of upsetting his friend.

'Well, then it seemed that I had conveyed merchandise out of France into Belgium. Owing to the time these Requisition people had taken to NOT pay for saving the lives of mules, old Vander what's-his-name the Brick-maker – ' Earnshaw stopped to masticate pork chop and haricot.

'Brickadier!' suggested Skene, but Earnshaw was past noticing.

' – had gone to his Deputy in the Chamber, and he'd told the Customs people – '

'Of course there was a Douane post – '

'I'm not saying there wasn't. I'm only saying it's war-time. I'm only saying that it's not worth while killing mules yourself with greasy feet and swelled hocks, when the Bosche will kill 'em for you with shrapnel. Well, they wanted another Court of Inquiry to satisfy the French Chamber and the King of the Belgians and God knows who, and I kept tearing the correspondence up. I'm on a Railway Laying Company, now, we've been doing a mile a day, all spiked, for this precious offensive up north. I was sent for, to Corps. I thought I was going to get the M.C. for Railway Laying under fire, and instead, it was all about this Customs-house business. A dam' young swine who'd been out here about ten minutes wanted to know why I didn't reply to his chits. I told him all right!' Earnshaw nodded. 'I told him what I thought of him, and this offensive and the army and the War. I told him I'd see one of the members for Lancashire. I told him to go to hell.'

Skene reached for his friend's dirty plate, gave him a clean one full of fruit salad, and pushed over the biscuits.

'He said it was mutiny, and all that, so I told him where to find me and cleared off. Now if you'll put me under arrest, I'll wait until they come for me . . .'

Then queerly, almost emotionally:

'You know Skene, if I've got to be arrested, I'd rather be arrested by you. I'll go quiet.'

Skene wiped his mouth, and swung out of the dug-out. On his way across to the Signal dug-out, the voice of Earnshaw pursued him, high and excited, the voice of a man who seldom uses it, its verbiage starred with Americanisms, and trailing off very near a 'Ba Gom!'

'We've been out here two years and more; what's it been but waste of men and waste of animals and waste of materials and nothing done.'

Skene rang up Corps, asked for Colonel Castle and told him the whole story, ending:

## A MATTER OF BUSINESS

'He's such a useful officer, sir, surely something – '

The answer came.

'You might teach him manners, not to mention discipline. We can't have junior officers shouting and storming all over Corps Head-quarters.'

'No, sir!'

'He ought to go to Mesopotamia, but send him in your box car to railhead. I'll have a warrant to meet him at R.T.O.'s. We want some Railway men for Forestry. Mind, I don't promise.'

Skene was beginning thanks, but the receiver was replaced. In half an hour Earnshaw went to railhead in the box car. An hour after that a young man in a Vauxhall staff car came to inquire for him. Uncle interviewed him.

'And who might you be?'

'Deputy Assistant Provost Marshal Umpteenth Corps!'

'Ho, well we don't keep spare officers here. Try the first turn to the right before the bridge. He may be that way.'

Twenty minutes later, Skene saw that young man in the same Vauxhall, still alone, going Corpsward.

'You've been misleadin' Corps staff, Uncle!'

'Well, I gave him the road straight to the trenches,' Uncle said. 'He'd never been there, and I thought it might do him good.'

*Chapter 20*

# Fly-by-Night

A fine evening, on the edge between summer and autumn, dim soft blue above, red glow on walls and trees, and along the ground, a filmy mist. Skene and his Quartermaster-Sergeant were putting together, from wires and telephone messages received from Corps and elsewhere, the evening's duties, so many parties of men and officers, so many loads of materials to be seen, checked and directed rightly. 'Bosche over, sir, arter the balloon!' At the same moment, the Lewis gun at the bridge struck up its demon rattle.

Skene turned to look. The enemy plane had made a sort of pecking dip at the grey shape of the 'sausage' balloon still clear in the dusk, against the pale sky. A whiff of smoke and a spurt of flame. ' 'Ere he come!' 'T'laad's joomped!'

Sure enough, high in mid-air, the shape of a parachute with its tiny burden had sprung like one of the magic flowers of the Japanese conjurer, and sailed with slow gyration, downwards, heading, it seemed, straight for the river. Then, swinging aside, the top-heavy-looking mushroom of pink silk settled slanting down the scarred avenue of the Béthune road. Skene and his corporal raced on signallers' bicycles over the pot-holed pavé. Some gunners from a neighbouring battery were already hanging on the cords and folding the unwieldy thing.

'T'laad' seemed tolerably bumped and bruised, and had sprained his shoulder when the parachute had taken his weight up with a jerk. Skene had the little Ford box car out and sent him off to his unit, just as a very clean and capable mechanic dashed up in a cycle-sidecar to take charge of the parachute. The fallen aeronaut called back: 'If I come back to this crush, I'll ask you to come and dine with us!'

Not many weeks passed before that invitation came, and on

the appointed day, at dusk, up rolled a sumptuous Crossley. Skene left his section and his conscience to 'Uncle', and went spinning over the Route Nationale, to where, carefully placed far from church, windmill, railway or main road, the aerodrome was spread on uncultivated clover, dotted with marquees, and striped with camouflage. His host explained: 'We're such a small mess at the Section, I thought you'd rather come here!' Waiting for the offensive, five squadrons and a balloon school were jammed together. The great hangars and workshops, the tenders, cars, cycles coming and going reminded Skene of a goods station. But no railway ever displayed such costly efficiency. He was taken to a marquee where a gramophone was being accompanied on the piano, and two smooth-faced schoolboys were playing diabolo. They all seemed schoolboys. Skene and the Doctor and the Quartermaster were the only men in the place over thirty. Yes, and the tragedy of that! There was an atmosphere of waiting. An orderly fixed a blue-pencilled list to the tent-pole. And one by one, these pale, slim boys, with their blue-circled eyes, went up and looked at it. Curiously matter-of-fact and fatalistic that quiet procession! Then those who were playing diabolo began again, those who were drinking drained their glasses, and ordered another; a new record was set on the gramophone. 'List of patrols for tomorrow!' said Skene's host, Carruthers of the balloon. They went in to dinner.

The faces round the table were impassive, eyes fixed on plates, very little conversation went on. Coffee appeared, two or three of them retired amid a chorus of 'Cheerio! old thing, I'll come and see you off!' 'They're the first lot; they'll be over Lille before it's properly light,' explained Carruthers.

Restraint seemed lifted. The Doctor and the Quartermaster were the next to go. Some one put a ragtime record on the gramophone. Some one else ordered a round of liqueurs. A tall boy, with Yeomanry badge in his lapel, whom everyone called 'Barney' (explaining: 'because he owns a bulldog'), leaned over to Carruthers. 'What about an evening off? I'm not on in this act!'

'Depends on what you mean by "off". I may have to go up tomorrow, and so may you!'

'Oh – tomorrow! It's tonight!'

In that 'tomorrow' was the reason why English air-fighting was so irresistible. Skene, thinking of the traffic on his bridges, with no better guidance than 'Uncle', said he must be home by midnight.

'Oh, but we'll drive you home!'

'I can walk really. I come from the Infantry!'

'So have heaps of us, but you can't possibly walk!'

Carruthers, wavering, put in: 'What'll we go in? They'll never give you a tender, Barney!'

'Simplicitas is my motto! There's a tender going into St Blanque with the mails – *compris*?'

To Skene it seemed like proposing to go to Boulogne or Folkestone.

'It's over twenty kilos back, and not even in the Army area!'

'My dear old Footslogger' (Barney took his arm), 'nothing can stop the R.F.C.'

Skene buttoned his British-warm with a certain zest. To avoid attracting attention they were to walk in twos down to the Motor Transport park, a few hundred yards away. The night was dark and fresh, and the breeze rising. Some one stood a last round of drinks. A high square tender swung off its asphalt stand. Barney was driving. In they scrambled. Past a British sentry and a French gendarme, the steel-studded double wheels of the tender hissed pleasantly along the Route Nationale, over a railway crossing and along an avenue, through villages, past camps, under the shadow of a high tower, into the narrow streets of St Blanque. They were dropped in the square at another mess, some lines-of-communication Head-quarters, where they drank whisky. Then out again, through narrow streets, to a spiked door over which shone the Red, White and Blue of one of those establishments to which, in deference to bishops at home, British officers were forbidden to go. About as much attracted as by a butcher's shop, Skene saw nothing for it but to follow into a big, square room, where, to the grinding of a desolating waltz, some officers were giving an exhibition of the then novel Jazz. Skene took a tumbler of champagne that had never seen Épernay, from a houri in a garment swathing her from below the breasts to the thighs. The noise, the smoke, the fumes of alcohol and scent made him want to vomit, but he sat squarely on a dilapidated ottoman, keeping those unattractive attractions at a distance by fluent French, which drove them to describe him as 'mufle' or 'mauvais farceur'. A quarrel had arisen. Skene saw his chance, unbolted the door and slipped out into the clean night air. He had hardly got outside before two red-capped English military police and a couple of French gendarmes filed into the house. The English Sergeant, an immense Metropolitan policeman, called over the mob's heads: 'Meenwee, Madame, fermee!' The French 'Brigadier', with the special surliness of his kind, grunted: 'Fermez votre boîte, nom de Dieu!' thumping the floor with his scabbard.

Some had to find clothes, others to settle for wine, or conclude arguments. Skene, smoking his pipe outside, watched. He found Carruthers, bemused with drink, at his elbow, and Barney, as alert as if he had never had a drop. 'Where's young Cumming?' (a youngster from a county regiment who had come with them in the tender). 'Did he go upstairs?'

'I didn't see him. Besides, he was keen on the dark one – what's her name? – wears a yellow thing! She was booked tonight, I heard Madame say!'

'Then he's not upstairs; he's a regular little thing in his habits!'

'Bet you he's gone back to the tender!'

'Let's go and look!'

Skene went too. Uncle must keep awake for once and see to things. The tender was standing in the Square, like a bathing machine on a promenade. The driver was singing gently to himself; going round to flood the carburettor, he fell across the bonnet and lay there, laughing.

'Tight!' commented Barney: 'here you, get into the tender!' The man obeyed with the sketch of a salute. A sleepy voice under the hood protested. 'Is that you, Cumming?' called out Carruthers. 'No, I'm going!'

They thrust the tipsy driver on one side, and peered in with

Barney's torch. An Infantry officer was lying across the seat with his feet on his pack. 'Lord!' cried Barney, 'who are you, and what the devil are you doing here?'

'You said you'd take me on to Boulogne . . .' Then, with weary wakefulness: 'Oh, it wasn't you, it was another chap!'

They stood and stared. Overhead, a night bomber droned. The drunken chauffeur snored. The clock of the baroque church struck – 'one'. Then Carruthers said:

'134 were sending down to pick up one of their fellows. I bet you Cumming's got into their tender. He'll be half-way to Boulogne by now!'

Barney said: 'Hell! Cumming and I are due out together at nine. We can do it and we d—d well must. Come on!'

Skene protested feebly. 'Look here, I must leave you chaps and get back on my own. I really can't take a trip to Boulogne when I ought to be back with my Clearance Post!'

'You awful old slop,' was all the answer he got. 'How d'y' think you're going back to your billet through a dozen police posts? And you can't stop here. You'll get arrested. Get in!'

Out over the cobbles, under an archway, and away on a wide road between trees. Skene could tell by the gradients that they were out of Flanders, further from the Line than he had often been. Under the hood next the sleeping chauffeur, he talked to their 'guest', as Barney called him. The boy was dazed and worried. He had had no leave for over six months, no sleep for two nights. He wanted to get home. 'D'you think we'll get there before the boat goes?' he kept asking Skene, 'because I don't want to miss it!' with a quiet fatuity which the War had taught to a whole generation.

Suddenly, round a bend, their headlights encountered another pair as strong. The brakes shrieked. It was the other tender with young Cumming. The chauffeur had found him asleep behind, assumed that it was his proper passenger, and started. When Cumming awoke and realized with a pilot's 'sense' that he was going the wrong way, there had been a scene, almost a panic. Now there was corresponding joy. They said 'good-bye' to their 'temporary gentleman', as Barney called him, and started back.

At three they were crossing the Grand Place of St Blanque. At four they were at the aerodrome, having hot coffee and sausages in the nipping cold of dawn.

While they were eating off tin plates in the Mess Kitchen, one of the quiet boys who had gone to bed early came and put his hand on Barney's shoulder.

'All right, old thing?'

'Tight as a rivet – I mean right as a trivet,' Barney spluttered. 'Such a game, believe me, friends, is hardly worth the playing!' And nodding 'good-bye' to Skene, he went across to bathe and sleep.

'A rum pair!' commented Carruthers. 'Division of labour. Barney does all the drink and devilment, and his chum stays at home and looks at the clock. But neither will go on patrol without the other!' Then, as if he had been guilty of an exhibition of intelligence, he hastily added: 'Very glad you were able to come; good-bye for just now!'

\*

At five Skene was slipping along to his billet. It was too light to take the tender nearer the line than Deporter's farm, and he walked the last half-mile. His faithful Corporal was awake, at the entrance of the Garden City. All was well. Skene thanked God. He felt very cold and sleepy. Overhead, two planes were droning out towards the enemy, two little bright-coloured insects crawling on the breast of the soft-lit dawn. The grey shape of the observation balloon bellied up to the end of its attachment, like some monster pursuing them. Skene thought of the men up there and somehow envied them. In the cold fit of dawn, tired and empty, he wished with all his heart he were one of those thoughtless boys, fooling away the dull hours of the evening and riding the clouds of the morning to imminent death.

Stale scent and tobacco on his clothes – a dab of powder where one of the 'attractions' of St Blanque had leaned against him, it was like some grinning mockery of the one woman he wanted, then, at the cold hour, to put her arms round him.

*Chapter 21*

# The Cousin of my Uncle

At dusk one evening, autumn dusk, grey, misty, still, Skene, off duty for once, was moodily smoking his after-tea pipe when he heard a hail from the northern shore 'Hi, digger!'

Across the darkening water were two high-shouldered, slouch-hatted figures – 'Anzacs', famous already at Gallipoli and Bullecourt, about to achieve greater fame at Paschendaele and Villers Brettonneux.

All Skene knew of them, then, was their splendid physique, their fine fighting qualities, and the tact needed to manage them behind the Line. He hailed back, 'Hallo!' and waited.

'We are coming across!' And sure enough they came on a sort of raft, propelling themselves with a spade and a bit of board, to the remains of the model suburb's plaster steps.

Quite against orders to cross corps boundaries in this fashion!

'What do you want?' hailed Skene.

'We are looking for my Uncle Jake.'

'Well, you won't find him here. This is the Umpteenth Corps post.'

'Is it now?' came the reply. 'If you'd only said that before, we'd have written and asked King George before we ventured to approach.'

The other added: 'Steady her, will you! I don't want to swim!'

Skene made no movement. The less voluble of the two, balancing the craft with difficulty, added:

'Don't mind him, digger. He's been drinking out of a bottle marked "fixatif" in the hopes it contained vin blanc. It's a real uncle we're after.'

'Well, who are you, anyway, and what do you want?'

The voluble one with the spade answered:

'I'm Sam Dakers and my servant here is Andy Dakers, my

## THE COUSIN OF MY UNCLE

brother, and we are looking for our Uncle Jake, –th Canadians.'

'Oh, that's all right. You'll find *him* here.'

'Now, how clever you are! We knew we should. We've known it for weeks, only your brass policeman wouldn't let us over the bridge.'

'No, those are his orders,' said Skene.

'You needn't tell me. Well, we've been obliged to take the door off the estaminet with the Greek name.'

'Greek name?'

'Well, it looks like the sound of the name of the old man who used to keep donkeys at Cairo.'

They got ashore, and hitched what Skene saw to be, in truth, a large yard-door from some agricultural building, to the steps, with a piece of barbed wire.

Sam, the talkative one, whom Skene perceived to be an officer, walked on one side of him on their way to the billet, while Andy, the private, walked with no more ceremony on the other. Sam continued sweetly:

'So you thought we were practising for the cinema?' Skene coughed. Perhaps what was called the cinema element did not come from the influence of the cinema on the colonies, but from the influence of the colonies on the cinema!

Uncle no sooner saw the visitors than he lifted his curved pipe from beneath his shaggy moustache and said slowly:

'Blank me, if it ain't Alf's boys!'

'So it is, Uncle Jake – and fancy your dragging your sixty years into the great European conflagration!'

'I'm as good as most. Burnside: Tea – a lot, quick!'

Such tea-drinking and whisky-drinking! Skene sat in the background and listened and mused.

'Well, how's Sis?'

'Last time Mum wrote, she said we was to give her love when we saw you; do you remember when you fastened the Chinaman's wooden collar on Shepheard!' How many meetings like this – since the War began – of nephews with uncles, from thousands of miles apart! And there it was, the simplicity, the shy good-temper, the sufficient brutality ready to show on cer-

335

# SIXTY-FOUR, NINETY-FOUR!

tain pretexts, the individual self-reliance. Those two went back very late, and after seeing them safely past his policemen on the bridge, Skene went his evening round warmed all through.

Two days later, the two nephews were back again, this time with wire netting and cable.

'We thought it was such a pity your lovely tennis court should be wasted, Uncle Jake, and Andy had to go to St Omer, so he brought these back.'

From a sack they drew four racquets and a box of balls a year old. With broom and shovel they cleared the required space, marked out the court, and strung their net on two pit-props won from the nearest dump.

Then began for Skene one of the happiest months of the whole War. At night, his rounds were long and heavy. In the morning there were reports, orderly room, detail of all kinds. But as the sun climbed high above the grass-grown streets and deserted marshes, there was silence and abandonment. The Bosches were quiet at this hour, his own men asleep or on duty. Then would come the whistle of Sam or Andy and the hauling of the raft across, and instead of a restless afternoon of brooding and boredom, a hard, fast game that made him sweat, and sent him happy and quiet-minded to the evening's work.

All too short those weeks of jolly comradeship and indomitable good-humour. More men were wanted, and more men; the Australian Corps went off and Sam and Andy with it.

From Ypres to the sea, there was raging a new bombardment greater in extent if not in intensity, than the historic gunfire of Verdun and the Somme.

The fabled German artillery was not only equalled, but outmatched, by day; the ground shook all night; thirty miles of horizon were lit by flashes. Andy, returning from duty in the north, had seen the French pouring through above Poperinghe.

The weather broke again on the very morning of the Australians' assault; and the peace of Skene's sector, a byword in France for three years, was broken too. The Bosches, how nearly beaten few then guessed, began their systematic retaliations.

## THE COUSIN OF MY UNCLE

Skene was called out one drizzling afternoon to find one of his bridges half-blown down and his policeman lying in the road with his head a little further on. This was only the prelude. Having failed, by some tiny detail, to become a final victory, the great offensive of the North sank and wallowed between the muddy ridges of Paschendaele and Moorslede. The weather became more uncertain, the Germans more obstinate and resourceful. Bombardment by day, bombing by night, exceeded the Somme offensive of the previous year, the so-called Line became nothing more than an impassable chequer of gas-sodden, water-logged craters defended by machine-guns. Thousands of all races, from all corners of the earth, were working on the roads. The traffic in men and materials was enormous.

As the low ridges of Flanders were conquered yard by yard, hopes rose, wavered and rose again. Uncle Jake was always confident. Skene was merely thankful that their billet lay out of range of the lesser artillery, and was too inconspicuous for the great guns that were turned on railway depots and rail-heads, miles in their rear.

One rain-washed morning, the post orderly brought a thin-papered besmudged note in indelible pencil. It was from nephew Sam.

'Andy has got it bad, in the Countess' Hospital near St Omer.' Uncle Jake, who hated death-beds, would rather Skene went, and they were still talking it over when a hail came from the northern bank, and Sam himself on a raw-boned, mud-caked mule shouted in the teeth of the wind that he had forty-eight hours leave...

That settled it. Skene jumped on a civilian bicycle that had been won no one knew how, pedalled across the bridge and joined Sam on the Aire road. They reached railhead and a friendly Colonial R.T.O. within an hour.

In a soiled and broken-windowed first-class compartment Skene brooded over the strange, vivid, absorbing life so many millions were living in conditions varying from those of the Garden of Eden on a wet day to those of a broker's man in a bankrupt boarding-house. It seemed to him that never could the intimate associations of the two years he had thus passed go from him, and that for always after there would be two races of men – those who had been in it, and those who had not.

It was still early afternoon when they stood in the pale twilight of a marquee, before a narrow bed, where what seemed but the skeleton of the big-boned Andy was propped against his pillows, breathing little short breaths with great difficulty.

Nurse and Doctor were there. But why the padre in the corner, and an obviously English girl in neat, dull-coloured clothes, whose face Andy never quitted with his glazing brown eyes, while she leant over him, supporting him with her left arm, and holding his clasped hands with her right?

On being brought into the casualty clearing-station, the injuries to Andy's backbone and lungs had been recognized as fatal. When he had with difficulty comprehended this, he had made it understood that he wished the nurse who had been on night shift, when he was brought in, to marry him then and there.

So, that great gaunt man, whose hair and eyebrows appeared impenetrably black against the sunken pallor of his flesh, whose great powerful bones protruded through the moist, flaccid skin, was married to a plain, kindly girl from the suburbs of a manufacturing town, the last beautiful thing his primitive, boylike spirit was to desire in this world, while she guided his trembling fingers through the changing of rings, and sealed her promise with a kiss on his forehead.

The nurse on duty put a screen round them; others withdrew. After a few hurried words about the necessary papers, Skene and Sam went out to the poplar-lined road leading to Hesdin.

They plodded along towards the railway station, Sam crying into an enormous khaki handkerchief.

And just then they were hailed from a Flying Corps tender by Carruthers of the balloon section, who was going down Skene's way with supplies.

Sitting in the back of the tender, going about twenty miles an hour through the autumn dusk, Sam dried his eyes and maintained a silence broken only by gruff monosyllables.

'Luckier I than he,' thought Skene. 'To him the extinction of life must seem horrible, he has so much of it; to me – what do I care?'

Indeed it seemed to him that the fading out he had just witnessed was a fortunate release. What would he not give to discard his aching nerves and rheumatic bones in the arms of some one who at least looked as if he were all-important?

Carruthers was saying, 'Old man Fritz is beat – he can't hang out more'n another fortnight!' Skene thought: 'A good job, too; everyone's had enough!' To this had the crusade against Germany dwindled – the War for Civilization!

Next evening, by candlelight in the dug-out, while Uncle and Sam, with some gunners from the neighbouring battery, played poker, while the shells whistled and the planes droned overhead, he sat down and wrote to Madeleine.

He found great difficulty in beginning. And when he had begun, he found great difficulty in going on.

He was sitting on his bed, a wire mattress scrounged from a derelict house. The circle of light from a wangled lamp fell on the players' cropped heads and soiled waterproofs. Sam's hands looked enormous. Uncle uncorked another bottle of whisky. At a louder crash than usual outside Skene called the duty orderly.

'Where was that?'

'Right over, sir, near the old bath-house!'

'Clear of the bridge?'

'Yes, sir, a good bit!'

Skene turned back to the paper which he had headed 'Ma chère Madeleine,' 'Madelon chérie,' and now, in a last attempt, 'Chère Made!' He got no further. Some one turned on the gramophone; it made him think of those early days when 'Tonight's the night!' had been all the go. And back came the ghostly armies of the first year, the men not only dead but buried and forgotten. Ah! Well! He gulped his whisky and watched the players. More in a game of poker than in any comfort he could get from Madeleine! What was the good in writing to a woman and asking her to comfort him? What could she do? – what had she done? – be nice to him, perhaps, see him on leave, tantalize him, use him for her own inscrutable ends with that so simple cunning of an unreflective woman living a hard life. He wrote: 'It's a long while since I heard from you. I am sick of this, and would like to see you again!' crossed it out, tore up the paper, and leaning forward, began betting on Uncle's cards.

*Chapter 22*

# The Third Birthday

The Canadians delivered the final attack on Paschendaele in October. By that time the town in which Uncle and Skene were quartered had begun to be deserted. The civilians were leaving in a steady stream. The gas-shelling was every day more regular and the cellars were becoming sodden. Only in patches on the outskirts was any inhabited house to be found. Gradually, even these were abandoned and the whole place became a great empty sepulchre, where feet rang on the stones of grass-grown streets and voices echoed from the walls of houses where no one lived. Pathetic, those last dregs of civilian evacuation! An old, half-paralysed man pushed before him an invalid's chair in which sat an older and more helpless woman.

'Courage, Father,' Skene said to him, taking his pass on the bridge.

'I have courage enough, thank you, sir. It is Mother who makes herself bad blood because she has had to leave behind all her things! This is all she can bring.'

The old lady was nursing a pink vase, some knitting, and a portrait of the Pope.

Next came the poor prostitute – the girl who went with mechanics and gendarmes in peace-time and with British Tommies during the War, too poor, and too damaged to bribe the necessary authorities to get her papers to Boulogne or Amiens, or one of the better pitches of her trade, or even to get taken out in a British car to Béthune, Abbeville or Hazebrouck. She had often tried, and had, amongst others, come up against Skene. With the undying courage and humorous philosophy of her sort, she bore no grudge.

'So they'll let you go at last, Sylvie,' said Skene, holding out her *carte* stamped and signed.

'Yes, old friend, they always said they wouldn't, but you see, in the end it is I who have won.'

This was the extent of her malice, just a child's 'So there!' She plodded off, on her cheap, thin, heel-twisted boots, her slack, much-corseted figure bent over by the wicker dress basket she was carrying, the unhealthy white of her skin showing through all artifice, turning her head left and right, even in that parade of misery, because it was her business. The last to go was the little white-haired, apple-cheeked Secretary of the Mairie. Skene had been associated with him in investigating a dozen cases of military looting or civilian stealing. Portfolio under arm, he was carrying away the matrix of the Cadastral map; tears were running down his face. He could only say, 'Oh, mon bon Monsieur!'

So they went. It was not like the panicky evacuations in the early months of the War. For three years they had been supporting conditions that grew steadily worse, and now at last were impossible. They were leaving behind a whole history of sacrifice and endurance, going to the cold charity of people a little more fortunate than they, but already sick to death of the War, and very likely themselves being shelled or bombed.

They left an empty shell of a town filled with gas. Skene wandered about it a little in the bright autumn midday, but the place had already passed beyond the looting stage. Some of it was stripped by the owners, some surreptitiously by soldiers, some was securely locked up and some already half-destroyed by shell-fire. He gathered plums from outlying gardens, grapes from a hot-house where the last splinters of glass were falling.

To east and south was the thin ring of British trenches. Inside – nothing.

So another winter crept on, and people said to themselves, 'A year ago I was doing such-a-thing with old so-and-so,' or 'two years ago', or 'three years ago', and now 'so-and-so is dead – let's see, was it 1915? How time goes!'

To Skene and Uncle all the difference was the shorter daylight, which should have meant less shelling but more bombing, instead of which everything seemed to grow more, and nothing less.

They had one great gain – a new Town Major. He was one of those young Scotchmen who appear thirty whether they are nineteen or thirty-nine, loose-limbed, long-striding, hard in build and fibre, great in width of loin, pale and often unkempt-looking, not from lack of blood or shaving, but from a great thickness of skin and wiry toughness of hair. A young gunner who quarrelled with this Captain Gilmour, 'Gillie' as he was immediately called, about bridge, or stores, or passes for the men, or some such trifle, called him: 'A wild Jock with heather growing out of his ears.' He paid no heed. In his personality there was something completely unbeatable, comforting in those days when disappointment gradually deepened into apprehension. Mobilized on the outbreak of war, in one of the old Scottish Territorial units, he had brought to the business a ferocity and cunning scarcely to be hoped for from an educated and well-mannered chartered accountant. Wounded early, he was sent, on recovery, to Gallipoli, and his stories of that epic, of personal valour and hand-to-hand combats, were entirely refreshing. He came to France in time to get his second wound on the Somme, and his third at Vimy, and was now allowed, by a thankful country, to take the comparatively 'soft' job of Town Major.

He had arrived just as news of Cambrai had set ringing the bells of London. It had also set 'reacting' all the German guns on the Front. For three days Uncle and Skene lost all their sleep, many of their meals, and five men. The shelling was indiscriminate, on account of the mists, but perfectly constant. On the third morning a hatless apparition, with a gas-mask strung round his neck, had halted a party of police, scavengers and storemen in the Garden suburb.

'Good morning,' said the apparition with a nice manner and a Glasgow accent. 'Can I use your telephone?'

Skene had conducted him to the 'Signal Dug-out', of which he and Uncle were very proud. He could not help hearing the beginning of the conversation on the telephone.

'Army Head-quarters – Army Head-quarters – yes, Army – d'you think I said Hind-quarters? – Hallo, Army Ten – is that you, Major? – yes – well, I have! I've got 'em all here at A19 at the Clearance Officer's – and now what the hell do you want me to do with 'em?'

Skene touched him on the shoulder. 'Come over and have breakfast when you've done! My Quartermaster-sergeant will billet your men!'

He came over. It was an hour before he was washed and shaved and breakfasted, and seated before a whisky, just as the Bosche shells began getting unpleasantly close on the road. His men were fed and housed on a derelict barge until accommodation could be found.

He never moved away, but formed part of their mess. His old job of billeting, etc., being completely gone, the Army did not seem to know what to do with him, and let him be. It was a good job they did, for Skene's work had more than doubled, and Uncle took less and less interest in anything.

Normally the Town Major was responsible for all that went on in the town, irrespective of change of unit or situation; Skene was not supposed to go beyond his dumps and bridges and the direction of traffic towards its proper unit.

All this was obsolete. In the streets where workpeople had gossiped and children played, nothing was now heard but the clank of hurried men and animals anxious to get away from those toppling houses and high walls that held the gas, the crash of falling wall or roof and the curious squashy explosion of the gas shell, whose tone differed completely from the crack of the old shrapnel, or high explosive's short dry sound. Now both officers made a journey a day into that deserted rubbish heap to see what road was clear, what had 'fallen in', or been 'stunk out', in the last few hours.

The echoes of Cambrai and Caporetto died away; no one knew exactly how many divisions had gone to Italy. The winter became strangely silent, strangely empty. Instead of being merely an incident in a considerable civil and military population, the post where Gillie the Town Major lived with Uncle and Skene had become an isolated little camp, without a soul within call, between the trenches that girded the empty town on one side, and some two or three miles of well-shelled roads and farms on the other. First one and then another farm or cottage, where gunners or engineers, Balloon Section men, or medical units had succeeded each other for years, was shelled out and abandoned. Christmas passed; and then in that queer silence came the first rumours of the great Bosche offensive.

Uncle, Gillie and Skene had seen such a lot of offensives that, to them, it seemed unlikely this new one would go any farther than the others. Offensives at Ypres and Loos, at Verdun and the Somme and Champagne and Arras! They had all ended – where? In stalemate. No, it was not taken very seriously in their little mess.

Sometimes they entertained Infantry officers going to the line, or field-gunners on their way to their unsavoury positions. The little mess had become well known throughout the Corps, and divisions changing over, in rest areas within sight of the sea, would ask each other, 'Are they still all right at Uncle's?'

From these visitors little or nothing could be learned. The Front was abnormally quiet. The trenches in most places had almost disappeared. 'We hold shell-holes with camouflage net over us and precious little wire in front. Can't keep anything repaired – we hold 'em with patrols and live in the support line!' said the Infantry. Skene thought of his report on the state of the front line he had written in October 1915. 'Our battery positions are full of gas – every shell seems to contain some!' said the gunners. But both agreed about the enemy: 'We can't find him – can't see him. He's miles back. We think he's got the wind up!' 'Like our people at home!' they added.

February came, fairylike with its wonderful early weather, clear skies, and all the promise of spring. Aconites and anemones bloomed in Plug Street Wood, in the deserted battlefields of the Somme, in the parks of Vlamertinghe or Trois Tours.

March came in, and with it that great apotheosis of Prussianism – that greatest effort at window-dressing which advertisement has ever devised.

To Skene, of course, it was all danger and discomfort. After weeks of publicity, that great bombardment opened over most of the British front, deeper in reach and greater in volume than any yet, and behind it deployed the rested, heartened, full-fed German troops from the collapsed Russian front, while thousands of labour battalions and gangs of civilian or captive labour prepared their roads and emplacements, their railways and jumping-off positions.

The day came at last; and that great avalanche of guns and men was launched.

To Skene, who had been able to sleep little, and that only in the daytime, it was almost a relief to hear that the great blow had fallen. It brought to the front of him all that was most English.

By night, watching from the door of the dug-out the far-reaching barrage of enormous guns; by day, watching the stream of divisions going south, to hold the Bosche at Ham or Peronne, and then to stop him at all costs from entering Amiens, Skene's feelings toughened and hardened and he could only feel what his Corporal said, when he saw his brother brought home, with legs from the knee downwards a mass of bloody rags: 'By God, I'll land them one for this!'

The night after he definitely knew that the Somme breakthrough had been frustrated, Skene woke a little after midnight, leapt out of bed, and shook himself.

No dream. Super-bombardment! Scrambling into gum boots and British-warm, he got out of the dug-out and looked round.

The desolation of the Garden Suburb was lit by one continual conflagration from Ypres around the whole horizon, dwindling into the flats towards La Bassée. The ground shook and tiles were flying off the buildings, though the actual shells were falling some thousands of yards away, except for a steady, punctual crash every two minutes in the direction of the bridge. He found his Sergeant beside him, the men all standing-to, and nothing to be done but wait.

Diving back into their resting-place, Skene woke Uncle. The old man came out, shivering with night air and whisky, and murmuring the headline of the Daily Paper of the previous week:

'All is quiet on the Western Front, but the situation is not without danger!'

'Where's Gillie?' Skene shouted in his ear.

'Dunno. Suppose he's run away. Fool if he hasn't!'

'Who's that on the road there?'

'Go and see while I have a tin-hat and gas-mask parade for our lot!'

Skene found two people in British-warms who said they were Canadian Demolition Engineers, looking for Captain Dakers.

'We've got to blow up his bridges, the Bosche are "through"!'

'Is that what all the noise is about? Captain Dakers is busy; I'll come along to the bridge with you, to see that our sentry don't shoot you.'

The atmosphere was chokier by the bridge, and Skene loosened his mask. His eyes watered from the whiffs of gas and the bridge seemed all out of shape. Then he saw that the brick pillar on the near side of the step-off was gone, with the sentry's shelter, all down into the dark, flash-reflecting water.

He bawled in the Canadian's ear: 'They've done our man in; here's your bridge; come and have a drink at the dug-out, by where you met me, when you can!'

He left them, stepping quickly aside. An old familiar rushing filled the air. A big 'un had just missed the bridge, and plunging into the river sent water and debris over everything. By the time he had wiped his face and head, he found a tractor on the top of him, lugging a six-inch howitzer. Behind came Gillie and an orderly confirming the news 'The Bosche are through!' 'Better get everything north of the river,' they agreed, and went back to Uncle, who had packed his own valise, and was giving directions to get out the barge. 'No go,' commented Gillie, 'they're through that side too!'

'Very well. The morale of the troops is excellent!' quoted Uncle. 'Wheels and animals over the bridge, we'll ferry the personal estate!' He pointed to Skene's valise that Jerry had just dumped, properly strapped, by the door.

'Thank God, the dumps are nearly empty!'

'What have you got?'

'Shovels and pick-handles and sandbags and camouflage, all trench stuff.'

'Put a match to it, take a tin of petrol. I'm just going to see what Corps is up to. I'll be back in an hour!' No one doubted Uncle for an instant. 'Where shall we meet?' asked Gillie.

'The old brigade bombing ground, at White Farm!'

After setting light to all that was inflammable, Skene got to the bridge in time to join in the cheers for the ambulances going through to try and reach the wounded from the battalion dressing station. Walking wounded, guns, and stragglers were coming the other way; Gillie was turning the latter back with a shovel.

Skene gazed. A New Army man, he had never seen anything like it. Regulars of Mons, and early Canadians of the second battle of Ypres, had seen it before; but not Skene; not the New Armies. Presently, whole units began coming over, Brigade Signals with their instruments, trench mortars, a whole platoon of Infantry, then the ambulances, all but one having failed.

The shelling was replaced by machine-gun fire, nearer and always nearer.

About half a mile to the north of the bridge was the old 'White Farm', where, after Skene had come to the sector, old Josef Deporter had gone on planting beet and pulling flax in fields ever more and more pitted with shell-holes and the curious flat saucer-like mark of the shrapnel bomb. The brigade then holding the line coveted his home pasture for a Bombing School. There, authorized by an enthusiastic Staff, some R.E.s had constructed trenches and a model pill-box, to show young soldiers the use of the smoke bomb. Old Deporter had gone to Skene, who offered compensation, then to the French Mission, who referred him back to Skene, finally to his Deputy in the Chamber. That worthy, hoping to be in the next Government, had made a violent attack on the present Government, whose parrying inquiries, percolating from Whitehall through Montreuil to Skene's corps, had caused the abandonment of the Bombing School just as the Bosche long-range fire made farm and pasture alike untenable.

Just as the grey morning pierced the drizzle (the weather had broken the very hour it ceased to be of use to the Bosche) Skene found Uncle getting out of the Ford car at the bombing ground, and Gillie placing the men and siting the Lewis guns. 'Beaten old Deporter, anyhow!' said Skene, and Uncle grunted.

'I've been up to Corps. They're gone!'

Skene whistled. Corps gone! It was like saying that King's Cross Station had run away.

'That means railhead and I dunno what!'

'Look!' Gillie pointed back over their right shoulders. The glare of burning dumps was dying in the lighter sky and becoming clouds of dim smoke. The inevitable Jerry, who had carried a 'Queen' stove on his back, now produced tins of hot tea. It was nectar. The humour of it touched Skene.

'This isn't the first time *you've* run away, is it, Jerry?'

'No, sir,' and then, in the same matter-of-fact voice: 'Did you wish to sleep in the pill-box, or in the Farm?' And looking at the skeleton timbers and gaping walls of Deporter's farm, they all laughed.

Uncle stopped first. 'Your friend Colonel Castle is at the Station, at least I think it's Castle, but he's got a tin hat. He's making things shift with Italian labourers, and Zulus, and some railway people. Railhead's like a fortress. He told me to stick on as long as we could. He says the French are coming and he's tired of being shelled.' It was a sentiment that found a general echo. Exasperated by mechanical routine, carried on under long-range fire, neither Skene nor anyone else felt much discomfort or panic. Let the Bosche come, man to man, and see.

He was coming.

One of the men Gillie had left under a Corporal at 'hedgerow' some hundreds of yards nearer the bridge, which they commanded with a Lewis gun, put his head round the corner of the trench.

'They're going to blow up the bridge, sir!' A roar and rain of fragments echoed him. Gillie, standing on the parapet, swore under his breath. 'Bossed it! the girders are still standing! Look here, I'm going to watch with that Lewis gun!'

In a few minutes the gibber of the Lewis was heard. Two men crawled up the ditch, with a stretcher, carrying a third. The Corporal had a message. 'Mr Gilmour sent this Canadian, who's wounded, sir; the other's killed trying to reset his charge, and 'ave you any ammunition?'

They put the collapsed Demolitions officer away in the box car, and sent three boxes of S.A.A. by hand down to Gillie. They were not short of it, thanks to the dumps about. Let the Bosche cross the bridge on the girders if he could!

Uncle had set everyone to work, roofing in here, digging out there, dividing the time into watches, until the dummy trenches, the model pill-box, and the ruins of the farm were 'not too bad to die in!' as he put it, wiping his eyes that the gas had made to water.

The day wore on, with some gas-shelling. Gillie and his gun seemed to be keeping the bridge, and the Bosche, not as yet too sure of what he was up against, had still to gather himself for his second stroke. An aeroplane, dipping like a swallow, was machine-gunning the opposite bank of the river.

Once Skene turned to Uncle:

'What do you reckon we've lost?'

'Ten miles of line and most of the Infantry of two divisions.'

'Bad as that?'

'Well, there was a brigade in the town and one each side. What have we seen come back?'

'The worst isn't opposite us!'

The April dusk drew down in grey showers; Skene walked up the road and found an N.C.O. and some men standing in front of Deporter's gate under the notice 'Private! Entry Forbidden!' They were the billeting part of a labour battalion, sent forward by some order never countermanded, and then hurriedly armed and told to do their best. Presently an officer and nearly two hundred men turned up, mostly grey headed. They confirmed Skene's worst fears. His men and they were the only troops between the advancing Bosche and the half-fortified railhead.

The night that followed was the queerest Skene had ever spent. On all sides, rumours, a sense of thousands in motion;

darkness and silence where was usually lights and traffic; lights and the rumble of machine-gunning or shelling, where darkness and silence should be. During his turn of duty, he walked round and round their little fortress with Jerry. Gillie had gone to the next farm, where the labour battalion were digging in, back across the road to Deporter's and the pill-box where the spare Lewis was. There came to him bursts of English song:

> 'I want to go home,
> No more I want to roam,
> Oh my, I don't want to die,
> I want to go home!'

from cheery souls eating and drinking round smothering braziers; then the certainty that the firing was dead behind him.

Uncle took his turn, but awoke Skene at dawn. 'Who's that on the road?'

'Skene took Jerry and crept along the hedge, a 'Mills' in each hand, shaking the sleep out of him and trying to subdue his breathing. The approaching figures were a great Australian and a small bandy-legged Jock, smoking and snuffing the air. As Skene came out on the road, the Scot gave him 'Good morning, sir!' and the Aussi: 'Hallo, digger, seen any Fritzes?'

'I thought I heard him your way!'

'There were some, but we settled 'em. Show the gentleman your watch, Jock!'

The little Scot produced a beautiful chronometer from his shirt: 'We'd sell it for a drink. 'Tis an officer's.'

'Are there any more of you?'

'Bags of us coming, and the French. Well, we'll be getting on. We'd like some more watches!'

Skene looked down the road and saw another couple, Jock and Aussi. Back at Uncle's trench he found Gillie shaking hands.

'Good-bye, old lads. This is good enough for me, I'm going on with this crowd!'

So passed Gille from their ken, with that motley band, chasing Ludendorff's deadly 'tactics of permeation'.

The next visitors were French Cavalry, on foot, with musketons and machine-guns.

'Two nights one day we came from Soissons!' the officer told Skene. 'We kill all our 'orses!'

Uncle and Skene and the Labour officer gathered their men and marched them to railhead. At the railhead were orders from Corps. They could 'pull out'.

They did. From railhead, a whole countryside plus an army was retreating.

In the fine spring rain, they trudged up the pavé, between heavy guns, farm carts, cows and ambulances, going the same way, and an opposite stream of English lorries full of sardonic French gunners, with their seventy-fives rattling behind. Skene was busy counting his men, looking out for the lame, scrounging a lift for this one or that, seeing that a collapsed civilian cart was cleared out of the road, helping to unload a ditched lorry. Now that he was again out of actual touch with the Bosche, his forebodings returned upon him and he worked with a heavy heart.

Not so the private soldier. With little or no grasp of the realities of the business, content to be in motion, going somewhere to do something, he inevitably sang. A limping, slouching crowd, nearly all freshly wounded, or lame with old wounds, marching or carried in vehicles, bearing or surrounded by God knows what collection of impedimenta, and all singing:

> 'Mademoiselle of Armentières
> She hasn't been worried for forty years.'

While the women and the old men who led the cows and drove the carts joined in the chorus: 'Vinky, Blinky, parley-vous!'

Apocalyptic, biblical, the crowd moved on. Behind it, a pillar of smoke by day, of flame by night rose from the burning dumps.

*Chapter 23*
# Colonel Werner's Revelations

All very well for Corps to say 'Pull out,' meaning 'Come out of the zone taken up by the French, where we lost half our Infantry and a third of our guns, and come back here, where we are, and reorganize!' All very well. Corps had twenty-four hours start. Skene and Uncle brought along their details – all unfit men – at the best pace they could.

Passing beyond railhead they met increasing streams of French men and guns, taking up the new line. They found some deserted horselines for billets, but were roused by shelling all round them, and tumbled out in the dark, to find the French coming back. The thin film of a labour battalion here, a Scotch machine-gun company there, and an Australian tunnelling company anywhere, had not sufficed to stem the Bosche, who had now moved up his guns and was coming on again. Mixed up with the debris of the Corps and the civilian refugees of fourteen communes, it took them three days' marching to get clear.

In the very long run, of course, the Bosche was stopped. Uncle had always known the reason, since that April day in 1915 when the handful of the original Canadians had outlived even the surprise of gas. The reason was simple: give him the finest chances in the world, the individual Bosche could not or would not fight. April petered out in shelling and reorganization. May came, but British and French were now reorganized and the gaps closed. The Bosche tried other sectors, in the French line – got a little way and stuck.

The corps to which Skene belonged took up a part of the new line, that ran through the old railhead. It seemed a queer topsy-turvy world to Skene, working his advanced area where the aerodrome and the rest billets used to be. Uncle had found a billet in the Estaminet de la Couronne, in the village of Bertezeele, on the edge of the Flemish-speaking plateau. Here they pursued their old habits as far as possible, taught the French units to play football, and in return learned a good deal about field cookery such as the British Army had never dreamed of.

One of those American divisions incredible to Ludendorff, and incredibly cheering to the tired French and English troops to whose support they came, appeared in the corps area, in size and spirit a complete surprise to minds stunned by nearly four years of continuous battle. Nearly fifty per cent stronger in numbers than either the French or English divisions, and composed exclusively of young men between twenty and thirty, selected for physical fitness from millions mobilized, they overflowed the old camping grounds, horselines, depots, manoeuvre areas and battlefields. Their officers, well-read, short-haired, spectacled young men of earnest and inquiring minds, less hampered than the English by regular army associations, and without the conscriptive tradition of the French, let loose a torrent of inquiry, experiment, and endeavour. The few experienced officers spared to them by the older armies for instruction and guidance were soon swept completely off their feet, and Skene, like many another of those semi-fit, odd-job-detachment officers, was impressed to give such instruction as might be possible in the few days before the new division went up into the Line.

He was accosted one morning by a tall, spare officer with tanned cheeks and grizzled hair – a Colonel Werner, U.S. Infantry, attached for instruction.

To have a Colonel attached to him, arriving before the order under which he moved, without servant or groom, off-saddling himself and putting up his own horse, did not surprise Skene at all – he had been too long in France. Moreover, he was genuinely thankful to see the Americans and curious to make their acquaintance.

Colonel Werner neither spat, nor touched strong drink, nor began his sentences with the 'See here, Stranger,' of the comic papers. He resembled nearly in face, voice, and manner that miniature of Skene's maternal great-grandfather, Quaker, banker, brewer, and Mayor of Overwater during the Peninsular

War, touched, say, by the influence of ten years' residence in the larger colonies.

The tight, stock-like collar of the American tunic, the clean-shaven lips and chin, faint suggestion of whisker, old-maidish precision in thought and speech, scrupulous care taken of a pair of long, fine hands unblistered by manual labour – such exterior details contributed to the illusion. But there was more than this – a clean freshness of the mind, great patience, respect for material means and for decisive action.

They soon became fast friends.

At this period of the War stale weariness had brought almost complete uniformity to the Sunday afternoon procedure of units not actually in the front line. Skene did nothing on Sunday morning that was not strictly necessary, lunched rather better than usual, then sat in a wicker chair that a thoughtful orderly had plundered from surrounding desolation, and took his ease, till the 'stand-to' at dusk and the increasing traffic again brought duties that could not be neglected.

Colonel Werner was an agreeable addition to these occasions. Seated in a corner of that Flemish meadow over which guns from Essen and Skoda were raging and ramping against guns from the Tyne or St Etienne, smoking an endless succession of long butt-ended cigars – his only indulgence, his one claim to be the real American of cinema and comic story – he would talk of his country, township, estate, home, wife and children, business and place of worship. In the long weeks of summer-lit suspense before Mangin's flank attack of July ushered in the final phase, he brought before Skene's imagination an ample wooden house in rolling wooded hills, where big, healthy, plain-minded people did, more than any other human beings perhaps since the world began, just what seemed good to them.

Once the Colonel was talking of the natives, their endurance, their passionate love of the soil – above all of the heroism of the women.

'There's a farm,' he said, 'in J34. I went there while I was attached to that — Corps' (he pointed northward, beyond the French), 'to see about the burial of fourteen of our men, killed by a long-range shot right in the yard — I expect you know the place — an ancient building — our Quartermaster, who's a professor of history, says it was built by Dagos.'

For half a minute Skene tried to persuade himself that he did not know, but the blood rushing to his temples gave him the lie — he held tight to the left arm of his chair and pulled at his pipe. The American went on:

'There's a girl there that has a history, I should say, but you can hardly ask her what it is, and it beats imagining. She lives there — it's so near the Line — she billets in her own home, so to speak — and borrows artillery horses, to pull her old buggy to market. Yes, I assure you, she drives from her home in a gun emplacement, in a buggy that Noah must have driven out of the Ark.'

Skene puffed his pipe; he could see every crease in the varnished leather cover of the so-called 'Buggy'.

'She wanted our fellows buried in the small patch next the road, and not in her home paddock where the Quartermaster had begun to dig. She wasn't getting on too well with our "Quarters" on account of having said that there were graves enough in France without having to walk over them every time she went to milk the cows. Quarters didn't take it very kindly, and neither did I, at first, until I had been talking to her for some minutes, and then her face kind of got me. I knew her trouble, through the difficulty we had in finding out how to make up the billeting return. It seems they were well-to-do until the Bosche broke through. She had lost her father, too, under unusual circumstances. It seems she had a married sister down Laventie way, carrying on a farm, as they all do, the man being mobilized, and the children going to school in gas-masks. Then the Bosche came round each side — you know.'

Skene did know. He could see the stream of wounded and stragglers getting over the bridge between the shells.

'When the news got up here — news travels among these people as if they were Indians — the old man apparently thought he must go and see to the married daughter. Partly affection, partly they'd got — I don't know how much land under potatoes — potatoes for manufacture, not to eat. Anyhow, the girl says,

## COLONEL WERNER'S REVELATIONS

he harnessed the old hoss with his three-cornered tumbril – you know, the sort with an iron rudder on the front wheel, and off he went, plumb into the battle! Can you imagine it!'

Skene nodded. Perfectly plain to him! The old, big-limbed, bent figure, going snail's pace beside the old horse in the tumbril, down roads at first empty, then full of refugees and wounded, then empty again, past burning farms and dumps, over shelled crossings of road, river or railway – down into the rattle of machine-gun fire and the stench of gas.

'So she lost her father!' Colonel Werner went on. 'Think she was beat? Not she! The farm was too far forward for much work to be done. A line of reserve trenches was dug through it, and marked the zone from which civilians were evacuated. The labourers were all gone, and the place in such a state one would have thought she couldn't live there. But could she be kept away? Not for a day! Every morning at "stand-to" we heard her out and about, issuing orders to the men – telling them "Don't!" like a pack of children. We arrested her twice, but what could you do? The French Mission wouldn't prosecute, the civil power had moved to Évreux, in Normandy, the A.P.M. said it wasn't in his jurisdiction. Every evening, she shut the place up, like a shop. We got accustomed to her, the men used to do odd jobs for her – they got to washing down the buggy – repairing the shrapnel holes it got, harnessing up for her on market days. She spoke good English and ruled that billet with a rod of iron. No outstanding claims for damage there! Then she got to cooking for the men. They got to saluting her. In my country we have one tradition of which we are proud!' ('Only one!' thought Skene, who, though he admired the Colonel's manners, had noticed how right America always was.) 'It's that of the civil war. That girl reminded me of tales my father used to tell of some of our women, in the old days. She might almost have passed for an American girl, I tell you. However pale and tired she grew, however the weather or the shelling might be, there she was, well-dressed and quiet, and mistress of the situation! Not from any high principle, but simply, as she said, because she had lost enough, and couldn't afford to lose any more. Yes, sir, the women are fine I reckon!'

*Chapter 24*

# Victory

In the middle of July the Bosche made what history now knows to be his last effort – the drive at Soissons. The French who lay next Skene's corps were summoned south. Uncle and Skene paid little attention. Besides being now permanently sceptic regarding all offensives, they knew that, submarines or not, the Americans were in France, some hundreds of thousands of them. English statesmen talked of 'fighting on three, or five years if necessary!' Such sentiments, uttered in London, passed over the heads of those who had lived for years east of Amiens and St Omer. Besides, for a long while everyone had been hearing rumours that Foch, now Commander-in-Chief, had many divisions in reserve. In their journeys backwards and forwards, Skene and Uncle both found that as a fact there were, not only American, but English and French divisions, far back, being 'saved up' for something, and their stoicism took again the rosy tinge that seldom deserted it for long.

To arrange for billeting the English troops that came to relieve the French, Skene had to go as far as St Firmin to see a French Head-quarters about detail. He found the dry, hard old French regulars, in their little temporary office, unusually elated, moving little flags on a big-scale war map, and *Moving Them Forward*. He was shown a communiqué. It told of what is now called Mangin's flank attack.

'Better news this morning?'

'I believe you, the news is better – and it is about time.'

'What does it mean?' asked Skene – 'the turn of our luck?'

'It shows we have still some strength!' was all the dry answer. 'Now, about these special units of the British Army for which you require space in our our area . . .'

Presently, his business done, Skene went across to the Coq

## VICTORY

d'Or Restaurant. The place was full of Frenchmen, dismounted cavalrymen turned into machine-gunners, but still the aristocrats of their army, with money in their pockets, doing themselves well, ransacking that little market-town inn, used to quiet English subalterns who would take what was put before them, not having sufficient command of the language to ask for anything better. Skene saw the red piping on their service-blue uniform, and remembered that they must be Cuirassiers, and that he had once asked news of one of that lot.

By this time the best wine of local hostelries was labelled 'Pontet Canet'; in earlier days it had been 'La Rose'. Skene ordered some, and invited the cooperation of a nice young Frenchman. If a celebration was forward, why not an allied celebration? The nearest young Frenchman was not unwilling. Like Skene, he had been too long in the War to refuse a possible drink.

Skene ordered a second bottle, and as the crimson liquid shrank behind the label asked casually:

'You didn't have a D'Archeville in your lot?'

'I believe you, we had D'Archeville. He was, like myself, a Cuirassier, and went to the Flying Corps. He was a type!'

Skene knew that this meant, not that D'Archeville was typical, but that he was 'some lad'.

'Was? He's gone, then?'

'Died in Champagne in 1917 — as I should have been, if I hadn't had a leg all in marmalade.'

'That's a pity; I had good wishes to give him, from an acquaintance.'

'You must give them now at the cemetery, at Avenant-le-Petit. He was a type, I tell you, Georges — cared for nothing but sport — I knew him well ... I had made sport with him, on his father's land, up in the north there, where one is nearly in Belgium ... The War breaks out ... A changed Georges ... everything in life left behind him. Nothing for Georges but Glory, Patriotism, and the regulation tobacco allowance!'[1] Skene filled up the young man's glass and nodded.

'Well! He was not a philosopher, as I am. One can't smoke

359

glory in one's pipe. Georges is full of devotion, repents his past life, and carries on. But he forgot one thing. Among his *amies* was the daughter of the gamekeeper of his sport in those parts – an old Fleming living in a farm of his father's. They have that system there. Giving up the various things Georges gave up, meant giving up that woman. Ah! but one is never finished with women!'

Before Skene's eyes there seemed to rise the dirty little railway station of his first railhead, and a figure with face turned towards the *décrets* and *arrêtés* that papered the walls – and a voice begging him to telephone to an English hospital, about a Frenchman.

'There was Verdun. You know where we were, in shell-holes out of whose sides ran little dribbles of blood.

'Both Georges and I were invalided, I with my leg, he with his lungs. I did not see him again until the following February. He and I were down at the great camp at Mailly, beginning the rehearsals of that *sacré* offensive of May 1917. We both took influenza, and they sent us to the hospital that used to be at the Hôtel Vitzman, Avenue Kruger, Paris!

'That woman found Georges. I used to see her when I visited him during his convalescence. She was not like the girl one used to see at Vanderlynden's farm, when one went shooting. She was still not quite Parisienne, but well-arranged. She had lived and learned. He took an apartment for her. But then he went back, of course. He was wounded at Chemin des Dames, and took consumption. He died. Poor Georges! He was a type!' The young man rose to go, with an elaborate English 'So long, chum!'


So he had found Madeleine's 'fiancé' at last, with the fatal appropriateness of war-time.

Jolting home in the box car Skene felt as if every word of the young Frenchman had stroked the hardened scars of an old wound.

Once back at his post, however, he had little time for

reflection – at last the old Bosche line, which Skene had first seen three years before, gave way before the attacks of English, French, Belgians and Americans. From below Lille up to Nieuport on the sea, it suddenly melted away. The frontier that had split the world in half just ceased to be, one fine morning.

Uncle was amazed. A real victory, won in battle! He gave it up. But to Skene there came an afterglow from his early enthusiasm. Of all those laughing boys who, in the great training camps of the New Army in 1915, had sung with such zest 'The only step the Kaiser's got to learn is the quick-step back to Germany', how few, how very few, were seeing the fruit of all those years of effort and unceasing bloodshed! And he was one.

His job had almost ceased. The battle suddenly lengthened out into a pursuit in which English patrols had all they could do to find the retreating enemy. Corps itself was preparing to move. Skene and other minor details received their orders. On a bright October morning, he stopped the Ford in which he and Uncle were travelling, within sight of the morass in which young Murdon had been killed.

'There,' he pointed to Uncle, 'that's where I was, three years ago, this blessed day.'

The Line had shifted at most a few yards since Skene's time. But the whole place had a look of decay. The continuous trenches, gradually abandoned, had fallen in or been blown flat. The last traces of trees had disappeared. Old landmarks, such as the remains of a cottage, or a length of paved road, had been dispersed. The coarse foliage – dock and ground-ivy and grass mixed with wild corn – stank of gas, and concealed grenades and pieces of shell. At every turn Skene noted with envy the concrete pill-boxes that would have saved so many lives, and the light, concealed, trench tramway that would have spared so many weary hours of fasting vigil. Standing just inside the old Bosche line, he could see how exposed was the angle of the British communication trench from his old dump to his old Head-quarters dug-out – 'How many times,' he thought, 'have I come round that corner! They must have seen my head and had a pot at it. I remember the splintered "A" frames of the re-

vetment; we couldn't think where they were enfilading from!'
He had a sensation of not being really there – of being dead with Murdon and Corporal Ames and the rest, of having returned from death to visit the place.

Uncle was poring over his 5A map of Belgium.

'Wasn't there a conservatory at the corner of the wood and a bit of kitchen garden?'

'Gone before my time – practically front line!'

'Well, that's where *we* were – first Canadian division, July 1915. Our horses used to go in the stables – here – and the château and the heavy gunners' mess was in the cellar!' Another war that Skene had never known, the war of the first few months – regular divisions with Colonials and Territorials attached, before trenches and the New Army. 'But the stables,' Uncle went on, 'were stone and very solid!'

They walked on. Nothing but spongy mud, coarse grass, scrap iron, stench!

Was this what they had fought for, this draggled scrap-heap; bereft now even of the comradeship that had once made it bearable – robbed now even of its importance as the frontier where Justice and Fairplay stood at issue with Oppression and Greed? This was what he had won through to – these dregs!

Uncle wiped his mouth and fastened the stopper of the flask.

'You ain't going t' buy the site, are y', Skene?'

Skene got back into the box car and dropped into a discussion as to whether there was not, in fact, money in the idea of buying and reclaiming the front line in Flanders.

\*

The Umpteenth Corps did not share the Allied entry into Lille. Instead they had an entry of their own into a Flemish manufacturing town, with a core of old market-place, cathedral and town hall, and an old bridge with dropsical flanking towers, surrounded by a rind of new red-brick suburbs. For a moment the old enthusiasm flared up. Flemish mechanics and shopkeepers and womenfolk, who had heard but never seen the English soldiers fighting for them all these four years, suddenly saw in their own streets khaki and tin helmets, and a young officer of the Intelligence collecting municipal officials. Sober twentieth-century people, from offices and shops, wearing the shawls of mill-hands, the bowlers and black coats of a laborious life, danced, shouted, wept and wrung the hands of officers and men. Ladies with every appearance of invincible propriety kissed perspiring R.E.s putting up the bridges the Bosche had destroyed, and dragged out materials for their work from unsuspected hiding-places.

Skene, borrowed by Intelligence to help straighten things out, sat in the magnificent 'Salle des Chevaliers' of the Town Hall, interrogating and docketing batches of Bosche prisoners. When he came out he was set on by troops of children who clung all over him, demanding to be kissed, and would soon have left him buttonless in their thirst for souvenirs. Struggling to his billet in the front room of a miner's cottage, he sat with Uncle over a bottle of whisky, waiting for news of the Armistice terms that had been sent to the Bosche. It was the evening of November the tenth.

The field telephone stood on the treadle sewing machine in the window. Corps Signals had been duly bribed.

The man of the house came in from work, and passed by them, with doffed cap, to the back kitchen where his family were collected round the stove.

'Have ye explained to him about the billeting?' said Uncle, doctrinaire in his cups.

Skene called the man back. The Frenchman protested. It was payment enough to have English in the house: but his wife struck in. It was too good, no doubt, but acceptable. 'Give 'im a drink!' said Uncle.

Man, wife, old aunt, and little daughter Simone all came, and from liqueur glasses drank 'to our deliverers' with tears and smiles, partly joy, partly unaccustomed whisky.

In the pitiful bare respectability of the little room, a cheap clock ticked, Uncle snored; Skene sat with his hand on the field telephone.

Before his tired eyes came faces from the great training

camps, peopled by happy boys, now dust and decay in any corner from Dunkirk to Baghdad – visions of fine light-hearted mornings, or wet benumbing twilight in Bailleul and Villers Brettonneux, of which no stone now rested on another – visions of the waste of No-Man's-Land, in the dreary machine-gun punctuated dawn, of Christmas dinners in the Officers' Restaurant at Amiens, when a hundred and fifty officers from all corners of the world with hands crossed sang 'Auld Lang Syne' – visions of all that great cataclysm which had turned the ease-loving, sport-following manhood of England into the New Armies – turned the New Armies into Armed and Fighting England stretching through France and Italy, half across Asia and the oceans of the world – the cataclysm which had caught him, Skene, like a straw, whirled him out of the quiet certainty of his office life in the Close of an English cathedral town – bumped him against this and that until he had become a person unrecognizable to himself, with all the landmarks of his existence changed; caught him too against Madeleine and wrenched the heart out of him.

The telephone bell buzzed. He took up the receiver.

'Umpteenth Corps Clearance Officer!'

'Speaking! Who are you?'

'Corps Signals. Is that Mr Skene?'

'Speaking!'

'We've just intercepted Bosche wireless, sir. They are going to sign in the morning!'

'Thanks! Good night!'

Reaching over the little table, he shook Uncle. The old man opened his eyes, owl-like, and sat up.

'They're going to sign!'

'Who? – what? – oh! the Bosche!'

The old man looked at Skene and then away.

'Well, that's the end of it then!' he said.

'That's the end of it!' repeated Skene.

And suddenly he could not look at Uncle. He could only struggle with an emotion not admissible in an officer. The end of it! This little mean room, in a Flemish slum! The laconic printed 'Order' that would appear on the morrow. Victory!

# VICTORY

Rounds! He went outside into the chill and darkness of that November night. At the small factory where his men were billeted, he found his sentry; in the little pay-office, his superior New Army Corporal, reading a paper-covered novel over a brazier; – beyond, in the low sheds where his men were sleeping, his mules tied up and his carts stacked, all was in darkness and silence. 'Celebrations!' he thought. Emerging again into the little paved street, he met what to him was typical of war as he had waged it. In the lampless glimmer of the night, a string of square boxes on wheels, known as limbers, was being drawn with a springless rattle over the pavé, by weary mules, beside whom were men just sufficiently awake to guide them. At the head a muffled figure, for all the world like the leader of some North Pole Expedition, was plodding beside a somnambulistic horse.

Abreast of Skene he muttered:

'This'll get me to Werlies, I s'pose! Is it true they've chucked it?'

Skene nodded. 'I believe the Bosche are going to sign the Armistice terms in the morning!'

'Good job. We should have chucked it, if they hadn't!'

And he stumped on.

Skene pulled off his boots and got into his blankets. 'Too long,' he thought. 'Who cares now?'

He had forgotten that this was Victory.

## Chapter 25
# Glory

Then over Skene, as over many of his kind, within a week or two of the armistice, a great black cloud seemed to shut down. Try as he would, he could not shake it off. It had gradually dawned on him, that he had come to regard war as the normal condition of things, that it had become a habit.

His extraordinary luck, that had never allowed him to sink below a certain level, stuck to him to the very end; though he knew, no more than any of us, what luck is! Is it a perfectly equable shifting of pieces on a chessboard by a player with superhuman knowledge of each piece and a definite ordered plan? Does the player know and care, or does he merely upset the board in a drunken sleep – or can the pieces, by a sort of latent facility of their own, take some part in the game? Anyway his luck held. Skene's Corps was not one of those that moved up to the Rhine; certain units and individuals went, but the bulk remained, a skeleton of its former self, just where it had left off fighting, among mining villages on the edge of a wooded plain. The people, though hard up for all the small comforts of life and daunted by years of a foreign occupation, tried to be hospitable.

When the demobilization scheme was made public, his one thought was to get out of it, away from it all, at once – from this War into which he had thrown himself with such enthusiasm, which had used him, to the point almost of extinction, and which now suddenly had ceased – and left him high and dry. Lying in a too-short bed in the ground-floor bedroom of a workman's cottage, he read Murray's version of the Hippolytus. Ah! but some who loved the gods didn't die young, and – wished they had! That was his mood, waiting for demobilization.

Uncle, of course, had no difficulty in placing himself in half a dozen different categories for instant demobilization. Skene filled up the same papers. Why not? Thomas's death had removed the last person who was more than a mere mess acquaintance. Jerry, his servant, with an old soldier's instinct, had gone sick and got himself demobbed. Burnside had taken a Commission, as Education Officer, to the Corps.

\*

A train more incredibly slow-moving even than the average military train, passed across battlefields already green round their evil-smelling pools.

It was a grey damp winter, whose frosts had begun early; and anything more desolate than that wilderness of coarse weed slowly obliterating shell-hole and trench, was inconceivable. Nothing moved over those hummocks of tortured soil that had swarmed with agony and effort, but the rat and the crow. Rounding the corner of a skeleton wood, Skene looked out of the window on a place he knew too well.

In the first battle of the early days a Midland Yeomanry regiment, flung desperately into the fight, had held the advancing Bosche, at the price of two-thirds of its men. 'Market Harbro' they had called it, and the name had stuck. It was still just recognizable. And today, it was alive. A Chinese labour company had been sent to remove explosives from the spot. The curious Celestials, moving inimitably about what had been an outpost of England – one of those stubbornly held mounds that had prevented London perhaps from having a German governor like Brussels – amused Skene. It reminded him of a Bible illustration by Doré, where the less-exemplary characters were working out destiny in terms of manual labour. In the midst of those flat-faced, shuffling, guttural Celestials, stood a figure different as West from East.

There was something familiar in the prominent nose and jaw, the square shoulders, humped in the British-warm, the sturdy, almost bandy legs in good breeches and boots, the hands thrust out of sight, the bridle of the horse trailing from one arm. Earnshaw, by George!

The train was in a doze characteristic of military trains after the armistice. The driver and one of those R.E. corporals who used to spring out of the soil, like a natural growth, were smoking and chatting together over the alleged subsidence of a piece of the line.

There seemed no hurry; Skene dropped from the carriage. It astonished him to find what affection he had for that bullet-headed, square-shouldered body. Earnshaw was not effusive, but he kept smiling and his eyes were very blue. 'Come over to my dug-out, and have a drink!'

He called a 'Chink' to hold his horse, but as they moved off over the morass Uncle could be heard shouting from the train: 'She's off!'

'It's no odds,' muttered Earnshaw, 'she's through every day – come and stay the night and bring your friend!'

So they turned and both began to shout across that waste: 'Get down and come and have a drink!'

Heads popped out, English, Scotch, Welsh, Colonial, French heads, amused, interested, uncomprehending. A private who had been giving a ventriloquial entertainment, held up his improvised dummy at the carriage window and made it say, 'Go to hell! Give my love to Kitchener, when you get there, and ask when the three years will be up!'

The train was on the move. With a final shout: 'See you in Dunkirk!' Skene turned away with Earnshaw.

Near by they lighted on one of those quiet polyglot men who used to officer the Chinese Labour Contingents in France – a Missionary by calling. The kindly spectacled face in that forlorn place seemed to Skene one of the most cheerful yet lost things he had ever seen. Farther on were German prisoners at work and the transport section which was Earnshaw's special care.

Standing on the shell-pocked ridge, covered with French grenades and German long-barbed wire, above the neat huts where Earnshaw's formation was encamped, Skene stopped and pointed.

'There – hospital farm – where that machine-gun emplacement is – there the Ypres road – and you're in the white château!'

Earnshaw nodded. Three years the War had surged backwards and forwards within a few thousand yards of the road from Ypres to Béthune, which had lined the original front of the B.E.F. in October 1914. Nearly every officer in the earlier divisions had at one time or another been billeted in that white château which, because it was owned by an Austrian, some said, was never shelled. Its very boundaries were gone, as a footmark fades on wet sand. Skene and Earnshaw went into the big mess hut. This was the Head-quarters of a formation composed more of Chinese and Bosches than of English. At lunch and dinner, a field-grey Fritz stood statue-like behind his chair and doubled to execute an order. In Skene's bunk were electric light and an electric bell – on the floor, walls, windows, and from one door to another were wonderful mats, woven of twigs, of wire, of anything, by squatting 'Chinks'.

In the dusk that drew down after tea, they played badminton, and after dinner, sat, pipe in mouth, drink at elbow, not referring to their common past, while officers from the ends of the earth, and officers who had spent the whole War at training camps in England, officers from Straits Settlements, or Glasgow, put records on the gramophone, played bridge, and told yarns. Skene realized how much of the War he had missed. Italy, Salonika, Dardanelles, Palestine, 'Mespot', China, Samoa, the naval shows.

It was Earnshaw who said:

'What about that girl at the farm!'

Skene swallowed with an effort.

'What about her?'

'We've got to ride to the station – we could call there on the way!'

'My dear fellow!' began Skene.

'May as well. We've got to pass the door.'

Skene put the matter out of his mind. A thin bent officer, lecturer at some Colonial University, was describing the experiences of Plumer's army sent to Italy to help the Italians in the dark hour of Caporetto. He described the arrival of the English and Scotch regiments among the Italian villages full of old men in cloaks and leg-wrappings, like Shakespearian or biblical characters, full of magnificent women, and sprawling statuesque children – and how they were all jumbled up with cockney or north-country Tommies, khaki-clad, hatchet-faced, jocular – he described the Italian dignity and shiftlessness and dramatic bombast, cheek-by-jowl with that indomitable sporting desire to 'larn' the Austrians even as the Germans had been 'larned'. And then Earnshaw spoke the words that were afterwards to be most often in Skene's ears. He had bought some land in Nairobi. Skene did not know where it was. 'It's where you're still let alone,' said Earnshaw.

At eleven next morning Skene was riding, as he had ridden more than three years before, with the same companion, towards that gravelly ridge, to north of which lay the railhead town whence he had first detrained, on coming out to France. The battle of 1918 had washed right up to the south of the ridge. The trees were gone, the land still covered with the rank waste to which the crops had run. They crossed a road. On a new English signboard were the names Calais and Courtrai. Earnshaw stopped and turned to the left. Skene recognized the familiar road and looked for the old red-brick tower above the thatched roof. There were buildings, but the shape was strange. Something jibbed in Skene's heart. Did he want to go, or not? Was he curious – angry – what? After all, it was he who had broken off the connection – for what? For a matter of taste!

Earnshaw was saying: 'Come on, they'll give us a drink!'

Perhaps she wasn't there.

A 'five-nine' must have hit the top of the old shot tower, and the delicate fuse, bursting the charge at once, had only flung down some cubic feet of the solid old brickwork. A smaller field-howitzer shell had dropped vertically through the great ridge of the thatched roof. The wallflowers were dead, and the dirt and neglect that trailed wherever battle had been, hung as the smuts hang after snow. But most of all Skene missed the rough bark of the old half-blind watchdog, who used to drag his chain like a lost spirit, at fall of foot or hoof.

They tied their horses by the bridge, and walked over the dinted cobbles, among neat stacks of wire and pickets, harvest of many trenches, towards the shutterless kitchen windows blocked with army canvas. Something like an uneasy ghost in dark clothes shuffled along the cobbles by the wall. Yes, yes – old Vanderlynden! 'Good morning, patron, how goes it?' But the old bowed figure only shuffled on, and passed out of sight round the corner of the house.

'The old boy seems to have forgotten us,' said Earnshaw.

'You know what happened to him!'

'Walked straight into the Bosche, going to rescue his married daughter's goods, but he must have got back weeks ago!'

He was evidently not moved by what, to Skene, was one of the most pathetic stories of the War.

'Good morning, Mam'selle.'

Skene looked up. There stood Madeleine, framed in the dark doorway . . .

The pallor he had found so charming was gone. She was browned and reddened by hard work. The great bunch of dark hair was more closely and simply done – her nondescript blouse rolled to the elbows, her dark skirt looped up. Her boots, alone, on the cobbles, had that sort of solid elegance he had first noticed, distinguishing her from her kind, the unaesthetic elegance of one who always chose the best, because it gave her more for the money! Earnshaw spoke again.

'Good morning, Mam'selle, how's the patron!'

'As he always is, now, since the Bosche took him prisoner!'

'You remember my friend?'

'Certainly I remember!' She did not even turn her head. 'Enter then, and have some coffee. We have no wine, your troops stole it all!'

In the half-dismantled, war-worn kitchen, Skene surveyed her filling the cups. She still moved with the grace of limbs toughened and stretched with hard work, and of healthy nerves working like well-oiled machinery.

Her voice was harder, her expression more severe – trouble, no doubt, and the responsibility of the farm! When she had finished an argument with Earnshaw on the price of eggs, she turned to Skene as though divining his thoughts.

'You know, I lost my fiancé after all!'

Skene replied:

'I am sorry!' She leaned on the table, musing.

'What a horror of a war, all the same!'

'Well, it's finished now!'

That seemed to excite her. She raised her voice: 'Yes – it was time. There's my brother Marcel dead now, the other was killed at the beginning. My father going about like a lost dog. Out of fifty hectares, ten or more are flooded – on the remainder there are tons of wire and filth. No labour, no tools or horses – what the Bosche didn't destroy, the Allies stole . . .'

Skene gazed. Was any other motive behind that unaccustomed vehemence? The final loss of D'Archeville – irritation against Skene himself? Such vindictiveness in one so self-contained, so ready to forget her troubles in any passing entertainment! . . .

' – and we can get no labour, and now every one is going away, to leave us to it . . . and they have not started paying us our reparations that are due to us from the Bosche – and no one cares – '

She folded her arms and stared out of the doorway at the grey and sodden landscape.

'But we shall do it. Everything will be put right; we will see ourselves paid, to the last halfpenny!'

Earnshaw was getting fidgety under this tirade of which he understood perhaps a sixth. He got up and made a remark in English. She did not reply.

'Come on!' he said, and moved out into the yard to unhitch his horse.

Skene followed. Madeleine was standing there and staring, obstinate, intractable. Whatever she was looking for, it was for nothing from him. He was forgotten. Whatever had once made her give herself up to him, had vanished as though it had never been. And this was right! She and he alike were part of a former phase, of a time already history, and long-past history at that!

Mounting his narrow hairless veteran of a horse, he looked back; she was turning from the doorway, without word or sign. But she was to haunt him many a year – symbolic of post-war France – a woman still young, pushing aside even her attractiveness, to toil and bargain ruthlessly – a woman widowed and childless, wrestling with Fate for the uttermost sou of compensation due to her.

*Chapter 26*

# The End of a Perfect Day

They had said nothing at parting, except: 'So long, old man!' 'Good luck!' Through the glassless window of his railway carriage, Skene saw Earnshaw leading away the spare horse, solid, unreflecting, absorbed in the matter in hand. And with him real England seemed to turn its back and go on to something else.

Thus he came to Dunkirk, to that grey Flemish town, last outpost in the marshes open to the North Sea and its mists. He hadn't been in the place since he had gone buying white shifts for patrols going out in the snow of 1916. Then it had seemed civilization itself, now just a dingy obstacle to freedom.

He inquired for Uncle. It took him all the afternoon. By accident he heard that he was in that Canadian hospital on the dunes where hundreds lay, stricken by influenza, while they waited for the boat to take them home.

Of that pestilence some said one thing, some another. Skene wondered if the real cause were not the sudden slump in the vitality of men, who, strung up to war for years, and suddenly hurled into peace, stood, as it were, beside themselves, searching in vain for the men they had once been.

The doctors attributed Uncle's collapse to his having gone ten hours without whisky. He was sinking when Skene arrived and did not recognize him. Skene stood there until the hard, free, good-humoured old spirit had passed; and was told: 'We must clear up, you know, heaps more waiting! Funeral in the morning!' Skene shuddered, and passed out of the tent, and as he went a bugle rang out in that call – the first he had ever heard in France:

> 'Sixty-four – ninety-four,
> He'll never go sick no more,
> The poor beggar's dead.'

## END OF A PERFECT DAY

The great demobilization camp with its thousands of men and hundreds of officers lay at the greyest depth of the Marsh, separated by sandhills only from the sea. It had all the marks of emergency like everything else in the War. There was the atmosphere that hangs about great docks after the launch of a ship, or street decorations after a procession. Gleaming arc lights on telegraph poles shone green on the multitudes being shifted hither and thither, sorted, registered, docketed, housed, fed and prepared for the boat and freedom on the morrow. Skene found his way to an officer to whom he had provided himself with an introduction. He knew too much to get mixed up with the unfortunate mob that went through the official treadmill. His new friend, a limping infantry major, greeted him kindly and inquired about the corps. 'We'll get out of this, if you'll wait for me a moment!'

Skene waited, and they caught a tram back into the town to a noisy restaurant, full of officers celebrating night after night the morrow they had been longing for during anything up to four years; full of Frenchmen and Belgians, greeting, laughing, drinking, or in low tones, at little side tables, reckoning up the loss of properties, and landmarks, the break-up of families, and industries, and forming plans for the future.

'We're better here!' he was told. 'Our camp is rotten with flu, the fellers are going sick in shoals. Have some of this Château Yquem, it's the last of the real stuff and there'll never be any more they say!'

They returned early to the camp; and Skene philosophic with food and drink walked up and down to finish his pipe, in the muggy darkness of the Flemish winter night.

From the N.C.O.s' mess, a gramophone was roaring out a tune. It was an old worn record, one of the songs of recruiting days ground out on a powerful new machine.

> 'For we don't want to lose you,
> But we think you ought to go,
> For your King and your Country,
> They both need you so!'

'Cut it out!' came a thick voice, 'it's worn out! Any road, I'm sick of it!' The tune stopped with a jerk.

Skene moved quickly away. That music-hall tune had rung through every parish hall in England, in the great days when the New Armies were enlisting and training by the hundred thousand. What hurt was the truth of the remark. Worn out – the emotion that it recorded. He was sick of it; every one was sick of it. A new record now was spinning out its song: 'When you come to the end of a perfect day.'

Skene went to bed, for the last time in that atmosphere of disinfectant, brazier-smoke, mules and tarpaulin.

Next morning dawned with the muggy cold and wet that reaches its perfection in Dunkirk. It was the third anniversary of Skene's first attack of trench fever and a fine ripe rheumatism gripped his bones. He managed to avoid being picked for duty, and made his way down to the quay.

He left the street through which was already flowing the long dun-coloured river of English soldiers, with its good-humour, and invincible school-treat unmilitariness; and came suddenly on a commotion to which Babel must have been child's play.

A broad quay ran before one of the old Napoleonic barracks, and all about it men were swarming, in French, German, Austrian, Italian, Serbian, Russian and who knows what other uniforms, parts of uniforms, civilian suits with military cap or pair of field boots. Blue, blue-grey, slate-grey, grey-green, grass-green, ivy-green, with flat, peaked, feathered or merely shapeless headgear – one in a thing like a lady's muff – one in a bowler, sweating and stinking, talking in tongues of all races, they were eddying, forming and breaking around banners, interpreters, and gendarmes.

It was one of the great clearing houses set up by the French to collect and redistribute to their homes the masses of prisoners – allied prisoners, enemy prisoners, interned of all nations, Flemish civilians who had been haled away for who knows what forgotten and defeated purpose, to some strange place within the cordon of the German trenches – Russians from Siberia, captured in some great Galician or Caucasian drive – every type

## END OF A PERFECT DAY

of German-speaking male – from Tyrolese to Hamburger – all mixed up with men of appearance and speech indistinguishable from Skene's own – who might have come – and probably did – from London, Glasgow or New York.

Leaning on a stone coping, Skene gazed and discussed the scene with one of those disillusioned, well-educated middle-aged corporals that could exist in no army but the French, and who summed it all up thus:

'One would almost say that the Devil had mixed all these poor souls expressly for the pleasure of seeing us comb them out again! This pot-pourri of races and tongues is the remnant escaped – and has had the good luck to preserve life, without home or family, existing like beasts for years. What have they learned? Nothing, my lieutenant, give them rifles and rum, a flag to follow and a master to drive, and they would start another war tomorrow!'

Skene delighted him with a present of English cigarettes, and left him explaining the difference between a Pole and a Jugo-Slav.

The homeward-bound boat was getting up steam. Skene made his way on to the upper deck. And then she slid out of the narrow bottle-necked harbour, past the destroyers tied up to the shell-and-bomb battered quays, he turned his back on the low shore, that rose from the Belgian sandhills where the Bosche guns used to stand, towards the downs which made a shadow on the sky-line beyond Calais. He did not want to look at it just then.

Below, on the main deck, the men were singing to a well-known hymn tune the doggerel:

> 'When I get my civvy suit on,
> Oh, how happy I shall be.'

'Good-bye, B.E.F.,' muttered Skene.

England hove grey-white out of the mists to meet him – a tender parent no doubt, but occupied for the moment with other things. It hurt him afresh to see those scraps of the victorious army disembark, without a cheer, without a sign – the lucky percentage of the New Armies – the biggest, most hastily gathered body of volunteers that had ever flocked togeher.

Demobilization had already been going on some weeks – every one had seen too many of the crowds in those hurrying trains to feel enthusiasm. The War had outlasted all patience, and all interest, become a cosmic stupidity like bad weather or high rates.

Dispersal Station in England was even more breathless and hasty than Demobilization Camp in France. Hundreds poured through it daily – shed all but their bare uniform, and passed away into civil life. The great machine of five years was reversing, spilling out civilians as it turned. So, in the grey twilight of a winter afternoon, Skene in a first-class carriage made his last journey. He was 'released' – with permission to wear uniform for twenty-eight days, would be given 'Special Instructions' if he were required.

Homewards!

But in his heart was a nasty qualm, a feeling that he was not really going home, that home lay behind him, in the rough-and-ready, meagre-hearty 'mess' – even further, in some well-groomed graveyard on the Belgian frontier, where most of his friends and comrades lay.

The train paused at a wayside station. He saw in the dusk a half-finished munition works already abandoned – endless new sidings full of queer devices – very young soldiers on the platform.

The train moved on again, and he seemed to be moving too. The railway carriage faded round him into another and a wetter twilight – the twilight of a dawn in which he had been relieved in the front line by Mansfield. The cold of filthy water seemed rising round his knees. The everlasting crackle and swish of machine-gun fire was soothing to his ears. The dawn showed bleary in the sky; he would have spoken to the ghost of Mansfield, but another voice spoke in his dream: 'Medal! 'ow can they give a medal to the 'ole world – we'll just get a bit o' brass with "I was there" on it!' – the voice of his servant, Jerry,

## END OF A PERFECT DAY

speaking to Sergeant Strood. And Skene awoke, awoke to gathering shadows in a railway carriage. The draught was whistling round his knees, the train moved with a rattle and a swish.

But that dreaming moment had brought its comfort. He saw things in proportion. After all, four years and more of service and discipline, of risk and discomfort – that was something.

He had gone into the thing neither because he was paid, nor because he was forced – and that was something. Processions and speeches were empty show – even the eventual effect on Europe was irrelevant – but deep within himself he had fulfilled a need, worked out a destiny. In what an abyss of self-contempt would he now be sunk had he not gone to that War – he, fit and of age?

That was it – the call had come, and he had answered; surely he had his reward in: 'I was there!'

# The Winner

# The Winner

He began by beating us – the 'C' Mess of Divisional Head-quarters – completely. It was no mean feat. We were perhaps the most hard-bitten, deeply-stained set you could find. Higher appointments fell to great skill, great influence, or great impertinence. But the sort of technical specialist who got pulled out of the Infantry and attached to Divisional Head-quarters, and messed in 'C' Mess, was a survivor of so much, chosen by the Gods from amongst so many of his equals and betters. Why 'Uncle' should have been so chosen, and how he arrived among us, we never discovered. But there he sat, one gloomy evening of 1916, with the Somme fiasco grumbling all along the horizon. He volunteered no information. He did not look the sort of man one could catechize. He just sat and smoked, and drank a good deal of whisky, not attempting to ingratiate himself, nor even to be agreeable. He beat us from the start. He went on sitting, smoking and drinking. He won. We adjusted ourselves to him, as he had not to us. He became a feature, then a boast, finally a byword. His outward appearance gave no clue to his personality. It was prosaic in the extreme. Bald, with a dirty grey moustache, of the kind which Tenniel attributed to the Walrus, broadish for his medium height, astonishingly spare, hard and agile for his years, which appeared to be nearer sixty than fifty, his maple-leaf badges showed the number of one of the battalions of the 1st Canadian Division and the rank of Captain. His name was Dakers. Beyond these vague indications he was a mystery. But he became an institution. We took to calling him 'Uncle'. It does not matter who first thought of it, or why. It suited him exactly. There is something of authority and responsibility connected with the title Father. But Uncle – that semi-detached relationship in which one can be kind without condescension, and humorously affectionate above the clash of antipathetic generations! Now, no one would have dreamed of receiving an order from Uncle. He never gave such a thing. On the other hand, we all contracted the habit of going to him for advice. This added immensely to his reputation. For whatever reason, good, or probably bad, he had been given the post of Clearance Officer at Divisional Head-quarters, it was soon discovered that Uncle was a man of parts. When everything failed, as it did, in those increasingly enormous and useless offensives, about once a week, Uncle always had some expedient ready. The further we departed from all the known rules of War, the better he grew. At his own job of Clearance Officer, he was pretty useless – anyhow, he left it all to young Skene, his Second in Command. But he was on surer grounds when called in to help the Deputy Assistant Director of Veterinary Services, with sick mules, or the Assistant Provost-Marshal with Colonials. And when the worst happened, when we had to retreat ten miles, and the whisky ran out, his efforts were remarkable, were crowned with success, and met with the fullest recognition (for by the middle of 1917, whisky was one of the few things one was still certain of wanting in a crumbling world).

On darkest days he would be found sitting (he never made heavy weather of his job) with his drink, over a tee-to-tum, or roughly carved horses, a paper racecourse, and dice: 'Spot a winner!' he would invite. We spotted him.

Thus, from being a mystery he became an institution. His fame spread far beyond our little 'C' Mess. Very high personages, who could not ask his advice, obtained his opinion by circuitous means. It was owing to some mumbled remark of his that the Australians were taken right back after the massacres of Paschendaele. It was because he said: 'You 'av been a long while thinking of it' that the new mark VIII non-galling ammunition-carriers were served out to all the machine-gun units for their teams.

He was entirely unconscious of the weight he carried. He never smiled when, as was fitting, he was eventually enshrined in an epigram.

It was young Kavanagh, that brilliant Irish schoolmaster, who said it. When Rest had fallen upon us, and the last excuse for the irksome discipline and bewildering boredom of soldiering was gone, Uncle still sat in the Mess, always smoking a pipe, and perhaps drinking a little more. One by one, as we exhausted the few poor alleviations of our lot, for there was not even enough work to occupy our minds, risk had been eliminated, and the amusements available to us had been worn to the bone, we dropped in, found that there was still an hour before they would bring us our tinned dinner, and sat down beside him. Kavanagh came in last, swallowed his drink at a gulp, coughed, stared and burst out: 'There sits Uncle, looking like a prairie!' None of us knew what a prairie looks like. But if unlimited and perpetual sameness is its characteristic, the simile is apt indeed. He had changed less than any of us in these four years or so. He did not blink on hearing the description, but suggested, in his voice, hoarse, as Kavanagh also had said, from drinking out of damp glasses, that we should play one of those childish gambling games in which he excelled, and which enabled him to pay his spirit-laden mess-bill. In this, as in everything else, he had us beat.

This concludes the direct evidence about him. As has been shown elsewhere, the increasing disintegration of the fourth year removed him from our little Mess, which broke up shortly after, as if he had been its central rivet. We went off to do our special jobs in special holes and corners, he went with Skene, who discovered that there were real nephews of his in France, justifying his soubriquet. But more than that, not even Skene discovered.

Yet the student of human nature can make a few shrewd deductions. How did the man come to be what he was? He had a reputation as wide as, and far more creditable than, that of most Generals. But he was an obscure insignificant old fellow. People called him ignorant, but Skene said No, primitive rather. It was not merely that he understood horses. The A.D. Veterinary Services did that. Uncle very nearly was a horse. He looked at things from a horse's point of view. He understood the tongue-tied, pocket-full-of-money insolence of Colonial troops. He understood a Massey-Harris reaper and binder. From the way he spoke to French mechanics who mishandled these almost human machines, one might almost say that Uncle looked at things from the Massey-Harris point of view. What sort of man has these thoughts, so rudimentary that they rank next to dumb instinct? Well, one must suppose some one born in and bred up to agriculture, leaving England at the earliest possible age, long before sophistication, and spending forty years without a break in Canada. Now the most primitive, entirely agricultural county in England is Wiltshire. It has no big town, not even a port. Its people have a slowness of speech and breadth of face that rather fitted Uncle's. As he never alluded to his childhood, never went to England on leave, never wrote to anyone, one may assume that he left in disgrace and never cared, perhaps never was able to go back. But that he was not Canadian born is pretty certain. He had no accent. His attitude to the War was too instinctive. He had no Imperialism. Nothing less than August 1914 could ever have brought such a truant home to the Mother he had saddened. If she has a consciousness, that queer Mother of us all, that sits between Ireland, and the Channel and the North Sea, she must think that he made good.

Most of us never knew of his death until years later. Then one or two came together, with Skene, and he told us. Then it was that one of us thumped the table with his fist crying: 'By Gad, he always won!'

We knew what was meant. We had been comparing notes, trying to make out how, after War so bad, the Peace could possibly be so much worse. We had admitted that for the best part of 1917 and 1918 the real enemy had been not the Germans, but the War. It beat most of us, but not Uncle. Just as he had always won at cards and drunk up his winnings, so had he swallowed the Armistice, lain down and died, of flu. Certainly, he was unbeatable.

And amid the toppling of crowns and thrones, and creaking of new nationalisms there glimmered our admiration for him. Of all the old and shaky and the new and gimcrack forms of civilization that may not outlast a decade, the England of which Uncle was a specimen will survive. Who else could hang on with so little fuss, and pass out so quietly?

# The Crime at Vanderlynden's

'Oh, my, I don't want to die,
I want to go home!'

Song of Kitchener's Army

# The Crime at Vanderlynden's

High up in the pale Flemish sky aeroplanes were wheeling and darting like bright-coloured insects, catching from one moment to another the glint of sun on metallic body or translucent wing. To any pilot or observer who had opportunity or gift for mere speculation, the sight that lay spread out below might have appeared wonderful. From far away on the seaboard with its coming and going of ships, there led rail, road, and wire, and by these three came material, human material, and human thought, up to that point just behind the battle-line where in dumps, camps (dumps of men) and Head-quarters (dumps of brains) they eddied a little, before streaming forward again, more slowly and covertly, by night, or below ground, up to the battle itself. There they were lost in that gap in life – that barren lane where the Irresistible Force dashing against the Immovable Post ground such a fine powder, that of material, very little, of men, very few, and of thought, nothing came splashing back.

But pilots and observers were too busy, adding to the Black Carnival, or saving their own skins from those puffs of Death that kept following them up and down the sky, to take any such a remote view; and even had they been interested in it, they could not have lifted the roof off the Mairie of the village – almost town – of Haagedoorne, and have seen, sitting in the Mayor's parlour, a man of middle size and middle class, a phenomenon in that place, that had been shocked in its village dignity so many times in those few months. For first it had been turned from one of those haunts of Peace, of small slow-moving officialdom, into the 'Q.' office of Divisional Head-quarters. It had become inhabited by two or three English Staff Officers, their maps and papers, their orderlies and clerks, policemen and servants; and now, last of all, there was added to them this quiet, absorbed young man – whose face and hair, figure and clothes had all those half-tones of moderate appropriateness of men who work indoors and do not expect too much. A young man who had neither red tabs nor long boots about him – and who seemed to have so much to do.

The old walls stared. The Mairie of Haagedoorne, half wine-shop, half beadle's office, had seen soldiers in its four hundred years, had been built for Spanish ones, and had seen them replaced by French and Dutch, English and Hessians, in bright uniforms and with a certain soldierly idleness and noise. This fellow had none of it. Sat there with his nose well down, applying himself to maps and papers, occasionally speaking deferentially to Colonel Birchin, who, a proper soldier, his left breast bright with medals, his face blank and slightly bored with breeding, would nod or shake his head. This was all part of the fact that this War was not as other wars. It was too wide and deep, as if the foundations of life had come adrift on some subterranean sea, and the whole fabric were swaying; it had none of the decent intervals, and proper limits, allowing men to shut up for the winter and to carry on their trade all the time.

The dun-coloured person attached to Divisional Staff, whose name was Stephen Doughty Dormer, indulged in none of these reflections. He just got on with it. He was deep in his job when an exclamation from his temporary Chief made him look up. The Colonel was sitting back in his chair (iron-bottomed, officers, for the use of), his beautiful legs in their faultless casings stretched out beneath his army table. He was holding at arm's-length a blue printed form, filled up in pen and ink.

Dormer knew it well. It was the official form on which Belgian or French civilians were instructed to make their claim for damages caused by the troops billeted on them.

The Colonel's mouth hung open, his eyeglass had dropped down.

'You speak this – er – language?'

'Yessah!' (with a prayer it might not be Portuguese). 'What language, sir?'

'This is – er – French.'

Yes, he could speak French, and hastened to look. Dormer was a clerk in a bank. Like so many of that species, he had had a grandmother with views as to the improvement of his position in the world, and she had insisted that he should learn the French language. Why she desired this was never discovered, unless it was that she considered it a genteel accomplishment, for she dated from the days when society was composed of two sorts of people, gentle and simple. She belonged to the former category and was in no danger of allowing any of her descendants to lapse. As she paid for the extra tuition involved, her arguments were irrefutable, and the boy intended for no more romantic a career than is afforded by a branch office in a market town, had, in 1900, a fair knowledge of the tongue of Voltaire and Hugo.

He had hardly reflected upon the matter again until, in the midst of a European War, he found that the War was being conducted in a country where French was the chief language, and that familiar-sounding words and phrases assailed his ear on every side. This was of considerable service to him, enabled him to add to his own and his brother officers' comfort; but he never boasted of it, having a profound uncertainty, after years of clerkdom, about anything so foreign and out of office hours. The legend of his peculiar ability persisted, however; and when after more than a year of incredible fatigues and nastiness, his neat methods and perfect amenity to orders were rewarded by the unofficial job of helping in the A. and Q. office of a division, he found his legend there before him. It was therefore with a sigh, and a mental ejaculation equivalent to 'Spare me these useless laurels,' that he got up and went over to his Chief's table, to be confronted by the sentence:

'*Esquinté une vierge chez moi!*'

'What's *Esquinté*? It's not in Cassell's Dictionary!'

'I should say – knocked asquint, sir! Spoiled, ruined; they often say it, if the troops go into the crops.'

'Well, how does it read, then? Knock asquint; no, that won't do; ruined, you say. Ruined a Virgin in my house. This sounds like a nice business, with the French in their present mood!'

Dormer simply could not believe it and asked:

'May I see the claim?'

'Certainly. Come here. Stop me wherever I go wrong.'

He knew more French than Dormer gave him credit for. He read the blue form, printed question and pen-and-ink reply to the end. It went like this:

Q. When was the damage committed?

A. Last Thursday.

Q. What troops were responsible? Give the number and name of the English detachment.

A. A soldier of the 469 Trench Mortar Battery (T.M.B.).

Q. Were you present and did you see the damage done?

A. No, but my daughter knows all about it.

Q. In what conditions was the damage done?

A. He broke the window (*vitrage*). She called out to him, but he replied with oaths.

Q. Can you prove responsibility (*a*) by witness?

A. My daughter.

Q. (*b*) By *procès-verbal*.

A. They insulted the Mayor when he came to do it!

Q. (*c*) By admission of the culprits.

A. Not necessary. It is visible.

Q. Did you complain to the officer commanding troops?

A. He would not listen.

And so on.

Deposed and sealed at the Mairie of Hondebecq, Nord, as the claim for compensation of Mr Vanderlynden, cultivator, sixty-four years old, by us Swingadow, Achille, Mayor.

'What do you say to that?' asked the Chief.

Dormer had a good deal to say, but kept it down. 'I can't believe it, sir. I know the billet. I remember Miss Vanderlynden. She's as strong as a man and much more determined than most. It's a mistake of some sort!'

'Pretty circumstantial mistake, isn't it? Look at this covering letter received with it.'

He held out a memorandum headed: 'Grand Quartier Général,' in French, to the effect that one desired it might be given

## THE CRIME AT VANDERLYNDEN'S

appropriate attention. And another from a department of English General Head-quarters with 'Passed to you, please.'

'The French have had their knife into us for some time. This'll be a nice case for them to take up. We must make an arrest at once. Sergeant!'

That Sergeant was a famous London Architect. He came to the door of the anteroom in which he worked.

'In what Corps Area is Hondebecq?'

The Sergeant spotted it in a moment, on the big map pinned up on the wall.

'Very well, wire them to take this up, and make an arrest.'

'There is just one point I should like to put, sir!'

As Dormer said it, he felt it to be 'cheek'. His Chief turned upon him the eyeglass of a regular officer who found it rather difficult to imagine how a junior temporary officer could put a point. But Dormer had seen two Courts-Martial, and the thought of some poor brute hauled out of a trench, and marched about for no better purpose than that, kept him firm.

'If an arrest is made, you will have to go on with the proceedings.'

'Naturally.'

'Then you will need a statement from the victim. If we had that first, we should know the truth!'

'Well, you'd better go and get it, as you know the people. You can see Corps and insist on an arrest. But, most important of all, try what a little money can do. He says a thousand francs. Well, you must see what he will come down to.'

Outside Divisional Head-quarters, Dormer turned to the right, to go to his billet, but a military policeman, stepping out from the shelter of the buildings, saluted.

'They're shelling that way, sir!'

It gave Dormer a queer familiar feeling in the pit of the stomach. Shelling, the daily routine of that War. But being a very punctilious temporary officer, and taking his almost nonexistent position in Divisional Staff very seriously, he pulled himself together.

'Oh, well, they'd have hit me long ago, if they could!' He

passed on, followed by a smile. He said those things because he felt them to be good for the morale of the troops. Sure enough, he had not gone many yards before the air was rent by a familiar tearing sound, followed by the usual bump and roar. It was well in front of him, and to the left, and he went on reassured. A few yards farther on, close to the side street where he was billeted over a pork-butcher's shop, he noticed people coming out of their houses and shops to stare, while one elderly woman, rounder than any artist would dare to portray, asked him:

'O Monsieur, is the bombard finished?' in the Anglo-Flemish which years of billeting were beginning to teach the inhabitants of the town. But the centre of excitement was farther on, where the little street of houses petered out between small, highly cultivated fields. Here the first shell had fallen right upon one of those limbers that were to be found being driven up some obscure street at any hour of the day or night. Two dazed drivers had succeeded in cutting loose and quieting the mules. A horse lay dead in the gutter. Against the bank leaned the Corporal, his face out of sight, as if in the midst of a hearty laugh. It needed only a glance, however, to see that there was no head upon the shoulders. It was just one of those daily disagreeable scenes which to Dormer had been so utterly strange all his life, and so familiar for the last year. Dormer made no fuss, but took charge. He knew well enough that the drivers would stand and look at each other. He sent one of them for a burial party from the nearest Field Ambulance, saw that the other tied up the mules and made a bundle of the dead man's effects – paybook, knife, money, letters – the pitiful little handkerchief-ful of all that remains for a soldier's loved ones – while he himself pushed his way into the orderly room of the nearest formation, that showed any signs of telephone wires. He had not many yards to go, for the camps lay along each side of that Flemish lane, as close as houses in a street.

He was soon inside an Armstrong hut, with the field telephone at his disposal, and while waiting to be given the orderly room of the Brigade Transport to which the casualty belonged, he happened to close his eyes. The effect was so striking that he immediately opened them again. There, on the underside of his eyelids, was the headless body he had just left. Curiously enough, it did not lie against the bank, as he had seen it, but seemed to swim towards him, arms above his head, gesticulating. Once his eyes were open again, of course it disappeared.

About him was nothing more wonderful than the interior of an Armstrong hut Orderly Room, an army table, an army chair. Some one's bed and bath shoved in a corner. Outside, trampled mud, mule-lines, cinder tracks, Holland elms, flat, stodgy Flanders all desecrated with War. He got the number he wanted, told the Brigade to fetch their broken limber, gave his rank and job, and put up the telephone. The impression he had had was so strong, however, that walking back along the cinder path, he closed his eyes again. Yes, it was still there, quite plain, the details of the khaki uniform all correct and clear cut, spurred boots and bandolier, but no head, and the arms raised aloft, exhorting or threatening.

If he went on like this he would have to see a Medical Officer, and they would send him down to the Base, and he would find his job filled up, and have to go elsewhere and start all over fresh, trying to do something that was not desperately boring or wholly useless. He had been doing too much, going up at night for 'stunts', and working in Q. office all day. He would have to slack off a bit.

By the time he got back to Divisional H.Q. the car stood ready. The feelings of one who, having been hauled out of the infantry, had then to return to the Forward Areas, were curiously mixed. Of course no one wanted to be shelled or bombed, to live where the comforts of life were unpurchasable, and the ordinary means of locomotion out of use. And yet – and yet – there was a curious feeling of going home. That great rowdy wood and canvas and corrugated iron town, miles deep and nearly a hundred miles long, was where one belonged. That atmosphere of obvious jokes and equally obvious death, disinfectant, tobacco, mules, and wood smoke had become one's life, one's right and natural environment.

His companion on this joyless ride was Major Stevenage, the

A.P.M. of the Division, an ex-cavalry officer of the regular army, in appearance and mentality a darker and grimmer edition of Colonel Birchin.

Dormer showed him the Vanderlynden dossier as they bowled along. He surveyed it with the weariness of a professional to whom an amateur exhibits a 'masterpiece'.

'Colonel Birchin thinks it's rape, does he?'

'Yes!'

'He's wrong, of course. Q. office always are! What do you think it is yourself?'

'A nasty snag. What happened doesn't matter. You and I could settle it for forty francs. But the French have got hold of it. It's become official.'

'What do you suggest?' Major Stevenage put in his monocle.

'We must go and see the Maire, and get it withdrawn. Let's see. Hondebecq? It's the Communal Secretary Blanquart we must see. Shrewd fellow and all on our side. These schoolmasters hate the peasants.'

Dormer knew the area well. Hondebecq was the typical village of French Flanders. That is to say, it was a cluster of cottages in which *rentiers* – peasants who had scraped a few savings out of the surrounding fields – lived on about forty pounds a year English; in its centre, a paved *grand' place* held a few modest shops, a huge high-shouldered church, carefully refaced with red brick, and a big, rambling 'Estaminet de la Mairie', next to the village school.

It was here that they found Blanquart, Communal Secretary, schoolmaster, land surveyor, poor man's lawyer, Heaven only knows what other functions he used to combine. He was the only man in the Commune handy with pen and paper, and this fact must have substantially added to his income. But, like all his kind, he could not forget that he came from Dunkirk or Lille; he had moments when his loneliness got the better of his pride and he would complain bitterly of the 'sacred peasants'.

They found him seated in his little front parlour – he only functioned in the official room at the Estaminet on State occasions – busy with those innumerable forms by which the food

## THE CRIME AT VANDERLYNDEN'S

of France was rationed, her Army conscripted, her prices kept in check and her civil administration facilitated. In the corner between the window and the clock sat an old peasant who said only, '*Bonjour.*'

Blanquart greeted them effusively, as who should say: 'We others, we are men of the world.' He made polite inquiries about the officers' health and the weather and the War, leading up to the introduction: 'Allow me to present you to Mister our Mayor! And now what can I do for you?'

Major Stevenage, a little lost in the mixed stream of good French and bad English, left it to Dormer.

'It is with reference to the claim of Vanderlynden! Can one arrange it?'

Blanquart had only time to put in: 'Everything arranges itself,' before the Major cut him short.

'You have some nice ideas, you others. Arrange it, I believe you. You will arrange it with our Deputy.'

Blanquart put in: 'Mister the Mayor was insulted by the troops. We wrote to our Deputy!'

Major Stevenage fidgeted. He had found it most difficult to go through this sort of thing, day after day, for years. He had been trained to deal with Asiatics. He turned on Blanquart:

'Why didn't you write to me first?' but the Mayor cut in again. His general outlook on life was about that of an English agricultural labourer plus the dignity of Beadledom. This latter had been injured, and the man, who seldom spoke a dozen sentences a day, now was voluble. He understood more English than one gave him credit for.

'Why write to you, officer, you are all of the same colour!' (By this time not a German attack could have stopped him.) 'My Garde Champêtre comes to tell me that there is a crime of violence at Vanderlynden's They demand that I go to make *procès-verbal*. I put on my tricolour sash. I take my official notebook. I arrive. I demand the officer. *Il s'est foutu de moi!* (Untranslatable.) He says he has orders to march to the trenches. His troops hold me in derision. They sing laughable songs of me in my official capacity –'

397

'It is very well, Monsieur the Maire,' Dormer broke in. 'We go to make an arrestation. Can you indicate the culpable?'

'But I believe you, I can indicate him,' cried the old man.

Dormer waited breathlessly for some fatal name or number which would drag a poor wretch through the slow exasperation of Courts-Martial proceedings.

'It was a small brown man!'

'That does not lead us very far!' said Dormer icily.

'Wait!' The old man raised his voice. 'Achille!' The door opened, and Achille Quaghebeur, the Garde Champêtre, in attandance on the Maire, stepped in and closed it behind him. He had, in his dark green and sulphur-coloured uniform, with his assumption of importance, the air of a comic soldier out of 'Madame Angot'. 'Produce the corroborative article!'

Achille found in his tail pocket surely the oldest and most faded of leather pocket-books. From this in turn he produced a piece of A.S.C. sacking, on which the word OATS was plainly printed in black.

'Voilà!' said the Maire.

'Totally useless!' growled the Major, turning red.

This made the Maire furious; he grasped the intonation and expression if not the words.

'You others, you are enough to send one to sleep standing up. One produces the *corroborative* pieces and you treat them as useless.' And there followed a tirade during which Dormer drew the Major outside, with profuse *Bonjours*! He thought that Blanquart was trying to sign to him that he wanted to say something to him privately. But the Major was upset, his dignity was hurt. A soldier by profession, he had reduced the settlement of claims to a fine art. He was said to have settled three thousand between the time he was made A.P.M. to the division on the Aisne to the day of his death at Bailleul. He told the chauffeur to drive to Vanderlynden's. The man seemed to know the way, and had probably been to the place many times. As the car jolted and ground over the cobbles into the yard, Dormer said:

'I shall ask for the daughter, Madeleine.'

'Just so!'

'I don't believe – '

'Nor do I,' said the Major stoutly.

Neither of them could pronounce the word 'rape'.

They got out, knocked at the door and knocked again. The place seemed not so much empty and deserted as enveloped in one of those encompassing noises that only sort themselves out on investigation. Too deep for a separator, too near for an aeroplane, Dormer diagnosed it: 'They've got the Government thrasher in the back pasture, next the rye!' (He had a good memory and could tell pretty well how most of the people distributed crops and work.)

They recrossed the bridge of the moat and skirting the latter entered the back pasture. There against the gate that gave on to the arable 'plain', as it was called in those parts, was the Government thrasher, the women labourers, and right on the top of the stack, old Vanderlynden.

Dormer shouted! Vanderlynden paid not the slightest heed. Perhaps he was deaf, no doubt the thrasher buzzed loud enough; but above all he was one of those old peasants whose only reply to this unheard-of War in which all had been plunged was to work harder and more continuously, and to show less and less consciousness of what went on round about them. There he stood, black against that shy and tender blue of Flemish sky, the motions of his body mechanical, his face between collarless shirt and high-crowned, peaked cap, expressionless. Finally, Dormer took one of the short stout girls that were employed in raking the straw away from the travelling band, and shook her roughly by the arm.

She was, of course, a refugee Belgian. No one else would work like that, not even a Chinese woman. Like a clockwork figure, she began to speak in 'English':

'No bon offizer billet all full you go Mairie!' without stopping for one moment her raking.

Dormer held her forearm rigid, and stopped her.

'*Saagte patron heer t'kom!*'

That reached her consciousness. Throwing down her implement, she put both hands to her mouth and began shouting

'Hoi!' at old Vanderlynden, and might have gone on shouting indefinitely if Dormer had not gone round to the French Army mechanic who drove the machine and given him an English canteen cigarette. That would have stopped an offensive. It soon stopped the thrasher and Vanderlynden looked down at his visitors.

'Good day, Patron!' called Dormer; 'can we see Mademoiselle?'

The old man got down with unexpected agility. 'Good day, my officer, what is it that there is?'

Dormer held out the blue claim form. At the sight of it, there came into Vanderlynden's face the look that a mule gives its feed, when, expecting and even enjoying bits of wood, leather, and nails, it comes across a piece of tin: not so much protest as long and malevolent calculation of the unknown. As a matter of fact he could not read more of it than his signature. He muttered once or twice, '*myn reclamorsche*', but got no further.

'Can we see Mademoiselle?' repeated Dormer.

The old man stared at him with the incredulity of a villager who finds a stranger ignorant of village news: 'But, my officer, my young lady is gone!'

At that moment the French mechanic, who had lighted his cigarette and now only wanted to be done with the job, put his lever over, and set the thrasher buzzing again. As if spellbound, old Vanderlynden gave one leap and regained his place on the stack. The Belgians fell to at their several jobs. The corn flew, the wheels whizzed, the grain rattled in the hopper, the straw swished in long swathes beneath the rakes. Dormer and the Major were left standing, idle and forgotten, with their War, while the real business of the farm went steadily forward, only a little hastened because the thrasher had to be at Watten next day.

They walked back to the car, in a black frame of mind. Neither spoke, from war habit of not mentioning the omnipresent perversity of things. But Madeleine Vanderlynden's departure from the farm, coming after the wording of the claim, was ominous indeed.

Travelling by motor has many disadvantages, but against all these it has one crowning advantage: to those who are weary and overspent, it provides more immediately and completely than any other physical sensation the feeling of escape. What magic lies behind that word! To get into the car and go, no matter whither, and to leave at any rate one incomprehensible muddle behind him: that was the illusion while the chauffeur was starting.

No farther off than the gate of the pasture, swaying at slowest speed over the unevenness of the entry, the car stopped. A motor-cyclist slithered up beside it, saluted the A.P.M. and produced one of those scores of messages that fluttered about just beyond the end of the field telephone. Dormer might have passed unknown, but the A.P.M. was unmistakable. Having handed over the flimsy envelope, the pocket Hermes threw his leg over the saddle of the gibbering machine that carried him, and was away up the lane and out on to the *pavé* road, out of sight before the A.P.M. could get out the words 'No answer'.

The A.P.M. sat frowning at the pink Army message form. The chauffeur sat frowning, one hand on the wheel, his foot keeping the engine going by light continual touches on the accelerator, his face screwed round to catch the order to proceed. The Sergeant of police sat perfectly still and impassive, looking before him, the sunlight glinting on the tiny fair hairs of his clipped moustache. The cyclist had gone, the chauffeur wanted to go, and, after a moment, quietly slipped into first gear and let the car gently gather way. The policeman did not have to want. He had simply to sit still and his morning would pass as his other mornings did, in passively guarding law and order in the organization of the British Armies in France and Flanders. It was not until the car was already moving at more than walking pace that the A.P.M. spoke, and Dormer got the queerest sensation from the sequence of such small events. For the first time it seemed to him that the A.P.M. was not in possession of the initiative. It was these private soldiers, waiting, coming and going, that forced him to give an order. The impression lasted only a moment, but it was disturbing. Decidedly, Dormer felt, he was not well, having such notions. Then he had no more time to think, for the A.P.M. was holding out the pink wire for him to read. He read:

'Corps requires signed statement of withdrawn claim.' The illusion of escape was gone. The botheration was not behind, it was ahead of them.

'No use saying she isn't there. We shall have to concoct something.' He was obviously waiting for Dormer to suggest.

'I think, sir, we might go back to Blanquart, and find out the girl's whereabouts. The Maire will be gone by now!'

'Thank goodness. To Hondebecq Mairie.' The car flew from second to top speed.

Back at the Grand' Place of the village, the car stopped, the chauffeur folded his hands, at the order to wait, the A.P.M. and Dormer entered the Estaminet. It was empty, as Dormer had foreseen. The Maire and his Secretary were not people who had time to waste, and were both gone about their jobs – the Maire to his farm, the clerk to his school, the classes of which were plainly audible through the wall, grinding out some lesson by heart, in unison, like some gigantic gramophone with a perpetual spring. It was the hour at which all France prepares for its substantial meal.

Outside, the Grand' Place was empty, save for the sunshine, not here an enemy, as farther south, but the kindly friend that visits the coasts of the North Sea all too rarely, wasting its pale and tepid gold on the worn stones, on the green-shuttered, biscuit-coloured façades of substantial two-storied houses, with steep roofs and tall chimneys, behind which protruded the summits of ancient Holland elms. For a long while there was no movement, save the flutter of a straw caught in the cobbles. The A.P.M. fidgeted. There was no sound but the classes next door, the wind in the street, the faint tremor of the window-panes, in response to some distant inaudible shelling.

'You wouldn't think there was a war going on within twenty miles?'

'Twenty kilometres, sir!'

'Is it possible? Are we going to wait all day, Dormer?'

'No, sir, only a moment; the people of the house can't be far off, but the door behind the bar is locked. I don't want to go into the school myself, Blanquart won't like it, and one wants to keep on the right side of him.'

'Why won't he like it? He'll have to.'

'The children get out of hand, sir, at the sight of a uniform. I've noticed it when I've been billeting.'

'Do they?'

'Yes, sir; it's all fun to them still.'

'Is it?' The A.P.M. grimaced and began reading the signs over the little shops: '*Charcuterie* – what's that?'

'Baked-meat shop. Pork butcher's we should call it, sir!'

'*Quincaillerie.*'

'Hardware!'

'Who's this, coming across the square?'

'Belgian refugee, sir!'

Dormer had no doubt about it. The heavy round-shouldered figure, the mouth hanging loosely open, the bundle carried under the arm, the clumsy boots, the clothes apparently suspended round the waist by a string. Her story was written all over: turned out of some Walloon or Flemish farm or town, at the approach of the Germans – tramping along a road with a retreating army all mixed up with a nation on the move, she had lost home, parents, occupation, all in a few hours, and was glad to get board and bed and any odd job that she could do.

'Is this the sort of person we have to interview?'

'Oh no, sir. Different type!'

The woman showed some mild interest at the sight of the car, and exchanged banter in pidgin English with the chauffeur and policeman. The invitation from the latter 'promenade', and the smiling, flattered refusal 'promenade no bon!' could be heard. Then she entered and stood before them.

'*Bonjour*, offizer, what you want?'

'Will you kindly tell the Maire's Secretary one waits to see him.'

'You want billets?' in English. 'Billets na poo!'

'No!' Dormer was always piqued when his French was disregarded or misunderstood. 'We want M. Blanquart!'

'All right.' She returned with him in a moment.

403

'M. Blanquart, we have been to the farm and seen Vanderlynden. He's very busy, and we didn't get much out of him, but we gather his daughter has left home. Do you know her address?'

A look of incredulity visited the face of the schoolmaster. He pointed across the square. 'There. She has taken the "Lion of Flanders". She gives lunch to officers!'

When this was conveyed to the A.P.M. he was considerably annoyed. 'Why couldn't that old fool Vander what's his name say so?'

Blanquart understood perfectly, not only the words, but the feeling. 'Ah, Monsieur, there you have the peasant. I have lived among them all my life. I am not of them, I am from St Omer, but I know them well. They are like that. They are thrashing. They are sowing. They cannot attend to anything else, even if it be their own business. You and I shall be treated like the weather, something to be used or avoided ...'

But the A.P.M. had stepped out of the Estaminet de la Mairie. Dormer lingered, just sufficiently to say:

'We are much obliged, M. Blanquart, we will attend to the affair.' For he had been brought up to behave as a little gentleman and knew that politeness cost nothing and that he might require the Secretary of the Mairie again.

Outside, the chauffeur was busy underneath the car, the policeman stood beside it, legs apart, hands clasped behind his back, face expressing absolutely nothing. In a few strides Dormer caught up to the A.P.M.

'This lady speaks good English, sir. No doubt you will conduct the inquiry yourself?'

'I hope so, if we really have found the person at last. We've wasted nearly the whole morning.'

Dormer was relieved; his mind, always inclined to run a little in advance, had already arrived at the point at which some one would have to ask this woman:

'Are you the victim of this shocking crime?' He didn't want to do it, for he felt that it was the A.P.M.'s business.

The two officers entered the Café-Restaurant of the 'Lion of Flanders'. The whole of the ground floor, a long, low room looking out into the Grand' Place, had been cleared and set with little tables. Round the desk from which the Patronne supervised the business, one or two officers from neighbouring billets were drinking mixed vermouth. The air was redolent of preparation, and it was only because they remained standing that the A.P.M. and Dormer attracted attention. Finally, a rough middle-aged woman in an apron asked what she could do for these gentlemen. Feeling the subject to be increasingly delicate, Dormer ordered two mixed vermouths and then asked if they might speak to Mademoiselle Vanderlynden upon business. The drinks were served, and behind them came the person required. No sooner had she come and inquired what was wanted, than Dormer wished to goodness she had not. He realized more than ever how difficult it would be to say to such a person, 'Are you the victim of the unmentionable crime?' But there she stood, quite good looking, imperturbable, a little impatient perhaps, obviously wanting to know without delay why she had been sent for in the middle of a busy morning. This was comforting in a sense; it showed there was something wrong with the whole atrocious story. On the other hand it was awkward, one had to go on and explain. So he pulled out the blue printed claim: the A.P.M. in spite of what had been said, left it to him.

'It is about this claim of your father's.'

She took it, scrutinized it a moment, and handed it back:

'Ah, that.' She was not helpful.

'You are of course familiar with the whole story?'

'Yes, I remember it all.'

The A.P.M. was listening attentively, impressed by her glib, adequate English, and even more so by her personality. Dormer, on the other hand, was occupied with his own feelings.

'There is some mistake, is there not?'

'No, there is no mistake.'

'The Major has come to see the – er – the damage!'

'I shall be pleased to go with you to the farm, after lunch.'

'That's a jolly good idea,' the A.P.M. broke in. 'We'll have lunch here, and go and look at the damage afterwards.'

'Very good. Will you take a chair, sir?' and she was gone.

'You see, it wasn't what you thought,' the A.P.M. went on,

finishing his drink at a gulp, and making Dormer feel, for the twentieth time, what a grossly unfair War it was.

The lunch was long, far more of the Flemish midday dinner than the French déjeuner. The A.P.M. took the lot, commented freely, enjoyed himself immensely. There were *hors d'oeuvres* (sardines, beans in oil, some sort of sausage, a kind of horse-radish, 'Wonder where the devil she gets 'em?' said the A.P.M.), soup (ordinary, but enlivened by parsley and bits of toast fried in fat and something, third cousin to a piece of garlic, 'scrumptious'), veal and spinach (very good, but 'no fish, pity!'). In a moment Mademoiselle Vanderlynden stood over them. 'I am sorry, we have only sardines, they will not let the fish come by train!' Chicken and salad ('Excellent. Ah, they understand oil, the French'), little biscuits, coffee that dripped through a strainer into glasses, rum ('That's English, I bet!'), and Dormer, shy in such matters, and without social code, began wondering whether he could offer to pay.

He had learned during bitter years, one rule: 'Always treat an A.P.M. if you can!' This had not been his preoccupation during the meal. He had been haunted by a tag of verse – from the 'Ingoldsby Legends' which he certainly hadn't read for twenty years. He was not one to read 'poetry'. But neither had he a regular soldier's trained indifference. He knew where it was going to end, this quest on which they were engaged. Some poor brute who had volunteered to come to this blessed country to fight the Germans, would be hauled out of some ghastly apology for a 'rest' camp – if he were lucky – more likely out of some dug-out or cellar, or even from Hospital – placed under arrest – frightened dumb, if by any chance he had any speech in him, and finally tried by a court to whom he was a 'Tommy' (the sort of person who enlisted in the regular army because he was out of work), and sentenced to some penalty. And here was the A.P.M. eating and drinking with gusto. It reminded Dormer of:

> Run to M'Fuze, and Lieutenant Tregooze,
> And run to Sir Carnaby Jenks, of the Blues.
> Cries, 'What must I fork out to-night, my trump,
> For the whole first-floor of the Magpie and Stump?'

the rhyme of the drunken swells who couldn't even keep awake to see a man hanged. It was, however, the ideal state of mind for making war.

The A.P.M. was saying to Mademoiselle Vanderlynden: 'The bill please, Madam,' and when he got it, 'By Gad, did we drink all that? Well, I don't grudge it.'

So he was going to pay. The room was emptying now, there were no troops in the village, and most of the officers lunching there (with shy propitiatory looks towards the A.P.M.) had some way to ride to get back to their units. Here was Mademoiselle ready to go and show them the damage. She wore no hat, but her clothes were good of their kind and she carried the day's takings clasped to her breast, in a solid little leather dolly-bag, far from new. The A.P.M. allowed her the rare privilege of a lift in the car. They went back over the same road that the two officers had followed in the morning. Once more Dormer had his queer feelings. There was something wrong about this. Three times over the same road and nothing done. As they turned into the by-road, Mademoiselle Vanderlynden held up her hand. 'Stop here, please!'

They were at the corner of the big pasture before the house. There was an ordinary hedge, like an English one, thickened at this angle into a tiny copse, with a dozen young poplars. Mademoiselle soon found a gap in the fence and led them through, remarking, 'The troops made this short cut!'

They found themselves in Vanderlynden's pasture, like hundreds of others over a hundred miles of country. There were no troops in it at the moment, but it had the air of being continuously occupied. In long regular lines the grass had been trampled away. Posts and wire, and a great bank of manure marked the site of horse-lines. Nearer the house, tents had been set up from time to time, and circles, dotted with peg and post holes, appeared half obliterated. At the corners of the field were latrines, and at one spot the cookers had blackened everything.

'Billets for the troops!' reflected Dormer, to whom the idea of lodging in the open had never ceased to be a thoroughly bad joke. 'Stables for horses, stables for men!' Obviously enough the machinery of War had been here in full swing. Dormer (a man of no imagination) could almost see before him the khaki-clad figures, the sullen mules, the primitive vehicles filing into the place, tarrying ever so briefly and filing out again to be destroyed. But Mademoiselle Vanderlynden was occupied with the matter in hand, and led to the other side of the coppice, where there had been built by some previous generation of pious Vanderlyndens a little shrine. It was perhaps eight feet high, six feet thick, and had its glazed recess towards the main road. But the glazing was all broken, the altar torn down, and all those small wax or plaster figures or flowers, vases, and other objects of the trade in 'votive offerings' and *objets de piété* which a Vanderlynden would revere so much more because he bought them at a *fournitures ecclésiastiques*, rather than made them with his own hands, were missing. Army wire had been used to fasten up the gaping aperture.

'There you are,' said Mademoiselle. She added, as if there might be some doubt as to ownership: 'You can see that it is ours. Here is our name, not our proprietors!'

Sure enough, on a flat plaster panel was a partially effaced inscription: 'Marie Bienheureuse – prie pour – de Benoit Vanderl – femme Marthe – Juin 187–'

The A.P.M. lighted a cigar and surveyed the ruins. He was feeling extremely well, and was able to take a detached unofficial attitude. 'Oh, so that's the Virgin, is it?'

'No. That is the place for the image. The image is broken, as I told you, and we removed the pieces.'

'Very good. Then I understand you claim a thousand francs for the damage to the brickwork and the – er – altar furniture which was – ah, broken – it seems too much, you know!'

'Perhaps, sir, you are not well ack-vainted with the price of building materials!' (Ah, thought Dormer, she speaks pretty good English, but that word did her.)

'Oh, I think so, I'm a bit of a farmer myself, you know. I have a place in Hampshire, where I breed cattle.'

Mademoiselle's voice seemed to rise and harden:

'Yes, sir; but if you are rich, that is not a reason that you should deny justice to us, who are poor. I do not know if I can get this altar repaired, and even if I can there is also the question of the *effraction* –'

'The what?'

'Legal damages for breaking in – trespass, sir,' put in Dormer, alarmed by the use of French. He could see she was getting annoyed, and wished the A.P.M., the lunch, the claim, the farm and the War, all the blessed caboodle, were with the devil.

'Oh, I see.'

'*Et puis*, and then there are *dédommagements* – what would you say if I were to knock down your Mother's tomb?'

'What's that. Oh, I can't say, I'm sure. I really can't go into all this. Captain Dormer, there is obviously no arrest to be made. It is purely a claim for compensation. I will leave it to you. I must be getting back. *Comprenez*, Mademoiselle, this officer will hear what you have to say and will settle the whole matter with you. Famous lunch you gave us. Au revoir. If you care for a game of bridge this evening, Dormer, come round to B Mess!'

Dormer took out his field notebook and conducted the inquiry partly in English, partly in French.

They sat in the cavernous old tiled kitchen, half-filled with the stove and its stupefying heat, half with the table, scrubbed until the grain of the wood stood out in ribs.

Mademoiselle Vanderlynden had dismissed the A.P.M. from her mind with the remark that he was a droll type, and gave Dormer her full attention, rather as if he had been a dull boy in the lowest class, and she his teacher.

'When did this occur?'

'Why, in April. It was wet, or he would not have done it!'

'Did you see it done?'

'Yes. I even tried to stop it!'

'Where were you?'

'Why naturally I was at that hole in the fence. One cannot always hire a boy to keep the cattle from straying.'

'Well?'

'Well, then the troops came in. They were not pretty to see!'

'What troops were they?'

She turned over a dirty dog-eared memorandum book.

'469 Trench Mortar Battery.'

'So they had had a bad time?'

'One gathered that. They were very few, and some of their material was missing. At the last came this man with his two mules. One was sick, one was wounded. Most of the men, as soon as they had put up their animals, fell down and slept, but this one kept walking about. It was almost dark and it was beginning to rain. I asked him what he wanted.'

'What did he say?'

' "To Hell with the Pope!" '

The shibboleth sounded so queer on her lips that Dormer glanced at her face. It was blank. She had merely memorized the words in case they might be of use to her. She went on:

'He did not like the images on the altar! Then he began to break the glass, and pull down the woodwork. One saw what he wanted. It was shelter for his mules.'

'You cautioned him that he was doing wrong?'

'I believe you. I even held him by the arm.'

'That was wrong of you, Mademoiselle. You should have informed his officer.'

'Oh, you must understand that his officer was asleep on the kitchen floor. But so asleep. He lay where he had fallen, he had not let go the mug from which he drank his whisky. So much – (she held up four graphic fingers) – ah, but whisky you know!'

'I see. You were unable to report to the officer in charge of the party. But still, you should never touch a soldier. He might do you an injury, and then, at a court of inquiry, it would be said against you that you laid hands on him.'

'Oh, you understand, one is not afraid, one has seen so many soldiers these years. And as for the court of inquiry, we have had four here, about various matters. They all ended in nothing.'

'Well, well, you endeavoured to prevent the damage, and being unable to report to the proper authority, you made your claim for damage in due course. But when the officer woke up, you informed him that you had done so?'

'Why necessarily, since we had the Maire to make a *procès-verbal!*'

'So I hear, from the Maire himself. But apparently the Maire did not do so, for the *procès-verbal* is not included with the other papers.'

'No, the Maire was prevented by the troops. (A grim smile broke for a moment the calculated business indifference on the face of one who excluded emotion, because it was a bad way of obtaining money.) Oh, la-la! There was a *contretemps!*'

'Do you mind telling me what occurred?'

She seemed to regret that brief smile, and apologized to herself.

'All the same, it was shameful. Our Maire is no better than any other, but he is our Maire. One ought to respect those in power, ought not one, sir?'

'In what way were the troops lacking in respect?'

'They sang. They sang – *casse-tête* – enough to split your head, all the way to the village!'

'Oh, they were on the move, were they?'

'It was pitiable, I assure you, sir, it was shameful to see. *Ces pauvres êtres*. They hardly had any sleep. Only a few hours. Then it seems the Bosche made a counter-attack, and paff! here comes a motor-cyclist, and they were obliged to wake up and fall in. Some of them could only stand up with difficulty. But at length, they were ready; then the Maire came. We had sent for him *d'urgence*, when we saw the troops were going, because you can't make a *procès-verbal* of a person who is no longer there!'

'No, quite right. But why did they sing?'

'Ah, *ça tombait d'accord*. Just as the officer gives the word, the Maire arrives. We had informed him it was a crime of violence, and he had taken it very serious. He is old, our Maire. He had put on his – *écharpe*.'

'What is that?'

She made a vivid gesture with her hands.

'It goes so! It is tri-colour. It is the Maire's official dress!'

'Ah, his official scarf!'

'That is it. Also, he had mounted his hat!'

'How did he do that?'

'The usual way. But it was a long hat, a hat of *grande tenue* – like a pot of confiture.'

'Mademoiselle, this will not do. I cannot settle this matter here and now, I must pass on all the papers to my superior officer, who will place them with the proper authority. They will ask "Is there no *procès-verbal*?" Am I to say: "The Maire went to make one. He put on his hat and the troops began to sing." It sounds like a joke.'

'Ah, you others, you are always the ones to laugh. It was just exactly as I have said. They sang!'

'But you told me just now that they were tired out!'

'Quite true!'

'It will never sound so. What did they sing?'

'Old Hindenburg has bought a hat!'

In a moment Dormer was convinced. The words painted, framed and hung the picture for him. He had just been beginning to hope that the whole thing would break down from sheer improbability. He now saw it stamped and certified with eternal truth. There was no need for her to add: 'They were not gay, you understand, they were *exalté*!'

'Excited!'

'Ah! Excited, like one is after no sleep and no food and then something very strange. They were excited. They called the Maire "Maréchal Hindenburg", and "Bosche", and "Spy". Those are words that ought not to be used between allies!'

'No, Mademoiselle, they ought not.'

But for a moment, the hardness left her face, she became almost impersonal.

'It was curious. They sang that – *sur un air de psaume*, to a church tune.'

'Yes, yes!' agreed Dormer. Out of the depth of his experience as a churchwarden welled up the strains of Whitfield, No 671, and out of the depths of his experiences as a platoon commander came a sigh: 'They will do it.'

He went through his notes to see if there were anything more he wanted to know, but from business habit he had already possessed himself of the essentials. He did not like the way the thing was shaping. He knew only too well what happened in the army. Some individual being, besides a number on a pay roll, a human creature, would do something quite natural, perhaps rather useful, something which a mile or two farther on, in the trenches, would be worth, and might occasionally gain, the Military Medal. This business of breaking down a bit of wood and plaster, to shelter mules, had it occurred a little farther on, had it been a matter of making a machine-gun emplacement in an emergency, would have earned praise. It showed just that sort of initiative one wanted in War-time, and which was none too easy to get from an army of respectable civilians. But at the same time, in billets, there was another set of rules just as important, which in their essence discouraged initiative and reduced the soldier to a mere automaton. The otherwise excellent thing which he did broke those rules. That again did not matter much, unless it was brought into accidental prominence by colliding with some other event or function – this Maire and his dignity for instance, would play the very devil, make a mountain out of a molehill, such was the perversity of things. Fascinated against his better judgement which told him 'The less you know about the business, the better,' he found himself asking:

'What was this man like, Mademoiselle?'

There was no answer, and he looked up. She had left him, gone into the back kitchen to some job of her own. She had left him as though the War were some expensive hobby of his that she really could not be bothered with any longer. On hearing his voice she returned and he repeated his question. He never forgot the answer.

'Like – but he was like all the others!'

'You couldn't pick him out in a crowd?'

'Perhaps. But it would be difficult. He was about as big as you, not very fat, he had eyes and hair like you or anyone else.'

'You didn't, of course, hear his name or number?'

'They called him "Nobby". It was his name, but they call

every one "Nobby". His number was 6494. I saw it on his valise.'

'On his pack?'

'Yes.'

'Thank you, Mademoiselle. You have told me all I want.' In his heart he feared she had told him much too much, but she had gone on with her work. He rose to go, but passing the dark entry of the back kitchen, he stopped, as though to avoid a shell. He thought he saw a headless figure, but it was only a shirt which Mademoiselle Vanderlynden had flung over a line before putting it through the wringer. He went out. She did not accompany him. She was busy, no doubt.

He had to walk to the main road, but once there, found no difficulty in 'jumping' a lorry that took him back to Divisional Head-quarters. On the steps of the Town Hall he crossed the A.P.M. It was very late for that functionary to be about. He had not even changed into 'slacks'.

'Hullo, young feller, you got back then?'

'Yes, sir.' Dormer rather wanted to say, 'No, sir, I'm not here, I'm at the farm where you left me.'

The A.P.M. passed on, but turned to call out: 'No bridge to-night. We're on the move!'

So it seemed. The interior of the old building was in confusion. The Quartermaster-Sergeant was burning orders, schedules, rolls and parade states of the Corps they were leaving. Signallers were packing their apparatus, batmen were folding beds and stuffing valises. Policemen were galvanized into a momentary activity.

To Dormer it was the old, old lesson of the War. Never do anything, it is always too late. He had been bound, by a careful civilian conscience, to try to get to the bottom of the matter. He might just as well have torn it up and let it take its chance. No, the Vanderlyndens would never let it rest until they got some sort of satisfaction. The Mayor and the French Mission and Heaven knows who else would have something to say. He wrote a brief but careful report, and sent the thing off to an authority at Boulogne who dealt with such matters.

\*

The weeks that followed were full of education for Dormer's detached, civilian mind. Accustomed to be part of a battalion, almost a close family circle of known faces and habits, then associated with the staff of a division that stuck in one place, he had never before seen an army, and that army almost a nation, on the move. Under his eyes, partly by his effort, fifteen thousand English-speaking males, with the proper number of animals and vehicles, impedimenta, movable or fixed, had got into trains, and got out of them again, and marched or been conveyed to a place where Dormer had to take leave of all preconceived notions of life.

No-Man's-Land, with trenches beside it, he was familiar with, but here were miles of had-been No-Man's-Land, grassless, houseless, ploughed into brown undulations like waves of the sea by the barrages that had fallen upon it; covered with tents and huts, divided by wandering rivers of mud or dust, which had been at some distant time, weeks before, roads. Into this had poured, like the division to which he was attached, forty other divisions, always in motion, always flowing from the railhead behind, up to the guns in front, shedding half the human material of which they were composed, and ebbing back to railhead to go elsewhere.

He came to rest in a tiny dug-out on a hillside of loose chalk, which he shared with a signal officer, and past which, at all hours of the day and night, there passed men, men, men, mules, men, guns, men, mules, limbers, men, men, men.

At least this is how they appeared to him. Forced by Nature to sleep for some of the hours of darkness, and forced by the Germans to be still for all the clearest of the daylight, it was at the spells of dusk and dawn that he became busiest, and that infernal procession was ever before his eyes. It was endless. It was hopeless. By no means could his prim middle-class mind get to like or admire anything so far from the defined comfort and unvarying security to which he belonged and to which he longed to return. It was useless. With the precision of a machine, that procession was duplicated by another moving in the opposite direction. Lorries, ambulances, stretchers, men, men, guns, limbers, men, men, men. The raw material went up.

The finished article came back. Dormer and his companion and their like, over twenty miles of line, sorted and sifted and kept the stream in motion.

That companion of his was not the least of his grievances. The fellow was no Dormer, he was opposite by name and nature. His name was Kavanagh, and one of the meagre comforts Dormer got was by thinking of him as a d—d Irishman. He was, or had been going to be, a schoolmaster, and next to nature (or nationality), the worst thing about him was he would talk. And he would *not* keep his hands still. Two things that Dormer most gravely disapproved of, and which he attributed in equal shares to lack of experience of the world, and too much signalling.

His talk was such tripe, too! He never lost a moment. He started first thing in the morning. All the traffic that was going up forward was gone. The earth was empty, save for anti-aircraft guns pop-popping at planes high in the Italian blue. Dormer had shaved and breakfasted and hoped to catch up some of the sleep he had lost during the night. But would that fellow allow that? No. Listen to him now, under the tiny lean-to they had contrived, by the dug-out steps, for washing purposes. He was – reciting – would one call it?

> 'The last tattoo is beating, boys,
> The pickets are fast retreating, boys,
> Let every man
> Fill up his can
> And drink to our next merry meeting, boys!'

'Do you call that poetry?'

'No.'

This was rather awkward. Dormer had intended a snub. Not caring for poetry himself, he had tried to take a high line. He went on lamely:

'Oh! What do you call it then?'

'A most amazing picture of the mentality of 1815. Compare it with that of 1915. In that old war of ours against the French, we swore, we drank, we conquered. What do you think that same fellow would have to write about us today?'

'He wouldn't,' put in Dormer, without avail.

'Something like this:

> 'Z day is fast approaching, boys,
> In gas-drill we want coaching, boys,
> Our iron ration
> Will soon be in fashion.'

What rhymes to coaching?'

'How should I know?'

'Joking apart, Dormer!' (As if Dormer had been joking.) 'Do you catch the impulse of the slogan? Of course, iron rations and gas helmets make a much more efficient soldier than drums and bayonets and rum, but the zest is all gone!'

Dormer did not reply; a belated party of engineers of some special service were passing up the road, and from where he lay in the dug-out he could see khaki-covered bodies upon dusty legs, but no heads, the beam of the entrance was too low. Suddenly he said:

'Did you ever dream that the army was like a giant without a head?'

'What did you say?'

Good gracious, what had he said? He replied, 'Oh, nothing,' and bit his lips. It must be want of sleep. Fortunately Kavanagh did not hear. He was going on with his poetry.

> 'The Colonel, so gaily prancing, boys,
> Has a wonderful way of advancing, boys,
> Sings out so large
> Fix bayonets and cha-a-a-rge,
> It sets all the Frenchmen a-dancing, boys!'

'What days they must have been, Dormer! You ought to have been a Colonel. Can't you see yourself on a big brown horse, gaily prancing? There ought to be a school for gaiety, just as there is for bayonet fighting and bombing. Can't you imagine yourself in a shako, like a top hat, with the brim in front only, glazed, with whacking great numerals?'

Dormer wanted to say: 'You've got a marvellous imagination!' which would have been intended as an unfavourable criticism. But the words stuck on his lips. Instead he said:

'It's all very well. You don't seem to see the serious part of all this – waste!'

'Waste, my dear fellow!' And to Dormer the harsh, cheerful voice had all the officious familiarity of a starling, gibing at one from an apple tree. 'Waste is not serious. It is nature's oldest joke. It used to be called Chaos. From it we came. Back to it we shall go. It will be called Immortality. The Graves Commission will give it a number, a signboard, and a place on the map, but it will be Immortality none the less. From Titans to tight 'uns, "each in his narrow grave".'

'Oh, chuck it,' said Dormer, disgusted and having no memories of that quotation. 'You've evidently never been in charge of a burying party!'

'I have. I did twelve months in the line, as a platoon commander. How long did you do that?'

'Twelve months about!'

'I believe you, where thousands wouldn't. Twelve months was about the limit. In twelve months, the average Infantry subaltern got a job, or got a blighty! I know all about it!'

'Then you ought to know better than to speak so. It's not a joke!'

'My dear Dormer, if it were not a grim joke it would be utterly unbearable.'

'I disagree entirely. It's that point of view that we are suffering from so much. You don't seem to see that this army is not an army of soldiers. It is an army of civilians enlisted under a definite contract. They aren't here for fun.[1]

'Oh, come, Dormer, don't you believe in enjoying the War?'

'I believe in getting it done.'

'You never will, in that frame of mind.[2]

'Oh, shan't I? What would happen if I didn't see that the right people get to the right place, with the right orders and right supplies, including you and your blessed flagwaggers?'

'Nothing to what will happen if the troops once begin to

regard the show as a matter of business! You haven't got a shako and a big brown horse, but you must play up, as if you had!'

'What rot you talk. I have a tin hat because it will stand shrapnel better than a shako. I have mules because they stand the life better than a horse.'

'Yes, but do you admire your tin hat? Do you really care for mules!'

Something made Dormer say in spite of himself:

'I did once come across a man who cared!'

'There, what did I tell you. He was winning the War!'

('Whatever did I tell him that for?' Dormer asked himself vexedly. 'A nice song he'll make of it.') But he only said:

'You're all wrong, as usual. He did nothing of the sort. He just made a row in billets!'

'Quite right too. Most of 'em deserve a row!'

'Possibly, but he went the wrong way to work!'

'Ah, that depends!'

(Irritating brute!)

'No, it doesn't. Were you ever at Ypres?'

'Was I not. I was hit at Hooge stables, and had to walk nearly a couple of miles to get to a dressing station!'

'Well, then, you remember, in the back billets, a place called the "Spanish Farm"?'

'Don't I just. Great big old house, with a moat, and pasture fore and aft.'

What a way to put it!

'Well, this chap I'm telling you of, was billeted there. He was attached to a Trench Mortar Battery. He was in charge of the mules. He didn't talk a lot of rot about it, as you suggest he should. One of his mules was wounded and the other sick. He broke down the front of the shrine at the corner of the pasture to get a bit of shelter for them!'

The effect of this recital was not what Dormer expected.

'That was an unspeakably shocking thing to do, worse than losing any number of mules!'

## THE CRIME AT VANDERLYNDEN'S

'I suppose you're a Catholic?'

'Yes, I am!'

'I thought as much. Well, I'm not, nor was this driver I'm telling you about. He just hated the waste and destruction of it all.'

'So he destroyed something more precious and permanent.'

'He thought a live mule was better than a dead saint.'

'He was wrong!'

And then the fellow shut up, got quite sulky. Dormer was delighted with his prowess in argument, waited a moment, turned on his side, and slept, as only men can who live in the open air, in continual danger of their lives, and who lose the greater portion of the night in ceaseless activity.

\*

When his servant woke him, with tea and orders and the nightly lists of traffic and stores, it was a wonderful golden and green sunset, tremulous with the evening 'hate'. The purple shadows were just sufficiently long to admit of getting the wounded back, and the road was filled with ambulances, whirring and grinding as they stopped, backed, and restarted, while a steady punctual crash, once a minute, showed that the Bosche were shelling the road or one of the innumerable camps or dumps along it, in the neighbourhood. Amid all this clamour, Kavanagh was not silenced, but recited at the top of his voice, and Dormer had a suspicion that the real reason was that it helped to keep down the nervousness that grew on men, as the years of the War rolled on, and the probability of being hit increased. Especially as, far overhead, the planes that circled and swooped like a swarm of gleaming flies, were attracting considerable anti-aircraft fire, and all round, big jagged bits were coming to earth with a noise almost echoing that of the ambulances.

Dormer's tidy mind was soon called into action. Some wounded who had died on the way to the dressing station, had been laid out beside the road as the ambulances had enough to do without carrying corpses ten miles. He went to make sure the M.O. had arranged for a burial party, as he had the strongest belief that casualties lying about were bad for the morale of the troops. When he got back to the dug-out, Kavanagh was 'going on', as he bent over a map of the extensions of the divisional cable lines, like a crow on a gate.

'See those chaps, Dormer?'

> 'Qui procul hinc – the legend's writ
> The – er – Picard grave is far away,
> Qui ante diem periit
> Sed miles, sed pro patria.'

'Do you believe in pronouncing Latin like Julius Caesar or like Jones Minor?'

'I don't believe in it at all. Pure waste of time!'

'Dormer, you are a Utilitarian!'

'Have it your own way so long as you get that cable line of yours sited. I've got parties coming up tomorrow to dig it in!'

'I shall be ready for them. Think of all that language, and language is only codified thought, buried in the ground, Dormer!'

'I have all the thinking I want over all the men buried in the ground. We're losing far too many!'

The 'victory' of the Somme had been a saddening experience for Dormer.

'That shows how wrong you are. We are mortal. We perish. But our words will live.'

'Rot! Do you mean to say that "825 Brigade relieve you tomorrow Nth Div. Ack, ack, ack" will live! Why should it? It'll be superseded in four days. Who wants to perpetuate it?'

'I disagree with you, Dormer, I really do. Here we are at the great crisis of our lives, of the life of European Civilization perhaps. Some trumpery order you or I transmit may mean in reality "Civilization is defeated, Barbarism has won!" or it may mean, I hope, "Lift up your eyes unto the hills from whence – " '

'I wish you wouldn't joke about the Bible!'

'I'm not joking, and you'll find it out before long. Men will fight so long as they've got something to fight about!'

'Well, they have. They want to get home. They'll fight fast enough about that.'

'Not they. That isn't the thing to make 'em fight. It's more likely to make 'em run away. They want an idea.'

'They've had enough ideas, I should think. I seem to remember the walls covered with posters, with an idea a-piece.'

'Those ideas were much too superficial and temporary. They want to feel that they are something, or that they do something so important that it doesn't matter whether they live or die!'

'That's all wrong. It does matter. This War will be won by the side that has most men and most stuff left.'

'Nonsense. It will be won by the side that has the most faith.'

'Oh, well, you go and have faith in your cable line. I've got to have it in these working parties.'

It was now dusk enough for the main body of troops to get on the move. The broad valley below was in ultramarine shadow, the round shoulders of the down touched with lemon-coloured afterglow. Up the drift of chalk dust that represented where the road had once been, an insignificant parish road from one little village to another, but now the main traffic artery of an Army Corps, there came pouring the ceaseless stream, men, men, men, limbers, men, mules, guns, men.

The longer he looked at them the more certain he became that he was right. Not merely the specialists in mechanics, engineers, ordnance, signals, gunners, but the mere infantry had taken months to train, and could be knocked out in a moment. The problem, of course, was to save them up until the moment at which they could produce the maximum effect.

How docile they were. Platoon for this, platoon for that, section of engineers, then a machine-gun company. Then rations, then limbers, wagons, hand-carts full of every conceivable kind of implement or material. Very soon he was obliged to stand in the middle of the road, with the stream of traffic going up, before him, and the stream of traffic coming back, behind, so that in addition to checking and directing one lot he had to keep an eye on the other to see that they did not begin to smoke until they were well down the side of the hill. Gradually the darkness thickened, and the crowd thinned, and the thunder of the front died down. At length he was left with only a belated hurrying limber or two, or ambulance, sent back for the third or fourth time to clear the accumulation of casualties. At last he felt justified in getting into his bunk and shutting his eyes.

Thank goodness that fellow wasn't back. He, Dormer, would be asleep, and would not hear him. He counted the khaki shoulders and dusty wheels that went round and round beneath his eyelids, until he went off.

Unfortunately for that particular *malaise* which the War occasioned to his precise and town-bred spirit, that was not his last sleep that he slept that night. Many a one never woke again to hear the earth-shaking clamour of the barrage, to see that eternal procession of men, men, mules, limbers, men, guns, ambulances, men, lorries, going on and on like some gigantic frieze. But Dormer did. He was one of those who, had he been born in the Middle Ages, would have been described as under a curse, or pictured as working out an atonement for his own or some one else's misdeeds. He had to go on doing his very best, and the more he disliked the whole business the harder he worked. The harder he worked the longer it seemed to that desired day when he might return to the quiet niceties of a branch bank in a provincial town. And all the time Kavanagh kept up that ceaseless argument as to one's mental attitude. Dormer didn't really believe in having such a thing, for he felt bound to join issue with the absurd ramblings of the other, and he could not escape, because their jobs naturally threw them together and because he secretly admired the way that Kavanagh did his work.

So the days turned into weeks and the weeks into months, the casualty lists grew longer and longer, the visible fruits of the immense effort grew smaller and smaller, and as the year wore on, the weather broke, and the only conditions that make life in the open tolerable, light and drought, disappeared, and they dwelt in the sodden twilight of tent or hut, while what had been the white powdery dust, became the cement-like mud that no scraping could remove. Sitting dejectedly over some returns he heard

> 'Still, be still, my soul, the arms you bear are brittle!'

'It's all very well to sit there and sing. This offensive is a failure, we shall never get through.'

'I'm afraid you're right, Dormer. I told you how it would be. I hope we shall learn the lesson.'

'It means another winter in the trenches.'

'Evidently.'

'It's very bad for the men. They've nothing to show for all that's been done.'

'That's nothing new.

> ' "I'm sick of parading,
>   Through cold and wet wading,
>   Or standing all day to be shot in a trench!
>   I'm tired of marching,
>   Pipe-claying and starching,
> How neat we must be to be shot by the French." '

That's what the men thought of it a hundred years ago. Then, they had to pipeclay their belts, two whacking great chest-constricting cross-belts. And their officers didn't arrange for them to play football, every time they went out to rest. In fact they didn't go out to rest. They just stayed in the line.'

'It wasn't very dangerous, was it?'

'There wasn't the shell fire, of course, but what about disease?'

'They were regulars.'

'My dear fellow, when is a soldier not a soldier?'

'I don't like riddles.'

'This is a serious question. How long will the War last?'

'Oh,' cried Dormer bitterly, 'another two years, I suppose.'

'You're about twenty wrong. We shall have conscription shortly, then the real strength will be put into the fight and will compensate for the losses of France and the inertia of Russia.

We shall then settle down to the real struggle between England and Germany for the markets of the world.'

Dormer frowned. 'You're a Socialist,' he said.

'Never mind my opinions. It won't matter by the time we get back into civvys what we are!'

Something rose up in Dormer. He said with certainty:

'You're wrong. The men'll never stand it. Two years at most.'

'The men stood it very well in the Peninsula for six years, and most of them had been fighting somewhere or other for the previous quarter of a century.'

'Once again, they were regulars.'

'Once again, so are you.

> "'For gold the sailor ploughs the main,
> The farmer ploughs the manor,
> The brave poor soldier ne'er disdain,
> That keeps his country's honour.'"

That's you to the life, Dormer. Twenty years hence you'll be a bronzed veteran, in a dirty uniform, with a quarter of a century's polish on your Sam Browne. You have already had more iron whizz past your head than any regular soldier gets in a lifetime, or even the lifetime of two or three generations. You've had a practical experience of war that any general might envy. The only complaint I have to make against you is that you're conducting the whole business as if you were back in your beastly bank, instead of, as the song says, behaving as one "That keeps his country's honour!"'

'That's all nonsense. I've just sent the 561 Brigade to occupy the new line that was taken up after the stunt last Thursday. You know what it's like. It's the remains of a German trench turned round, so that they have all the observation. They've strafed it to Hell, and we are firing on photographs of trenches that are probably empty. It's all nonsense to say the defending side loses more men than the attacking. That's true while the attack is in progress, but an attack in its very nature cannot last long, and then the defenders get their own back.'

As he said the words they were enveloped in an explosion that shook the wet out of the canvas upon them, and whose aftermath of falling débris was echoed by stampeded traffic in the road.

'The Bosche seem set on proving you right,' laughed Kavanagh. 'They forget, as you do, that, sooner or later, an attack gets through and ends the War.'

'Not this one. Nothing but no more reserves will end this. And that may happen to both sides at once. It may all end in stalemate!'

'If it does, we shall fight again. We represent Right. The enemy represents Wrong. Don't you ever forget that for a moment.'

'I don't. I believe we are in the right, or I should never have joined up.' When really moved, there came into Dormer's grey inexpressive face a queer light, that might have made the Germans pause, had they seen it. He was a man of few theories, but he was literally ready to die for those few, when they were attacked. He went on shyly: 'But I don't believe in war as a permanent means of settling "disputes".'

'Bravo!' cried Kavanagh. 'I like you when you speak out. I only wish you did more of it. You're quite right, but what you don't see is that modern society is so rotten that it can only be kept alive by violent purges, credit cycles, strikes, and wars. If it were not for such drastic remedies people of the twentieth century would perish of ease and comfort.'

'Come, ease and comfort never killed anyone.'

'Spiritually!'

'Oh, I don't go in for spiritualism!' Dormer was saying, when his servant brought him his tea. There was bread, that had rolled on the floor of a lorry until it tasted of dust, oil, blood, and coal. There was butter. There was marmalade. There was some cake they had sent him from home. Leaning his elbows on the board on which they wrote, he held his enamel mug in both hands and swilled his chlorinated-water, condensed-milk tasting tea. For the first time, as he clasped the mug and filled his gullet he was warm, hands, mouth, neck, stomach, gradually all his being. He put the mug down nearly empty and shoved the cake over to Kavanagh. 'Have some?' he mumbled.

\*

They found themselves in a village of the Somme country, hardly recognizable for the division that had come there for the offensive, five months before. Just infantry, with the necessary services, without artillery, or cavalry, they were billeted in barns and cottages up and down a narrow valley, with cliff-like downs rising each side and a shallow, rapid stream flowing between poplars and osier beds at the bottom. Dormer was entrusted with the critical military operation of organizing Football, Boxing and entertainment, and spent his time to his great satisfaction, up and down the three miles of road that ran through the Divisional Area, notebook in hand, listing the battalions or companies as entering for one or another of these sports. He liked it and it suited him.

Mildly interested in sport as such, what he liked about his job was that it kept his feet warm and his mind employed, and he arranged so that his daily journey ended sufficiently far from Head-quarters for some hospitable unit to say, 'Oh, stop and have lunch!' It would then be a nice walk back, a quiet hour or so, getting the correspondence into shape before the Colonel returned from the afternoon ride, by which he shook down his lunch and made a place for his dinner. After that would be tea, orders to sign and circulate, mess, a game of cards, and another day would be done. He had long found out that the great art of war lay not in killing Germans, but in killing time.

Over and over again, every day and all day, as he moved up and down those wintry roads, he looked at the faces of the men who knew now that the great offensive had resulted in infinitesimal gains, enormous losses, and only approached the end of the War by so many weeks. He failed entirely to make out what was going on in their minds. Officers were always officially pleased to see him because he was attached to Divisional Head-quarters, because he came to talk about games, not about work, because he was, as he was perfectly conscious, one

## THE CRIME AT VANDERLYNDEN'S

of the most difficult fellows in the world to quarrel with. He had never had any great bitterness in life, and was so averse to official 'side' that he made an effort to appear as informal as possible. Sometimes N.C.O.s would be produced, consulted as to whether a team could be got together, what amount of special training could be allowed intending pugilists, without interfering with necessary drills and fatigues, what histrionic, (or to put it frankly), what music-hall talent could be found. The N.C.O.s were (of course) keen, smart, attentive, full of suggestions and information. They had to be. They kept their jobs by so being, and their jobs gave them just the opportunity to live about as well as lumbermen in the remote parts of North America, instead of existing like beasts in barns, not pet animals, not marketable produce, but just beasts, herded and disposed of, counted and controlled, for such was the fate of the average infantryman, and war being what it is, there came a gradual acquiescence in it. It could be no other.

But all those plain soldiers, of whom only one or two per cent had even a voice in their entertainment, of what they thought, who knows? Dormer wondered. He wondered even more at himself. Why on earth, in the midst of a European War that had changed his whole existence so dramatically, he should want to go bothering his head about what was happening to other people he couldn't think, but he went on doing it. Otherwise the life suited him rather well, and with every fresh week that separated him from the offensive, a sort of balance so natural to the thoroughly balanced sort of person that he was, went on adjusting itself, and he found himself thinking that perhaps in the new year there might be a new chance, the French, the Russians, the Italians might do something, so might we. Then it would be over, and one could go home.

It was then that the inevitable happened. He knew it as soon as he got into the room at the Mairie that served for Q. office. He was so sure that he stood turning over the correspondence on his desk, the usual pile of returns, orders, claims and indents, without reading them, certain that the Colonel was going to speak to him. At last the Colonel did speak:

## THE CRIME AT VANDERLYNDEN'S

'Look here, Dormer, I thought we settled this?'

There it was, the blue questionnaire form, the other memorandums, Divisional Corps, Army, French Mission, Base Authority, all saying 'Passed to you please, for necessary action.' With an absurd feeling that it did not matter what he said, or did, and that the whole thing was arranging itself without him, he got out:

'What is that, sir?'

'This – er – civilian claim for compensation. Something about a girl in a hayfield. What did you do, when we were up in Flanders?'

He rebelled so against the unfairness of it.

'Major Stevenage had the matter in hand. I went with him to the spot.'

'What did you find?'

'It was not what I – you – we thought, sir. The words "*La Vierge*" were intended to convey that a shrine had been damaged.'

'A shrine? Really. How odd the French are? It was accidental, was it? Bad driving?'

'No, sir, not exactly. A driver wanted shelter for his mules –'

'Quite right, quite right.'

'So he broke into the shrine –'

'Ah, that was a mistake, of course. Whatever were his unit about to let him?'

'The matter was not reported until later.'

'Then they placed him under arrest and stoppages?'

'They were moved immediately, sir. But I didn't gather that any action was taken.'

'But when Major Stevenage found it out?'

'It had happened so long before that he thought it was impossible to pursue the matter. So I made a report and sent it to the proper authoritity, to see if an ex gratia payment could be made.'

'And they have done nothing, of course. So the French Mission have dug it up again.'

'Indeed, sir.'

'Yes. Oh, I can't wade through all this. But I tell you what, young Dormer. You've got yourself involved in this correspondence, and I shouldn't be at all surprised if you didn't ever get out. I shouldn't really.'

'I can't see that I've done anything wrong, sir.'

'Can't you? Well, it's no good your telling the French Mission that, I'm afraid. You might go and try to persuade them that there's a mistake, or an exaggeration, and get them to drop it. You'd better go and see them anyhow. They're at Flan! Take what's-his-name with you.'

From this, Dormer, by long experience, understood that he was was to go to Army Head-quarters and to take the Divisional French Liaison Officer with him. He neither liked nor disliked the job. It was the sort of thing one had to do in war-time and he was used to it. So he went down the little stony street to the pork-butcher's, where, upon the swing-gate that admitted one to the dank, greasy, appetizing interior, where every sort of out-of-the-way portion of the pig lay cooked and smelling 'sentimental', hung the placard 'French Liaison Officer', with the number of the Division carefully smudged out. Here, bluecoated, booted and spurred, sat the French Liaison Officer, innumerable small printed sheets of instructions before him, carefully arranged on this pile or on that, while in between lay the cardboard-covered *dossiers*.

Dormer's immediate impression was: 'Not enough to do. Passing the time away,' but he had too much sympathy with such an attitude to say so. He was greeted with effusion:

'My dear Dormer, to what do I owe the pleasure?'

Dormer never liked effusion. He replied briefly:

'This,' and threw the papers on the table.

It amused him to watch the change in the other's face from purely official politeness to perfectly genuine determination to keep out of it.

'Well, Dormer, you've heard of System D?'

He had to think whether it was Swedish gymnastics or a patent medicine.

'It means "*Débrouillez vous*," or "Don't get mixed up with

it." That is my advice to you. In any case I shall leave it alone. It is a matter of discipline purely.'

'Quite so.' Dormer did not care whether the sarcasm was obvious. 'But I have received orders to go and see your Chief at Army Head-quarters, and to take you with me. I suppose you don't mind going. It'll be a ride.'

'I shall be delighted. I will go and tell my servant to have my horse round. I will introduce you to Colonel Lepage. He is a man of excellent family.'

'I thought you would,' said Dormer to himself.

Accordingly, they rode together. The Frenchman rode with style, being bound to show that he was of the class of officer who could ride, a sharp demarcation in his army. Dormer rode as he did everything else. He had learned it as part of his training, without enthusiasm, knowing that a motor-bike was a far better way of getting about. But he was careful of a horse as of anything else. They arrived at Flan. It was another little stone-built village. The only difference he could see between it and Louches, which they had just left, was that it stood on the top of a hill, the other along the bottom of a valley.

Its present temporary occupants, however, he could soon see to be a vastly different category. Every little house was placarded with the signs or marks of the offices or messes it contained. Very-well-groomed orderlies and signallers strolled or waited. Big cars and impeccable riding horses were being held or standing. They found the French Mission, got their horses held (instead of turning off the petrol, and kicking down a stand, thought Dormer) and entered.

It was the little Picard parlour of some small *rentier*, who, having sold beetroot to advantage during fifty years, found himself able at last to fold his shirt-sleeved arms, and from his window, or often from his doorway, to watch other people doing what he had done in the little paved Place.

He, of course, had gone to Brittany, Bordeaux, the Riviera, to be out of the sound of the guns that had killed his son, and his vacant place had been scheduled by a careful Maire as available for billeting. The French army, more impressed by orders, better trained, more experienced, had carefully removed every picture, book, or cushion and stored them in safety – where a British Mess would have left them – at least until they were broken or disappeared. At small tables sat two or three officers in azure, with three or more bars on the cuff. Dendrecourt halted before one of these, clicked his heels, and saluted, and asked if he might present the Captain Dormer, of the English Army. Colonel Lepage rose with effusion, excessively English:

'My dear Dormer, charmed to meet you. Sit down. What can we do for you?'

'I have been sent to see you about a civilian claim for compensation.'

'*L'affaire Vanderlynde!*' put in Dendrecourt.

'Aha!' The Colonel tapped his blotting-pad with a paper knife, and knitted his brows, 'What have you to propose?'

'My General' – Dormer was sufficiently practised to avail himself of that fiction – 'wished me to explain that this matter has been fully investigated.'

'Ah! so we may shortly expect to hear that the guilty individual has been arrested?'

'Well, not exactly an arrest, sir. The whole affair rests upon a mistake.'

'What sort of mistake?' The other officers gave up whatever they were doing, and gathered round at the tone of the last question.

'Upon investigation, it appears that the claim is not for – er – personal violence.'

'I should be obliged if you would define personal violence.'

'That would take us rather far afield, sir. All I want to point out is that the expression "*La Vierge*" does not refer to Mademoiselle Vanderlynde, but to an image in a shrine.'

There were some beginnings of a titter and Dormer was conscious that he was blushing violently. But Colonel Lepage quelled the others with a look. He had the matter so well in hand that Dormer began slowly to feel that he must be one of those political soldiers, whose every act and speech is dictated by the necessities of some policy, hatched high up among

Foreign Offices and their ante-rooms, and worked out in detail by underlings dealing with underlings. Moreover, Dormer was perfectly conscious that he was a junior officer, and therefore a splendid target. Colonel Lepage would not meet him that evening at Mess. He resigned himself, and the Colonel drew a long breath, and let himself go.

'Upon my word, it is all very fine for you others. We are much obliged for the information as to the meaning of the word *Vierge*. And also for being told that no arrest has been made and that no compensation has been offered. Unfortunately the matter has gone a good deal further than you suppose, and we have to furnish a report to a higher authority, to the French War Office in fact. The matter is a most serious one. The claim is for trespass upon private property not demarcated for billeting under the law of 1873. You follow?'

Dormer held his peace. With the exception of the word demarcated, the Colonel's English was as good as his own and many times more voluble. He contented himself with thinking 'Cock – cock – cock – cock pheasant!'

'Then there is the actual damage to the fabric. You may not be aware that such an object is held in great veneration by the owners, more particularly in Flanders where they are very devout. But the most serious thing of all was the treatment accorded to the Mayor when he was – with the most perfect legality – called in by the claimant to take official note of the damage. This functionary was grossly insulted by the English troops and I regret to say that these occurrences are far too frequent. Only last Easter at Bertezeele, the procession of the Religious Festival was the object of laughter of the troops, who may not be aware that the inhabitants attach great importance to such matters, but who should be so instructed by their officers. And at Leders-cappell only last week, the Mayor of that Commune also was insulted in the middle of his official duties. These incidents are very regrettable and must be checked. Therefore I regret to say that your explanation is valueless. Perhaps you will be so good as to convey this to your General?'

Dormer had a feeling that whatever he said would make no earthly difference, so he merely muttered:

'Very good, sir,' and turned on his heel.

Walking their horses down the hill from Flan, Dendrecourt said:

'My word, he was in a state of mind, wasn't he? our Colonel.'

Dormer had the clearest possible presentiment that the moment the door closed upon them, the Colonel had said "Pan" in imitation of a cork being snapped into a bottle, and that all the rest of the officers had laughed. So he said:

'What on earth is behind all this, Dendrecourt?'

'Why, nothing, except the dignity of France.'

'The whole job is only worth a pound or two. I'd have paid it out of my own pocket rather than have all this about it.'

'Well of course, you may have enough money to do it, but, my dear Dormer, a few pounds in England is a good many francs in France, not only in exchange value, but in sentiment. Then, no one likes having his grandmother's tomb broken into —'

'I suppose they will get over it, if they are paid enough money,' rejoined Dormer, bitterly, for it was exactly what he had heard before.

'Certainly!' replied Dendrecourt, without noticing, 'but it is most unfortunate at this moment. There is a religious revival in France. A new Commander-in-Chief and a new spirit, and these insults to the religious sentiment are very trying. Then there is the insult to the Mayor.'

'Oh, devil take the Mayor!'

The Frenchman shrugged. 'The devil has taken all of us, my friend. We are a sacrificed generation. You find the Mayor of Hondebecq annoying. So do I. But not more than everything else. You would not like it if French soldiers laughed at an English Mayor!'

'My dear Dendrecourt, in England a Mayor is somebody. Not an old peasant dressed up in a top hat and an apron, all stars and stripes.'

'Well, here is lunch!' (He called it lernch.) 'I will not join with you, Dormer, in the game of slanging each other's nationality.'

Dormer dismounted and handed over his horse, and went in to lunch, walking wide in the legs and feeling a fool. The only pleasure he had had was the male-game-bird appearance of Colonel Lepage.

Of course he said nothing about his morning's work, and of course Colonel Birchin had forgotten it. At the end of the week the Division moved into the line and he had to go forward with that fellow Kavanagh to check the workings of communications. They were 'in' four weeks, and came out in the great cold of January 1917, and were moved up near to Doullens. They had not been out a week before the Colonel sent for him. He knew what it would be about, but the whole of his mind being occupied with keeping warm, he did not care. They were in huts, on a high plateau. White snow obliterated every colour, softened every outline as far as the eye could reach, except where the road to Arras lay black with its solid ice, the snow that the traffic had trodden into water, refrozen into a long black band, scattered with cinders, gravel, chalk, anything that made it negotiable.

Dormer looked at the collection of huts, with the obvious pathways between, the obvious, inevitable collection of traffic, lorriers and limbers, motor-cycles and horses, that accumulated round any Head-quarters. He wondered how long it would take the Bosche to discover it in some air-photo and bomb it all to blazes. Inside Q. office, in spite of two big stoves in the tiny box of a place, it was so cold that every one breathed clouds of steam, and the three officers, and the clerks, sat in their coats.

'Look here, Dormer!' – the Colonel sounded as though he had a personal grievance – 'just look what I've got from the army.'

It was an official memorandum, emanating from Army Headquarters and duly passed through the Corps to whom they had belonged, and by the Corps to the Divison, inquiring what results had been arrived at in the Vanderlynden affair, and whether it could not be reported to the Minister of War that the matter had reached a satisfactory conclusion.

'I thought you settled all that, while we were at Louches?'

'Well, sir, I went to see them at Army Head-quarters and explained, or tried to.'

'You don't seem to have done any good at all. In fact it looks as though you and Dendrecourt had a nice morning ride for nothing.'

'I couldn't get a word in. It suited somebody's politics to blackguard us just then, and I left it at that. It didn't seem any use arguing, sir.'

'Well, this must be stopped somehow. We shall have the French War Minister taking the matter up with Whitehall, directly, and a nice figure we shall all cut. I've known men sent to Salonika or Mespot, as company commanders, for less than this.'

'Very good, sir. What shall I do?'

'Get on with it. Find out who did the beastly damage, and strafe him. Strafe somebody, anyhow, and bring the remains here in a bag. We can show it to Corps, and they can write a sermon on the efficiency of the Adjutant-General's Department.'

'Yessir. If you refer to the correspondence you will see that the name of the unit is mentioned.'

Dormer stood perfectly still, while his superior officer turned over the closely written, printed or typed sheets. His face was carefully veiled in official blankness. He had an idea.

'Well, here you are,' the Colonel was saying, '469 Trench Mortar Battery. You'll have to go and see 'em. You ought to have done so long before!'

Dormer could not help adding, maliciously:

'Wouldn't it be sufficient if I were to send 'em a chit, sir?'

'No, it wouldn't. We've had quite enough of this procrastination. It'll land us all in a nice hole, if we're not careful. You go and see them and insist on getting to the bottom of it.'

'Yes, sir. The order of battle will give their position.'

'I'll see to that. I'll have it looked up and let you know in the morning.'

'Yes, sir.' He went back to his hut, delighted.

Escape. Escape. Even the illusion of escape for a few hours, it must be at least that, for if the 469 Trench Mortar Battery were

## THE CRIME AT VANDERLYNDEN'S

in the same Division, the same Corps even, he would have heard of them. They must be at least a day's journey away, and he would be able to get away from the blasting and withering boredom for at least that. Colonel Birchin, a regular, who had been on various Staff appointments since the very early days, had no conception how personnel changed and units shifted, and unless he (Dormer) were very much mistaken, it would be a jolly old hunt. So much the better. He would have his mind off the War for a bit.

The reply came from Corps that, according to the order of battle, 469 Trench Mortar Battery was not in existence, but try Trench Mortar School at Bertezeele. It was all one to Dormer. He might simply be exchanging one cold hut for another, he might travel by rail and lorry instead of on horse or foot. But at any rate it would be a different hut that he was cold in and a different mode of conveyance that jolted him, and that was something, one must not be too particular in war-time. So he jumped on a lorry that took him into Doullens and at Doullens he took train and went through Abbeville and the endless dumps and camps by the sea, up to Étaples, where the dumps and camps, the enormous reinforcement depots and mile-long hospitals stretched beside the line almost into Boulogne, where was a little pocket, as it were, of French civilian life, going on undisturbed amid the general swamping of French by English, on that coast, and of civilian life by military. Here he got a meal and changed and went off again up the hill, past Marquise, and down a long hill to Calais, in the dark, and then on, in the flat, where the country smelled different from the Somme, and where the people spoke differently and the names of the stations sounded English, and where there were French and Belgian police on the platforms.

He slept and woke at St Omer, and slept again and woke to find all the lights out and a general scurry and scatteration, with the drone of aeroplanes and the continual pop-popping of antiaircraft fire. Then came the shrieking whirr and sharp crash of the first bomb, with its echo of tinkling glass, barking of dogs, and rumour of frightened humanity.

Like most people accustomed to the line, Dormer regarded the bombing of back billets as a spectacle rather than as one of the serious parts of warfare, and got out to stroll about the platform with officers going up as reinforcements. They exchanged cigarettes and news and hardly stopped to laugh at the horrified whisper of the R.T.O., 'Don't light matches here!' It was soon over, like all bombing. If you were hit you were hit, but if you weren't hit in the first minute or two, you wouldn't be, because no plane could stay circling up there for very long, and the bomber was always more frightened than you were. Then the train moved on, and Dormer could feel on each side of him again the real camp life of units just behind the line, mule standings, gun parks, and tents and huts of infantry, and services. It was midnight before he got out at Bailleul. He had left the camp on the Arras road in the morning, had made a great loop on the map and reached a railhead as near the line as he had been twenty-four hours before. He stumbled up the stony street to the Officers' Rest House, drank some cocoa out of a mug and fell asleep, his head on his valise.

In the morning he got a lift out to Bertezeele, and found the Trench Mortar School. He reflected that it would really be more correct to say that he took a lift to the Trench Mortar School, and incidentally touched the village of Bertezeele. For the fact was that the English population of the parish exceeded the French native one. Men of all sorts and conditions from every unit known to the Army List (and a good many that had never graced the pages of that swollen periodical) were drawn into this new device for improved killing. Dormer himself, one of those who, since the elementary home camp training of 1915, had been in or just behind the trenches, wondered at the complicated ramifications with which the War was running. Apparently those curious little brass instruments, the bane of his life as an infantry platoon commander, which used to come up behind his line and there, while totally ineffective in the vital matter of beating the Germans, were just sufficiently annoying to make those methodical enemies take great pains to rob him of his food and sleep for many ensuing days, were all done away with.

Stokes, whoever he was, but he was certainly a genius, had effected a revolution. Owing to him, neat tubes, like enlarged pencil-guards, with a nail inside the blind end, upon which the cap-end of the cartridge automatically fell, were being used, as a hosier might say, in all sizes from youths' to large men's. Stokes was branded with genius, because his invention combined the two essentials – simplicity with certainty. He had brought the blunderbuss up to date.

What else were these short-range, muzzle-loading, old-iron scattering devices? Just blunderbusses. History was not merely repeating itself. As the War went on it was moving backwards. Tin helmets of the days of Cromwell, bludgeons such as Coeur de Lion used upon Saladin, and for mere modernity, grenades like the original British Grenadiers of the song. He had never had any head for poetry, but he could remember some of the stuff Kavanagh had sung in the dug-out. Not tow-row-row. That was the chorus. Ah! he remembered.

> 'Our leaders march with fusees,
> And we with hand-grenades,
> We throw them from the glacis
> About the enemy's ears.
> With a tow-row-row,' etc.

Well, now we didn't. If we had grenades we carried them in aprons, like a market woman, with a skirt full of apples. And if we had a blunderbuss, like the guard of the coach in the 'Pickwick Papers', we kept it, and all the ironmongery that belonged to it, on a hand-barrow, and pushed it in front of us like fish-hawkers on a Saturday night. What a War! Kavanagh was quite right of course. There was neither decency nor dignity left in it. Wouldn't do to admit that though! And putting on his very best 'Good - mornin'-Sah-I-have-been-sent-by-Divisional-Headquarters' expression, he asked his way to the 'office' as they were beginning to call the orderly room in most detachments, and inquired for 469 Battery. Yes. They were to be seen. Orderly room, as a Corps formation, was distant and slightly patronizing, but the information was correct. He could see the Officer commanding the battery. Certainly he could, as soon as morning practice was over. That would do. He made himself as inconspicuous as possible until he saw the various parties being 'fallen in' on the range, and heard the uncanny ear-tickling silence that succeeded the ceaseless pop-pop of practice and then drifted casually into the wooden-chair-and-table furnished anteroom, where the month-old English magazines gave one a tremulous homesickness, and men who had been mildly occupied all the morning were drinking all the vermouth or whisky they could, in the fear of being bored to the point of mutiny in the afternoon.

There was, of course, the usual springtime curiosity as to what the year might bring forth, for every one always hoped against hope that the next offensive would really be the last. An orderly wandering among the tables appeared to be looking for him, and he found himself summoned before the Officer commanding the School.

Although his appointment was new, Colonel Burgess was of the oldest type of soldier, the sort who tell the other fellows how to do it. The particular sort of war in which he found himself suited him exactly. He had the true Indian view of life, drill, breakfast, less drill, lunch, siesta, sport, dinner, cards. So he ruled the mess cook with a rod of iron, took disciplinary action if the stones that lined the path leading to the door of the anteroom and office were not properly white, and left the technical side of the business to Sergeant-instructors who, having recently escaped from the trenches, were really keen on it.

He received Dormer with that mixture of flattery due to anyone from Divisional Head-quarters and suspicion naturally aroused as to what he (Dormer) might be after. He was annoyed that he had not heard of Dormer's arrival, and hastened to add:

'Not a very full parade this morning, units come and go, y'know. We can never be quite sure what we are going to get! What did you think of our show?'

Dormer realized that the old gentleman was under the impression he was being spied on:

'I really didn't notice, sir. I have been sent to see the Officer commanding 469 Trench Mortar Battery. Matter of discipline arising out of a claim for compensation.'

'Oh, ah! Yes indeed. Certainly. See him now. Sergeant Innes!'

The efficient Scotch Sergeant to be found in all such places appeared from the outer office.

'Have we anyone here from 469 T.M.B.?'

The officer required was duly produced, and the Colonel retired to the Mess, leaving them together. Dormer sized up this fellow with whom he was thus brought into momentary contact. This became by necessity almost a fine art, during years of war. Dormer was fairly proficient. The fellow opposite to him was of the same sort as himself. Probably in insurance or stockbroking, not quite the examination look of the Civil Service, not the dead certainty of banking. He had obviously enlisted, been gradually squeezed up to the point of a Commission, had had his months in the line and had taken to Trench Mortars because they offered the feeling of really doing something, together with slightly improved conditions (hand-carts could be made to hold more food, drink and blankets than mere packs) and was getting along as well as he could. He heard what Dormer wanted and his face cleared.

'Why, that's last April. I couldn't tell you anything about that. I was in Egypt!'

'You don't know of any officer in your unit who could give some information about the occurrence?'

'No. There's only young Sands, beside myself. He couldn't have been there.'

'Some N.C.O. then?'

'Heavens, man, where d'you think we've been? All the N.C.O.s are new since I was with the crowd!'

'But surely there must be some record of men who were with your unit?'

'Well, of course, the pay rolls go back to Base somewhere. But I suppose you can pick the name and number up from the conduct sheet.'

'You see, I don't know the man's name. His number was given as 6494.'

'That's a joke, of course. It's the number that the cooks sing out, when we hold the last Sick Parade, before going up the line.'

'Of course it is. You're right. I ought to have remembered that, but I've been away from my regiment for some time.' Dormer pondered a moment, relieved. Then the thought of going back to the Q. office with nothing settled, and the queries of the French Mission and the whole beastly affair hanging over his head, drove him on again. He made his air a little heavier, more Divisional, less friendly.

'Well, I'm afraid this won't do, you know. This matter has got to be cleared up. It will be very awkward if I have to go back and inform Head-quarters that you can't furnish any information. In fact, they will probably think it's a case of not wanting to know, and make a regular Court of Inquiry of it.'

He watched the face of the other, and saw in a moment how well he had calculated. The fellow was frightened. A mere unit commander, and a small unit at that! To such a one, of course, Divisional Head-quarters were something pretty near omniscient, certainly omnipotent. Dormer watched the fellow shift in the chair without a qualm. Let some one else be worried too. He himself had had worry enough. The face before him darkened, smirked deferentially, and then brightened.

'Oh, there was old Chirnside. He might know.'

'Who was he?'

'Chirnside? He was a sort of a quarter bloke. It was before we were properly formed, and he used to look after all our stores and orderly room business. He had been with the battery since its formation. We were just anybody, got together anyhow, chiefly from the infantry, you remember?'

Dormer saw the other glance at his shoulder straps and just refrain from calling him sir, poor wretch. He took down the information and thanked his friend. Chirnside had apparently gone to some stunt Corps, to do something about equipment. That was all right. He wouldn't be killed.

Having got thus far, Dormer felt that he had done a good deal, and went to take his leave of Colonel Burgess. But he soon found that he was not to be allowed to get away like that. He was bidden to stay to lunch. There was no train from Bailleul until the evening and he was willing enough. The lunch was good. Food remained one of the things in which one could take an interest. He did so. After lunch the Colonel took him for a walk over the golf course. This was the margin of land around the range, on which no cultivation was allowed, and from which civilians were rigidly excluded, for safety's sake. At least during range practice, which took place every day more or less, in the morning. After that, of course, they could be without difficulty excluded for the remainder of the day for a different, if not for so laudable a purpose.

The Colonel was a fine example of those qualities which have made an island Empire what it is. Having spent most of his life from sixteen years old at Sandhurst, then in India or Egypt, and finally at Eastbourne, he knew better than most men how to impose those institutions which he and his sort considered the only ones that made civilization possible, in the most unlikely places and upon the most disinclined of people. Dormer had seen it being done before, but marvelled more and more. Just as the Colonel, backed of course by a sufficient number of his like, and the right sort of faithful underling, had introduced tennis into India, duck-shooting into Egypt, and exclusiveness into Eastbourne, against every condition of climate or geographical position, native religion or custom, so now he had introduced golf into Flanders, and that in the height of a European War.

At the topmost point of the golf course, the Colonel stopped, and began to point out the beauties of the spot to Dormer. They were standing on one of those low gravelly hills that separate the valley of the Yser from that of the Lys. Northward, beyond Poperinghe, was a yet lower and greener ridge that shelved away out of sight towards Dunkirk. East lay Ypres, in an endless rumour of war. Southward, the Spanish towers of Bailleul showed where the road wound towards Lille, by Armentières. Westward, Cassel rose above those hillocks and plains, among the most fertile in the world. But the Colonel was most concerned with a big square old farmhouse, that lay amid its barns and meadows, at a crook in the Bailleul road.

The Colonel's eyes took on a brighter blue and his moustache puffed out like fine white smoke.

'I had a lot of trouble with that fellow.' He pointed to the farm. 'Wanted to come and cultivate the range. I had to get an interpreter to see him. Said he could grow – er – vegetables in between the shell-holes. At last we had to order afternoon practice to keep him off. Then he wanted this part of the land. Had to move the guns up and make some new bunkers. Four rounds makes a bunker, y'know. Come and have tea?'

It was very nice weather for walking, dry and clear. The Mess had seemed tolerable at lunch, but Dormer had not been long at tea before he recollected what he seldom forgot for more than an hour or so, that it was not tea, one of the fixed occasions of his safe and comfortable life. It was a meal taken under all the exigencies of a campaign – chlorinated water, condensed milk, army chair, boots and puttees on one, and on this particular afternoon a temperature below zero, in an army hut.

The Colonel, of course, occupied the place of warmth next the stove. The remainder of the Mess got as near to it as they could. The result was, that when the Colonel began to question him as to the object of his visit, and how he had progressed towards attaining it, everybody necessarily heard the whole of the conversation. He now realized that he was telling the tale for the fourth time. He had told it to Kavanagh, then to Colonel Birchin. Now he had told it to the Officer commanding 469 T.M.B. and finally here he was going over it again. He resented it as a mere nuisance, but was far from seeing at that moment the true implication of what he was doing. The matter was not a State secret. It was an ordinary piece of routine discipline, slightly swollen by its reactions in the French Mission, and by the enormous size and length of the War.

If he had refused to say why he was there the Colonel would certainly have put him down as having been sent by the Division, or some one even higher, to spy on the activities of the School. He didn't want to be labelled as that, so told what he knew glibly enough. The Colonel waxed very voluble over it, gave good advice that was no earthly use, and dwelt at length on various aspects of the case. The French were grasping and difficult and superstitious, but on the other hand, drivers were a rough lot and must be kept in check. They were always doing damage. The fellow was quite right of course to look after his mules. The animals were in a shocking state, etc., etc., but quite wrong, of course, to damage civilian property, tradition of the British Army, since Wellington all the other way, the French naturally expected proper treatment, etc., etc.

Dormer had heard it all before, from Colonel Birchin, Major Stevenage and others, with exactly the same well-meant condescension, and the same grotesque ineffectiveness. This old Colonel, like all his sort, couldn't solve the difficulty nor shut the French up, nor appease G.H.Q.

Presently, the old man went off to the orderly room to sign the day's correspondence, the Mess thinned and Dormer dozed discreetly, he had had a poor night and was desperately sleepy. Some one came to wake him up and offered him a wash, and he was glad to move, stiff with cold, and only anxious to pass the time until he could get the midnight train from Bailleul. They were very hospitable, made much of him at dinner, and he ate and drank all he could get, being ravenous and hoping to sleep through the discomforts of the long train journey in the dark. He was getting fairly cheerful by the time the Colonel left the hut, and only became conscious, in the intervals of a learned and interesting discussion of the relative theories of wire-cutting, that a 'rag' was in progress at the other end of the room.

A gunner officer, a young and happy boy who was still in the stage of thinking the War the greatest fun out, was holding a mock Court of Inquiry. Gradually, the 'rag' got the better of the argument and Dormer found himself being addressed as 'Gentlemen of the jury'. A target frame was brought in by some one to act as a witness-box, but the gunner genius who presided, soon had it erected into a sort of Punch and Judy Proscenium. Then only did it dawn on Dormer that the play was not Punch and Judy. It was the Mayor of Hondebecq being derided by the troops, with a Scotch officer in a kilt impersonating Madeleine Vanderlynden, and receiving with the greatest equanimity, various suggestions that ranged from the feebly funny to the strongly obscene. O.C. 469 T.M.B. found a willing column formed behind him which he had to lead round the table, an infantryman brought a wastepaper basket to make the Mayor's top hat, and in the midst of other improvisations, Dormer discovered the gunner standing in front of him with a mock salute.

'Do you mind coming out of the Jury and taking your proper part?'

It was cheek, of course, but Dormer was not wearing red tabs, and beside, what was the use of standing on one's dignity. He asked:

'What part do I play?'

'You're Jack Ketch. You come on in the fourth Act, and land Nobby one on the nob!'

'I see. What are you?'

'Me? I'm the Devil. Watch me devilling,' and with a long maproller he caught the players in turn resounding cracks upon their several heads.

They turned on him with common consent, and in the resulting struggle, the table broke and subsided with the whole company in an ignominious mass. The dust rose between the grey canvas-covered walls and the tin suspension lamp rocked like that of a ship at sea. Everybody picked himself up, slightly sobered, and began to discuss how to get the damage repaired before the Colonel saw it in the morning.

O.C. 469 T.M.B. stood at Dormer's elbow:

'We've just got time to catch your train.'

'Come on.' Dormer had no intention of being marooned in this place another day. Outside a cycle and sidecar stood panting. Dormer did wonder as they whizzed down the rutted road how long such a vehicle had been upon the strength of a Trench Mortar School, but after all, could you blame fellows? They were existing under War conditions, what more could one ask?

\*

He woke to the slow jolting of the train as it slowed up in smoky twilight at Boulogne. He bought some food, and sitting with it in his hands and his thermos between his knees, he watched the grey Picard day strengthen over those endless camps and hospitals, dumps and training grounds.

He was retracing his steps of the day before, but he was a step farther on. As he looked at the hundreds of thousands of khaki-clad figures, he realized something of what he had to do. With no name or number he had to find one of them, who could be proved to have been at a certain place a year ago. He didn't want to, but if he didn't, would he ever get rid of the business?

The 'rag' of the previous evening stuck in his head. How true it was. The man who did the thing was 'Nobby' with the number of 6494 that was beginning to be folklore. Of course he was. He was any or every soldier. Madeleine Vanderlynden was the heroine. O.C. 469 T.M.B. was the hero. The Mayor of Hondebecq was the comic relief, and he, Dormer, was the villain. He was indeed Jack Ketch, the spoiler of the fun, the impotent figure-head of detested 'Justice', or 'Law and Order'. And finally, as in all properly conducted Punch and Judy shows, the Devil came and took the lot. What had Dendrecourt said: 'The Devil had taken the whole generation.' Well, it was all in the play. And when he realized this, as he slid on from Étaples down to Abbeville, he began to feel it was not he who was pursuing some unknown soldier in all that nation-in-arms that had grown from the British Expeditionary Force, but the Army – no, the War – that was pursuing him.

When he got out at Doullens, and scrounged a lift from a passing car, he found himself looking at the driver, at the endless transport on either side of the road, at the sentry on guard over the parked heavies in the yard of the jam factory, at the military policeman at the crossroads. One or other of all these hundreds of thousands knew all about the beastly business that was engaging more and more of his mind. One or other of them could point to the man who was wanted.

He found himself furtively examining their faces, prepared for covert ridicule and suspicion, open ignorance or stupidity.

He had, by now, travelled a long way from the first feelings he had about the affair, when he had thought of the perpetrator of the damage at Vanderlynden's as a poor devil to be screened if possible. He wouldn't screen him now. This was the effect of the new possibility that had arisen. He, Dormer, did not intend to be ridiculous.

On reaching the Head-quarters of the Division, he found the War in full progress. That is to say, every one was standing about, waiting to do something. Dormer had long discovered that this was war. Enlisting as he had done at the outbreak of hostilities, with no actual experience of what such a set of conditions could possibly be like, he had then assumed that he was in for a brief and bitter period of physical discomfort and danger, culminating quite possibly in death, but quite certainly in a decisive victory for the Allies within a few months. He had graduated in long pedestrian progress of Home Training, always expecting it to cease one fine morning. It did. He and others were ordered to France. With incredible slowness and difficulty they found the battalion to which they were posted. Now for it, he had thought, and soon found himself involved in a routine, dirtier and more dangerous, but as unmistakably a routine as that in which he had been involved at home.

He actually distinguished himself at it, by his thoroughness and care, and came to be the person to whom jobs were given! Thus had he eventually, after a twelvemonth, found another false end to the endless waiting. He was sent to help the Q. office of Divisional Staff. He had felt himself to be of considerable importance, a person who really was winning the War. But in a few weeks he was as disabused as ever. It was only the same thing. Clerking in uniform, with no definite hours, a few privileges of food and housing, but no nearer sight of the end of it. The Somme had found him bitterly disillusioned. And yet even now, after being two days away from the Head-quarters where his lot was cast, he was dumbfounded afresh to find everything going on just as he had left it.

They were all waiting now for orders to go into a back area and be trained. For, as sure as the snowdrop appeared, there sprang up in the hearts of men a pathetic eternal hopefulness. Perhaps nothing more than a vernal effusion, yet there it was, and as Dormer reported to Colonel Birchin, in came the messenger they had all been expecting, ordering them, not forward into the line, but backward to Authun, for training. It was some time before he could get attention, and when he did, it seemed both to him and to the Colonel that the affair had lessened in importance.

'You've asked 3rd Echelon to give you the posting of this Chirnside?'

'Yessir!'

'Very well. That's all you can do for the moment. Now I want you to see that everything is cleared up in the three Infantry Brigade camps, and don't let us have the sort of chits afterwards that we got at Lumbres, etc.'

So the Vanderlynden affair receded into the background, and Dormer found before his eyes once more that everlasting mud-coloured procession, men, men, limbers, cookers, men, lorries, guns, limbers, men.

He looked at it this time with different eyes. His Division was one-fiftieth part of the British Army in France. It took over a day to get on the move, it occupied miles of road, absorbed train-loads of supplies, and would take two days to go thirty miles. The whole affair was so huge, that the individual man was reduced and reduced in importance until he went clean out of sight. This fellow he was pursuing, or Chirnside, or anyone who could have given any useful information about the Vanderlynden claim, might be in any one of those cigarette-smoking, slow-moving columns, on any of those springless vehicles, or beside any of those mules.

He gazed at the faces of the men as they streamed past him, every county badge on their caps, every dialect known to England on their lips, probably the best natured and easiest to manage of any of the dozen or so national armies engaged in the War. He was realizing deeply the difficulty of discovering that particular 'Nobby' who had broken the front of the shrine at Vanderlynden's. It was just the thing any of them would do. How many times had he noticed their curious tenderness for uncouth animals, stray dogs or cats, even moles or hedgehogs, and above all the brazen, malevolent army mule. He was no fancier of any sort of beast, and the mule as used in France he had long realized to have two virtues and two only – cheapness and durability. You couldn't kill them, but if you did, it was easy to get more. He had been, for a long while now, a harassed officer, busy shifting quantities of war material, human, animal, or inanimate, from one place to another, and had come to regard mules as so much movable war stores. Added to the fact that he was no fancier, this had prevented him from feeling any affection for the motive power of first-line transport. But he was conscious enough that it was not so with the men – the 'other ranks' as they were denominated in all those innumerable parade states and nominal rolls with which he spent his days in dealing.

No, what the fellow had done was what most drivers would do. That queer feeling about animals was the primary cause of the whole affair. Then, balancing it, was the natural carelessness about such an object as a shrine – this same brown-clothed nation that defiled before him, he knew them well. As a churchwarden, he knew that not ten per cent of them went inside a place of worship more than three or four times in the whole of their lives. Baptism for some, marriage for a good proportion, an occasional assistance at the first or last rite of some relative, finally, the cemetery chapel, that was the extent of their church-going.

A small number, chiefly from the North or from Ireland, might be Catholics, but also from the north of Ireland was an equal number of violent anti-Catholics, and it was to this latter section that he judged the perpetrator of the outrage to belong. No, they would see nothing, or at best something to despise, in that little memorial altar, hardly more than an enlarged tombstone, in the corner of a Flemish pasture. It was strange if not detestable, it was foreign; they never saw their own gravestones, seldom those of any relative. He sympathized with them in that ultra-English sentimentality, that cannot bear to admit frankly the frail briefness of human life. And so the thing had happened, any of them might have done it, most of them would do it, under similar circumstances?

The tail of the last column wound out of B camp, the N.C.O. he took with him on these occasions was reporting all clear, and might he hand over to the advance party of the incoming Division. Dormer gave him exact orders as to what to hand over and obtain a signature for, and where to find him next, for he did not believe in allowing an N.C.O. any scope for imagination, if by any possibility such a faculty might have survived in him.

The weather had broken, and he jogged along in the mud to C camp and found it already vacated, but no advance party ready to take over, and resigned himself to the usual wait. He waited and he waited. Of course, he wasn't absolutely forced to do so. He might have left his N.C.O. and party to hand over. He might have cleared them off and left the incoming Division to shift for itself. That had been done many a time in his experience. How often, as a platoon commander, had he marched and marched, glancing over his shoulder at tired men only too ready to drop out, marched and marched until at length by map square and horse sense, and general oh-let's-get-in-here-and-keep-any-one-else-out, he had found such a camp, a few tents subsiding in the mud, a desolate hut or two, abandoned and unswept, places which disgusted him more than any mere trench or dug-out, because they were places that people had lived in and left unclean.

He had never experienced such a thing before he came into the army. His nice middle-class upbringing had never allowed him to suspect that such places existed. And now that he was Captain Dormer, attached H.Q. Nth Division, he endeavoured to see that they did not. So he hung about intending to see the thing done properly. He got no encouragement. He knew that when he got back to the Division Colonel Birchin would simply find him something else to do, and the fact that no complaints followed them, and that the incoming Division had a better time than they would otherwise have had, would be swallowed up in the hasty expedience of the War. Still, he did it, because he liked to feel that the job was being properly done. To this he had been brought up, and he was not going to change in war-time.

As he hung about the empty hut, he had plenty of time for reflection. His feet were cold. When would he get leave? What a nuisance if these d—d people who were relieving him didn't turn up until it was dark. The February day was waning. Ah, here they were. He roused himself from the despondent quiescence of a moment ago, into a crisp authoritative person from Divisional Head-quarters. Never was a camp handed over more promptly. He let his N.C.O. and men rattle off in the limber they had provided themselves with. He waited for a car. There was bound to be no difficulty in getting a lift into Doullens, and if he did not find one immediately there, he would soon get a railway voucher. As he stood in the gathering dusk his ruminations went on. If it were not for the War, he would be going home to tea, real proper tea, no chlorine in the water, milk out of a cow, not out of a tin, tea-cakes, some small savoury if he fancied it, his sister with whom he lived believing in the doctrine 'Feed the beast!' After that, he would have the choice of the Choral Society or generally some lecture or other. At times there was something on at the local theatre, at others he had Vestry or Trust meetings to attend. Such employments made a fitting termination to a day which he had always felt to be well filled at a good, safe, and continuous job, that would go on until he reached a certain age, when it culminated in a pension, a job that was worth doing, that he could do, and that the public appreciated.

Instead of all this, here he was, standing beside a desolate Picard highway, hoping that he might find his allotted hut in time to wash in a canvas bucket, eat at a trestle table and finally, having taken as much whisky as would wash down the food, and help him to become superior to his immediate circumstances, to play bridge with those other people whom he was polite to, because he had to be, but towards whom he felt no great inclination, and whom he would drop without a sigh the moment he was demobbed.

Ah! Here was the sort of car. He stepped into the road and held up his hand. The car stopped with a crunch and a splutter. They were going as far as Bernaville. That would suit him well. He jammed into the back seat between two other people, mackintoshed and goggled, and the car got under way again. Then he made the usual remarks and answered the usual inquiries, taking care to admit nothing, and to let his Divisional weight be felt. Finally he got down at a place where he could get a lorry lift to H.Q.

His servant had laid out some clean clothes in the Armstrong hut. For that he was thankful.

\*

The Division now proceeded to train for the coming offensive. 'Cultivators' had been warned off a large tract of land, which was partly devoted to 'Schools', at which were taught various superlative methods of slaughter, partly to full-dress manoeuvres over country which resembled in physical features the portion of the German line to be attacked. The natural result was that if any area larger than a tennis court was left vacant, the 'cultivators' rushed back and began to cultivate it. Hence arose disputes between the peasants and the troops, and the General commanding the 556 Brigade had his bridle seized by an infuriated female who wanted to know, in English, why he couldn't keep off her beans.

The matter was reported to G. office of Divisional Head-quarters, who told the A.P.M., who told the French Liaison Officer, who told an Interpreter, who told the 'cultivators' to keep off the ground altogether, whether it were in use or not. In revenge for which conduct the 'cultivators' fetched the nearest gendarme, and had the Interpreter arrested as a spy, and tilled the land so that the C.R.A. Corps couldn't find the dummy trenches he was supposed to have been bombarding, because they had all been filled up and planted. So that he reported the matter to Corps, who sat heavily on Divisional Head-quarters, G. office, for not keeping the ground clear. Tht A.P.M. and French Mission having been tried and failed, Q. office had the brilliant idea of 'lending' Dormer to G., upon the well-tried army principle that a man does a job, not because he is fit, but because he is not required elsewhere.

So Dormer patrolled the manoeuvre area, mounted on the horses of senior officers, who were too busy to ride them. He did not object. It kept him from thinking. He was, by now, well acquainted with manoeuvre areas, from near Dunkirk to below Amiens. It was the same old tale. First the various schools. The Bombing Instructor began with a short speech:

'It is now generally admitted that the hand-grenade is the weapon with which you are going to win this War!'

The following day in the bayonet-fighting pitch, the instructor in that arm began:

'This is the most historic weapon in the hands of the British Army. It still remains the decisive factor on the field!'

And the day following, on the range, the Musketry expert informed the squad:

'Statistics show that the largest proportion of the casualties inflicted on the enemy are bullet wounds.'

Dormer was not unkind enough to interrupt. He did not blame those instructors. Having, by desperately hard work, obtained their positions, they were naturally anxious to keep them. But his new insight and preoccupation, born of the Vanderlynden affair, made him study the faces of the listening squads intently. No psychologist, he could make nothing of them. Blank, utterly bored in the main, here and there he caught sight of one horrified, or one peculiarly vindictive. The main impression he received was of the sheer number of those passive listening faces, compared with the fewness of the N.C.O.s and instructors. So long as they were quiescent, all very well. But if that dormant mass came to life, some day, if that immense immobility once moved, got under way, where would it stop?

It was the same with the full-dress manoeuvres. Dormer had never been taken up with the honour and glory of war. He was going through with this soldiering, which had been rather thrust upon him, for the plain reason that he wanted to get to the end of it. He considered that he had contracted to defeat the Germans just as, if he had been an iron firm, he might have contracted to make girders, or if he had been the Post Office, he would have contracted to deliver letters. And now that he watched the final processes of the job, he became more than ever aware that the goods would not be up to sample. How could they be? Here were men being taught to attack, with the principal condition of attack wanting. The principal condition of an attack was that the other fellow hit you back as hard as he could. Here there was no one hitting you back. He wondered if all these silent and extraordinarily docile human beings in the ranks would see that some day. He looked keenly at their faces. Mask, mask; mule-like stupidity, too simple to need a mask; mask and mask again; one with blank horror written on it, one with a devilish lurking cunning, as if there might be something to be made out of all this some day; then more masks.

He wondered, but he did not wonder too unhappily. He was beginning to feel very well. Away from the line, the hours were more regular, the food somewhat better, the horse exercise did him good. There was another reason which Dormer, no reader of poetry, failed altogether to appreciate. Spring had come. Furtive and slow, the Spring of the shores of the grey North Sea came stealing across those hard-featured downs and rich valleys. Tree and bush, blackened and wind-bitten, were suddenly visited with a slender effusion of green, almost transparent, looking stiff and ill-assorted, as though Nature were experimenting.

Along all those ways where men marched to slaughter, the magic footsteps preceded them, as though they had been engaged in some beneficent work, or some joyful festival. To Dormer the moment was poignant but for other reasons. It was the moment when the culminating point of the Football Season marked the impending truce in that game. He did not play cricket. It was too expensive and too slow. In summer he sailed a small boat on his native waters. Instead, he was going to be involved in another offensive.

The Division left the manoeuvre area and went up through

Arras. Of course, the weather broke on the very eve of the 'show'. That had become almost a matter of routine, like the shelling, the stupendous activities of railways and aeroplanes, the everlasting telephoning. Again Dormer saw going past him endlessly, that stream of men and mules, mules and men, sandwiched in between every conceivable vehicle, from tanks to stretchers. When, after what communiqués described as 'continued progress' and 'considerable artillery activity', it had to be admitted that this offensive, like all other offensives, had come to a dead stop, Dormer was not astonished. For one thing, he knew, what no communiqué told, what had stopped it. The Germans? No, capable and determined as they were. The thing which stopped it was Mud. Nothing else. The shell-fire had been so perfect, that the equally perfect and necessarily complicated preparations for going a few hundred yards farther, could not be made. The first advance was miles. The next hundreds of yards. The next a hundred yards.

Then the Bosche got some back. Then everything had to be moved up to make quite certain of advancing miles again. And it couldn't be done. There was no longer sufficient firm ground to bear the tons of iron that alone could help frail humanity to surmount such efforts.

For another thing, he could not be astonished. For weeks he worked eighteen hours a day, ate what he could, slept when he couldn't help it. Astonishment was no longer in him. But one bit of his mind remained, untrammelled by the great machine of which he formed an insignificant part. It was a bit of subconsciousness that was always listening for something, just as, under long-range, heavy-calibre bombardment, one listened and listened for the next shell. But the particular detached bit of Dormer was listening and listening for something else. Watching and watching, too, all those faces under tin helmets, and just above gas-mask wallets, all so alike under those conditions that it seemed as difficult to pick out one man from another as one mule from another. Listening for one man to say 'I am the one!' to be able to see him, and know that at last he had got rid of that job at Vanderlynden's. But nothing happened. It was always just going to happen.

At length the Division moved right up into the coal-fields and sat down by a slag heap near Béthune. Then Colonel Birchin called to him one morning across the office: 'I say, Dormer, I've got the whereabouts of that fellow Chirnside. He's near Rheims. You'll have to go.'

Dormer went. For two whole days he travelled across civilian France. France of the small farm, the small town, and the small villa. Far beyond the zone of the English Army, far beyond the zone of any army, he passed by Creil to Paris, and from Paris on again into a country of vine-clad hills above a river. He was in a part where he had never been as a soldier, never gone for one of those brief holidays to Switzerland he had sometimes taken. It caused him much amusement to think of the regular Calais–Bâle express of pre-War days. If they would only run that train now, how it would have to zig-zag over trenches, and lines of communication.

He entered the zone of a French Army. On all sides, in the towns and villages, in the camps and manoeuvre areas, he saw blue-coated men, and stared at them, with the same fascinated interest as he now felt, in spite of himself, in spite of any habit or tradition or inclination, in his own khaki variety. These fellows carried more on their backs, had far less transport. His general impression was of something grimmer, more like purgatory, than that which English troops gave him. The physical effort of the individual was greater, his food, pay and accommodation less. And there was none of that extraordinary volunteering spirit of the Kitchener Armies, the spirit which said: 'Lumme, boys, here's a war. Let's have a go at it!' The French had most of them been conscripted, had known that such a thing might, probably would happen to them, had been prepared for it for years. They had not the advantage of being able to say to themselves: 'Well, I jolly well asked for it. Now I've got it!'

A saturnine fate brooded over them. He noticed it in the railway and other officials he met. They were so much more official. R.T.O.s and A.P.M.s – or the equivalent of them, he supposed – who surveyed his credentials, and passed him on to the place where he was going, did so with the cynical ghost of amusement, as who should say: 'Aha! This is you. You're going there, are you? You might as well go anywhere else.'

Eventually, in a stony village, beneath a pine-clad ridge, he found the familiar khaki and brass, the good nature and amateurishness of his own sort. He stepped out of the train and across a platform and with a curious pang, almost of homesickness, found himself in England. Here was the superior corporal in slacks from the orderly room. Here were the faultless riding horses, being exercised. There was nothing like them in all the blue-coated armies through which he had passed. The Commandant to whom he reported, treated him partly as an officer reporting, partly as a nephew, asked amused questions about billets in Flanders, who was doing such-and-such a job with Corps, what were the prospects of leave, and above all, did Dormer play bridge? He did. Ah! Then the main necessities of modern warfare were satisfied.

And as he found his billet and changed his clothes, Dormer reflected how right it all was. What was the good of being officious and ill-tempered? What was the good of being energetic even? Here we all were, mixed up in this inferno. The most sensible, probably the most efficient thing to do, was to forget it every night for a couple of hours, and start fresh in the morning. Chirnside was away with his detachment, but would be back shortly. In the meantime the Commandant hoped Dormer would join his Mess. The billet was comfortable and Dormer made no objection. On the contrary, he settled down for a day or two with perfect equanimity. It was always a day or two nearer the inevitable end of the War, which must come sometime, a day or two without risk, and actually without discomfort. What more could one ask?

The Commandant, Major Bone, was a fine-looking man, past middle age, with beautiful grey hair and blue eyes with a twinkle. His height and carriage, a certain hard-wearing and inexpensive precision about his uniform, suggested an ex-guards Sergeant-major. It was obvious that he had spent all his life in the army, took little notice of anything that went on outside it, and felt no qualms as to a future which would be provided for by it. He was one of those men with whom it was impossible to quarrel, and Dormer pleased him in the matter of blankets. The Major offered some of those necessities to Dormer, who was obliged to reply that he had six and feared his valise would hold no more. He had won the old man's heart.

The Major had fixed his billet in a little house belonging to the representative of some firm auxiliary to the wine trade. The little office had become his office. Orders, nominal rolls, lists of billets and maps hung over the advertisements of champagne, and photographs of Ay and Épernay. On the other side of the hall, the little dining-room suited the Major admirably, as his Mess. It had just that substantial stuffiness that he considered good taste. The chairs and table were heavy, the former upholstered in hot crimson, as was the settee. Upon the mantelpiece, and upon pedestals disposed wherever there was room and sometimes where there was not, were bronze female figures named upon their bases 'Peace', 'Chastity', 'The Spirit of the Air'. Dormer did not admire them. They were nude. As if this were not enough they had their arms either before them or behind them, never at their sides, which seemed to him to aggravate the matter. Together with a capacious sideboard, full of glass and china, *couronnes de noces* and plated ware, all securely locked in, these decorations made it almost impossible to move, once the company was seated at table.

Indeed, during the winter, the Major complained he had been in the position of having one place frozen at the door, and one roasted next the Salamander anthracite stove. But with the milder weather, things were better, for the two big casement windows could be opened, and filled the room with sweet country air in a moment; they gave on to the street which was merely a village street, and across the road, over the wall was a vineyard. The Mess consisted of the Major, Doctor, Ordnance Officer, and Chirnside, whose place Dormer temporarily took. There they were a happy little family, removed far from the vexations attending larger and smaller formations, isolated, with their own privileges, leave list, and railway vouchers, as pretty a corner as could be found in all that slow-moving mass of discomfort and ill-ease that was the War.

On the third day, Dormer's conscience made him inquire how long Chirnside would be. 'Not long,' was the reply. 'You can hear what's going on?' He could indeed. For two days the earth and air had been atremble with the bombardment. French people in the village, and the French soldiers about the place had a sort of cocksure way of saying *'Ça chauffe?'* Indeed, the offensive had been widely advertised and great things were expected of it.

Then finally Chirnside did return. Dormer had been doing small jobs for the Major all day, because idleness irked him, and on coming back to change, found a grizzled oldish man, thin and quiet, a slightly different edition of the Major, the same seniority, the same ranker traditions, but memories of India and Egypt instead of Kensington and Windsor. Dormer listened quietly while the two old soldiers discussed the offensive. There was no doubt that it was an enormous and costly failure. That hardly impressed him. He was used to and expected it. But he had never before seen an offensive from outside. He had always been in them, and too tired and short of sleep, by the time they failed, to consider the matter deeply. But this time he listened to the conversation of the two old men with wonder mixed with a curious repulsion. They were hard working, hospitable, but they had the trained indifference of the regular soldier that seemed to him to be so ominous. In the regular army, where every one shared it, where it was part of a philosophy of life derived from the actual conditions, and deliberately adopted like a uniform, all very well. But no one knew better than Dormer that none of the armies of 1917 contained any appreciable percentage of regulars, but were, on the other hand, composed of people who had all sorts of feelings to be considered and who had not the slightest intention of spending their lives in the army. Not for the first time did he wonder how long they would stand it.

The Doctor and Ordnance Officer being busy sorting casualties and replacing stores, there was no bridge that evening and he was able to approach Chirnside as to the object of his journey. The old man heard him with a sort of quizzical interest, but was evidently inclined to be helpful, twisted his grey moustache points and let his ivory-yellow eyelids droop over his rather prominent eyes.

'Spanish Farm. April 1916. Oh, aye!'

'Could you recall an incident that occurred there. Damage to a little chapel in the corner of the pasture where the roads met. A driver wanted to shelter his mules and broke into the place?'

Chirnside thought hard, looking straight at Dormer. It was obvious to Dormer that the old man was thinking, with army instinct, 'Here, what's this I'm getting involved in? No you don't,' and hastened to reassure him.

'It's like this. The case has become unfortunately notorious. The French have taken it up very strongly. You know what these things are, once they become official test cases. We've got to make an arrest and probably pay compensation as well, but at present our people at Base are sticking out for treating it as a matter of discipline. The unit was the 469 T.M.B., but there have been so many casualties that no one can tell me the name of the driver who did it.'

Dormer was thinking: 'There, that's the umpteenth time I've told the yarn, and what good is it?' When suddenly he had a stroke of genius:

'Of course, they've got hold of your name.'

It succeeded remarkably well. A sort of habitual stiffening was obvious in the Army-worn old face in front of him. Chirnside shifted his legs.

'I can't tell y'much about it. I don't know the chap's name or number, and I expect all the rolls are destroyed. Anyway he might not be on them, for he wasna' a driver!'

Chirnside was relapsing into his native Scotch, but Dormer didn't notice. He had got a clue.

'What was he then?'

'He had been servant to young Fairfield, who was killed.'

'You don't remember Fairfield's regiment. That might help us?'

'No, I don't, and it wouldn't help you, for he came out to Trench Mortars, and not with his own crowd. This servant of his he picked up at Base, or from some employment company.'

'What on earth was he doing with those mules?'

'What could you do with 'em? The driver was killed and the limber smashed to matchwood. The feller had nothing to do, so he did that!'

'You don't remember what happened to him after that?'

'Um – I think he went as young Andrews' servant.'

'Ah! What did he come from?'

'Andrews? Gunner, he was!'

'Thanks. That may help. You saw the row when the Mayor of the village came to certify the damage?'

'Aye, there were some blethers about the business. You couldna' wonder. The old feller was got up like a Tattie Bogle. The men had had no rest, and were going straight back to the line. They marched all right, but you couldn't keep them from calling names at such a Guy – young troops like that!'

'You couldn't describe Andrews' servant to me?'

'No. He looked ordinary!'

A mistake, of course, no use to ask old Chirnside things like that. A third of a century in the army had long ago drilled out of him any sort of imagination he might ever have had. He was just doing a handsome thing by a brother officer in remembering at all. His instinct was obviously to know nothing about it. But, piqued by the novelty of Commissioned rank, he went on: 'Yes, I can tell you something. That feller had a grievance. I remember something turning up in one of his letters, when we censored 'em. Lucky spot when you think how most of the censoring was done.'

'I should think so. What was it?'

'Couldn't say now. Grievance of some sort. Didn't like the army, or the War, or something.'

Dormer sat down and wrote out the information obtained and made his preparations to rejoin the Division. The Major said: 'Oh, no hurry, stop another day, now you're here!' And all that evening, as he thought and wrote, and tried to believe this fatal business a step nearer completion, he heard the two old soldiers, like two good-natured old women, gossiping. Each expected the other to know every camp or barrack in which he had lain, each named this or that chance acquaintance, made any time those thirty years, anywhere in the world, as though the other must know him also. Often this was the case, in which they both exclaimed together, 'Ah, nice feller, wasn't he?' Or, if it were not the case, the other would rejoin, 'No, but I knew So-and-so, of the sappers,' and probably the second shot would hit the mark. It could hardly fail to do so in the old close borough of the Regular Army. And then they would exclaim in unison again.

Dormer was as impressed as he ever was by any member of the Professional Army. They knew how to do it. He would never know. The army was their God and King, their family and business. In a neat circle they went, grinding out the necessary days to their pensions. The present state of Europe, while verbally regretted or wondered at, did not scratch the surface of their minds. How could it? It had been a golden opportunity for them. It made the difference to them and to any human wife or family they might have accreted, between retiring on Commissioned pay-scale, or taking a pub or caretaker's place, as the ex-Sergeant-major they would otherwise have been. But there was charm in their utter simplicity. Nothing brutal, very little that was vain, and some nicely acquired manners.

The offensive of the French Army, in the machinery of which they had their places, moved them not at all. Chirnside casually mentioned that he gathered it had been a big failure. Dormer expected to hear him recite some devastating tale of misdirected barrage, horrible casualties or choked communications. Nothing so graphic reached him. The old man had simply attended to his job, and when he found that the troops were returning to the same billets, drew his own conclusions. That was all. Dormer was horrified, but no one could be horrified long with Chirnside. Of course, he didn't mind how long the War went on.

Having completed his preparations, Dormer went up to his little room and was soon asleep. He was in fine condition and thoroughly comfortable, and was astonished after what appeared to be a very short interval, to find himself wide awake. There was no mistaking the reason. It was the row in the street. He pulled on his British-warm and went to look. It was quite dark, but he could make out a confused crowd surging from side to side of the little street, could see bayonets gleaming, and could hear a clamour of which he could not make out a word. It was like nothing he had ever heard in the War, it recalled only election time in his native city, the same aimless shuffling feet, the same confusion of tongues, the same effervescence, except that he had instinct enough to know from the tones of the voices that they were raised in lamentation, not triumph. He was extremely puzzled what to do, but clear that no initiative lay with him. For ten minutes he waited, but the situation did not change. He opened his door very quietly. Not a sound from the Major. From Chirnside, opposite, heavy regular breathing. Above, in the attics, the low cockney brevity of soldier servants discussing something with the detachment of their kind. Reassured, he closed the door, and got back into his blankets. The noise was irritating but monotonous. He fell asleep. He next awoke to the knocking of his servant bringing his morning tea, and clean boots.

'What was all that row in the night?'

'Niggers, sir.'

'What do you mean?'

'French coloured troops, sir. They got it in the neck seemingly. They don't half jabber.'

Major Bone was more fully informed. There was no doubt that the French had had a nasty knock. Black troops were coming back just anyhow, out of hand, not actually dangerous, the old soldier allowed it to be inferred, but a nuisance. What struck him most forcibly was the dislocation of the supply services. Defeat he accepted, but not unpunctuality.

'These Africans are besieging the station, trying to board the trains, and get taken back to Africa. I can't get hold of an officer, but Madame says they're all killed. She's in an awful state. I don't suppose you'll get away today!'

He was right enough. Dormer's servant shortly returned,

humping the valise. The station was closed, the rolling stock had been removed. The black troops were swarming everywhere, collapsing for want of food and sleep, disorganized and incoherent. Dormer went out shortly after and verified the state of affairs. He was not molested, so far had the breakdown gone, but was the object of what appeared to him most uncomplimentary allusions, but all in pidgin French, too colonial for his fair, but limited, knowledge of the language. There was clearly nothing to be done, so far as transport went, that day, and he resigned himself to spending his time in the little Mess.

The Doctor and Ordnance Officer appeared at dinner with reassuring news. The failure of the offensive had been bad, but the French had never really lost control and were getting their people in hand immediately. There was a rumour that a General who tried to restore order had been thrown into the river, but it might be only a tale. Major Bone was contemptuous of the whole thing. Do – what could they do, a lot of silly blacks? The French would cut off their rations and reduce them to order in no time. Thus the old soldier. But he did not prevent Dormer going to bed with a heavy heart. To him it was not so much a French offensive that had failed. It was another Allied effort, gone for nothing. His life training in apprehension made him paint the future in the gloomiest colours. Where would fresh men be obtained from? Whence would come the spirit – what they called morale in military circles – to make another attempt? If neither men nor morale were forthcoming, would the War drag out to a stalemate Peace? He had no extravagant theories for or against such an ending to it. To him it meant simply a bad bargain, with another war to make a better one looming close behind it. And his recent military training had also received an unaccustomed shock. A new army enlistment, he had seen nothing of the retreat from Mons, and was far from being able to picture March or April 1918, still twelve months in the future.

For the first time in his life he had seen panic, confusion, rout. True, it was already stopped, but that did not expunge from his mind the sight, the noise, the smell even, of that crowd of black soldiers who had suddenly ceased to be soldiers, numbers standing in line, and had so dramatically re-become men. The staring eyeballs, the physical collapse, the officer-less medley of uncertain movement were all new to him, and all most distressing. Of course, the fellows were mere blacks, not the best material, and had probably been mishandled. But under a more prolonged strain, might not the same thing happen to others? The Germans were the least susceptible he judged, the Russians most. What would he not see, some day, if the War dragged on?

Whatever narrow unimaginative future his unadventurous mind conjured up, his far stronger faculty for getting on with the matter in hand soon obliterated. He was no visionary. Contemplation was not in him. Directly the trains were running he left that cosy little Mess of Major Bone's to rejoin. He left off thinking about the War, and took up his job where he had, for a moment, allowed it to lie, disregarded under the stress of new events and strange emotions.

As the train moved on and on through French lines of communication he was wondering again about the fellow who had done the trick at Vanderlynden's, of how he was to be found, of how the whole thing would frame itself. These French chaps, whose transport he saw each side of him, Army Corps after Army Corps. Biggish men, several of them, in a round-shouldered fashion, due partly to their countrified occupation, partly to their uniform, with its overcoat and cross-straps. Browner skinned, darker of hair and eye than our men, they confirmed his long-established ideas about them, essentially a Southern people whose minds and bodies were formed by Biscayan and Mediterreanean influences. They would not be sentimental about mules, he would wager. On the other hand, they would not laugh at a Mayor. They did not laugh much as a rule, they frowned, stared, or talked rapidly with gestures, and then if they did laugh, it was uproariously, brutally, at some one's misfortunes. Satire they understood. But they missed entirely the gentle nag, nag, nag of ridicule, that he used to hear from his own platoon or company, covering every unfamiliar object in that foreign land, because it was not up to the standard of the upper-middle classes. To the French, life was a hard affair, diversified by the points at which one was less unfortunate than one's neighbour.

To the English, life was the niceness of a small class, diversified by the nastiness of everything else, and the nastiness was endlessly diverting. For the French were mere men, in their own estimation. Not so the poorer English of the towns. They were gentlemen. If they lapsed (and naturally they lapsed most of the time) they were comic to each other, to themselves even. How well he remembered, on the march, when the battalion had just landed, passing through a village where certain humble articles of domestic use were standing outside the cottage doors, waiting to be emptied. A suppressed titter had run all along the column.

A Frenchman would never have thought them funny, unless they fell out of a first-floor window on to some head and hurt it. Again, to a Frenchman, Mayor and Priest, Garde Champêtre and Suisse were officials, men plus authority and therefore respectworthy. To Englishmen, they were officials, therefore not gentlemen, therefore ridiculous. If a big landowner, or member of Parliament, or railway director had walked into Vanderlynden's pasture, just as 469 T.M.B. fell in for their weary march back to the line, would they have laughed? Not they. But then those members of England's upper classes would not have worn tricolour sashes to enforce authority. So there you were. With this philosophic reflection he fell asleep.

Dormer returned to an army which was at its brightest. It had held the initiative in the matter of offensives for over a year and a half, and if no decision had been come to, a wide stretch of ground had been won, and hope on the whole was high. From time to time there were rumours of a queer state of things in Russia, but it was far off and uncertain. The matter of the moment was Messines, the famous ridge which had been lost at the very beginning of the War and which was now to be regained. In this affair Dormer found himself busily engaged. Here were no waste downs of the Somme, but some of the most fertile land in the world.

Among other matters confronting the Generals was the problem of how to keep civilians from rushing back to cultivate land of which they had been deprived for three years. The day came, the explosion of the great mines, so Dormer was told, was heard in London. If he did not hear it, it was because a well-directed long-range artillery bombardment, complicated by a bombing that was German and German only in its thoroughness, deafened and bewildered him, took his sleep, killed his servant, and stampeded the horses of all the divisional ammunition columns near him, so that his tent was trampled down, his belongings reduced to a state hardly distinguishable from the surrounding soil. However, the blow, such as it was, was successful. Irish and Scotch, Colonial and London divisions took that battered hillock that had defied them so long, and Dormer in spite of all his experience could not help thinking: 'Oh, come, now we are really getting on.'

But nothing happened. Dormer heard various reasons given for this, and twice as many surmises made about it, but well aware how much importance to attach to the talk that floated round Divisional Offices and Messes, relied upon his own experience and arithmetic. According to him, nothing could happen, because each offensive needed months of preparation. Months of preparation made possible a few weeks of activity. A few weeks of activity gained a few square miles of ground. Then more months of preparation, grotesquely costly, and obvious to every one for a hundred miles, so that the enemy had just as long to prepare, made possible a few more weeks' activity and the gain of a few miles more.

This was inevitable in highly organized mechanical war, fought by fairly matched armies, on a restricted field, between the sea and the neutral countries. He admitted it. But then came his lifelong habit of reducing the matter to figures. He roughed out the area between the 'front' of that date and the Rhine, supposing for the sake of argument that we went no farther, and divided this by the area gained, on an average, at the Somme, Vimy and Messines. The result he multiplied by the time taken to prepare and fight those offensives, averaged again.

The result he got was that, allowing for no setbacks, and providing the pace could be maintained, we should arrive at the Rhine in one hundred and eighty years.

For the only time in his life Dormer wished he were something other than Dormer. For a few moments after arriving at his conclusion, he desired to be a person of power and influence, some one who could say with weight that the thing ought to stop here and now. But this very unusual impulse did not last long with him.

All that remained of Belgium and wide tracts of French Flanders adjoining it, became one huge ant-heap. Never had there been such a concentration, Corps next to Corps, Services mosaiced between Services, twenty thousand men upon roads, no one could count how many handling munitions, as, from Ypres to the sea, the great offensive of 1917 slowly germinated.

Dormer was soon caught up and landed in the old familiar blackly-manured soil of the Salient. He was not disgusted or surprised. He was becoming increasingly conscious of a sensation of going round and round. Now, too, that troops were always pouring along a road before him, he had again the feeling that his head was an empty chamber, round which was painted a frieze, men, men, mules, men, limbers, guns, men, lorries, ambulances, men, men, men. It might be just worry and overwork, it might be that he was again forced to share his limited accommodation with Kavanagh. They were in a dug-out on the canal bank, just by one of those fatal causeways built to make the passage of the canal a certainty, instead of the gamble it had been in the days of the pontoon bridges. The passage became, like everything else in the War, a certainty for the Germans as much as for the Allies. The place was registered with the utmost precision and hit at all times of the day and night. It probably cost far more than the taking of any trench.

Amid the earth-shaking explosions that seldom ceased for long, in the twilight of that narrow cavern in the mud, Kavanagh was as unquenchable as he ever had been on the high and airy downs of the Somme. During the daylight, when nothing could be done outside, he bent over his map of cables while Dormer perfected his plan for getting first-line transport past that infernal canal. He purposed to send an N.C.O. a good two miles back, with small square pieces of card, on which were written 9.0 p.m., 9.5 p.m., and so on, the times being those at which the unit so instructed was to arrive beside his dug-out. He thought rather well of this idea, no jamming and confusion, and if the enemy made a lucky hit, there would be fewer casualties and less to clear away. In the middle of his calculations he heard.

> 'Why, soldiers, why
> Should we be melancholy,
> Whose duty 'tis to die!'

He could not resist saying:

'If you must make that d—d noise, I wish you'd put some sense into it.'

'Sense. I was trying to cheer you up!'

' "Duty 'tis to die" is jolly cheering, and quite untrue.'

'Oh, is it? What is our duty then?'

'Our duty is to live if we possibly can. And I mean to do it. It's the people who keep alive who will win the War.'

'According to that, all one has got to do is to get to Blighty, or preferably the United States, and stay there?'

'Not a bit. You exaggerate so. All I said was, that it is foolish to make it a duty to become a casualty.'

'Dormer, I shall never get you to see things in the proper light. You're like a lamb trying to leap with joy, and never able to get its hind legs off the ground.'

'This is all rot. What connection is there between lambs and leaping, and our jobs? Mine is to see that various people and things are in the position where they will be wanted, at the moment at which they will have most effect in winning the War. Yours is to see that they can speak and be spoken to when required.'

'Lovely, lovely! What a teacher you would have made.'

'I had a better job.'

'There is no better job, except perhaps the one we are doing. I do admire your descriptions of them. All you want is to put in a personal allegorical note. You might condense the whole thing by saying that you will be Minerva if I will be Mercury. Yep?'

'Whatever are you talking about?'

'Yours to see that all is in order. That is a matter of reason. You are the Goddess. I am merely a lesser God. Mercury was God of Communications. I wonder whether they'd let me design a cap badge for signallers. Mercury playing on a buzzer. You may have your Owl!'

'Oh, shut up.'

'I fear I must, the bugle calls, and I must follow, or my watch shows it is time I was looking after my chaps. But you've had a brilliant idea, Dormer.'

'I?'

'You've had the idea of fighting the War allegorically. Wisdom and Light we are. That would do away with half the horror. So long!'

Then queerly, instead of feeling relieved from an annoyance, Dormer felt more despondent than ever. What could it be? Was the fellow right? Surely not! All that nonsense! And yet – and yet what would not he, Dormer, conscious of his own probity, have given to be conscious instead, of Kavanagh's lightness of heart? That very probity drove him out in the all-too-late summer dusk to see that everything was going right. Yes, here they were; details of transport, parties to dig, parties to carry, details of services, engineers of all their various grades. Punctual, incredibly docile, honest English in their gestureless manner of getting on with the job. They took care of their mules – (look at these beasts pulling as though they were English too, instead of the Argentine crossbreds he knew them to be) – not because it was a duty, although it was, and not because the mule was a miracle, like a tank or an aeroplane, but just because it was a mule, that meant, to English soldiers, and to English soldiers only, a fellow-creature, a human being. On they went, reporting to him, and pushing on, sometimes with a hurried question as to map square, or other crucial uncertain detail, sometimes with only a grunt. That endless procession had not been in progress many minutes before, amid the considerable and gently growing shell-fire, there came a bang that seemed to go right through his head. He knew from old trench experience what it was. Nothing but a gun pointing straight at you could make that particular hrrmph.

He set his feet, not a moment too soon. It was a five-nine, the sort the French called '*Grande Vitesse*'. A whirlwind, a small special whirlwind pointed like an arrow, hit the causeway so that it shook and then went up with a wheel of splintered bits. He was glad he had devised his patent card system. The units were not too close together. He had time to shout to the next, 'Come on, you've two minutes to get over!' and over they went, as if the Devil were after them, instead of a lump of Krupp steel fitted with lethal chemicals. They were hardly over before the second came, whump! To say that Dormer was frightened, was to fail to describe the matter. He was stiffened all over, his hair stood up, his heart thumped so that it hurt him, his feet were stone cold, but he knew his job and did it.

The next lot to come was a whole field company to do some special duty, and although he hurried them, the tail of the brown column was still high and exposed when the shell came. They ducked and darted into any cover that was available, and he heard his voice, as the voice of some one far away speaking to a public meeting, like a voice on the wireless, saying:

'Come on. Get out of that and come on. If I can stand here, surely you can get out of it.'

They did so. Behind them came a special party to dig in the Meteorological Officer. What a menagerie it was! Every trade, every nation too, Chinese, Zulu, West Indian, Egyptian. He did not blame the Germans who had chalked in blue on the bare back of a Portuguese, whom they captured and stripped. 'The Monkey House is full,' before they drove him back into English lines.

Even truer did Dormer find it when he had to go back for any reason, to Corps H.Q. or beyond. French and Belgians he knew, he had found them in the trenches beside him years before. Portuguese he had become accustomed to, Americans he looked forward to with anticipation. But farther back, he found Chinese, Africans of all descriptions, Indians, East and West, while the French, in addition to their black troops, had Spanish and Italian labour.

It did not please his parochial mind. He felt increasingly that there was something wrong when you had to drag in all these coloured people from every remote quarter of the globe, without even the excuse the French had, that they were 'Colonials'. But no one could tell, least of all Dormer himself, whether his feelings were the result of a strong belief in the Colour Bar, or whether it were merely the futility of it all. For in spite of the omnium gatherum of race, tongue and religion, the offensive failed. As a matter of routine, the weather broke on Z day. Within forty-eight hours it was obvious that the affair had stuck. Apart from a feeling of the hand of Fate in it, a sinister feeling of great incomprehensible forces working out his destiny for him, without his having the least power to influence the matter for better, for worse, which was so desolating to his pre-War habit of mind, where a certain line of unostentatious virtue had always carried a reward that could be reckoned on with the greatest exactitude, there were other disturbing elements in the situation.

Of course the Bosche was ready. He was bound to be ready, couldn't avoid it. He had immensely thickened his depth of defence, which was now composed not of the old obvious trenches full of men, all of which could be blown to pieces, but of small isolated turrets of ferro-concrete, where two or three machine-gunners (and who made better machine-gunners than the careful Germans) could hold an army at bay, until dislodged by a direct hit by a shell of six-inch calibre or over, or laboriously smoke-screened and bombed out, at the rate of perhaps a mile a day, on good days. He saw his computation of one hundred and eighty years altogether insufficient for getting to the Rhine. Moreover, for such work this medley of nations was of no good at all. It reminded him of a book by Anatole France he had been compelled by a friend to read, wherein a great conqueror enlisted in his army all the men of his nation, then all the men of the neighbouring nations, then all the savages at the end of the earth, and finally the baboons and other combatant animals. That was all very well. That was just story telling. But it horrified Dormer all the more to see such story telling coming true before his eyes. As coloured-labour company after coloured-labour company filed past his tent, guttural and straggling, he was able to pull himself together, and see that it was not true after all.

These people, little better than beasts, uglier in some cases and far more troublesome, were no good. They couldn't fight. You couldn't trust them to stand the shelling or to obey an order. Then just as he was feeling rather relieved, he saw the logical result of his conclusions. All the fighting would have to be done by those very men who had volunteered or been conscripted and who had been so generously wasted ever since. They were sticking it, and sticking it well, but this new offensive that had just opened promised to try them pretty high. Would they stick that? Would the day ever come when he would see them a mere mob, like those French black troops he had seen in May? Perhaps peace would be made. Such is the eternal hopefulness of men, that he even hoped, against all previous experience. That quenchless gleam common to all human souls, one of the basic things that makes war so long, and peace, where it is so much less necessary, just that much less attractive, added to work for fifteen hours a day, kept Dormer sane and healthy for weeks, in spite of worsening conditions, and the steady increase in enemy shelling. It was with a return of that uncanny feeling of being haunted that he found himself called up to Divisional Head-quarters. He knew quite well what it was, but he had relied on the difficulty of finding Andrews, on the tremendous strain of this most costly and urgent of all offensives, to keep the matter out of his path, or rather to keep him out of its path, for he had long dropped into the habit of feeling himself as in a nightmare, pursued by something he could not see or even imagine, but which was certainly sinister and personally fatal to him.

When he got to the office his feeling of nightmarishness was rather aggravated than allayed. Colonel Birchin was talking to the A.D.M.S. The fact was that the A.D.M.S. was a new one, patently a Doctor who had been fetched out from Doctoring, had been found capable of organization and had been shoved into the job *vice* someone else gone higher up. Beside him, Colonel Birchin shone, as it were, with the glamour of another world. Dormer had seen him in camp and hut, and château and Mairie for a year and a half, just like that, handsome and sleek, filling his plain but choice khaki with a distinction that no foreign officer could gain from all the blues and reds and yellows and greens and blacks, varnished belts and metal ornaments of other armies. And in that moment of sharpened nerves and unusual power of vision Dormer seemed to see why. Colonel Birchin was not an officer of a national army in the sense that any French, German, Italian or Russian Colonel was. There was nothing of the brute and nothing of the strategian about those nice manners, that so easily and completely excluded everything that was – what? Unmilitary? Hardly. There was nothing consciously, offensively military about the Colonel, 'regular' or professional soldier that he was. He would never have swaggered in Alsace, massacred in Tripoli, Dreyfused in France. He would never have found it necessary. For Colonel Birchin was not a state official. He was an officer of the Watch, the small band of paid soldiers that Stuart and subsequent kings kept to defend themselves from mobs, national armies, and other inconvenients. Colonel Birchin might write himself as of 'The Herefordshire Regiment', but it made no difference. His chief, inherited, and most pronounced quality was that he was a courtier. He represented the King. Preferably, at home, of course, where one could live in all that thick middle-class comfort that had ousted the old landowning seignorial dignity and semi-starvation. But upon occasion, Colonel Birchin could betake himself to Africa, India, and now even to this France, sure that even in this most tedious and unpleasant of wars, he would be properly fed and housed.

So here he was, representing the King even more exactly than before he was seconded from the King's Own Herefordshire

## THE CRIME AT VANDERLYNDEN'S

Regiment. He spoke and looked, in fact, rather as if he were the King. Ignorant and unused to the immense transport, the complicated lists of highly scientific equipment, he judged rightly enough that his one safe line was to represent authority, and see that these semi-civilians who did understand such things got on with the War. So he listened in a gentlemanly way to the A.D.M.S. (who wore beard and pince-nez) explaining at great length a difficult alternative as to the siting of Forward Dressing Stations, and contributed:

'You do what is best, Doctor, and we shall back you up!'

Then he turned to Dormer, hunted a moment among the papers on the table, and spoke:

'Look here, Dormer, about this affair of yours?'

It took all Dormer's training to keep his mouth shut. He saw more clearly than ever how Colonel Birchin and all like him and all he represented, were divesting themselves of any connection with what looked like a nasty, awkward, tedious and probably discreditable business. But he had not grasped it.

'They've found Andrews – this – er – gunner, who will be able to give you information. And – look here, Dormer – this affair must be cleared up, do you understand? Andrews is in hospital. You can go by car to Boulogne, but we expect you to get it done this time. Corps are most annoyed. There's been a nice how-d-y-do with the French.'

Dormer swallowed twice and only said:

'Really, sir.'

'Yes. Car starts at seven.'

Accordingly at seven, the big Vauxhall moved off from that little group of huts, in the meadow that was so regularly bombed every night. Dormer, sitting next to Major Stevenage, did not mind. As well Boulogne as anywhere, while this was going on. All the roads were full of transport, all the railways one long procession of troop and supply trains. It was about as possible to hide it all from the Germans, as to conceal London on a Bank Holiday. In fact it was rather like that. The population was about the same, if the area were rather larger, the effect of the crowd, the surly good humour, the air of eating one's dinner out of one's hand was the same.

There was very little sign of any consciousness of the shadow that hung over it all. Hospital trains and ambulances abounded, going in the opposite direction, but no one noticed them, so far as Dormer could see. The type of man who now came up to fight his country's battles was little changed. The old regular was hardly to be found. The brisk volunteer was almost gone. Instead there had arisen a generation that had grown used to the War, had had it on their minds so long, had been threatened with it so often that it had lost all sharpness of appeal to their intellects.

Right back to St Omer the crowd stretched. Beyond that it became more specialized. Air Force. Hospitals. Training grounds. Then, across high windy downs, nothing, twenty miles of nothing, until a long hill and the sea.

Up there on those downs where there was no one, never had been anybody ever since they were pushed up from the bed of some antediluvian ocean, and covered with short turf, Dormer had one of his rare respites from the War. Briefer perhaps, but more complete than that which he experienced on his rare leaves, he felt for a while the emancipation from his unwilling thraldom. It was the speed of the car that probably induced the feeling. Anyhow, on the level road that runs from Boulogne to Étaples – the ETAPPS of the Army in France – he lost it. Here there was no escaping the everlasting khaki and transport, that State of War into which he had been induced, and out of which he could see no very great possibility of ever emerging. He had no warning of what was to come, and was already well among the hospitals and dumps that extended for miles beside the railway, when a military policeman held up a warning hand.

'What's the matter, Corporal?'

'I should not go into Etapps this morning, if I were you, sir.'

'Why not?'

The man shifted his glance. He did not like the job evidently.

'Funny goings-on, there, sir.'

'Goings-on, what does that mean?'

Dormer was capable of quite a good rasp of the throat, when required. He had learned it as a Corporal.

'The men are out of 'and, sir!'
'Are they? The A.P.M. will see to that, I suppose.'
'Very good, sir.'
'Drive on!'

Dormer didn't like it, to tell the truth. But he was so used to bluffing things he didn't like, and his own feelings, and other people's awkwardness, that he could not do otherwise than go on. Also he didn't realize what was on foot. A certain amount of daily work was being done in among the dumps and sidings where the population was of all sorts of non-combatant, Labour Corps units, medical formations, railway people, and others. But from the rise by the Reinforcement Officers' hut, he began to see. The whole of the great infantry camp on the sandhill – and it was very full, he had heard people say that there were a hundred thousand men there – seemed to have emptied itself into the little town. Here they sauntered and talked, eddying a little round the station and some of the larger estaminets, in motion like an ant-hill, in sound like a hive of bees. The car was soon reduced to a walking pace, there were no police to be seen, and once entered there was no hope of backing out of that crowd, and no use in appearing to stop in it.

'Go slow,' Dormer ordered, glancing out of the corner of his eye at the wooden face of the chauffeur. Nothing to be seen. Either the man didn't like it, or didn't feel the necessary initiative to join in it, or perhaps considered himself too superior to these foot-sloggers to wish to be associated with them. Most probably he hadn't digested the fact that this mob, through which he drove his officer, was Mutiny, the break-up of ordered force, and military cohesion. It might even be the end of the War and victory for the Germans. All this was apparent enough in a moment to Dormer, who was careful to look straight again to his front, unwinking and mute, until, with a beating heart, he saw that they were clear of the jam in the Market Place, and well down the little street that led to the bridge across which were the farther hospitals, and various sundry Base Offices, in the former of which he was to find Andrews. Now, therefore, he did permit himself to light a cigarette. But not a word did he say to his chauffeur. Now that it was behind him he had the detachment to reflect that it was a good-humoured crowd. He had heard a gibe or so that might have been meant for him or no, but in the main, not being hustled, all those tens of thousands that had broken camp, chased the police off the streets, and committed what depredations he did not know, were peaceful enough, much too numerous and leaderless to make any cohesive threat to an isolated officer, not of their own unit, and therefore not an object of any special hatred, any more than of any special devotion, just a member of another class in the hierarchy, uninteresting to simple minds, in which he caused no immediate commotion.

Here, on the road that ran through the woods to Paris Plage, there were little knots of men, strolling or lying on the grass. They became fewer and fewer. By the time he arrived at the palace, mobilized as a hospital, for which he was bound, there remained no sign of the tumult. Here, as on the other flank, by the Boulogne road, Medical and Base Units functioned unmoved. But the news had been brought by Supply and Signal services and the effect of it was most curious.

Dormer had to pass through the official routine, had to be announced, had to have search made for young Andrews, and finally was conducted to a bed in Ward C., on which was indicated Captain Andrews, R.G.A. Dormer of course wanted to begin at once upon his mission, but the other, a curly-haired boy, whose tan had given place to a patchy white under loss of blood from a nasty shrapnel wound in the leg, that kept on turning septic, had to be 'scraped' or 'looked at', each of these meaning the operation table, and was only now gradually healing, would not let him.

Once away from the theatre and the knife, Andrews, like any other healthy youngster, soon accumulated any amount of animal spirit, lying there in bed, adored by the nursing sisters, admired by the men orderlies. He was not going to listen to Dormer's serious questions. He began:

'Cheerio! Sit on the next bed, there's no corpse in it, they've just taken it away. Anyhow, it isn't catching. Have a cigarette, do for God's sake. They keep on giving me the darned things, and they all end in smoke!'

'Sorry you got knocked out.'

'Only fair. Knocked out heaps of Fritzes. I gave 'em what for, and they gave me some back. I say, have you just come from the town?'

'I have just motored through.'

'Is it true that our chaps have broke loose?'

'There's a certain amount of disorder, but no violence that I could see.'

Dormer was conscious of heads being popped up in all the surrounding beds. So that was how it took them! Of course, they were bored stiff.

'How topping. Is it true that they've killed all the red-caps?'

'I didn't see any signs of it.'

'Cleared up the remains had they? Picked the bones, or fallen in proper burying parties.'

'I don't think there was anything of that sort.'

'Oh, come now, first we heard they had set on a police-corporal that had shot a Jock.'

'What did he do that for?'

'Dunno. It isn't the close season for Jocks, anyhow. Then it was ten police-corporals. The last rumour was that they'd stoned the A.P.M. to death –'

And so it went on. Lunch-time came. A Doctor Major, impressed by Dormer's credentials, invited him into the Mess, and asked a lot of questions about the front, the offensive, and the state of Étaples. Dormer always liked those medical messes. It seemed so much more worth while to mend up people's limbs, rather than to smash them to bits. The Doctors had their professional 'side' no doubt, but they had a right to it.

After lunch Dormer made his way back to Ward C. He was met by a hush, and by a little procession. The Sergeant-major came first and after him bearers with a stretcher covered by the Union Jack. The hush in the ward was ominous. They were all so close to what had happened. It was not like the open field where the casualty is a casualty and the living man a different thing. Here the dead were only different in degree, not in kind. They were worse 'cases' – the worst, that was all. So there were no high spirits after lunch. They had gibed about Death in the morning, but Death had come and they had ceased to gibe. In the silence, Dormer felt awkward, did not know how to begin. When he had made up his mind that he must, he looked up and found Andrews was asleep. So the day wore on to tea-time, and after tea he was not wanted in the ward, and was wanted in the Mess. He himself was not hurrying to return to any regularly bombed hut near Poperinghe. The Commanding Officer was even more emphatic. Étaples was not safe. Dormer let it go at that, and got a good game of bridge.

In the morning he found young Andrews as young as ever and got down to his job at once:

'Do you remember joining 469 T.M.B.?'

'Yes, sh'd think I do.'

'Do you remember the man you had as servant while you were with them?'

'I do. Topping feller. Gad, I was sorry when I had to leave him behind. Of course, I dropped him when I went to hospital. Never was so done!'

At last!

'You couldn't give me his name and number, I suppose?'

'I must have got a note of it somewhere. I say, what's all this about? Do you want to get hold of him?'

'I do. He's wanted, over a question of damage in billets. They've sent me to find him out.'

'Then I'm damned if I'll tell you. Because he was a topping chap!' rejoined Andrews, laughing.

'You'd better tell me, I think. The matter has gone rather high up, and it might be awkward if I had to report that the information was refused.'

'Lord, you aren't going to make a Court of Inquiry affair of it, are you?'

'It may come to that, and they've got hold of your name.'

'Gee whizz! I don't like landing the chap. I may not have got any particulars of him, now, my things have been so messed about.'

'Well, look and see!'

'All right.'

Andrews fumbled out from the night-table beside his bed, the usual bedside collection. Letters in female handwriting, some young, some old – from one or more sweethearts and a mother, thought Dormer. Paper-covered novels. The sort (English) that didn't make you think. The sort (French) that make you feel, if you were clever at the language. Cigarettes, bills. One or two letters from brother officers.

'Blast. It's in my Field Note-book, in my valise, in store here. I shall have to send to have it got out. Wait half a mo' and I'll get an orderly.'

As they waited, he went on:

'What's he wanted for? Some dam' Frenchman going to crime him for stealing hop-poles?'

'Something of that sort. You wouldn't remember it, it happened before you joined the Battery.'

'Then it jolly well wasn't my man Watson. He'd only just come up from Base!'

'Come, the man was of middle size and ordinary to look at, and had been servant to an officer of the name of Fairfield, who was killed!'

'Oh, that chap. I know who you mean now. I don't call him my servant. I only had him for a day or two. His name was Smith, as far as I can recollect. We were in the line, and I never got his number. He disappeared, may have been wounded, or gone sick of course, we were strafed to Hell, as usual. I should have got rid of him in any case. He was a grouser!'

'Didn't like the War?'

'I should say not.'

Hopeless, of course. When Andrews saw Dormer rise and close his note-book, he apologized:

'Beastly sorry. Afraid I'm no good.'

'That's all right. I don't want to find the fellow, personally. It's simply my job.'

'Fair wear and tear, so to speak?'

'Yes. Good morning.'

'Don't go – I say, don't. You're just getting interesting!' Heads popped up in the surrounding beds. 'Do tell us what it's all about.'

'Merely a matter of damage in billets as I said.'

'Go on. There's always damage in billets. You must ha' done heaps, haven't you? I have. There's something more in it than that.'

'Well, there is. Perhaps it will be a lesson to you not to go too far with other people's property.'

'I say, don't get stuffy. What did the feller do?'

'He broke into a shrine.'

'I say, that's a bit thick.'

'It was!'

'What did he do it for? Firewood?'

'No. He wanted to shelter a couple of mules!'

'Good man. Don't blame him!'

'No!'

'But they can't crime him for a thing like that?'

'They will if they catch him.'

'Go on!'

'It didn't stop at that.' Once more it seemed to Dormer that a good lesson might do no harm to the light-headed youth that Andrews represented, and several of whom were listening, anxiously from that corner of the ward.

'Did G.H.Q. take it up?'

'Yes. They had to. The Mayor of the village came to make an official inquiry and the Battery made fun of him.'

'Lumme! I bet they did!'

'They should not have done so. That made the French authorities take it up. Goodness knows where it will end!'

'End in our fighting the French,' said some one.

Dormer felt that it was high time to put his foot down. 'You may be privileged to talk like that while you're in hospital. But I don't recommend you to do so outside. You ought to have the sense to know that we don't want to fight anyone, we most certainly don't want to fight some one else after Germans. In any case, we don't want to do the fighting in England!'

There was a dead silence after he had spoken, and he rose, feeling that he had impressed them. He stumped out of the ward without another word, went to the Mess, rang and demanded his car. The Orderly Office would have liked to detain him, insisted on the possible state of Étaples, but he would not hear of it. In those few hours he had had enough and more than enough of the Base – the place where people talked while others Did – the place where the pulse of the War beat so feebly. He felt he would go mad if he stayed there, without sufficient occupation for his mind. His car appeared and he soon left the palace and the birchwoods and was rattling over the bridge into Étaples. 'Now for it!' he thought. But no policeman warned him off this time. He soon saw why. The streets had resumed their normal appearance. He might have known. That fancy of his, about the Headless Man, came back to him with its true meaning. What could they do, all those 'Other Ranks', as they were designated? Just meander about, fight the police, perhaps. But they had no organization, no means of rationing or transport. Of course, they had had to go back to their respective camps with their tails between their legs in order to get fed.

There was nothing to show for the whole business but a few panes of broken glass and some splintered palings. By the time he got to St Omer and stopped for lunch, no one seemed to have heard of it. By tea-time, he was back at Divisional H.Q. And none too soon. A fresh attack was to be made the following day. He went straight up to the canal bank, where Kavanagh was as busy as ever, and dropped into his work where he had left it. There was just the same thing to do, only more of it. A desperate race against time was going on. It was evident enough that this most enormously costly of all offensives must get through before November finally rendered fighting impossible. There was still some faint chance of a week or two of fair weather in October. Fresh Corps were massed and flung into the struggle. Engineers, Labour Corps, anyone who could throw a bomb or fire a rifle must do so. What had been roads of stone *pavé*, had been so blown about with shell-fire that they were a honeycomb of gaping holes, repaired with planks. More and more searching were the barrages, denser the air fighting. Progress there undoubtedly was, but progress enough?

Through the sleepless nights and desperate days that followed, Dormer's feelings towards Kavanagh were considerably modified. The fellow still talked, but Dormer was less sorry to hear him. He even recited, and Dormer got into the way of listening. They were now in an 'Elephant' hut. No dug-out was possible in that sector, where eighteen inches below the surface you came to water. No tent could be set, even had they wished for one. Their frail house was covered with sandbags, of a sufficient thickness to keep off shrapnel, and presumably they were too insignificant to be the object of a direct hit, but in order to leave nothing to chance they had had the place covered with camouflage netting. Outside lay mile after mile of water-logged runnels that had been trenches, on the smashed and slippery parapets of which one staggered to some bit of roadway that was kept in repair at gigantic cost in lives and materials, guided by the lines of wire that either side had put up with such difficulty, and which were all now entirely useless, a mere hindrance to free movement. But they were 'in' for a long spell, and could not get away – did not want to, they were less bombed here than farther back. Rations reached them, that was as much as they had time to care about. Otherwise, the night was well filled for the one with counting off the parties that filed past into this or that attack, for the other in picking up those signal lines that had been smashed by shell-fire during the day, and replacing them.

As that endless procession went past him once more, Dormer felt that he now knew of what its component parts were thinking. Australians, Canadians, Welsh, Scotch, Irish, English, they were thinking of nothing in particular. Like the mules that went with them, they went on because they couldn't stop. Food and sleep each day was the goal. To stop would mean less food and sleep, mules and men knew that much, without use of the reasoning faculty. It had become an instinct. All the brilliant casuistry that had induced men to enlist was forgotten, useless, superseded. Even English soldiers were conscripts now, the War had won, had overcome any and every rival consideration, had made itself paramount, had become the end and the means as well.

A man like Dormer, accustomed to an ordered and reasoned existence, who could have explained his every act up to August 1914, by some good and solid reason, was as helpless as any. Stop the War? You wanted to go back half a century and alter all the political and business cliques in which it had been hatching. To alter those you wanted to be able to alter the whole structure of society in European countries, which kept those cliques in power, was obliged to have recourse to them, to get itself governed and financed. To do that you wanted to change Human Nature. Here Dormer's imagination stopped dead. He was no revolutionary. No one was farther than he from being one. He only hated Waste. He had been brought up and trained to business, in an atmosphere of methodical neatness, of carefully foreseen and forestalled risks. Rather than have recourse to revolution he would go on fighting the Bosche. It was so much more real.

Somewhere about the point at which he reached this conclusion, he heard, among the noise of the sporadic bombardment, Kavanagh's voice:

' "Now that we've pledged each eye of blue
And every maiden fair and true,
And our green Island Home, to you
The Ocean's wave adorning,
Let's give one hip, hip, hip hurrah!
And drink e'en to the coming day,
When squadron, square,
We'll all be there,
To meet the French in the morning!' "

That's the stuff to give the troops, Dormer!'

But Dormer, although cheered, was not going to admit it. 'You'd better go and sing it to the Seventy-Worst. They go in at dawn!'

'Good luck to them. Listen to this:

> ' "May his bright laurels never fade
> Who leads our fighting Fifth Brigade,
> These lads so true in heart and blade,
> And famed for danger scorning;
> So join me in one hip hurrah!
> And drink e'en to the coming day,
> When squadron, square,
> We'll all be there,
> To meet the French in the morning!" '

How's that for local colour. Is there a Fifth Brigade in tomorrow's show? They'd like that.'

'I bet they wouldn't. Anyhow, it's silly to repeat things against the French.'

'Man, it's a hundred years old.'

'Like my uncle's brandy.'

'You and your uncle!'

'I had an uncle once who had some brandy. It was called "Napoleon", and was supposed to date from 1815. When he opened it, it was gone!'

'There you are. That's your materialism. But you can sing a song a hundred years old and find it's not gone!'

'It's not a bad song. Only silly!'

'Well, try something older:

> ' "We be
> Soldiers three,
> Lately come from the Low Countree,
> *Pardonnez moi, je vous en prie;*
> We be
> Soldiers three." '

That's nearer three hundred years old. That's what fellows used to sing coming back from Ypres in those days!'

'You talk as if we'd always been in and out of that mangey hole.'

They both leaned on their elbows and gazed out of the tiny aperture, under the sacking, away over the sea-like ridges of pulverized mud, into the autumn evening. Between the rainclouds, torn and shredded as if by the shell-fire, watery gleams were pouring, as though the heavens were wounded and bled. They spilled all over the jagged stonework of that little old medieval walled town, compact within its ramparts, for the third time in its history garrisoned by an English Army. Kavanagh told him of it, but Dormer remained unimpressed. The history of the world that mattered began after the battle of Waterloo, with Commerce and Banking, Railway and Telegraph, the Education and Ballot Acts. Previous events were all very well, as scenery for Shakespeare's plays or Wagner's Operas. But otherwise, negligible. Yet the interlude did him good. He felt he had brought Kavanagh up short, in an argument, and he went to his night's work with a lighter heart, and a strengthened confidence in himself.

Of course, a few weeks later, the offensive was over, with the results he had foreseen, and with another result he was also not alone in foreseeing. Once back in rest, near Watten, he heard people talking in this strain, in G. office:

'I suppose, sir, we shall go on fighting next year?'

'Um – I suppose we shall. But perhaps some arrangement may be come to, first. There's been a good deal of talk about Peace!'

That was the mood of Divisional Head-quarters. A growing scepticism as to the continuance of the War. At the moment, Dormer missed the motive at the back of it. Away from H.Q. while the Division was in action, he had lost a good deal of ominous news. The talk about the transference of German Divisions from one front to another was old talk. He had heard it for years. He did not at the moment grasp that it had now a new significance. Then something happened that put everything else out of his head. He was not feeling too well, though he had nothing to complain of worse than the usual effects of damp and loss of sleep. Colonel Birchin had got himself transferred to a better appointment, and his place was taken by a much younger officer, glad to take it as a 'step' up from a dangerous and difficult staff-captaincy. They had been out at rest less than a week and Dormer had assumed as a matter of course that he would be put in charge of organized sports for the winter, as usual. But he was only just becoming sensible of the change that had come over H.Q. Colonel Birchin used to have a certain pre-War regular soldier's stiffness and want of imagination (which Dormer had privately deplored), but he had kept the Q. office well in hand. This new man, Vinyolles, very amicable and pleasant, and much nearer to Dormer's new army view of the War (he was in fact younger than Dormer, and than most of the clerical N.C.O.s in the office) had nothing like the stand-off power of his predecessor. Also, the office, like everything else, had grown, half a dozen odd-job officers were now attached, and without wearing red, sat and worked with Dormer. So that when Dormer went to show his Football Competition Time Table and his schedule for use of the Boxing Stadium, he found that he had to explain how these things were usually done. Colonel Vinyolles had no idea. Dormer ought to have been warned. But his head was not working at its very best. He had a temperature, he thought, and wanted to go and lie down at his billet for a bit and take some aconite, a remedy he had carried with him throughout the War. Colonel Vinyolles was quite nice about the Sports, and just as Dormer was turning to go, said to him:

'Perhaps you can help me in this matter. I see your name occurs in the correspondence!'

Of course, he might have known. It was the familiar *dossier*, as the French called it, the sheaf of papers, clipped together, at the bottom the original blue Questionnaire form that old Jerome Vanderlynden had signed. At the top a fresh layer of official correspondence, 'Passed to you please, for necessary action.' 'This does not appear to concern this office.' 'Kindly refer to A.Q.M.G.'s minute dated July 1916.' And so on. Dormer knew quite a lot of it by heart and the remainder he could have 'reconstructed' with no difficulty. The only fresh thing that had happened was a minute from the new chief of the French Mission enclosing a cutting from a newspaper – a French newspaper of all conceivable rags – from which it appeared that some deputy or other had 'interpellated' a minister about the matter, asked a question in the 'House' would be the English of it, Dormer supposed.

'What am I to tell the Mission?' Colonel Vinyolles was asking.

Dormer was not a violent man by habit, but he felt that he was getting to his limit with this affair. He thought a moment, wanting to say: 'Tell them to go to the Devil!' but held it in reserve, and substituted: 'Tell them the matter has attention!'

'Thanks very much!'

Dormer went and rested.

The following day he felt no better and did not do much. He had the Sports well in hand, and there was no movement of troops. The day following that he felt queerer than ever, and jibbed at his breakfast. He went along to see the D.A.D.M.S., always a friend of his, who put a thermometer under his tongue, looked at it, shook it, looked at Dormer, gave him an aspirin, and advised him to go and lie down for a bit. On his way to his billet Dormer put his head into Q. office to tell the Sergeant-major where he was to be found if wanted. He was called by Colonel Vinyolles from the farther room. It was again full of people he considered (as rank counted for less than experience) to be his juniors. He could see something was 'up'. They were all highly amused except Vinyolles.

'I say, Dormer, I consider you let me down on this.'

'What's the trouble?'

'Trouble! I've got a nice chit back, in reply to my saying "the matter has attention". They say that any further delay is "inadmissible" and that they will be obliged to carry the matter higher.'

'Let 'em!'

'Oh, that won't do at all. The General has seen this, and he wants to know what you mean by it.'

'He ought to know by this time!'

'Captain Dormer!'

Of course he was wrong, but he felt rotten. It wasn't Vinyolles' fault. He pulled himself together.

'Sorry, sir. I mean that the case has been going on for nearly two years, and has certainly not been neglected. I think every one who counts is familiar with it.'

He meant it for a snub for some of those chaps who were sitting there grinning. He saw his mistake in a moment. Vinyolles was as new as any of them, and naturally replied: 'I'm afraid I have no knowledge of it. Perhaps you will enlighten me?'

'It must have been June 1916, when we first received the claim. The late A.P.M., Major Stevenage, took it up as a matter of discipline, but on investigation considered that it was rather a case for compensation, as damage in billets. The French Mission insisted that an arrest must be made, and I have made every possible effort to trace the soldier responsible. But formations change so quickly, during offensives especially, that it is impossible.'

'I see. What exactly did he do, to cause such a rumpus?'

At the prospect of having to retell the whole story, Dormer got an impression that something was after him, exactly like the feeling of trying to get cover in a barrage, and wondering which moment would be the last. He put his hand to his head and found some one had pushed a chair against his knees. He sat down vaguely conscious of the D.A.D.M.S. standing near by.

'An officer of 469 T.M.B. was wounded and his servant was given two mules, sick or wounded, to lead. He got to the billet mentioned and seems to have taken a dislike to the horse-lines. He found one of those little memorial chapels that you often see, in the corner of the pasture, and knocked in the front of it to shelter the beasts. The farmer didn't like it and sent for the Mayor to make a *procès-verbal*. By the time the Mayor got there, the Battery was on the move again. It was about the time of one of those awkward little shows the Bosche put up to contain us during Verdun. The Battery had been badly knocked about, and the men were excited and made some sort of a scene! The Mayor told his Deputy and his Deputy told some one at French G.H.Q. It all keeps going round in my head. I don't want to find the chap who did it. He's no worse than you or I. He was just making the best of the War, and I don't blame him. I blame it. You might as well crime the whole British Army.'

What had he said? He fancied he had given the facts concisely, but was not sure of himself, his head felt so funny, and he was aware that people – he could no longer be sure who they were – Q. office seemed crowded – were tittering! – Some one else was talking now, but he was not interested. He rested his head on his hand and heard Vinyolles: 'Well, Dormer, you go along to your billet, and we'll see what can be done!'

He got up and walked out. The D.A.D.M.S. was at his elbow, saying to him:

'Get into this ambulance, I'll run you across!' but he never got to his billet. He got into a train. He did not take much notice, but refused the stuff they wanted him to eat. After that he must have gone to sleep, but woke up, under a starlit sky, with an unmistakable smell of the sea. They were lifting him under a canvas roof. Now, from the motion, he perceived he was at sea, but it did not seem greatly to matter. He was out of it, he had cut the whole disgusting show. He had done his bit, now let someone else take a turn.

\*

Dormer had not been home on leave since early spring, and the leave that he got for convalescence gave him not only some idea of the vast changes going on in England, while he, in France, had been engaged in the same old War, but a notion of changes that had gone on in that old War without his having perceived them. He was let loose from Hospital just before Christmas, at that unfortunate period when the public at home were still feeling the reaction from the Bell-ringing of Cambrai, were just learning the lengths to which the collapse of Russia had gone and were to be confronted with the probable repercussion of that collapse upon the prospects of the campaign in the West. There was no escaping these conclusions because his own home circumstances had so changed as to throw him back completely on himself. His father having died while he was in France, his mother had taken a post under one of the semi-official War organizations that abounded. The old home in which he had grown up had been dispersed, and he found his only near relative in his native town was his sister, a teacher by profession, who had moved the remnants of the old furniture and his and her own small belongings to a new house in one of the high, healthy suburbs that surrounded the old town. She was, however, busy all day, and he fell into the habit, so natural to anyone who has lived in a Mess for years, of dropping in at one of the better-class bars, before lunch, for an *apéritif*, and a glance at the papers. Here he would also pick up some one for a round of golf, which would keep him employed until tea-time, for he could not rid himself of the War-time habit of looking upon each day as something to be got through somehow, in the hopes that the morrow might be better.

These ante-prandial excursions were by far the closest contact he had had with anything like a normal, representative selection of his fellow-countrymen, since they and he had become so vitally altered from the easy-going sport-loving England of pre-War, and he had to readjust his conception considerably. He soon grasped that there was a lot of money being made, and a lot of khaki being worn as a cover for that process. There was plenty of energy, a good deal of fairly stubborn intention to go on and win, but a clear enough understanding that the War was not going to to be won in the trenches. And when he had got over some little spite at this, his level habit of mind obliged him to confess that there was a good deal in it. There were many signs that those who held that view were right.

Sipping his drink, smoking and keeping his nose carefully in his newspaper, in those bars lighted by electric light, in the middle of the dark Christmas days, he listened and reflected. The offensives he had seen? How had they all ended? How did he say himself they always must end? Exactly as these chaps had made up their minds! Would he not see if there did not remain some relative who could get him one of these jobs at home, connected with supplying some one else with munitions? No, he would not. He understood and agreed with the point of view, but some very old loyalty in him would keep him in

France, close up to the guns, that was the place for him. He had no illusions as to that to which he was returning. He knew that he had never been appointed to Divisional Staff, had merely been attached. There was no 'establishment' for him, and directly he had been sent down as sick, his place had been filled, some one else was doing 'head housemaid' as he had been called, to young Vinyolles, and he, Dormer, would go shortly to the depot of his regiment, from thence to reinforcement camp, and thus would be posted to any odd battalion that happened to want him. The prospect did not worry him so much as might have been supposed. He felt himself pretty adept at wangling his way along, and scrounging what he wanted, having a fine first-hand experience of how the machinery worked. He did not want to go into the next offensive, it was true, but neither did he want the sort of job he had had, and even less did he want to be at Base, or in England. Boredom he feared almost as much as physical danger. Accustomed to having his day well filled, if he must go to War he wanted to be doing something, not nothing, which was apparently a soldier's usual occupation. But he did not feel his participation in the next offensive very imminent. He had heard them all talking about 'Not fighting any more,' and now here was Russia out of it and America not yet in, and Peace might be patched up.

The most striking thing therefore that he learned was this new idea of the Bosche taking the initiative, and attacking again. A new army officer, his knowledge of the Western Front dated from Loos, and was of allied offensives only. He had never seen the earlier battles of Ypres, the retreat from Mons was just so much history to him. When he heard heated arguments as to which particular point the Bosche would select for their offensive, in France, or (so nervous were these people at home) in England even, he was astonished, and then incredulous. The level balance of his mind saved him. He had no superfluous imagination. He had never seen a German offensive, didn't want to, and therefore didn't think he would. As usual, the barparlour oracles knew all about it, gave chapter and verse, could tick off on their fingers how many German Divisions could be spared from the Eastern Front. He had heard it all before. He remembered how nearly the cavalry got through after Vimy, how Moorsledge Ridge was to give us command of the country up to Courtrai, how Palestine or Mespot were to open an offensive right in the Bosche rear, not to mention all the things these Russians had always been said to be going to do. This might be another of what the French so well called 'Canards' – Wild Ducks. He would wait and see.

He was impressed in a different way by the accounts that now began to filter through, of what had been happening in Russia. Officers shot, and regiments giving their own views on the campaign. That was what happened when the Headless Man got loose! No doubt the Russians, from all he had heard, had suffered most, so far as individual human suffering went. And then, Russians were, to him, one of these over-brainy people. Had anyone acquainted with his ruminations taxed him to say if English people were under-brainy, he would have said no, not necessarily, but brainy in a different way. Left to himself he felt that all the opinions he had ever formed of the Russians were justified. Look at their Music. Some of it was pretty good, he admitted, but it was – awkward – beyond the reach of amateurs, in the main. This appeared to him, quite sincerely, to be a grave defect. He was conscious – more, he was proud – of being an amateur soldier, and knowing himself to be modest, he did not fear any comparison between the actual results obtained by English amateurs like himself, and the far more largely professional armies of other countries. And now these over-brainy ones had gone and done it. He knew as well as anyone the hardships and dangers of soldiering, had experienced them, shared them with the ranks, in the trenches. Why even in this beastly Vanderlynden affair, it would have puzzled him to say if he were more sorry than glad that the private soldier had never been brought to Justice. But English – and even Frenchmen – as he had seen with his own eyes, if they mutinied, got over it, and went on. It was only people like the Russians that went and pushed things to their logical conclusion.

He had a hatred of that, being subconsciously aware that the logical conclusion of Life is Death. Naturally, from his upbringing and mental outlook, he had no sympathy with the alleged objects and achievements of the Russian Revolution. He could not see what anyone wanted with a new social order, and as for the domination of Europe by the Proletariat, if he understood it, he was all against it in principle. He was against it because it was Domination. That was precisely the thing that had made him feel increasingly antagonistic to Germany and German ideas. It had begun long ago, during brief continental holidays. He had met Germans on trains and steamers, in hotels and on excursions. He had grudged them their efficient way of sightseeing, feeding and everything else. But he had grudged them most their size and their way of getting there first. If it had not been for that, he had a good deal more sympathy with them, in most ways, than with the French. Subsequently he had found Germans infringing on the business of his native town, selling cheaper, better-tanned hides than its tanners, more scientifically compounded manures than its merchants. Then they invaded politics and became a scare at election times. And after the false start of 1911, in 1914 they had finally kicked over the tea-table of the old quiet comfortable life. He did not argue about this. He had felt it simply, truly, directly. Under all the hot-air patriotism and real self-sacrifice of August 1914, it had been this basic instinct which had made him and all his sort enlist. The Germans had asked for it, and they should darn-well have it. If they didn't they would go on asking. They were after Domination.

That craze had started something that would be difficult now to stop. Dormer saw very well that other people besides Russians might find grievances and the same wrong-headed way of venting them. The Russians would probably go on with their propaganda, all over the world. The Germans, on the other hand, had probably set the Japanese off. And so we should go on, all the aristocratic classes calling for Domination by their sort, all the ultra-brainy democracies calling for their particular brand.

So when he was passed as fit and told to rejoin the depot of his regiment, at a seaport town, he went without any panic fear of the future, German or otherwise. He went with a deep conviction that whatever happened, life had been cheapened and vulgarized. It was not by any means mere theory. He had seen what sort of a home he might hope to make after the Peace, with his mother or sisters, or if, conceivably, he married. Not a bad home, his job would always be there, and certain remnants of that bourgeois comfort that had grown up in all the old quiet streets of the provincial towns of England during the nineteenth century, privileged, aloof from the troubles of the 'continent', self-contained. But remnants only, not nearly enough. He and all his sort had been let down several pegs in the social scale. Without any narrow spite, or personal grievance, he felt that the Germans had caused this upset and the Russians had put the finishing stroke to it, made it permanent, as it were. He happened to be opposite the Germans in the particular encounter that was not yet ended, and he was able to draw upon an almost inexhaustible supply of obstinate ill-will.

He went to the depot in its huts on a sandy estuary. It was commanded by a Major of the usual type, and no one knew better than Dormer how to keep on the right side of such a one. He was, of course, a Godsend to the Major. He had all the practical experience and none of the fussiness. He merely wanted the job finished. That suited the Major exactly, who didn't want it to finish in a hurry, but wanted even less to have to find ideas for training troops. Dormer, with his two and a half years in France, was the very man. He looked trustworthy. He was set to instructing the raw material, of which the camp was full. He disliked it intensely, but, as always, took what was given him in his sober fashion and did his limited best with it. He was amazed to find such reserves of men still untouched. His own recollections of early 1915 were of camps filled with an eager volunteer crowd of all ages and conditions, who were astounded when it was suggested to them that certain of them ought to take a commission. Now he found that his sort went a different way, direct to O.T.C. or Cadet Corps. There was a permanence about the camp staff that he had never seen in the old days. But most of all he was impressed with the worn appearance of the camp. Thousand after thousand had passed through it, been drafted overseas, and disappeared. Thousand after thousand had followed. In the town and at the railway, there were no longer smiles and encouragement. People had got painfully used to soldiers, and from treating them as heroes, and then as an unavoidable, and profitable incident, had come to regard them chiefly as a nuisance. He forgot how he had wondered if the men would stand it, he forgot how often he had heard the possibility of an early Peace discussed. He began to wonder now if people at home would stand it – the lightless winter nights, the summer full of bombing, the growing scarcity of comforts, the queues for this, that, and the other, the pinch that every gradually depleted family was beginning to feel, as one after another of its members had to go. He had been so long out of all this, up against the actual warfare, glad enough of small privileges and of the experience that enabled him to avoid the more onerous duties, the worst sorts of want, that he only now began to realize what he had never grasped, in his few short leaves, that there was still quite a considerable, probably the greater portion of the nation, who did not share his view of the necessity of going on. Another avenue of speculation was opened to him. What if all the people at home made Peace behind the backs of the Armies? Yet, being Dormer, he did not submit to this homegrown philosophy. He just went on and did the next thing that his hand found to do.

Of one thing he became pretty certain. All these people at home had 'got the wind up'. He didn't know which were the worst, the lower middle class, who were beginning to fear invasion, as a form of damage to their shops and houses. He thought of those ten departments of France that were either occupied by, or shot over, by the Germans. Or against the newspapers, with their scare-lines, their everlasting attempt to bring off this or that political coup. Or again the people in power, who were keeping this enormous number of troops in England, presumably to defend the beaches of the island from an armed landing. He had become during the three years that had contained for him an education that he could not otherwise have got in thirty, a more instructed person.

An offensive was an offensive, could be nothing more or less. Every offensive had been a failure except for some local or temporary object, and in his opinion, always must be a failure. The idea of an offensive conducted across a hundred leagues of sea made him smile. It was hard enough to get a mile forward on dry land, but fancy the job of maintaining communications across the water! He attended enough drills to fill in the time, organized the football of the Brigade to his liking and let it go at that. At moments he was tempted to apply to be sent to France, at others to try and join one of these Eastern expeditions, Salonika, Palestine or Mespot. But the certainty of being more bored and of being farther than ever from the only life he cared for, made him hesitate. He hesitated for two long months.

Then on 21 March he was ordered by telegram to proceed to France. He felt, if anything, a not unpleasant thrill. With all his care, he had not been able to dodge boredom altogether. The depot camp had also been much too near the scenes of his pre-War life. He had gone home, as a matter of duty, for several week-ends and had always returned finely exasperated, it was so near to and yet so far from home as he had pictured it, in his dreams. Now, here was an end to this Peace-time soldiering. The news, according to the papers, seemed pretty bad, but he remembered so well the awful scurry there was for reinforcements on the morning that the nature of the Second Battle of Ypres became known. This could not be so desperate as that was. Practically the whole of the rank and file in the depot were under orders. He took jolly good care not to get saddled with a draft, and spent the night in London. People were in a rare stew there. He had a bath and a good dinner and left it all behind. He took a little more note of the traffic at the port of embarkation. On the other side, he found lorries waiting and went jolting and jamming away up to Frecourt, forty miles. He rather approved. It looked as though our people were waking up.

At Corps reinforcement camp – a new dodge evidently – he

got posted to a North Country battalion; and proceeded to try and find their whereabouts. He was told that they were going to Bray, but it took him some time to understand that they were falling back on that place. When, by chance, he hit upon the Division to which they belonged, they were on the road, looking very small, but intact and singing. He soon found plenty to do, for he grasped that practically the whole battalion was composed of reinforcements, and had only been together two or three days. They set to work at once to strengthen some half-completed entrenchments, but after two days were moved back again.

It was during those two days that he saw what he had never to that moment beheld, an army in retreat. The stream of infantry, artillery and transport was continuous – here in good formation, there a mere mass of walking wounded mixed up with civilians, as the big hospitals and the small villages of the district turned out before the oncoming enemy. He thought it rotten luck on those people, many of whom had been in German hands until February 1917, and had only had a twelvemonth in their small farms, living in huts, and had now to turn out before a further invasion. The bombardment was distinctly nasty, he never remembered a nastier, but as usual, the pace of the advance soon outdistanced the slow-moving heavy artillery, whose fire was already lessening. He had no feelings of sharp despair, for as he had foreseen, a modern army could not be crumpled up and disposed of. What he did now anticipate, was any amount of inconvenience.

Amiens, he gathered, was uninhabitable, that meant many good restaurants out of reach. New lines of rail, new lateral communications would be necessary, that meant marching. Just when they had begun to get the trenches fairly reliable, they were entrained and sent wandering all round the coast. The wonderful spring weather broke with the end of March, as the weather always did, when it had ceased to be of any use to the Bosche, and had he been superstitious, he might have thought a good deal of that. It was in a cold and rainy April that he found himself landed on the edge of the coal-fields, behind a canal, with a slag heap on one side of him, and a little wood on the other, amid an ominous quiet.

The company of which he had been given command was now about a hundred and fifty strong and he had done what little he could to equalize the four platoons. He had one officer with him, a middle-aged Lieutenant called Merfin, of no distinguishable social status, or local characteristics. The day when a battalion came from one town or corner of a county, under officers that were local personages in the civil life of its district, was long past. Dormer placed his second-in-command socially as music-hall, or pawnbroking, but the chap had been out before and had been wounded, and probably knew something of the job. The men were satisfactory enough, short, stumpy fellows with poor teeth, but exactly that sort of plainness of mind that Dormer appreciated. They would do all right. Perhaps a quarter of them had been out before, and the remainder seemed fairly efficient in their musketry and bombing, and talked pigeons and dogs in their spare time, when not gambling.

The bit of line they held was Reserve, a bridgehead over the canal, a strong point round a half-demolished château in the wood, and some wet trenches to the right, where the next battalion joined on. Battalion Head-quarters was in a farm half a mile back. Dormer and Merfin improvised a Mess in the cellar of the Château, saw that the cooker in the stables was distributing tea, and let all except the necessary guards turn in. He had some machine-gunners at the strong point, and across the canal were two guns, whose wagons had just been up with rations and ammunition. His own lot of rations came soon after and he told Merfin to take the first half of the night, and rolled himself in his coat to sleep.

As he lay there, listening to the scatter of machine-gun fire, and the mutter of officers' servants in the adjoining coal-hole, watching the candle shadows flicker on the walls that had been whitewashed, as the draught stirred the sacking over the doorway, his main thought was how little anything changed. Two and a half years ago he had been doing exactly the same thing, a few miles away, in the same sort of cellar, in front of an enemy with the same sort of advantage in ground and initiative, machine-guns and heavy artillery. He was as far from beating the Germans as ever he had been. He supposed that practically all the gains of 1916 and 1917 south of Arras had been lost. On the other hand, the Germans, so far as he could see, were equally far from winning. What he now feared was, either by prolonged War or premature Peace, a continuance of this sort of thing. And slowly, for he was as mild and quiet-mannered a man as one could find, his gorge began to rise. He began to want to get at these Germans. It was no longer a matter of principle, a feeling that it was his duty as it had been in the days when he enlisted, took a commission, and had come to France. He was no longer worrying about the injustice of the attack on Belgium or the danger of a Germany paramount in Europe. He had now a perfectly plain and personal feeling. But being Dormer, this did not make him cry out for a *sortie en masse* like a Frenchman, nor evolve a complicated and highly scientific theory as to how his desire was to be realized. The French and Portuguese who fought beside him would have found him quite incomprehensible. The Germans actually invented a logical Dormer whom they had to beat, who was completely unlike him. If he had any ideas as to what he was going to do, they amounted to a quiet certainty that once the enemy came away from his heavy and machine-guns, he, Dormer, could do him in.

So he went on with the next thing, which was to turn over and sleep. He woke, sitting bolt upright, to the sound of two terrific crashes. One was right over his head. The candle had been blown out, and as he struggled out of the cellar, barking his shins and elbows, he was aware that the faint light of the sky was obscured by a dense cloud all round him. Instinctively he pulled up his gas mask, but the sound of falling masonry and the grit he could taste between his lips, reassured him. It was a cloud of brick dust. Across the canal, the barrage was falling on the front lines with the thunder of a waterfall. The Bosche had hit the Château, and if he were not mistaken, had put in another salvo, somewhere near by. At the gate of the little park-like garden he ran into a figure he recognized for Merfin, by the red light of the battle, just across the canal.

'What is it?'

'Aw – they've knocked in the bridge!'

'Every one standing-to?'

'Can't help 'emselves.'

They went to look at the damage. The bridge was a small, one vehicle affair, with steel lattice sides, and an asphalt roadway. The bridge piers at the near end had been blown away, and the whole had settled down some four or five feet, on to the mud of the towpath.

'Can you get across?'

'Aw – yes – easy!'

'Better get across and wait a bit!'

He himself went back to find up his stretcher-bearers, who, he had always noticed, wanted an order to get them in motion. The guard on the bridge was dead so far as he could see, but some one was shouting, behind, at the Château.

He found the C.S.M. with two men digging out the servants whose coal-cellar had been blocked. One of them was badly crushed, but his own man only shaken. Then there were horses on the road. Gunners, trying to get their teams up to the advanced guns. Hopeless, of course. Then came a runner from battalion. Send Merfin with two platoons. He saw to that, and rearranged his depleted company. It took some time. The barrage appeared to be creeping nearer. The ground shook with the continuous concussion and whiffs of gas were more and more noticeable, but the heavier stuff was already falling farther to the rear. Then came a runner from across the bridge. There was a crowd on the road. Dormer went and found just what he expected. Walking wounded and those who wanted to be treated as such. He sorted them out, directing the former down the road to the dressing station, and setting the others to dig. If he had got to hang on to this place, and he supposed he had, he meant to have some cover. The stream of people across the broken bridge increased. Trench mortars and machine-gunners, platoons of his own regiment. The Bosche was 'through' on the left, and they were to come back behind the canal. The barrage died out, to confirm this. The machine-gun fire came nearer and nearer.

In the cold grey light of a wet April dawn, a tin-helmeted figure dashed up on a borrowed motor-cycle. It was the Brigade Major. What had Dormer got? He heard and saw, and took a platoon and all the sundries. His last words were: 'Hang on here, whatever you do!' Dormer heard the words without emotion. He realized that it meant that he was expected to gain time. He got hold of his Sergeant, and overhauled the rations and ammunition. They were not too badly off, and the cooker lay stranded in the stable yard. That meant hot water, at least. He took a turn round the place. The Château grounds had once been wired as part of some forgotten scheme of defence of 1915 or early 1916. That was all right. On the other hand, the 'bridgehead' – a precious half-boiled concoction – was full of gas and the barrier on the road blown away.

He got his few men out of it, with their several casualties, and started them carting brick rubble from the dilapidations of the Château to make an emplacement for a machine-gun on the near side of the bridge. He stood looking at the road by which the Bosche must come – a mere lane that led from one of the neighbouring coal-pits, and was used, he imagined, for transport of coal that was required locally. It meandered out of sight, among low fenceless fields, until the shallow undulations of the ground hid it. In the distance was the steamy reek of last night's battle, but nothing that moved, amid the silence broken only by long-distance shots, and fusillade somewhere on the left. Then, down that road he saw a party advancing, led by an officer. There was no doubt that they wore khaki. He waited by the bridge for them, and shouted directions to them how to cross. He got an answer:

'Hallo, you old devil, what are you doing?'

It was that Kavanagh. There had been an advanced signal exchange, and he had gone to bring his men in. They were tired, hungry and disgusted, but Kavanagh had the jauntiness of old. He wasn't going back to Division, he was going to stay with dear old Dormer, and see this through. Dormer thought a moment, then said: 'All right.'

'All right. I should think so. I don't suppose I could catch

Division, even on a motor-bike. They must be nearly at Calais. It's all rot. The Bosche are done!'

'Are they?'

'Sure. What are they waiting for now?'

'Bringing up their artillery?'

'That won't blow the water out of the canal.'

'Possibly not. But we may as well have some food while it's possible.'

'You old guts. Always eating!'

'Yes, when I can. Aren't you?'

'Now, Dormer. You know me better than that. Glory is my manna.'

'Will you take cold bully and tea with it?' asked Dormer as they dropped into the cellar.

Kavanagh made no objection, and they ate in silence, fast, for ten minutes. Then they saw the men were being fed, and relapsed, in their hiding-place, into pipes, and whisky out of Kavanagh's flask.

'How did you get into this show?' Dormer asked.

'The Division – your old Division, my boy, left me here to hand over! They might have spared themselves the trouble. But I'd got a most lovely scheme of lateral communication. Corps gave me a lot of sweet words about it. I suppose I shall get the M.C. Now the silly old Hun has gone and blown it all to bits. What about you?'

'You know I got wrong and was sent home sick.'

'I heard all that. It was about that Vanderlynden affair, wasn't it?'

'It was!'

'Well, you've no idea what a sensation you created. Vinyolles got simply wet behind the ears with it. Some French Deputy said, after the Somme show, that English troops did more damage to France than to Germany. Of course every one on Divisional H.Q. has changed in the last few months. They all established an alibi or Habeas Corpus or something. It was one of the things that made the French Press go for unity of command! You were a boon to them!'

'I wish them joy of the business. I don't know why you mix me up with it.'

'Why, it was your pet show, wasn't it?'

'It got fathered on to me because I could understand what it was about.'

'Yes, you told Vinyolles, didn't you?'

'The ignorant brute asked me.'

'I know. He's all fresh. I find him trying also. Well, he knows all about it now.'

'Tell you the truth, I've no idea what I said, Kavanagh! I was feeling queer!'

'Vinyolles thought you'd gone potty.'

'He wasn't far wrong.'

'He said you told him the whole British Army was guilty of the Kerrime at Vanderlynden's!'

It was the first time Dormer had heard it called that.

'Well, in a sense, so they are.'

'In a sense, War is a foolish business!'

'I thought you liked it?'

'I was trying to talk like you – '

Before Dormer could reply, the sacking over the door was lifted, by Dormer's Sergeant.

'Cop'l Arbone is back, sir!'

'Very good. Did he get in touch with the Major?'

'He only found a Lewis-gun section, sir. The Major moved most of the men along the canal, where there's more trouble!'

'All right!'

'Well, I suppose I may as well go and have a look at my lot.' Kavanagh stretched himself. 'I told 'em to hunt round and see if they could get this place wired up!'

'Umpteenth Corps ought to have thought of that, long ago!'

'Did you ever know Corps think of anything?'

While Kavanagh was so engaged, Dormer took a turn round the various guards and posts he had established. There appeared to be fair cover from view, and even from small-arm and field-gun fire. Of course when the Bosche really wanted to get the place, nothing Dormer and Kavanagh and some forty men could do would stop it. In coming round to the stables behind the Château he found his Sergeant with two men, laboriously trundling on a hand cart what he soon verified to be slabs of marble. What would they think of next? The explanation was, 'There was a champion bathroom, sir, an' I thought we could set up our Lewis better with these!'

When Kavanagh saw what was going on, he laughed.

'More damage in billets, Dormer!'

'Well, the stuff will be smashed up anyhow, won't it?'

'Two blacks don't make a white. I understand why you told Vinyolles the whole army was guilty. You're doing just what your friend did about his mules.'

'Why will you drag in that beastly business? This has nothing in common with it.'

'To the common all things are common. You tell the owner of the Château that when he finds out.'

Dormer was going to say 'He won't find out!' but refrained. He disliked arguing. This seemed a particularly bad argument. Also, at that moment, a Lewis gun began, just below. Then another. He went to the garden wall, and peered out. Nothing visible, as usual. He thought of all the battle pictures he had ever seen. The prancing horses, the gay uniforms, the engrossing action of figures that pointed muzzle or bayonet at each other, that wielded sword or lance. Here he was, an incident in one of the biggest battles in the world. All he could see was neglected arable, smashed buildings, a broken bridge and a blocked byroad, all shrouded in steamy vapour. He made out that it was the Lewis opposite the end of the bridge that was firing. He crawled along the gully that had been dug from the Château gate to the roadway, and so to the emplacement by the step-off of the bridge. The Corporal in charge of the section turned to him.

'Got 'im, sir!'

'What is it?'

'Bosche in the ditch, under them bushes!'

Dormer waited a moment, but nothing happened. He crawled back, and sent his Sergeant round to see that every one was under cover. Back in the cellar he found Kavanagh, and told him.

'I know. Once more into the breach!'

'It's not poetry, Kavanagh. This is the start. Once they find we're stopping them here, they'll shift us, you may bet!'

'I shouldn't wonder. My lot are trying to get into touch with Brigade. They're running a line back behind the wood. There's no one on our left, as far as can be found.'

'Must be some one.'

'Why should there be? Brigade have probably moved by this time.'

'Ah, well, can't be helped.'

No use telling the chap that it was all useless. He just sat down and lit his pipe. He perceived clearly enough that they were being sacrificed – just left there to hold the Bosche up for a few hours, while the Division went back.

During the day there was sporadic machine-gunning. The Bosche was feeling his way for crossing the canal, but had found it far less easy than in the sectors farther north. Tolerably certain that the main attack would come at dawn, Dormer and Kavanagh got what rest they could, though proper sleep was out of the question. Their servants had found a well-upholstered sofa, and a superior brass bedstead, which now adorned the cellar, causing Kavanagh to gibe about damage in billets. Their vigil was lightened by the sounds of song from the stables where such men as they had set apart as reserves were lodged.

> 'Old soldiers never die,
> They only fade away,'

to a well-known hymn tune, made Dormer homesick, but delighted Kavanagh.

'Listen to that!'

'I can't help it, unless I send and stop them.'

'Never, man, never stop men who can sing at such a moment. It means philosophy and courage!'

'It means foolishness and rum!'

'Dormer, I fear you are no born leader!'

'No, of course I wasn't.'

'But you've got to lead men now, and lead 'em to victory.'

'I don't mind much so long as I lead 'em to Peace!'

'Yes, but don't you see, mere Peace will mean Revolution!'

'I don't believe it. I saw that affair at Étaples. I saw the trouble among the French troops in May. Those chaps prefer to take orders from you and me rather than from their own sort.'

'How do you account for Russia, then?'

'I can't. But it's an object lesson rather than an example, I should say.'

'You used not to talk like that. You used to say that the men wouldn't stand it.'

'I've lived and learned!'

'Both, I am sure.'

'You needn't be so superior. No one knew what any of this would be like until it was tried. We've something to go by, now! This War depends on turning a crank. The side that goes on turning it efficiently the longer will win. Our chaps look like lasting!'

'So do the Bosche. No, Dormer, you're all wrong –'

At that moment a fresh burst of song came from the stables. A Cockney voice to a waltz tune:

> 'Orl that I wawnt is larve,
> Orl that I need is yew –'

'There,' cried Kavanagh, his voice rising into his excited croak. 'That's what we want!'

Dormer did not reply. With dusk came a few long-range shots, gradually broadening and deepening into a bombardment towards dawn. Both of them had to be out and about all night. They had several casualties, and the whole place reeked with gas. As the grey light of another day began to change the texture of the shadows, movement was discernible about the road. It was their chance and with a higher heart and the feeling of relief, they were able to let loose the Lewis guns, which they had managed to save intact. For more than an hour, Dormer crawled from one to the other, seeing that they did not overheat or jam, for the fact that they were killing Germans pleased him. Then there was a slackening of fire on both sides.

They waited and the suspense from being irksome, became tolerable. There was a good deal of noise each side of them, and Dormer began to wonder if his detachment were surrounded, especially as the servants whom he had sent back to get into touch with Brigade, had not returned. It was a dull rainy afternoon prematurely dark, and the rain as it increased, seemed to beat down the gunning, as water quenches a fire. He must have been in that half-waking state that often superimposed on sleeplessness and the awful din, when he was thoroughly roused by trampling in the trees round the Château. He called to Kavanagh but got no reply. Then there was a pushing and scrambling at the wall behind the stable, and English cavalrymen came swinging over it. Dormer and Kavanagh were relieved, and were shortly able to hand over and prepare to march their command back to rejoin their Division, which, depleted by four weeks of continual mauling, was being taken out of the line.

The battle was by no means over. They next went in farther north, and Dormer had the queer experience of going into trenches where Corps H.Q. had been, of billeting in rooms where Major-Generals had slept. Gradually he became aware of lessening tension, reduced shelling, and slackened machine-gun fire, but it was the end of May before he found, when sent to raid an enemy post, that there was no one there. He had been right after all. The German offensive also had failed. Anticlimax was the rule of the War. He was glad that he had parted from Kavanagh, who had gone back to his proper job with his Division, goodness knew where. He felt that the fellow would remind him that for several hours while they lay together in those scratched-out trenches round that little Château by the canal, he had given up hope. He need not have bothered. If the Bosche could not win on that day, he never would. Slowly now the British lines were creeping forward. Then he found American troops behind him.

It was during this phase of things that he found himself upon familiar ground. Except on Kavanagh's lips, he had not heard of the crime at Vanderlynden's since before Christmas. It was now September. Here he was, detrained and told to march to Hondebecq. He passed what had been Divisional Head-quarters in 1916 and noticed the shell-holes, the open, looted, evacuated houses. He passed along the road which he and Major Stevenage had traversed all those years ago. The Brigade were in Divisional Reserve, and were quartered in a string of farms just outside the village. He looked at the map squares attentively, but on the large scale map he found it actually marked Ferme l'Espagnole. Being Dormer, he just saw to the billeting of his company and then learned that the Battalion Head-quarters were located at the Vanderlyndens', and had no difficulty in finding good reason to walk over there, after tea.

The place was not much changed. It was soiled, impoverished, battered by War, but the German advance, which had stopped dead a few miles short of it, had been spent by the time it reached its limits in this sector, and had early been pushed back. Trenches had been dug and camouflage erected all round the place, but it had not suffered damage except by a few long-distance shots, the routine of trench warfare had never reached it. In the kitchen, darkened by the fact that the glass was gone from the windows, which were blinded with aeroplane fabric, stood the familiar figure of Mademoiselle Vanderlynden. He asked for the Colonel, and was civilly directed to the parlour on the other side of the door. Not a word of recognition, hardly a second glance. He did not know if he were sorry or glad. He would have felt some relief to hear that the claim that had caused all the trouble had been settled. But he did not know what he might bring down upon his head by inquiry and held his tongue. His business with the Colonel was the usual regimental routine, nominal and numerical rolls, reinforcements and indents, training and movements. It did not take long. On his way out he passed the kitchen door and said just:

'Good night, Mademoiselle!'

'Good night, M'sieu!' And then calmly: 'They are going to pay us for the damage to *La Vierge*!'

'I am glad to hear it.'

'I thought you would like to know. It has been a long time.'

'Yes, a long time. I hope it will soon be settled.'

'Ah, not yet. I know these offices at Boulogne! They have a good deal to pay for, no doubt.'

'No doubt. Good night, Mademoiselle!'

'Good night, *mon capitaine*.'

Walking back to his billet, he had once more that sensation of escape. Was he really going to get away from that business, this time, for ever? True, Mademoiselle Vanderlynden seemed little enough inclined to be vindictive. He could not help feeling that her view of the affair was after all reasonable and just. She bore no malice, she wanted things put right. Money would do it. She was going to get the money, or so she seemed to think. She had no animus against the man who had broken a piece of her property. She had neither animus against nor consideration for himself, the representative of the British Army, who had so signally failed to hasten the question of compensation. She took it all as part of the War, and she was seeing it correctly. It was the British Army that had done it. Her home, where she was working so peacefully in 1914, had become first a billet, then all but a battlefield. The Crime at Vanderlynden's was the War, nothing more nor less. That was exactly what he felt about it. No damage had been done to any furniture or valuables that he owned, but he had still to get out of it with his body intact, and resume the broken thread of existence, where it had been snapped off, all those four years ago. True he had not been badly paid, but he had taken a considerable risk – it was much more dangerous to be an officer than a private, more dangerous to be a private than a civilian. She had gauged the whole thing correctly, right down to the necessarily slow and complicated process of getting it adjudicated by some set of fellows down by the coast, who ran these things off by the hundred and had a whole set of rules that had to be complied with. He turned at the end of the farm road and took a look back at the old place. There were worse billets than the Spanish Farm and people more awkward to deal with than the Vanderlyndens. In the Somme he had come across farms where they charged you for the water and people who removed everything right down to the bedsteads. Vanderlynden had only wanted to be paid for what was wantonly damaged. They were French, you couldn't expect them to be sympathetic about other people's mules. What a queer world it was, he would never have suspected all the crotchets that human nature could present, had he not been thrust nose-foremost into this infernal show.

All his philosophy forsook him, however, on entering the billet where his company was lodged. The woman had been selling not merely beer, which was connived at, but spirits, to the men. Two of them had got 'tight' and had been arrested, and he would have them up before him in the morning. Then there would be the question as to where she got the spirits from, whether some Quartermaster-sergeant had been making away with the rum, or whether she had induced some one to buy it for her at the Expeditionary Force Canteen. It all came back to the same thing. Men kept under these conditions too long.

No one had been more surprised than Dormer, when the Allied Armies took up the initiative again in July, and appeared to keep it. With a lugubrious satisfaction he found himself retracing the advances in the Somme district of 1916. It was an ironical comment on his hard-earned War-wisdom, two years devoted to doing precisely the same thing at precisely the same place. Of course, he had learned some lessons, but his estimate of one hundred and eighty years was still too small. But when the movement became perpetual and he found himself on ground he no longer recognized, among villages that showed all the signs of methodical German occupation, he began to wonder. A slight wound in the forearm threw him out of touch for a week or two, and when he went back, he found himself in a more northern sector again, and for the first time found cavalry in front of him. It suited him all right, he didn't want to have the job of bombing out little nests of machine-gunners, that marked each step in the line of advance. His feelings were pretty generally shared. Men began to ask themselves whether there was any glory in being knocked out at the moment of victory. When his battalion was again obliged to move in advance of the cavalry, against obstacles which, although always evacuated, were out of the sphere of cavalry tactics, he found for the first time a definite unwillingness among his command to obey orders in any but the most perfunctory manner.

He had sufficient sense to see that it was very natural. In the early days the job had been to keep men under cover, to avoid useless and wasteful casualties. The lesson had been learned at length with a thoroughness that he could never have instilled. The old, old boast of the Territorial Colonel who had first enlisted him, and whose tradition was actually of pre-Territorial days, from the period of the Volunteers of before the Boer War, was better founded than he had ever supposed. He had been inclined to scoff when he had heard the old boy talk: 'Our motto was Defence not Defiance!' He did not scoff now. It was deeply, psychologically true. The army that had survived was an army that had been made to fight without much difficulty, while its back was to the sea, with the knowledge that trenches lost meant worse, if possible, conditions of existence, and it was moved by some rags of sentiment, as to holding what one had got; an army which displayed all the slowly aroused, almost passive pugnacity of the English working class, so docile, yet so difficult to drive out of a habit of mind, or an acquired way of living. They had no real imperialism in them, none of the highfalutin' Deutschland über Alles, none of the French or Italian bitter revengefulness, nor peasant passion for acquisition. The Rhine had never figured in their primary school education. They had no relatives groaning under Austrian or German domination – no rancorous feelings bred from the attempt to force alien language or unassimilated religious forms down their throats.

He had always regarded the boast about an Englishman's House being his Castle as so much claptrap. He knew by daily experience of business, that any Englishman was governed by economic conditions. Religious and racial tyranny were so far removed from the calculations of all his sort, and all above and below it, that the very terms had ceased to have any meaning. This War had no effect on the lightly borne if real tyranny of

England, the inexorable need to get a permanent job if possible and keep it, with constant anxiety as to the tenure of one's lodging, and the prospect of old age. These fellows who fell in with blank unmeaning faces, in which there was no emotion, and who marched with the same old morose jokes, and shyly imitated the class standards which he and those like him handed down to them from the fount of English culture and fashion in the Public Schools, had done what they had promised to do, or had (the late comers) been conscripted to do. They had engaged or been called up for duration. That was a typically English slogan for a European War. Their Anglia Irridenta lay in the football fields and factories, the music-halls and seaside excursions that they talked of, and now hoped to see once again. Their Alsace Lorraine lay in the skilled occupations or soft jobs that women or neutrals had invaded. When he listened to their talk in billets, and occasionally caught some real glimpse of them, between their mouth-organ concerts, and their everlasting gamble at cards, it was of the keen Trades Unionists who were already talking of purging this, that or the other skilled industry from all the non-union elements that had been allowed to flow into it, behind their backs, while they were chasing Fritz across this b— country, where Belgium, France, or Luxembourg were simply 'billets', and the goal was 'dear old Blighty' – behind them, over the Channel, not in front, still ringed about by German trenches.

There were elements of hesitation, he noticed, in the Allies. The French felt they had done much too much, and wanted to be back at their farms and little shops. The Belgians wanted to march into their country without the tragic necessity of knocking flat all its solidly built, hard-working little towns. All three nations shared the inevitable sense that grew upon men with the passage of years, of the mechanical nature of the War. Thus the cavalry, where the greatest proportion of regular soldiers lingered, were still keen on exploiting their one chance. The artillery, buoyed up by the facilities that their command of transport gave them, fired away their now all abundant ammunition. The machine-gunners, containing some proportion of picked men, and able to feel that they could easily produce some noticeable effect with their weapon, were still game. But the mass of infantry, tired enough of the bomb and the rifle, and probably unfitted by generations of peace, for any effective use of the bayonet, were rapidly adopting the attitude, unexpressed as always with the humbler Englishman, of 'Let the gunners go on if they like. We don't mind!'

On a grey November morning, Dormer went to his billet in the suburb of a manufacturing town. It was the most English place he had set eyes on in all his three years. It was not really suburban, very nearly, not quite. There was no garden before the door, it was close to the factories and workshops where the wealth that had built it was made, instead of being removed a decent mile or so. In fact, it just lacked the proper pretentiousness. Its owner had made money and was not in the least ashamed of admitting it, was rather prone to display the fact and his house looked like it. It was a villa, not a château. It was the home of a successful manufacturer who did not want in the least to be taken for a country gentleman. He, poor fellow, had been called up and promptly killed, and his home, with its stained-glass windows, expensive draping and papering, clumsy if efficient sanitation, was inhabited only by his widow.

Dormer thought there could not be in the world any person so utterly beaten. Broken-hearted, exposed during four years to considerable bodily privation, being in the occupied area, she was no Mademoiselle Vanderlynden of the Army zone that Dormer knew, making a bold front against things. She was a delicate – had been probably a pretty woman – but it was not from any of her half-audible monosyllabic replies that Dormer was able to discover to what sort of a country he had come. A little farther down the street was the factory, long gutted by the Germans and used as a forage store, where his company were billeted. The old caretaker in the time-keeper's cottage told Dormer all that was necessary, and left him astonished at the moderation of tone and statement, compared with the accounts of German occupation given by the Propagandist Press. Possibly, it was because he addressed the old man in French – or because he had never parted with his English middle-class manners – or because the old fellow was nearly wild with delight at being liberated. This was what Dormer heard:

'Enter, my Captain. It is a Captain, is it not, with three stars? The insignia of Charles Martell!' (Here wife and daughter joined in the laugh at what was obviously one of the best jokes in father's repertory.) 'You will find that the Bosches removed everything, but that makes less difficulty in the workshop. You have only to divide the floor space between your men. I know. I was a corporal in the War of 'Seventy. Ah! a bad business, that, but nothing to what we have now supported. You will do well to make a recommendation to your men not to drink the water of the cistern. The Bosches have made beastliness therein. Ah! You have your own watercart? That is well done, much better than we others used to have, in Algeria. It is always wise to provide against the simple soldier, his thoughts have no connection. You say you are accustomed to Germans and their mannerisms? I do not wonder. We too, as you may judge, have had cause to study them. I will tell you this, my Captain, the German is no worse than any other man, but he has this mania for Deutschland über Alles. It comes from having been a little people and weak, and so often conquered by us others. So that to give him some idea of himself, since he cannot invent a culture like us other French, he must go to put all above below, and make a glory of having a worse one. That shows itself in his three great faults – he has no sentiment of private property – what is others', is his. He must be dirtier than a dog in his habits – witness our courtyard – and he has to make himself more brute than he really is. You see, therefore, he has stripped the factory, and even our little lodging, down to my daughter's sewing-machine, and the conjugal bed of mother and myself. You see also, that we had our grandchildren, our dog Azor, our cat Titi. Now many of the Bosches who lodged here were certainly married and had their little ones and domestic animals. Yet if they found a child or a beast playing in the entry when they entered or left, they must give a kick of the foot, a cut, with the riding-whip. Not from bad thoughts, I assure you. It is in their code, as it is in that of us others, English and French, to lift the hat to make a salutation. The officers are the worst because in them the code is stronger. For the German simple soldier, I have respect. They sang like angels!' (Here the old man quavered out the first bars of:

'Ein feste Burg ist unser Gott.')

Dormer wanted to get away, but could scarcely forbear to listen when the daughter broke in:

'But, Papa, recount to the officer the droll trick you played upon those who came to demolish the factory!'

'Ah, yes. Place yourself upon a chair, my officer, and I will tell you that. Figure to yourself that these Bosches, as I have explained, were not so bad as one says in the papers. They had orders to do it. I know what it is. I have had orders, in Algeria, to shoot Arabs. It was not my dream, but I did it. I will explain to you this.

'It was the day on which they lost the ridge. One heard the English guns, nearer and nearer. Already there were no troops in the factory, nothing but machine-gunners, always retreating. A party of three came here with machinery in a box. One knew them slightly, since they also had billeted here. They were not dirty types; on the contrary, honest people. Sapper-miners, they were; but this time one saw well that they had something they did not wish to say. They deposit their box and proceed to render account of the place. They spoke low, and since we have found it better to avoid all appearance of wishing to know their affairs, we did not follow them. Only, my daughter had a presentiment. Woman, you know, my officer, it is sometimes very subtle. She put it in her head that these would blow up the factory. She was so sure that I lifted the cover of their box and looked in. It was an electric battery and some liquids in phials. I had no time to lose. I placed myself at the gate and ran as fast as I can to where they were, in the big workshop. I am already aged more than sixty. My days for the race are over. Given also that I was experiencing terrible sentiments — for you see, while we keep the factory there is some hope we may be able to work when the War is finished, but if it is blown up, what shall we others go and do – I was all in a palpitation, by the time I reached them. I cried: "There they go!"

' "Who goes?" they asked.

' "The cavalry," I cried.

'They ran to the entry, and seeing no one, they feared that they were already surrounded. I saw them serpentine themselves from one doorway to another all down the street. The moment they were lost to sight I flung their box into the big sewer!'

\*

Dormer billeted his company in the factory. He did not fear shell-fire that night. He himself slept in a bed at the villa. It was the first time he had left the night guard to a junior officer. In the morning, he paraded his company, and proceeded, according to plan, to await the order to move. The days were long gone by when a battalion was a recognizable entity, with a Mess at which all the officers saw each other once a day. Depleted to form Machine-Gun Companies, the truncated battalions of the end of the War usually worked by separate companies, moving independently. There was some desultory firing in front, but his own posts had seen and heard nothing of the enemy. About nine he sent a runner to see if his orders had miscarried. Reply came, stand to, and await developments. He let his men sit on the pavement, and himself stood at the head of the column, talking with the two youngsters who commanded platoons under him. Nothing happened. He let the men smoke. At last came the order: 'Cease fire.'

When he read out the pink slip to his subordinates, they almost groaned. Late products of the at last up-to-date O.T.C.s of England, they had only been out a few months and although they had seen shell-fire and heavy casualties, yet there had always been a retreating enemy, and fresh ground won every week. The endless-seeming years of Trench Warfare they had missed entirely. The slow attrition that left one alone, with all one's friends wounded or killed, dispersed to distant commands or remote jobs, meant nothing to them. They had been schoolboys when Paschendaele was being contested, Cadets when the Germans burst through the Fifth Army. They wanted a victorious march to Berlin.

Dormer read the message out to the company. The men received the news with ironical silence. He had the guards changed, and the parade dimissed, but confined to billets. He heard one of his N.C.O.s say to another: 'Cease fire! We've got the same amount of stuff on us as we had two days ago!'

It made him thoughtful. Ought he to crime the chap? Why should he? Had the Armistice come just in time? If it hadn't come, would he have been faced with the spectacle of two armies making peace by themselves, without orders, against orders, sections and platoons and companies simply not reloading their rifles, machine-gunners and Trench Mortars not unpacking their gear, finally even the artillery keeping teams by the guns, and the inertia gradually spreading upwards, until the few at the top who really wanted to go on, would have found the dead weight of unwillingness impossible to drag? The prospect, though curious, was not alarming. In a country so denuded and starved, one could keep discipline by the simple expedient of withholding rations. He had already seen, a year before at Étaples, the leaderless plight of all those millions of armed men, once they were unofficered. He was not stampeded by panic, and his inherited, inbred honesty bade him ask himself: 'Why shouldn't they make Peace themselves?' The object that had drawn all these men together was achieved. The invasion of France was at an end, that of Belgium a matter of evacuation only. 'Cease fire.' It almost began to look like an attempt to save face. Was it the same on the German side too?

In the afternoon he proposed to walk over to Battalion H.Q. and have a word with the Colonel. He knew quite well he should find the other company commanders there. Naturally every one would want to get some idea of what was to be expected under these totally unprecedented circumstances. He was met at the door of his billet by a message from the youngster he had left in charge. He had got a hundred and forty prisoners.

Dormer went at once. He could see it all before he got there. All along the opposite side of the street, faultlessly aligned and properly 'at ease' were men in field grey. At either end of the line stood a guard of his own company, and not all Dormer's pride in the men he had led with very fair success, with whose training and appearance he had taken great pains, could prevent his admitting to himself that the only point at which his lot could claim superiority was in a sort of grumpy humour. The machinery of War had conquered them less entirely than it had conquered the Germans.

In the little time-keeper's box, turned into the company office, he found a tall, good-looking man, who immediately addressed him in perfect English, giving the rank of Feld Webel, the quantity and regiment of his party and adding: 'I surrender to you, sir.' Dormer gave instructions that the party should be marched to Brigade Head-quarters. He wanted to send some report as to the capture, but his subordinate replied: 'We didn't capture 'em. They just marched up the street. The post at the bridge let 'em through.' Dormer let it go at that, and having seen the street cleared, he walked over to see his Colonel, who was billeted in a big school in a public park. His story was heard with that sort of amusement that goes with the last bottle of whisky, and the doubt as to when any more will be obtainable. The Adjutant said: 'Simply gave 'emselves up, did they?'

But the Captain commanding C Company, a man of about Dormer's own sort and service, voiced Dormer's thought.

'I believe, in another week, we'd have had both sides simply laying down their arms.'

'Oh, nonsense, soon stop that!' The Colonel spoke without real conviction. He had to say that officially.

With regard to the object for which he had come, Dormer found every one in his own difficulty. No one knew what was to happen, except that arrangments were already on foot for enormous demobilization camps. But the immediate steps were not even known at Brigade. Every one, of course, aired some pet idea, and were interrupted by noise outside, shouts and cries, the sound of marching, and orders given in German. The room emptied in a moment. The part was at one end of the town, and abutted on the smaller streets of artisans' dwellings that, in every town of the sort, goes by the name of Le Nouveau Monde. This quarter had apparently emptied itself into the park, to the number of some hundreds, mostly people of over military age, or children, but one and all with those thin white faces that showed the long years of insufficient and unsuitable food, and the spiritual oppression that lay on 'occupied' territory. They were shouting and shaking their fists round the compact formation of Dormer's prisoners, who had just been halted, in front of the house. The N.C.O. in charge had been ordered by Brigade to bring them back. A chit explained the matter: 'Prisoners taken after 11.0 a.m. to be sent back to their own units, on the line of retreat.'

The Feld Webel enlightened the Colonel's mystification: 'We refuse to obey the order, sir. Our regiment is twenty miles away. All the peasants have arms concealed. We shall just be shot down.'

It was a dilemma. Dormer could not help thinking how much better the Feld Webel showed up, than his own Colonel. The latter could not shoot the men where they stood. Nor could he leave them to the mercies of the natives. How difficult War became with the burden of civilization clogging its heels. The first thing to do was obviously to telephone the A.P.M. for police. In the meantime a French Liaison Officer made a speech, and Dormer grinned to hear him. Fancying apologizing for the War. But what else could the fellow do. He did it well, considering. The crowd quieted, thinned, dispersed. The police arrived, and had a discussion with the Adjutant. Still no conclusion. The Feld Webel strode up and down in front of his men, master of the situation. At length, some one had an idea. Six lorries rolled up in the dark, an interpreter was put on board, and the party moved off in the November dusk. The Commander of C Company and Dormer left H.Q. together. Parting at the corner that separated their scattered companies, they both exclaimed together:

'What a War!' and burst out laughing.

*

It was perhaps, to a certain degree, Dormer's fault, that during the remainder of November he became conscious of a dreary sense of anticlimax. No doubt he was that sort of person. The emergencies of the War had considerably overstrained his normal powers, which he had forced to meet the need. The need had ceased, and he had great difficulty in goading himself up to doing the bare necessary routine of Company office parades. He managed to avoid being sent up to the Rhine, and even secured a reasonable priority in demobilization, but beyond this there was nothing for it but to 'continue the motion' of waiting for the next thing to happen.

His principal job was to extract from an unwilling peasantry, enough ground for football. How often did he go to this farm and that village shop, with his best manner, his most indirect approach, liberal orders for any of the many commodities that could be bought, and in the last resort, cheerful payment of ready money out of his own pocket in order to obtain a grudging leave to use this or that unsuitable meadow, not to the extent that the game of football demanded, but to the extent that the small proprietors considered to be the least they could make him accept for the most money that he could possibly be made to pay.

Then, in the long dark evenings, there was the job of keeping the men away from the worse sorts of estaminet. His own abilities, limited to singing correctly the baritone part of Mendelssohn's Sacred Works, or Sullivan's humorous ones, was not of any practical service. What was wanted was the real star comic, the red-nosed man with improbable umbrella, the stage clergyman with his stage double-life and voice that recalled with such unintentional faithfulness, the affected mock-culture of the closed and stereotyped mind. Any deformity was welcome, not, Dormer observed, that they wanted to laugh at the helplessness of the bandy leg or the stutterer, the dwarf or the feeble-minded. On the contrary, the sentimentality of the poorer English had never stood out in brighter relief than on the edge of those devasted battlefields, where in their useless khaki, the men who had perpetuated the social system that had so blindly and wantonly used so many of them, waited patiently enough for the order of release from the servitude that few of them had chosen or any of them deserved. No, they liked to see the cunning and prowess of the old lady, or the innocent boy, applauded the way in which all those characters portrayed as having been born with less than normal capabilities showed more than normal acquisitiveness or perspicacity.

Dormer could not help reflecting how different they were from the New Army in which he had enlisted. In the squad of which, at the end of three months' violent training and keenly contested examinations, he had become the Corporal, there had been one or two labourers, several clerks from the humbler warehouses and railways, others in ascending scale from Insurance Offices and Banks, one gorgeous individual who signed himself a Civil Servant, three persons of private means, who drove up to the parade ground in motor-cars. He well remembered one of these latter going surreptitiously to the Colonel and applying for a commission, and being indignantly refused, on the grounds that the Colonel didn't know who (socially) he (the applicant) was. But when the news got out, the section were even more disrespectful to that unfortunate individual because they considered he had committed a breach of some sort of unwritten code that they had undertaken to observe. So they went on together, the immense disparity of taste and outlook cloaked by shoddy blue uniforms and dummy rifles, equal rations and common fatigues.

But the first offensive of the spring of 1915 had brought new conditions. The loss in infantry officers had been nothing short of catastrophic. Very soon hints, and then public recommendation, to take commissions reached them. The second meanwhile had altered. Two of the more skilled labourers had got themselves 'asked for' by munition works. Of the remainder

Dormer and four others applied and got commissions. He could see nothing like it now. There was more of a mix-up than ever. For some men had been exempted from the earlier 'combings out' of the unenlisted for skill, and others for ill-health. There was now only one really common bond, the imperative necessity to forget the War and all that had to do with it. This was the general impetus that had replaced the volunteering spirit, and it was this that Dormer had to contend with. He mastered the business of amusing the men pretty well, and his subordinates helped him. A more serious difficulty was with the skilled mechanics. Fortunately, an infantry battalion demanded little skill, and except for a few miners who had been out no time at all, and were at present making no fuss, there was plenty of grumbling but no organized obstruction.

He found a more advanced state of affairs when he went at the appointed time to supervise a football match between a team representing his own Brigade and that of a neighbouring Brigade of Heavy Artillery. Crossing the Grand' Place of the village to call on the Gunner Mess he found a khaki crowd, but it took him some minutes to realize that a full-dress protest meeting was in progress. Senior N.C.O.s were mounted upon a G.S. wagon. These, he gathered, were the Chairman and speakers. Another soldier, whose rank he could not see, was addressing the meeting. More shocked than he had ever been in his life, he hastily circled the square, and got to the Mess. He found most of the officers in; there was silence, they were all reading and writing. After the usual politenesses came a pause. He felt obliged to mention the object of his visit. Silence again. Eventually the Captain with whom he had arranged the preliminaries of the match said rather reluctantly:

'I'm afraid we shan't be able to meet you this afternoon.'

Dormer forebore to ask the reason, but not knowing what else to do, rose and prepared to take his leave. Possibly he spoke brusquely, he was nervous in the atmosphere of constraint, but whatever may have prompted the Gunner Captain, what he said was a confession:

'Our fellows are airing their views about demob.'

'Really!'

'Yes, perhaps you noticed it, as you came along?'

'Well, I did see a bit of a crowd.'

'You didn't hear the speeches?' The other smiled.

'I heard nothing definitely objectionable, but it's rather out of order, isn't it?'

'Well, I suppose so, but we get no help from up-atop!' The Captain nodded in the direction of the Local Command.

'No, I suppose not,' Dormer sympathized.

The young Colonel interposed. 'It's very difficult to deal with the matter. There's a high percentage of skilled men in our formation. They want to be getting back to their jobs.'

'It's really rather natural,' agreed the Captain.

Dormer tried to help him. 'We all do, don't we?'

There was a sympathetic murmur in the Mess which evidently displeased the Colonel.

'I'm not accustomed to all this going home after the battle. Time-expired men I understand, but the New Army enlistments – ' He left it at that, and Dormer felt for him, probably, with the exception of a few servants and N.C.O.s, the only pre-War soldier in the Mess, uncertain of himself and trying not to see the ill-suppressed sympathy if not envy with which most of the officers around him regarded the affair.

'Awfully sorry, Dormer,' the Captain concluded, 'we simply can't get our crowd together. You see how it is. When this has blown over I'll come across and see you, and we will fix something up.'

Dormer went.

The Gunner Captain came that evening. In Dormer's smaller Mess, it needed only a hint to the youngsters to clear out for a few minutes. Dormer admired the good humour with which the other approached him. It was obviously the only thing to do.

Over drinks he asked, modelling himself on the other's attitude:

'So that business blew over, did it?'

'It did, thank goodness. Awfully decent of you to take it as you did. I hated letting you down.'

'Don't mention it. I saw how you were placed.'

'The Colonel very much appreciated the way you spoke. I hope you had no trouble with your chaps?'

'They were all right. I pitched them a yarn. They didn't believe it, of course. Some of them were at the – er –'

'The bloomin' Parliament. Don't mind saying it. It's a dreadful shock to a regular like our old man.'

'Naturally.'

'He spoke the plain unvarnished truth when he said he was unused to all this demobbing.'

'Well, well, you can comfort him, I suppose, by pointing out that it isn't likely to occur again.'

'He's a good old tough 'un. Splendid man in action, that's what makes one so sorry about it. Otherwise, of course, one knows what the men mean. It's only natural.'

'Perfectly.'

'His trouble is not only the newness of it. It's his utter helplessness.'

'Quite so. Absolutely nothing to be done. The – er – meeting was as orderly as possible. I walked right through it. They simply ignored me.'

'Oh yes, there's no personal feeling. They all paraded this morning complete and regular.'

'That's the end of it, I hope.'

'I think so. They came up to the Mess – three N.C.O.s – a deputation, if you please. They brought a copy of the resolution that was passed.'

Neither could keep a straight face, but laughter did not matter because it was simultaneous. The Captain went on, finishing his drink:

'I believe the old man had a momentary feeling that he ought to crime some one – but our Adjutant – topping chap – met them in the passage and gave them a soft answer, and cooked up some sort of report, and sent it up. It pacified 'em.'

'Did they need it?'

'Not really. 'Pon me word, never saw anything more reasonable in my life, than what they had written out. It's too bad, hanging 'em up for months and months, while other people get their jobs. They know what they want so much better than anyone else.'

'It's impossible to please every one.'

'Yes. But when you think of what the men have done.'

Dormer did not reply. He was thinking of the Infantry, with their whole possessions on their backs, always in front in the advance, last in the retreat. The Gunner took his leave. Like everything else, either because of the incident, or more probably without any relation to it, the slow but steady progress of demobilization went on, those men who had the more real grievance, or the greater power of expression, got drafted off. The composition of units was always changing. Even where it did not, what could 'other ranks' do? To the last Dormer felt his recurrent nightmare of the Headless Man to be the last word on the subject. But it was becoming fainter and fainter as the violence of the first impression dimmed, keeping pace with the actuality of the dispersal of that khaki nation that lay spread across France, Germany, Italy, the Balkans, and the East. The Headless Man was fading out.

\*

It was mid-April, the first fine weather of the year, when his own turn came. Of course the Mess gave him a little dinner, for although nothing on earth, not even four years of War, could make him a soldier, his length of service, varied experience, and neat adaptability had made him invaluable; again no one had ever found it possible to quarrel with him; further, his preoccupation with games had made him perhaps the most sought-for person in the Brigade.

Had it not been for these reasons, there was little else to which he had a farewell to say; casualty, change, and now demobilization removed friends, then chance acquaintances, there was no one with whom he was in the slightest degree intimate. He might almost have been some attached officer staying in the Mess, instead of its President, for all he knew of the officers composing it. There was nothing in the village that lay on the edge of the battlefield that he wanted to see again. It was not a place where he had trained or fought, it was not even the place at which the news of the Armistice had reached him. It was just a place where the Brigade of which his battalion had formed a part had been dumped, so as to be out of the way, but sufficiently within reach of rail, for the gradual attrition of demobilization to work smoothly. An unkind person might have wondered if the mild festival that took place in the estaminet of that obscure commune was not so much a farewell dinner to old Dormer, as an eagerly sought opportunity for a little extra food and drink that might help to pass the empty days. Slightly bleary-eyed in the morning, Dormer boarded the train, waved his hand to the little group of officers on the platform, and sat down to smoke until he might arrive at Dunkirk.

On a mild April evening, he paced the port side of the deck of the steamer that was taking him home. He was aware that he might have to spend a night in dispersal station, but it did not matter in the least. The real end of the business to such an essential Englishman as Dormer was here and now, watching the calm leaden sea-space widen between him and the pier-head of Calais. Prophets might talk about the obliteration of England's island defences, but the sentiment that the Channel evoked was untouched. After years of effort and sacrifice, Dormer remained a stranger in France. He might knows parts of it tolerably well, speak its language fairly, fight beside its soldiers, could feel a good deal of intelligent admiration for its people and institutions, but nothing would ever make him French. It would perhaps have been easier to assimilate him into Germany. But on the whole, in spite of his unprovocative manner, he was difficult to assimilate, a marked national type. Lengthier developments and slower, more permanent revolutions were in his inherited mental make-up, than in that of any of the other belligerents. In a Europe where such thrones as were left were tottering and crashing, nothing violent was in his mind, or in the minds of ninety per cent of those men who covered the lower deck, singing together, with precisely the same lugubrious humour, as in the days of defeat, of stalemate, or of victory:

> 'Old soldiers never die,
> They only fade away.'

He turned to look at them, packed like sardines, so that even the sea breeze could hardly dissipate the clouds of cigarette smoke, just as no disaster and no triumph could alter their island characteristics, however much talk there might be about town life sapping the race. As he looked at them, herded and stalled like animals, but cheerful in their queer way as no animal can ever be, he remembered that somewhere among all those thousands that were being poured back into England day by day (unless of course he were buried in one of those graveyards that marked so clearly the hundred miles from Ypres to St Quentin) was a private soldier, whom he had been told to discover and bring to justice for the Crime at Vanderlynden's, as Kavanagh had called it. He had never even got the fellow's name and number, and he did not care. He never wanted the job, nothing but his punctilious New Army spirit, that had made him take the War as seriously as if it had been business, had kept him at it. Now he had done with it, the man would never be found. But in Dormer's mind would always remain that phantom that he had pursued for so many months – years even, over all those miles, in and out of so many units and formations. It had come to stand for all that mass whose minds were as drab as their uniform, so inarticulate, so decent and likeable in their humility and good temper. Theirs was the true Republicanism, and no written constitution could add anything to it. He had not thought of that affair, during all these last months that had seen so many Empires fall, so many nations set upon their feet, but he thought of it now.

He turned once again and surveyed that coastline, somewhere behind which he had made that pilgrimage; there it lay, newly freed Belgium on the left, on the right the chalky downs that ran from Gris-Nez far out of sight, down to Arras. Between the two, on those marshes so like any of South-Eastern England, had taken place that Crime at Vanderlynden's, that typified the whole War. There, on those flat valleys of the Yser and the Lys, the English army had come to rest after its first few weeks of romantic march and counter-march. There had the long struggle of endurance been the longest and least spectacular. It was there that the English Effort, as they called it, had played its real part, far more than on the greater battlefields farther south, or away on other continents. The Crime at Vanderlynden's showed the whole thing in miniature. The English had been welcomed as Allies, resented as intruders, but never had they become homogeneous with the soil and its natives, nor could they ever leave any lasting mark on the body or spirit of the place. They were still incomprehensible to Vanderlynden's, and Vanderlynden's to them. Dormer was of all men most unwilling and perhaps unable to seek for ultimate results of the phenomena that passed before his eyes. To him, at that moment, it seemed that the English Effort was fading out, leaving nothing but graveyards. And when he found this moving him, his horror of the expression of any emotion asserted itself, and he elbowed his way down the companion, to get a drink.

When he came up again, that low shore had passed out of sight, but ahead was visible the moderately white cliffs of England, beyond which lay his occupation and his home, his true mental environment, and native aspiration. He experienced now in all its fullness the feeling that had been with him with such tragic brevity from time to time during those years. This last passage of the Channel was, this time, real escape. The Crime at Vanderlynden's was behind him. He had got away from it at last.

# The Stranger

If the dispersing crowd in the Grand' Place notice him at all, it is only with the most cursory interest. Food for gossip he may be, but even gossip is not very important. The important thing, this Easter Sunday in Hondebecq, is the prospect of planting the potatoes shortly. That is what all the men and a good many of the women are thinking about. Easter of course is a festival, the young communicants will walk in procession this afternoon, boys in dark suits and peaked caps, girls in white, like little brides, priest and beadle, Maire and schoolmaster will marshal them about the portable image of the Virgin under its little canopy. This was done during the War even. But it is a very brief respite from the real business of life, and a matter of routine, and directly it is over, if the weather serve, one can get on with the potatoes. It is not the Easter procession that the stranger has come to see. Stranger he is, because everyone knows everyone else in the village, and his face is strange. Also he wears tweed jacket, flannel trousers, and a shapeless hat, and carries a stick. The only strangers known to the village are English. Without doubt he is an Englishman, come back, as one has known them to do, queer people, any time these ten years. What for? To look at the place where they came to fight the War! Something to look at, that is. As if one did not chiefly require to forget all about it. But being English he is, one remembers from what one saw of that nation ten years ago, incredibly rich and idle, and can afford such follies.

Of course, Camille Vanacker, the village 'mutilé' will make up to him, in the hopes of getting a tip. Quite right. The English are rich and Camille is a poor devil who has lost both arms at Verdun. There they go.

The Englishman listens, and gives money, but does not pursue the matter. Verdun is only a name to him. He moves with a sort of uncertainty across the Place. One takes a look at him, but one saw so many, it is very odd if one can recognize him, in civilian dress. He goes into the Lion of Flanders, orders a drink of white wine, in his strange French, stands by the counter smoking his pipe, scrutinizing all the faces, as though he expected to be greeted by some one. But no one greets him. What with death and change, refugees coming in and old inhabitants who have made their fortunes moving out, ten years is enough to obliterate any acquaintance he had. The middle-aged men were all away too. No, no one knows him. Presently he goes. As in all these villages, a few steps take him off the cobbles of the village, out of the sound of children, pigeons, cocks, and church bells, into the green country. To his left, the flat arable, cut chess-board-wise with tiny ditches crossed by diminutive roads, lined by trees, stretches from a slow-moving stream, up a low ridge, out of sight. To his right, pasture, then a windmill above a tiny wood. That wood is the only uncultivated piece of land to be seen, and even it has been planted, and is being cut for timber. The stranger takes a good look. It is not because he forgets the road. It would be truer to say the road has forgotten him, it is so changed, utterly lonely and forsaken, all those little signboards 'D.A.C.' 'Lorries this way' 'C.C.S.' 'No Tanks' are gone.

He walks along, listening to the stillness, as another would listen to an unaccustomed noise. It is not only the bump-bump of lorries, the pit-pat rattle of limbers drawn by mules, the slog-slog and dusty chatter of infantry he misses. Nor the drone of aeroplanes going right back to St Omer. There ought to be something behind all these, dull and low, a mere background of noise, but always there, the murmur of the battle that went on, year after year, over hundreds of miles. It is the lack of that which makes him strain his ears until they feel a sort of ache.

Gazing in the direction from which it ought to come, he sees, beyond the mill, a line of telegraph poles, running out of sight. He knows what it is. The *route nationale* to Lille, thirty kilometres away. But the thing which stuns his imagination is the fact that today, if he wanted to, he can walk right along to Lille.

No one will stop him. There will be no gradual lessening of glass in the windows, and roofs on the houses, no camouflage netting beside the road, no place where cheery voices will hail him with advice to walk in the ditch. No final scramble in upturned earth, to the brink of that weed-grown river of death, dammed between the two hastily-thrown-up banks called trenches, where men live like rats in holes. There will be nothing there, nothing. Roads and bridges have been rebuilt, wire and posts pulled up, trench and tram-line filled in and smoothed down, and cultivated. He knows. He has already been to Ypres. He does not want to go again. The War may have been 'legalized murder' as it was now called. But Post-War is murder on show, with a small price for admission to defray expenses. Even then they cannot show you War. With a sudden descent from lunatic waste to careful meanness, they can only show where War has been. He may walk to Lille, and a good deal farther; he may walk off the earth, and never see War again.

And there is one other physical sense, which memory makes to crave something it cannot recapture. He sniffs the air. Smell of country, of green crops just showing, of rich damp earth turned over and ready for roots. Even if it were not too early, there will not be any wild flowers here, like the wild flowers he remembers in the Somme before June 1916. And none of that is what his nose is asking for. What it misses is the proper smell of that road, the Flemish border lane that for so long was the main street of a great straggling camp of fifty thousand English-speaking men. The proper smell is brazier smoke and manure and disinfectant and tobacco. It had to be discovered, because no story and hardly a history book mentioned the fact, that to fight, a man must live. The usual heroics about dying for one's country are not merely idle. They are the reverse of the fact. To fight one must not die. To fight for a few minutes, one must live for weeks. Even Wellington's Hundred Days did not contain ten of fighting. So, with a great modern War you get cooking, sanitation, transport, and comforts just as in a great modern Peace. Or, as his nose more briefly describes it, brazier smoke and disinfectant, manure and tobacco.

His reflections are interrupted by one of those deep-seated habits that are all the stronger for being so unconscious; he can only feel something in the slope of the road, that makes his feet want to turn to the left. He is beside a bit of hedge, almost an English hedge, ending in a gate. He goes to it and peers over. Yes, there was no doubt about it. It is the big pasture at R33 on the map. How often he came back there, he cannot think, but it is the place he remembers best, in all those wanderings from camp to billet. It is what he has been looking for, the reason of his detour by out-of-the-way Hondebecq, instead of following the usual route of tourists, visiting the Front. The thing they call the Front, pre-eminently a place where men have died, soon saddened and sickened him, but at R33 perhaps one might catch a glimpse of the place where men had lived. Better here than anywhere else. The biggest and best known camp was only a war-time affair, inhabited by soldiers, cleared away since the Armistice. But the low two-storied old house, there at the back of the pasture, under the elms and round its cobbled-edged manure heap, is a place that had kept its civilian character all through the War, and has survived, more or less intact, now that War has gone. He looks and looks and slowly he understands why it seems so strange. The pasture is empty. Not a soul stirs. Not even a pig is in sight. Leaning on the gate, he closes his eyes, to recall how it used to look. Slowly the picture comes back. The quagmire about the gate, the 'road' built of faggots and brick-ends from bombarded buildings, that led to the house, the tents to the left, the transport parked to the right. He can feel the rough surface under his feet, can hear the lugubrious jollity of men doing odd jobs, the squawking and fidgeting of the mules, being as awkward as possible. At the corner of the barn, to the left, the cookers blacken everything, but on some of the hard ground just by the entry, the lip of the old dry moat it may have been, a party of men are falling in, to go up to the line for some special duty. He passes in front of them, watching the N.C.O. checking their equipment.

He knows, before he gets there, that the third file from the left is that lanky boy who never seemed to have hardened to the life, nor to have swallowed the nature of the business in hand, a boy with brown eyes always trying to see something beyond their scope, like an animal. That boy had once asked him: ' 'Ow long is this War goin' on, Sir!' 'Oh, two or three months. Year, maybe!' 'A Year?' with a gasp of horrified incredulity. That boy was going to be killed and knew it. There were men like that. In his dream he tries to warn the boy to go sick, get told off for other duty, anything, and the effort wakes him from his day-dream. There is nothing there. He has not moved. He has but closed his eyes for a moment. The pasture is empty. Right back there, as if stubbornly wedged in a corner, the old house stares him out of countenance. He stares back. He bears no grudge. It was watertight. You could get cooking done well, and washing done there. What else did a soldier want? It wasn't home, it could have no permanent relation to him. But there had been order, discipline, some sort of civilized restraint there. And looking at the barn where he had so often forbidden men to smoke, he derisively lights his pipe. The worst misfortunes pass. Wars do end, some time.

Something is coming along the lane, he hears the flop-flop of hoof and rattle of springless wheel. How often has he not heard it, rations, or tents, or some odds and ends of impedimenta being brought up. How often has he not waited for some such slow moving vehicle, at that very gate, spinning out the vacuity of soldiering, by seeing something done right, which otherwise would only be half done, because it was everybody's business. Here comes a farmer, in black Sunday best, with the big horse in a tumbril, doing some small job that must be done, on these farms, whatever the day. He swings the gate open for it and gets:

'Merci, M'sieu!' from the man, whose face is strange. Nothing else. The man thinks him a fool if he thinks about him at all, idling there.

But as the horse and tumbril recede towards the house, they become once more part of the dream, the rattle and hoof-fall become the sound of transport moving. He stands at that gate, as the battalion comes back from the Somme, for Messines. The

G.S. Wagon has been to railhead and brought back, among other things, the post-bag from Brigade. In the guard tent there, by that very gate, let the R.Q.M.S. sort it out. The battalion is of course three-quarters new drafts, there are a lot of letters, and a fair number for men who would never get them unless the angels turned post corporals. But the deliverable ones are passed to the N.C.O.s, one per company, who are waiting, and then arises, all over the pasture, the boisterous sardonic fun inseparable from the New Armies, the banter of men who would never take a War quite seriously, and who, instead of being sentimental at such a moment, are calling to each other:

'Look what Mother's sent her blue-eyed boy!'

' 'Ere's an illustrated. Pictures of our last Show. O Lor! (shy deprecation) Fat lot they know!'

'Father's wounded. He is, I tell you. He's a Special. He sat on a spiky railin' to rest 'is pore leg!'

'She says she's going to have another, she reckons!'

'Well, what d'you expect, going home on leave!'

The smell, the noise, the look of Khaki sprawling on trampled grass besets him. It had been so real, so absorbing. He, no less than all those fellows, had adjusted himself to it, had sat on some old bit of board (if he could get one) in somebody else's field, to read little bits of news from an England to whom the War was somewhere else, some one else's; an England which like himself and all those men could never take such a preposterous affair quite seriously.

He opens his eyes, and the sound, the sight, the odour vanish. Nothing! there is nothing there. Some birds are chattering in the elms, the greyish spring day is waning. It is no good standing there waiting for something to come back, which will never come back. At least one hopes not. He has still some time to put away before his train, he will follow the lane down to the *pavé*, have a last glance from the high land there, and so back to the village and the station. That will be a good wind-up, for he feels that he will not come that way again.

So he goes between pasture and arable, here a cottage, there a farm, hiding well back behind elms, with the gleam of pond or moat about it. The crossroads look lop-sided. Then he recollects that the oaks that line the *pavé* were gapped by shell fire, in the final flurry of 1918. That, of course, had been his last sight of the place, two streams of retreating divisions and evacuated civilians all mixed up, and his battalion coming up to relieve, jammed in the crush, and the Brigade Major borrowing him from his Colonel and posting him there with an N.C.O. to sort things out. He must certainly have a drink in the Estaminet de la Croix (In t'Kruyshook they call it more often) – in memory of the five-nine that had just missed him and hit the gable above his head. He pushes open the door. A woman with an apron over her Sunday dress gives him good day. He must have white wine – the rasping vinky-blinky of that immortal song about the Mademoiselle of Armentières. Here it is, strong and sour as ever, but good stuff to march on. Between glasses, he asks:

'Were you here, in the War?'

'No, Monsieur, we are refugees installed here!'

Of course. The proprietors, he might have known, had either lost all the males of the family or made so much money, and anyhow gone elsewhere. He has nothing to talk about to this woman, no common memory or wonderment. He drinks and muses. And there comes over him an odd feeling of someone wanting him, just outside the window. He stares. Nothing. Surely there is the shuffling of feet, murmur, the grating of heavy boots and rifle butts on the cobbles, just as though his platoon were standing easy, waiting the order to move. He goes to the window.

'What is it that there is, Monsieur?'

'Some one?'

'No, Monsieur!' she replies. But he is so certain that he goes out of the door, round the corner of the house, and a few yards down the *pavé*. He is not so far wrong. They are waiting for him, 'properly at ease' in the drill-book phrase, if ever men were. Without even reading the little Notice Board of the Graves Commission, he leans on the fence of the little cemetery and scans their names. They are not really his platoon, they are a mixture of all sorts, gathered from one of those last actions in the fields below there – Private This, Sapper That, Gunner Someone. And he understands why he is a Stranger. These have not relapsed into Peace and England, as he has. The War has survived them. He feels their appeal, almost their reproach, warning him that, sooner or later, he must follow, for all his luck.

After a few minutes, he leaves them, goes back into the Estaminet, finishes his wine, and pays. The woman has not been anxious. She knows the English are mad, but honest. As he leaves the place she says, as though certain that he will not return, 'Adieu, Monsieur!'

He replies 'Adieu,' partly to her and partly, as he closes the door, to that straight road, along the low ridge above the shallow valley that he had traversed time and again, the tide-mark to and from which the battle had flowed, ebbed, flowed again, and finally ebbed. He glances at his watch. Just time to catch his train, to Calais, to England, home. Into the dusk the stranger hurries away.

## MORE ABOUT PENGUINS
## AND PELICANS

*Penguinews*, which appears every month, contains details of all the new books issued by Penguins as they are published. From time to time it is supplemented by our stocklist, which includes around 5,000 titles.

A specimen copy of *Penguinews* will be sent to you free on request. Please write to Dept EP, Penguin Books Ltd, Harmondsworth, Middlesex for your copy.

*In the U.S.A.*: For a complete list of books available from Penguins in the United States write to Dept CS, Penguin Books, 625 Madison Avenue, New York, New York 10022.

*In Canada*: For a complete list of books available from Penguins in Canada write to Penguin Books Canada Ltd, 2801 John Street, Markham, Ontario L3R 1B4.

*In Australia*: For a complete list of books available from Penguins in Australia write to the Marketing Department, Penguin Books Australia Ltd., P.O. Box 257, Ringwood, Victoria 3134.